Devil's in the Details

A Novel by
Sydney Gibson

Edited by A.E. Vikar and Associates.

This novel is dedicated to the supportive readers who keep encouraging me to write more of what's inside of my head.

To my parents, who were surprised that my days spent in a dark room was because I was writing a book, and still wonder why I don't ever go outside.

To Donna, thank you for entertaining me when I ranted and reading the super early drafts of this mess and helping me fix the grammar mistakes.

To Kimberley, you know what you did! This is all your fault! Thank you for everything!

This story is told in two point of views. Look for the below images to signify a change in the character's point of view.

Alexandra Ivers

Victoria Bancroft

Chapter 1

"Please, please, just work for me one more time." I turned the key in the ignition for the hundredth time, groaning and slamming the steering wheel with my fist when it clicked and did nothing else. Telling me that the old beat up mini cooper wanted me to give up like it already had. "Shit." I ripped the car keys out of the ignition and threw them into my bag.

I would have to take the damn metro home.

Sliding out of the old car, I slung my bag around my shoulders and kicked the rusted door closed. I was still three months away from being able to look at buying, or leasing a new car having just moved back to D.C. I let out a heavy breath looking around the hospital parking garage, hoping I could spot Stacy's car to try and hustle a ride home out of her. But her shiny red Honda was missing from its usual spot next to the elevator. I groaned, pulling out my cell phone and texting her to see if she was close by. It was almost three in the morning and I really did not want to take a late night adventure on the metro or play taxi cab roulette.

I started walking towards the bank of elevators when the phone beeped with Stacy's reply.

-I left the hospital at one after the last rush. I can come back and get you if you want, Alex.-

I rolled my eyes. Stacy lived up near Springfield and it would take her at least an hour to get back to the hospital just to take me for a fifteen minute ride back to my apartment on the fringe of the capital. I sent her a reply to not worry, that I would take a cab. At least I wasn't still in my scrubs. Just a loose jacket, white V-neck and comfortable jeans, clothes I knew wouldn't draw too much attention from the night crawlers that lived only in the darkness of late night hours.

Dropping my phone back in my bag, I dug around until I felt my pepper spray and pulled it out. Linking the keychain canister on the strap, I rode the elevator down to the front lobby and left the stuffy, sterile confines of the hospital.

Outside on the streets of Washington D.C., I took a deep breath of the cold night air, letting the crisp cool air sting my lungs, removing the last pieces of stale hospital air from them. I was tired. It had been my fourth twelve hour shift this week and as much as I liked and needed the overtime, I still needed to get unpacked and settled in at my new apartment.

Turning right, I kept my eyes forward, smiling to the handful of paramedics and nurses smoking in the ambulance bays as I walked towards the metro station staircase. I was familiar with the city, having been born and raised just outside of it until I moved to New York in search of a big exciting life. Only to end up getting burned out and moving back to the smaller big city I was used to.

I trotted down the stairs, relieved but nervous to see the metro platform was deserted aside from a small group of men laughing over cigarettes by the bathrooms. There were two other people with me. A tired looking senate intern in a rumpled white dress shirt and khakis, balancing an overstuffed briefcase while his fingers flew across a cell phone screen. The second person, was a tall figure sitting on a bench reading a Popular Science magazine. I couldn't distinctly tell if they were male or a female since the aviators, USN ball cap and hooded sweatshirt covered most of their face. I sighed and turned back to the empty tracks, leaving them to their magazine and opted to move closer to the intern who looked safe.

I moved to stand near the intern, glancing back at the group of men laughing obnoxiously from their spot. Glaring at me with lecherous eyes when they noticed my attention was on them. I shifted my bag closer to my chest, gritting my teeth. I had my fair share of stares in subway stations, metro stations, bars, and even the occasional examination room while inserting a catheter.

I shifted in my stance, smiling softly at the young intern next to me who was staring at me with tired eyes. He returned my smile with a bashful one and focused back on his phone. My skin began to prickle as the air suddenly shifted around us, making me nervous. I glanced over to the group of men and saw they were staring harder at me, starting to push away from the wall they all leaned against to make their over to where I stood.

I turned back to the dark tracks, my right hand moving to unclip the pepper spray to palm it. I was too tired for this shit. Leaning forward a step I could hear the rush of wind signifying the incoming metro. All I had to do was take the front car and sit behind the driver where I knew there was a camera, and I would be okay. Maybe the douchebags that looked like white rapper wannabes would back off and return to hanging outside the piss smelling bathrooms.

Eyes forward, Alex, keep your eyes forward, the train is coming. I took steps closer to the edge when I felt the group come closer.

"Looky, looky, what do we have here?" The voice was heavy with false ego and cheap cigarettes. The voice fell directly behind me, and I flinched at the smell of a rancid mix of stale cigarettes and cheap cologne. "You lost? You need some help with directions?"

I clenched my jaw, staying silent. I knew from my past that being nice, or rude, would just egged these shit heads on.

The train was moving closer. I could see its bright front light reflecting along the dirty off white tile lining the tunnel.

I went to take a step closer to the edge, when I was surrounded and the face that went with the voice fell in front of me. He was a typical sleaze. Greasy looking with a thin mustache and beard, wearing a baseball cap with an unbent brim and layered clothing sprouting the logos of mixed martial arts fighters and obnoxious sports teams. He had beady brown eyes that squinted at me. The red edges of those beady eyes told me he was coming down from Oxy and would not give in very easily when I rejected his attempts of asking me out on a date or offers to safely escort me back to his place.

I flicked my thumb over the trigger for the pepper spray, feeling his other friends move closer and bump into me as they surrounded me. Shoving the scared as shit intern away from us.

The sleaze leader moved closer, "You a mute?" He scanned down my body in a way that made me want to take a scalding hot shower the moment I got home. "You a hot piece of ass. You looking for a date tonight honey?" He reached out to run his hand down my arm. I took a step back, bumping into one of the others behind me. Pulling laughs from all of them. "Ohh! Looks like she's a little stuck up." The sleaze moved inches away from my face, "You ain't no better than us." He smirked, running his tongue over dry, cracked lips.

When he reached up to run his filthy hands down my face, I reacted and kicked him hard in between his legs. I watched him fall to his knees, his mouth was agape in the shape of a wide silent O, as he struggled for air, clutching at his balls. I half smirked at the small victory when he recovered enough to gasp out, "Fuck her up, boys."

I spun lifting my hand up to spray all of them when a hard fist caught me in the stomach, making me double over in pain. A hand suddenly yanked at my hair, lifting my head up to set it up for the hard open palm slap that struck me across the mouth. Splitting my lip open, making me cry out in pain and see stars.

I closed my eyes as I felt hands start grabbing at my arms and clothes, hands and fists striking me and sending jolts of pain through my body. One hard strike sent the pepper spray out of my palm and bouncing down the platform, disappearing behind a trash can.

I looked up to see the train come to a stop, the doors open and stare at me as if to beg me to break for it and run. But I didn't, I couldn't. I was being held back by the filthy hands of drug addicts.

I fell to my knees when my feet were knocked out from under me and closed my eyes, begging to whoever would listen that I wouldn't cry in front of these assholes.

Just read your magazine, Victoria, just ignore the shit heads in the corner. That's what I kept repeating to myself over and over. Ignore the shitheads who smell like piss, cigarettes, and burnt heroin. I had sized them up the moment I walked down the stairs to the platform. Them, and the poor overworked kid wearing the typical uniform of a tired intern. He was harmless, too busy swiping left or right on the dating app on his phone.

I normally didn't take the metro, but I had to tonight. The job I just finished had forced me to take unusual routes back home. A bus, a cab, a quick jog through the national cemetery, and now a quick three stop ride before I could collect my car and go home. I hated the metro, no matter the time of day or night. It was the true definition of a sardine can. People shoved together to share their smells, fluids, and worst of all, their life stories if you offered up a kind smile.

The brunette had caught my attention the second she stepped off the staircase. She did not fit anywhere in this scene. Clean clothes, nice messenger bag around her shoulder and the pepper spray clutched in her right hand like it would be a life saver when called upon, gave her away. Never mind the fact it was three in the morning in one of the most dangerous metro stations in the city.

I peered at the brunette through my aviators. She was beautiful, another thing that struck me right away. I rarely ever thought that about anyone, but this woman was beautiful. Her long dark brown hair was tied back and draped down her back. The angles in her face told me she had some sort of European blood running through her veins. The bright dark blue eyes held so much even in the tiny glance she gave me as she surveyed her surroundings. She had eyes that could be kind and fierce all at once, something I had not seen in a long time. It made me want to look at her again and for a little longer.

And even though her clothes were a bit loose on her, I could tell she worked out and kept her body in shape. Leaving me to believe that she was either an actress or a medical professional, considering the late hours and both professions had a hub on this side of town.

I turned back to the pages of my Popular Science when the brunette glanced back at me, I didn't need to draw attention. I would continue reading about solar satellites and wait for the train. Shuffle to the same car as the intern, and hope the shit heads didn't follow. I just wanted to go home, shower, burn my clothes and send off for my payment to be deposited while I ate ice cream.

But that's not what happened. The shit heads, as predicted, couldn't keep it in their pants and made a bee line towards the brunette. Cat calling, whistling and surrounding the poor woman.

Sucking in a breath, I kept my head down. Not wanting to get involved as they shoved the poor intern, who was on the verge of pissing his pants, away. Giving them more room to go after their target.

I clenched my jaw at what I saw, I couldn't get involved and hoped the shitheads would just harass her until the train came, chase her into a car and then giggle like fools as they took another hit of whatever shit they were on. It was a terrible thought process, but I had a long night finishing up a messy job and didn't want blood stains on my clean clothes.

The train came and I stood up. After rolling the magazine up under my arm, I took a few steps closer to the edge of the platform. Glancing at the group of men, one of them shot me a look, flipped me off and growled at me to keep my nose on my face. I clenched my jaw when I heard the disgusting words come out of the mouth of the one right in front of the brunette. I rolled my neck, my gut telling me that I couldn't walk away while my brain was telling me this wasn't any of my business.

Then the shriek of a man who just had his privates smashed, pulled all of my attention to the group. The brunette had kicked him hard in the testicles, dropping him to his knees to cry like a baby. I smirked and laughed at the sight, mentally giving her a high five. Then I turned to see the first punch strike her in the stomach and the hard slap that followed.

I didn't think, I just acted after that. I didn't have sympathy for men like them.

I tightly gripped the rolled up magazine in my right hand and started walking quickly towards the group. As I moved closer the train arrived and stopped and when the doors opened I walked behind the intern, shoving him into the car, I heard him grunt as he fell onto his ass. Scattering the papers that escaped from his overflowing briefcase around the platform and train car.

When he was out of the way, I rushed towards the first man who flipped me off. Grabbing him by the shoulder, I spun him around. By the time he faced me to utter whatever nonsense, the heel of my palm met his nose with deadly force. Smashing the cartilage into the nasal bone, driving both into his brain. Killing him instantly.

Throwing his lifeless body out of my way, I grabbed the owner of the hand that slapped the brunette. Wrapping my fingers around his, I yanked and twisted. Hearing the delightful snap of his wrist, he screamed and went to hit me while shouting for his friends to help him. I glanced at his hand in mine and swung the tightly rolled up magazine against the inside of his forearm, shattering the bone in two. The sharp edges pierced through his skin, he fell to his knees screaming at the sight of his bones poking out. This offered me a clear shot to swing the magazine at his throat, shattering the hyoid bone with enough power, the bone shards sliced through his carotid artery.

He would be dead in seconds.

I turned to the third man, ignoring the gurgling sounds of the second choking on his own blood. This shithead still held onto the brunette, his face sheet white as he witnessed what I had done to his friend. He dropped the unconscious brunette, raising his hands up in surrender as her limp body hit the floor with a slap and a thud.

"Hey man, I ain't got no fight with you!" He stumbled back to run from me. I pushed my hood back, revealing my long pale blonde hair in a ponytail and hissed at him, "I am no man. And you need to learn that you never lay a hand on a woman."

His eyes widened and he turned to run. He only took a few steps before I snatched the red fire extinguisher from the wall next to us. Throwing it with deadly accuracy at the back of his head, I smirked when I heard the crack of his skull breaking open from the impact of the heavy metal can. I watched as he fell face first, hitting the floor with another crack. Breaking his own nose on impact and ending his misery like his other friend.

Looking down at the beaten brunette, I spotted the ring leader trying to get up and run from me. Clutching between his legs from the pain, I took a deep breath. My heart was still beating at slow, normal rate just as if I was back sitting on that bench and reading my magazine.

The train had left the station the second I pushed the intern in it, leaving me and the ring leader in stale silence. I walked up to him, kicking the back of his Achilles tendon hard. Dropping him back to the floor with a shriek, I crouched down to him. Tucking my aviators away and pulling off my hat, I set it on the floor next to him and away from the small pools of blood growing around us.

Staring at the piece of shit, I already knew what I was going to do. I stood back up, walking over to the trash can, I bent down and pick up the small can of pepper spray. Looking it over to see that it was police grade, I smiled. I then moved to stand on the side of the groaning man who was now crying as he looked around at all of his dead friends, "Please, man, please! You gotta let me go, I'm sorry! I won't tell no one about this!"

I sucked in a deep breath, the stink of blood heavy in the air starting to mix with the smell of death. A scent that was oddly calming when I was surrounded by it. Only for the reason that it was the one constant in my life I had known the longest. Bending down to the man I looked him dead in the eyes, watching his widened as he saw that I was a woman. "You're a girl? Holy shit...what are you? A soldier of fortune?"

I clenched my jaw, flicking the safety cap off the pepper spray, "I wish I could tell you that this is a lesson learned for you, but you won't be alive in the next five minutes to learn anything from it."

Aiming the tiny nozzle right at his eye line, I pressed the red button and emptied the canister in his face. I barely heard his screams, I had learned to tune them out a few years ago so I could focus on what came next. I grabbed his arms, twisting his wrists until they snapped, for no other reason than it made me feel better. I then dragged the screaming man to the edge of the platform.

Not bothering to look twice, I rolled his body onto the track, looking up to see the quick flicker of the next train's light on the tunnel walls. I stepped back, picking up my USN hat and tucking it in my back pocket before bending down to the brunette. When I went to check her for a pulse, I glanced up to see the black domed security cameras at each end of the platform. "Dammit."

Digging out my cell phone, I pressed my third contact as I checked to see if the brunette still had a pulse. She had one, it was light and thready, but there was one. Reaching up to brush her hair away, I cringed when I saw the purple marks forming around her eyes and cheeks. My stomach churning at the sight confused me. I never had a reaction to anything like I was now, looking down at this woman.

"What's what Victoria?" The hyper female voice helped to drown out the muted groans from the tracks.

"Platform 3 at the Federal Triangle station. I need you to wipe the security footage then run a protocol echo with the police." I waited until it was confirmed and clicked the phone to the Bluetooth settings, pressing the small headphone into my ear, "I also need a car sent to this location on the surface a half a block away." I scooped up the brunette in my arms, hearing her whimper as her head rolled to settle against my chest. "No driver, just leave the keys in the visor."

"You got it Victoria." The voice paused, filling the air with the clicks of a keyboard. "Do I want to know why I am doing all of this?"

I clenched my jaw, shifting my arms to get a better hold on the brunette, hating the way she felt cool and clammy in my arms, telling me she was going into shock and I would have to take her to a hospital and not just drop her off outside the ER. "I got involved in something I shouldn't have, Dani." I climbed the stairs quickly, turning to the right just as I heard the train bellow through the platform and end the groans with a rush of wind.

The night was still cool and I welcomed the fresh air. I glanced down at the brunette, the small beads of sweat forming on her forehead made me rush towards the black sedan pulling up under a distant street light. The headlights flicked twice and the driver got out, disappearing down the street under the guise of a late night jogger. I too started jogging towards the car, wanting to get this woman to a hospital before she grew worse and fell deeper into shock.

Setting her gently in the driver's seat, I reached across to buckle her in when I heard a struggled whisper, "Who are you? What happened?"

I cursed under my breath and leaned back to face the hazy, half opened eyes staring directly at me. Reaching up, I brushed some of her hair away, smiling even though I knew she could see my entire face since I had left my hat and aviators off, "You're going to be okay. I am taking you to the hospital now." I pressed my palm against her cheek, "You're safe now."

The dark blue eyes held mine for a moment before she nodded painfully, tears gliding down her bloodied and bruised cheeks. "Okay." Her voice trembled and I saw that she was still scared but, for whatever reason, she trusted my words.

I let out a breath, standing up and closing the door I rushed to the driver's side as I heard the distant sirens coming towards us. Dani popped in my ear again. "The cops are on their way, Victoria. All of them are familiar with protocol echo, you won't have a problem." She blew out a breath, "I ran the faces through facial recognition. You didn't kill four innocents, that's for sure." She had an indignant tone in her voice, as if she was trying to find some justification for what I had just done.

I cut her off, "Dani, I don't care. You know that. I never care about who they are or what they've done right or wrong. Just clean it up and leave it alone." I clicked off the Bluetooth and started the black sedan, squealing off in the opposite direction of the flashing red and blue lights.

Why the hell did I get involved, especially when I had a morning class to teach in less than five hours.

"Oh, Alex, I feel terrible for not telling you I left early." Stacy sat next to my bed, picking at the standard issue white thermal blanket covering me. "I was going to text you, but my mom called and I was stuck listening to her ramble on about her new crochet class." She looked up at me, her eyes running over the bruises and cuts on my face. "I should have come back for you."

I smiled weakly, feeling the corners of my mouth tug at my still swollen cheek, "It's okay, Stacy. I should have taken a cab or gotten one of the guys to help me with the mini." I sat back against the stiff pillows. Every inch of my body was sore and felt like it was broken, but nothing was broken. I was just bruised, scraped and full of muscle strains. I rolled my head towards the television playing the afternoon soap operas with the volume muted. "Do you think Dr. Owens will sign off on letting me out today?"

"I overheard him talking to the X-ray tech, he just needs you to answer the call of nature to make sure there is no internal damage and he will cut you loose." Stacy grabbed my forearm, "Alex, you should at least stay overnight. You had a rough night." Her voice faded off near the end.

I kept my eyes on the television, "I know, but I'd rather be at home in my own bed." I turned to look at her, "When did you say the detective will be in to talk to me?" I bit the inside of my mouth. I really wanted to go home so I could cry in peace. I had held it together from the moment I woke up in the emergency room with all of my co-workers rushing around my gurney asking a thousand different questions with fearful looks in their eyes.

Stacy leaned back in her chair, "In a half hour. I guess the other officers who hounded you while Kathy stitched you up was not good enough." She shook her head, "I swear to god, I hope they find those bastards and throw them in cells with big angry convicts that hate men who beat up women."

I gave her a small smile at her frustration. Stacy was my closest friend at the hospital, we connected within minutes of my first shift and she was a huge help as I readjusted to living in D.C. again. "I'm sure they'll get theirs."

A soft tap on the doorframe made Stacy and I both look up at the tall woman with brown hair wearing a bland grey pantsuit, standing half in and half out of my room. "Excuse me, Ms. Ivers? I'm Detective Jennifer Scarlett. Is this a good time to ask some follow up questions about last night?" She had a polite smile on her face trying to make it feel like her presence wasn't so much of an unwelcomed intrusion.

I nodded, "Sure."

The detective ushered into the room, setting a thick black binder on my tray, glancing at Stacy as she dug out a pen, "Do you mind if I speak to Ms. Ivers alone?" She smiled tightly as Stacy stood, whispering that she would be back to check on me in a five minutes to chase the stiff detective out of the room, we both hated when cops did this and Stacy was in protective best friend mode. She winked at me, shot the detective a mean stink eye and left the room, leaving the door open a crack.

When we were alone, the detective sat in the now vacant chair, pulling out notes and a few photographs from her binder. "I apologize for bothering you while you are still recovering, but the more information I can collect the faster I can close this case." She clicked her pen, "Can you start from the beginning? I know you told the boys yesterday everything you remembered, but if I could hear it again, it would help."

I scooted further up in the bed, already irritated by the lack of overall care most police detectives exhibited when they did hospital visits. Not really caring about the injured person on the bed, the physical and emotional pain they were in, just if they could offer up clues and statements to speed up the case.

I always hated it and would always keep the cops out of the rooms as long as I could. I motioned to the bottle of water Stacy left on my tray, "Can you hand me that?"

Detective Scarlett nodded, handing me the bottle then stared at me, waiting.

I blew out a breath, fidgeting with the bottle cap. "All I remember is going down to platform 3 at Federal Square to wait for the metro. There were two other people besides the group of men over by the bathroom." I furrowed my brow as my memory slowly replayed last night. "I did nothing to provoke the group. I stood next to a kid that looked like he was an intern." I paused trying to control my emotions that were begging me to cry as I shifted and felt pain in every inch of my body.

"Can you describe what he looked like?" Detective Scarlett jumped on the quick pause.

I gave her a shitty look, "He was tall, maybe six one. Brown hair, and looked like a thousand other interns swarming around the capital at any given day." I squeezed the water bottle before taking a slow sip.

"You mentioned to the officers that there was a man sitting on a bench reading a magazine. Can you describe him?"

God was this woman cold, "I don't know if it was a man or a woman. I couldn't tell. They were wearing a blue baseball cap with letters on it, sunglasses and they wore a hood over their head. I only noticed they were reading Popular Science." I glared at the woman, "Aren't there cameras in the station? Why can't you review the tape? See all of us on the platform and stop bothering me? Isn't it clear to you detectives that I was just a random attack by bored drug addicts? Drug addicts that I am sure will be back in the same spot tonight looking for their next target." I was getting angry, trying to hold back my tears and from shouting at this woman to piss off and find the men who beat the hell out of me and beat the hell out of them.

Detective Scarlett smiled tightly, clicking her pen closed she pulled out a few photographs, "Normally, yes, each station has cameras placed at the entrances and exits. Allowing for full coverage of the platforms and the tunnels." She held the stack of photographs in her hands, "As for finding the men who attacked you, we don't need to do that, Ms. Ivers." Handing over the photographs, she continued, "All four men who attacked you were murdered. Brutally murdered, and by the looks of it, by someone who knew exactly what they were doing."

I stared in the woman's brown eyes before drifting to look at the crime scene photographs. Three bodies were scattered on the concrete floor, pools of blood dotting underneath them. There was a puddle of an orange red liquid that wasn't blood, leading towards the edge of the platform, disappearing down onto the tracks.

There were no close-up images of the fatal injuries on the men, only wide shots of the whole scene. I looked over the photographs, not feeling much of anything. I had seen worse in my days as an emergency room nurse and it would take a lot more to make my stomach turn. Then there was one small fact, I felt no remorse for these men. They had gotten what they deserved. I set the photographs down next to the uneaten jello on the tray table in front of me, "Am I suspect?"

Detective Scarlett shook her head, noting the lack of any reaction to the death of my attackers, she glared back at me before speaking, "Not at all. I spoke to the doctor treating you and he informed me that your injuries were debilitating. Meaning you were barely able to get away let alone inflict the immense amount of physical damage these men endured." She looked at me for a minute, "You don't remember anyone coming to your aid? Anyone coming into the station at the last second?"

She reached over and pointed at the first man, "This man died from choking on his own blood. The bones in his throat were shattered and sliced through his arteries, after his forearm was broken in two like a dried piece of wood." She then pointed at the next one, face down with a pool of blood under his head, "This one. The back of his skull shattered by the fire extinguisher that appears to have been thrown at him. He fell on his face and died instantly when the force of the impact snapped his neck. The Medical Examiner found pieces of skull imbedded into his brain." She moved to point two more times, continuing with the vivid descriptions, "This man had his nose shoved up into his brain, he was dead before he hit the floor. And here, well, let's just say after the train ran over him, there wasn't much left to identify him by."

Detective Scarlett stared at me, again waiting for a reaction from the gruesome details, but I didn't give her one. "So, you don't recall maybe seeing a police officer, a solider, or someone that carried themselves like they could be a professionally trained fighter, walk onto the platform?

I shook my head, "I blacked out after the one asshole clocked me across the face." I shoved the photographs away, suddenly wanting to be done with this interview since I felt like I was being treated like a suspect or an idiot, not the victim. "Are we done? I'm just going to repeat what I told the officers last night. I don't remember anything else other than what I told them and you."

Picking up the photographs and sliding them back in her binder, Detective Scarlett spoke, "The woman who brought you into the emergency room last night. How do you know her?"

My head shot up to look at the detective. My memory flashing a crystal clear image of the blonde with the soft slate grey eyes, looking at me as I sat in the passenger seat of a car. The way her voice was kind, strong, and made me feel safe when I came to and felt how hurt I really was from the attack.

I also remembered for a split second, through the throbbing of my cheek and the sting of the tears rushing down my face, how beautiful the woman was. How warm her hand was against my cheek when she whispered that I was safe now. I closed my eyes, trying to draw out smaller details that would help me recognize the good Samaritan that took me to my hospital and carried me into the emergency room. Handing me off to the staff and disappeared without leaving a name.

I shook my head, "No, I don't know her. I just moved back to the city and the only people I know around here is Stacy and the rest of the staff I work with." I turned to look at the detective, "If you can find out who she is, I would like to thank her."

She nodded, writing a few notes in her binder, "Thank you Ms. Ivers, I think you've given us a few leads to follow up on." Detective Scarlett stood up, pulling on her sleeves, "I will leave my card and if you think of anything, please call me. I'll be in touch as we work on this case." She smiled tightly, "And I hope you get well soon, Ms. Ivers." With that, she hustled out of my room, leaving the door open.

I fell back into my pillows, closing my eyes and letting a few tears slip out. I was tired, sore, in pain, and every time I stopped thinking for more than a second, I would see their faces. I could feel their hands grab at me then, hit me. Hear the disgusting laughter as I hit the concrete floor hard, falling to the mercy of violent drug addicts.

I took a few deep breaths, forcing my brain to find anything else to think about to calm my turning stomach and racing heart. I tried to think about my current patients, work, the piles of boxes I still had to unpack. None of it helped. Then I let my mind fall to the blonde woman who knelt in front of me, buckling my seat belt. The way she smiled softly, her eyes never leaving mine until the last possible second. The way her voice calmed me down and took the edge off my shock.

I focused on her and my heart rated slowed, my stomach stopped turning, and I began to breathe easier.

I kept her in my head even as I heard Stacy shuffle back into the room, "Dr. Owens said if I can get you to pee, I can take you home in an hour. So I brought a pitcher of water and a straw." She set the pitcher down, "I eavesdropped a little, that detective is a bitch."

I chuckled, keeping my eyes closed with the blonde hovering behind my eyelids. As I went to open them, my mind picked up on something in the memory of the blonde. When she stood up to close my door, I caught a glimpse of a hood hanging over the back of her jacket and a quick flash of the blue brim of a baseball cap hanging out of her back pocket.

My eyes flicked open, reaching for the pitcher of water I half barked at Stacy, "Can you call Roger in security and ask him for a favor? Ask if he'll let me take a look at the security footage of when I arrived in the emergency room?"

I dropped the straw in the pitcher and started drinking the water. "Tell him I will buy him doughnuts for a month."

Stacy shrugged, picking up the in room phone, "I don't think he needs the doughnuts, but yeah I can ask. I'm sure he'll do it since he has a crush on you." She dialed the security office, looking back at me, "What are you looking for? The cops are trying to get a warrant for the same footage."

I licked my lips, "A blonde. A blonde who I think saved my life."

"Can any of you give me three quick tactical facts that made Erwin Rommel so successful in the North Africa campaign of World War Two?"

Half of the students in the room shot their hands up, making me smile and point at the eager Ensign in the back, "Ensign Christenson."

The young man in the black short sleeved uniform the Academy allowed the Midshipmen to wear during the spring, stood up straighter than a board, "Yes ma'am. Rommel was successful because he was willing to put himself in the front lines and lead his troops. He utilized the speed of his tanks over his enemies to an advantage and he often caught his enemies by surprise before they had a chance to organize their own defenses."

I nodded, "Thank you Ensign. You may be seated." I walked over to the white board, scribbling the three answers I was just given under the handful of other lecture notes I had written over the last hour. "Even though Field Marshal Rommel was a part of the German army, and an enemy to the Allies, he still was one of the greatest military tacticians of the war. And as they always say, history repeats itself. I believe that we all can learn from our enemies as much as we can our allies."

I set the black marker down on the small desk, looking at the clock, "Alright, that's the end of class. For next week, I would like you all to read chapters ten to twenty one in your text, as well as pick one great military leader throughout history and write their greatest tactical successes and failures."

Folding my arms across my chest, I scanned the room of future naval officers in front of me. Intense with giving me their full attention, "I will be extending the due date until next week as well. I know it's a drill weekend and I would much rather have you all focus on getting a good night of sleep versus staying up late to get a paper written."

The buzzing bell cut me off. The entire room stood up at full attention, waiting for my command. I waved my hand, "Class dismissed."

A unified yes ma'am filled the room before they all filed out in an orderly fashion. I smiled, thinking back to my days here and how I was so high strung that I could probably turn coal into diamonds in my palm for how hard I clenched them on a daily basis.

I wiped the white board clean before collecting my notes and dropped them in my briefcase, noticing that my right palm had a small purple bruise growing from where I drove it into a face last night. I stretched out the hand, feeling that it was a little sore, but not anything that would hinder the rest of my day or need further attention. Picking up my briefcase, I exited the room and headed towards my office. Nodding at the rushing students who cast firm ma'am's my way.

It was the end of the class day for me and I was exhausted. Only managing two hours of sleep before having to get up and make it to my eight o'clock class. The impromptu trip to the emergency room had taken more time than I wanted. I barely escaped without being cornered to give up my information and why I was bringing in the battered brunette.

I stared at the frosted glass of my office door, *Commander V. Bancroft, USN Ret. - Military History and Tactics*, painted in gold on the pebbly glass. I hated that I had to have my formal title on the door instead of just my name, but tradition and protocol ran deep in the Naval Academy.

Pushing the door to my office open, I frowned at the sight of the redhead in the khaki colored Navy uniform sitting on the edge of my desk, flipping through the stack of graded papers. "Dani, don't mix those up. They're in alphabetical order by class."

She rolled her eyes and set the stack down, "Sorry Professor Bancroft." She moved to flop down in the chair facing my desk as I closed the door and locked it. Dropping my briefcase on the floor next to my desk, I took off my dark blue suit jacket, "I'm not a Professor, just an instructor."

She raised her eyebrows at me, "Well I can't call you Commander since you are retired and refuse to wear a uniform." She brushed at her gold Lieutenant bars, "And I can't call you by your first name in the sacred halls of the Naval Academy, so Professor it is."

I rolled my eyes, pulling up the sleeves of my button down as I sat, "Why are you in my office anyway? I thought they rarely let you out of your cave over in the basement." I leaned back in my leather chair, scanning over all the paperwork I would have to take home. Midterms were in a week and I would have to submit grades soon.

Dani squinted at me, "I'm here because I did what you asked last night and scrubbed the security footage from the station. But we have a small problem."

I didn't look up from the stacks I was mentally organizing, "Did the old man get wind of the request?"

She shook her head, "Nope. You know he doesn't care what his freelance artists do. As long as the interests of Voltaire are kept intact, you can do whatever you want. They will just wash their hands clean of you if the time ever came."

Dani leaned forward, her green eyes staring at me until I finally looked up. "Then what is it Dani?" She was beginning to irritate me.

She smiled, "I love it when I irritate you. Anyway, the problem is a rookie detective over at the Metro Police Department. She is attached to one of the old guys going through her FTO for the homicide division and didn't quite understand why they were all brushing it off as a gang on gang crime. That those shit bags all took a little too much oxy and turned on each other. She is poking around at the morgue, noticing that the damage you inflicted was more than just high-ons bashing each other." Dani paused, "I intercepted the warrant request for the hospital security footage, rerouted it to the bottom of every pile of every judge in town. It will take her until at least next Christmas to have a judge even look at it."

I nodded, "You didn't scrub the hospital." It wasn't a question. I knew Dani would avoid scrubbing private security systems. It would draw too much attention and in a month's time, the hospital would recycle the tapes and any footage collected would be recorded over.

"Nope, more work than its worth. I figure this hotshot will keep running into walls with our guys inside the department. She'll eventually bend and give up to the bullshit ways of police cover ups. Then she can move on to the cases she thinks she can solve." Dani stood up as she finished her sentence and smoothed out her uniform, "I have to get back to the basement, the old man has sent over a new job for you and I need to run the usual on it before I hand it over." She turned to head to the door, pausing with her hand on the doorknob, glancing over her shoulder at me, "I watched the footage before I scrubbed it. You saved that woman's life. What ever happened to your rule of never getting involved, Victoria?"

I looked up in her green eyes, hesitating to find a reason why I did get involved. Finally, I shrugged, "I just did."

Dani gave me a strange look, "Fair enough."

She pulled the door open and went to step out when I blurted out, "Can you find out who that woman was and if she's okay?" I swallowed slowly, wondering why I was asking for this information. I really never did get involved but over the last day, I couldn't stop thinking about the brunette and the way she looked in my eyes in the car. I couldn't stop thinking about her and who she was.

Dani grinned at me, pointing at me with her thumb and forefinger like a gun, "You got it Professor. I will have something for you tonight." She skipped out of my office, closing the office door behind her.

Leaving me in the cool silence of my office, I reached for the stack of papers, picked up a red pen and set to grading the essays on General George S. Patton and his influence on modern military history

Chapter 2

"I'm sorry Alex, but these cameras ain't high grade. I can only get what you're looking at." Roger wiped at his mouth, smearing the powdered sugar on his chin, as I leaned painfully forward in my wheelchair.

Roger ran the monitoring system of the security department and spent his days sitting in a dark room in a comfortable chair. Watching the three hundred plus cameras the hospital had. Roger was big man, in height and girth. A big nice guy, in his early forties, with a kind heart and a weakness for pretty girls and doughnuts. Two things I was taking advantage of in asking for a favor. I needed to know what the blonde looked like and it was worth the twenty dollars I spent on doughnuts.

I had Stacy get me a wheelchair and roll me to the elevator before she started her shift. She rolled me in the elevator and left me with another bottle of water. Emphasizing that I should spend more time working on peeing and getting home, rather than digging in things I shouldn't.

But I had to know who this woman was. This woman who came out of nowhere to scoop me up, take me to the hospital and left me feeling a small trace of something I had never felt before. It was as if my gut was driving me to find her, as if she held some sort of answers I had been looking for in life. If anything, maybe she knew who took care of the four assholes and I could find them and thank them for exacting vigilante justice.

"Is there any more footage from the ER's west entrance?" I squinted at the blurry screenshot of myself being carried through the sliding glass doors in the arms of a woman with long blonde hair tied up in a ponytail. I swallowed down a dry throat, squeezing the water bottle in my hands. I was suddenly very anxious the moment Roger began plucking through last night's footage.

He rolled the black mouse with a chubby hand, tapping the play key and setting the blurry screenshot back into motion. "There's a little from the main entrance, but nothing that was any good." He clicked a few more times, "There is this, the pole camera that looks down on the ambulance lane."

I sat and watched as a plain black sedan stopped in front of the ER. The blonde climbed out of the driver's seat and as she went to move to the passenger side, she looked up and made direct eye contact with the camera. Frowning and dropping her head down to tuck it away from the camera. "Pause it! Right here!" I jutted my hand out, frightening Roger mid bite of his third jelly doughnut. He slapped the keypad, pausing the video. I waved excitedly, "Rewind a few seconds to where she steps out of the car."

Roger did as I asked, and when he paused the footage, I let out a ragged breath. Staring at the face of my savior. "Can you print this up?" I glanced hopefully his way.

Roger looked at me, "Alex, I could get in a ton of trouble having you down here and accessing the DVR." He glanced at the doughnut in his fingers, then back at me. I smiled as best as I could around my split, swollen lip, "Roger, please? I just want to thank her for saving my life." I nodded to the half empty box of doughnuts. "I will buy a dozen a week for a month straight."

Roger sighed, hitting the print button, "Don't tell anyone that I did this for you. I could lose my job. And don't you take that to the police, I heard some detective lady was asking about our footage, but was denied until she gets a warrant." He grabbed the piece of paper as it whispered out of the printer, handing it over to me.

It was still warm and when I looked at her face, I felt shivers run through my hands and up my arms. The paper was warm like her hand had been. Like her voice and her eyes. I smiled looking up at Roger, "My lips are forever sealed." I bent over the side of the wheelchair, giving him a quick kiss on the cheek before I folded up the screenshot and tucked it in my pocket. I laughed lightly at how much Roger blushed as I rolled the wheelchair out of the security room and back towards the elevator.

I had to find Stacy and I had to pee. Then I could go home and start looking for the blonde.

I had to find her and I wasn't exactly sure why.

I loved my house.

My medium sized craftsman house with grey siding with white trim, and the perfect amount of trees and flowers to give it a very cozy feeling. My nice little house sat on a quiet street in a quiet suburb across the harbor from the Naval Academy. My neighbors were quiet older retirees from the Navy, or other branches of the military, and left me alone.

I had one lovely older couple next door to me, Dale and Mary, who kept an eye on my house, picked up my newspaper and mail if I was out of town for a few days.

More often than not, I would end up talking to Dale for hours over the fence on Sunday afternoons discussing lawn fertilizer and how the Navy has changed since he served in the Vietnam War.

I had Dani immediately run both of them the second I bought the house and moved in. Mary was a retired elementary teacher who was clean as a whistle. Not even a traffic citation or contact with the police, other than bringing cupcakes to the local police department a few times a year to thank them.

Dale was a retired Navy Captain who was drafted during Vietnam and proudly served his country until he retired five years ago to tinker with his classic '63 Mustang and cultivate his impressive flower garden. Digging into Dale, he was harmless. Never indulged in the intelligence side of the Navy and was also clean as a whistle, if not cleaner than his wife. The two were just living the true American dream, married high school sweethearts who served their community and took the lonely single woman next door under their watchful eye.

I enjoyed Dale and Mary, they made me feel normal. Or at least they helped me maintain the shell of a normal person. Smiling, waving and helping take the trash cans in for my arthritic neighbors. Then I would retreat into my beloved home, into my den and sit in front of my heavily secured laptop to open up the other side of my life.

The one side where I killed without hesitation and discretion. Doing it for money and my country.

Waving at Mary as she stood out on the driveway, watering the lawn, I walked into my house. Closing the front door behind me and locking it, I let out an exasperated sigh as I hung up my jacket. I was close to exhaustion and wanted nothing more than to change into my comfy sweatpants and a t-shirt then relax for a few hours before diving into grading papers or whatever new job was waiting for me on the laptop.

Walking through the living room towards my den, I mentally noted tomorrow's lesson plan that still needed to be typed up. I would finish the last handful of papers to grade and then I could collapse on my giant couch in front of my giant TV. Setting my briefcase on the old mahogany wood desk, I glanced at the nondescript black laptop. Sitting there as lifeless as an inanimate object would, but it wasn't so inanimate. It was ominous. Ominous because of the things I knew would be waiting for me the second I started it up.

I turned away from the desk and headed to my bedroom, eager to strip out of my Professor business suit. Unbuttoning the dress shirt with every step, stifling a few yawns, I debated just going to bed. It didn't matter that it was only half past three in the afternoon, I was tired and nothing sounded more appealing than curling up under my blankets and getting a good night's sleep. Hoping some sleep would chase away thoughts of the brunette.

It only took one look at my big soft bed, and I was done for. I changed into my pajamas of linen shorts and a big baggy sleep shirt. I set my cell phone on the nightstand, drew the room darkening curtains closed and fell into bed. Snuggling deep into the rich down pillows, I reached for the remote and turned on another massive TV hanging on the wall across the room from the bed.

The screen lit up the room and I smiled as I heard the smooth, giddy voice of Katherine Hepburn fill the room. Her face in black and white quickly following as she traipsed around the screen chasing Cary Grant in *Bringing up Baby*. I let out a deep breath, pulled the blanket up closer and eventually drifted off to the sounds of her unique laughter.

Two hours later, I woke up to the sound of my phone wiggling around the nightstand. Groaning, I rolled over and grabbed it without looking at the display. There was only one person who ever called me. "Dani." I half yawned around saying her name.

"Professor. Did I wake you?" I rolled my eyes as I sat up in the bed, Dani clearly did not care if she had woken me up. She rarely cared about much in our love hate relationship.

I pushed my hair back, squinting at the TV to see Maureen O'Hara in the Quiet Man, "Why ask if you don't really care?" I sighed, "Let me guess, I need to get the laptop."

"First, yes, you need to get online. I have your next job and I need to go over it with you, per the request of the old man." I could hear the others she worked with in the basement murmuring in the background, "Second, I care. Sometimes. Well, not all the time, but you are my favorite plumber so far."

I stood up from the bed, stretching as I walked to head back downstairs, "Should I take that as a compliment?"

"You should, because you are the one who has lived the longest out of the others." Dani's voice changed to sincere and serious for a split second before she returned to obnoxious, "Anyway, Professor, are you at your laptop? I would like to get home before rush hour."

"Give me a minute." I jogged down the final few steps and rushed into the den. I had learned over the last few years that Dani could be impatient and the more impatient she became, the more driven she became to irritate me. She was already doing a stellar job by calling me Professor.

Sliding into the old leather chair, I fired up the laptop. Punching in my password and ensuring that the ISP rerouted and the encryption was operating at a high level, I clicked on the small envelope icon. "Okay I'm online."

"Copy. Let me go secure the phone line." I heard a series of three clicks, "Okay, all set. Open up your email and let's get started."

Once I clicked on the icon, the dossier spilled out over the screen. Filling it with photographs ranging from close ups on a driver license to wide shot surveillance images.

"Thomas H. Emerson. Thirty two years old, single white male. He lives up in King George, and works for the Congressman out of Delaware, district nine. He fell onto our radar per the request of the tea drinkers overseas. It appears he has been doing a little bit of inside trading in regards to drug smuggling. Since his kind older boss is rallying for DEA reform, Tommy here has been using those classified memos sent back and forth between the Congressman and the DEA to help the Colombian cartel spread their business out to the England and Ireland markets. Primarily trafficking heroin over there in mass quantities and leaving overdosed bodies everywhere."

Dani paused as she pulled up the DMV photograph of Thomas. He was a typical blonde hair, brown eyed, political science major. He had a car salesman smile and a cockiness that dripped from his eyes and made me frown. I hated cockiness. I also hated the graphic photos from the police crime scenes, primarily the ones of young kids dead in pools of their own vomit from the uncut heroin the cartel flooded their neighborhood with. All because Thomas was a son of a bitch working under the guise of serving his community and country proudly. He was a cocky lying shit, and I despised liars.

I clicked on his records, primarily his banking records. Instantly picking up on the spontaneous large withdrawals after multiple medium sized deposits. "What is his vice? Drugs, hookers, gambling, booze?" I scrolled through the records, he was a typical idiot drug smuggler informant. The cartel would take great care in depositing money in reasonable amounts that would not send off alarms, but Thomas would pull out of his money in large chunks.

Dani chuckled, "You are good at this game, Professor. Tommy has expensive tastes in prescription pills and middle class escorts. We have surveillance of him in his condo outside of D.C. getting high on Suboxone, Xanax, OxyContin and running through a handful of internet ladies of the night. He just indulged in a weekend binge that looks like he barely survived it."

I leaned on my palm, scrolling through more records. "Send me the address and tell the old man it will be done Saturday night." I clicked the files closed, already having memorized everything I needed, "I want the usual payment an hour after I send out the completion notice." I leaned back in the chair, yawning slightly, rubbing my growling stomach. "Goodbye Dani."

"Whoa now, Professor. I have that little extra you asked for last night. Check your email, the message marked creeper." Dani chuckled, "Goodnight Professor, I will be eagerly awaiting your phone call."

She hung up before I could grumble out a retort.

I hesitated opening the email. Chewing on my bottom lip as I debated why I wanted to get further involved with the brunette. It had been a spontaneous request that I had forgotten about after grading endless essays. I sat staring at the screen, trying to find any justification to open the email and learn everything about the stranger I saved last night.

I sighed, standing up from my desk, I walked to the kitchen. Digging in the refrigerator for sandwich making components, I continued to internally debate what to do.

Yes, she was beautiful and intriguing. Her strength and sassiness in the face of four men was admirable. Then there was the way she looked at me, the way her dark blue eyes gave me shivers in the strangest way. But then there was the fact I had killed those four men and that my life was not one easily inhabited by me, let alone another. My past failed relationships were proof of that. I was always hiding something and letting my significant other think I was a cheating whore. Leaving at odd hours of the night or for days at a time, always coming back to shower immediately and saying I had to work late. My life had become very solitary and I liked it. It made it easier to pretend when I only had to pretend for one.

Slapping bread on the roasted chicken and Havarti sandwich, I threw it on a plate and grabbed a beer from the fridge and searched out my briefcase, before returning to the den. Continuing to ignore the still on laptop, I pulled out the last of the papers I had to grade and turned on the TV across from the desk.

I smiled as another of my favorite classics was on, surrounding me in the classic sounds of movies that were of a simpler time. Just silly love stories or stories of the heart, no violence, car chases, graphic love scenes. Just gentleman and ladies swooning respectfully over each other in black and white. I busied myself with eating the sandwich and grading papers in between quick glances at the TV. When finally, as I was on my last paper, a woman sauntered onto the screen to mingle with Ava Gardner. A woman who had the same angles and same dark eyes as the brunette.

I found myself staring at the screen and not paying attention to the dialogue, just watching the woman as she spoke her three lines and disappeared from the screen. Leaving Ava and I both curious about a mysterious brunette who just whisked in to our lives for a handful of minutes.

Blowing out a breath, I tossed the last half of my sandwich down on the plate and reached for the laptop. I didn't blink as I clicked the tiny little white envelope. Filling my screen with driving record, current mailing address that placed her in the not so good parts of D.C., her college transcripts, banking files and ending with her direct deposit account that had her working at Capital City Hospital. Which was a short walk from the metro station where we happened across each other. At the end of the files telling me everything I needed to know about the brunette, her driver's license ended the small flood of information I had sifted through.

It was a driver's license issued by New York State and was about a year old. The brunette was grinning, her bright blue eyes smiled with her. I felt my stomach wiggle when I looked over the undamaged face. She was even more beautiful without the bruises and blood I first saw her in. My eyes drifted to her name, Alexandra A. Ivers.

Squinting at the screen, I whispered, "Nice to meet you Alexandra."

I winced as I sat down on the rickety metal chair in front of my equally as rickety metal desk I had pilfered from the city dump back in New York City. I was still very sore and getting worse as the mild painkillers Dr. Owens prescribed me, began to fade away.

Reaching for my laptop, I unwound the USB cord to hook up my all in one printer, dropping the image of the blonde Roger had gotten me on the glass top. I was going to try an old trick the one NYPD cop I dated for minute, had taught me. Scan a person's picture into your computer and then do a Google image search. Nine times out of ten, you would find a match since the entire world was addicted to over sharing.

I shifted in the cold chair, waiting for my laptop to warm up and the scanner to finish. Looking around my small apartment that had an industrial feel, I felt very alone. The cold exposed steel beams in the ceiling and the exposed brick work had felt cozy and hip when I first viewed the place, but now it felt too sterile and lonely. I knew it was a side effect of being attacked and coming down off all the painkillers they had forced into me to keep me awake and calm to tell my story. But that knowledge did very little to cure the feeling of wanting someone to come home to and talk to. Whether it was a roommate or a lover, I really could use someone right now.

I wiped away the few tears that escaped, leaning forward to focus on the laptop and not my pity party. I clicked the dialog box telling me the scan was successful. The security image was fuzzier on my computer but the image was still clear enough I could dump it into Google and have it accepted. After clicking and dragging the image to the search bar, I leaned back as it searched through the endless information super highway. While the search engine did the work, I removed my cellphone from the clear plastic patient's belongings bag I was sent home with.

There were only four missed calls from my mother. I groaned, Stacy had told me she called my mother since she was the emergency contact on my paperwork. I couldn't get upset with her about calling my mom and then having her call me incessantly.

No one at work knew my past or that I was a loner by choice. My family lived down near the Tennessee border in Virginia and I had always had limited contact with them since I graduated from college and struck out on my own. My true family was just mother and I, and she lived up in Sperryville, still a lengthy drive away. When I was five, my real father pulled the typical, "I'm running out for cigarettes" routine and never came home. Leaving my mother and I to do the best we could.

Tapping the call back button, I closed my eyes and stood up, hobbling over to sit on the edge of my bed where it would be softer on my sore body. Three rings and my mother's voice bellowed in my ears, "Alexandra Ava Ivers! Why haven't you returned any of my calls? I have been worried sick and almost drove up there to see if you were okay." I could hear the worry, heavy and thick, in her voice and for a split second, it made me feel terribly guilty.

"Sorry, mom. I just got home from the hospital and turned my phone back on." I winced again sitting on the bed and scooting back to lie against the pillows. I sucked in a breath to steady my voice, "I'm fine. Just a few scrapes and bruises." I reached up to run my fingers over the still swollen cheek under my left eye, grazing my fat lip with butterfly bandages keeping it together.

"Please don't lie to me, your friend Stacy sounded scared when she called me. What happened?" I could hear my mother pacing around the island in her kitchen.

"I was mugged. The stupid mini died on me and I opted to take the metro. I was in the wrong place at the wrong time." I frowned realizing that the stupid mini was still at the hospital, lifeless. A reminder that I now couldn't take the metro and would have to waste money on cabs. "It's okay, a Good Samaritan took me to the hospital and I'm fine, mom. I promise." I glanced at the laptop, the hourglass icon still spinning as Google continued to search.

My mother sighed, "Maybe it's time you leave the big city. The hospital down here is hiring. They always need good nurses."

"Mom, you know I would wither away in a small town." I picked at the edge of the afghan laying on the corner of the bed, "I'll be fine. I just need a new car." I paused. I hated having these kind of conversations because it always felt like I was disappointing my mother by not settling down in the small town she lived in. Marrying a handsome doctor, popping out three grandchildren and living the dream she wanted for me.

"Alexandra, please. You know we are all each other have in this world." Her voice trembled before she sniffled.

I sighed, "You have Bill and the dogs, mom." I tried my best to comfort her. I was her only blood family and felt all of the guilt she was handing down. "How about I rent a car and drive down for the weekend? I've been given two weeks off to rest up and heal."

As my mother eagerly agreed, I saw the search had ended. A small box telling me that there were three possible matches for my submitted image. Swinging out of the bed, I hobbled back to the desk and hurried an earnest goodbye and I love you to my mother before hanging up and dropping the phone on the desk.

Sliding gingerly back onto the metal chair, I clicked the results and felt a wave of nervousness rush over my entire body. The first close match was a tall man who was an online organic produce seller. Tall, lanky, lean and long blonde hair that made him look female if you squinted. The second result was a twenty two year old girl who had a million and half selfies of her surfing out in Southern California. Lean, lanky and long blonde hair, but clearly too young and too far away to be the blonde I was looking for, that and she had blue eyes.

The third search result brought me to the faculty page of for the Naval Academy. To a portrait shot of a woman with light blonde hair in a full dress uniform of the United States Navy. I gasped as I recognized the slate grey eyes in the portrait as the same ones that were my lighthouse in the storm that terrible night. Staring at the photograph, I felt myself shivering. From nerves, excitement and a thousand other things I couldn't place. The woman was even more beautiful in her naval uniform, slightly smiling at the camera in a way that was professional, but kind.

I scrolled down to look for her name, my nerves boiling to the edge as I took my time. Worried that there wouldn't be a name, that this would be too easy to find her, but at the bottom, there was a name.

Commander Victoria Bancroft, USN Ret. – Instructor of Military History and Tactics.

I leaned back in my chair, curling up and rubbing my arms to chase away the shivers. "Victoria. Your name is Victoria."

Thomas sat next to me on the gaudy leather couch that he no doubt paid for with his cartel money. We continued watching the action movie he had playing on the impressive large screen television when I broke in through his back door near the kitchen. He had the sound up so loud on his movie theater grade sound system, that he never heard, or saw me, as I stuck the needle in his neck. Injecting him with a tranquilizer that would get muddled in with the rest of the prescription drugs I was about to force feed him.

"How can you watch this crap, Thomas?" I looked over at him, reaching up to drop four more pills down the thick tube I inserted in his throat to make the delivery of pills and booze that much more natural. I followed the pills with a chaser of nice bourbon I had bought just for the occasion. "It's all digital effects, no real talent in the acting. And look? I mean a car physically cannot do that. Physics just doesn't work that way."

Thomas was alive for the moment, but with every minute that passed, he was sliding deeper into an overdose coma and by the end of this terrible movie, he would be dead. I glanced at my watch, pulling back the edge of my black rubber gloves, I was right on schedule. Reaching into my bag, I flicked the top off another prescription bottle of suboxone. Shaking out a small handful of the pills, I sprinkled the rest around Thomas and on the floor. Standing up, I started dropping pill after pill down the tube and looked around the living room. I spotted his briefcase tucked in the corner by the coat rack near his front door. I walked over to it and rifled through it, easily finding the burner cellphone, some bank receipts and a plane ticket to Colombia, hidden in a side pocket. I sighed, looking over at Thomas, "You're really dumb, Thomas. You've made this far too easy for me."

I haphazardly tossed the items around the living room for when the police showed up, they could close the case quickly with all the evidence laid out for them. Chalking it up to another untraceable cartel hit and leave it at that. The old man and the tea drinkers would be happy with the lack of attention brought by Thomas's death being labelled an overdose and having the cartels information link to Congress, severed.

I moved back to Thomas, picking up the bourbon and reaching to dump the rest of the pills and the bottle down his throat, when he suddenly lurched forward. Coughing, gagging, his hands flailing up to grab at his throat and the tube I had shoved in there. "Shit."

I rushed over to the man, wrapped my fingers around the tube and yanked it as hard as I could. Ripping it out of his throat, I stepped back as I heard the ominous sounds of him about to throw up. And he did. Thomas began throwing up all over the couch and the coffee table in front of him. Throwing up all of the pills and booze I had force fed him.

I clenched my jaw, hesitating as I hated getting dirty, but if I didn't do what I was about to, Thomas would live and I would have to take a messier route. I wasn't interested in giving him a Cuban neck tie tonight, too bloody for what I was wearing.

I rolled my neck and knelt down next to the still vomiting man. He looked up in my eyes with panic and hope. Hope that I would help him, but instead I smiled as I slid my left hand to the back of his and tangled my fingers in his thinning hair. Yanking his head back up, making him whimper in pain, I clamped my right hand over his mouth and pinched his nose shut, cutting off all of his air supply.

Thomas clutched at my arms, trying to get a hold on me but was far too intoxicated to do so. Limp hands and rubbery fingers just slapped at my arms as I held tight, watching his face turn purple. I stared in his eyes, watching the life drain out. I didn't even look away when I heard him gurgle and throw up. My hand holding his mouth closed caused him to start choking on his own vomit. Through it all, I felt nothing but mild annoyance this was taking much longer than I had planned.

It only took three more minutes before Thomas finally gave in and fell limp. I released him and stepped back, letting his head fall forward and smash into the corner of the coffee table. The coroner would write this up as an overdose gone horribly wrong. Thomas threw up so violently that he fell forward, split his forehead open and ended up suffocating himself in his own vile. It would be a messy, embarrassing death that would have his family and neighbors whispering about how he was such a good boy, that they could never believe him to be a drug addict or a drunk.

Wasting no more time, I collected my bag and walked back out the back door. I locked it up and retraced my steps through the condominium complex, keeping my head up and eyes forward so I would not garner too much attention. I would just look like a run of the mill female, carrying an overnight bag, smiling and giggling as she spoke to her lover about being excited to spend the weekend at their place.

I kept the image up until I was back at my car parked in the side lot of the convenience store next to Thomas's complex. Dropping the bag in the trunk, I walked inside to pick up a gallon of milk and a pint of strawberry ice cream. I smiled at the older lady clerk, rubbing my stomach as she looked at the two random items, "Pregnancy cravings are a bitch. I don't even like strawberries."

The lady smiled at me warmly, "Oh honey, I know how that is. I have three daughters and we all had the same strange late night cravings. But next time you should have your husband go out for you. You should be at home resting." She chuckled shaking her head about my fictional husband not being as doting as she wanted.

I laughed with her, "He's next door getting me tacos to go. Divide and conquer the cravings." I took the bag from her, "But I'll make sure he gets the next round." I waved at her and left the store. My fake smile dropping from my face the second I walked out of the door.

I dropped the plastic bag in the passenger seat and pulled out of the lot. I didn't need the milk or the ice cream, but I needed an alibi since the convenience store had cameras on the exterior. The older lady would not remember the nice friendly pregnant lady on a Saturday night. Instead she would tell the police about the five different shady customers who came in that night, if they ever came to question her about Thomas and his death. It was a little extra effort on my part to cover my bases, but it was one of the reasons why I was the old man's favorite. I left nothing to chance.

Pulling out on to the main road that would take me to the freeway, I looked up at the street sign as I sat at a red light, instantly recalling the brunette. Alexandra's apartment was less than two blocks away. Tapping my fingers on the steering wheel, I debated it. Debated driving to her apartment and seeing if she was alright from a distance. Her discharge papers had been in the file Dani sent me. I knew she would be home, and I suddenly wanted to go and see if her apartment was safe since the neighborhood she lived in wasn't.

I sighed, "Don't get involved, Victoria. Go home. Make a milkshake and go to bed." I murmured the words in the quiet of the car. "You've already done too much."

The light turned green and I started driving towards the freeway. I clenched my jaw in awkward silence, my thoughts twisting together as to why I should and should not being doing this until I smashed the radio power button, chasing out the silence and my thoughts with today's top 40 hits. Chasing away the white noise before my heart and my gut forced my hands to turn the car back around and drive to her apartment.

I couldn't get involved.

I repeated that phrase over and over in my head the entire drive back to my house.

I couldn't get any more involved.

But I knew I would, it was only a matter of time before I did. A matter of time before I searched out why her face would show up every time I closed my eyes in the last forty-eight hours.

Chapter 3

"Let your mother do her thing. You know she won't stop." Bill spoke softly as he sat kitty corner from me at the small dinner table in the kitchen. I moved in the chair, trying to smile and not wince as I pressed on very sore and angry bruises.

"I know. I just don't want her to worry." I looked over at my mother, plating the giant sandwiches she was making for Bill and I, rambling nervously about what the neighbors were up to and whatever gossip she felt was necessary to pass on.

"She is going to worry, kid, and looking at you in person, I'm kind of worried too." Bill sighed and leaned forward, picking up his glass of water. "You said you were mugged?"

I turned to look in the soft, yet concerned hazel eyes of my mother's longtime boyfriend. I could see how gruesome my bruises and cuts were in the way he ran his eyes over them, cringing at spots.

Bill had been a part of our lives since I was nineteen and had oddly become my step father even though my mother never wanted to remarry. Bill was good to me, better than good, but still tended to tread lightly. It's as if he knew he wasn't my father and didn't have the right to act like one. I shrugged, patting him on the shoulder, "That's what the police tell me. All I remember is waking up in a strange car, then waking up in the ER with my coworkers hovering over me."

Bill smiled tightly, "The police have anything?"

I shook my head as my mother whisked over, setting her massive creations down in front of us. "Not really. There's a rookie detective on the case. A real stiff woman that has no tact, but I can tell she has nothing to go on." I motioned to the sandwiches, "Let's eat. We can talk more after dinner." I winked at him and turned to my mother to compliment her on the size of the turkey and cheese sandwich in front of me.

After lunch, and after Bill and my mother embarked on their hour long Sunday afternoon walk with the Scotties, Annie and Barney, I snuck out to the back patio with my laptop. Sitting on the cushy chaise to stare out at the massive backyard. The view was my favorite part of my mother's house, sitting on an acre of land that rolled up into the high mountains of Sperryville, Virginia. It was still cool, but there were hints of spring starting to settle in as the treetops were filling in with green leaves. Making me want to take deep breaths of the cool, clean mountain air and continue to chase out the stink of the city and the occasional smells of that night that still lingered in my nostrils.

Curled up in an old blanket. I stared out into the backyard. My mind returning to the blonde and the image from the security cameras. Her eyes, I always returned to her eye and the way they looked at me.

I had come to my mother's house in hopes of trying to forget that night and the crazy idea of finding the blonde who carried me to the hospital. But after a day, I couldn't. I only found myself thinking about her more. To the point that I barely paid any attention to the conversation going on around me or when the dogs happily climbed up on my lap and napped away as I zoned out. I wasn't even able to pay much attention to my mother's insistent requests to stay a few more days until it was settled upon. I apparently had said yes to staying until Wednesday under her watchful eye and care. Which was fine, the longer I was away from the city, the better.

But with every minute I sat in the chaise, burying my nose in the blanket, I grew anxious. My thoughts running to different ways of reaching out to the mysterious woman. Whether it was to email her at her faculty email address, hustle the admissions office for a phone number, or call on a police favor and get an address. Then there was the extreme option, going to the Naval Academy and meeting my savior face to face.

I chuckled to myself, looking up at the evening sky, "You are crazy Alex, you don't even know this woman." I didn't know her, and I should be more concerned with helping that cold detective find the clues to close this case. Not chase after a woman who was there in my moment of need.

A very beautiful, blonde woman with eyes the color of expensive granite.

I fidgeted with the frayed edges of the blankets, turning to the sounds of Barney barking his way back to the house, when spontaneity struck. I dug out my phone, tuning out the sounds of Annie and Barney barking together, showing Bill and my mother the way home, and sent Stacy a text.

-Stacy, want to go to sightseeing at the Naval Academy with me on Wednesday? I will buy you a lobster roll.-

-The Naval Academy? I thought you were over men in uniform?-

I smiled, I was over men in uniform since I broke up with the NYPD cop, but there was something about a woman in uniform that had caught my interest.

–I am, but I'm off for two weeks and Bill tells me it's a must see? There's also an outlet mall outside the campus. –

-Sold. I will pick you up Wednesday morning. –

I shook my head, Stacy was a sucker for shopping, bargains or no bargains. I replied to her and before I locked up my phone, I drifted to the picture gallery. Pulling up the security image I had sent to my phone for quick reference.

The longer I looked over the blurred edges and mottled colors, the more I felt the need to find this woman. It was like I was being driven by a force other than a need to thank her. I wanted to know this woman in a way that had me questioning a lot of things.

Sunday was always my favorite day of the week. It felt slower than the rest of the week and gave me an immense sense of calm. Like the one I was feeling now as I leaned on the top of the wooden fence, listening to Dale tell me about his first few days on a river boat in Vietnam.

"I grew up in Louisiana, Victoria, that's a hot tropical heat on its own. But sitting on those rivers in that metal tub, it felt like I was sitting on the sun and Jesus was dumping hot water over my head." He smiled at me, propping his hand on the top of his rake, "Everything smelled like rotting vegetation. I can't look at cooked spinach without feeling like I am right back on that damn boat." Dale shifted, "I don't imagine it was any better for you at the beginning of your war."

I smiled softly at the old veteran. I had found a strange connection with him, one that came with having seen the things he and I had in our respective wars. "I don't think I will ever like sand again. Especially on a hot day. Hot sand has a smell to it that can haunt you if you let it." I stood away from the fence, looking over my yard and how it lacked the bright colors dotting around Dale's. "I only spent a little bit of time in Iraq after Baghdad fell, then it was back on the boat to keep the kids in line. You know how it is, Captain."

Dale chuckled with me, "Always a babysitter, never really a soldier."

Dale and I both looked up to see Mary pop her head out the patio sliding door, "Victoria, you're more than welcome to join us for dinner. Pot roast and leftover cobbler?" She smiled warmly at me like my own mother would if she was still alive.

I raised my hand politely, "Thanks Mary, but I have a large stack of essays to read before morning. The midshipmen would not understand why their grades were delayed."

Mary grinned, "They would if they had my pot roast." She waved at me, "Leftovers will be there if you want it. Stop on over in the morning and I will send you off with a hearty lunch." Mary then pointed at Dale, "Ten minutes and you better be washed and sitting at the table."

Dale saluted his wife, "Yes ma'am." He then turned to me, "If you change your mind." He raised an eyebrow my way as a silent plea for me to come inside for more war stories.

"I know. Thank you again." We parted ways, entering our houses at the same time. Dale to sit down to a lovely dinner with his wife and I to sit in my den watching old movies with essays, eating leftovers.

Sitting at the desk, I half debated going next door and indulging in a moment of normal. Sit with my neighbors and pretend for an hour or two. Live a normal life, one that was taken away from me against my will.

Pressing the power button on my thin remote, I reached for the first essay on top of the smaller stack I had left to grade before morning. The television lighting up with Cary Grant in *I Was a Male War Bride*, showing in glorious black and white. I smirked to myself, reciting the lines as they were spoken, having seen this movie almost a hundred times. I could recall it in my sleep like I was feeding the lines to Cary from the sidelines. I had also decided on finishing off the lasagna I had made when I got home from my late night job with Thomas. Thinking of how nice the thick, gooey cheese would end this day on a high note.

Flipping open the first page of Ensign Christenson's essay on Patton, I faded into grading mode, barely hearing my phone ring from the far corner of the desk. Blindly reaching for it and answering it, I frowned when I heard Dani's voice.

"Happy Sunday, Professor." Dani sounded less than cheery, but then again she never sounded overly cheery unless she was actively irritating me.

"Dani." I set my red pen down, leaning back in the chair and letting my eyes drift to the screen in an attempt to tune the woman out. "How can I help you?"

Dani laughed softly, "It's more like how can I help you?" The quiet clicks in the background told me she wasn't in the basement, but probably at home. "The old man just sent me confirmation of payment. Should be in your account now and ready for you to spend it on school supplies. He also wanted me to pass on that he and the old lady are very happy with the end result." I heard the obnoxious chuckle under her breath.

I rolled my eyes, it only took thirty seconds for her to irritate me, "Thank you. Is that all?" I looked at the clock, I could only think about the leftover lasagna I had in the fridge, waiting for me to reheat and eat the other half with a big glass of red wine.

Dani sighed, "Actually, no. There is a slight problem." She clicked a few more times making me wonder if the woman was forever in front of a computer, "You popped up late last night on my web search alerts. Looks like someone did an image search for your ugly mug." She paused, "The image looks like it came from the security footage from the hospital where you dropped your brunette damsel off. Why the hell did you look right at the camera? You of all people know better."

I clenched my jaw, "What is your point?" I was agitated now. I had looked up at the one far off parking lot camera. Gauging the distance, I was sure that it was a fixed one that only watched the upper level of the concrete parking structure.

"The point is, I had to go in and scrub the hospital footage before pining it on a fumbling security guard who was deleting last month's footage. I just dumped that night's footage into it right before he hit delete. The poor guy will probably be fired when the hospital has to pull out that footage when that warrant request is finally granted." Dani was rambling before she paused, "If the old man got wind of this..."

I cut her off, "I know." I leaned forward to rest my elbows on the desk top, "Thank you, Dani."

"No problem, Professor. Like I said you are my favorite." I heard her sigh quietly, "Do you want me to have the cleaning crew go check out your brunette's apartment? See how much she has on you?"

I twirled my red pen. I knew that a cleaning crew being sent in would raise some concerns that I would have to sweep under the rug. It would also put a target on the woman, one that would cycle back to me with orders to eliminate her. "You said she only ran my picture?"

"Yup, and it took her right to the Naval Academy website, straight to your horrid faculty photograph. I dug around in her web history and there's nothing more than a handful of visits to a Netflix account and then a map to a small suburb up in Sperryville from her loft in the city." I heard Dani click a few keys, "It's waiting in your email." Dani's voice told me she already knew what I was intending to do.

"Thanks. I can take it from here. I'll let you know if I find anything, but please..."

It was Dani's turn to cut me off, "Got it, Professor. Loose lips means we both end up dead." Dani hung up after issuing a quick goodbye.

Throwing the phone on top of the essays, I opened up my laptop and waited for it to power up. I was internally chastising myself. I never, ever, made mistakes. I had made one mistake a long time ago that led me into this life I now lived.

Clicking on the email from Dani, I opened the file. Looking over this Alexandra's internet browsing history for the last forty-eight hours, stopping as I stared face to face at the blurry image from the parking lot. I shook my head, "This is why you don't get involved." I hit print, grabbing the full address and small map that would take me to her apartment. Dani had also sent over the brunette's phone records, telling me that she had just made a phone call from Sperryville in the last five minutes that traced back to an address where a woman by the name of Katharine Ivers lived.

Running a quick background check on the woman as I walked back upstairs to change, I found the sixty-one year old woman to be her mother.

Giving me hope that Alexandra had returned to her mother's to recuperate for a few days.

Stripping down out of baggy old jeans and loose USN sweatshirt I had worn all day, puttering around the house and the yard, I pulled out the ubiquitous uniform of tight black running pants and black long sleeved running shirt from the closet. Walking past the large mirror on the back of the closet door, reflecting the image of my naval uniforms lined up perfectly to form a muted rainbow of khaki to dark blue and ending in the crisp snow white of my full dress uniform, I also caught the reflection of a memory that I always did my best to ignore whenever a mirror and I were in the same room.

A memory that I couldn't erase, but only cover up with clothing and hide from my direct thoughts. Which I quickly did before I gathered my hair in a ponytail and rushed back downstairs. Only pausing on the way to the garage to pick up the well-worn black duffel bag that Dani called my "plumbers toolbox" from the coat closet, before rushing out the side door to the garage.

Flopping down into the plush burgundy leather seat of the silver BMW X5 SUV, I set my duffel on the passenger seat instead of tucking it into the trunk like I normally did. I would only have to drive three blocks in my personal car before switching it out at the small rental car place where my employer had set up for all of us "plumbers" to utilize the company cars with ease and discretion. Making it even harder to be traced if things went to shit on a job.

I was grateful for this little perk, only for the fact that I had once taken my personal car to a job and ended up having to torch it after I got blood all over the upholstery. Now I only ever drove the company cars for jobs or anything that might result in me using my unique talents.

After quickly switching out the BMW for a plain black sedan, I raced over to the seedy side of the capital city. My jaw clenched as the streets degraded from clean and shiny, to graffiti ridden and full of the night walkers that made my skin crawl. I also felt my stomach turn when I realized that this was the neighborhood Alexandra chose to live in. A wave of wanting to protect her washed over me out of nowhere. I squeezed the steering wheel, funneling out the feeling into the hard plastic. It was a feeling I didn't welcome because it meant that not only was I continuing to get involved, but I was also getting attached.

And getting attached was far worse than getting involved.

Twenty-five minutes later, I was standing inside a half assed attempt to turn a shitty apartment into an industrial hipster loft. There was exposed brick and metal duct work all around the small one-bedroom loft, trying to give off the appeal of deconstructed construction. It only succeeded in exposing the foundation and structure issues of the worn down apartment building. I shook my head and made a note to dig into the landlord's records to see how bad he was gouging his tenants. Then send in one of my city inspector friends to check up on how well the building met up to city codes.

Setting my duffel bag down right next to the front door, I pulled on a pair of leather gloves and started scanning around the loft. There were stacks of brown packing boxes with girly, curvy handwriting in black marker directing the eye to pick out which one had kitchen items and which one had books. There was a full sized bed pushed against the eastern brick wall with white and purple blankets tussled about and left as they laid. There was a medium sized rusted metal desk pushed over and under the large cloudy windows on the southernmost wall. On top of that desk was an older white laptop and a handful of papers scattered around it. There was a tiny kitchen in the far corner of the room. It held nothing more than a refrigerator, a cabinet or two, with an industrial sized sink with clean dishes stacked to one end of it. I noted there was no overflowing trash can of takeout containers. Which meant either this Alexander never ate or she cooked at home a lot.

I wasn't interested in the laptop. I knew Dani would have already had done everything on her end to keep tabs on Alexandra and every little thing she did online. I was more focused on finding out who this woman was and what I would have to do to make her lose interest in me.

I shuffled around the room, picking through many of the boxes. Finding nothing but old medical texts, a handful of romance novels, and a few bestselling nonfiction books I had seen line all the shelves in all of the airports I frequented in my life. I poked in another box, smirking when I saw it was her movie collection, finding a few of the old classics I also carried in my personal movie collection.

In a small box pushed next to the bed, I found picture frames and albums mixed in with framed diplomas from high school, college, and nursing school. I picked up a large stack and sat down on the edge of the bed, looking over the diplomas first. Alexandra A. Ivers had gone to a small town high school in Winchester, Virginia, then moved on to the University of Virginia to graduate with honors in nursing and then moved on to New York City where she received her nursing license. All of the diplomas and degrees were perfectly matted and framed with care. Telling me that the woman was proud of her achievements that took her out of the small town she lived in and on to one of the biggest cities in the world.

I set the diplomas to the side with care and went through the picture albums. The first two documented the woman's life from her high school cheerleading years as a teenager to her big move to New York. Grinning with friends, family, and a few men who looked like boyfriends or suitors. A few of the old Polaroid's had handwritten scribbles on the white band under the glossy image. There was a picture with '*Alex and Jess '00*' written in the open white space. I found another one with a handsome man draped over the brunette labeled, '*Alex and Billy take Brooklyn*' and a handful of other quick notations of fun memories.

I furrowed my brow, smiling as the nickname clicked in my head. "Alex. I kind of like it better than Alexandra." I continued to sift through the plastic covered pages until a sudden pang of guilt fell into my thoughts. Forcing me to slap the albums shut and set them back in the box.

I never ever felt guilt when rifling through people's things. Especially the things of my marks. It was all a part of the job, a part of the research process and getting to know the person. Find the perfect way for them to die and have it mean very little to those investigating it. Granted, those were the marks that I had the time to investigate and set up a perfect scenario like Thomas had experienced a night ago.

But right now I felt guilty.

Guilty that I was sitting in this woman's home. Probably the only place she really felt safe now in this city. Here I was, picking through her things like a nosy neighbor, trying to figure out what kind of threat she was. Well, I was trying to figure out if she was actually a threat, but my gut was telling me she was far from a threat like I understood the true meaning of the term. But then my heart would pipe in and tell me she was a threat, a threat to the foundation I stood on if I continued to get involved.

I took a heavy breath and stood up from the bed, looking for anything that would give me something to chase her away from me. To make her believe I was a last minute superhero that took her to the hospital and nothing more. I turned to the kitchen when my eye caught a small notebook on the black metal nightstand by the bed. The top of the notebook was covered by a thin yellow piece of paper that looked to be an auto mechanic's quote slip. I picked up the yellow paper unfolding it. It was a repair quote for a 1974 Mini Cooper. I smiled at the image of the brunette tooling around in the tiny sports car. As I read over the quote, I saw she was being taken advantage of. She was given a quote that was well over three times the amount it would normally cost to replace the air filter and fix fan belts.

Without thinking, I took a picture of the slip, particularly the address of the shop and phone number. I would make a phone call in the morning and make sure that her car was taken care of and at a reasonable price. I hated when men thought women were ignorant to life on a whole.

Setting the slip to the side, I reached for the small, worn red leather notebook that was bound together by a single black rubber band, doing its best to hold the overstuffed book closed. Picking it up, I flipped to the back without a second thought. Ignoring the postcards stuffed in the crease, the little news clippings, and other tiny mementos one kept in a journal as their life documentation. Knowing that any most recent entry would be in the back.

The last page had a small entry dated from this morning in the same curvy handwriting that was around me on the boxes. A white piece of paper folded in half was tucked on the next page.

"Her name is Victoria Bancroft. I think she is the one who, not only saved me, but could be responsible for those pictures the detective showed me. I haven't told anyone about her since I found her on the internet, because I know I will sound crazy.

All I know is that no matter how much I try to fight it. I want to find her. I need to find her. To say thank you and look in her eyes. Look in her eyes and see if what I felt that night, is still there."

I chewed on the inside of my lip, reading over the private musings of this Alex. I moved a gloved finger to the white paper, flicking it open to reveal it was a print out from the security footage. A hard copy of me staring directly in the camera.

"Shit." I replaced the paper and closed the journal. Setting it back on the nightstand as I found it, I scanned around the loft. My mind working a thousand miles a minute only to settle on a single hard thought.

She felt the same thing I did. She was feeling the same things I was now.

This was not good.

"Alex, are you sure? I can walk with you a little longer?" Stacy looked at me with a semi-concerned look.

I smiled, "It's okay. I can tell how bored to death you are with all of this history." I shoved her gently on the shoulder, "Go and take a break. I saw you staring at the small shops across the street." I shifted on the wooden cane twisted into a spiral Bill gave me when I left this morning, "I have my cane." I waved my hand around the large campus of the Naval Academy, "And a million sailors that will rush to my rescue if need be."

Stacy shrugged, smiling back, "Okay Alex, I'll be back in maybe a half hour and then lunch?"

I nodded, "Sounds like a plan. I just want to check out the admissions building. Bill said something about scheduling a guided tour in there."

Stacy gave me a look, "Who knew you were one for military history Alex." She turned to walk across the street, visually picking out her first destination. "Call me if you need me, and make sure you tell people you won the fight." She motioned to my still healing face. The bruises had turned to a lighter shade of yellow and green at the edges. The swelling around my eye had gone down, and my split lip was fine without needing a small piece of tape to hold it closed.

After we picked up my newly repaired mini cooper, I would have to offer to drive Stacy around for the next week to pay her back for everything.

The mechanic had called while we were on our way to Annapolis, telling me that they were able to finish up a few days earlier than the two weeks he promised me and that the repairs were so minor they were on the house. A far cry from the thousand dollar quote I was handed after towing my car there before heading to my mother's house. It made me curious, but not curious enough to question it. Even though the mechanic sounded frightened when he told me that if I had troubles with the car in the future, he would take care of them for free.

Maybe my luck was turning around.

I half smiled, watching Stacy run across the street and get swallowed up in shopping bliss, before I turned back to the large white building towering in front of me. Removing the small map of the campus I had downloaded and printed out before Stacy picked me up, I glanced at it. I was right in front of the admissions building where I would be able to find out where the blonde was teaching or at least where her office was.

Walking as fast as my sore body would let me, I smiled at a young female sailor who held the door open for me. Her eyes roaming over my injuries as she held her smile, I shrugged at her as I passed, "I don't think boxing is the profession for me anymore. Can you point me in the direction of the Student Advisory Office?"

The girl's smile grew honest, and her eyes less worried, "Yes ma'am. Go to the left right after the visitor's desk. Captain Pegg is not in today, but his secretary can help you out."

I nodded my thanks. I attempted to stand up straighter and do my best to walk steadier. I suddenly felt the need to be proper and a little more mindful of my manners as I walked around the most primly pressed people I have ever come across. The lobby of the admissions was bustling with men and women in uniforms, walking with a sense of purpose that made me admire them.

Going left after the visitor's desk, I came to a wood and glass door with *Captain S. Pegg* painted in gold letters. It made me smile and think of all the old movies I saw with doors just like this. I tapped on the open door once, drawing the attention of the young man sitting at an old metal desk. He stood up when he saw me, smoothing out his khaki uniform, "How can I help you, ma'am?" He smiled at me, his eyes taking the same journey over my face everyone else had since I stepped out of Stacy's car.

I grinned at the way he said ma'am. "I was told that you could help me out finding information on how to become a student here? My nephew is interested in joining the Navy after high school. I want to see him to go to college first. We both agreed this is the best of both worlds."

The young man nodded, walking to a filing cabinet across from his desk, "I can help you out some, ma'am, but Captain Pegg would be the one to speak to. He knows far more than I do about the academic requirements and the programs available for a new student."

He pulled out a thin folder with the USNA logo on the front. "I can give you this and set up an appointment for you and your nephew if you would like? By the way, I'm Ensign Peters."

I took the thin folder, "Nice to meet you, Ensign. My name is Alex." I flipped open the folder pretending to look over the cover sheet in hopes of distracting the young man from asking for a last name, "I will call back later for an appointment. Can you tell me if there is a decent military history program here? My nephew is a savant when it comes to military history and tactics, always reading biography and history books like they were comic books." I smiled at the young man, doing my best to put on the charm to help my fake backstory stick.

He grinned, "We do. Actually we have one of the best instructors in the country." He walked back to his desk, tearing off a sheet from his note pad and scribbling on it before handing it over to me, "Commander Victoria Bancroft. She is in today if you'd like to speak with her." The Ensign looked up at the clock, "And her open office hours just started. Feel free to head over to her office, I know she would be more than willing to discuss her class and the program with you, ma'am."

I took the paper from him with Victoria's office location and phone number, "How do I get to her office?" I looked up at him, shifting my weight on the cane, wincing as my legs were starting to tell me it was time to sit down and not walk another step.

His eyes grew wider and he reached for me, "I should have offered you a seat, ma'am." He motioned to a chair, "I can get a midshipman to take you over or I can find a wheelchair, ma'am."

I waved him off, "I am fine to walk, thank you Ensign Peters." I looked over my shoulder at the open door, "Can you give me directions?"

The Ensign nodded, holding his hand out for the piece of paper he had given me, "I can write them down for you, ma'am. Commander Bancroft's' office is in this building." I handed the paper over and let the kid draw out a quick map before handing it back. "She is up on the second floor, ma'am, straight down from the elevators."

Looking at the little perfectly drawn map, I smiled, "Thank you Ensign Peters. I should get moving if I want to catch her before her next class."

"Yes ma'am." He smiled back at me, walking with me to the door, "If you need anything, ma'am, I also wrote my desk phone number on the bottom. I can come up and help you if you need it, ma'am."

I whispered a thank you and headed back out to the bank of elevators, suddenly feeling like I wanted to cry. Everyone on this campus had been so kind and concerned, that it overwhelmed me.

I was not used to strangers caring, let alone making eye contact with me and offering to help me, and yet, I just had at least five people in the last few hours genuinely care about my well-being. All starting with the blonde two floors above me.

I had to swallow down the rising nerves as the elevator doors closed on me waiting for me to choose a floor. I stared at the old steel elevator door, wondering if this was a good idea to find my savior and thank her in person. I could easily back out, go back outside and find Stacy. Have her take me home and resort to sending a nice little thank you card to the blonde named Victoria and let her fade out of my thoughts.

I took a deep breath, my hand moving on its own to mash the two button.

There was no way she could fade from my thoughts no matter how hard I tried to make her.

I flinched when the elevator dinged and the doors whispered open. My nerves had me on edge as I sucked in a slow breath and stepped out. I was beyond nervous, my stomach was twirling in knots like a carousel gone ballistic.

I never got nervous. Even in my first days as a nurse, I never got nervous. I was always one who was completely confident about life and lived based on the idea that spontaneity was necessary to live a full life. It was one of the things that spurred me to follow through on this crazy idea of coming to the Naval Academy and searching out a total stranger.

I shuffled slowly out of the elevator, looking around the hallway lined with office doors. I tucked the small piece of paper from the Ensign in my pocket, when I felt my phone vibrate. Stacy was sending a text to check on me. I replied quickly and shoved the phone back into my pocket, noticing that my hands were trembling. I shook my head, "Get it together Alex."

I ran a hand over my hair, then gripped the top of my can tighter and started walking down the hall, looking at the glass office doors I passed. Reading the names one by one.

Captain F. Georges.

Lieutenant P. Smithers.

Lieutenant Commander W. Alvin.

All the titles looked the same with the tiny differences of a USN or a USMC under the name, or a Ret. next to the service branch abbreviation.

All names that when painted in gold, made me feel even more nervous. I was completely out of my element.

I paused and for a second, debated turning around and hobbling back to the elevator and leaving. Then my eyes settled on the door two steps ahead of me.

Commander V. Bancroft. USN – Ret.

I blew out a slow breath. There was no turning back now.

I raised my hand, still shaking, and knocked lightly on the pebbled glass under her name.

Propping my chin up with my hand, I checked over the pop quiz I had just given my last class. I was satisfied that most of the class had passed with flying colors. Only one or two had a below ninety percent score, but it was nothing to get upset over. The entire class was on track to passing the class with honors and a full understanding of what I was teaching them.

The quiz was written last night right before bed to try and distract my thoughts when all I could think about was Alex and her journal entry. The only time she wasn't in my thoughts was when I was teaching and reading essays, or sitting down with midshipmen to discuss their progress and future.

It also didn't help that I had no side work from Dani. Which gave me more time to sit in my house, watching old movies and comparing every brunette that walked on screen to the one in my head.

After searching her loft, I left and tried my best not to look back. Only calling Dani to tell her that Alex was clean and no one to worry about. Dani seemed satisfied with that and told me her minor cleanup had ensured that my cock up of looking at the hospital camera would never go any further than her and I. Meaning Alex was safe from the prying eyes of my employer.

Scrawling a 100% on the quiz in my hand, I set it off to the side and reached for another. My eyes scrolling over the answers, I debated calling Dani and asking for a quick side job that would take me out of town. I was starting to get anxious and I didn't like it. When I became anxious, I would think too much and begin analyzing the things I couldn't understand, mainly my feelings towards the brunette and why I was drawn to her and why she was drawn to me.

I leaned harder on my hand, checking off wrong answers in red ink. In reality, if I was a little more normal, I could probably just call the woman and talk to her, or run into her at the coffee shop down the street from the hospital that her bank records showed she frequented.

I rolled my eyes at myself, as if creeping up on someone with the knowledge I had about Alex could ever be played off as normal.

Shifting in my desk chair, I tugged at the khaki uniform I was in, hating the way the material felt on my skin and the way the white t-shirt I had to wear felt too thick. I avoided wearing my Navy uniform any chance I could, but I had a full faculty meeting today with the Commandant and I had to be in full uniform. Not only did I hate the material, I hated that the uniform told my military history in bold colors of the rainbow, highlighted by the silver oak leaves on my collar.

It was a part of my history I wanted to leave to the history books and not on my body where everyone could see and ask far too many questions.

Flipping to another quiz, I looked at the clock. I had another hour and a half of open office hours until I could go to lunch. Then I could bury my mind in afternoon classes followed by droning out all coherent thoughts during the meeting. Hoping all of it would keep Alex free from my mind until I could get home and find more distractions.

A soft knock on the glass of my office door pulled my chin away from my hand. Forcing me to straighten up and set down my pen, I called out, "Come in."

The door creaked open as I turned to picked up the grading book from my briefcase. There were still five midshipmen I was expecting to speak with. I kept my eyes on the spiraled black notebook, standing up to go through the formalities of saluting and ma'am's. "You can sign in on the way out." I looked up from the gradebook to see which of my students it was.

But when my eyes locked on my visitor, I had to clench my jaw to prevent from showing any outward emotion.

She looked better than when I had dropped her off in the ER. Her bruises were fading and the lack of blood staining her skin, gave me a clear view of her and reflected the same beauty I saw in the photographs at her loft. I still found myself gripping on to the edge of my desk to funnel out the emotions I felt as Alex slowly walked into my office with a sheepish, shy smile on her face. She stopped to stand in the middle of the room in fitted blue jeans, a thin dark blue jacket covering a soft grey shirt. Her hair was up and away from her face, begging me to look at her when it was the last thing I wanted to do.

Alex looked around the office, her cheeks pinking up in embarrassment, "I know this is, um, a bit unusual, but I just really had to find you." Her head turned, her dark blue eyes locking on mine in a moment of silence. It was just her and I staring at each other, and yet, my heart began to accelerate like a finely tuned sports car with every second this woman stared back at me. Her perfume, one I knew well and liked, filled the air around me, making me grip harder on the wood edge of the desk.

Alex finally looked down at the cane she was propped against, "Are you Victoria Bancroft?" She winced as she took another step forward. Her body still healing from the beating she took at the hands of the men I killed for her.

I knew she knew the answer. She knew it the second she made eye contact with me, but I could also see how nervous she was and how completely out of character it was for her to be standing in my office like this.

I cleared my throat, "I am, yes." Letting go of the desk, I moved towards her. Moving to the side she wasn't leaning on, and gently grabbed her elbow, "Let's get you seated."

Alex didn't flinch when I touched her, but I did. I felt how warm she was under the thin, washed out dark blue jacket she wore. It was a warmth I had not felt in a long time and I had to fight not to let go of her arm like I wanted to. I could see her look at me in the corner of my eye, her eyes running over my face and her memory putting pieces together. There was also something else in her eyes that had my skin warming up to the point I could feel the sweat build at my temples.

It was a look I had not seen in very long time, one of admiration wrapped in lust and something more. The something more I dared not explore further, ignoring it by looking at the pale grey blue carpet as I guided Alex towards my desk.

I smiled, looking up at her, walking her to the chair in front of my desk for students, doing my best to avoid looking in her eyes. "Can I get you a glass of water before we discuss why you had to find me?" I kept my professional tone, knowing if I showed any emotion, Alex would run with it. I honestly wanted her to run away, away from me, and I would do it by putting my best efforts to be cold and professional to her.

It was going to be mild torture to sit across from her and not look at her like the stunning woman Alex was. Stunning, strong, and ballsy enough to come to my job and talk face to face with me. This was unexpected and it made the foreign things I felt for her grow with every minute she sat across the desk. This was not good and I knew it was going to get me in trouble the longer I was around this woman. My will starting to crumble with the cold mask I put on when I recognized it was her knocking on my office door.

"I'm fine, thank you." Alex set her cane against the front edge of the desk.

I returned to my seat, shuffling up the graded papers and setting them to the side, "If you change your mind, please don't hesitate to ask." When my desk was clear, I looked up at Alex, still staring at me with blue eyes that started to glass over.

I went to open my mouth to deliver some dry, firm questions if she was a family member of a student, or if she had questions about enrollment since I spotted the corner of Ensign Peters letterhead in her front pocket, when Alex started talking.

"I know that it's probably crazy to come to your office, you will probably think I am crazy, but I had to find you, Commander Bancroft." My rank came out of her mouth with awkwardness.

I held up my hand and smile softly, "You can call me Victoria."

She nodded, swallowing hard and looking down at her hands, "My name is Alex Ivers and I know it was you who took me to the hospital after my incident. I really." Alex paused, looking up to make direct eye contact, "I really had to find you and thank you for helping me that night." The poor woman was so nervous I could almost see her heart pound under her clothes.

I smiled tightly, looking at my pen holder and not those soulful blue eyes, "You don't need to thank me, Alex. I did what I did, because you needed the help."

Alex nodded, "I know, but I really appreciate you doing that. People rarely ever want to get involved these days, let alone help me. I don't have many friends in the city, really only one and a bunch of coworkers, but no one who would go out of their way like you did." Alex looked at the ceiling. I could see in her eyes and body language that she was lonely and it might have been one of the reasons why she was so driven to find me. She sighed, "I can't believe I'm sitting here. Sitting in front of a woman I don't even know. I never do things like this."

I could hear the tears rising in her voice. "Alex, it's fine."

I looked up at the clock, about to mumble how I was about to start class and should go. I was beginning to feel uncomfortable with what my heart and my head wanted me to do as this woman sat across from me. My head wanted to treat her coldly and send her on her way to never be heard from, while my heart begged me to stand up, go to her and hug her like she clearly needed. Hold her and tell her that I couldn't stop thinking about her from the moment she looked in my eyes in the car. That having her here in my office, gave me something I never thought about, but now ached for as she looked at me embarrassed for being this bold.

Alex shook her head, "Can I be honest?" She wiped at her eyes before a tear slipped free. I nodded once, giving her the go ahead to continue. "Victoria, I searched you out because for some crazy reason I had to find you. I had to find you because there's something driving me to find you. To thank you in person and tell you that I can't stop thinking about..." Alex suddenly stopped her words. Shaking her head again, she struggled to stand up from the chair, "Never mind, this was crazy." I stood up and walked over to help her, but she waved me off when I went to reach for her, smiling weakly. "I got it."

Alex tugged at her jacket, "I should go, my friend is probably worried about me." She went to turn back towards the door, but stopped, looking back up at me with cloudy eyes, "Thank you for helping me, Victoria." She smiled and picked up her cane.

It only took two painful steps before the words rolled out of my mouth faster than I could stop them. "Alex, wait." Her unfinished sentence drove me to do something. Only because it was the same thing I was struggling with. Thinking about her constantly.

Alex looked over her shoulder as I reached for my business card. Scribbling my cell phone number on the back in red pen, I handed it over to her. "If you need someone to talk to, a friend, or you need anything. Please call me." It was my turn to swallow hard. My gut was shaking its head at me while my heart was giving me a high five.

Alex's face lightened, a small half smiled formed as she turned back to me, reaching for the card. Her fingertips brushed across mine and sent shivers down my spine. Our eyes connected again in a long silent moment, so many things said that betrayed my stone cold demeanor and her nervous one. There was something brewing between us, something mutual and something that was beginning to scare me about the way it felt.

Scared me how much I liked the way it felt.

Alex held the card in her two fingers before looking down over my number. She quickly tilted her head back up to look at me, "Can I borrow your pen?" The air around us eased away from the tension that hung heavily in the air from the first word she spoke.

I held it out to her, watching her, confused, as she slowly took the battered red pen from my hand. Alex wrote a number beneath mine and handed both the pen and card back to me, "That's my number. I have already been the crazy one, so I'm going to leave you my number. You can call me if you want to talk, Victoria." She turned to walk back towards the door.

I looked at her confused, "You don't want my number?" I was taken aback. No one ever refused my phone number, my personal cell phone number, when it was given to them. Suitor or not. I knew the way men and women looked at me enough to know that my phone number was coveted by many. It suddenly felt like the tables were turned on me and I had inadvertently given Alex the upper hand.

Alex turned back to me with a small smirk on her face, "I'd rather you have mine." She then tapped the side of her temple, "Plus, I kind of have a photographic memory." Her smirked turned into a knowing grin, "Have a nice afternoon, Victoria."

I stood there in awe as Alex walked out of my office, looking down at the red digits written in the curvy handwriting from her loft. Alex was certainly unlike anyone I had ever met and I wanted nothing more than to get to know her. Regardless if it meant playing with the proverbial fire that was the foundation of my life.

"Daydreaming Professor?" Dani's voice shattered the silence I let slip in around me.

I shot my head up, tucking the card in my pocket before scowling at the redhead swaggering into my office. "What do you want?" I half growled it, turning away from her to hide my flushed cheeks by staring out the office window.

I felt Dani stop to stand next to me, "I came here for two things. First, to irritate you, which I can see I have succeeded in doing." She held out the thick dark blue envelope, "And second, the old man has a job for you. You leave tonight for Toronto, details are in the package. Call me when you land." Dani glanced at the side of my head, "That wasn't the brunette from the other night I saw hobbling towards the elevators, was it?"

I snatched the blue envelope from her hands, "Mind your own business, Dani." I moved to drop the envelope in my briefcase when I heard her firm tone.

"I would if you didn't make it my business by being careless." Dani moved to the edge of the desk where Alex's cane had just sat, "I don't care if you want to fulfill some perverse superhero fantasy, Victoria, but be fucking careful. You know what happens when people find out about the old man's plumbers." She raised an eyebrow at me until I closed my eyes.

"I do, Dani."

She smiled at me, "Good. Like I said, I don't care, and to be honest you look like you could use a good lay." Dani turned to leave, "Oh, by the way, you do make that uniform look good. It's a shame you don't wear it more often, Professor." She waggled her fingers at me in an exaggerated goodbye, "Call me later, Professor."

I groaned and flopped down in my chair as the door clicked shut.

I leaned forward, covering my face with my hands. I had gotten involved, breaking my number one rule, but I was strangely glad I did as much as I regretted it. The way my heart pounded when Alex was near, told me the stupid decision I made that night to save her was the best one I had made in a very long time.

Now, I only hoped it wouldn't cost me everything I had.

Chapter 4

Walking out of the admissions building I couldn't wipe the smile off my face, or hold back the nervous laughter. I couldn't believe that I had just done what I did. I must be borderline crazy.

I shuffled towards the bench under a tree, sliding over the white wooden slates to sit as comfortable as I could. I shook my head still laughing to myself. I had just done the ballsiest thing I had ever done in my life. Waltzed into a complete stranger's office, spoke my mind and gave her my phone number like we were in a seedy bar on a Saturday night.

I leaned back against the bench, staring up at the long branches of the oak tree. It was full of new green leaves, providing me with plenty of shade. Giving Victoria my phone number was a last thought, a totally crazy and spontaneous move. It came over me as I saw the look in her eyes as we shared the intense awkward moment of silence right before she handed me her business card.

It was her eyes again. The warmth radiating from them. They melted away her attempts to hold a cold, tough exterior. I knew she was hoping I would get discouraged and run away, like I wanted to the second I sat in the chair in her office. The woman was very stoic, very practiced in her demeanor, and mysterious. Then to top it all off, she looked beyond amazing in that stiff and perfectly tailored khaki uniform that fit her better than any glove could.

Victoria was more beautiful than I had remembered from the night of my attack. She had the long pale blonde hair pulled up and away from her face, as the military demanded of all women. It didn't help in keeping me focused on thanking her and talking to her. Instead it forced me to scan over the hard angles and soft edges of her face. I could easily see the traces of a smile that could cover her entire face if provoked properly.

The longer I looked over the fine details of her face, studying her, the more I began to feel my body heat up. Letting my brain drift to idle thoughts of what she would look like first thing in the morning before she put herself together for work. What her laugh would sound like and what I could do to draw them out of her. All of it was pure, idle, silly thoughts that could be played off as an instant attraction born out of loneliness, or the simple fact she was there to help me when so many others would have stepped over me. Maybe it was so much more that I couldn't quite explain in the handful of minutes Victoria and I shared making terribly awkward small talk.

I sighed hard, dropping my eyes from the tree branches to look across the large campus stretched out before me. I knew that no matter how hard I tried to talk myself out of the crazy idea, I did indeed have a connection with this woman. There was a hard reality and truth, when I would find her eyes looking directly in mine, there was a connection and chemistry there. That feeling made it harder to not be drawn back to stare in her grey eyes, and pick apart the way she made me feel. The way Victoria looked at me, was as if I held some sort of secret she had been searching for a very long time.

I moved my cane to rest against the side of the bench, taking in a deep breath of the afternoon air. The chemistry that hung thickly in the air between the blonde and I grew exponentially from the moment she helped guide me to the chair. Her hand shaking as it gently fell to my arm. I could also easily see Victoria's struggle to not directly right at me. The small beads of sweat forming at her temple before she hastily wiped them away. Then there was the way the pulse in her neck throbbed, cluing me in that her heart was racing just as fast as mine.

And then came the moment where we stood face to face. A pocket of silence dropping between us like an anvil, and as I looked in her soft grey eyes for the fiftieth time in that office, I felt my heart skip one beat. One single beat before it felt like it stopped then started again when she looked away.

That alone was something my heart had never done in my entire lifetime. Never for another, but it did for this incredibly beautiful, kind woman. There was something about her that kept her firmly in my thoughts and driven me to act a little crazier than I normally would. That's why I took the chance. Writing my number down and throwing the ball in her court. I thought it would backfire until I saw the astonished look in her face that I was refusing to take her phone number.

As I walked out of the office, I knew I would be hearing from the blonde sooner than we both thought, or wanted.

Stacy appeared out of the corner of my eye, shopping bags filling both hands, "Alex! You should have called me. You look flushed and tired." She plopped down next to me, setting the bags on the ground between her feet. "Did you get what you came here for?" Stacy had a sarcastic tone as she nudged me with her shoulder, mumbling about not knowing I was a history buff.

I tried hiding my grin by looking down at the tops of my worn running shoes, nodding, "I think I did." I glanced back up at the admissions building, "I think I got more than I expected." I reached for my cane, pushing on it to stand up with my eyes still on the building in the area where I imagined Victoria's office was. "Let's go get that lobster roll I promised you."

Linking my arm into Stacy's for extra support I shook my head and half listened to her prattle on about the shops and what cute things she bought.

My thoughts were only wrapped around the image of Victoria in her uniform and her phone number. Blazing in bright red ink as a possible warning sign of what I might be getting myself into. Those red digits burned into my memory, mingling with the tiny twitch in my gut, telling me that I had better hope to hell that my crazy idea wouldn't backfire on me.

"Are you online?"

Sitting down behind the cheap wooden desk in the company apartment, I clicked on the laptop to light up the screen, "Yes Dani. Let's get started."

Dani huffed, emphasized by the hard click clack of a keyboard being pounded in the background, "We're already a half hour behind. I'll have to go faster than usual." I heard the distinct staccato of Dani's fingers moving faster than lightning over the keyboard. I didn't bother to interject my usual sarcastic comment at her huffing like a spoiled brat, or try to explain the delay with how customs was backed up when I landed in Toronto, or that the company car was not in the lot like it was supposed to be when I left the terminal. All minor details that were screwed up by using the tea drinkers set up crew in Canada and not the one Dani and I both wanted to travel with me as I left D.C. A crew her and I both trusted and knew exactly how I needed, and liked things setup before I started a job.

Resting my elbows on the edge of the desk I stared at the screen, watching as Dani remotely opened the files and dumped them all over the screen of my laptop.

"Okay. First, let me direct your attention to the lovely thug you see before you. Sergei Boykov, a low level warrior for the Grekov family who operates out of Canada and Ukraine." Dani moved the image of a very typical looking Russian man to the side of the screen.

Sergei had large Russian mafia tattoos that covered his neck and distinct features that would tell even a blind man he was Eastern European. The massive tattoo of the Kremlin on the left side of his neck that would make it easy for me to find him quickly. He had greasy black hair styled in a messy but fashionable way, his face was acne scarred and his plain brown eyes held very little soul or personality. Telling me right away what type of person he was, a selfish shitbag.

Dani continued as I memorized the face of my target. "Sergei has been running the human trafficking side of things for the Grekov's for the last six months. Buying, selling, and trading men and women of all ages. Sometimes, he tests out his product before moving them onto the final buyers. He loves his cocaine and cannot get enough of it lately. This has him on the bad side of his Captain since he is spending more time snorting up his profits instead of sending them home. Sergei also has a history of keeping male and females that suit his fancy, as personal entertainment. If you get my drift." Her tone had turned hard and full of disgust at the end.

I sighed, "I do, Dani, but try and keep the personal commentary to a minimum. You know I hate developing an opinion about a target."

Dani took in a breath, "I know Victoria, but sometimes it's hard to bite my tongue with some of these shit heads." She clicked and a new photograph filled my screen. A young girl, who had to be no more than seventeen years old, with long strawberry blonde hair and a bright smile on her face. A smile that showed everyone she was confident about having the whole world ahead of her. "So this is where we come in, well, you come in. Seems the old man and the old lady received a frantic phone call from one of the biggest and baddest arms dealer in the Ukraine, asking for a favor." Dani paused. I could hear her struggle with keeping her comments to herself. "The girl you are looking at now, is the youngest daughter of one of the most infamous black market arms dealer in Europe, Katrina Dovzhenko. She just turned seventeen last month."

My ears perked up when I heard the last name of the girl, forcing me to interrupt Dani's diatribe, "You don't mean Yuri Dovzhenko's daughter. The black market arms dealer the UN and every peace loving country have tried to take down for the last decade?" I began to feel the frustration boil up.

I knew my job and my employers kept to playing the neutral party, but sometimes it was hard to digest. Especially when it came to doing a favor for a man who was primarily responsible for arming the same enemies I had fought in the desert against, who also had weapons that often outweighed mine. Let alone, being the main supplier of weapons, arming both sides of the ongoing war in his own country. The man was only loyal to money and would do anything for it. I had to clench my jaw as Dani continued.

"The one and only." Dani sucked in a breath, "Focus, Professor." She waited until I groaned at her using the horrible nickname, "Daddy came to Voltaire a few days ago asking for help, laying quite a bit on the table as payment for our services. I won't get into this because, its well above my pay grade and at a classified status, and no one has told me what he's offered us. Anyway, it seems Yuri's daughter was at a dance club in Odessa three weeks ago and was slipped a little extra boost juice in her drink. She was kidnapped at the end of the night and ended up over in Toronto in Sergei's personal collection. None of the kidnappers or Sergei knew who Katrina's daddy is. It looks like daddy just found out when one of his own thugs was enjoying a little paid action at Sergei's brothel, and recognized the girl when she was offered up to him for an extra charge."

I stood up from the chair, moving to the large window of the expansive apartment. Looking out on the nightscape of Toronto, my eyes drew up to the CN tower. "Why didn't Yuri just have his men take care of the issue?" I was getting more frustrated by the details of Sergei and his business than I was about the fact I was about to do a favor for another dirt bag.

"He can't. Seems if he did step in to retrieve his daughter, it would upset some sort of peace treaty with the Grekov family. Something in the back chatter about the two being in bed together in the arms business. I don't really know Professor. I just get the case files for the jobs, do the research, and send you on your way."

Dani paused for a second, waiting for me to comment. "But the old man and old lady have agreed to help Yuri regardless of where he falls in the morality scale. They want you to go in and do what it takes to eliminate Sergei. Just like daddy is paying for. Get the girl safely out of there, then Voltaire gets access to things the UN has tried to get to for the last ten years. Leaving it for the great Voltaire to ride on in, waves its magical black ops wand, and save the day in the eyes of the UN. When in reality, here we are, doing business with war criminals and street thugs." She clicked again, grumbling under her breath, the sound making me return to the laptop. "Sergei is holed up at the fancy apartment building two blocks from you. He's up in the penthouse and the last intel I had from the security cameras, Katrina is currently in there with him."

I roamed over the security footage and the blueprints of the building Dani had laid out on my screen. "How many guards?" I wanted to clear out my growing frustration and move towards getting into the right mind frame to do this job and leave any personal feelings out of it.

"Five on the penthouse floor, that's it. Sergei keeps a light crew at the penthouse. Usually one by the elevator, two at the door and the other two milling about inside the penthouse making sure Sergei doesn't go completely off the rails with all the cocaine he has been ingesting lately. I've been monitoring the security footage over the last twenty-four hours to find patterns and the only one I find is Sergei raging out at his men when there isn't enough cocaine in the penthouse. It also looks like he keeps his personal objects of desire high as kites along with him." I could hear the disgust return in her voice. Something I heard very rarely from the very cut and dry woman. Dani paused one more time before sending me the confirmation instructions. "The old man and the old lady have both given you dealer's choice on this one, Victoria. You can go about it anyway you want as long as you make it look like his own family turned on him."

Another series of photographs filled my screen like a card dealer dishing out the next hand of poker. The photographs were of crime scenes from all of the Grekov hits spanning over the last five years. "These crime scene photos were pulled from Toronto Metro Police to give you a better reference point. They love guns and knives."

I scanned over the images, quickly developing my strategy, "How much time do I have?"

"They want you in and out by three a.m. Sergei's Captain is expected to meet him at around eight in the morning. The police need to be there before then and rope the scene off, hopefully scaring back the Grekov family until Yuri is satisfied and I can spin the gossip that it was an internal hit." Dani clicked a few more times, moving security footage images around on my screen to bring up the side alley of Sergei's apartment building. "There will be a van waiting at the first floor service entrance. It will be our clean-up crew this time, and they will take the girl from you and ship her back off to Daddy. After that, both you and the cleaning crew need to send confirmation the job is done and, as usual, I will be your eye in the sky rerouting the security cameras and getting you where you need to go. Keep your blue tooth on. When it's all done, all you have to do is disappear like you usually do and I will see you Monday morning at school." Dani clicked a few more times, "There's a bag in the mattress with everything you'll need."

I mumbled a thank you and hung up on Dani. I looked at the time on my laptop, noting that it was edging closer to quarter to two in the morning. I now had less than an hour to complete this job, making me a bit agitated that I didn't have more time to prepare properly.

I rushed to the bed I would not sleep in tonight and lifted the heavy mattress up to find a square black backpack. I removed it and unzipped to find a silenced Walther PK380 and a nice set of lightweight tactical throwing knives with two push daggers at the bottom. All of the weapons matched up perfectly to what the Grekov family's thugs preferred to use as their tools of disposal and how I had seen them used in the crime scene photographs. The Grekov's loved brutal close quarters, exactly what I had in mind for Sergei.

Setting the backpack on top of the bed, I moved the overnight bag next to the granite fireplace in the center of the apartment and took out the usual black clothes I wore on all of my jobs. I dressed as I silently ran through the blueprints and visualizing every little movement I would be making.

After changing out the t-shirt and jeans I wore on the flight, and into my "work" clothes, I threw on a solid black pair of sunglasses and pulled up the hood on my thin jacket before leaving the hotel room. Grabbing the backpack and slinging it over my shoulder, I shoved a pair of thin black leather gloves into my front pocket. I kept my head down and avoided eye contact as I slowly slid into work mode.

Stepping out onto the city streets I sucked in a few calming breaths before starting to jog down the two blocks to Sergei's apartment building. I would look like a typical late night jogger, a wealthy lady or actress who was hiding from the bustling nightlife as I tried to sneak in a quick run before the bars let out and filled the streets with drunks.

Less than ten minutes later, I was standing in the elevator of Sergei's apartment building, watching the digital readout count down the floors on the way up to the penthouse. I tapped on the ear bud in my left ear, "Dani, I'm in."

"I see you. Try not to look directly at any cameras tonight, alright Victoria?" Her tone was back to the typical sarcastic one Dani always had when we worked together.

I rolled my eyes under my sunglasses, "You won't ever forget that, will you?"

"Nope. It was a stupid mistake and I will hold that over your head until you've learned your lesson Professor." She accentuated all of the syllables in Professor.

I shook my head, "I'm going to mute you until the job is done. You have my back?"

"Always have, Victoria. Always will." Dani was genuine with her words as she was every time she spoke them when I went into a job where she was my eyes in the sky. "You're clear. The cameras have been rerouted and are on a loop. All anyone will see from this point on is big dumb guard walking in circles."

I chuckled softly before whispering "Thank you." I hit the ear bud again, muting Dani out unless I needed her. It was against protocol, but it was hard for me to focus if I heard anything in the background that could distract me. It had gotten me hurt on the first few jobs after I started working for Voltaire. Hearing Dani's breathing, or her soft clicks was too much, and eventually we both agreed that muting was the best option for both of us.

I stared at my blurred reflection in the steel of the elevator doors as I put on the black leather gloves. I then reached into the back pack, wrapping my hands around the silenced PK380 and stepped out of the elevator.

Walking directly towards the first big Russian standing against the wall across from the elevator reading a newspaper, I tried to smile at him like I imagined a normal person would. He didn't even give me a second look before uttering in a thick Russian accent, "You have wrong floor."

My smiled fell to a smirk as I kept walking towards him, fully removing the handgun from the backpack, "I don't think I do." I fired two shots in his chest and one between his eyes before he had a chance to look at me. The large man slid down the wall to land on his ass, the paper in his hands propped up as if he was still reading it. It would have looked quite normal if it wasn't for the large red smear of his blood on the wall behind him and the gaping hole in his forehead.

I moved past him, swinging the back pack around my left shoulder and moved down the hall, the smell of blood already filling the air and my nose, making the little bit of nerves I had felt in the elevator disappear completely. I fell into the perfect zone I always did when I started working and I made a mental note to research why the smell of blood had such a calming effect on me at the strangest times. Maybe I could talk to my therapist about it at my yearly psyche exam for the Naval Academy.

Moving silently down the hall, I stopped right behind the second guard. He was also leaning against the wall outside of the shiny black double doors. He was engrossed in his cell phone, watching motorcycle racing videos and laughing like a drunken donkey.

He dropped to the floor on his stomach with one shot to the back of his head right at the base of his skull. Blood and tissue splattering on the leaves of the poor fern plant that sat directly across from him.

I leaned over the body to look at the silver magnetic door lock. A bright red light staring right at me above the card slot. I tucked the PK380 back into the backpack and waited for Dani to give me the green light. Digging around in the backpack I wrapped my right hand around three of the throwing knives that lined the interior. When the light on the lock blinked green, I pushed the door open, startling the third guard carrying a stack of clean white towels.

He fell to his knees, the white towels tumbling to the floor around him as he clutched at the black steel knife lodged in the middle of his throat. His hands scrambling to stanch the blood pouring out as he gurgled from the red fluid sliding down his windpipe, quickly seizing up his lungs.

I didn't give him a second look as I stepped over him, kicking his hand free from my ankle as he feebly tried to stop me. His voice coming out in choked wet garbles, trying to yell for help.

Walking through the large, gaudy black and white marbled penthouse I spun another knife around my index finger, looking for the fourth and fifth guard. I craned my neck when I could hear loud techno music playing, mixed with a few angry shouts coming from a man off to my direct right. Sergei had to be in that room. I raised an eyebrow in amusement, this was easier than I expected.

I swung the backpack on to my shoulders after dropping another knife into my right hand, and proceeded to creep around a corner, quickly coming face to face with wide eyes of the fourth guard. He scrambled, reaching for the gun holstered on his hip, but failed.

I had to step to the side as his blood spurt out of his jugular at an unusually high angle. I kicked him onto his back, pushing the knife to the hilt into the side of his neck to finish the job quickly as I pulled back the sleeve of my jacket to look at my watch. Glancing at the digital display, I had less than twenty minutes to meet Sergei and find Katrina. I had to hurry this up.

I opted to go right to the room with the techno music instead of searching for the last guard, knowing Sergei's screams would draw out the final guard and I could finish them both off at once.

I took three steps towards the white wooden double doors when I felt two tree trunk sized arms wrap around my waist and lift me up, followed by cursing in Russian.

I tugged at the arms, but found them to be too thick and strong for me to wiggle free from. I moved quickly, slamming my left hand holding the throwing knife into the thick forearm trying to squeeze the life out of me.

I hit the floor as a loud scream filled the room. Rolling on my back I saw the fifth guard, grabbing at the knife in his arm, trying to pull it out, but the blood made everything slippery. I smirked as I watched him fall to his knees, desperately trying to yank the knife out before he looked up at me.

A quick look of confusion crossed his face when he saw that I was a woman, the confusion rapidly turned to anger. I raised an eyebrow watching him scramble for the gun on his hip. I shook my head, smirking wider and jumped to my feet to lunge at him. Throwing a hard angle kick to the edge of his jaw and hearing the loud snap of success as I landed on my knees. He crumbled to the ground dead on his gun side. I reached out, pushing him off his side, shrugging when I saw he had at least gotten the gun halfway out of his holster before I snapped his neck.

I patted his cheek, looking in his lifeless eyes. "You almost got me."

Standing up, I removed the backpack. Tucking the PK380 in my back waistband, I grabbed the two push daggers sitting in the bottom. Tossing the empty backpack on the floor, I took a deep breath and headed towards the white double doors holding back the blaring techno music.

Kicking the double doors open I found Sergei sitting on a large circular bed wearing silk boxers and a black silk robe. He sat facing me, snorting white, mountain sized piles of cocaine on a piece of broken mirror he held in his hand. The techno music was at an ear piercing level, making it clear that Sergei had been oblivious to everything that had gone on around him and that I was now standing in the room with him. I stared at the piece of shit for a second before I started walking towards him, hollering, "Hello Sergei."

His head shot up when he heard my voice. He threw the mirror to the floor, throwing up clouds of cocaine, "Who the fuck are you?" He looked around for his guards, shouting in a thick broken accent. "Nikolai! Vladimir! Get in here!"

I chuckled, "They won't be coming anytime soon, Sergei." I continued to walk towards him with my hands at my side, the dagger hilts firmly in my palms and ready to strike like lightning.

Sergei's eyes dropped to the blood dripping from my gloves. Sergei was a foolish junkie, but he knew why I was there and what I had just done to his guards. He growled at me as he turned to look at the large silver handgun on the brass and granite table just out of reach to his left, "I fucking kill you."

I shrugged, "You can try." I half smiled at him, moving closer.

Sergei did try and went to get up to go for his gun. I sighed hard and ran the few steps to him. Moving faster than he expected, I drove the two push daggers deep into the crease of his thighs, immediately severing the deep femoral artery. He screamed out in pain and went to reach down to pull them out of his legs.

I shook my head, snatching both of his wrists before his fingers had a chance to graze the hilts, "Oh no, no, Sergei. You don't want to do that, unless you want to bleed out." I nodded to the daggers in his thighs, sticking out and twitching with him, "You see the blades are actually preventing you from bleeding out. You move one of these a millimeter and you will be dead in three seconds as your heart pumps all of your blood out of the sliced femoral arteries."

Sergei tried to rip his wrists from my hands, I shook my head again, twisting them both back until I felt them snap. I waited for his screams to lessen before I dropped his maimed hands to crouch down in front of him. I pulled back the sleeve of my jacket, looking again at my watch, "I have ten minutes, Sergei, so let's make this quick. Where is Katrina? You tell me where she is and I might let you live."

Sergei turned his head away from me, trying to figure out a way to still get to the gun from the table. I sighed harder, standing up and walked to the table to pick up the gun. After stuffing it next to the PK380, I returned to kneel in front of him, slapping him hard across the face, "Stop wasting my time. Katrina, where is she?"

Sergei looked dead in my eyes with big dilated black pinholes for pupils, trying hard to see through the dark lenses of my sunglasses. "Whoever sent you is coward. Send woman to do a man's job."

I clenched my jaw, reaching for the daggers to pull them out, "I don't like it when my time is wasted. Say goodnight Sergei." I linked my finger around the hilt of both daggers and began to pull them out slowly.

"No, wait, wait! I give you money, drugs, men, women, whatever you want." Sergei was frantically pleading with me.

I shook my head, pulling the dagger out slowly. I hated when they begged. "I told you what I want."

When he felt the first tingle of blood escaping his femoral, Sergei shouted, "Fine! She is in other room. Sleeping. I didn't hurt her!"

I nodded once, shoving the dagger back in place before I stood up and walked towards the side room off of the main bedroom. Pushing the white door open slowly, I saw a half-naked girl wearing only a tiny pair of underwear, curled up in the middle of the bed. I didn't have to look twice to know it was Katrina. Her strawberry red hair was a tangled mess. Her lipstick was smeared with the rest of her heavy makeup, making her look like a morbid clown. The girl was visibly high on something by the way her dilated pupils looked straight through me.

I rushed to the bed, shaking her awake enough to get her to stand up and walk with me towards the front foyer. I didn't care she could see my face, she was far too high on cocaine and god knows what else to ever remember this night. It bothered me deeply that Katrina didn't try to fight me or say anything. Instantly telling me that her abuse had been violent, and lengthy at the hands of Sergei. Driving her into a dark hole of simply surviving no matter what the cost.

I looked at her as I wrapped her in a blanket to cover her, pushing her away from the screaming and yelling Sergei, "Wait for me by the front door, Katrina, I'm taking you home to your father."

She nodded numbly looking in my eyes with a strange confusion, "Poppa here?" Katrina tried to focus her drug induced vision but gave up, nodding as I whispered again for her to go wait for me in the foyer. I watched her walk out, stepping over the dead guards as if they were children's toys strewn around the floor. The anger rose quickly in me and came from nowhere with immense force. Something that rarely happened on jobs, but there was so much about this one that ate at me.

When Katrina was out of the room, I turned back to Sergei. He tried to smirk at me with confidence as he spoke, "I will find you and I will kill you, woman."

I looked up at the ceiling, sucking in a deep breath before I took the two steps to stand in front of the man again. I lifted my sunglasses up so he could look in my uncovered eyes. I wanted him to watch me as I reached down, wrapped my hands around the two daggers, intent on removing them, and watch the man bleed out, but my rage wouldn't allow me to let Sergei have the easy way out.

I began to push down hard on to the daggers with my palms, pushing them deeper into Sergei's groin. Smiling with satisfaction as I felt them break through the flesh on the back of his legs. His screams of pain and rage did nothing but egg me on. I began to slowly twist the daggers, feeling them rip through tendons, ligament, and muscle until I felt, and heard, the blades scrape against his femurs.

I turned away from Sergei spewing and spitting curses in my face, and yanked up hard on the daggers. Ripping them free from his flesh, I held his eyes intently. I wanted him to see in my eyes that I was killing him, with no other reason than I wanted him to die, and die painfully.

I continued to stare at Sergei as his screams turned from angry to panicked, looking down at the blood pouring out of his thighs. Unable to do a damn thing as he watched his life fade away with every beat of his heart.

I took three steps back, dropping the bloody daggers on to the floor in front of him. I turned away from him and walked away, closing the white double doors behind me to drown out the sounds of a dying man's last breaths and words.

I felt nothing. My heart rate didn't increase and I barely broke a sweat.

I calmly walked back to Katrina sitting on the edge of a white leather chair by the front doors. I said nothing as I lifted her up and walked her out of the apartment, and into the elevator. In less than two minutes, I handed her off to the cleaning crew waiting for me in the side alley, also handing off the PK380 and Sergei's weapon to be disposed of.

The cleaning crew drove off as I walked away, stripping off the blood soaked gloves and tucking them deep in my pockets. I pulled up my hood and turned right at the end of the alley. Calmly jogging back down the street to the company apartment, reaching up when I was a block away from the apartment to press on the ear bud, "Dani, it's done. Cleaning crew has the girl."

"Roger that Professor, you finished five minutes early, well done. I'll call you in the morning to confirm your payment. Your flight leaves in an hour and half." Dani sounded relieved and tired. "Have a safe trip."

I tapped the ear bud, shutting off as I picked up my pace. Running off the rest of the adrenaline and clearing my senses over the last few blocks back to the company apartment.

Two hours later, I sat in front of the fireplace in my living room. A large fire was burning as I tossed the black garments into the flames. Standing in the middle of the room dressed in only a baggy old shirt and underwear, I held a half glass of bourbon. My skin was still prickling from the boiling hot shower I took to scrub the last remnants of Sergei from my body as I stared aimlessly at the orange and red flickers of light. The warmth of the fire soothed my mind and the bare areas of my skin that the oversized and faded USNA Lacrosse shirt didn't cover. I was tired, exhausted and a thousand other things I didn't want to analyze in this moment.

The one thing I did feel was lonely.

Lonely that I had no one to talk to as I left the apartment with my carry-on bag gripped tightly in my hand. No one to talk to as I drove to the airport and dumped the company car at the rental lot, then walked in to smile blankly and nod at the CATSA officers. Flashing my Navy Intelligence identification card that allowed me to bypass the usual security measures and searches.

It was almost seven in the morning. The slivers of late morning light coming through the wooden slats of the shades covering the windows around me, cast striped patterns on the hardwood floor to my right. I had to get ready for my morning class at nine as soon as all of the equipment and clothing I used was burned to my satisfaction.

Seven in the morning and I felt like I was the only person in the world who was awake and it dug under my skin more than I thought it should. More than I wanted it to.

Draining the rest of the bourbon, I threw the last piece of clothing into the fire and walked to my desk. I traded the empty glass for my cell phone and moved to go to my bedroom to pick out which suit I was going to wear for today's classes.

After selecting a plain grey pinstripe pair of pants and a light blue button down collared shirt, I laid them out on my bed. I then turned to grab my wallet from the bedside table and place it in my briefcase when I caught the off white edge of my business card poking out of the top.

At the sheer sight of the edge, I felt my heart ask something from me. To go and remove the card and call Alex.

I hesitated, the wallet in my fingers. I knew calling her would mean getting more involved, which would lead to getting further attached to the woman. Then that would develop into all the other relationships and friendships I'd ever had before in my life. Quickly wilting away as the duality of my life kept everyone at an arm's length no matter how much I cared for them.

What I should do is remove the card and throw it in the fire and move on. Settle for Dani, Dale and Mary being the only people in my life that I could almost call friends or companions.

Instead of following through on what I should do, I plucked the card from my wallet. Dropping the simple brown leather bi-fold to sit next to my clothes for the day, I grabbed my cellphone and dialed.

Sitting down on the edge of the bed, perched nervously with my elbows resting on the tops of my bare thighs, I slowly began to talk myself out of making this phone call on the second ring. On the third ring I began hoping she wouldn't pick up, by the fourth ring I started to drop the phone away from my ear and leave this last second phone call as a moment of weakness, one to never return to.

Then I heard, "Hello Victoria."

I had been up since five. Old habits of working the late shift kicking in and I couldn't fall asleep if my life depended on it. I finally gave up and decided to unpack and alphabetize my movie collection before moving on to unpacking and hanging up my clothes in the closet.

Leaning against the front of my couch, I was stacking DVD's in piles. Ones I wanted to keep and ones I wanted to donate to the local library. It was all painfully boring and I was looking forward to nine o'clock to strike so I could drive over to my favorite coffee shop and get out of the apartment. Cabin fever was hitting me hard since Stacy and I got back from our road trip and now that I was feeling better and moving better, I wanted out. I wanted to go back to work, but had to wait at least another week before the head nurse would even think about letting me back in. More than anything, I wanted to return to being and feeling normal instead of this semi helpless woman who would receive stares, and hushed whispers, when people saw the bruises and cane. I was getting antsy and I hated it because I was alone and had nothing but occasional texts from Stacy about work gossip, a few calls from my mother to check in, and my Netflix queue I was quickly blowing through.

But more than that, I was getting antsy because every time I looked at my phone, I hoped I would see Victoria's number pop up on the screen. It had been almost three days and nothing, leaving me to believe that I had been a bit too crazy and forward and my plan back fired. Karma's way of telling me that some gut feelings were better left in the gut and not acted upon.

I shook my head as I glanced at my phone sitting next to me on the floor. I really needed to get over the blonde and look for something or someone else to consume my thoughts. Grabbing my coffee cup, I focused on sifting through my television show collections, debating which ones I wanted to keep.

It was a quarter to eight in the morning. I would give myself another twenty minutes with the DVD's before I changed out of my pajamas and headed out on the town. Maybe I would go to a bookstore, or be a tourist down at the Mall and stroll around the Smithsonian.

I was lost in reading the back of one DVD of an old movie I hadn't watched in years, when my phone started to vibrate next to me. I reached for it and turned to look at the screen, half expecting it to be another text from Stacy about the midnight orderly getting caught having sex with the afternoon intern in the MRI room again.

When I saw the ten numbers I had memorized, flash in white on the screen, I couldn't hold back the grin as I tapped the green call button, "Hello Victoria."

"Alex, hi. I hope I didn't wake you."

Victoria's voice was soft, warm, smooth and sounded tired, but none the less, it made me blush to hear her say my name. "You didn't. I've been up for a few hours working on unpacking and cleaning." I pushed myself up to actually sit on the couch as a heavy pause filled the line. I bit my bottom lip, about to start a conversation with a silly polite opening of how are you? How's work?

"I'm sorry for calling so early, but I'm going to be down in D.C. tomorrow for a quick trip for work and I was wondering if you would like to grab lunch or coffee?" Victoria paused, it was evident she was not very good at idle talk that didn't have a clear purpose or directive. Her stumbling made me grin wider as she continued, "I want to apologize for being standoffish and rude the other day in my office. And I think that I could use another friend." Her words ended abruptly.

I chuckled at how adorable it was to listen to this strong and fiercely put together woman bumble like a teenager asking out their very first prom date. "I'm totally free tomorrow, Victoria. There is a really great sandwich place down on Jackson Avenue on the north side of Arlington Cemetery. We can meet there at like one?" I tried hard to keep the excitement out of my voice, since I had no idea why I was getting as excited as I was. I had no idea who this woman was, she could be a killer or a freak for all I knew, and yet, I found myself drawn to her like a bug to the bright blue light of a bug zapper.

"I think I know of the place you are talking about, Monument Meats?" I could hear the smile in her voice, making me laugh hearing her say the ridiculous name.

"That's the place. They have the best roast beef I have ever had." I leaned against the thin cushions of the couch, feeling the tension ease between the blonde and I.

"How about we meet at Lee's house in the cemetery and walk over. I know the parking over on Jackson is nonexistent." Victoria now sounded more confident, like I had experienced in her office.

I nodded to no one, "Sounds like a plan."

"Okay." Another awkward heavy paused fell before, "Well, I need to get ready for class. I'll see you tomorrow Alex."

"Yes you will, Victoria."

We both issued goodbyes and when I hit the red end call button, I sighed. Still grinning like idiot without knowing exactly why. It wasn't a date. It wasn't anything more than two people meeting up for lunch in hopes that a new friendship could be created. That was it, just two people looking to be friends.

But as I set my phone down on the arm of the couch, I felt deep down in the pit of my stomach, the hope that there was something more between Victoria and I than a possible friendship. Something more that I didn't know I really wanted. Until I heard her voice on the phone saying my name, as if she was the only person in the world who knew how to say it in just the right way.

I groaned, rolling my eyes at myself. I was getting out of hand with the way I thought this woman made me feel. Any psychologist would tell me that I was still harboring a deep form of hero worship for the woman.

That in time after my injuries healed and my bruises faded away, I could be left looking at a dirty penny hiding under the shiny gold coin image I had placed on Victoria since that night. She could easily be a dirty penny, but she would be the most gorgeous dirty penny I had ever met.

I shook my head, pushing up from the couch to make a fresh cup of coffee, muttering to myself. "Maybe you really are crazy."

Dumping out the cold coffee, I decided to work on alphabetizing my pantry to stop the daydreams of how lunch would go tomorrow.

Chapter 5

The cemetery was busy even for a Saturday. There were tons of tourists milling in and around the old historical house, snapping pictures as they ooh'd and awed over the expansive view from the front porch. It all made me want to second guess arranging this lunch get together and having Alex to meet me at Lee's house. I didn't think about the fact that it would be filled with so many people on a sunny, warm weekend day in spring.

I didn't like to be in crowds, there are too many things to watch out for and too many things that would catch my overly detailed oriented mind. Analyzing every movement everyone made as they smiled politely, stepping around me to enter the house.

I moved to sit on the far corner of the porch, well away from the entrance and people. Far enough away that the tour guides voices fell to muted murmurs of rehearsed dialogue. Rehearsed speeches intended to educate the groups of tourists on who Robert E. Lee was and his impact on the world and how he shaped the city below them. Some of the speeches were so painfully inaccurate, I had to bite the inside of my cheek to keep my tongue in my mouth. Opting to keep my head down and focusing on reading the battered copy of Casino Royale I had put in my bag last month.

I had read the book a million times, but it still kept me entertained and at ease when I was stuck waiting. Waiting in a growing pool of unusual anxiety and nerves.

I stuck my finger to hold the pages where Bond begins the epic card game to look at my watch. I had arrived at Lee's house forty-five minutes early and that had quickly whittled down to ten minutes. Deep down in my nervous stomach, I was hoping Alex wouldn't show.

I almost didn't bother to show up myself, but when I got up this morning and looked out the bedroom window to see Dale and Mary's family over for an early spring barbecue, I felt the strong need to get out of the house. I needed to get away from the happy, laughing normalcy of next door. I didn't want to be trapped in my house, listening to the happy sounds of family. Knowing that it would just make me ache inside to have something I couldn't have.

I also knew that the second I stepped outside to water the lawn or shove the trash cans in the garage, Dale or Mary would be all over me, haggling me to come over and join them and their family.

Then they would segue into introducing me to their one still single son who worked for a congressman and who they felt would be a perfect match for me.

As I pulled the BMW out of the garage, that is exactly what happened. Mary waved me down and I couldn't ignore the kind older woman. Mary did her best to bargain with me through the open driver's side window, but eventually I won out with exasperated excuses of midterm papers drowning me. I was sent on my way with a small bag of brownies to tide me over as I worked in my office with promises of picking up leftover barbecue when I came home.

I did almost reroute the BMW and head off to my office and send Alex a ubiquitous text that I had a last minute work thing, but I didn't. For whatever reason, I drove down to Arlington. I started eating all of the brownies out of pure stress, wanting to chase away the strange nerves I had with a sugar high. I was over-thinking and over-analyzing what the hell I was doing. Going to lunch with Alex would lead to getting in deeper with her. The devil's advocate in me kept heavily hinting at the fact I could use a friend that wasn't tied to work and one that wasn't tied to endless lies, while the logical advocate in me heavily suggested that there was so much more to why I was doing this. It was the "why's" that I wanted to drown out with thick, gooey, double chocolate squares of heaven and loud music.

Now here I was, sitting on the porch steps of an ancient house, looking out on the best view this city had to offer, trying to find the courage to stand up and go back to my car and go home. I wanted to forget this crazy idea and the woman with genuine blue eyes and just continue operating my life as I had for the last ten years or so. I blew out a slow breath, and flipped my book open to stick the worn business card I used as a bookmark to save my spot. Maybe by the time I got home, Mary would have some still warm leftover pulled pork sandwiches I could wash down with Dale's home brew.

"A quarter for your thoughts?"

I swung my head up to catch Alex walking up the gravel path, grinning at me as she held her hand up to shield her eyes from the bright sun. I involuntarily swallowed at the sight of her. Her cane was gone, she was moving easier and most of the bruises had faded away enough to be hidden under minimal makeup, even the split lip looked just like an extra dab of lip gloss. The lack of bruises and evidence of the violence she endured, finally gave me a true view of how stunning this woman was. I dropped my head back to the book on my lap, very glad that I was wearing sunglasses and had the sun to use as an excuse for the blush I knew was creeping over my face. "A quarter? I always thought quote was a penny for your thoughts?" I stood up, grabbing my bag and dusting off the back of my jeans.

Alex shrugged as she stopped to stand in front of me, "It is, but my mom's boyfriend always offered up a quarter knowing it would take more than a penny for me to pay attention or spill the beans. I made at least forty dollars off of him in my freshman year of college." She turned to look out across the front yard, "This view, it's incredible."

I nodded to no one looking in the same direction she was, shouldering my bag, "It is. It's the one place in the city that someone can go and feel completely separated from the hustle and bustle of the nation's capital." I turned to sneak another look at Alex.

She was wearing the same light blue jacket she had worn in my office, a loose fitting white t-shirt with a generous scoop neck that offered up a revealing view of her skin and a bit of cleavage. I skipped my eyes over that detail to scan over her loose jeans and an old pair of boots that were once black, but were now more scuffed than black. The light spring wind fluttered around her, forcing her clothes to billow and hug around her curves as it also teased small pieces of her dark brown hair around her face. My jaw clenched at the sudden rush of warmth in my body from the ideas in my head about those clothes and what could be underneath them.

I turned back to dropping the old book in the bag, glancing at my watch. Alex was five minutes early, making me smile to myself. I was stuck now. I cleared my throat, "Are you hungry?"

Alex turned back to me, her eyes clearly roaming over my dressed down look of loose blue jeans with a few holes in them, and the old tattered pair of white converse. The haphazard outfit I threw on, was topped off with a light blue linen shirt that was one size too large for me, but did its job in covering the almost see through old white V-neck t-shirt. A shirt that had definitely seen most of the laundry compartments in the Navy's fleet of ships.

"It's nice to see you dressed down, Victoria." I could hear her cautiously test out using my first name, wondering if it was still okay to do so. "I don't feel the overwhelming need to salute you or make up a lie about my dog eating my essay." Alex grinned as she squinted against the sun.

I smiled nodding, "Thank you. Weekends are the only time I can leave the suits and uniforms in the closet and dress like a bum." I motioned over her shoulder, trying to ignore the silly joking banter Alex was attempting. It was out of habit, not out of purpose, to get this lunch meeting started so I could end it sooner. I just wasn't good at first impressions if it wasn't in a classroom or in a mark's house with their blood on my hands, "If you want, we can take the back path to the restaurant. It will be less tourist laden." I rolled my eyes under the sunglasses, could I be more stiff and rude? Probably.

Alex laughed lightly, turning to where I had directed, "That sounds good." She waited for me to step next to her before she leaned closer to me, "Victoria, I'm just as nervous as you are."

I glanced at her, her eyes boring right through my sunglasses made my heart skip and my gut tell me that I needed to decide what I was going to do from this point on. I didn't say anything, just smiled again, then fiddling with my bag strap as I started to walk down the gravel path with Alex falling in line next to me.

"Why did you pick Lee's house to meet?" Alex's voice was soft, an attempt to ease the strange tension between us with casual conversation starters.

I lifted my head up, focusing on the path ahead, "It's close to the sandwich shop and everyone knows where it is." I trailed off before I admitted out loud that the house was one of my favorite places in the city. There was something about this woman that made me want to tell her things that I kept locked up, and do it without thinking twice. I smiled softly, looking over at her, "Why did you pick Monument Meats?"

Alex chuckled, trying her best not to reach out for me as her steps would get a little wobbly on the downhill slide of the loose gravel path, "It's honestly the first place that popped in my head. I used to eat there on the weekends during my first and last years in college." She paused, "To be even more honest, I haven't been there in years, but I do remember that they had a massive corned beef sandwich." Alex suddenly grabbed my elbow as she stumbled. "Shit, sorry. I probably should have brought my cane. I didn't expect this path to be such trouble." Her brow furrowed in frustration that her body was still lagging on getting over her injuries.

Alex went to pull her hand away from my elbow, when I shook my head, gently grabbing onto hers, "It's okay. Use me if you need to. Some have told me that I am as stiff as a wooden board." I smiled at her, hoping the joke would ease the tense air around us.

Alex laughed, moving closer and gripping onto my arm right above my elbow as I dropped my hand from her. Her hand was warm, soaking into the thin, ragged material of my old shirt. Sending a shiver up through my arm and right to my chest. I clenched my jaw to fight through the sensation and focus on the way she squeezed ever so slightly. Telling me that Alex already trusted me far more than I did her.

"I wonder why anyone would say such a thing about you." Alex smirked at me, "I did want to ask if you took etiquette classes, I had never seen anyone stand up as straight as you did in your office the other day."

I sighed, "Blame the Navy." I then laughed lightly, "And that I'm actually a bit stiff and not much of a people person." I rolled my eyes, "Again, you can blame the Navy for that."

Alex laughed with me as we walked down the back path, past the park stations and maintenance huts. "You're a teacher Victoria, how can you not be a people person?"

I shrugged, guiding Alex out of the cemetery and out on to the bustling city street. I could feel my guard go up immediately as I subtly scanned the crowds out of habit and instinct, "I'm a teacher in a military academy. It's the one place, probably the only place, where a teacher can be just a teacher and not a person." I pointed down the street, "It's just one more block, are you okay to walk a bit further?"

I felt Alex's hand squeeze my arm again, "I am." Her voice was so quiet, another clue that Alex was possibly a bit more interested in me than just seeking out a new friend.

I swallowed down the feeling of her hand on my arm, and how that simple act of her squeezing it was bringing up so much warmth through my body. I resisted the urge to look down at the woman who I could feel looking at me.

This was going to be a long lunch.

There was something about Victoria that was mysterious. It was the type of "mysterious" that went past an idea brought on by James Dean or television shows. It was sexy but frightening at times. Yes, her mysteriousness did add to her overall attractiveness and drew me deeper into her, but there was something there that had my gut sniffing around like a bloodhound looking for clues. It was that small thing that kept me from completely swooning openly over the woman the second I saw her sitting on the porch steps reading her James Bond book like an aloof college student in holey jeans.

Victoria was beautiful, beyond beautiful, bordering on gorgeous, and I couldn't stop myself from looking at her in the worn out bum clothes she wore. A far cry from the perfectly tailored Navy uniform I last saw her in. One that had left me and my thoughts going in directions I never thought I would venture into, especially in regards to the woman wearing that uniform. Then again, uniforms were always a weakness of mine.

I held onto Victoria's arm as she guided us out of the cemetery and down to the city street. Making me a bit giddy at how chivalrous she had been to offer up her arm and check on me. Chivalry was a lost and forgotten art, and for a romantic like me, any sliver of that came my way made me giddy, and it did leave me at a loss for words. I was only able to grin like a dope as Victoria walked us to the hole in the wall deli that I had indeed pulled out of thin air under pressure when Victoria suggested meeting up for lunch. I glanced at the bright red, white, and blue facade as she quietly announced we had arrived.

Monument Meats was exactly as I remembered it from my college days. A patriotic sandwich place that served huge portions cheap to the locals and the tourists who flooded this street every day. The huge, cheap portions had been the main reason why all of us nursing students hit the place weekly. I looked over at Victoria, "Hasn't changed one bit in almost fifteen years."

Victoria had pulled her sunglasses off, palming them to reach for the door. Opening it for me, she gently held on to my arm to keep my balance steady, "I guess that's a good thing?" She smiled softly at me, guiding me into the half empty restaurant.

I nodded, walking in and heading towards the closest booth that was also the furthest away from the handful of lunching tourists. "It is if the portions are still the same size." I slid into the creaky red vinyl seat, smiling at Victoria as she waited until I was safely seated before letting me go and taking the seat across from me.

I set my bag next to me and began fidgeting with the placemat with presidents on it, in hopes of preventing from looking or staring at the blonde. When that didn't work, I ended up roaming my eyes over the tacky Americana décor. There were pictures of presidents and monuments plastered over the walls and faded by the sun. I let out a slow nervous breath, catching a hint of a delicate perfume coming from her side of the booth. God, Victoria even smelled good and it was stewing up more feelings in my stomach towards my lunch companion. I quickly grabbed two menus, setting one in front of her, "The Jefferson corned beef sandwich is the best I have ever had, next to that is the double bacon club sandwich. Also known as the Reagan club special."

Victoria nodded, scanning over the menu before setting it down as a middle aged waitress waltzed over to take our order. "What can I get yous twos today?"

I grinned at her thick New York accent, trying not to laugh at how ridiculously thick it was for the area we were in. I set the menu down, "I will have the Jefferson corned beef sandwich, with fries and a large sweet tea. Please and thank you."

The waitress scribbled on her pad, "How's about you sweetheart?" She waved her double chin in Victoria's direction.

Victoria smirked, catching my eyes and giving me a look, "I will have the Reagan club special with coleslaw and a large coke. Please." She picked up my menu, handing both over to the waitress, who snatched them up and waddled away. Mumbling that our order would be ready in a flash.

"Is that accent real or just for show?" Victoria set her sunglasses down with her phone before looking up at me questioningly.

I chuckled, "It's real. The owner is from Brooklyn and I think that's his wife, or daughter. I can't really remember. The last time I was here, it was dollar pitcher night and I had just passed my finals." I leaned back against the booth, "So, needless to say, I don't remember much from that entire week."

The blonde nodded, looking down at the table top, she began playing with the red, white, and blue plastic tablecloth. The poor woman was terrible at hiding her nerves.

Cluing me in that I would have to be the ice breaker no matter how nervous I also was. I waited until the waitress dropped off our drinks before pulling out the icebreakers. "I liked Casino Royale, but I think To Live and Let Die is my favorite Bond book."

I watched as Victoria looked up at me with wide curious eyes. I pointed at her bag, "You were reading Casino Royale when I walked up." Squeezing the lemon into my tea, I sat forward, "My mom's longtime boyfriend had all of the books when I was growing up. I ended up reading them out of curiosity and attempt to get to know him better. I do like the lengthy card game scenes in Casino Royale and how Bond feels borderline deviant."

Victoria sighed, laughing quietly, "That's because he is borderline deviant. It's why I prefer the books to the movies. The books always give the impression that Bond could just let go one day and turn to the wrong side of life. While the movies do their best to creatively turn Bond into the dashing white knight." She picked up her coke, sipping some of it, "You are quiet observant, Alex."

"It comes with the job. As a nurse I have to be the first set of eyes for the doctor, and in most cases, I have to be the doctor's eyes when their arrogance blinds them." I let out a short breath, Victoria was beginning to physically ease up. "I will admit that the doctors down here are far more arrogant than the ones in New York. Maybe because the hospital I work at treats most of the nation's politicians who work down in the capitol building. They think they are gods for treating the government. That maybe in a way they are the ones keeping the country running." I rolled my eyes, reaching for another lemon.

"The city in general is laden with arrogance and self-entitlement." Victoria's voice had a tone to it that told me that she had firsthand experience in those two personality traits. She cleared her throat, "Why a nurse and why come back to the nation's capital?" She suddenly turned to look out the window, "I'm sorry if that's a little personal for a first question."

I shook my head, "It's not. It's the standard starting a new friendship question." Good god was Victoria adorable right now. This hero worship I felt for the woman was turning into one hell of a tempest of attraction for her. I would have to sort out the feelings conjuring in me before I could attempt a friendship, especially when I looked at her hands and wanted nothing more than to hold them. I bit my bottom lip, pretending to think of a grand answer to her question. "Why a nurse? Hmm, I don't have some life changing story sized answer to that. I've always wanted to be a nurse since I was a kid. Maybe it was the soap opera my mom watched about the one hospital were nurses filled the screen and saved the drama of the day. Or maybe, it was that nurses were the ones always giving me candy when the doctor wasn't looking, or something else. Either way, I was drawn to it, and to be honest, I am really good at it."

I smiled a bit wider when I looked up to see Victoria's grey eyes staring intently in mine. She was actively listening and that was a rarity in the world, especially in my world.

I held her eyes for a second before continuing on, "As for the why I came home, it was simply that. I wanted to come home and maybe settle down. My mom is getting older and I missed seeing her whenever the mood struck. That, and New York can wear a person down to the nubs if you let it. It almost wore me down to the nub and beyond. I was an emergency room nurse at Bellevue and then at Mt. Sinai." I shrugged, "I became burned out and wanted a slower pace."

Victoria raised an eyebrow, "And so you come home to work at George Washington Hospital, with one of the busiest emergency rooms in the city?"

I laughed, "It's far slower than Bellevue. Trust me." I picked up my tea, taking a large sip as the waitress dropped off the mountains of meat, cheese, and bread. I grinned watching Victoria's eyes widen at the sheer size of her sandwich. "Yep, the portions are still the same."

"This is quite possibly the biggest sandwich I have ever come across." Victoria picked up her napkin, laying it across her lap, trying to figure out where to start. I watched her, noting how carefully she moved no matter what she did. Whether it was holding my arm to steady me, picking up a piece of paper, holding a pen with precision, or try to size up how to lift the pile of food in front of her, Victoria was exact as well as precise and it was endearing to me.

"Ever? Even in your time in the Navy? There wasn't a port down in Italy or Alabama that had baby sized sandwiches?" I picked at my sandwich separating the halves into smaller chunks. "And by the way, why the Navy? Why a teacher?"

Victoria looked up, catching my sandwich strategy and mimicking it, "Why the Navy? Simple reason, the Naval Academy offered me a full scholarship when my ACT and SAT scores were released in my senior year of high school. They won me over with the incredible educational program and the offer of having a job the day I graduated was too hard to pass up. I took it, and since my family didn't have the means to pay for college, it seemed to be a perfect match." I waited for Victoria to take her first bite of the Reagan club, watching as she quickly smiled around a messy mouthful at how good the sandwich was. She covered her mouth with a napkin, "This is exceptional!"

I laughed, picking up my first chunk, "Surprisingly good isn't it?" I wanted to make a political joke, but held back. Remembering the cardinal rules of topics to avoid when meeting someone. Politics, religion, number of sexual partners.

Victoria nodded, chewing fully before setting the food down, "To answer the second part, why a teacher? I fell into it. As my time with the Navy came to an end, I was offered a teaching position since I had minored in military history. I took it. Again, the attraction of having a job the same day I was discharged was too hard to ignore."

I watched Victoria sigh and turn back out the window, pausing for a moment, her eyes fluttering around the traffic as it drove by.

When she turned back to me, looking dead in my eyes as she spoke, I saw that she was telling me something she probably never told anyone. "I missed the innocence of my days at the Naval Academy. Going back gave me an opportunity to teach the next generation of officers to learn from history's mistakes. Then take those mistakes to heart and learn to avoid making mistakes that would cost them so much if they allowed it."

Something in her words told me she was speaking from personal experience, and it made me curious, "Did you serve in the war, Victoria?" I bit into my arm sized pickle. It was a run of the mill question that anyone would ask anyone who was in today's military. In this day and age, it felt like every soldier had been to the desert and back.

Her slate grey eyes turned cloudy, a far cry from the soft and kind ones I had enjoyed since the moment we sat down. The blonde nodded once, "Yes, but I left right after the fall of Baghdad." Victoria cleared her throat, picking up her sandwich, "Your turn, Alex. What's your favorite old movie?"

I watched the tiny clouds swarm around the woman as she kept her head down and focused on the wads of bacon in her grips. I smiled, taking the obvious change in topic, "I would have to say my all-time favorite old movie has to be *Bringing Up Baby*. I had one fierce crush on Katherine Hepburn when I was younger. I even asked for a tiger for one Christmas. Didn't get it, but I did get my own copy of the movie on VHS to watch endlessly."

In that small sentence, the clouds around the blonde that I was developing a mighty crush on, disappeared. Victoria raised her head up to meet my eyes with clear and sparkling ones. A smirk pulling at the far corner of her mouth, "That is one of my favorite movies ever." She then set her own giant pickle on my plate, "I hate pickles."

And with that revelation, the ice and tension melted away. Victoria became a different person wholly. Warm, open, wickedly intelligent, and funny. She continued to relax around me and our conversation turned from forced and struggled, to easy and never ending. I told her how my mother gave me the middle name Ava, in honor of Ava Gardner. Then how I was still a New York Giants fan living in a city where the Redskins were the only football team in the world, and would proudly wear my Giants shirt to any Redskins home game.

Victoria in turn told me about how she would write pop quizzes that had patterned answer keys to trip up her students, hoping that at least one would notice that all of the answers were A's or B's in a multiple choice offering. She divulged how envious she was of her neighbor's expansive flower garden and that she was determined to one day have at least one flower bloom in her yard, come hell or high water.

Through it all, the silly tidbits and the short stories of growing up as awkward teens in high school, I could see Victoria was sharing things she rarely did, but at the edges I could see she was still holding back.

That mysterious effect of hers coming into play. It was as if she was living a double life and had to be careful not to reveal her second identity. It was all intriguing and I played it off as her being nervous and awkward in a first impression setting. I also shoved it down because of what I was starting to feel more and more for this woman. Wanting the mysterious to stay a mystery for a little longer.

We sat and talked for hours. Victoria kept her full attention on me, only breaking once or twice when she received a phone call that made her smile weaken, but she ignored those calls and kept her focus on whatever nonsense I was rambling about.

When the bill came, Victoria snatched it away before I could look to see what my half was, saying that the next lunch would be on me. She then helped me up to leave when the waitress threw us evil looks for taking up a booth for most of the day when the tourists began to pour in. Victoria continued to hold on to my elbow without me ever suggesting I needed the steadying, which I really didn't, but who was I to refuse the kindness of a beautiful stranger. By the time she held the door open for me, I was beyond smitten with this woman and it excited me as much as it confused me.

Standing back out on the street, I looked up in the sky before looking at the giant street clock a few blocks down. "Wow, it's almost six in the afternoon. Talk about a long lunch." I smiled looking over at Victoria, catching her looking at me in a way that told me that she was clearly checking me out.

She turned away, her cheeks turning a soft pink, "It was an enjoyable long lunch." She shifted the bag on her shoulder nervously, "Can I walk you to your car?" Victoria turned back to me, spotting the small frown on my face that the day was coming to an end, "I'm sorry Alex, I really did enjoy today. This. It was, needed." She smiled the widest I had ever seen her, "Thank you for stalking me and cornering me in my office."

I couldn't hold back the shy laughter, "I didn't stalk you, but I did corner you." I leaned into her arm, hearing her gasp softly, "I should thank you for calling me, even though I waltzed into your office like a crazy person." I sighed at how happy I suddenly felt in this moment. Standing next to my new friend, one that I was starting to think about what it would be like to kiss her. "This was also needed, I needed to spend time with a non-work friend."

I couldn't stifle the yawn before it escaped, I was tired. Exhausted. This was the most I had been out and about in over a week since leaving the hospital. Moving a still healing body and being void of painkillers or even aspirin, my body was starting to protest and hint that it was time to go home, lie down and take a nap while passing out with the television on. Victoria laughed, patting my arm, "You look like you could use a rest." She pushed on her sunglasses to block out the bright, low hanging, afternoon sun, "Where did you park?"

I pointed towards the giant clock, "The structure two blocks over. It was the only place that wasn't full."

Victoria turned us to head in the direction of my car, "No wonder you're tired, I had you walking for miles to meet me. You should have called me. I would have come to meet you here instead of up at the cemetery."

I shrugged, "I could have, but then I wouldn't have been able to sneak a peek at a beautiful blonde reading spy novels mixed with the best view in the city." I bit the inside of my mouth, hoping my blunt attempt at flirting didn't backfire. When I glanced at Victoria, I couldn't get a read off of her, just noticed the deepening pink on her cheeks telling me that my flirting did indeed have some effect on her.

We walked together towards the parking structure. Victoria filling the air with typical idle chatter about the weather, the influx of tourists in the city, and when I was going back to work. Her tone had shifted back to the closed off one that had reigned at the start of our lunch. I answered her, finding small victories when I could make her laugh or get her tone to change back to the warm one that was sweeping me off my feet.

Entering the parking structure, I dug out my keys, pointing to the rusted blue back end of my Mini Cooper, "That's me over there." I palmed my keys, letting Victoria walk me to the driver's side door. I really didn't want this day to end. I wanted to ask her to go have a drink with me, go to a movie, troll down the dairy aisle at the grocery store. A hundred different things I could suggest, all of them included spending a handful more hours with her. I opened the driver's door, throwing my bag onto the passenger seat, "I go back to work on Monday, the night shift. But I do have Friday and Saturday off if you wanted to grab lunch or go to a museum?"

I cringed at my awkward stumbling. I was always a smooth operator when it came to dating, but then again I primarily dated men who asked me out first and could barely tear their eyes away from my chest. Not the stunning blonde woman who was pushing her sunglasses up so she could hide from looking in my eyes after scanning over my piece of crap car. I blew out a nervous breath, "I know you're busy, but you can call me, text me if you want to talk or hang out? I think we just barely grazed the surface of this friendship, I mean I have a ton more awkward high school stories I can tell you."

Victoria laughed, "I'll call you Monday after I get my midterm break schedule. I would like to try the Washington chicken salad sandwich." She turned back to my rusty bucket, "Is this a '67? How does it run?"

I looked over the hood of the rust bucket, "It's a '74, but there are some '67 parts on it." I tapped the edge of the door, "It runs like it is brand new these days. The mechanic down the street from me fixed it up at no charge, gave me free lifetime maintenance on it too. And here I thought he was trying to gouge me when I hobbled in with it on the back of a tow truck." I turned back to Victoria, catching the hint of a smirk on her face.

She nodded, "It's hard to find decent mechanic's these days." She then turned back to me. A heavy silence fell between us when our eyes met.

A silence that spoke volumes when neither of us could find a simple word, let alone a vowel to utter towards one another. I watched as she visibly swallowed hard, "I should get going. If you don't leave now, you'll hit traffic, Alex."

I reached out, gently grabbing her wrist as she went to turn away from me. I held on to her tightly, moving closer, "There's always traffic in D.C., Victoria." I waited until she faced me, it was now or never. I moved closer, "Victoria, I, today was amazing and I really think you're amazing and I have been wanting to do this since you gave me your pickle."

I broke into her personal space, feeling and hearing her heart pound as my hand moved from her wrist to the side of her neck. I looked up in her eyes, our faces inches apart, Victoria kept looking down at my mouth and back up in my eyes. She wanted this as much as I did. Definitely a good sign to continue what I was about to do. I smiled softly and leaned in to kiss the woman, my lips brushing hers softly. I could hear her gasp, and it did nothing but spur me on as I went to close the gap hovering between us.

Victoria suddenly turned her cheek to me. I could feel her breath on my ear as she whispered, "I can't Alex. I...just can't."

I squeezed my eyes shut, biting my top lip as I nodded slowly before backing away. Taking a deep breath to reform my rejection into acceptance, I smiled at the blonde woman who was clutching to the strap of her bag like it was a life line. I nodded again, sticking out my left hand to her, "I understand, Victoria. Friends? I can do friends." I tried to keep the waver out of my voice.

I glanced at her, seeing the storm return in her eyes. Her jaw clenching as she struggled with whatever was in her thoughts at this exact moment. Victoria shot her hand out after a moment of leaving mine hanging in the space between us, wrapping it up in a tight grip, "Yes. Friends, Alex."

I held her hand for a moment, trying to get that damn storm to break and release the woman I knew was hiding under the firm grip and the professional facade she just threw on in hopes of making the rejection of my advances, easier. "Then friends it is." I dropped her hand against my will and turned back to get into my car, "Call me Monday, Victoria."

Victoria nodded, shutting the car door for me before taking a step back. She stood there straight as a board, waiting for me to start the car and drive off. I took one look in the rear view mirror to see her pull out her cellphone and get on it immediately. I groaned, squeezing the steering wheel out of embarrassment and frustration.

Of course I had to crush on a woman who was already taken. It was just the trend of my luck these days.

"Professor! What did I do to deserve a Saturday night call from you? Are you going to ask me out for drinks or tacos?" Dani's chipper voice added to my frustration.

I was half walking and jogging out of the parking structure. Trying to control the overflow of feelings from the day and Alex almost kissing me. "Dani, you're beyond annoying today. I'm returning your phone calls."

"Oh those. Those were just the confirmation of payment and a quick side job offer coming in from the old lady. She wanted me to offer it up to all of the plumbers before she sanctioned it back down to the B teams." Dani huffed, "What has made you a cranky pants today? The library didn't have the copy of Washington's boring-ography you wanted?"

I groaned, clutching the strap of my bag until it felt like it was cutting into my palm. The emotions I currently felt, made it feel like I was drowning. I wanted to kiss Alex. I had wanted to kiss her halfway through our lunch when I saw how her eyes grew brighter with her smile and when she laughed at my dumb Navy jokes, but I couldn't. I couldn't do anything more than be friends with her, no matter how much my heart pushed against my chest, begging me to let it go, so it could welcome Alex in with open arms. That this was my chance to have a normal life, make an attempt to have a normal relationship.

But I wasn't normal. I couldn't be normal.

"What's the side job?"

Dani huffed again, tapping on a keyboard, "It's a quick sniper hit up on the edge of northern Cuba. Some militant is threatening to take over the Cuban establishment as we know it. It's resulted in both sides of Voltaire's interests getting their panties in a big twist. It's an in and out job. Pays a quarter of your usual. Probably why none of you plumbers want it. Greedy bastards you all are." Dani's mocking tone was not helping me.

I ran around the corner, hitting the unlock button on my BMW parked outside of the parking structure, "I'll take it. I will be at the airport in fifteen, have the flight ready."

"Whooooaaa Professor. Are you okay?" Dani's tone shifted away from active irritation to active curiosity, "You never take the last minute side jobs, what's wrong?"

I sighed, dropping down into the seat, "I need to clear my head before I do something stupid." I threw my bag on the passenger seat, catching the corner of the Bond book. I clenched my jaw as it continued to remind me of Alex and how I should be calling her right now, apologizing and telling her that I did want to kiss her. I wanted her to kiss me. That during our lunch I had been more open and honest with her than I had with anyone, even my gentle harmless next door neighbors.

I pushed the bag on to the floor before starting the SUV, "Did you hear me Dani? Fifteen minutes and I'll be at the airport."

"Copy that Professor asshat." I heard Dani click a few more times, "You are a go. Hangar five. The cleaning crew will meet you and hand over the equipment. I'll brief you when you land."

I hung up on Dani before she could utter another asinine remark. Pulling out on to the street, I raced through traffic and towards the airport. I knew exactly what I was doing, running from my feelings. Running towards the one thing that had stolen all of the things I felt for a long time ago, all because a brunette woman was sweeping me off my feet every time I turned around to look in her dark blue eyes.

Dark blue eyes that begged for me to stop hiding behind the veil of my double life and let her in.

But I couldn't.

And I wouldn't.

Chapter 6

~One Month Later ~

Walking into the hospital, balancing two cups of coffee and my briefcase, I smiled and nodded at the handful of nurses who brushed by me. It was half past seven in the morning and I was headed towards the nurse's station right inside the first level trauma ward. I grinned softly at the yawning younger nurse leaning against the filing cabinets, "Morning Stacy, is Alex still here?"

Stacy covered her mouth quickly, nodding and reaching for the cup of coffee I extended to her. "Yup. She should be over in a second to drop off her charts from rounds." She took a deep sniff of the hot coffee, moaning in delight, "You are a lifesaver Victoria. The cafeteria coffee tastes like burnt tar."

I laughed, watching the woman sip heavily from the paper cup, "It's the least I can do." I tilted my wrist to look at the time. I would have plenty of time to make it to the academy and prep for the morning's class.

Stacy smirked at me, "The least you can do is bring some fresh bagels the next time?" Her eyebrows raised in a display of hope.

I gave her a playful dirty look as Alex popped around the corner, arms full of charts. Regardless of the fact that she was wearing faded green scrubs and bright blue tennis shoes, Alex still looked beautiful with her hair up and in nurse mode. Her tired blue eyes brightened up when she saw the coffee I held out towards her. "Oh! I had hoped you would stop by this morning." She took the cup from my hand, dropping the charts in hers, and grinned at me, "Good morning, Victoria."

I rolled my eyes slightly at the over exaggerated way she said it, "Good morning, Alex." I shifted my briefcase, "Why wouldn't I stop by? It's Thursday, and I always bring you coffee on Thursday because you always buy my first drink on Fridays." I looked over at the brunette, my friend, smiling at how happily she sighed as the caffeine gave her the extra energy she would need to finish out the last two hours of her shift. Alex chuckled, setting the cup down as Stacy grabbed a stack of charts and hustled away, hollering a thank you and her bagel request. "I'm so ready for the weekend. It's been a long couple of nights on the ward and I want nothing more than to sit in my pajamas and swim in piles of popcorn, binge watching movies."

She ran a hand over her hair, "You know you don't need to bring me coffee every week, Victoria." She said it halfheartedly. I knew she liked it when I brought her coffee and I liked bringing it to her.

After the debacle that was our first lunch, I had tried my best to find ways to apologize to Alex. I did call her that following Monday in between classes. Wanting to explain why I politely rejected her advances, but I couldn't find the right lies, and ended up telling her that I just wasn't in a place to date and was only looking to be friends. Insert a handful of other piss poor it's not you, it's me reasons. Alex bought the bullshit nonsense I spewed forth, sort of, or she just moved on past whatever she saw in me and we fell into an easy friendship.

We went out that following Friday for drinks and pizza at a local sports bar by her apartment. It was my test to see if I could be friends with her, nothing more, and I found that I could. Alex was easy to be around and she made me loosen up. I was still very careful about leading her on or giving her the wrong signals. She bought dinner and drinks that night, even as I protested, and then I promised I would bring her coffee on the way to work every Thursday to pay her back. Thursday being Alex's longest shift of the week.

Both had slowly become a tradition between us over the last month. I would stop in for a quick visit on Thursday at the hospital, then Friday we would go eat pizza and people watch at the sport bars. On the days I was out of town on a job, we would at least share a phone call. Usually, I would call her at the clean-up part of the job just to hear her voice and chase away the loneliness before it had a chance to sink its teeth in me.

I really liked Alex as a friend. I liked what she brought into my life, this almost normal balance that came from Alex just purely being herself. I liked all of the stupid jokes and her easy outlook on life no matter how hard of a night she had putting people back together. Alex was always smiling, putting others first and it made me feel normal and less of a monster in the closet.

Then there was the battle I still fought every day to keep my feelings hidden. The feelings for Alex were growing every day for her were getting harder to keep a secret. Alex was clearly moving on from whatever she saw in me. She would sometimes mention talking to one of the male doctors she worked with or about the ones that would hit on her mercilessly, trying to flirt with her. I would listen to all of it with a smile on my face, hating the fact that I wasn't those male doctors or any of the ones catching her attention. At the same time, my heart was shouting at me to do anything to tell Alex that I wanted more from her. Instead, I opted for the continuing silence and motioned to the steaming cup next to her hand, "I don't have to, but I like drinking for free on Friday's."

Alex laughed, slugging me softly in the shoulder, "Somehow, I think you're getting the better end of the deal." She looked up in my eyes, her smile growing wider as we made eye contact, "You up for tomorrow night? The usual?"

I hated when she looked in my eyes. It always took my breath away and made my stomach wiggle. I sighed and looked down at the tips of my black heels, "I can't tomorrow. I'm flying out to Connecticut until Sunday for another recruitment fair for the academy." In truth I had a Colombian drug lord to gut and string up in his mansion by early Sunday morning, but that was beside the point.

I glanced back up at Alex, her smile fading but still holding strong. "Crap, I work a double Sunday. What about next week?"

I looked up at the ceiling, pretending to go over an imaginary calendar, "I think I might be free on Saturday." I peered back down at the brunette, "Brunch Saturday morning? Then a lunch of astronaut ice cream at the Air and Space Museum? It'll be on me to make up for missing this week's pizza party."

Alex laughed, shaking her head at me, "They aren't pizza parties. Stop calling them that." She scooped up her coffee cup, "But you have a deal, Victoria. Only if you bring bagels next Thursday with the coffee." Alex squinted at me like a hardened contract negotiator would in the heat of negotiations.

It was my turn to shake my head, " I see you and Stacy have been conspiring against me, but yes, bagels and coffee next Thursday." I stole a look at my watch, "I should get going, I have two students to meet before class." I gave Alex a look, "Text me when you get home?"

Alex rolled her eyes, "Yes mom, I will unless I pass out in my scrubs like I did last week." She winked at me, "I'll walk you to the front." Alex moved to my side, her hand pressing on my upper back, "And you will call me when you land in Connecticut?"

I smiled tightly at how her warm hand soaked into the fabric of my thin suit jacket, sending shivers down my spine, "Yes dad, I will." We walked together back out to the front sliding doors and I was very grateful for the cool morning air rushing through each time the doors whisked open.

"Alright, I have to get back and do my last rounds so I can finish off the night's paperwork and head home." Alex's voice was soft and I could feel how tired she was. I turned to face her, "Tell Stacy I said goodbye and that she will get her bagels." Smiling at the blush of victory that covered Alex's cheeks.

Alex grinned, dropping her hand from me, "I told her tag teaming you would work." She then held her arms out like she did each and every time we parted ways, signaling she wanted a hug. "Bring it in Bancroft."

I sighed dramatically and moved into her arms. Clenching my jaw as the hug was perfectly warm. Dreading how Alex smelled amazing even after working twelve hours, and lastly the way we fit together. Like we were meant to be this close regardless of the reason. All of it made it harder for me to accept that I had been the one to push her into the friend zone.

Wrapping my arms around her waist, pulling her tighter into me, I whispered against her ear, "Alex, have dinner with me?"

Alex laughed and stepped out of my arms, raising an eyebrow as she shook her head, "You couldn't afford me, Victoria." She then rolled her eyes at the small joke I had come up with to ease the fact I had rejected her. I told her would ask her every time we said goodbye to have dinner with me, and in turn Alex would respond with how I couldn't afford her. I thought it was a way to level the playing field and it stuck. It soon became our own way of saying goodbye.

I nodded, smoothing out my jacket and shirt, "I know." I turned to walk out to my car, waving over my shoulder at the brunette, "I will call you later, Alex."

"You better, Victoria."

I didn't look back. Just kept my eyes forward on the silver car. For a split second, I wondered why I was keeping Alex in the friend zone. Why was I keeping the incredible woman that I cared about and was caring more for every day, at arm's length? Was I being foolish and ridiculous? Not logical and sensible?

My phone started ringing in my front pocket, as I pulled it out and saw Dani's name, reality struck hard. This was all of the reasons and more of why I had to keep Alex where she was. Answering the phone, I set my briefcase in the back of the BMW, "Dani."

"Pro-fess-or."

I huffed, "Can't you ever be normal on the phone?"

"That's a funny one. You do know what we do to bring home the bacon right? It's definitely not sitting in offices, doing taxes and other boring shit." Dani was in full agitation mode. "Anyway, I think I need to make this a quick phone call. Classes have been canceled for you today, Professor. You need to get your stodgy ass over to the airport and head to Argentina. The old man pushed up the deadline on your job."

I groaned, sitting in the driver's seat. "Do I still have the same amount of time to prepare?"

"Yup, but you need to be done by Saturday night. Seems Senor Cocaine Valdez has plans to leave Argentina first thing Sunday morning. If we don't move now, it will be months until we get another chance like this." Dani paused, "Old man has tripled the usual for you. Meaning you can buy your brunette bestie a big ole latte."

I jabbed the start button on the BMW. "Didn't I tell you to stop monitoring my personal life?"

Dani laughed, "Oh Professor, my job is nothing but monitoring your personal life. And have you forgotten about how you met nurse blue eyes? Remember how I helped destroy evidence? Yeah, that case is still open and it's in my best interest that I keep at least one eye on you and your fumbling attempts at dating or whatever you two are doing. Not that a court would ever dare to touch me, but I love reminding you of how imperfect you can be, Victoria."

I squeezed the phone, "Can we talk about this when I get back?"

Dani laughed again, "Certainly not, but I will make sure to email you schematics of the hospital so you know where not to look directly in the cameras. Toodle loo Professor, call me when you land in Argentina."

~Thirty-six hours later ~

It had been a knockdown, drag out fight. A straight up bar room brawl with my mark for the last fifteen minutes and I was running out of gas. The knock out injection did nothing to stop the man since he was so full of cocaine laced with PCP. It only made him angrier that I had interrupted his evening. Now I was going toe to toe with the bastard in the middle of his terra cotta covered atrium.

"Who the fuck sent you! Rodrigo? Carlos?" He wiped the blood from his chin where I had split it open with my right knee. "Was it the Americans?" He glared at me with hazy drug filled eyes, stumbling in his steps as he tried to catch his breath.

For the last fifteen minutes, the drug lord and I had danced. Traded hard punches and kicks, followed by his irritating form of the guess who game. It didn't even faze him when he ripped my mask off and saw that it was woman kicking his ass. I didn't care what he thought about me being the one to kill him. I hadn't even bothered to remember his name. Only his face and that he smoked a nightly Cuban cigar on his expansive patio, where we both now stood in front of each other like panting prize fighters.

I didn't answer his slurred, stunted questions. I only tightened my fists as I ran my tongue along the inside of my mouth, tasting blood. At least he didn't knock out my teeth with that last hard right hay-maker that grazed my cheek.

I blew out a heavy breath. I was done playing games and wanted to be done with this. I charged the jacked up drug lord, spearing him at the waist with all of my body weight propelling me, dropping him to the hard tile beneath us. I smirked when I heard the back of his head smack the tile with a loud and satisfying crack. Knocking him out to the point the PCP would not help him anymore. I hopped to my feet, digging in my front pocket to pull out the last two injection needles, and wasted no time in jamming them into his neck. Depositing a killing dose of the knockout drug into his system.

I knew the chemicals in the drug would mix with the cocaine and PCP and would basically cause his heart to slowly explode in his chest. Adding that extra oomph to the drama I needed to finish this job.

I stood up, taking in large breaths to clear my head and get ready to do what I had to next. Send a clear message to the others in the grandest way possible.

Turning away from the lifeless drug lord, I stumbled over to my backpack and removed the rest of my tools as I pressed against my side. Wincing when I felt at least two fractured ribs along with the fat lip he gave me. I had managed to escape any solid hits to the face, but when I wrapped my hands around the length of nylon rope, I could feel my knuckles were torn open. I took the rope out of the backpack and threw it at the feet of the dead drug lord, wincing more from the pain settling into my body.

Reaching back in for the large and very sharp knife, I spotted my cell phone light blinking in the front pocket. I removed the phone and tucked it in my back pocket, I would check Dani's message when I had strung the drug lord up and his blood was covering the floor.

It didn't take much effort to string the bastard up using one of the gaudy marble arches around the atrium as a fulcrum. I soon had him swinging like a rag doll in seconds and wasted no time drawing the knife across his midsection. Stepping back as his intestines, and blood, spilled out of the large gash. I knew I had to do this part quickly before the remaining blood in his body coagulated and any half assed police officer could tell the stomach wound was done after his death.

I laughed to myself, I was lucky that the knockout drug was a blood thinner and provided plenty of the red liquid to spill free from the drug lord. I stared up at the lifeless man, swaying in the archway as his guts hung out of him like gruesome paper streamers. A small sigh of relief escaping from my mouth as I turned away to start the clean up.

Dumping the knife back into the backpack, I took out my phone to call Dani to confirm the job was done, then call to clean up crew to have them meet me on the other side of the mansion wall. I needed a hot shower, clean clothes, an aspirin and a large glass of bourbon immediately.

I groaned when I pulled off the black leather gloves, revealing how skinned my knuckles really were. There were large chunks of skin missing from the first two on each hand, and luckily, the leather had helped to stanch the bleeding. I clenched my jaw as I swiped a shaky finger over the phone screen, I had one missed call from Dani, two more texts from her and one text from Alex.

Ignoring the one from Alex, I dialed Dani, only to tell her the job was done before she could utter a single snarky word. I was not in the mood for her shit tonight, especially after I had to play punch out with the drug lord. I moved slowly to grab the backpack, wincing when I bent down to pick it up. My ribs were definitely bruised or fractured from the hard kick my right side absorbed.

When the backpack was around my shoulders, I opened Alex's message.

-Victoria. I haven't heard from you. I hope your flight got in safe and you are boozing it up with some cute flight attendants in the hotel bar. But seriously, message me back. I really am looking forward to those bagels. :) -

I half smiled at the text. I couldn't message Alex back right now as I stood in a morbid display of dangling intestines in a pool of blood. A display I had created without a second thought.

I desperately wanted to keep Alex separate from this second life of mine in every way I could. I hated that it would only make her worry like she always did when I took trips and couldn't call her right away or tell her I had landed safely. I would always hear it in her voice when I did call her back. Feeling in the tone of her voice, how worried she was about how much I flew combined with the latest news reports of downed flights across the world.

Locking the phone, I shoved it in the front pocket of my black jacket and walked out the side entrance I had taken to access the drug lord's patio where he had sat smoking a cigar less than an hour ago.

I said nothing to the cleaning crew when they picked me up and dropped me off at the airport. I said nothing to the flight crew, not even a thank you when I was handed a fresh set of clothes and clean towels to use in the bathroom on the private plane. I had slipped into complete silence to process what I had I just done, and none of these people dared to speak to me. They knew I was a plumber and one of the most dangerous ones in Voltaire. They were just as afraid of me as I was of myself at times, giving me a stronger idea of how normal would never be in the cards for me.

I remained silent the entire flight home, alternating from staring out the window to the glass of bourbon clutched in my bandaged hands.

~Twelve hours later ~

It felt like Deja vu. Standing in the middle of my living room, fire roaring, as I tossed my work clothes one piece at a time into the flames. Numbly watching the fire destroy the blood soaked gloves and jacket I had worn while I sipped on a heavy glass of bourbon.

This was my life.

It was like a morbid wash cycle that only drove home the way I felt so lonely in the moments after a job. Blindly following through on my routine of destroying the equipment over a celebratory glass of expensive liquor.

Standing alone in the bright morning hours of a Sunday that would leave me sitting alone in my den and eating my neighbor's leftovers or whatever other food creation I found the energy to make. Listening to Dale and Mary chatter as they worked in the yard or sat in their patio chairs reading the weekend edition.

I shuffled away from the fireplace after throwing the last piece of clothing in the fire. My bare feet embracing the coolness of the wooden floor, I walked to my desk in the den. Sliding into the cold desk chair, I set the bourbon down and reached for my cell phone, re-reading Alex's first text message and then the second she had sent while I was in the shower.

-I'm heading to the hospital and might not be able to check my phone. But please, call me or the nurse's station when you get up. Tell me all about the wild night you obviously had last night. A.-

I sighed, swallowing down the tears that were coming from nowhere. I tapped the call back button and pressed the phone to my ear. Closing my eyes as the rings counted down until I heard her voice.

"And she arises from the dead! Connecticut that much of a party town you can't call your friend back to check in?" I could hear the relief in Alex's voice.

I smiled, running fingers around the edge of the glass in front of me, "Sorry about that Alex, I had a late day at the career fair, and then managed to sneak on the red eye home." I paused. I was tired and the sound of Alex's voice was having a profound effect on me.

"You're home?" The excitement in her voice was palpable.

I nodded to my empty den, "Arrived about an hour ago." I drifted off, biting my bottom lip to hold back the tears when I looked at the bloody and bruised hands. A gentle reminder of why I couldn't say what I really wanted to in this call to Alex.

"Are you okay, Victoria? You sound weird."

I sighed, trying to laugh and throw Alex off. "I'm just really tired." I cleared my throat, "Tell me how your popcorn and pajama Saturday went."

Alex chuckled and proceeded to ramble on about how she managed to get sucked into a television show recommended by Netflix that was solely directed at teenagers, but found herself watching all thirteen episodes in one day. Alex giggled, telling me how she fulfilled a bucket list item by going to the grocery store in her pajamas to get more popcorn, only to run into the chief resident at the hospital.

I sat and listened to her. Fighting the urge to interrupt her and tell her the only reason I called her was so I could hear her voice.

~Three months later ~

"You guys are like the cutest, oldest married couple ever, Alex. I hope when I'm married for twenty-five years, I will be as adorable as you and Victoria." Stacy smiled at me as she sipped the fresh cup of coffee Victoria had delivered, since she was still in Seattle at a conference.

I threw a pen at the woman, "We aren't married, Stacy. We're just friends that happen to be very nice to each other." I slid up to sit on the desk at the nurse's station, taking a deep breath of the coffee in my hands. I looked down at the big box of bagels, trying to find the blueberry nut one Victoria always made sure I got. "What gives you the old married couple idea about us?"

Stacy rolled her eyes, grabbing an apple cinnamon bagel. "I don't know. Maybe it's that she brings us coffee every Thursday like clockwork. Then on Fridays and now Saturdays, you two get swallowed up in the Alex and Victoria bubble and no one can break into it. Then there's the tiny fact that you both check in with each other daily like my mom and dad do. Another cute old married couple." She took a large bite of the bagel, "I don't understand why you aren't dating already." Stacy moaned at the taste of the still warm treat in her hand.

I gripped my Styrofoam cup tightly. Stacy was right about all those things, but I played it off as being a perk of a close friendship. Our friendship had grown over the months and besides Stacy, my mom and Bill, Victoria was all I really had and I was okay with it. I shrugged, "That's just what best friends do." Trying to brush the topic to the side, I went to ask Stacy about who could pick up my Sunday shift so I could have dinner with mom and Bill.

Stacy stood up from her chair, "Yeah, but do best friends look at each other like I sometimes catch the both of you doing?" She patted my arm, "Like I said, why aren't you dating the mysterious Naval officer? Why aren't you two running off into the sunset indulging in your silly old couple ways that makes us all envious?"

I sighed, setting the coffee down. It was a question that randomly popped up in my head when I caught Victoria looking at me in a way that made my entire body blush, or when I couldn't fall asleep until she called me back, or texted me to tell me she had landed safely and was back home. Then I would always remember Victoria was the one who put me in the friend zone and showed no signs of ever pulling me from it.

I shrugged again, sliding off the desk to pick up some charts, "We're just friends, Stacy, and that's all it is. All it will ever be."

Stacy nodded at me, "That's good enough for me, but is it good enough for you?" She brushed past me, grabbing another bagel, "Has she invited you over to her house yet?"

Stacy struck a nerve with that last question. It had been a hot topic for me whenever I would ramble on about what Victoria and I did on my days off. It was a simple question that opened up a can of worms. No, I had not been to Victoria's house, still didn't have one idea where she lived. I only just recently found out what kind of car she drove when I had to show her where to park in front of my apartment building. Then there were the thousand other little things I didn't know about the mysterious blonde. Granted they were little things, but they were somewhat important in the whole scheme of building a friendship.

I shook my head, my mood darkening from the innocent questions. "No." I tucked the charts under my arm, "I'm going to hit up rounds and then double check that Deb is for sure up to switch shifts with me." I tapped the box of bagels, "Try to leave the blueberry one for me."

Stacy waved me away, "Like I would ever dare to touch the one bagel your mysterious best non-girlfriend friend always gets just for you. The bagel is safe, Alex. I'll see you in an hour for that intubation in room six."

I said nothing, just walked away from the nurse's station and down to the far end of the hall where there was a small supply closet. I pushed the door open and dropped the charts on a pile of towels. Letting out a breath, I scanned the room trying to remember what I needed, when all my mind wanted to do was pick apart the red flags of Victoria. She was mysterious, yes, and I had gotten past my hero worship after she rejected me. That simple rejection knocked me down a notch and took all of the wind out of my sails. I had been silly to try and make a move that day when I didn't even know the woman.

Then again, I still didn't really know Victoria. She rarely ever dove into talking about her out of town trips or anything else about her job. Only telling me that the trips were for boring recruitment fairs, history conferences and something else related to her teaching job. She would then usually move the conversation to me and how the hospital was.

Yes, I could get the blonde to talk about the things she liked. What her favorite books were, what old movies were her weaknesses and I could get her to ramble on about any of her favorites if given the opportunity. I knew her favorite foods, the beer she liked the most and that she would do just about anything if I gave her a bottle of expensive bourbon. Other than that, I didn't know when her birthday was, where she lived, or who her family was. All the things that friends who had known each other for almost six months would have hashed out by now.

I did notice that when certain topics were brought up, like why she looked so tired after a one-day trip to West Virginia, or when I mentioned her days in the war, her eyes would get cloudy and give off a dangerous, almost scary look.

Almost scaring the hell out of me if I looked at her too long. It was as if underneath the warm, kind, comforting, funny side I saw, there was a very dangerous person. Victoria would just smile tightly in a way that reminded me of those shit heads in the metro station and move the conversation to a different topic. Those strange moments would have scared me off if I didn't feel so safe with the blonde. Opting to use the experience of her time in the war as the reason why she had that dangerous aura about her sometimes.

Then there were the strange phone calls from her female co-worker, or ex-girlfriend, I hadn't figured out which yet, that would always take Victoria away from me for a minute or two. My friend seemed to disappear as she spoke in quick, angry tones or sent angry texts back. I had put together that whenever those calls came, Victoria would have to go out of town for a few days. Leaving me and my dime store detective skills leaning towards a shitty secretary who probably enjoyed flirting with the attractive blonde every chance she could.

I placed my hand on my hips, analyzing this friendship in a supply closet. Victoria did know almost everything about me. I had told her a thousand different stories over our pizza parties and movie nights at my apartment. I shared my dreams, my hopes, my embarrassments, the shitty days and the good days at work. There was very little Victoria had left to learn about me. It even got to the point that Victoria and I could communicate silently. She would know instantly what was wrong with me by the way I said hello or the way I sighed. Even my mom and Bill knew about Victoria, and they were eager to meet the woman who had rescued me and brought a smile back to my face.

All I truly knew was that I loved being around her. Deep down, I had a fantastical idea she was also miserable all week until she saw me on Thursday mornings. I loved the way she smiled. I loved how tightly Victoria would hug me when we first saw each other after one of her trips. How she would call me at late hours and just ask me to talk to her about random things. I loved the way she would put a protective hand on my back whenever we were in the city, walk me to my car and stand by until I drove safely away. I loved how the woman looked in her fitted pantsuits, like the professional she was and then shift to the relaxed and still gorgeous woman in her baggy, dirty jeans and the worn out USN shirt of the day. I loved that we were like an old married couple and it was the easiest relationship, or friendship, I had ever had in my life.

I loved everything about Victoria because deep down, I knew I was falling in love with her and there was nothing I could do about it until she let me in and took me out of the stupid friend-zone.

I sighed, grabbing a box of gauze pads and tape, I was falling in love with a stranger who was also my best friend.

I would have to do something about this soon.

Dropping the gauze and tape on top of the charts, I left the closet. I was headed towards my first patient of the day when I felt my phone vibrating in my back pocket. I tucked everything under my arm and pulled the phone out, unable to hold back the grin when I saw it was Victoria calling.

"We just got the bagels, thank you for doing that. You could've skipped a week, Victoria. I'm sure Stacy would've forgive you, eventually." I stopped walking, knowing that I was grinning like an idiot after giving myself the fifth degree about this strange friendship less than a minute ago.

"I didn't want to break tradition, Alex." Victoria sounded tired, her voice had a rough rasp to it, "I just got home and wanted to call you to let you know and ask if you would be interested in a movie marathon Saturday? I could use a quiet weekend after this last trip."

I couldn't resist, my heart had the advantage over my gut and the red flags it was waving at my heart, "Saturday works. I picked up tomorrow so I could have Sunday off." I gripped the charts in my hand, trying to hold back the urge to let out any emotion, but then my gut won and I slipped, "You want to have it at your house this time?"

Victoria's breathing changed ever so slightly, "Can we do your apartment? The neighbors are having a birthday party for their three-year old grandson. It's going to sound like the circus came to town, specifically right in my backyard." She paused, "I'll buy the popcorn and other junk food?"

I felt my grin fade a bit as I looked down at the floor. Victoria was definitely hiding something from me and it was, and had been, blinking in front of my face like a neon sign for months. "Yeah, that sounds good. See you at my place at noon? I'll make nachos for lunch and we can play dinner by ear?"

"I will see you at noon, Alex." Victoria cleared her throat. There definitely was something wrong, it sounded like she was about to cry or was in pain.

"Victoria, are you okay?" The nurse in me took over, "You sound...sick?"

"I'm fine Alex, it was a long trip and I really need this semester to be over with so I can have a break. It's a bitch going out of town and having to be back for morning classes." Victoria's voice turned from the soft, trembling one to the very practiced Navy officer I knew well. It made me angry that she was doing this and it was sending up another red flag. I heard her take a deep breath, "Alex, have dinner with me?"

I bit my bottom lip, looking up at the ceiling and squeezing my eyes closed, I forced it out, "You couldn't afford me, Victoria. Get some rest. I'll message you when I'm off." I dropped the phone away and hung up. I shook my head at how much I was letting my heart guide me when it was clear I needed to start listening to my gut. I jammed the phone back in my pocket and started my rounds.

Saturday.

Saturday would be the day I started peeling back the layers of Victoria Bancroft.

I sighed hard when I reached the nurses station and picked up a few new charts that had come in over the last five minutes. I tried to read the injuries I needed to monitor throughout the night, but couldn't focus on anything other than Victoria.

After a stalling and reading the word hypertension a thousand times, I huffed and threw the file on the counter. I covered my face and groaned in hopes of easing the frustration filling my body.

"Rough night?"

I lifted my head up to look at the owner of the smooth feminine voice. A tall, beautiful woman wearing a EMS uniform stood across the station from me. Grinning at me as she organized her medical bag. The woman had big expressive brown eyes, long dark hair tied back, and she had an attitude about her that screamed cocky. Nothing out of the ordinary for any of the EMS techs I worked with on a given day, but this woman didn't look familiar.

I frowned lightly, "Same old, same old." I gave her a soft smile and looked at her nametag. "Are you new here, Diablo?" I smirked at the name.

She glanced at her nametag, tapping it with her index finger, "I know, you can thank my dad for the last name." She suddenly moved around the corner and held out her hand, "Angela Diablo." She raised her eyebrows when I smirked again, "My parents had a sense of humor, and yes, I just moved over to this district yesterday with DCFD."

I chuckled and took her hand, "It's nice to meet you Angela. I'm Alex Ivers." I dropped her hand and moved back to the chart. "If you need any help finding your way around this place, let me know." I smiled at her, "Stay away from the cafeteria coffee and don't let the security boys in the ER hit on you too hard."

Angela laughed, "They won't stand a chance, but thank you, Alex." She then squinted at me, "Forgive me, but you look really, really familiar."

I shrugged, picking up the charts I had to work on. "I guess I have that kind of face." I kept my smile tight, this woman was clearly about to flirt with me and it was the last thing I needed tonight. "If you excuse me, I need to get started on my rounds."

I moved past her when I heard, "I'll see you around, Alex and be careful when you leave tonight. I heard there's been some trouble in the metro stations late at night. Some weird vigilante taking care of the shit head junkies."

I looked over at Angela, she grinned and winked, "Hate to see a pretty lady like you get slapped around." She then grabbed her bag, threw me a wave and left.

My stomach started doing a slow roll. There was something about Angela that bothered me and it wasn't that she had already dipped into the gossip pool of this hospital.

She creeped me out in the way she looked at me and spoke about the metro station.

~Saturday~

All of my plans to peel back Victoria's layers fell to the wayside the second I opened my apartment door and saw the blonde standing there. Her long, pale, blonde hair down and flowing over the faded USNA shirt she wore. Leading my eyes down to a pair of closer fitting blue jeans. Victoria was gorgeous as ever, and grinning at me like she always did when we missed a week of spending time together. Those plans then quickly dissolved when she handed over the popcorn and grocery bag of junk food, grabbing me into a tight, warm hug that almost left me breathless. I had to end the hug before she felt how hard she made my heart pound when I was in her arms, using the excuse that the nachos were going to burn in the oven to walk away from her.

I sighed, tucking the ice cream in the freezer, I would have to fight through this and try to talk to Victoria or ignore it and enjoy the day with my friend. Making a promise if I did, I would have to talk to her next week. Closing the freezer, I looked over my shoulder at her, "Did you want a beer or wine to start?"

Victoria moved to sit on the edge of the couch, smiling, "Beer please." Looking at the blonde I could see how tired she was, her eyes were not as clear and bright as usual. I glanced at her right hand and saw new lacerations on the knuckles right where the others had been from a few months back when she had fallen during a training exercise at work. I knew the kind of lacerations she had on her knuckles were not from falling onto brick walls. They were the ones I saw on patients who came in from bar fights or on boxers. They were the type of lacerations you got from beating the shit out of someone. She also appeared to be favoring her one side, wincing a tiny bit when she shifted on the arm of the couch.

Aside from the lacerations and bruises on her hands, Victoria had an air around her that was tense and on edge, no matter how hard she tried to cover it up with smiles. "You fall down chasing sailors again?" I motioned to her knuckles.

I watched her scan around the apartment, like she did every time she was over, instead of looking at me or answering my question. Picking out the little things I had done to make the apartment feel more cozy and homey. "Yeah. A few of the guys from the local recruitment office challenged me to a push up contest. I slipped and smashed my hand on the concrete. I should be fine, I had the medic look at it."

I knew she was bullshitting me. She would never look at me when she was bullshitting me or being vague. I had quickly picked that up about Victoria. When she was hiding something, she would never look in my eyes. Before I could ask her to clarify, Victoria grinned as she looked at the wall above my bed. "You hung up that old Go Navy! sign I gave you?"

I smiled, walking over with a beer in my hand. "Of course! It reminds me of you and it covers up the one hole in the plaster from when I tried killing a spider with a hammer."

She raised an eyebrow taking the beer from me, "I do remember that panicked early morning phone call. I told you to use a newspaper."

I rolled my eyes, "I told you I don't read the newspaper. So it was either the hammer or my shoe." I walked back to the kitchen to set up plates for the nachos. "The hammer won. I didn't like the idea of walking spider guts through the house or the hospital."

Victoria laughed, following me into the kitchen. Leaning her back against the counter, she looked over at me scooping the hot nachos from the cooking sheet, "I should buy you a subscription to the Times so you always have a newspaper handy to squish spiders."

I laughed and shoved her lightly. "Maybe you should. Or you could just keep giving me more of your Navy memorabilia to cover the hammer holes."

I filled a plate up with nachos when I heard Victoria say softly, "I'd give you all I had, if you wanted it, Alex."

My stomach flipped as my jaw clenched hearing the tone she used. It bordered on flirty, sensual, loving, all tones that just friends didn't use with each other. I focused on trying to fill the plate, but couldn't. My gut screamed at me, shoving the plans of clearing the air with Victoria back in my face. I sighed hard, leaning on the counter with both hands. I gave in. "Victoria, what are we doing?"

I felt her back away a few steps, "What do you mean, Alex? We're going to eat nachos and watch Hepburn movies. Audrey and Katherine." Her voice was still low. A feeble attempt to hide that I had caught her.

I turned to look at her. "No, I mean, what are WE doing Victoria?" I pushed off from the counter, motioning between her and I. "This. What is this? What are we doing?" I looked in her eyes and was thankful when I only saw them turn glassy. Not a cloud in sight. "This friendship. Is it just that?"

Victoria closed her eyes nodding, "Yes. It's a friendship. You don't have to ask that, Alex. You're my friend, I'm your friend."

I folded my arms across my chest, getting irritated and frustrated, "There's more between us, Victoria. I can see it. You have to see it, and everyone around us can see it. Stacy called us a cute old married couple the other day." I laughed nervously, "Matter of fact she pointed out a lot of things that got me thinking. Thinking what are we doing? You put me in the friend zone after that day at the deli. Telling me you aren't ready to date because of this or that, but dammit, Victoria." I paused, "What are we doing? I need to know so I can move on or move forward with whatever this is."

Victoria slowly set her beer down, looking down at the tops of her dirty white converse, "You are my friend Alex. You're probably the best friend I've ever had." She looked up at me, the clouds starting to form around the edges of her eyes, "That's all we can ever be." In her tone I heard a thousand different things that she wanted to say but never would.

I nodded, my jaw clenching, "Why? Can you at least tell me why?" I dropped my hands to my hips. My frustration quickly turning to anger, "Why won't you tell me anything about you? Everything about you is a damn mystery. I don't even know where you live, when your birthday is. Simple shit like that. Simple things that friends share with each other, but I don't know any of it. All I do know is the way I look at you and the way you look at me, that's not how friends should look at each other."

I looked at her hard again, my courage fading as I saw that what I was doing was about to change everything between us, but I couldn't do it anymore. "You know everything about me, Victoria, and yet I only get snippets in return. I do know that you're this amazing woman who helped me one night and as much as I want to be just friends, it's hard." I swallowed, holding back the part where I wanted to tell her I was falling in love with her. I suddenly wished I had a beer in my hand to guzzle for some extra liquid courage, "This is so hard because there is something more here, something incredible and something that isn't just a friendship."

Victoria pushed away from the counter, shoving her hands in her pockets, "I can't Alex. I don't expect you to understand or accept it. You wouldn't be the first or the last." She turned to walk towards the door, "I should go."

"Dammit Victoria, stop! Talk to me. Tell me something. I feel like you're walking away from me to avoid talking." I didn't want to plead with her, but it felt like I was about to lose her. "If you want to be friends, tell me. Tell me to move on from what I think is between us and I will." I went to grab her and stop her, when she turned around to face me.

There was conflict riddling her face, the clouds covered her eyes and yet she looked like she was about to cry. "Move on Alex. Move on from whatever you think there is. Because it isn't there. It isn't here." She let out a slow breath, "I will always be there if you need me. Call and I will answer. I'll always be your friend Alex." She smiled tightly and went to the front door. Grabbing the knob she hesitated, turning her head back to me, I heard in a ragged voice, "My birthday is November 6th."

With that she opened the door and walked out, closing it behind her with a soft click. Leaving me to let out the massive breath I was holding. The tears fell freely as I decided in that moment to move on. Forget ever having anything more with Victoria than a friendship.

A friendship I knew in the morning would be completely different for the both of us.

~*Six months later* ~

I knew walking out on Alex that day in her apartment would change everything, and it did to a point. After that day, we stopped hanging out every weekend and it took me almost three weeks to answer her texts or call her back. I only dropped off coffee in person once in a while now, but that was starting to fade away as Alex did seem to move on. She was never always there to meet me, just Stacy was. Eagerly taking the box of bagels and cups from me, telling me Alex was tied up with a patient and would be for a few minutes more than I could wait. When I did see Alex, things were not like they once had been. I saw in her eyes the sadness I had placed there. Gone were the constant phone calls at all hours, the text conversations, the checking in when either of us got home. All of it faded away, whittled down to simple 'hey, how are you', or 'want to grab a beer?' messages. Messages that felt flat and void of the emotion, or care that once filled every syllable.

When we did go out to dinner, we talked and had a good time, but there were walls up now. Gone were the goodbye hugs and the silly inside jokes. They were replaced by awkward waves and call you when I get a chance promises. Alex was now cautious about what she said, and did, while I retreated behind one of my masks and hated it.

I hated that I had decided to hide from Alex and not let her in like I wanted and needed that day.

I knew what I was saying when I told her I'd give her everything if she wanted it. I just wanted her to smile at me that day. Tell a dumb joke, hug me and then settle in with nachos and movies. I would then fall asleep on her shoulder and she would wake me up, offer for me to stay and then send me on my way. But instead, she called me out on the things that had been waiting to explode for months.

I had long picked up that our friendship had turned into a pseudo relationship and no matter how much I tried to fight it, I didn't.

I liked it.

I liked the way Alex felt normal and made me feel like I could do this. That in another month I could ask her to be more with me. That I was falling hopelessly and uncontrollably in love with her. I wanted her to love me as much as I wanted to love her.

But I didn't do that when she asked me what we were doing, what we were becoming. I walked away for the sake of my double life. Putting it first in the name of keeping her safe.

Those first few weeks after I told her to move on, I took every job Dani sent my way. Sniper hits, the usual planned out hits, quick interrogation jobs where I beat the hell out of someone for answers while I beat the hell out of feeling anything. Finding serenity and calm as I felt and heard bones crack under my hands, and smelling fresh blood as it filled the air. Clear signs that I couldn't ever be normal.

Even Dani noticed a change and eased up on being her snarky self. Leaving her comments to a minimum and only asking once if I needed to talk. I brushed her off and focused on the work. I took job after job to prevent myself from thinking about how lonely I was and how badly I wanted to call Alex to simply listen to her tell me about her day.

Adding in the end of the semester workload, I became so busy that I rarely had time to sleep before I was changing and driving to class. Soon I found my way back to the old calm, distant ways and was able to reply to Alex's calls and messages. Soon we fell back into a convoluted form of what our friendship once was.

And that's how it went for the last few months until I had a really rough job, killing another human trafficker in trade for secrets from a known biochemical terrorist. I had flown straight home from Bolivia, did the usual of burning my clothes and showering when I looked at the clock and saw that Alex would still be at work for another four hours.

I suddenly craved to see her, talk to her and maybe try to explain why normal wasn't in the cards for me. More than anything I wanted to hear her voice and ask her to hold me one more time. I wanted her to come home to and fight hard for a life with her. It all came out of nowhere and blindsided me. Pushing me to fix the shitty mess I made months ago, and try to at least get my best friend back.

I changed quickly and rushed to the BMW. Catching Dale to inquire if I brought beers and steak home, if he and Mary would be up to grilling them and joining me for dinner. Dale nodded with a grin, telling me he would be waiting with baited breath. I smiled, waving at him as I backed out of the driveway.

Maybe I could do normal.

Walking into the hospital I spotted Stacy backtracking her steps the second she saw the white box in my hands. Her smile covered her face, "Well now, it's been a minute since we had bagel day." She waved me over to the nurse's station, looking over my jeans and zip up blue hoody, "No class today, Victoria?" She smirked at her little joke.

I laughed, shaking my head, "The semester is done, and I'm off until September. The suits and uniforms have been all tucked away in plastic for the season." I handed her a tall cup of coffee, looking around as the nerves began to settle hard in my stomach, "Is Alex?" I didn't have to finish the sentence.

"She's here, pulling a double so this coffee will be much needed. Poor girl won't be off until eight tonight, but she's currently up in Ortho on break. Talking to her Doctor Dean." Stacy made a disgusted face, "Those two make me want to throw up, how stupid and giddy they've been lately." She lifted open the lid of the white box, "OOOOhh, pastries today?" She looked up at me for permission to dig in.

I handed her the box trying to hide the wave of emotions hitting me, "Yea, there's Danishes and strudel. The cheese ones are Alex's favorite." I cleared my throat, "Who's Doctor Dean?"

Around a mouthful of raspberry Danish, Stacy spoke, "Doctor Dean is this typical handsome orthopedic surgeon that has been after Alex since her first day here. She always brushed him off, rejecting his numerous date requests, until recently. The last two months they have been going out, sneaking off to make out in supply closets and what not. Alex keeps blithering on about this trip to the Poconos they're taking next week. I think she's finally going to either put out or he's going to ask her to marry him. Either way, its gross. Doctor Dean is gross and way out of Alex's league even for a surgeon" Stacy then looked up at me, "You've been missed around here."

I barely heard her as my jaw clenched so tightly, I could almost hear the tendons snap. My jealousy was rearing its ugly head in force. I curled my hands in fists, when I heard my name again. "Victoria? Did you hear me?"

I swung my head around to the woman, "Yeah, sorry. I had a long flight this morning." I smiled, "What did you say, Stacy?"

Stacy set her Danish down, moving closer to me, "I said you've been missed around her. Not just by me and my bagel neediness, but Alex too. She won't ever admit it to your face, but since you two had that falling out, she hasn't been the same. I think Doctor Dean is her way to get over you."

I forced out a laugh, "We're just friends."

Stacy rolled her eyes, "Yeah and I have an asshole on my elbow." She patted my shoulder, "Either give her up or get her, and do it soon before Doctor Dean gets into her scrubs." Stacy looked up, "Speak of the gross devils now."

I turned to look where Stacy was and saw Alex kissing a tall, dark haired man in a white coat, then giggle as he whispered something in her ear. The kiss and the hand holding between Alex and Doctor Dean was innocent, and yet it did nothing but ignite less than innocent thoughts in my head. Ones that bordered on what his screams would sound like as I castrated him. I had to force myself to look away as my jealousy continued to run rampant, "I should go." I turned to walk away, when I heard my name.

"Victoria?" Alex's voice was quiet, apprehensive, and had a hint of excitement. It had been almost three weeks since I last saw her. Three weeks ago when we had our last awkward pizza party where the conversation was so forced it became painful. I left early, claiming I was coming down with a cold. Hopping on a flight to Venice an hour later to dismember a rogue mafia member in his warehouse.

I forced my best smile on, "Alex. Hi." I waved to the white box and coffee cup, "I was heading in to work to clean up and lock up for the summer. Figured it's been a minute since I saw you." I looked up to see her dark blue eyes staring in mine the way that always made my heart skip. Hers were turning glassy and I could see her visibly swallow. Giving me a glimmer of hope that she hadn't forgotten about me like I once wanted her to.

I went to say something, when a delicate, callus free hand was thrust in my face. "Hi, I'm Dean. You must be the infamous Victoria I hear so much about. The Naval Academy Professor, right?"

Doctor Dean grinned a full set of shiny, glinting white veneers, my way. I grit my own teeth and took his hand, noting that he shook hands like a dead fish and not like a man. He was handsome, but had more ego than looks. I squeezed his hand a little too tight as I smirked, "That's me. Stacy was just filling me in everything I need to know about you, Doctor Dean."

He winced and released my hand, tucking it in the front pocket of his coat before throwing an arm around Alex, "Hope it's all good things." He glanced at Alex who was still staring at me with a completely unreadable look that made my heart ache, "Well, I should leave you two to catch up. I have a consult in five minutes." He bent and kissed Alex's cheek, "I will see you later, babe."

I sucked in a breath through my nose, folding my arms across my chest to hide the white knuckled fists I carried. "I should go too. I need to get to the office before Ensign Hall gets caught up with the others." I smiled at Doctor Dean, "Nice to meet you."

He nodded at me, kissing Alex once more before swaggering down the hall. I turned to say goodbye to Stacy, who was wide eyed watching what had just transpired like it was a soap opera, "Stacy, enjoy the pastries." I then turned to Alex who was breathing heavily with a flushed face, "Alex." I went to walk back to the front when I heard her.

"Victoria, we're just seeing each other." She paused when she realized that she was doing exactly as I had told her to do months ago. "He's a nice guy." It was her way of justifying that she was moving on. Looking for the life I could not give her, didn't seem to want to give her. I was also having a hard time standing in front of her. Trying not stare at her in her scrubs with her hair up, showing off the features that were my favorite on her. The same ones that I would see at night whenever I closed my eyes and let my mind drift to her. The way she folded her arms tightly to hide how hard her heart was pounding.

I knew in this moment this would be the last time I saw Alex. I couldn't do this, I couldn't fight for her when she was moving on and giving me clear signs that I had to let her go.

I nodded, "He seems nice. Has the handshake of a four-year old, but he seems nice?" I heard Stacy choke, holding back a laugh. Both Alex and I gave her a dirty look. She held up her hands, "I think I hear a pee bag that needs changing." She hustled out of the station, patting my shoulder, "Thanks for the goodies, and remember what I said." She looked over her shoulder, "You've been missed."

I smiled and watched her walk away before returning to Alex, "There's strudel in the box. Your favorite." I moved my hands to the front pockets on my hoody, struggling to find something to say as the air grew tense. Finally, I shrugged and smiled at the woman who held my heart, "I hope he treats you right and it looks like he can afford you." I smiled wider when I saw the small joke ease Alex.

She nodded, "He can, but I won't let him take me to dinner." She then looked over at the rack of charts, taking in a deep breath she spoke, "It was good to see you, Victoria. Maybe we can get together in a couple days for pizza." I felt the struggle in her. She was not expecting me to show up at her work, catch her with her new boyfriend and still feel the things she did.

I licked my lips, "I'm off for the summer. Call me when you're free." I glanced at the giant wall clock. I needed to find an excuse to leave this awkward moment. "I need to hit the road before rush hour." I turned around and started walking back down the hall.

"I won't let him take me to dinner because I'm still waiting for someone else to ask me to have dinner with them." Alex's voice was strong, but wavered as she called after me.

I paused my steps but didn't look back. I couldn't let her see the single tear escape as I blew out a sigh of relief. I nodded with my back to her, "Hopefully they'll be able to afford you." I continued walking towards the front door, wiping away the tears.

Outside I rushed to the BMW and called Dale, "Dale, I have a huge favor to ask of you. I need you to deliver something to George Washington Hospital. I'll fill you in when I get home." I hung up and tossed the phone in the console.

I sat on the edge of the bed in the on call room, I still had another three hours of my shift and I wanted nothing more than to drown out the pounding in my head with a large bottle of wine. I held my head in my hands as I stared at the lines in the tiled floor.

Seeing Victoria this morning had thrown my emotions in a blender and they had yet to stop spinning. It had been almost a month since I last saw her, two weeks since I last spoke to her and I was starting to get over her. At least I thought I was.

But then I saw her. Saw the pain in her eyes when she saw Dean and I, and instantly knew I would never be able to get over her. No matter how hard I tried with handsome doctors and half assed make out sessions in closets. Dean would never be her and whenever I closed my eyes and lost myself in kissing him, I would drift off and fantasize it was Victoria. That it was Victoria's soft lips against mine, her hands roaming over my hips and my back. Then I would feel the stubble on his chin and it would snap me back into reality.

He wasn't Victoria and he would never be.

It was because of those little big things, that I had yet to sleep with him or really give my all in dating him. Deep down I was hoping Victoria would rush in to the hospital, professing her love for me or at least tell me what her favorite color was.

I pressed on the sides of my head, Dean wasn't the answer. Victoria wasn't the answer. I had to move on, I had to forget Victoria. Especially when I blurted out the inside joke, hoping she would turn around. Grin at me, sweep me up in her arms and hold me like I had only recently stopped aching for every night. More than anything, I missed Victoria. I missed the way she just knew me without having to explain my moods like I had to with Dean.

I shook my head and stood up from the bed, going to my bag to pull out my phone. The only way this was going to end was if I cut Victoria off, told her to stop coming to the hospital and just let me fade into a good memory.

Opening up her contact page, I began typing up the starts of a polite but firm message to her when Deb poked her head in the room. "Hey Alex, there's a lady here that has a delivery for you?"

I frowned, "A delivery?"

Deb nodded, "Yep. She says you need to sign for it?" She then grinned, "It's flowers and a gift. Looks like Doctor Dean is a romantic."

I groaned, dropping the phone in my pocket, "His idea of romance is getting me fifty yard line tickets for a Redskins game." I rolled my neck and followed Deb out to the nurse's station.

She looked over at me, "You're a Giants fan, doesn't he know that?"

I shrugged, "I've told him at least a hundred times. He's not that great of a listener." I looked up at the station to see an older woman standing next to the one desk with a large bouquet of yellow tulips in one hand and a small brown paper wrapped package in the other. I furrowed my brow, "Flowers?"

Deb wiggled her eyebrows, "Flowers, maybe he's been talking to Stacy?"

I shook my head as we neared the older woman, "She wouldn't tell him shit, she hates him. Plus, there are only two people who know that tulips are my favorite flower." As I said it, my stomach dropped, Dean wasn't one of the two. This couldn't be.

The older woman smiled as I stopped in front of her, "Are you Alexandra Ivers?"

I nodded, still confused, growing more and more anxious. "I am." The woman handed me the small package and set the flowers on the edge of the desk, "My name is Mary and a mutual friend of ours asked me to bring you this." She dug in her pocket, pulling out a thin off white envelope, "Please read this after you've opened the package." Mary winked at me before turning and walking back down the hall.

Deb peered over my shoulder, "Open it! This is exciting!" Her giddy squealing drew the attention of a few other nurses and that one creepy paramedic, Diablo, to stop and gawk a moment before I gave them all dirty looks. Silently shooing them away. I gave Deb a hard dirty look before reaching for the package tearing open the corner. I gasped when I saw it there was a small stuffed tiger resting on top of a DVD copy of *Bringing Up Baby*. I clutched the tiger to my chest as my mouth went dry and I felt my heart begin to race. I picked up the envelope, my hand shaking as I ripped open the corner and pulled out the single sheet folded once over.

I bit my bottom lip as I read and tears began to fill my eyes.

"Alex,

I might not have doctor money or a mouth full of shiny white teeth, nor could I ever bring myself to call you babe, but I know what I want and I don't want you to move on. Unless it's with me. I'm ready to fight for you and give you everything you want from me.

So, will you have dinner with me? And maybe a movie after?

I mean it this time.

Also, my favorite color is, sadly, Navy blue.

Victoria."

I burst out in tearful laughter, crumpling up the note against my chest as I buried my face into the soft orange fur of the tiger. I looked over at Deb, "Cover me? I need to make a phone call."

Deb grinned, unwrapping the tulips to drop them into a beaker full of water. "Sure, go call your incredible man."

I shook my head, "This didn't come from any man." I ran back down to the call room, "It came from an incredible woman."

I barely made it into the on call room before I hit Victoria's contact. I swallowed a few times trying to shake out the tears so I wouldn't burst into them when she answered. I squeezed my eyes shut when I heard her voice.

"I tried to get you a real tiger, but the zoo looked at me like I was crazy. I hope the stuffed one is suitable." Her voice was tentative and nervous, something I rarely heard come out of her. It told me she was serious about her note and she was serious about giving us a shot. "Will you have dinner with me?"

I grinned, feeling the rush of tears cover my cheeks, "You can't afford me." I fought the words out around choked happy sobs.

Victoria sighed, "It's a good thing I'm making you dinner then. At my house." I heard her let out a breath. "Tomorrow? I'll send you my address."

I shook my head, "I'm free tonight." I didn't want to waste another minute like we both had over the last few months.

I could almost feel her grin through the phone, "I'll see you at my house at nine, Alex. I hope you like lasagna."

I chuckled, wiping away the rest of the tears, "I love it." I whispered a quick goodbye and slid down the door to sit on the floor. Laughing and shaking my head as my phone beeped and I saw Victoria's address fill my screen.

This was too good to be true, and I really hoped it wasn't, because it was almost perfect.

Chapter 7

It was either nerves or fear that kept me awake the entire drive to Victoria's house. I was constantly checking the GPS map a thousand times to make sure that I was going to a house in Annapolis. I was struggling to wrap my head around the fact that I was really, and truly, going to her house. When I thought about that minor fact, the nerves would overwhelm me. The nerves would force me to stay focused on the road and the map for the simple fear of crashing, and never making it to her house.

Oddly enough, being focused and nervous kept my eyes open. I was beyond exhausted having worked two doubles over the last two and half days. My body wanted me to find a warm bed and curl up in it for days. My heart wanted me to keep pushing, keep moving until I was standing in front of Victoria, standing in her house and finally have what it, and I both wanted for the last year.

It took me a little longer than I predicted, traffic was sticky and I wasn't used to driving on this side of town. The surrounding neighborhood was filled with quaint houses with addresses on mail boxes and not painted on dirty windows. My heart won out in keeping me calm and I quickly found myself in a small neighborhood filled with amazing old houses that I knew my nurse paycheck could never afford me. I slowed the old mini down to a crawl, craning my neck to read the lit up addresses on fancy mailboxes and up on fancy porches. Double checking the text from Victoria a thousand more times, feeling my stomach twist in anticipation as the numbers counted closer to my destination.

It all still felt like a dream from the moment I hung up until now. All of her actions had left me floating through the last few hours of the shift with a silly grin on my face. Deb was constantly asking me nosy questions about who my secret admirer was while I gazed at the tulips in between marking down patient doses. I would ignore her interrogation, smile and move on to the next set of rounds. Continuing to float around dreamily with the unique sensation in my stomach that came with a particular brand of excitement only love could offer up.

I was in love. It was certain now.

I was utterly and unabashedly in love with the mysterious blonde that had literally swept me off my feet in a handful of written words. Words that swept me up into a fierce tornado that I knew would consume me and be one hell of a ride.

Letting out a heavy sigh, I finally pulled up in front of a large craftsmen house that had the front porch light on, beaming down on the black and white address numbers affixed above the door. Biting my bottom lip, I paused. This was it, this was Victoria's house.

I hesitated for a minute, my nervous hyperactive mind creeping up on me with all sorts of doubtful thoughts and words. I shook my head to shake them away as I pulled the beat up mini into the driveway to park next to her shiny silver BMW. Turning off the old car, I sat for a moment, having to press my hand over my stomach as the butterflies began to turn into anxious eagles. Flapping their wings to encourage me to go further.

I shook my head again, blinking the exhaustion free from my eyes as I reached for my giant bag of extra clothes and other random necessities I needed on double shifts. I grinned when I saw the yellow tulips sitting in the beaker on the floor. For the hundredth time, I thought, this was it. The one stupid phrase circling in my head with every new piece Victoria offered to me. Pieces I had wanted for a year. This was what I was hoping for, and wanting, from the moment I saw her picture on the internet so long ago.

The beautiful stranger who had saved me and changed that terrible night into a series of beautiful memories.

When I shoved the heavy car door open, the night air was crisp and helped to wake up my body and senses. The air also held the lightest aroma of varying flowers blooming as spring was shifting into summer. It all increased the floating feeling I carried as I hoisted the bag onto my shoulder and started walking towards the front door.

Glancing around the yard in the darkness of night, I could still easily see how meticulous Victoria was outside of her uniform. Her lawn was pristine and not one thing appeared to be out of place. I chuckled softly to myself walking over the perfectly aligned cobblestones leading me up to a large grey wooden door, wondering if there was a crazy, or unplanned bone in the woman's body.

I looked up at the large door with a small stained glass window up at the top. Taking in another deep breath, I lifted my hand to knock on the door when it suddenly opened in a slow, yet quick manner. Victoria stood before me, pushing the door to the side as the light from the house encircled her in an elegant yellow glow. She broke into a huge grin as she looked right in my eyes, "Alex."

I bit my bottom lip to try and keep the grin on my face from growing any bigger. "Victoria."

Then came the ever present awkward silence, which had basically become our song over the last year. Falling between us to give me the perfect opportunity to look Victoria over like I had done a million times in secret, but now felt I could do blatantly. She wore a thin, loose and faded pink sweater that draped around her shoulders. Showing more of her skin than I had ever seen before. Her blonde hair was up in a messy ponytail and the baggy jeans drew my eyes down to see the woman was standing comfortably barefoot. This was clearly relaxed Victoria and it immediately put me at ease. I squeezed my bag strap tighter, "Is it laundry day?" I cleared my throat lightly to cover up the wavering voice caused by rising nerves.

Victoria gave me a look, "Excuse me?"

I laughed, pointing at the sweater, "For the almost year I've known you, I've only ever seen you in uniforms, business suits, the never ending supply of Navy shirts, or Navy colored hoodies you own. I have never, ever, seen you in a sweater. Let alone a pink one." I shrugged, feeling embarrassed that this was my opening line of this new foray into a relationship with her. "But, it looks great on you. You look really beautiful." My courage and normal bravado I carried in life, was quickly being replaced by this fumbling, mumbling flirting.

Victoria smiled softly, looking down at the stone porch. "I wore this for you, Alex. You mentioned a long time ago when we were shopping that you thought pink would look good on me." She cleared her throat, waving me inside. "Anyway, welcome to my home, please come in?"

God, she did remember everything. I smiled at the new level of awkwardness Victoria and I were reaching, "Thank you." I stepped into the foyer of her house, suddenly feeling like I had to put on all of my best manners and stand in one spot as she closed the door, shuffling to lean against it nervously.

"Did you find the house okay?" Victoria was a step behind me, closing the door.

I nodded, trying so very hard not to look around even as the smells of fresh baked lasagna in the oven had its hooks in my nose, "I did, but I must confess that I had some help from the GPS." I shifted my bag, "You have a nice house, Victoria." I internally rolled my eyes at how terribly forced this conversation was going. Victoria was my friend, my best friend and the woman I was in love with. Why was it so hard to talk to her when I told her just about everything? Even that one time I had the terrible stomach flu and was trapped in my bathroom for a day, calling upon her to bring me medicine and some sports drinks to fend off dehydration.

Victoria pushed off the door, moving quickly towards me "I'm sorry, I'm forgetting all of my manners. Can I take your bag and coat?" She smiled shyly as she looked over me, "Are you sure you want to have dinner tonight? You look exhausted, Alex. I can save dinner for tomorrow? It'll be just as good." Victoria nervously rambling was the cutest thing I had seen in a long time.

I slipped the bag off my shoulder, handing it over to her, shaking my head, "No way in hell would I pass this moment up, Victoria. You finally ask me to dinner and did it in the most incredibly romantic way." I met her eyes, feeling my heart melt at the sight of them. "I can sleep later, but right now all I want is to sit with you. Be with you."

I dropped my head to look at the ragged edges of my scrubs, "I waited a really long time for this moment. A really long time for you, Victoria." I whispered it, so fearful to say it any louder and scare the poor woman away.

I heard Victoria breathe out audibly as she took my heavy bag and coat. Leaving me in scrub pants and the old long sleeve shirt I often wore under the scrub shirt. I turned to look in the direction of the kitchen and the smells emanating from it to distract myself from wanting to grab her, kiss her, or just hug her until the world ended. "It smells amazing! I hope there is a glass of wine or two to go with it. Today was one crazy day." It was more than crazy. It was a roller coaster of emotions with a side trip on a tilt a whirl.

I went to take a step out of the foyer to loosen up the tension that was beginning to swarm around us again, when I felt Victoria's hand clasp gently around my elbow. Stilling my movements and pulling me back at the same time. I turned to her with a confused look on my face, "What is it…."

The rest of the words never made it out. Victoria's hand on my arm was followed by her other reaching up to my cheek and then sliding to the back of my head as she pulled me into her body.

When her lips met mine, it was as if the entire world stopped, exploded and then was rebuilt upon the first touch of those soft lips followed by the intense sensation it sent through my entire body.

It took me a second to respond and realize that she was kissing me. That this was the moment I had been waiting for, dreaming about, for months. I pushed back against her mouth, placing my hands on the edges of her jaw to hold her as I pressed our bodies closer. I felt her stumble one step back, causing her to release my arm to move both hers to wrap around my side. Steadying the both of us.

I kept my eyes shut as we kissed like our lives depended on it. Feverish, passionate, loving and consuming. Add in another thousand words to describe this kiss, it didn't matter, it was perfect and before I knew it, I felt her tongue on my bottom lip, silently asking me for more. I answered her silent request, moaning and smiling against her mouth as the kiss grew in intensity. Never in my life had I experienced a first kiss like this. Not even my very first kiss under the swing set in third grade with Bobby Stevens. Kissing Victoria felt like what I imagined it felt like when atoms split.

I soon felt Victoria pull back from me, hearing and feeling the soft pants of lungs needing air. As much as I wanted the kiss to go on for the rest of this night or my life, I knew air was critical. Victoria's hand moved from the back of my neck to rest on my cheek as she leaned back to look in my eyes with a shy smile, "I've been wanting to do that since I gave you my pickle." It came out as a whisper but held the same power as if she shouted it from a mountain top.

I burst out in laughter, feeling all of the tension around us dissipate. "Me too, Victoria, me too." I let out a heavy, happy sigh. "Care to show me around?" I covered the hand on my cheek, pulling it down so I could slide my fingers in hers, sighing again at the way her warm hand felt in mine. If this was a dream, I never wanted to wake up.

Victoria nodded, licking her lips and looking at me like she wanted to kiss me again, "Of course, but how about we eat something first." She looked down at our hands in a way that told me that she was surprised just as much as I was by this moment.

I nodded, feeling my stomach growl and gurgle, telling me that food was a desperately needed remedy at this moment, no matter how much I wanted to kiss the beautiful woman in front of me. I looked over her shoulder to see where she hung up my bag, "I brought the movie for after." I turned back to catch Victoria still staring at our hands together, "And little baby." I then brought up our hands to bring Victoria's eyes up to mine. "Thank you for that."

She smiled softly at me and I could see the tiniest edges of clouds forming around her irises appear and then disappear just as quickly. "You do know that baby in the movie was a leopard?" Victoria raised an eyebrow, "I almost got you a stuffed leopard but…."

"I told you that I wanted a tiger ever since I was younger because of that movie. Is there anything you don't remember?" I took in a slow breath, "I know baby is a leopard, but I confused it with a tiger as all little kids do with animals who look the same. My mother was just happy the movie could settle me down when I was acting up, so much so she bought me my first stuffed animal. A tiger that I named baby, to carry around whenever I was upset. " I shrugged, "I never really figured out baby was a leopard until I was a teenager." I paused looking at the woman in front of me. "I honestly didn't think you were listening that first day, during our first lunch. You seemed so nervous and distant."

Victoria squeezed my hand, "I was listening, Alex. That day and every day after." The blonde paused, looking over at the kitchen in an attempt to clearly change the subject, "Follow me. The lasagna should be perfect by now."

I let Victoria lead me into the kitchen, my gut telling me to be cautious while my heart was floating in pure bliss. I glanced at her hand in mine and told my gut to just let me have this one night, this one dinner, before it begged me to pay more attention to the bits and pieces that were still far too mysterious about Victoria.

I had always been in control of every single aspect of my life, throughout my entire life, from my first day at the Naval Academy until now. Never once did I allow control to slip away, or allowed myself to give it to someone else. I had done that once, a very long time ago in Baghdad, and it changed my life. Then came everything else that followed Baghdad and starting to work for Voltaire, it all forced me to keep a thick choke hold on control.

But now as I pulled the bubbling hot lasagna from the oven, one I had made solely because I knew it was Alex's favorite, I realized I had allowed her to have control over my heart without a second thought. Maybe it was seeing her with someone else, that limp fish of a doctor. Maybe it was seeing in her eyes, as I walked away this last time, Alex was about to give up on me and ask me to stay away through a text, or an awkward phone call.

I knew I would never be able to pin point the exact moment I handed over control to my heart and the brunette sitting in my house, nor did I want to. All I knew was that I was taking a huge chance with Alex. Taking a chance that I could be normal and have the life I never knew I wanted until it almost slipped out of my fingers and into the hands of that greasy doctor Dean.

I was about to hand Alex all of the control and pray to God I could do this.

Turning to set the hot pan on top of the stove, I looked over at Alex. She was leaning against the edge of the grey granite island, trying her best to hide the signs of exhaustion creeping in more and more around her eyes. The poor woman was about to collapse. "Are you sure you can make it through dinner?" I wanted to look in her eyes, but found myself drifting down to her lips. An overwhelming desire to kiss her again coursed through my veins, made it very hard to think, let alone speak.

I couldn't tear my eyes away from her lips. How the bottom one was fuller than her top lip and how it felt against the tip of my tongue, sending shivers of heat through my arms. I had kissed Alex in the foyer purely out of spontaneity and fear. I feared if I didn't in that moment, I would lose my courage and never do it. Leaving me to regret it like I had regretted not doing a hundred other things with Alex and for her.

The only thing left in my thoughts outside of wanting to kiss her senseless, was that I knew for certain, I was in love with Alex. I loved her with all of my heart and soul, and I would have to fight every day to keep her. Fight myself to keep from sliding into the usual modus operandi of letting my partner, or whoever I was dating, think what they wanted when I had to disappear. Eventually, allowing them to scream at me, call me names and stomp off without a second look. Giving up on me as I couldn't, or wouldn't, fight to keep whatever relationship alive just so I wouldn't have to answer questions and tell truths better left to the darkness they lived in. I would have to fight all of that with Alex. I knew it also meant I'd have to lie to her to keep her close and keep her safe. Safe from the truth I hid, and keep the killer I was, hidden from the world. Hidden from the woman I was in love with.

The human in me wanted to love and live normally more than it wanted to hide the killer I was. Deep down I knew it would lead me down a road that would cost me everything I had and was creating with Alex, but then again, I had almost lost everything when I asked Alex to let me go and move on almost a year ago.

I sucked in a breath looking up at Alex, the risk was worth it. She was worth it. Loving her was the one thing I would do because I wanted to. Because I had to.

Alex nodded, shifting to stand upright, "Of course I'm sure." She smiled softly, looking around the kitchen, towards the living room where the fireplace and another large television hung over the mantel. "Your house is really nice."

I chuckled as I reached for plates and wine glasses, "It's still a work in progress. I keep wanting to change the rugs or the furniture until it feels like a home, not just a place where I sleep." That was the truth. My house still had yet to feel like a home and not just a place where I slept and destroyed the evidence of my second life.

"Well, it's far better than my one room loft studio apartment with spiders and holes in the walls." Alex laughed, leaning her hands on the edge of the island. "How long have you lived here?"

Scooping out a thick piece of the pasta and meat creation to place it on a plate, I paused, thinking how long I really had lived in this house. "I want to say maybe five years? It took me awhile to save up and find the perfect neighborhood and house." I suddenly grinned, I was about to tell Alex something I had never told anyone, "I also bought the house because the back porch looks exactly like Susan's in *Bringing Up Baby*." I heard Alex laugh again, forcing me to look up at her and give her a pointed look, "What?"

She shook her head, "Nothing. I just find it amazing that we're both so attached to that movie." Alex eagerly took the plate with a massive piece of lasagna, "Why is it your favorite movie, Victoria?"

I shrugged, grabbing a bottle of red wine, "I think why I love that movie so much is because Katherine reminds me of my grandmother. From the crazy Connecticut accent all the way down to the wild antics." I smiled warmly as I filled a glass for Alex, "She was the one who made me watch the movie with her one summer, and after she passed while I was in the Academy, I would watch it to remember those summer days up on the beaches of Nantucket and center myself." It all fell out with ease, as if my heart had been waiting for this moment. A moment where I had finally found someone I trusted enough to set my double life to the side and be the woman I really was. It also didn't help that having Alex in my house felt so right, felt like she had belonged there from the start. She truly was the one piece that made my lonely house begin to feel like a home.

I looked up to see Alex smiling at me, her eyes dead set on mine and absorbing every snippet I spoke about my life. It hit me hard that I had really shut this woman out and gave her very little in regards to who I was underneath the two masks I wore. Especially since she had given me her all from day one in that deli over massive sandwiches and pickles. It made me swallow hard and blink back the tears before they could make a full appearance.

I cleared my throat, waving to the small table by the back porch doors. "We can eat over there or in the living room on the couch. I can put a movie on while we eat?" it was an ambiguous question, one I asked with the hopes a movie would distract conversation away from me.

Alex grinned, "Living room. You know that I can't ever eat a meal without the television on. Plus, I'm in desperate need of sitting on something soft and not made out of hard plastic." She picked up her plate and wine glass, following me into the living room.

I motioned to the large dark grey couch that looked like fluffy thunderclouds, "Pick a spot while I find the remote." I set my plate and glass down on the old dark wooden coffee table, picking up a stack of large naval history coffee table books to set them on the floor. I glanced up at Alex as she sat slowly down on the couch and carefully set her food down next to mine, looking for coasters to set the wine glass on.

It made me chuckle. "Alex, don't worry about spilling. I've had everything scotch guarded." It was true. I had scotch guarded every cushion and pillow the day I bought the furniture. Just in case I got blood on something as I went to burn the equipment I used or didn't clean my tools well enough before bringing them home.

I felt my smile fade slightly at the morbid thought. I waved my hand absently to wave the thought away, walking to the side table to grab the remote before moving to sit down next to Alex. After turning on the television, I set the remote back on the table to pick up my plate. I sat down next to Alex but left a polite amount of space between the two of us. "You can surf through the channels. I usually only have the movie classics channel on or the news." I glanced over at Alex and laughed. She had already shoved a healthy forkful of the lasagna in her mouth and seemed to be in food heaven by the noises she was making. "Is it really that good?"

Alex nodded with her eyes closed. Swallowing some of the food down before she spoke, "God yes! This is the best I think I've ever had, Victoria. That's saying a lot since Bill is Italian and can make one mean cheese and spinach lasagna." She opened her eyes and glanced at me, a grin covering her face. "What?"

I shook my head, looking down at my plate, "Nothing, it's just been a really long time since I've cooked for anyone." I smiled tightly and took a small bite of my food.

"You can cook for me as much as you want, Victoria." Alex's voice was so soft. It made my heart squeeze tightly in my chest. This delicate back and forth, bold, but cautious flirting, was creating a strange tension to hang heavily in the air.

Things were changing between us again, moving back to the ease of our friendship that I cherished, but now there was a giant elephant that neither of us wanted to push out of the room quite yet.

It was if we were dipping our toes in the water, waiting for the water to be just perfect. I sighed lightly at how ridiculous this was. I could kill a man with my bare hands, and yet here I was stumbling like a teenage boy removing his first bra.

I tilted my head in her direction to make a comment, catching *Roman Holiday* in black and white playing on the television, when I caught the way Alex was looking at me. It was exactly the same way she did right before she tried to kiss me in the parking structure after our first lunch and again when I left her standing in the middle of the hospital a few hours ago. It was a look of love, hope, fear, lust, and it consumed me. That simple look wrapped around my heart and told me all the things I had been ignoring for so long. This was the look of someone who loved me unconditionally and could love everything I was.

I went to say something when Alex suddenly reached up and swiped at the side of my mouth with her thumb, "You had some sauce...there." She awkwardly pointed at the spot she had just wiped.

I turned back to my plate, "Thanks." Nervousness filled me like the hoover dam had just broken inside of me, releasing wave upon tidal wave of nervous butterflies in my stomach. I set my plate down to get up and search out some napkins and some air. "I forgot napkins." I half mumbled it, looking up at Audrey Hepburn grinning at me in bold black and white.

Before I could push up from the couch, I felt Alex's warm hand glide across my cheek. "Wait, there's another spot of sauce."

I turned to face her, finding her inches from mine. Those big blue eyes looking in mine and down at my lips, asking for silent permission to move forward. I licked my lips and tilted my head towards her, sighing as I saw the huge grin on her face right before she bent forward and kissed me.

This kiss wasn't hard like the one I unleashed on her in the foyer. It was softer, far more delicate and tentative, but amazing nonetheless. Alex didn't take it any further than the innocence behind it, parting from me just as quickly as she started. Sighing contently as she leaned back and looked down at me, "I couldn't resist." Her face turned a bright red as she sat back down on the couch, reaching for her now empty plate.

I smiled, licking my lips, tasting pasta sauce and wine, "I don't want you to, Alex." My voice was a heavy whisper. I really didn't want her to hold back anymore as much as I didn't want to hold back. My body was coming alive as I breathed in her scent of the light perfume she wore every day. The perfume mixed with the cheap apricot shampoo she used, and the starchy smell of the color-safe bleach she used to wash her scrubs.

All of it was distinctly her, and it was the most intoxicating scent as she sat inches away from me. I had always been conscious of the little things that was solely Alex, but now everything was amplified and filtered into my heart.

Leaving a permanent mark with explicit sensory memories the second I opened my heart to her.

Alex looked up at me, the ever infamous Alex grin on her face, and pointed at my plate. "You going to eat that?"

I chuckled at Alex's way of chasing away the awkward tension that was beginning to grow heavier. I traded her empty plate for my very full one, "You can have it."

I leaned back against the couch cushions, picking up my glass of wine, I sat and watched Alex devour the rest of my lasagna as she scooted to sit closer to me. Her leg touching mine in a way that it felt truly like a first date where the parents were just on the other side of the room. I couldn't help but smile and lean into her, eventually allowing her to lean fully up against me when she was finally done eating. It was something both of us did without thinking as we sat and watched movies at her apartment. And just like usual, Alex was soon snuggled up against me. She let out a heavy sigh from being stuffed with lasagna. I smiled at how it felt to be back to normal with Alex. I looked down at the brunette to see her sleeping heavily with her head on my shoulder and a warm hand resting at the top of my thigh. Squeezing here and there as if she was checking I was still real and she wasn't dreaming. That was the new part of this scene. Her and I finally breaking past the half walls of just friends we had hovered around for far too long.

I pulled Alex closer against me. Shifting her into a more comfortable position with my arm around her, before covering her up with a blanket. Letting her sleep and enjoying how warm her body was against mine, while I watched Gregory Peck and Audrey Hepburn traipse about Rome.

If this was what normal felt like, I wondered why I hadn't bothered to find it sooner.

The sound of a chainsaw forced my eyes open. I had to blink a handful of times to get them to focus and stay open. By the time they had adjusted to the bright light filling the room from the windows across from me, I realized I wasn't in my tiny apartment. I was still in her house, laying on her couch, covered in her blankets.

I smiled, pushing myself to sit up against the back of the couch. I yawned and looked around the living room, smiling more as I saw the soft pillow I had slept on.

It was clear Victoria had placed it there along with the thick navy blue blanket that covered me. I was still tired, but I felt much better than when I had struggled to stay awake after eating three pounds of lasagna.

I knew at some point I had failed, and that was why I was tucked up on the couch.

I let out a happy sigh, pulling the blanket around my shoulders as I scanned around the living room, noticing the bookshelves along the walls that were filled with older books and some magazines. There were little Navy nick knacks tucked in the spaces between books with a few framed photographs that I couldn't make out who was in them or what they were of. All of the things in the room made me curious to poke around in an attempt to get to know the blonde better, but deep in my gut I knew it was better if I left her to tell me when she felt ready.

I yawned again, my eyes falling to the neat pile of clothes next to a thick fluffy towel, a washcloth with a small note and a fresh picked purple tulip sitting on top. I grinned and giggled softly, Victoria was beyond a hopeless romantic and I couldn't help but giggle at the way it made me feel.

Snaking my arm out from underneath the blanket, I picked up the tulip and the note.

"The shower is upstairs next to my bedroom. I found an old pair of your jeans you left in my car when I helped you do laundry. Sadly, all I have is old Navy shirts.

Coffee is in the kitchen.

V"

I dipped my nose into the tulip, inhaling its delicate scent before I set it back on the table and grabbed the two neat piles. I was more than excited to take a hot shower and find Victoria. Today was the beginning of something that I knew would change my life and I was eager to get the day started.

I found the staircase and her bedroom, resisting the urge to be very nosy and poke around in it, and headed directly to the bathroom after grabbing a few extra things from my bag.

One scalding hot shower later, in probably the biggest shower and bathroom I had ever seen, and that included the one in Dean's huge and gaudy house up in Springfield, I changed into the set of clothes Victoria left me. The shirt was a bit tight in some spots, but it still fit me. The faded Navy mascot of an angry goat made me laugh and shake my head as I gathered up my scrubs and wet towels.

I was very tempted to raid Victoria's closet and drawers to just see exactly how many Navy t-shirts she owned, since it appeared she had a new one just when I thought I had seen the entire collection.

After hanging up the towels neatly on the rack in the bathroom, I quickly brushed my teeth and went to head for coffee when I paused on the way to the door. Staring over at the big bed with the covers all neatly tucked into a perfect square to match the curves of the mattress, I felt my stomach wiggle.

Thoughts of what it would be like to share that bed with Victoria raced through my head. What it would be like to wake up on a Saturday morning after a late night of watching movies and eating dinner. Then what it would be like to wake up to her on a Sunday morning after a lengthy night of exploring what she kept hidden under her uniforms and old t-shirts. I clenched the ball of clothes tighter against my chest at the images of Victoria naked. It made my heart throb, along with other parts of my body.

I let out a heavy sigh and turned to head back downstairs. I had thought many times about what Victoria looked like underneath her clothes, what her skin would feel like under my fingertips and if her touch would be gentle or firm. Would she command control in the bedroom? Or allow me to take the lead like she so often did in our lives together. Waiting for me to guide her, tell her where I wanted to be kissed and touched.

I bit the inside of my cheek to bring my inappropriate thoughts back to reality and out of the gutter. Victoria and I were still friends and just because yesterday was a turning point, it didn't mean either of us was near the point of jumping into bed together. Bang away like bunnies, as Stacy suggested so many times Victoria and I should be doing.

Rolling my eyes, I shoved my scrubs into the bag. I grinned when my hand brushed across soft fur, and pulled out the stuffed tiger. I moved to set him on the coffee table before I folded the blankets and picked up the pillow I used. For whatever reason, being in Victoria's house made me want to be a little neater than normal. It was as if I was afraid to upset the gentle balance of finally being in Victoria's home and a further into her mysterious life.

Walking into the kitchen when I was done tidying up my makeshift bed, I spotted a large glass vase full of the purple tulips. I sighed happily, "Victoria, you're killing me slowly." I chuckled, moving to the coffee pot that was still warm and filled the kitchen with the rich of aroma of very good coffee. I laughed more when I saw the coffee mug shaped like a battleship the blonde had left out for me. Victoria was clearly in love with the Navy and anything Navy related.

Taking the first sip of the warm black coffee, I leaned against the counter. Letting the caffeine fill my veins and wake me up, I stole a look at the clock on the stove. It was a few minutes after ten in the morning. I quickly scrubbed my brain to recall what Victoria usually did on Saturdays at this time. The woman was hard core for routine and most times I couldn't get her to deviate from it. Gripping the battleship in my hand, I continued to search out what she could be doing that would leave me in her house alone.

Pushing away from the counter, I shuffled out of the kitchen and moved towards the small den where a large wooden desk sat facing another large television. I was surprised that the woman had so many televisions in her house, especially for a teacher, but I knew how much she loved her old movies.

The den was very warm and cozy, with more waist high bookshelves around the walls and under the television, filled with more books about military history. Moving to the large desk, I smiled when I saw the stacks of graded papers on one corner with a note reminding Victoria that she needed to file them by the end of the week.

I continued to scan over the desk. Finding every small thing with Victoria's handwriting made me smile and my heart beat a little faster. I shook my head at how I reacted to just seeing her handwriting, knowing that I was completely head over heels in love with the woman. If her handwriting had this effect on me, God help me if we went any further than stolen kisses and snuggles.

I continued to look around the den, skipping over the black laptop that sat on the far corner. It looked unusual and thicker than normal laptops, but I soon found my attention pulled in the direction of the wall behind her desk. The wall was covered in perfectly lined up diploma frames. Victoria's high school diploma, her Bachelor's degree and Master's degree from the Naval Academy. All set along the wall with a handful of other certificates she had received in her time serving with the Navy. Next to the diploma frames, sat a small shadow box propped against the wall on top of a bookshelf.

Setting the battleship mug down, I reached for the shadowbox recognizing that there were medals inside. Bill had a few from his stint in the National Guard, but the ones in the box were nothing like the good conduct ones he had. These medals I recognized from news reports about heroes and those websites I sometimes donated to help wounded veterans. One in particular that seemed to pull all of my attention, was the purple heart shaped one in the middle with a single bronze leaf on the ribbon above it. I felt my heart drop as my brow furrowed, I knew what the purple heart meant, and vaguely knew what the bronze leaf stood for.

I bit my bottom lip as my stomach swirled as I thought about Victoria being injured enough to earn one of these. I had run across many veterans and active soldiers in New York during fleet week when they drank a bit too much and got out of hand. Many would ramble my ear off as I stitched them up, laughing that they had survived rocket attacks or explosive devices, but could barely survive an angry hooker with a beer bottle. Then there were the few quiet ones who would recount to me what they survived, how they received the same purple medal I was looking at. None of the stories revolved around tiny paper cuts or twisted ankles.

I ran my fingers over the glass top of the shadowbox, wiping away the thin sheet of dust. My heart tightening in my chest as scenarios I had heard, flashed in my head with Victoria in them. I could understand now, why she was closed off or careful. She had been to war, and by the looks of it, seen far more than she wanted to speak of. I stared at all of the medals, recognizing most of them except for one tucked in the far corner. One was gold and looked like a golden starburst with a red, blue, white and yellow ribbon.

I went to hold the shadowbox in better light when I heard a grunt and groan from outside, followed by something heavy hitting the ground. Setting the shadowbox back in its place, I rushed back into the kitchen and towards the back porch doors.

Pushing them open I was given a clear and full view of a huge backyard that did indeed look like it fell straight out of *Bringing Up Baby*. I smirked for a moment before turning to my head in the direction of more groans.

Over the medium high white picket fence, I immediately spotted Victoria's blonde hair up in a ponytail. She and an older man were on each side of a large seedling, dragging it towards a hole in the ground. I walked slowly to the fence, my eyes never leaving Victoria. She was sweaty and dirty, and as she lifted her end of the tree's root ball, I could see the muscles in her arms flex and strain. Making me lick my lips and suddenly feel very warm on this cool spring morning. She was stunning, even in the sweat soaked grey t-shirt she wore with her hair sticking to the sides of her face. Victoria was entrancing, and the feelings I felt looking at her bed, tripled. My breath quickened and I had to resist the urge to climb over the fence, grab her and kiss her senseless. Forget this cautious route we were taking and take her to bed.

"Hello Alex!" A soft woman's voice pulled me away from my impolite thoughts. I turned to see the woman who had delivered the flowers and gift to the hospital. I swallowed hard to try and force the desire out of my voice, "Hi! Mary is it?" I cleared my throat, sneaking one more look at Victoria before walking over to the fence. I dipped my head down to try and hide my blushing face, before reaching the fence. "It is." Mary smiled at me in a way that told me she knew exactly what I was staring at, but didn't embarrass me by calling me out on it.

She motioned to the man with Victoria with a dirty garden glove, "That's my husband Dale, he wrangled Victoria into helping him plant the maple tree we bought yesterday." She shook her head, "He wanted to do it himself, but I talked him out of it. He can be a silly old man sometimes." Mary turned to look at me, her eyes scanning me like a protective mother would, "I see Victoria's surprise did the trick."

I blushed again, "Yes ma'am. Thank you for delivering it." I felt like I was center stage.

"You don't need to thank me. I volunteered to do it after Victoria explained the situation to us." Mary reached over and patted me on the shoulder. "I'm a sucker for romance." She let out a soft sigh, turning to look at her husband and Victoria finally succeeding in getting the root ball seated in the hole. "It's good to see someone bring a smile to that girl. She's lived here for years. Always alone. Goes to work and comes home at the same time." Mary turned to me, "I knew when she talked about you that there was more to this story than just friends."

I looked at the older woman, smiling at the way she was so forward and to the point. "There always has been on my side."

I smiled tightly. "I've liked Victoria for a very long time. Probably since the first day I met her and she saved my life." I suddenly laughed, rolling my eyes, "That sounded really cliché, sorry."

Mary squeezed my shoulder, "It's not cliché, it's a true love story." She winked at me just as Victoria straightened up, wiping her brow as she looked directly at me. A big grin spreading across her face as she waved lightly, taking long strides over to the fence.

"Morning Alex." She headed to the open gate next to where Mary and I stood, looking over her shoulder, "Dale, I think you're good. Call me if you need more help." Dale waved her off, thanking her and then waving at me before he hollered at Mary to follow him inside the house, claiming they needed to leave us kids alone.

I laughed, shaking my head before turning to look at the dirty grinning woman. I looked her over, shaking my head dramatically, "You're filthy."

Victoria laughed, wiping her hands down the front of her shirt, "It happens when you plant trees." She folded her arms across her chest, "How did you sleep? You were passed out and I didn't have the heart to move you from the couch."

I shrugged, "Okay I guess, I mean my couch is more comfortable." I grinned back at the woman who suddenly looked very concerned, "I'm kidding. I slept great." I wanted to reach for her, grab her hand, do something physical to feel closer to her, but I was nervous doing it out in the backyard.

Victoria nodded, "Good. You found the coffee and everything okay?" She turned to move towards the open back door.

"I did. And the flowers." I followed her, stepping closer to her side as we walked back to the house. "They're beautiful." I brushed against her bare arm with mine, "Thank you."

Victoria smiled, letting me go inside first, "They are, but nowhere near as beautiful as you, Alex." Her voice was soft but confident, making my insides melt into a puddle.

I closed my eyes, "You're just saying that to be polite." I tried a joke to push out the rising desire to follow through on lunging her, but she was making it harder and harder. I walked to the coffee pot, clearing my throat, "Did you want me to pour you a cup or make an iced coffee?"

"Alex." Her voice was right behind me, sending shivers down my spine as I turned to face her. Her hand reached up to the side of my face as she looked in my eyes, "I mean it. You're beautiful. You're intelligent, funny, kind, loving and a million other things that I will find the time to tell you." Victoria moved closer to me, her voice dropping, "You're very beautiful, and even though I smell like a dirty wet dog covered in mud, I'd really like it if you would kiss me."

The air was sucked out of my lungs and all I heard was the intense pounding of my heart. I held her eyes, taken aback by this bold side of Victoria I had never seen before. I felt my hands tremble, and the only thing I knew to do to steady them, was to grab Victoria's hips and pull her closer to me as I bent forward and honored her request.

I kissed her with everything I had, pouring all of the nerves, the excitement and lust I felt for her into that kiss. Squeezing her hips harder when I heard her soft moan as my tongue passed over her bottom lip asking for more. Victoria's hands soon found their way into my hair and held me in place as she kissed me back. Our tongues meeting as we both moaned at the feeling. The way our lips seemed to fit together in a way I knew I would never find the same in another man or woman. Victoria was the only who could kiss me like this and I would probably never want another to kiss me like she was now.

I felt myself being turned and pushed against the counter, still holding onto her hips as she pressed our bodies together. The kiss grew in intensity to the point that my body was slowly building an all too familiar pressure that started between my legs and went to my heart. I moved my hands from her hips to the small of her back. Holding her still and trying to keep my hands from roaming any further. I could smell the fresh dirt, her sweat and the lingering aroma of the tulips on the island behind us. All of it was intoxicating and I couldn't help but slide my hand under the edge of her shirt. My fingers brushing the warm and sweaty skin exposed to me right above the waist of her jeans.

I moaned against her mouth when I felt the one thing I had dreamt about for far too long, moaning harder when it felt exactly how I imagined. Victoria nipped at my bottom lip, pushing her hips against mine as our kiss turned into unrestrained making out. I wanted her, my body ached for her, and I was losing control of my thoughts and the promise I made to myself to wait.

My hand moved further to the side, reaching to grab the edge of her shirt when the side of my thumb moved from soft skin to a patch of bumpy, rough skin. Skin that felt puckered and a lot like a thick scar. I felt my brow furrow as my mind struggled to connect what I was feeling and pull me from the haze Victoria's kisses kept me in. I moved my fingers up to run it over the patch my thumb had just brushed across, when Victoria suddenly parted from me and stepped back out of my arms. She was red face, panting as heavily as I was and when I looked in her eyes, I saw the faintest set of clouds forming in them.

She licked her lips and smiled bashfully, pulling her shirt down as she took a step away, "Oh Alex, I'm sorry for losing my head there." She let out a heavy breath, reaching for my hand, winding her fingers in mine, "We should probably take it slow for a bit, I have so much to tell you."

I smiled back, semi grateful for the break, but now curious. Curious what Victoria was hiding under her shirt. I knew for certain it was scar tissue I felt, and it was the reason she stopped kissing me. "I'm just as much to blame, Victoria." I looked down at her hand, running my thumb over her knuckles, feeling the small patches of scars she had on the first three knuckles, "I can never say no to a sweaty and dirty woman when she asks me to kiss her."

I tilted my head up to her, smirking, "But I can and will wait for you." I leaned forward, kissing the corner of her mouth softly as I murmured, "Go and get cleaned up. You're taking me to brunch."

I leaned back still smiling as Victoria looked at me confused, "I am?"

I nodded, "You are." I then gave her a playful frown, "Have you forgotten our Saturday tradition? You take me to brunch after I buy you drinks all night on Fridays?"

Victoria laughed, bringing our hands up to kiss them. "Of course." She then dropped our hands, "I will only be fifteen minutes." She kissed my cheek, smearing some of the dirt on her face on to mine purposefully, laughing softly, "By the way, my shirt looks really great on you."

I groaned, wiping away the smudge of dirt, swatting her arm as she passed me to go upstairs, "I will not fall for your dirty tricks to get me to shower with you." I looked over my shoulder to see the heavy blush rise up her cheeks as she ran up the stairs.

I sighed at myself, if she only knew how badly I did want to shower with her.

Instead I retrieved the battleship mug from the den, rinsed it out and set to making iced coffees for both of us. Today was definitely a new beginning. I had already seen sides of Victoria I longed for and was excited she was showing me, but deep down, I knew there was more of a mystery to her and I wondered if she would reveal it to me, or if I would have to dig it out of her.

Chapter 8

"How many Navy shirts do you actually own, Victoria?" Alex raised an eyebrow as she lifted a forkful of her potatoes and egg mash, a favorite of hers, which she ordered at the diner down the street from my house. I had taken Alex there a handful of times, hoping that if I got her close to my house, I would eventually break through and actually bring her into it. Bring her into the parts of my life I so badly wanted her to be a part of, but couldn't figure out how to do it just yet.

I smiled, pouring syrup over my waffles, "Maybe a hundred, maybe two hundred?" I set the syrup bottle down. "It comes with the territory. The Academy always gives us faculty wearables as free advertising, add that on to my own little collection and it's literally become a wardrobe of its own. That, and I tend to be lazy about clothes when it's not about uniforms or business suits", I shrugged, "I'm more of a jeans and t-shirt kind of girl." I smiled, pointing at Alex's shirt with my fork, "And I'm pretty sure you have one or two of my shirts stuffed away in your laundry hoping I won't ever find them." I winked at her, "By the way, you can keep this one and the others you stole from me."

Alex's mouth fell open in mock surprise, "I would never steal from you!"

I laughed, "Really? I am pretty sure you have my grey Academy zip up that I let you borrow when you were cold after the movies last fall. Then my dark blue Go Navy, Beat Army shirt, and lastly, I still can't quite find my favorite faded USNA rugby shirt." I picked up a chunk of waffle, smiling at how red faced Alex had become.

"I can give them back." Alex mumbled softly, poking at her plate. She sighed looking up at me with slightly sad eyes, "To be honest, I wasn't sure if I was going to ever see you again. Considering how the last few months had gone and then seeing you at the hospital. Dean..." Alex shrugged as she realized that she was slowly filling the air with the inevitable elephant we both tip toed around for months until it sat squarely between us. I knew the second elephant, the one that was still hiding in the secret closet in my bedroom with the black gear bag, would eventually work its way out.

I had also taken full notice of how Alex ran her fingers over that one spot on my back as she kissed me in the kitchen. Her fingers moving over the scarred skin like they were investigating where it came from and not looking for the quickest way to get my shirt off so she could see me topless.

I knew in time, the nurse in her would eventually ask questions, and then I would eventually have to tell her the truth, or come up with convoluted lies. Regardless that the truth could be easily accessed by a simple public news search. I made a quick mental note to call Dani later and ask her to monitor any further internet searches so I could at least be prepared.

Sticking the fork under the waffle, I reached across the table and grabbed her hand. Picking it up so her fingers could fall into the spaces of mine, "Alex, look at me." Alex hesitated before making eye contact, I smiled softly, "I'll be honest with you, it took me seeing that limp fish of a man, have you in the ways I always wanted you, to help get me over the fear." I ran my thumb over the top of her knuckles, "I did want you to let me go. I wanted you to find someone else. When I saw him, holding you, my heart told me that it was the end and you had moved on. Then you told me you were still waiting for me."

I paused, squeezing Alex's hand as I looked up in her eyes to see them glass over, "My fear of losing you out of my own stupidity, and fear, that I couldn't be everything you wanted and deserved out of me, won. I walked out of the hospital set and determined to win you over." I smiled, "And steal you away from Doctor Dean."

Alex giggled, sniffling as she squeezed my hand back. "Victoria, you always had me. You didn't have to steal me." She then sighed, rolling her eyes, "I probably should call and tell him that I can't go to the Poconos next weekend."

"You can still go with him if you want." I gave her a playful smirk, "I know I didn't have to steal you, Alex, but I did have to do something to make sure you knew I am serious about this. About us." I laughed, reaching up to wipe away the single tear that began to escape out the corner of her eye. "But, I'll still be honest in telling you, I am not easy to be with. I work too much, I travel too much and have been alone for a really long time. Things you already know." I rested my hand against her cheek, feeling her sigh. I looked deeply in her eyes, seeing the proverbial light at the end of the tunnel. Alex was my lighthouse in the hell storm I had lived in for almost twelve years.

She pressed her palm against my hand on her cheek, "I do already know all of that. You also know that I also work too much, and easily become a cranky pants when I work back to back doubles." She pulled my hand down, kissing my palm before releasing it. "We can do this, Victoria."

I nodded, looking down at the plate of waffles, still holding on to Alex's other hand, "We can." It was a harsh whisper. On one hand, I believed we could do this, and I was starting to fully believe for once in my life. I had never felt like I did with Alex. Not with anyone else I have ever been with or close with. She made me want to hang up the black clothes and hide away all the killing tools. Embrace one life and not two. Embrace a singular life where I could be the simple history Professor looking forward, and not the killing machine that had to often look over her shoulder.

I motioned back to her plate, "Eat up before it gets cold, then think of what you want to do today." I smiled at Alex, watching her grin and let go of my hand so she could finish eating.

I managed one more bite before my cell phone rang in my pocket, I pulled it out to see Dani's name blinking at me. I clenched my jaw, as once again, reality made this moment convoluted. I smiled at Alex, "I'll be right back. I have to take this call, it's the Academy. I still haven't turned in my final grades."

Alex nodded, waving me off, "Go. I'll watch over your waffle." She waited until I stood up from the booth, before poking her fork into one very large chunk on my plate and popping it in her mouth.

Walking outside to lean against the silver side of the diner, I answered the phone firmly, "Yes."

"Well good morning to you, Professor." Dani seemed agitated, which was unusual since she was usually trying to agitate me.

I ran my hand through my hair, "Get to the point of why you are calling me, Dani. I want to enjoy my day off."

Dani blew out a breath, "Must be nice to be off for the summer while some of us have to keep working." I heard the familiar clicking of a keyboard, "Any shit, the old lady wanted me to reach out to you. She has a side job up in Northern Ireland that she needs a gentle hand to deal with it. Triple pay, in and out job. Leave Monday and back by Tuesday night."

I groaned, looking back through the window of the diner, catching a glimpse of Alex looking happier than she had been in months, making it harder for me to deal with this phone call. I didn't want to do the job, but I knew if I started refusing jobs it would bring attention to me. I had a perfect attendance record and deviating from it would alert Voltaire.

I also knew Alex had a double on Monday followed by her regular Tuesday shift. She would hardly notice I was gone, and it would still give me the rest of the day with her and part of Sunday before she went back to work. I sighed at the balancing act that had already begun. Balancing starting something with the woman I was in love with, and the job I felt nothing for.

"Are you listening to me, Professor?" Dani had a bite in her voice.

I snapped back, "What is it with you today? You're uncharacteristically assy."

Dani sighed, "This job just wears on me." She cleared her throat, "So are you in or are you out? If you're out, I have a job from the old man waiting for you. A three day trip to Brooklyn, eliminate a shifty mole in homeland security who has been selling secrets to anyone and everyone. A real piece of shit."

"Dani," I cut her off, rubbing at my temple, "If I take the side job, I want at least three weeks off. Use up some of my vacation time." Dani started laughing, "What's so funny?" I was beginning to get angry that she was truly wasting my time.

"Nothing, just the fact that Voltaire offers benefits and vacation time, still gets my skirt in a knot. We are in the killing business and yet we get our early physicals covered and a chunk of time to relax. It's a morbid society we live in, Victoria. Don't you agree?" She paused, "Wait, you never take vacation time. What's up?"

I clenched my jaw tighter, "Tell the old lady I will take the side job. Then dump the Brooklyn job on Dante, she loves moles." I waved lightly at Alex, catching her eating the rest of my waffle. "Look, I have to go."

I heard the keyboard clicks, "Fine. Old lady has approved it. Check your email later for the details and the other usual shit."

I went to hang up when I stopped, "Dani, can you do me a favor?"

"Oh! Now she wants a favor! These favors just keep piling up Professor." She laughed when she heard me grumble, "Go ahead."

"Can you monitor any internet searches tied to my service in the war, particularly the news reports and public records from that day?"

Dani let out a slow breath, her tone turning very serious, "Is that meddling detective back on the prowl for answers about the metro murders?" Dani knew what had happened to me during the war. When it was brought up, it was the only time she was not a sarcastic asshole, especially when I spoke of that day.

Dani had been there at the end of that day. She had been the key Naval intel officer that was able to find me and because of that she was eventually brought into Voltaire to act as my handler. Dani was the only person I could trust, and as much as I hated her at times, she had truly saved my life. Due to that tiny piece of history between us, she also knew the truth and had to hide it with me.

I shook my head to no one, "No. I just need you to monitor searches." I went to head back into the diner, "I will contact you as usual when it's done. Goodbye Dani." I hit the red end button and jammed the phone back into my pocket.

Reaching the diner door, I pulled it open and sucked in a deep breath, letting it out slowly as I walked back to the table. Allowing a slow smile to cover my face before I gave Alex a playful dirty look at how much of my waffle was missing.

She bit her bottom lip, "I ordered you another one, sorry."

I shook my head sitting down, pushing the rest of my food towards the eager brunette, "It doesn't matter. As long you're full." I picked up my coffee cup, "But you're now buying brunch." I cocked an eyebrow at Alex.

She sighed smiling, leaning forward on the table, "Anything for you." She winked at me, before slowly finishing the rest of my half devoured waffles.

I set the cup down, wrapping both of my hands around it, "I was thinking. That weekend you took off to go to the Pocono's?"

Alex looked up at me with curious eyes, "Yes, what about that weekend? I was going to call my boss and see if I can pick up the shifts now that I think Doctor Dean and I are better off just being co-workers."

I laughed, "Not even going to remain friends?"

"Nope, he barely remembers my middle name after I have told him a thousand times. Needless to say, it's better off if I downgrade him from possible suitor to co-worker status." Alex reached for her orange juice, "Anyway, what about that weekend I took off?"

I twirled the brown ceramic coffee cup. "I have some vacation time coming up after this last trip on Monday." I saw Alex's smile fade, "I'll only be gone a day at most. I have to head up to Rhode Island to the Officer Candidate School and meet with one of the instructors. It's all administrative nonsense. They want me to look over the next batch of candidates." I paused, hating the fact that the lie fell so easily from my mouth, "I'll be back Tuesday afternoon, and I was thinking that we could spend some time together. Go on that road trip to Richmond you always talked about or do other boring things."

I shifted in my seat nervously. This was all new territory for me, wanting to spend time with someone, being the one to initiate spending time together. I had always let the other person dictate and guide me through the nuances of being in a relationship, but here I was, wanting to be with Alex. Taking vacation time to be with Alex and becoming someone else for her. Someone a little more human.

I was letting down walls and opening up the steel doors I kept my heart, and life, behind for so long. All because of the woman sitting across from me.

Alex grinned, tilting her head and looking out the window to hide the blush forming around the curves of her cheeks, "I think I could probably fit you in somewhere, only if we do boring things." She glanced at me, her grin turning into a smirk, "Only if we go to the air and space museum for astronaut ice cream. I vaguely remember you promising me that a long time ago and it never happened. Your flight was delayed coming back from San Diego and I got stuck eating cold pizza with Stacy in my apartment."

I laughed, nodding. "I do remember that."

I did remember that day. I was late coming back from New Zealand, not San Diego. A tropical storm had flown over the island and I was stuck at a backwoods airport with my equipment and the cleaning crew.

We all had missed the exit window when the maniacal evangelist I was sent to kill and dismember, ran from me. I had to chase him for almost a mile before I shot him in the calves. I then had to cut him up in the heat of the sun, lugging the heavy body parts to the shore. Tossing arms and legs into the ocean to make it look like a shark had gotten to him during his morning swim.

I was stuck for a day with barely any phone signal and people who were paid not to acknowledge my existence. I had to break routine and destroy my clothes in a burning barrel of shit from the outhouse at the bar two doors down from the airstrip. It was one of the only times that it really bothered me that I couldn't call Alex for a day or more. Having to wait until we landed in Berlin to switch planes. Hearing the underlying fear in her voice had a very profound effect on me. It was the first time in a long time that I started to really hate my second job, my second life.

Looking up at the waitress as she set down my fresh plate of waffles, I smiled thanking her before turning back to Alex. "I need to pay up on the many rain checks I owe you, and I think next weekend would be perfect time to get a start on that."

"All you have to do is be here, be with me and tell me things. Things like where you grew up, what you were like in high school, your secret celebrity crush, what you did in the Navy and a thousand other things I can't think of right now." Alex paused, "Mainly, why no one has scooped you up and put a ring on it." Alex looked hard in my eyes, "There are so many things I don't know about you, Victoria." Her voice was kind, even, but it felt like a ton of bricks traveling across the table to my ears.

I clenched my jaw, opting to look away and down at the plate, "I guess I'm a bit too private sometimes." Cutting up the waffle, I kept my eyes down as I spoke, "But first, let's enjoy this breakfast and go from there. "

Alex sighed softly, her tight smile that told me she was mildly irritated that I was being vague. "Ok." She sat back in the booth, looking out the window, "I was thinking maybe we can go grocery shopping and I'll make lunch. We can stay inside today, watch movies, or that one new show on Netflix Stacy and the other nurses keep rambling about. The one with dragons and wolves." Alex rolled her eyes, "The orderlies can't stop shouting the one catchphrase as they clean gurneys."

I raised my eyebrows, "Let me guess, winter is near?"

Alex gave me a dirty look. "Don't tell me."

I shrugged, "I might have started watching the first episode the other night. It's surprisingly, really good." I sipped my coffee, "I think you would like it, Alex, or you can pick through my movie collection. Do up a Doris Day or Bette Davis marathon?"

Alex searched my eyes, her smile returning to normal, "It sounds like you are offering up your house this time for movie night." Her tone was a mocking one. Her way of easing the tension resulting from the fact that I had gone from very closed off to very open and eager to have her in my house, let alone in my life.

"I am." Poking at my waffle, I grew nervous, "I kind of like it when you're there Alex, and I still have to give you the tour of the place." I let out a slow breath, "You can stay again tonight if you don't want to drive home. I'm sure I can dig up another Navy shirt for you to wear before you head into work and I can wash the scrubs." I grimaced, realizing I was rambling.

She grabbed my wrist, leaning forward, "Victoria, you don't need to be nervous." She chuckled, "I mean I'm nervous too, but we don't have to be. We've known each other for a year now, been best friends. Whatever comes next, well, come what may." She ran her thumb over my pulse, smiling as she felt it quicken, "Of course I will stay if you want me to." Alex sighed, "I've missed you, Victoria." It came out in a barely audible whisper.

I covered her hand with my other, "I missed you too, Alex." I sucked in a breath, "So, you want to head to the grocery store next? Burgers? Your famous triple cheese with baked potatoes? I also have some leftover cherry pie from Mary and plenty of wine."

I kept my smile as Alex pulled out a pen and started making a list of ingredients we would need. I watched her laugh, holding my wrist as she went on to tell me about how her mother's boyfriend taught her how to melt the cheese just right before taking the burger off the grill. I listened intently, my heart also intently listening. Hoping that I had finally found the balance it so desperately needed. The perfect balance where it, and I, could live happily, peacefully and maybe look at the light at the end of the tunnel instead of looking away from it with sunglasses on.

"I know Dean, but I think it's better if we just stay coworkers. You work up on the tenth floor and I work in trauma four floors down. It would be impossible to maintain a friendship." I was in the middle of Victoria's backyard, staring up at the giant oak tree at the far end.

I dreaded making this phone call, but after Dean had called twice and sent a few salacious texts, that Victoria happened to see them, the white knuckles on her hands told me she was about to murder the ground beef in her hands. So, I decided now was best to rip the band aid off. "Dean, we had fun, but I don't think I'm ready for anything serious. A serious relationship."

I turned to look at Victoria removing the thick burgers from the grill. She gave me a silent look asking if I was okay. I rolled my eyes and waved her back to the grill as Dean droned and whined on. For a doctor, an orthopedic surgeon, he was as whiny as small child who wasn't getting their way. I had been on the phone with him for the last twenty minutes and it was like talking in circles.

I folded my arm across my chest, staring down at the faded, scowling goat staring back up at me. Dean was whining about the trip to the Poconos, followed by asking if he had done anything wrong. He was beginning to irritate me.

Turning to Victoria I saw her grin at me. It was the one grin that had melted my heart when I saw it for the first time in that deli. I couldn't hold back the sappy, happy sigh my heart shoved from my lungs. I had not felt like this for anyone, ever, and the last thing I wanted to do was waste my time on the phone with a whiny surgeon. I wanted to be over with the blonde who was poking holes in the foil around big potatoes.

I clenched my jaw and interrupted Dean, "Dean, stop talking." I smirked when I heard him stumble over the last syllable, "Here's the deal. I can't date you anymore because I have been in love with someone else for a year and you'll never be able to compare to her, on any level. She and I just decided yesterday that we are going to give this a shot and I would be stupid to pass it up, stupid to let her walk away from me again." I waited a moment, hearing Dean continue to stumble and stutter as he heard the word her. "I have to go. I hope you find someone you deserve Dean. I think Katie up in Oncology has a crush on you. You should ask her out." Without a second breath, I hung up on the man, shoved the phone in my back pocket and strode over to Victoria.

She was facing the grill, intensely focused on the task at hand. She didn't notice me walking over and I took advantage of it. Wrapping my arms around her waist, I pulled myself into her, grinning when I heard her heart pick up pace as I settled my chin on her shoulder. I took a deep breath in, soaking up the scent of her soap, the way the late afternoon sun warmed her skin and added a little extra oomph to the scent of her shampoo. I grinned wider when I felt her hand cover mine, pressing it against her waist.

She leaned back, "How did the phone call go?" There was an edge to her voice, one that hinted in the slightest towards jealousy.

I turned my face closer into her neck, "As good as expected. I eventually told him the truth. That I couldn't date him anymore. That someone incredibly amazing had fallen back into my life and there was not a damn thing he could ever do that could compare to her." I pressed a light kiss against her neck, "That could compare to you." I was surprised at how bold and comfortable I had become with Victoria in a matter of a day. It also didn't help that I couldn't stand to be away from her for very long, or go without touching he every five seconds.

I noted the flush I had caused to creep up her neck as I ran my lips softly down her neck. I loved the reaction she had whenever I did touch her. I was beyond addicted to it and made a promise to do it as much as possible.

"Alex, I don't think I'm anything amazing." She pressed against my hand once more before removing it to grab the rest of our late lunch. "I'm definitely not comparable to a surgeon." She turned smiling softly at me and pointing at the small plate next to the grill.

I reluctantly removed myself from her body to grab the plate, "No you're not a surgeon. You're right about that." I held the plate as Victoria placed the potatoes on it, "I don't think I would be that interested in you if you were." I smirked at the look on her face. "I can barely tolerate your ego as it is."

Victoria raised her eyebrows, a half smile on her face, "Really? You think I have an ego?"

I shrugged playfully walking towards the porch doors, "A little one," I looked back at her, seeing her squint critically at me. I decided to keep the ruse going, "Especially in your Navy uniform. You stand so tall with all those ribbons and your shiny rank insignia, it's like you are in a world of your own."

Victoria's face changed ever so slightly, so much so that if I didn't know her as well as I did, I would have missed it. "Alex, that uniform, my uniform, wearing it is like living in a different world for me." The smile faded completely as she held the door open for me, "That's why I don't like wearing it or using my rank." She glanced past me, into the kitchen and I saw the clouds forming in her irises.

I had to change the subject fast, "I was going to say that you also look devastatingly gorgeous in uniform and that everyone should be envious." I let out a sigh of relief internally when I saw the corner of her mouth curl up in a smile. I walked over to her, gently shoving her from the burgers and condiments sitting out on the island. "Sit down and get that dragon show of yours started. I'll finish the burgers." I cocked an eyebrow at her, "Still a triple cheese, extra mayo and no pickle, kind of girl?"

Victoria laughed out loud, chasing the strange tension out of the room, "I am. That has definitely not changed." She moved behind me to the refrigerator, pulling out two bottles of raspberry ice tea, "Can you put cheese on my potato?"

I shook my head, shoving her again, "I can, and I will. Now go, warm up my spot." I snickered, reaching for the large fresh baked buns.

I went to start on hers when I felt warm, soft lips kissing my cheek and her breath against my ear as she whispered, "I'm really glad you're here, Alex."

Victoria walked out of the kitchen before I could utter a word, leaving me to close my eyes and bite my lip in a feeble attempt to hold back the shit eating grin on my face. I sucked in a happy breath and returned to making lunch.

"Okay, okay, how about this one. First kiss." I sat facing Victoria on the couch, my legs tucked up underneath me and a bowl of popcorn sitting in between us. I shoved a handful in my mouth, laughing at how serious Victoria's face had become as she tried to think.

We had been playing the question game for the last few hours. So far I had learned that Victoria loved old movies because of her grandmother who babysat her during the summers. Her parents were long out of the picture from an early age and she had no contact with them since she graduated from the Naval Academy. She could recite all of the states in alphabetical order, then confessed she secretly always wanted to get a tattoo on her lower back, but didn't dare because of the tramp stamp stigma.

All of it was fascinating to me, no matter how trivial it might have seemed to anyone else, it was important to me. I was finally learning who Victoria was, getting all the tiny pieces that made up a person's character, and personality. I could see a shift happen in the woman as she told me facts about herself. It was as if she was letting all of the weight of the world slowly off her perfect shoulders and handing it over to me to carry some of the load.

I wanted to ask her about the Navy, the time she served overseas, the medals in her den, but I didn't. I had picked up that discussing the Navy, and what came with it, was something that would derail her instantly. Leaving me to believe that the worries and the fears I felt when I saw her purple heart, would break my heart if I heard them. I was also too caught up in how cute Victoria was telling embarrassing stories from her youth.

She nervously tugged on the drawstrings of her ragged hoody before letting out a dramatic sigh, "My very first kiss." She then looked up at me with bashful slate grey eyes, "Would have to be Brian Casper, in ninth grade, and I did it on a dare at a pep rally." Victoria rolled her eyes, "I was so embarrassed. I ran and hid out in the tennis courts until night fell then pretended to be sick for three days after."

I went to crack a joke when she held up her hand, "Now my first real kiss. That was Mindy Emerson, second year at the academy. We had been quietly flirting for months and finally, after watching the first years climb Herndon monument, we went out for pitchers of beer. She and I kissed in the alley behind the bar." Victoria smiled, looking down at her hands, "That was the first real kiss that meant anything to me."

Chewing slowly on the popcorn, I felt the subtle waves of jealousy roll in my stomach. "And what happened to Mindy?" I tried to keep the tone in my voice even.

Victoria furrowed her brow, "She met a third class midshipman. He was on the rugby team and I was quickly forgotten. The last I saw her was in San Diego at the naval station right before I deployed overseas. She happily hugged me and showed me her engagement ring." Victoria shot her head up, sucking in a sad breath and plastering a tight smile on her face, "Your turn." She scooped up a handful of popcorn. "How many times have you been in love?"

Tugging the blue blanket around my shoulders, I tapped the edge of the giant red plastic bowl, "Hmm. Good question. I think I've been in puppy love a million times, especially in New York. Everyone is so attractive there. All models, movie stars, Wall Street brokers and the like. I had a crush every other day on this guy or that one girl that would walk by in the most amazing dress I had seen all week, you know, the usual fare for New York City."

I chewed on the inside of my mouth, thinking about what I was going to say next, "As for real true love, the kind you see in soap operas and chick flicks? I would have to say three times. My first real boyfriend in high school, that took me into college, but fell apart when he transferred to a college in Seattle to follow his dreams of hemp growing for clothing." I smirked at Victoria as she laughed at me, "The second was the nice police officer in New York who brought in his injured partner after a car chase went wrong. He and I dated for a long time and I thought I was going to marry him." I felt my face fell as I thought about James. "But nurses and cops go together like oil and water. Both are always so high strung, overworked, over tired, and it fell apart. He found a lady cop he liked better and I found that I liked my job more than I liked being in a relationship."

I thrust my hand in the bowl, grabbing a large handful of the salty and buttery reprieve from my past. I was so lost in thoughts of the past that I forgot my silly trick to flirt with Victoria, telling her about the last person I was in love with. I wanted to play the vague game and test the waters to see if I could tell her what I felt about her and how long I had felt that way. That she was the third person I had fallen in love with, and probably the last one I ever wanted to fall in love with. That she was my heart, the air I breathed and everything else I had searched for in my pursuit of love.

But now I had deflated myself and wanted nothing more than to gorge on popcorn and end this stupid question game.

"And the third?" Victoria's voice was so delicate I barely heard it.

I glanced at her, chewing around the piles of popcorn in my mouth, "The third what?" I was hoping that if I acted dumb she would move on.

Victoria poked my knee, smiling, "The third person you were in love with. Who was the lucky dog?" She was trying to ease my mood, bring me back to the silliness I had indulged in since we started this game.

Shaking my head, "It's not important."

I swallowed the popcorn, reaching for the beer we had switched to a couple of hours ago, "All I will tell you is that the third isn't a were, but an is. Someone I am in love with." I quickly chugged the beer, avoiding looking at the blonde. "Anyway, we should stop. It's almost two in the morning and you're sitting on my bed." I motioned to the large clock hanging on the opposite wall from the television that had some random classic movie on, the volume muted.

I went to stand up and grab the half empty bowl, catching the way Victoria was looking at me. It made my heart skip a beat and drop into my stomach. Or course she would catch on to my vague word puzzle, and now I was dreading her reaction. "I can clean up and then head back home." I was nervous, the look in her eyes bore straight down to my soul and I couldn't get a read off of Victoria.

Hurrying into the kitchen, I dumped the popcorn in the trash and went to place the bowl in the dishwasher before I collected the empty tea and beer bottles. I grimaced as I tried to ignore Victoria as she walked slowly into the kitchen with the empties from the living room. What was I thinking? Professing my love to her after a day? It would just scare her back into the dark cave she had lived in for the last year. I knew I loved her with everything I was, but I also knew I was jumping the gun.

"Alex."

I smiled tightly, dumping out the last splashes of tea and beer, "It's okay. I only had two beers. I should be able to make it home."

I heard her huff in that way that told me she was gently irritated with me. "Alex, you had four beers, but that's not the point." I felt her hand on my upper arm, stopping me from cleaning, "I want you to stay."

Leaning on the edge of the island, I looked up at Victoria and felt all of my will dissipate. I bit my lip. "I don't want to impose, and I feel like I could wear out my welcome at any minute."

"Never happen." Victoria pulled me into her arms with a smirk, her silly Navy lingo making me roll my eyes. "You can take my bed and I will take the couch, or the fold out in the spare bedroom." She held me tightly, "Alex, this thing we are doing, starting, I know where it can lead to, will lead to. I'm just as scared as you are, but I'm in no rush." She leaned back to look in my eyes, "We have plenty of time to do things, say things, be something. All I know is that I want to take it one day at a time, with you. I don't see a need to rush anything with you." Victoria smiled at me, "Just so you know, you were my first kiss. The first kiss, from the first person that actually really meant something to me."

I bent my head down, blushing, "When did you become this hopeless romantic who continues to sweep me off my feet?" I pressed my palms against her back, wanting her to draw me back into her arms.

Victoria shrugged, "Blame Cary Grant, Rock Hudson, Gregory Peck, they all taught me the ways of winning a lady's heart." She bent forward kissing my forehead, "You also make it very easy." She backed out of my arms, picking up the rest of the empties. "You can have the couch or my bed, ladies' choice tonight."

Staring at the blonde, I wanted to blurt out that we should share a bed, but I didn't. "I'll take the couch. Baby will keep watch over me."

"Okay. If you need anything, you know where my room is." Victoria tossed the glass bottles into the recycling bin and went about checking all of the doors, "There should be an extra pair of sweatpants in the laundry room in the dryer with your scrubs. Feel free to borrow them." She raised an eyebrow at me, "But, in the morning, they stay here. I can't have you stealing all of my favorite Navy gear."

I held my hands up like a caught criminal, "You got me! I will promise that your sweatpants and this shirt with the angry goat will be here after I leave."

"He's not an angry goat, he's a fighting goat." She groaned mockingly at me, "You have so much to learn about the Navy, Alex." Victoria turned, moving to the staircase she looked over her shoulder, "If you need anything..."

I waved her off, "I know, you're right upstairs. Shoo! I need to get some sleep."

Victoria grinned, shaking her head as she laughed going up the stairs, "Goodnight Alex."

"Goodnight Victoria."

I watched her until she disappeared at the top of the staircase, letting out a heavy sigh when she was gone, I turned off the lights in the kitchen and headed to the laundry room she had shown me to earlier. After quickly changing into her grey Navy sweatpants, I curled up on the couch. Smushing the pillow into the perfect ball, I stared over at Baby. He stared back at me, giving me what I thought was a "What are you doing" look? "Why aren't you up in her bedroom?"

I flicked his tiny black tiger nose, "Knock it off, and go to sleep."

Baby seemed to glare back at me, and then it struck me.

I didn't kiss her goodnight.

Sitting up on the couch, I plucked at the edge of the blanket. I didn't kiss her goodnight. We had parted like friends, or friendly roommates, nothing more to it. This was not how I wanted to leave Victoria, thinking we were still in the friend zone.

I flung the blanket off after sitting and debating back and forth with the stuffed tiger for at least twenty minutes, and marched my way to the staircase.

Lying in my very large and very empty bed, I stared blankly at the far wall. The day had been exhausting in the most amazing way. I had given more to Alex than I had ever given anyone. I told her things that I never told anyone in my adult life, not even past partners. It was incredible how easy it was to shed off the layers of thick skin I had grown over the last few years. Hiding behind a stoic, cold and controlled persona.

It was the most comfortable I'd ever been, sitting with her and eating popcorn. Sharing secrets like two girls having a slumber party, but yet, there was so much more to it. It was me letting her in, hoping that the further I let her in, the more she could keep me centered. Distract me from thinking about who I was and who I had become. That in time, Alex could replace the smell of blood as my calming point.

Rolling up into my blankets, I settled deeper into the pillow. I knew what Alex was trying to tell me when I asked her about how many times she had been in love and for a split second, I wanted her to say it so I could say it back and tell her I was completely in love with her. In love with her from the first moment I decided to get involved that day she looked over at me while I hunched over a copy of Popular Science.

I sighed into the pillow, in time it wouldn't be this fumbly and new. I would find the confidence and she would find it as well, bridging the gap from being just friends to being more. It didn't help that I literally ached for Alex.

The ache intensified with every small touch of her arm against mine, fingers grazing fingers as I handed her a beer. The way she hugged me from behind at the grill, kissing my neck in a manner, that made me almost lose my senses and dragged her into the house and up to my bed.

Alex was different. She was worth more than a quick run to the bedroom. She deserved more from me before I even thought about taking it to the next step. Never mind the fact that not only did I have emotional scars, I had physical ones. Scars that I wanted to keep hidden from her for a bit longer. Even though it would be the hardest thing to do in my life, refrain from groping Alex and slowly removing her clothes to reveal the stunning beauty I knew was underneath.

I rolled over again, yanking the blankets over my head groaning louder as my sexual frustration mocked me, when I heard a soft knock on the door. I sat up in the bed, squinting in the darkness as the light from the hallway slid in. I easily made out Alex's shape in the shadows, "Alex? Is everything okay?"

I heard her take in a shaky breath, "Yes." She stepped inside my room, "No, no everything is not okay."

Moving to push up from the bed I paused when Alex suddenly rushed to the side of the bed, murmuring, "Everything is not okay, because I didn't kiss you goodnight."

I had no chance to react or counter her statement before her hands slid across my cheeks and her lips met mine in an overwhelming, yet perfect amount of force. I had to grab onto her side to prevent from falling back and taking her with me. When I was steady I kissed her back, pushing my mouth harder on hers as the day's desires began to take over. Wrapping my arm around her waist, I pulled her onto the bed to sit in my lap as we kissed. Teeth nipping at lips, tongues moving over the same spots, it quickly became a feverish game of give and take.

I had to break away from her when I heard a quiet moan fall out of Alex's mouth just as she pressed our bodies closer together. God, did I want this, but it wasn't right. Not now, not on the first day of our new beginning.

Lifting Alex up and away, I gently sat her back down on my lap. Her hands falling from my face to rest on the tops of my shoulders, I kept my firm grip around her. I had to swallow to catch my breath, "Um, wow."

Alex smirked, equally breathless, "Yeah, wow." She ran her hand across my shoulder to rest on my neck. "That was a first."

I cocked my eyebrow at her, trying so hard to keep my hands where they were and not move them to the edge of her shirt, "A first?"

She nodded, running her thumb over my pulse, "Mhmm." She stared down in my eyes for a moment before rolling off my lap to sit on the edge of the bed next to me. "My first real goodnight kiss where I didn't stay after to indulge any further." She stood up. It was obvious she was experiencing the same struggle I was in keeping it innocent. "Back to the couch for me." Alex paused, "I just couldn't fall asleep knowing that I hadn't kissed you goodnight like I should have."

Alex moved to walk out of the room when I grabbed her wrist, stilling her, "Alex. Stay with me?" I didn't want her to leave and I didn't want to go any further with the woman. I just wanted her near me. To feel the warmth of sleeping in the same bed with someone, the warmth of being in the same bed with someone I loved.

Nothing more, nothing less.

She looked at me, her lips pursed tightly together. I could still see her heart racing in her neck, "Victoria..."

I tugged her back to the bed, "Just sleep, Alex." I looked over at the empty side of the bed, "It's been a really long time since I innocently shared a bed." I half smiled at her, "All it will be is cuddles and snuggles." I rolled my eyes, "And maybe a little snoring on my end." Alex tilted her head down laughing. I wiggled her arm, having successfully chased out the sexual tension, and slowly began to pull her back to the bed, "And I will even let you choose which side."

She sighed, shaking her head at me, "Fine." Crawling up onto the bed, Alex slipped under the covers next to me. After adjusting her pillow, she pointed at me, "But no hanky-panky, Ms. Bancroft, or I will not be responsible for my actions."

I held up my hand, "Scout's honor." I laid down onto my back, pulling the blankets up, smiling at the way Alex's body heat created the perfect temperature and filled the bed. I closed my eyes to focus on sleeping and not curling up into the woman next to me, when I felt an arm sneak its way across my stomach followed by Alex snuggling her entire body up against mine.

She kissed my shoulder, mumbling against it, "Goodnight Victoria."

I grinned in the darkness, dropping my hand to find hers, linking our fingers together. I bent and kissed the top of her head, "Goodnight Alex."

Within five minutes, Alex was passed out. Breathing heavily as she held onto me like she owned me. In reality, she did. She owned my entire being and there was no turning back now.

Chapter 9

I had woken up a few hours after I passed out on Victoria. The beer had blended with the emotional highs of the day, and caught up to me. Allowing my body to relax just enough to fall asleep in the blink of an eye. Unlike like most nights when I fell asleep immediately, I would wake up a few hours later and sit in the dark. Convincing my brain that it was perfectly okay to go back to sleep for another six or seven hours, especially on a day off.

Normally that would have worked when I was alone in my loft apartment, sprawled out in the middle of my bed alone, but right now, my mind was on a mission with my eyes. There was enough ambient light in the room from the small night light in the bathroom that I could see most of Victoria's features as she laid on her side, sleeping peacefully under warm blankets and pillows.

I had moved to sit up in the bed against the headboard, trying not to disturb Victoria as I looked down at her. The first thing my eyes fell to were her hands. Lying next to her face on the pillow, they made me sigh at the memory of how they felt in mine. How whenever she and I held hands, I felt completely safe with her.

I leaned over further to focus on her knuckles. The tiny white scars from scrapes and cuts, the calluses. Her hands looked like hands that belonged on a boxer or a mixed martial arts fighter, not the gentle woman sleeping peacefully next to me. Victoria was a teacher, not a fighter. It was something about her hands that had bothered me for as long as I knew her. More on the days she would come home from one of her work trips and she would hide her hands from me any chance she could. I sighed softly, maybe I was thinking too much into it. Maybe her scars were from helping her neighbor Dale dig holes, fix his roof, or putter around working on that old Mustang in his garage.

Dragging the duvet up further, I let the curious questions I had about Victoria's hands, and the mysteries they often held, fade into the thoughts of how her and I had gotten to this point. How one terrible moment in my life became one of my most cherished friendships, then evolved into this love I was on the verge of professing. Even as my gut was poking at the bottom of my heart trying to tell me that there was something more to what my trained nurse eyes saw on her hands and in the way she tenderly moved her body sometimes after one of her trips.

Sitting in Victoria's bed, propped against her pillows, I couldn't pinpoint the exact moment that I knew I had fallen in love with her, and that somewhere along the way she began to feel the same. I could simply feel it in the air between us, the looks we shared while passing the salt or the popcorn or how she would pause her sentence as she looked up and met my eyes.

It was all cliché things written in the books from the dawn of time that led all humans to believe in love and that love was attainable if we felt it. I had spotted the signs in the second month of our friendship. In that second month of a newly formed routine, the idea I was smitten with Victoria only because she had been the Good Samaritan, fell to the wayside. It was quickly replaced by that slow burning and rolling feeling in the pit of your stomach that told you all the things you didn't want to hear or believe.

The whisper of love was slowly creeping its way into your life whether you wanted it to or not. Not caring if you were ready or not, pointing its big bold finger at the one who looked at me like Victoria did. It was that look that would carry me to the rest of my days finally believing in the bedtime stories and cheap romance novels my mother read on long road trips.

I did wish I had one particular moment where I would be able to sit and tell my grandchildren, 'and that was the moment I knew I was in love with her.' But there wasn't one exact moment, there were many. All little sections and pieces of time that snowballed into this feeling that sat heavy, happily heavy, around my heart whenever I was near the blonde.

We fell in love the old fashioned way as Bill would say, with small looks, touches and a deep rooted feeling of undying safety of giving one's heart to the other.

I smiled, reaching over to brush some of the hair that had fallen across her face. Maybe one day I would sit and try to figure it out. For now, I was content to live in the moment.

Victoria sighed heavily when she felt my hand skim across her cheek. Rolling over in the bed, she slid her hand across the mattress until it bumped into the side of my leg. Her eyes flicked open and squinted to focus in the dark. "Alex? Are you okay?" Her raspy voice was laden with worry.

I grinned, nodding as I scooted back down to lay next to her. "I couldn't sleep. My brain is still on double time." I moved the duvet to cover her up. "Go back to sleep, Victoria."

She nodded slowly, her eyes already closing as she moved closer to me. Resting her head on my shoulder before breathing out heavily and falling into the gentle rhythm of sleeping. I dropped my hand to rest on her shoulder, running small circles against the thin material of her sleep shirt. Eventually putting myself to sleep with the monotonous motion of my hand infused with the even up and down of her breathing.

I left Alex in the bed, laughing silently at the way she sprawled out into the middle of the bed the second I got up. Clutching to the pillow I used in one hand and hers in the other. She was sleeping like a dead rock with her face smashed into the pillows and her body buried under blankets. It was something Alex often did when she was beyond tired and had kept her body up longer than it needed. She usually achieved this level of exhaustion on the weeks when she worked endless doubles then tried to stay awake for my benefit to spend time with me.

It was an only a few minutes past eight in the morning, and like clockwork, I got up and went downstairs to start my morning routine. Start a fresh pot of coffee, stare at the pantry to decide if it was going to be a cold cereal, oatmeal, or bacon and eggs kind of morning.

As the coffee brewed, I picked up the morning paper from the porch, waved hello to Dale who was out as usual, watering the flowers in his front yard. I then would go back inside and head to my den while my internal breakfast choice debate continued. Then, I would sit down at the ominous black laptop and read through the next job I had in my queue.

But this time, the routine changed. Instead of sitting at my desk, I stood in the doorway to the den. Arms folded and peering over at the plain looking black rectangle perched at the edge of my desk. For the first time in a very long time, I didn't want to open it up, turn it on and dive into the emails or case files awaiting me.

Walking away from the den I returned to the kitchen, removing the semi faded index card with the berry muffin recipe Mary gave me months ago when I raved over them after she handed me a bag over the fence one morning. I had decided to busy my hands with trying not to mangle the simple looking recipe while waiting for Alex to wake up.

Setting up all of the items I would need to make the muffins, I allowed myself to indulge in the warm moments of last night. The intense and consuming goodnight kiss Alex launched on me, followed by me doing another first in my life, asking Alex to sleep with me out of the simple desire that I wanted to be close to her.

I wanted to finally know what it was like to have her warmth roll over me as we slept. How it finally felt to have her in my arms like I dreamt of far too many times when we were trying to be just friends and I was jealous of the stupid fuzzy blanket she curled up in on movie nights.

There had been so many diminutive things about Alex that many would have overlooked or paid no attention to. Like how she treated all of her patients like they were the only one she had. How she would always give her spare change to whoever needed it, or the way she just knew what was wrong with me within the first syllable I uttered. Then there was the way she looked at me, not like I was the person who saved her that night on the station, but the person who was saving her heart when so many others had failed. The way Alex cared about me, looked at me, all of it, was what brought the humanity I had lost so long ago back from the deep dark depths I had to force it into to do the job.

Then there was the way she would giggle at her favorite parts of a movie, covering her face to hide the fact that she was truly giggling and not laughing. The way she would always con me into watching whatever dumb TV show of the week she had gotten hooked on, and ask incessantly if I liked it. The way Alex was just Alex. Living life to the fullest and not letting the darkness of the world she often saw in the trauma ward, affect her.

I had only seen her cry once, a month before she called me out on our pseudo relationship and our friendship started on the path of fading into nothing. It had been after one of her patients that she spent days looking after when they came in after a car accident, passed. She gave her all to that patient, doing her best to make sure that they would be able to go home. But sometimes fate and medicine don't always agree, and Alex lost the patient. She called me that night, unable to speak through the sobs. I raced to her apartment and sat with her as she cried until she fell asleep in my arms on the couch. That was the moment I knew I had fallen completely and irreversibly in love with her, and I would do everything I could to take care of her. We never spoke of that night, but the tension between us grew incomprehensibly thicker and I knew what would be coming in time.

All these fragments of ridiculous and serious thoughts had carried me for a year as I tried so desperately to keep Alex in the "friend's only" category. Hoping that I wouldn't fail and I could keep her away from me, to protect her. Never mind that the woman was tough, tenacious, stunning, intelligent and had a heart that would make an iceberg melt with one of her infamous hugs.

As I slathered the muffin pans with butter, I thought back to how close I had come to letting her fade into the wind and into the arms of that doctor. I had meant it when I told her that it took me seeing her in the arms of another, receiving the attention and love I wanted to give her but had fought so hard not to do while I kept in her in the friend zone. All because I wanted to stick to my guns and not get any deeper involved with the woman.

Getting deeper involved with her would jeopardize her safety, it was a given. A given that I didn't know if I could stomach. Seeing her cry once was soul shattering enough. I didn't think I could endure being the reason, or the cause of her sobbing and broken heart, all because I had another life that was a killer of a job.

She was the woman from the metro station. The woman who I took one look at and knew that she would be the one thing that could change my life more than all the other life altering things I had experienced. The woman I cursed myself for getting involved so long ago, and now as I looked up at the ceiling, hearing her stir in the bedroom above me, I smiled happily.

Twenty minutes later, a yawning brunette straggled her way down the stairs and popped into the kitchen with a sleepy grin on her face. Tugging on the drawstrings of a very familiar dark blue and yellow sweatshirt. "Morning." Her voice was deeper than normal with the slight rasp that came with having just woken up.

I grinned back at her, pouring the last of the muffin batter into the pan, "I see your sticky fingers are back at it." I nodded with my chin to my Navy Seabees hoody that I never wore anymore. Turning to slide the pan into the oven, I moved to pour Alex a fresh cup of coffee. Adding the exact amount of milk and sugar she preferred. "How did you sleep?"

"I was cold and this sweatshirt was under my scrubs in the laundry basket." She came to stand next to me as I finished making her coffee. I could hear the smirk in her voice well before it showed on her face. "I slept really well, but then woke up when I realized you were gone after I rolled over and found nothing but cold pillows." She zipped the hoody up to the neck, smirking fully at me. "So I decided it was time to get up and find something warm to wear."

I shook my head, "What am I going to do with your grabby hands?" I turned to hand her the cup, but caught the dark look in her eyes. It was an innocent comment, but one that was probably not the best choice considering the amount of sexual tension hanging in the air between us over the last day.

"I could think of one or two things." She paused, looking down as her cheeks flushed, fiercely embarrassed by her bold comment. "Are you making muffins?"

I swallowed hard, nodding as I set the cup down and reached up to Alex's face. Gently cradling her face with both of my hands, I placed a slow, soft kiss to her one cheek. Then moved to the other, kissing her other cheek softly. Before I backed away I waited for her to look up into my eyes. When she did, and I saw the pure love swimming in her dark blue eyes, I leaned forward and kissed her fully on the mouth. It was a slow, delicate kiss that was full of intention. I wanted to kiss Alex slow and with purpose. Soaking up the way her lips felt against mine, how she would search out my bottom lip with her tongue and coax it towards her teeth so she could nip at it. Already knowing it would pull a moan from me and force me to kiss her harder.

I held her face in my hands, smiling against her mouth as I felt her hands fall to my hips, digging her fingertips into the small space of skin available to her as my sleep shirt lifted up a fraction of an inch. We kissed slowly, for what felt like half an eternity, until the warm berry muffin smell began to distract our bodies need to touch each other and redirect it to filling our stomachs.

I parted from Alex's lips, kissing the corner of her mouth one last time before dropping my hands from her face, "I almost forgot to kiss you good morning." I whispered it, smiling as she grinned and blushed, licking her lips. "Wow, I think that beats my goodnight kiss, Victoria." She squeezed my hips once more before letting go and tucking her hands into the front pockets of the hoody, clearly trying to control the urge to go further and put those grabby hands to good use. I knew that taking it slow would explode in our faces in the most glorious of ways, and I wasn't sure if I could wait much longer.

I picked up the coffee I made for her and motioned over my shoulder, "Sit down, the muffins will be ready in a minute." I glanced up at the clock on the oven, "What time does your shift start?"

Alex sipped the coffee, frowning slightly, "I have to be in by noon. Stacy called me while I was digging for the sweatshirt, um, I mean, looking for my scrubs. One of the other nurses called off sick and they want me to come in at twelve to cover lunches." She leaned forward on the island, watching me pull out the hot muffins.

"I will feed you a muffin or two, and then you should probably head upstairs. Start getting ready. I'll pack up some of the leftover lasagna to take with you." I suddenly started laughing at how domestic I sounded.

Alex shook her head, laughing with me, "Yes mom, and that sounds like a plan." She took the offered muffin, pulling it apart to cool it before popping a bite into her mouth. "When are you leaving for Rhode Island?"

I felt my smile fade when Alex mentioned my trip. Bringing back the reality I was so desperately trying to keep out of the day, out of the routine until Alex was on her way to the hospital and not sitting in front of me. Making me wish I really was just a silly military history Professor. "First thing tomorrow morning. I'll be back Tuesday night. Then I'm on vacation for a few weeks." I tried to turn my smile a little more genuine, "You have doubles Monday and Tuesday, so you won't even know I'm gone. Then on Wednesday we can get together for lunch and think about what boring things we can do this coming weekend."

Alex chewed on her muffin, pulling pieces off it as she looked up at me, "Promise me that you'll call and text me?"

I rolled my eyes playfully. "Yes, of course I will." I handed her another muffin, hoping to distract from the look in her eyes that told me so much more than a simple request to call her when I landed. "You better start getting ready, it's going to take you at least an hour to get back to the hospital from here."

Alex smiled, grabbed the second muffin and slid off the chair. Two steps out of the kitchen she paused, looking over her shoulder she met my eyes, "I always notice when you're gone Victoria, because a piece of my heart goes with you every time you leave, and I can't sleep until I know you're home and my heart is whole again." She said it so faintly that if she wasn't standing a foot away from me, I wouldn't have heard it.

I watched her smile tightly, turn back around and jog up the stairs.

After Alex had showered, changed back into her scrubs and packed up what little things she had brought with her, including discreetly shoving my SeaBees sweatshirt into the bottom of her bag, I had her lunch set aside and ready to be taken with her.

The leftover lasagna was in a glass container with one of those fancy sealing lids, a small container of the side salad I had made yesterday for our burger lunch, and a bag of muffins for her and Stacy. I even went so far as to set a bottle of ice tea and plastic utensils neatly on top of it all. The entire lunch was in a brown paper bag I had found in my pantry from my last grocery trip. I also couldn't help but set one of the purple tulips into the bag. I knew how much she loved the flower and I oddly wanted to have a piece of me with her when she went back to work, while I prepared to get back into my work mindset.

Setting it next to her purse, I smiled and rolled my eyes. This weird domestic side of me was out in full force and I actually enjoyed it. It helped keep what would come next after Alex was gone and I had to return to the morbid version of my reality. The one where I was due in Ireland to kill someone in less than twenty four hours.

As I packed up Alex's lunch, waiting to send her off to work with a kiss on the cheek and a cheesy wave from the porch, it made me feel like this was possible. The impossible I had thought for so long to be impossible, was now truly possible. Shit, I was still wearing my pajamas of baggy blue striped cotton pants and an oversized White Stripes tour t-shirt that I still had and slept in going back to before I started at the Academy. It was faded to almost nothing and one of the few things non Navy related. Alex did indeed, make relax and forget to worry about the little inconsequential details.

Alex came running back down the stairs, pulling her hair up into a ponytail, grinning, "I think I'm going to be late."

I raised an eyebrow, "You did take a forty five minute shower then dawdled around, looking for your scrubs and stealing my sweatshirt."

Alex's cheeks flushed as she walked over to the island where I had all of her things neatly lined up. "I didn't steal anything. I just had a hard time finding my long sleeve shirt I wore the first night I came over." She went to grab her large bag when my hand shot out and dug into it.

Pulling up a corner of the dark blue fabric, tilting up it to show the bee's face wearing a sailor's cap, I smirked at her, "This just fell in your bag?"

Alex gave me wide puppy dog eyes, "Sure did."

I shook my head, tucking the sweatshirt back into the bag, "You can keep it. I know your floor gets icy at night, but I do expect you to bring it back when you come over after I land Tuesday night."

Alex paused all of her movements, looking right up into my eyes. A soft smile curling around the edges of her mouth, "Are you inviting me over for another sleepover, Professor Bancroft?"

I had to bite the inside of my cheek when I heard Professor, immediately thrusting thoughts of Dani into my head and what was still waiting for me in my den. I picked up the brown paper bag and Alex's hand, guiding her to the front door, "Maybe. I still have to check the flight itinerary, but I should be home an hour after you get off work."

I felt Alex's hand slide into mine, squeezing firmly as she dropped her head and grinned, "Well maybe I'll accept the invite."

We walked slowly to the front door and I opened it to allow her to go first out into the bright sunny late morning sun, pouring down through the few clouds in the blue sky. I heard her sigh as she took a deep breath, looking over at her car parked next to mine. "For the first time in a very long time, I really don't want to go to work." Alex looked up, smiling softly.

I lifted her hand, "We have the weekend." Running my thumb over her soft skin, I also really didn't want Alex to go to work. I wanted her stay with me and continuing living in this little bubble we had created over the last couple of days. I turned to look over at Alex when the black sedan parked a few feet down the block caught my eye. My stomach began to turn and I clenched my jaw, but I plastered on a brighter smile and gently guided Alex to her car. I had the sudden urge to get Alex quickly out of my neighborhood. The urge struck my heart with a quick thump, like a flimsy gut punch that sucked my breath away. I kept my tone even so Alex wouldn't pick up on anything.

That my second was life hovering right around us, closer than I wanted it right now. "The quicker you get to work and the quicker I get to Rhode Island, the quicker we will get to the weekend of doing nothing but all the boring things you can imagine."

Alex laughed, leaning into my side as her other hand ran down my forearm, "You got me there, Victoria."

I helped Alex place her bags and her lunch in the old mini, smiling at the yellow tulips sitting in a glass beaker on the passenger side floor. The tulip bulbs had opened and tilted towards the light coming from the window. Looking up at me as if to say, "Finally! You finally opened your heart to the light."

After shutting the passenger door, I walked Alex to the driver's side, opening the door for her. I glanced around making sure that my BMW blocked the view of the black sedan that faced us. Alex turned to face me, opening her arms up wide, grinning, "Bring it in Bancroft."

I laughed and walked into her warm embrace. Breathing in deeply the smells that were all Alex, holding her close, so close I could feel her heart pound against my chest. I shut my eyes, murmuring against her ear, "Call me when you get to the hospital and when you get home, or whenever you're bored." Her arms tightened around me, her palms firmly flat against my back. Her silent request for me to hold her even closer.

I could feel Alex smile against the side of my neck as she leaned back just enough to look in my eyes, "I will, and I will text you whenever I'm bored." She reached up and brushing some of the hair back behind my ear, "You'll call me when you land in Rhode Island and when you've landed back home?"

I grinned, loving that we had already so easily fallen back into the groove of our old friendship. "I will."

The air grew thick as we both stood in each other's arm, staring like dreamy Shakespeare lover's. "You better get going." I motioned to the brown paper bag, "There's a small surprise in your lunch for you, help get you through the double tonight and there's a little something for Stacy." I grinned when Alex giggled, rolling her eyes.

"I almost forgot about her." Alex reached up with both of her hands, holding the sides of my face, "Thank you for this, Victoria. It's..." She paused, clearly searching for the words to say to avoid saying the words I knew she wanted to say.

I didn't allow her to search for very long, I bent forward and kissed her softly, holding her in my arms one last time as I felt her melt into them. Leaning back, I memorized the way she looked right after I kissed her. Flushed cheeks, a goofy smile that she tried to hide by biting her bottom lip and lastly the way her blue eyes grew brighter the longer she looked at me. It was a look I had seen a hundred times over our friendship. Mainly, when she was debating whether or not to get another scoop of ice cream, or when I turned quickly in a store to ask her a question and caught her looking at me like she was now. All signs that unnerved the foundation I had been living upon for so many years, but would now memorize and cherish.

Taking a step back I cleared my throat, "You need to hit the road." I knew if I didn't force Alex to get in her car and leave, I would drag her back inside and keep her and the bubble we created intact for the rest of my life. Damn the world around us and the second job that was looming. Damn Dani who was sitting in that black sedan down the block just out of sight of the untrained eye, who would think nothing about a plain black sedan with black window tint in a neighborhood full of nice family cars.

Alex sighed dramatically, stepping back and slowly getting into her car. I softly shut the driver's door. Alex looked up as she started the car, "See you late Tuesday night?"

I grinned at the way her voice was almost pleading, but in the cutest way, "You will."

Alex's face split into the biggest grin I had yet to see from the woman. I moved to the front of the mini as she backed out of my driveway and drove down the street, waving and blowing me a kiss as she took the last right turn, taking her out of my neighborhood and back out towards the freeway.

Walking down to the mailbox, I grabbed the morning newspaper and looked directly at the black sedan that was slowly moving towards my driveway.

I read the front page headlines as Dani pulled into the spot Alex had just left, not bothering to look up as she got out of the driver's side and walked around the front of the car to stand across from me.

"Is she going to be a problem?" Dani's voice had no emotion in it. She asked the question just like one would read a monotonous test question out loud.

Keeping my eyes on the headline about the upcoming primary election campaign battles, I furrowed my brow. "My house is not on the surveillance list. The old man and old lady signed off on that request when I brought it to them over five years ago." I glared at Dani, "Unless you are suddenly in the business of going rogue."

Dani rolled her eyes at me, shifting the black leather bag in her hand as she tugged at the collar of her khaki uniform, trying to get the gold bars on her lapels to lie flat. "I came by last night to drop off your next job. Old lady changed her request from email to hand delivery. She seems a little paranoid ever since the one mainframe firewall collapsed last week." Dani sighed, "All of us in the basement told her that it was one out of a thousand firewalls and it would take a genius hacker a week to break through them all." She moved towards the front porch, "Can we take this inside, Professor?"

Folding up the newspaper I tucked it under my arm and kept my glare on the redhead. Nodding once that she could go inside the house. I knew Dale would be out in the next five minutes to start his morning ritual of watering the plants.

Dani went directly to the kitchen and slide her leather bag across the island. Clicking open the small metal latches, she reached for a muffin, "I thought you and nurse blue eyes were on the outs? A friendship going down the drain after you pulled the plug." She removed a very familiar thick blue envelope, placing it on top of her bag as she took a bite of the muffin in her hand.

I walked to the other side of the island, tossing the newspaper on to the edge. "Things change." I moved to grab the envelope when Dani dropped her hand on top of it.

"Victoria." She waited until I looked up at her, "Is she the reason why you asked me to monitor internet searches? Is she why you look happier? Like you have actually been smiling for real and not faking it like you always do?" She lifted her hand and shoved the blue envelope my way. "Is she the reason why you want to finally take a vacation after almost three years of working nonstop?"

I clenched my jaw, picking up the envelope, "Why does it matter?" I didn't want to get into it with Dani. I knew the rules of Voltaire. They didn't frown on or discourage their operatives to find families or relationships, just as long as secrets remained secrets. I was the one who backed out of following that road, finding it far too difficult to lie to someone I cared about. Lying that I was going to a stupid conference when in reality I was off on a sniper hit in the far reaches of this country or another. I also knew the ultimate rule of Voltaire, that if anyone found out what I did, their face and background would end up in a case file and be slid across another plumber's kitchen table like Dani just slid one across mine.

A case file that had notes attached with requests to make it look like a car accident or something completely random and semi innocent. A death that would be written off as a random tragedy. Nothing more. All it would do was send a clear and solitary message to the operative that Voltaire's missions and secrets were to remain secret. At all costs.

Dani flicked a few crumbs from the top of her ribbons on her uniform, "It matters shit all to me personally, but professionally, well you know how it goes when Voltaire finds problems." She glanced up at me, "But I can tell you like nurse blue eyes a lot, and have from that first day you asked me to play Creeper McCreeps for you. It seems you two have breached the friend zone."

I sighed hard, growing agitated with Dani as I tore open the top of the envelope, "Again, Dani. Why does it matter to you?"

She paused, staring at me with a look that was far from business or the heavy sarcasm that always radiated from the woman's bright green eyes. When she spoke, her voice was different. A far reach from the usual tone I experienced and had from her on a daily basis for the last five or so years. "It matters to me, Victoria, because you're happy. I can see it. No matter how hard you try to plaster on more of the concrete mask you live behind, I can see in your eyes, you're happy."

She stood up, clicking her bag closed, "And I like that, because after everything you and I have been through. All the things I have seen in your eyes going all the way back to the dreadful day in that sandy shithole of an interrogation room we first met in, I finally see the beautiful human you once were before all of the world took a hot shit on you."

She smiled tightly at me, her own memories beginning to dim the bright green of her irises. "I need to get back to the basement, I have a meeting with the old man before lunch."

Dani snatched one more muffin and headed towards the front door, "The old lady has confirmation instructions in the case file. The usual protocol as always and I'll be in your ear throughout the duration."

I half followed her towards the front, the blue envelope still clutched in my hands. I was agitated like normal, but not because of Dani's abrasive nature, but because of what she just said. Her words sinking in deep, settling around my heart and my gut. I couldn't deny that she was right in what she saw in my eyes. I was happy and I knew it would be a problem down the road.

As Dani opened the door she looked back at me, her eyes settling on mine for a moment before she spoke, "Victoria, I will always have your back. And if nurse blue eyes is the one, I'll have her back as well." The last few words came out softly, but in a way that felt heavy and ominous.

Then again, nothing about the job Dani and I had was lighthearted and easy.

I nodded once, looking down at the floor before I half whispered out a thank you. I kept my eyes on the floor as I heard the front door close behind Dani, heard her car start up and drive down the same street, take the same right turn Alex had to head back into the city. Creating a morbid mirror image of how my two lives were starting on the slow path to an inevitable collision.

I practically skipped into the hospital, carrying my large brown paper lunch bag. Grinning and saying hello to everyone I passed. Security guards, orderlies, nurses and even the occasional comatose patient sitting in a wheelchair. The grin had appeared when I opened the bag to pick out another muffin to eat and saw the single purple tulip laying on top of the perfectly packaged lunch. A small note taped to the stem folded over, my name written in Victoria's precise handwriting.

I resisted the temptation to open the note right away, knowing that I would need the boost when lunch time came around in another eight or nine hours.

Yes, I was back at work and would not see the light of day outside of this hospital for another seventy two hours at least, but for once, I didn't care. I wanted to stay busy. The busier I stayed the faster time went, the faster I would be back with Victoria and we could pick up where we left off. Continuing the slow exploration of this new chapter we had started.

It didn't help that I was already starting to miss her and could not refrain from sending her a short message as I dropped my bag off in my locker before heading out to the nurse's station.

My grin only growing wider as she replied just as fast with cute message and a smiley face.

I tucked the phone in my front pocket and headed out to the nurse's station. Coming around the corner to come face to face with Stacy who was frowning as she flipped through the endless stacks of charts set before her.

Moving past her, I dropped the small bag of two muffins Victoria had packed especially for Stacy, on the pile she was staring at. "How many do we have today?" I bent over to sign in and look over the patient board behind the desk Stacy sat at.

Stacy held up the plastic bag, "You bake?" She eyed the muffins like they were an untrusted science project grown in my kitchen.

I laughed, leaning over the opposite edge of the nurse's station from Stacy, "Nope. Victoria made them." I flicked the bag with my finger, "She packed those just for you this morning."

Stacy's mouth hung open in mid-bite, her eyes squinting at me critically. "The Victoria?! The hot Navy teacher best friend who is not a possible girlfriend, but should be your girlfriend forever, Victoria? The Victoria that was slowly disappearing out of your life because of the gratuitous friend zone issue that has been hovering over your heads for the last year? "

I shook my head, moving to write my name up on the whiteboard, "Yes, that Victoria." I dropped the marker on the ledge and turned back to Stacy. "So how many patients do we have today?"

Stacy shook her head, taking a huge bite out of the muffin now that she knew it was made from a trusted source. A moan of delicious happiness, quickly escaped before she spoke, "Thirteen, but Deb is expecting more as the night carries on. It's going to storm later and there's a cherry blossom beer festival starting tonight and going on for the rest of the week."

I went to pick up a chart when Stacy's hand slammed down, "But first! Tell me everything." She looked me over, "You're still wearing the same scrubs and shirt you bolted out of here on Friday with. You never do that. You have at least a month's supply of scrubs before you recycle back to the first sets." She then waved her hand over my face, "And this. This whole grinning like an idiot and glow you have. Means one thing."

Shaking my head, "What is that one thing, oh wise Nurse Cavanaugh?"

"You broke through the friend zone and slept with the good Navy officer. I thought Doctor Dean looked like someone shit in his Audi when I saw him in the hallway." Stacy grabbed my wrist to still my fluttering of patient notes. "So?"

Rolling my eyes, I sighed heavily, "We didn't sleep together. Yes, I stayed at her house for the last two nights, and that's why I am in the same scrubs. Yes, we are out of the friend zone and I am no longer seeing Doctor Dean." I looked up at Stacy unable to hide the grin from forming, "She was the one who broke the friend zone walls down. Sent me tulips and a note to come have dinner with her at her house Friday night."

"Halle-fucking-lujah! About damn time one of you got off the pot or got hemorrhoids." Stacy raised her arms up in the air like a deep south snake charmer. "Deb had been prattling on about some romantic gesture dropped off for you, but I tuned it out, thinking it was from greasy Doctor Dean." She scooped up the charts, "Walk with me and tell me everything as we change out IV's in room eight and nine."

She looked back, "Oh by the way, that one weird DCFD EMS chick keeps asking where you've been. I think her name was Diablo? I think she's got a crush on you, I mean she's got a hot latin vibe about her, but she creeps me out."

I frowned, "She's just weird I guess. You know how some paramedics are when they reach job burnout." I sighed and looked at Stacy, "Just tell her I'm taken or married, anything to keep her away."

Stacy threw me a salute, "Will do nurse! But I did overhear her asking a few people about the night you had your attack. Keeps asking who the lady was that brought you in." She nudged me, "I took care of it, I threatened the security boys I'd tell administration what they really do at night instead of watching cameras." She waved her hand in the air. "Anyway, tell me everything about the great nonsexual sleepover you had."

I laughed hard, shaking my head at Stacy as she peppered me with questions. I answered them as we changed IV's, checked meds and finished out the first set of rounds. I told her the way Victoria asked me to her house and what her house looked like. How sweet her old neighbors were, and the other thousand and one things Victoria and I had talked about over the last two nights. Stacy grinned at me like a sucker, often whispering she wished her boyfriend was as cute or half the romantic Victoria was.

I continued to ramble, telling Stacy about the first kiss and how it literally was better than anything I could have imagined or seen in any movie. That I felt my brain short out and rebuild in the few seconds I kissed the beautiful blonde woman.

By the time we had finished checking the floor, Stacy was caught up on my new relationship. She flopped down in the rolling chair by the whiteboard and threw her feet up on the edge of the desk, "You're in love aren't you?"

My head nodded yes even before I could decide if I wanted to answer truthfully or play the vagueness game. "I am. Have been for a while now, but never knew if she felt anything for me or could." I looked up at Stacy. The gnawing gut feeling I had looking at Victoria's medals in her den returned, but it wasn't enough to distract me from sharing with my only friend the incredible shift in Victoria and I's relationship. "I want to tell her, but I know it's not the right time, yet. Everything is so new and tentative. There's so much we need to learn about each other."

Stacy spun in her chair, "There is, even I can tell that woman is a walking mystery novel. The kind where you never know who the murder is until the last chapter and then when you do find out, it's the sweet old next door neighbor. I can see it in her eyes, there's something more to her and I can't quite place my finger on it. Like it's the same look we see in the vets that come in after a bar brawl. The empty stares of having seen too much, but with Victoria there's a whole new level to that look."

She stopped spinning and looked up at me with a smile, "Don't get me wrong, I adore her and I think she is the best thing to ever happen to you and she would never do a thing to hurt you, but there's mystery there."

I sighed, signing off on the last few charts, "I know." I looked at Stacy, "I found a display in her den the first morning. A bunch of war medals filling a frame the same size I keep my college degree in. Full of ribbons and shiny medals, I could only recognize one or two. Mainly the purple heart with an oak leaf on the ribbon. The there was a silver star and one really weird one that looked like it came from the VFW. That one I couldn't tell what it was, I'd never see one like it before." I leaned on the edge of the stations high counter, "Whenever I bring up the war or her service, Victoria gets this look in her eyes and changes the subject. I hate to push, and I won't until much later, if at all."

Stacy scooted over to the computer, clicking and bringing up a search engine page. "Tell me what that one weird medal looked like, maybe we can look it up."

I moved to stand behind her, "It was a gold star with five points, a blue center with a gold star burst in the middle. The ribbon was white with black trim and a red and blue striped center."

Stacy's hands moved quickly and soon pulled up an exact image of the medal I had seen. She moved closer to the monitor and began reading off the dull description. "The National Intelligence Medal of Valor. An honor given to recognize heroism and courage in service to the intelligence community or to overall national security. Second only to the National Intelligence Cross and Intelligence star among the intelligence community's awards for bravery."

She clicked a few times on other images until another one caught my eye. "Wait, click on that one that looks like a silver coin. Victoria had one of those in the bottom of the frame, I think it's a challenge coin. Like the one that nice Marine we stitched up last week, showed us."

Stacy nodded with a smirk, "I remember him, he was a cutie and wanted my phone number." She clicked on the silver coin and read off that description, "The Distinguished Intelligence Cross. The highest decoration awarded by the United States Central Intelligence Agency. Awarded for voluntary act or acts of extraordinary heroism involving the acceptance of existing dangers with conspicuous fortitude and exemplary courage. " Stacy paused and turned to look right into my eyes as I stared at the screen wide eyed. My stomach starting to get the kind of butterflies that came from discovering a secret that was better left alone.

I whispered, "Close the window. I don't want to read anymore." As I looked, I saw the list of recipients on the page. At the bottom of the short list was one name that stuck out, "Lieutenant Victoria C. Bancroft, USN." I folded my arms across my chest and stared at the whiteboard, my gut was right. There was something more about Victoria. Something like the mystery novel character Stacy had compared her to. Something that involved the CIA and military intelligence community. A set of words that was a far cry from the words Professor of Military History and Tactics I had seen on her office door.

The more I thought about it, all of the tiny details I had noticed over the last year about Victoria were gradually falling out of my memory like the lost pieces to a puzzle found under the couch. Revealing themselves to me and offering up a chance to fill in the big blank spots I had about the woman I was falling for. Had fallen for.

"Hey Alex, you okay?" Stacy's voice was soft as she came up from behind me.

I turned to her with a tight smile on, "Yeah, totally. I think I'm just absorbing the fact that Victoria was in the war and my mind is running wild with ideas of how she got her purple heart and what she went through." I shrugged, "You know the stories we hear from the vets we take care of, old and young, they never end up to be happy stories."

Stacy patted my shoulder, "It'll be okay. I bet she got a paper cut filing some secret letter to a General about issuing more chocolate rations. She's an officer, and we have heard all of the vets complain about the officers only getting calluses on their asses from sitting in the back" She smiled, trying to break up the tension, "Come on, let's go start on the second half of the floor, and then you can buy me coffee in the cafeteria."

I laughed, nodding, "You're right. It's probably nothing. I'll just ask her about it when it feels right. I kind of want to live in this little bubble of happiness, muffins and amazing good morning kisses from Victoria for as long as I can." I let Stacy link her hand into my elbow to guide me towards the elevator when the doors opened. The smile faded from my face the second I saw Detective Jennifer Scarlett step out and look directly in my eyes. She forced on a smile as she walked towards me, "Excuse me, Ms. Ivers. I was looking for you. I was wondering if I could have a moment or two of your time?"

Stacy gave me a look, one that asked if I needed her to shove the detective back into the elevator with a hearty boot to the ass. I shook my head and patted her hand, looking back at the mousy woman. "I only have a moment."

Detective Scarlett looked at Stacy then back to me, "Is there somewhere private I can speak to you?"

I frowned, "Is this about my incident? That was almost a year ago, and nothing has changed on my end. Obviously your police department never found any evidence to link me to anything other than being the victim of a senseless attack." I gripped tighter to Stacy's hand on my arm, "So whatever you need to say, say it, privacy is not needed on my behalf."

Detective Scarlett sighed hard, irritated, "I understand Ms. Ivers. You were cleared of any suspicion a while ago, but I actually came here to talk to you about the woman who helped you that night." She removed a small notebook from her interior blazer pocket, opening it up to a page, "A Victoria Bancroft?" She looked up at me and caught the way my jaw clenched at the sound of Victoria's name, "Do you happen to know her or maybe had any contact with her in the last year? I'm trying to find her and question her about that night. Some new evidence has popped up on this now cold homicide case of the men who attacked you."

I heard Stacy whisper, "What the fuck?" She then looked at me, "I can call Nick and Jay up here, they'll remove this cold fish bitch in a heartbeat."

Shaking my head, I moved away from Stacy's hand, "It's okay." I dug a twenty out of my back pocket and handed it to her, "Go get the coffee and meet me back here in ten minutes." I stared right in Detective Scarlett's eyes, "This will only take a minute." I motioned to the file room to the left of the detective, "We can talk in there, but again, I don't think I can help you with much it's been a year since my attack."

Detective Scarlett nodded, closing the notebook and waiting to follow me to the room, "I appreciate whatever you can offer, Ms. Ivers." As we both entered the file room, I shut the door and closed my eyes. My gut starting to swirl at the idea of having to go over that horrible night was bothersome enough. Combine that with having to tread lightly with this detective and whatever questions she had about Victoria was going to be very difficult. Especially now that I had the start of a sinking feeling that there was something Victoria was either hiding from me, or avoiding telling me about her past.

Chapter 10

"Would you then say that you and Ms. Bancroft are friends?" Detective Scarlett was staring at me as she sat at the small desk we used to stack released patient files. I stood against the far wall, doing my best to be the farthest away I could from the mousy, yet intense looking woman.

I folded my arms across my chest, trying very hard not to lash out at this woman. "We are acquaintances." It was the half-truth. A couple of days ago Victoria and I were truly just acquaintances on the verge of being less than that. I waved my hand at the notebook she had been scribbling in, "Read over your notes. I met Ms. Bancroft shortly after my incident to say thank you for her help. We became friendly and like everything else in life, things faded away without constant attention. The only people I keep as friends are my coworkers and family. Even then, I have little time for them." I raised my eyes at the detective, "And I'm running out of time for these questions."

Detective Scarlett smirked, "I understand, I just need five more minutes." She made another few swirls and curls with her pen before she leaned back in the chair, "How did you find Ms. Bancroft?"

I rolled my eyes, "Through luck and a thing called the internet. You can find anyone on the internet if you look hard enough."

The detective nodded, "And how exactly did you go about it? I recall that you couldn't remember many details about the woman who brought you in to the hospital. How did you manage to get an image of Ms. Bancroft that allowed you to find her?" She tilted her head in a way that told me she was baiting me.

I pushed off the shelves, sighing hard. "I bribed the one security guard to get me a screen shot from when I was brought in. The rest Google did for me, but it was fruitless. It only led me to Ms. Bancroft's teaching position at the Naval Academy, which you already know. I don't even really know more than that about the woman." I moved closer to the detective, "Now, answer a few of my questions. Why are you bringing this case back into my life? I've moved on, I've healed and I am doing my damnedest to forget that night."

She closed her notebook slowly, standing up as she tucked it back into her blazer pocket, "The case went ice cold after we cleared you and found the one intern who was there with you on that platform. Both of you stating that the only other person on the metro station that night was a tall lean man sitting on a bench away from the show. The case was closed on your end, but the death of your attackers still hangs open."

She folded her arms over her chest, "But a year later, I finally get my warrant request approved for security footage of the metro station and of the hospital approved. Only to find out that all of that footage has been mysteriously destroyed and or recorded over. So, I went back over the evidence collection and happened to find a plethora of DNA evidence recovered from the bodies. A thousand plus people go through that station a day, so you can imagine how much DNA was soaked into the blood stains on the floor and on the bloody clothing of those men." She turned to head out the door, "But one hair strand stood out. It had been buried into a plastic bag with a handful of others. The evidence tech clearly didn't care that night, but when I saw it, it stood out from the rest. A single blonde hair in a mix of brown and black hairs, so I ran it."

Scarlett smiled tightly, "Led me to a Victoria Bancroft. A woman I am having a hell of a time tracking down. No address on the books over the last five years, just one that leads me back to the Naval Academy and then disappears into the red tape of government nonsense." She shrugged, "It got me thinking. Military woman, military training, an impressive history of service for her country. Things I found on the internet just by running her name." The detective gave me a raised eyebrow and a shitty look I wanted to slap off her face. "I thought maybe she could help me piece together the injuries those men received. Tell me if it was done by a trained hand or hands fueled by adrenaline."

The way she implicated Victoria, told me she knew that I knew more than I was telling her, but she wasn't going to push. A good detective always knew if they pushed too hard, too fast, they would lose their leads quickly and never get them back.

She pulled the door open, "I'm sorry to bother you, Ms. Ivers. I'm just trying to chase leads to close the only case I still have hanging over my head as unsolved." She took one step out of the door, before digging in her back pocket for a business card. "If you do happen to see Ms. Bancroft or know how to get a hold of her, tell her I would like to talk to her." She set the card on the edge of the desk and tapped on it, "Thank you for your time, Ms. Ivers."

I stared at the white square, my mind working a thousand different angles at once. There were too many strange things happening at once that gave my gut feeling everything it wanted to start forcing me to ask questions I wasn't sure I wanted the answers to.

Rushing to the edge of the desk, I snatched up the business card, ripped it into two and headed back out on to the floor. Dropping the pieces of card-stock into the biohazard bin right outside the door.

If Detective Scarlett wanted to find Victoria, she would have to do it without my help. Victoria had saved my life that night and I wasn't going to let what we had become, and what we had started over the last few days, be interrupted by an eager detective wanting to close up a case. A homicide case of four pieces of shit that got exactly what they deserved.

I made my way back to the nurse's station, trying to picture Victoria being capable of creating the injuries I had seen in those crime scene pictures. Each time I tried to place her there, I couldn't imagine Victoria doing it. She was far too gentle, quiet, reserved and a bit too OCD to get blood on her hands let alone on her clothes. She almost had a panic attack the other night when I spilled melted butter on her faded, and torn Navy shirt I slept in. Rushing me to the kitchen to run warm water and soap on it before the grease set in.

I blew out an irritated laugh as I saw Stacy who was giving me the, "Tell me everything." eyes she always did. I shook my head, "It was nothing. The detective is trying to earn her stripes. I guess my attack last year is the one thing holding her back." Scooping up the coffee Stacy had sitting waiting for me, I took a large drink. I dug out my phone to text Victoria, but stopped when I saw I had a message from her.

-Leaving now. Flight leaves in an hour. I'll call you when I land and will be thinking about you the whole flight. I hope you enjoy lunch and tell Stacy I said hi. Is it too early to say I miss you already?-

I sent a quick reply back. *-It's not too early, because I feel the same way. Hurry home.-*

Dropping the phone in my pocket, I sighed heavily. I would tell Victoria about the detective's visit when she got home, then maybe lead into the other questions I had about her medals and her name at the bottom of the web page Stacy and I stumbled across. But, for right now, I saw no reason to start corrupting the happiness no matter how much my gut wanted me to.

"Hello nurse Ivers?" Stacy was waving her hand in front of my face, "You keep zoning out on me like that and I'll leave you to change out the colostomy bag in room two instead of passing it off on to one of the medical students." She grinned as I groaned.

"Not room two. Old man Thatcher constantly forgets to open up the exhaust valve. I literally smelled like shit for a week after the last time I changed it. My shoes, my hair, everything." I picked up the last half charts we had, and followed Stacy to the end of the hall to start the next set of rounds.

At least for a few hours, my mind would be distracted by work and not meddling about in the idle thoughts of what I had seen on the internet and what Detective Scarlett had placed there. I knew in a few hours into this double shift and the rush hit, I would be so tired I would forget what my own face looked like. Let alone the crazy hypothesis of what happened to me, followed by a stupid game of guess who in regards to who Victoria Bancroft was.

In my eyes, all of it was pointless. It happened a year ago, a lot had changed in this last year and I didn't want to look back. I wanted to look forward.

Even if my gut told me not to.

~Twelve hours later – Outside of Dublin, Ireland~

"Sorry we have to do this in the car, professor, but the old lady is being paranoid and wants to make sure out conversations are kept between the two of us." Dani sighed lightly through the earbud. "You have the package with you?"

I nodded to no one, laying out the case file on my lap as I sat in the black Land Rover a few miles away from my targets house. "I do." I shifted in the driver's seat, looking in the rear-view mirror at the pub entrance I had parked across from. I knew I wouldn't stand out in a packed pub lot, especially as busy as this one was, "I glanced over the file before I left, but do your thing."

Dani laughed, "I like how you care very little about the old lady's growing paranoia."

"The old lady has gone through worse phases over the years. This growing paranoia of hers isn't very minor if she wants me to hide in one of our safe cars, but again, I don't really care. You do remember how much she lost it when that one mainframe based in the south of France went tits up?" I shook my head. The old lady was the one boss of mine who was as fragile as she was heartless and it confused me for a long time until I finally just stopped caring.

She laughed harder, "I do. Even after we all tried to explain to her that it was just the mainframe for the legitimate business cover for Voltaire. A woman's exclusive lingerie company serving the needs of the rich and ultra-famous. All that was lost was catalogue mailing addresses sold off to junk mail companies, and yet she still wanted to burn the Paris office to the ground." Dani took a deep breath to refocus, "Back to the task at hand, Professor."

I rolled my eyes, opening the blue file folder and revealing a clear photograph of a middle aged woman with rosy cheeks and the typical crazy, curly, red hair of an Irish woman. I smirked as I thought of how much the woman looked like that one cartoon character from that movie a few years back. I picked up the sheet as Dani began to speak in her very monotone briefing voice.

"This lovely gal is Maura O'Hara. Forty eight years old and the head of this new Irish liberation movement she created a few years ago. The woman is leading the charge to reinvent the IRA on a level that even the old IRA members are beginning to grow nervous of her intentions."

I heard a soft click and beep in the background, looking up as the touch display in the Land Rover lit up, "Sorry, I hacked into your car. This is so much easier and I cannot stand how slowly you turn pages. The sound is like nails on a chalkboard to me."

I huffed, throwing the now useless case file on top of my black bag, "Your voice often has the same effect one me."

Dani chuckled, "Love you too, Professor." A few more clicks and beeps filled the touch screen with the case file. "The last two years Maura has been nothing but a blip on the radar, but now she is casting out a very wide net. Striking out to the youth of Ireland who are rebelling like the rest of the world's youth against their governments. And like many other nut job terrorist group leaders, she is using them to do her dirty work. Keeping her hands clean so she can be the politically correct face of her new group and movement. Rumor has it, she is eyeing the Prime Minister spot in the next election. Lady O'Hara is using the LOIR, the Liberation of Ireland's Republic, as a front. Much like Voltaire's fancy lingerie front. Hide the truth under dirty laundry." Dani paused, hoping I would get her joke and laugh at it.

I ignored it.

"Anyway, Maura has been driving the tea drinkers mad with her threats to run for political office, let alone the backdoor politics she's popular for. Making deals with the shit of known terrorist groups in the Middle East to fund and arm her movement. She needs to be eliminated before she follows through on her open threats of linking up with our favorites in the Middle East. Creating a multifaceted terrorist group that may not be able to be contained. The woman is smart, evil, charismatic and has a vengeful mission. Her parents were imprisoned in the eighties due to their membership in the IRA. They died shortly after being release when the IRA disbanded in the early 2000's. Maura was raised with hate towards the world, so she's picked up the torch but not in a fun vigilante superhero way."

I tapped at the screen, scrolling through crime scene and media photos of graphic car bombings, buildings, and schools firebombed to hell and back. The result of the utter bloody violence caused by the LOIR. I sucked in a breath as many of the photographs began to trigger my own memories, "How does the old lady want this one to go down?" I swiped through more of Maura's background, not caring to read anything more about the woman. I knew what Dani meant when she mentioned our favorites, bringing a quick flash of the first day Dani and I met racing to the front of my memory.

"It seems Maura has her own ritual. She downs a bottle of wine every night as she soaks in a bubble bath, reading the day's headlines of what her movement has accomplished, or will accomplish." Dani sighed, "That's why you were requested. You have a gentler hand than all of the others. The tea drinkers want this to look like a pure and simple accident. Something that cannot be pinpointed back to any group or anyone."

I bit my bottom lip, already forming the plan. "Right. How much time?"

"The cleanup crew has eyes on the house. Looks like the red headed she-devil is getting her nightly routine started. Old lady wants you to be done and the house cleaned in three hours, not a minute over. Gives the body plenty of time to go through the start of rigor mortis and have the local coroner sign off without too much interest as to what really happened to the woman."

I reached over to turn the car on when Dani spoke, "Gentle hands Victoria, both the old man and old lady have started to get worried about the amount of force you've been using in the last few jobs. They're happy with your work, but are happier when you don't go super hands on."

I leaned my head against the steering wheel, knowing that I had begun to lose control as I dealt with my feelings and everything else that was back home. Mainly thinking I was going to lose Alex out of a dumb decision I had made to let her go. I whispered to Dani, "I know, but I also know that I now have a reason to be careful. I can't go home with my own bruises and cuts. I'm running out of excuses about sailors challenging me to push up contests or whatever."

Dani laughed, "I can't believe blue eyes ever took any of those excuses as legit ones. When is the last time you actually physically did a push up? Professor flabby pants?"

I smirked in the darkness of the car, starting it up. "Dani, I'm turning you off now. I'll click in when I'm at the house."

"Ha! I knew it. Retirement is giving the good Commander Bancroft a belly." Dani hollered a toodle loo as I clicked mute on my earpiece and started to back out of the parking lot.

Maura lived in Maynooth, a small town right outside of Dublin. A smaller town that had the quaint typical feel of Ireland with its older building and homes. The woman's house was set up on a hill, and was a decent sized modern house made to look like the old cottages that dotted the rolling countryside of Ireland.

I found her house with ease using the pre-programmed GPS in the Land Rover. I parked a few houses down and did the usual, covering my head and most of my face with the deep black hood, before I slung a small bag around my shoulders.

Stepping out into the car, I shoved a set of headphones in so I looked like a late night jogger. I ran to Maura's house and was able to utilize the stone walls that surrounded it, climbing them with ease under the cover of the overgrowing ivy that tangled among the stones.

When I was in the yard I scanned around, un-muting Dani in my ear, "Speak."

"Yes master." Dani half growled the words out. "The only cameras are at her front door, garage and rear entrance. The other ones that covered the perimeter magically went out during last week's thunderstorm. The repair men have to replace all the units, meaning the cleaning crew was able to get you a large span of room to move in. Your best option is the side door that leads into her dining room from the backyard." Dani paused, "And it looks like she is moving into the bathroom to get her wine and bubble on."

I rolled my eyes, tugging the hood over my face, "I'm going to move now. I will keep you in my ear this time, but keep it to a minimum."

"You got it. I will only speak when spoken to. Good luck Professor."

With that, I took a deep breath and ran across the yard. The tall grass keeping my footsteps soft as I rushed to the side door. Dani had already disabled the home's electronic locking system, wasting no time in allowing me to gain entry.

I wiped my feet on the rug and with a kitchen towel that was close by, removing any traces that someone from the outside had been inside after the nightly dew fell. I tossed the towel into a laundry basket off in the mud room as I crept towards the stairs that would lead me to the bathroom and bedroom I was searching for.

Edging around the corner I stopped at the bedroom door and listened. I could hear soft music playing and the hum of a woman's voice trying to sing along. There was the slow slosh of water followed by a clink of glass being set on porcelain. I closed my eyes as I brought up the layout of the bathroom I had studied in my kitchen and again on the flight over. The bathtub would be slightly to the left underneath four large windows that looked out onto the expansive hills that Maura's house backed up against.

I opened my eyes when Dani chirped in my ear softly, "She's on her third full glass of wine. The bottle is pretty much done for, so you're good to go."

I nodded, reaching for the doorknob and opened it slowly. I wanted to catch the woman by surprise and make it look like an accident. That she startled herself as she drunkenly slipped reaching for the last remnants of her wine. Losing balance on wet porcelain from an overfilled bath running over.

I peered in, catching the full view of Maura O'Hara soaking in a massive white claw foot tub. Holding an even larger wine glass filled to the brim with deep red wine. Her head, with her bright orange red hair piled on top of her head pinned in a loose bun, was swaying to the gentle sound of a slow Rod Stewart love song. I could easily see from the blush in her cheeks, the wine was taking hold in her blood and doing so quickly.

Pushing the door open just enough to slip in, I heard in a thick Irish accent, "No need to tip toe, I have been expecting this for a while now." Maura opened her hazel eyes and looked right at me, "Feel free to come in and join me." She waved a pudgy, wobbly hand towards the wine bottle. "Have a drink?"

I said nothing, and continued to walk towards the tub. I already had what was going to happen in the next few minutes planned out. I kept the hood up as I moved closer to the woman who continued to talk to me as if I cared about anything she had to say.

The woman continued to drink and sway to the music, "So. CIA? MI6? NSA? GARDA? Or are you one of those freelancers I often use myself." She raised an eyebrow at me, wholly expecting I would answer her and carry on a conversation.

When I didn't answer she rolled her eyes. "You hit-men types and your strong and silent ways. So cliché." She pointed at me with her half empty wine glass, her words now starting to slur a bit, "It is the twenty first century, traditions are broken every day. Take me for example, a woman in charge of a new terrorist cell that has the first world about to shite their pants." She giggled, slapping at the bubbles sitting around her chest.

I continued moving slowly to the tub, gauging the proper distance I would need to make this quick, and very painful for her.

Maura turned to me, her wine clouded eyes meeting the shadow covering mine, "Before you kill me, can I ask you a question?"

I stood still as I crouched slowly down in front of the tub, eye level away from the woman. Reaching into my pockets for my black gloves with the carbon fiber knuckle guards.

She giggled again, "I see this is going to be a one sided conversation." After taking another large sip from her wine she shifted to rest her chin on her forearm on the edge of the tub. "I started this mission of mine after my parents were taken from me. Mind, body and soul. I watched their spirits broken by the so called "just government" that put them in prison for speaking out on their feelings. I held my mother as she died in my arms, suffering from the side effects of being starved by the harsh political prison she was in. My father died shortly after her, his mind whittled away to nothing from the solitary confinement they kept him in for decades."

She peered down to try to look at my face hoping to see if her words had any effect on me. I felt nothing, and cared nothing for her sob story. I tilted my head down so she wouldn't see my face. I wanted to get this over with and get back to the pub for a pint before I flew home. "Oh dearie, just let me look at your face. Since it appears it will be the last one I'll ever see."

I sucked in a breath. I needed to get this done, and I knew the only way I could distract the rambling drunk was to indulge her rants. I lowered my voice, "Ask your question."

Maura's eyes widened, "A woman? They sent a woman to kill me? How very gender equal of them." She clapped her free hand on the side of her arm on the tub's edge. "I'm rather impressed, to be honest, and a little honored."

She slid back in the tub, her hand moving to rest right next to the large bottle of red wine that had maybe one, or two sips left, "The question. I think your answer might be worth hearing now, since you're a woman." She tilted her glass to her lips, "Have you ever loved something or someone with everything you had, that no matter what, you would destroy the world and everyone in it, in their name? For them?"

I clenched my jaw when the word loved fell over my ears, sending a clear picture of Alex to settle in my mind. Allowing my mind drift for a split second to the fact I knew she was at home by now, tucked up in her messy bed with the messy purple and pink sheets she loved, and probably wearing one of my shirts as she slept hard from the night's double shift. I had to squeeze my eyes shut, unconsciously shifting on the balls of my feet as the collision of my human life and my killer life, struck hard.

"Ah, I hit a nerve. The hit woman has a heart. There is someone, isn't there? A handsome beau back in France or England? A banker perhaps? I see you with a banker. They never pay mind to anything but money and how often they can get their dick wet. Or maybe it's a she? I am all about equality." Maura's tone changed, telling me that she thought she had found a chink in my armor. She must have seen my jaw twitch when she said it, and ran with it. "Ah it is a she! How very modern."

Maura sighed dramatically, "She will never love you like you want, or need to be loved. I've seen your type a thousand times. Hoping someone will love you." She grinned sloppily at me, "But, she will never love you. When she finds out the truth, she will despise your meager existence." I hated that she had hit a nerve and in some way, brought Alex into this moment. Brought Alex where I couldn't keep her safe, even if it was just in thoughts and words.

In reality she did, it felt like Alex was right around the corner. Waiting to see this side of me. It shook me to the core and I wavered for a millisecond and it forced me to look down at the floor. As I began to look up and tell the woman to shut the hell up, I caught that her right hand behind the wine bottle, her fingers curled around something.

Whispering a "Fuck." I launched up from the crouch I was in, grabbing her right wrist as she rushed to raise the .38 caliber revolver to shoot me. I then grabbed a thick handful of her red curly hair right at her temple, yanking back so hard I felt the hair rip out of the scalp as she screamed, small droplets of blood beginning to form from where I pulled harder.

As I slammed her wrist on the granite table she had her wine bottle on, forcing the gun out of her hand, I moved to her forearm, bending it until I felt the bone snap.

Maura screeched at me, "You filthy cunt! My people will find you and destroy everything you own! Everyone you love!"

Yanking her hair harder I dropped her broken arm, pushing my hood off so she could see my full face. I smirked at her, "I dare them to try. I am nothing but a ghost that doesn't exist." I twisted her hair harder, tearing out more or the thick red hair. "And you, my dear, are nothing but a ghost in a machine. A machine that wants you dead. Your desire and pleasure to avenge your parents through the pain of others dies with you right now. No one will care that you ever lived, they will only care that you are dead."

Using all the force I had, I slammed Maura's face into the edge of the tub. Smirking when the satisfying sound of her skull cracking against the hard porcelain overran the vocals of Rod Stewart.

Lifting her head, I saw that I had split her forehead open to the bone, blood poured out of the gash and mixed with the bathwater. Creating almost the same color of wine she had drank. Maura was still alive, and could survive the blow I gave her. I let out a slow breath, grabbing the sides of her jaw and face, and as I sucked in slower, steadier breath, I snapped the woman's neck. Killing her instantly.

Checking her pulse and satisfied there was none, I dragged her limp, wet body out of the tub. Ensuring that I spilled enough water on the floor to make it look like that as she went to grab her last few sips of wine, she overreached. Slipped out of the tub and tried to stop herself, breaking her arm and then slipping further on the water everywhere. Hitting her head on the edge of the tub before tumbling out and landing in a way that it twisted her neck until it snapped.

The coroner would label it an accident. That Maura O'Hara, had been drunk and had taken a terrible drunken spill. The town would gossip about it for a few months, the news media would pick it up for a day or two and the world would continue to spin madly on. The next maniac would take her place and Maura O'Hara would fade into a memory. A woman who had all this power, but couldn't handle her booze and a bubble bath.

And, yet, her words had sunk in a little too deep. Her words about love and if my truths were discovered, I would never be loved. I would be looked at as a monster and no better than the ones I murdered in the name of God and country.

Turning towards the door, I retraced my steps and exited through the same door I came in. After climbing over the wall and running back to the Land Rover, I clicked into Dani as I sat in the driver's seat. "It's done." I coughed, trying to clear out the tremble in my voice that appeared without my permission. "The cleaning crew will only have to go in with the police under protocol alpha to make sure only Maura's DNA is at the scene. I used gloves, but I need to start being extra careful these days."

I could hear Dani breathing slowly before she spoke, "I know Victoria. I saw and heard it all." She paused, the air between us growing thick.

She cleared her throat, before speaking again. "I can have a flight ready for you in a half hour if you want it. After the usual debrief and payment process, I can have you home by seven p.m. our time." I knew in the tone of her voice what she was telling me, without actually telling me.

Alex would be done with her last shift at the hospital by eight. I wondered for a second if Dani could see inside the Land Rover, see my hands tremble as I pulled off the black gloves and shoved them in my bag, if she saw my heart pounding when I reached for my cellphone and saw the handful of messages from Alex.

Lastly, I wondered if Dani could just read my mind and know how badly I needed to hear Alex's voice right in this exact moment, to confirm that I had someone who loved me. Loved me and was waiting for me. No matter what.

"Do it. Send me the directions to the second airport we use here. Have the cleaning crew take the car when I arrive, burn it clean." Dani confirmed my requests and updated the GPS the second I started the car. I tossed the cellphone onto the passenger seat, ignoring Alex's messages for now

Driving back to the isolated airfield we used, I struggled to prevent from crying. What I had done to Maura and what I had said to her was out of pure emotion. Not out of a sense of duty to my job, but emotion. Emotion because she had found the sliver in my walls and pushed too far in.

She had found that the killer in me had a heart and it could be used against me.

The 72 hours at the hospital went in the blink of an eye. The shifts at the hospital were nothing but a blur of bloody patients, gauze and bandages being thrown everywhere on top of orders being hollered over the sounds of life saving machines being rolled in and out of trauma bays.

For the start of a week, the hospital was busy. Whether it was the cherry blossom beer festival or something else in the cosmos, I barely had time to think, let alone sit down for more than a minute. Car accidents, bar fights, shootings, stabbings, etc. All of them came in in droves. At one point Stacy whispered she would give me her next two month's paychecks if she could switch vacations. Cracking a morbid joke that if this was how a Monday and a Tuesday were going to be, heaven help us all when the weekend came.

I laughed, and told her no way in hell would I pass up a week off now. I would need at least a day and a half to catch up on sleep.

I worked through the doubles that quickly became triples, and last night, I opted out of actually driving home and crashed in an on call room. Curling up on a lumpy mattress and passing out the second my eyes closed.

I was released of my nursing duties after helping an intern stitch up a little girl who had fallen down the steps of the Lincoln Memorial, splitting her shin open. As I finished wrapping her leg, telling her a funny story about how I had fallen out of a tree, I felt my phone vibrate and knew it was Victoria telling me she was on her way home.

I walked out of the stuffy hospital with a smile. Feeling lighter having made a little girl smile, as well as getting closer to seeing the girl who made me smile. I had cleared out my thoughts the second the cool, clean air entered my lungs. Helping to clear out the thoughts I had over the last few nights as I struggled to put people back together and sit by them, hoping they would make it through the night for one reason or another. Taking one deep breath of the clean air, I grinned, instantly thinking of how the clean night air also made me think of Victoria.

Bustling out to my car I, dug out my cellphone from the bottom of my bag. Grinning wider when I saw that I had a couple messages from Victoria. Swiping open the phone I read the short one from when she landed in Rhode Island then read the two others talking about how boring reading the candidates files were and that she had to go to lunch with a few other faculty members.

There was one last one that had come in about an hour ago, telling me that she was at the airport and on her way home. There also was a voice mail waiting for me, I hit play zealously and pressed the phone to my ear. It suddenly hit me hard how much I had missed the woman already. Three days felt like a lifetime.

"Alex, hi. I should be landing a bit after nine. I wanted to know if it was okay to come over to your apartment when I landed." Victoria's voice sound off, strained and sad, making me worry, "I really want to see you. I miss you." She cleared her voice of the hidden tears I could hear in the low octaves of her tone, "I have to go, the plane is boarding. Message me if you don't want me to stop by, I know you'll be exhausted."

I heard hushed male voices in the background, ushering Victoria through the terminal, causing her to utter a hurried goodbye before hanging up. My fingers flew like lightning, typing out a quick, "See you at my place." message to her.

Dropping the phone back into my bag after hitting send, I checked my watch. It was half past eight at night. I had maybe an hour to get home, shower, clean up my mess of an apartment and maybe get started on a quick dinner or snack for the both of us.

Hopping into the old mini, I raced out of the parking structure. Weaving through the early evening traffic, I gripped tighter to the old steering wheel. There was something in Victoria's voice that had me thinking a million different things.

Maybe that detective had gotten to her, told her the half-truths I answered her questions with, and maybe she somehow found out that I had gotten a bit nosy in her den and saw the fingerprints in the dust on her medals. I bit the inside of my cheek as I drove faster, whatever it was that was bothering Victoria, I knew it wouldn't be good and that it would lead to a conversation that could overshadow the best two and half days of my life.

Standing in the center of my tiny and poor excuse of a kitchen, I scanned around the loft, checking that everything was in order. The dishes were washed and put away, my bed was actually made for once and I had shoved the laundry I ignored into a closet. My shitty apartment almost looked decent.

I knew Victoria had been here a million times over the last year and never ever cared that I was a bit messier than she was, but for some reason I wanted her to come to my apartment and feel calm within a warm, clean home. Whether or not it was just a one bedroom loft apartment, it was my home and I wanted her to feel at home here with me.

Bending down to peer into the greasy brown window of the oven, I saw the nachos I had thrown together melting nicely. I stood up and went to grab plates, when I heard the soft knock on the door. Victoria's knock. She would always knock twice in a row, pause and then knock once more.

I smiled at the simple things about her I had memorized, calling over my shoulder, "It's open."

Turning to the door, I could not help but grin when I saw the blonde push through the door slowly, her head down as she had her hands full of a bottle of wine wrapped up in a brown paper bag. She looked beautiful to me, like looking at the first bloom of the cherry blossoms on the trees that lined the Mall. Something so beautiful it was almost ethereal and hard to believe it was real.

She was wearing a pair of jeans that were so big they almost hung off her hips, revealing the faint curvature of her hipbones with a plain faded black t-shirt with the Navy seal logo across her chest. Closing the door behind her, Victoria turned to look at me. A delicate smile drew her mouth into a curve the moment we made eye contact. She held up the brown bag, "I brought wine."

Nodding, I waved her over to the kitchen, noting that her tone was still as it was on the voice mail from earlier. "I made nachos."

She moved to the small counter top next to me, setting the bottle down. Silence quickly filled the air along with a heavy dose of tension. Something was seriously wrong and it made me nervous. I shifted slightly to lean on my side facing her, "You look tired, Victoria."

She nodded slowly, her arms folded against her chest with her head down. I could see her thinking as if she was writing her thoughts down on paper in front of me, her eyes were cloudy at the edges of the irises. I took in a breath and moved to get the food ready, "They should be done in a minute, and then you can fill me in on all the boring details of your trip."

I turned too quickly to see her jaw clench up and her face twist. The next thing I knew, her hand was on my bicep, gently pulling me back to her, to face her.

"Victoria?"

The last few syllables of her name were muffled as she covered my mouth with hers, kissing me hard and deep, as she pulled me into her body. I half grunted when our bodies met, but didn't stop kissing her. Reaching up, I ran my hands over her neck and to the back of her head, holding her as we kissed hungrily. Something was different about Victoria in the way she kissed me. It was if she needed to kiss me, that she needed to feel connected to me. I tried to think about what could be bothering her, but lost all train of thought when her tongue met mine at the same time she grabbed my hips.

Pushing me towards the kitchen counter, Victoria lifted me up in one quick movement and sat me on the counter. My legs instinctively opened to allow her to stand between them. Her hands moving from my hips to the edge of the plain white tank top I wore.

I moaned against her mouth when I felt her warm hands slide up underneath the material, gathering it as she slid her hands and the thin tank top up my body. Making me shiver from the cool air hitting my skin and what I knew was coming. I pushed harder against her mouth, my hands moving to her sides and then to her back, pushing Victoria forward, deeper into me. Only moving them when Victoria's hands motioned for me to lift my arms up to remove the tank top.

We broke apart, breathing heavily as she threw my tank top on the floor, her eyes roaming my body with so much intensity, it made my throat dry. I tried to look her in her eyes, but couldn't catch them. "Victoria..."

My voice broke her trance, she glanced up to look in my eyes. There was a storm of desire, fear, pain, love and something else hiding in the slate grey irises of the woman. I went to reach for her face, when she lunged at me again. Kissing me hard again, not in a way that hurt, but in a way that she needed this and the only way she could communicate it was silently. I couldn't resist and melted back into her as I felt her fingertips graze the skin on my back and up to where my bra clasp sit. I grabbed her sides harder when I felt the bra release and Victoria's hands move it forward.

I was on the verge of losing control, my body was becoming overwhelmed with the sensations of her kissing me, her bare hands on my bare skin and how it felt exactly as I imagined it. I bit her bottom lip, hearing her moan into my mouth and slip her hands under the bra.

When her palms fell to the side of my breasts, I couldn't hold back. I wanted to feel her against me, skin to skin. I ached to feel her breasts against mine, run my fingers over her stomach and further down. I wanted to know if I was doing the same things to her that she was doing to me, lighting my entire body on fire in ways no one else could. I wanted to know what she felt like, tasted like, and I wanted her to do the same to me.

I dropped my hands to the waist of her jeans, reaching for the hem of her shirt. I wanted to tear it off, but didn't. My hands moved slow due to the overload of pleasure the rest of my body was experiencing. My fingers dipped under Victoria's shirt, grazing the thick patch of skin I had felt a few days ago. Making my brain shift out of pleasure town and back into logical nurse brain. I suddenly had a curiosity that could not be avoided.

Pressing my fingertips against the one ridge, I could almost feel it was a burn scar, but as quickly as my hand touched the rough patch, it was covered by Victoria's and pulled away from her skin. She placed my hand on the edge of the kitchen counter, and returned to the business of slowly removing my bra.

Even through the haze of her delicious and intoxicating kisses, my mind was still curious. I bit her lip again, pushing my mouth hard against hers to distract her and moved my hands back to her shirt, once again moving to that part of her back that was as much of a mystery as she was.

And once again, Victoria's hand covered mine and move it back to the counter. This time holding it there as she used one hand to try and remove my bra. This was where my gut, my brain, and the other body parts that were on fire and needed release, all came together and threw up a red flag.

I bent away from Victoria's mouth, breathing heavily, and kissed up her neck until I was next to her ear, whispering, "Let me touch you, Victoria."

I instantly felt her body stiffen up and her movements hesitate, but she said nothing. Moving back into my space, holding my hand tighter against the counter she moved away from my bra and towards the top of the loose sweatpants I had thrown on. It was her way of distracting me.

This time it was I who grabbed her hand before it dipped to where I ached for her, gently holding her hand from going any further. I leaned back away from the woman. Her face was flushed just as much as mine was. The air thick with heat and desire, but there was something off. Bending to look at her eyes, I found the courage to ask, "What are you hiding? It's just a scar, nothing more."

I watched as Victoria's jaw twitched tightly. "Alex." Her voice was soft but had that same tone it did that day I tried to kiss her and she rejected me. "Please don't."

I squeezed her hand as I pulled it up to place it on my almost bare chest over my heart. "Do you feel how hard you make my heart race?"

Victoria's hands trembled as I held it there, "You're safe here. You're safe in my heart and my arms." I swallowed hard, fighting so many emotions, fearing that Victoria was about to retreat like she had so long ago. Retreat because I was getting to close to something that scared her. "There's no reason to be afraid of this, of me. I won't ever hurt you."

Victoria went to step away, slowly pulling her hand free from under mine, "I'm not worried about you hurting me." Her voice was a half whisper as she kept her head down.

I caught her wrist before her entire arm was lost to me, the words rushing out faster than I could stop them, "You can't hurt me, Victoria. I love you."

It was as if an anvil had fallen between us, sucking all of the air out of the room. I felt her stiffen up in my grasp as she pulled my hand free from her arm, not daring to look at me, Victoria shook her head as I saw the tears stream down her face, "Don't Alex." The way she said it, sounded like a warning mixed with a plea.

Reaching out to her, I realized my mistake in telling her I loved her so soon. I had loved her for as long as I could remember her being in my life, but I spilled it out of my mouth in the heat of passion like a silly teenager. "Victoria, wait...I."

I couldn't finish, Victoria shook her head, "It's not safe to love me." She suddenly turned away from me and rushed out of my apartment, slamming the door behind her. Leaving me half naked and disheveled on the kitchen counter as the smell of burning nachos and confusion filled the air.

I sat on that counter for what felt like hours, staring off into space. Tears filling my eyes before I slid off it, picked up my tank top and put it back on before turning off the oven. After I set the blackened nachos on the top of the stove, I walked straight to my laptop and turned it on.

My fingers trembled and stumbled as I typed her name and the name of the silver coin into the web search engine. Hesitating only a second before I clicked on her name and let the monitor fill up with news articles that were almost ten years old, all of them about a Lieutenant Victoria Bancroft and her actions in Baghdad.

I clenched my jaw, knowing this would add fuel to the fire I didn't start, but it was time. I had to know who I was in love with.

I had perfected the art of silent crying years ago, but was failing at it now as I raced back to my house, letting out all of the emotions I had bottled up from the job and from what just happened in Alex's apartment. I sobbed openly for the first time in years, gasping for air as I drove the BMW as fast as I could back home.

I pulled the car into the garage so I could avoid Dale and Mary poking their heads out or coming over to drop off the mail. I grabbed my bags and went inside. After throwing them into the laundry room I headed down into my basement, only pausing to drop my phone on the desk in the den.

My basement was the one place I would go to when I wanted absolute peace from the world I lived in. It was finished as a library and small bar area. It was where I kept my extra text books for class and the other texts I used to write tests and hand out assignments to my students. It was also where I buried my past in the far closet next to the bar.

Alex would be calling and texting in the next few minutes and I knew it would be best to leave it, and her, alone for a while. If I didn't, I knew I would say something, or do something, that would ensure Alex would never love me. I was afraid that I would return to being the woman she had almost given up on a few days ago. As much as the one side of me knew it was what I should do, hearing her say that she loved me and that she would always keep me safe, frightened the hell out of me.

Then Maura popped into my head, her Irish accented voice repeating the words she had said moments before I killed her.

"When she finds out the truth, she will despise your meager existence."

Then my heart spoke up and told me to prove her wrong. I had to prove to everyone including myself wrong. I could love Alex and I could keep her safe, I just had to figure out how, and that's why I left. Instinct from years of being alone and keeping people at a distance took over, and I walked away.

Walking over to the bar when I was in the basement, I grabbed the large bottle of vintage bourbon on the top shelf. After pouring a very full glass, I moved to the closet and opened it. Revealing all of my old uniforms, fatigues and the other remnants of the war I had shoved in there when I moved in. After taking three or four large sips of the bourbon, I grabbed the grey plastic bin on the bottom of the closet and dragged it out to the middle of the room. I dragged it over to the large leather couch and sat down. Drinking more of the bourbon, I flipped open the lid and stared at the contents.

Large stacks of newspaper clippings from that day on top of the framed certificates from my medals. I lifted them out one by one, my jaw clenching tighter as each old memory was brought back. Tucked in with the stack of memories, was a plastic bag full of my unit's patches I cut off my destroyed uniform, and saved, as I was taken out of Baghdad and back to a safe zone.

Underneath that was another plastic bag of my old Lieutenant bars, and ribbons from my dress uniform tucked in with a picture of the day I received my last two medals from the President and the current CIA Director. In the picture, I still had the bruises on my face, the stitches on my forehead and bottom lip. I had to lean on Dani who stood next to me, for support. I tried to smile that day, but was still in pain. Mentally and physically to want to pretend any harder than I was.

I ran my finger over the image, stopping as I saw the old man and the old lady in the background standing next to the Secretary of Defense and that one Colonel from the Army Intelligence Unit, who I still hated to this day.

After tossing the pictures and bags to the side next to me, I reached deep into the bottom of the bin, pulling out the copy of the mission that had gone so wrong. A copy only one other person knew I had, because they gave it to me. Opening the file, I felt the tears rise as I read my medical file from the US Army doctors who treated me, reading terms such as *"Excessive second degree burns, puncture wounds from a knife or spike in lower back, with heavy loss of blood. There are also lingering signs of starvation and dehydration."*

Followed by the psychiatrists notes of, *"Severe case of PTSD evolving, also a severe case of detachment from psychological manipulation or torture. As if the patients ability to feel empathy or apathy was removed leading to the frenzied state the rescue team found her in. Will have to look further into the mission notes, patient was held in grueling conditions for a lengthy amount of time."*

My heart felt like lead, my eyes began to well up and I let the tears free. How would I ever explain any of this to Alex? Show Alex any of this? And then tell her what followed after. Who I became. What I became.

Flipping to the pictures of my injuries, I heard my side door creak open. I shot my head up as I reached under the couch and wrapped my hand around one of the .40 caliber handguns I kept hidden around the house. Pointing it up at the staircase, I listened as the steps moved closer.

"FedEx delivery, I found the garage door and side door open. I've called the police."

I dropped the handgun on the couch after hearing Dani's voice. I called up to her, "In the basement. Close and lock the door behind you, please."

She rushed down the stairs in her uniform, tucking her own handgun back into the black briefcase she carried, giving me a dirty look, "For fuck's sake, both doors left open?" She tossed her briefcase on the bar and picked up the bottle of bourbon, giving me another look before walking back over to me with a thick manila envelope. "Old lady sent me over with the payment. She was too afraid to send it over the wire." Dani dropped the envelope on the side table next to me. I caught her looking at the mess of memories I had spread out.

Her face dropped slightly, "I see why the bourbon." Dani sat down next to me, filling up my glass before taking a swig from the bottle. She let out a breathless curse at how strong the bourbon was, "Phew, that shit is strong." Motioning to the mess in front of me, "Why do you want to remember?"

I looked up at her with red, teary eyes. "Alex." Shrugging I picked up the bourbon and drank.

Dani sighed, her hand falling to my shoulder, "What happened?"

Dani was the last person I wanted to open up about Alex or anything else in my private life, but I had no one else that would understand. I held the glass in both hands, "Ireland went bad. The mark got into my head and found a chink in my armor." I stared at the brown liquid that was sinking into my veins, making me feel numb as I needed and wanted to be, "I came home and went right to Alex. I needed to feel something, to connect to something and someone to prove that old bitch wrong, but when Alex kept reaching for my scar, I kept stopping her." I glanced at Dani as the tears clouded my eyes. "She told me she loved me."

Dani let out a slow breath, pulling me to lean against her as she wrapped an arm around me, "And you love her." She said it as if she had known from the moment I asked her to find the woman I helped that night. A night that now felt a lifetime ago.

I nodded silently as I leaned against her, "I told her I wasn't safe to love, and left." I waved at the mess in front of us, "Dug all of this out to try and figure out a way. A way to be able to love Alex and hide this. Hide the monster I am, the hero I am, the stupid fucking asshole I am for thinking I could..."

"It took me thirteen days to find you, Victoria." Dani cut me off, "Thirteen days because the walls of the cave they kept you in were so thick, the signal from the chip you hid in your boot would come and go. They all told me to quit, to give up, to let you go. That you and the rest of the unit were lost to us days ago, but then you would blip up on my radar, giving me hope."

She looked down at me, her own memories of how we met filled her green eyes. "I went to the old lady and old man, not having any idea who they were. Begging them to give me a team of six to go in and get you out. I was the one who sold them on how smart you were and how much smarter I was than you." She smirked as I shook my head at the bit of arrogance coming through in the heartfelt moment. "If anyone is to blame, it's me. I look back now and see that I dragged you into this, along with that asshole Colonel."

I sighed, wiping my eyes, "You saved my life, Dani. They would have killed me the next day."

Dani reached up, wiping my cheek with the back of her hand, "And you saved mine. You saw that guy behind me." She stopped speaking, she didn't have to finish, we both knew. We both had the same memories from that day.

I frowned, "The only reason I was able to stop the frenzy I was in, was because I saw your green eyes. They all had brown eyes and the only thing I could understand was to kill everyone with brown eyes, because of what they did to me and my team." I squeezed my eyes shut when I heard the pops of gunfire, the flashes of the knife I had in my hand followed by the blood spurting here and there as I cut and slashed my way out. Then came Dani's bright green eyes, highlighted by the dirt and mud covering her face and helmet, making me stop for a split second. Realizing she was out of place, her voice telling me I was okay, that I was safe. Far different from the harsh male voices screaming at me for days on end in broken English, Farsi, and Arabic.

She dropped her head down, "We both did things and saw things that day. I'm certain both of our brains are rewired in ways I don't think I ever want to understand." Dani reached over and tapped the file she had gotten for me two years ago when I began to ask the old man and old lady for my original case file to review out of curiosity. "Our secrets lie in here, Victoria."

I nodded slowly, sipping at the bourbon that was starting to give me a heavy buzz. My tears coming back as I thought about Alex, "What do I do about her?" It came out so soft, I almost didn't hear my own voice.

Dani grabbed my wrist gently, pulling my attention to her phone. The screen was lit up with ping notifications, my name popping up on internet searches of that day. The polished up news reports, and media releases of the mission, and how I received the medals sitting in my den. "I think if you love nurse blue eyes as much as you clearly do. I think the only route to take is the truthful one, since she has already begun searching out the mystery that is the brooding Professor."

I looked at the phone as my name moved across the screen, Alex clearly reading every little news report she could about a Lieutenant Victoria Bancroft and her actions on a day in May, 2004. "But maybe leave out the part about Voltaire and becoming a killer for a black ops agency within our own government."

Dani set her phone in her lap, standing up she scanned over the memories, "Because you know I'm still looking for the truth from the inside out. The less you and I pop up on their radar, the easier it will be for me to keep digging and keep you and nurse blue eyes safe."

I looked up at the tall redhead, "I thought you gave that up a few years ago, looking into who we work for." I was confused, especially since Dani had seemed to be more of a company woman and far more dedicated than she had been since the beginning days of us becoming partners in Voltaire's projects.

Dani bent down to my ear, whispering, "Never. They destroyed my life, I want to destroy them even if it takes me until my very last breath." She stood back up looking around the basement, "By the way, I encoded bug zappers into your house, so if you do tell nurse blue eyes the truth, do it here. Even I won't hear a thing."

She moved around the couch, picking up her briefcase she looked back at me as she stepped up on the first step leading back up to the kitchen. "Victoria, I mean it. I will always have your back and if you decide that you want to do this with Alex, I will be there for her as well." She stared in my eyes for a lengthy second to ensure that I understood.

I nodded once, biting back the tears, "Thank you Dani."

Dani saluted me, "Till next time Professor. I'm taking the leftover muffins on my way out."

After I heard the side door close, followed by my garage door, I cleaned up most of the pieces I had pulled out of the bin. Leaving it open, I placed the file on top and slowly closed it. I knew Dani was right. The truth was the only way at this point. If Alex decided that this was too much, that my past was too much to bear and she walked away from me. I knew she would be safe. Only hearing terrible war stories from a veteran that would not link back to Voltaire in any way. I also knew that Dani would make sure Voltaire would never know about Alex's existence if this all went south and Alex left me.

Walking back upstairs, I grabbed my cellphone. My heart twitching when I saw there were no phone calls or texts from Alex in the last two hours. I set my bourbon down and hit Alex's contact button. Chewing on my lip as I waited through the rings until I heard her trembling voice, "Victoria."

I could hear and feel that she had been crying, that I had possibly broken her heart again. I bit deeper into my lip to keep myself on track, "Alex, can you come over to my house? I think I have some things I need to tell you."

Chapter 11

My eyes were glued to the screen of my laptop. Reading news report after news report, watching all the video clips of real time war footage followed up by the medal ceremony a few months later. All of them showing a very young Victoria covered in mud and blood being rushed to a helicopter as reporters chased after her in what looked to be like the center of a city that could have been Baghdad.

The reports that accompanied the clips had the basics. A unit of Army Rangers and Navy Seals had gone in for what was supposed to be a successful rescue mission. Rescuing a group of three survivors of a citizen support envoy trying to establish a place for refugee help weeks after Baghdad finally fell. The unit of six had been captured and taken hostage by a lingering group of insurgents.

After that, the report fell into the patriotic propaganda of the time. Pushing ideas that America was winning the war, bringing peace and freedom to the people. There were no details of any mission or rescue, just Victoria's name and rank. There were two other medals included in a report that was issued a few days before her medal ceremony, but I wasn't able to track those down. The most detailed report I did find, only named the Purple Heart and the Silver Star she had received, but there was no other mention of the other medals I had found in the box. The ones that the internet attached to the CIA as being the organization who handed them out.

The one video clip that broke my heart the most was watching her receive her medals from the President. She was standing in a line with a handful of other soldiers who had done more than their fair share in a senseless war and were receiving the tokens of our country's appreciation. It was this Victoria, the clean woman in her dress uniform, covered in faded bruises, holding on to the arm of shorter red head standing next to her, that crushed my heart. The way she looked around the room like she was scared and lost, not knowing how to act and flinched whenever someone brushed her arm, or when the President shook her hand.

It was the look in her eyes that made me fall apart and cry. I could see in them that there was more to the story the news fed to the world. There was more to her envoy being attacked and her unit being kidnapped. All because I had seen that look in thousands of others over my time as a nurse. Whether it was in police officers, firefighters, paramedics or veterans, they all had a look that told you that they had gone past the limits humans can endure. They were humans who have seen more than anyone ever should and came out of it. Seen things and done things to survive that could be covered up by clean uniforms and shiny medals, but would poke its head out whenever you stared in their eyes for too long.

My strong Victoria, the woman who had been nothing but tender, soft, kind, and giving since the moment I met her, was hiding ten years of pain and hurt underneath the mask all survivors build and put on so they could pretend as long as they could. Never wanting to show or talk about the hell they endured. It now made sense why she was so guarded.

I kept reading and watching clips until my eyes wouldn't allow me to see through the tears. Forcing me to cover my face and rest my elbows on the edge of the metal desk. I was still angry at Victoria for walking out on me like she did. Especially right after I said the three little words that held so much power, but now I understood some of the reasons why she was like she was.

I sniffled and looked up, hearing my phone ring from over on my bed. It was Victoria's ring tone, the Navy fight song.

Slipping out of the old metal chair I walked to the bed, feeling the anger rise with my tears. Victoria knew I could handle hearing her past in the war, handle hearing the hell she had been through. She had to have known it the second I told her I loved her, that I wasn't ever going anywhere. Taking a deep breath, I answered the phone, "Victoria."

"Alex, can you come over to my house? I think have I some things I need to tell you."

My jaw clenched on its own. Her voice was feathery, as if she could barely get the words out, it was so thick with apprehension. I struggled, picking at the edge of my deep purple comforter. I wanted to go to her, but I knew if I faltered and let Victoria hide away, I would be lying to myself and allowing her to continue to hide whatever she thought she had to from me. The only way I saw to do this was to lay it all out, be honest and force more of it from the both of us.

Clearing my throat, I glanced at the Go Navy! Sign hanging over my bed, "I looked you up on the internet Victoria. I read about what happened on May 7th, 2004. Well, what the news wanted to tell the world about that day."

I heard her let out a heavy breath, "Can you come over? I don't want to do this over the phone." Her voice now had the slightest quiver to it.

Moving to the closet, I started unconsciously grabbing the clothing I had stolen from her, dumping them into a bag. I had been down this road more than once, twice, three times, shit it had been a lot of times that I was returning borrowed clothes and facing the inevitable, it's not you it's me, talk. Followed by the stupid break up speech that would always come next.

I knew what would come next after hearing, I don't want to do this over the phone or over text. "Yes, but only if we talk honestly. Lay it all out, Victoria. You don't need to hide from me. I can't keep doing this if you want to keep hiding from me." I paused, knowing I was back to where we were the last time I made nachos in my apartment.

I was fighting a hopeless battle, but at least I would go down in flames, "I meant what I said. All of it." I drifted off, zipping up my bag and catching Baby sitting on the edge of my one pillow.

I almost went to reach for him too, to add him in with the rest when Victoria's voice filled my ear. "Then honesty you will get. It won't be pretty, and it won't be polished up like the news has done. There are things missing in all of those reports and video clips I know you watched. It will be brutal, harsh, painful, but it will be me, Alex. You will be getting me." Victoria cleared her throat, "I will see you in an hour." She hung up before I could reply or comment on the fact I caught the tail end of a sob as she pulled the phone away.

Victoria never cried.

Pulling into her driveway, I didn't get out right away. I sat for a moment, staring at the front door with the porch light on, and then staring at the time on my watch. It was close to two in the morning, and like the saying went, nothing good happens after midnight. Granted, the saying generally referred to getting wasted and having one night stands, but sitting in my raggedy mini, the saying felt heavier to me. Like a foreshadowing phrase of what was actually waiting for me. What could be so bad that Victoria had to warn me? Prepare me for? She knew I was a nurse and had more stories of gore and graphic debauchery than a B horror movie.

Then the one thought that got me here and kept me motivated to actually come to her house fell into my head, I loved her. I loved Victoria like no one before and for the many red flags and gut feelings that told me to leave it, I couldn't. I loved her more than anything and I would always regret it if I let her fade away out of fear of what was waiting for me. The horrid truths that kept Victoria locked away from the world and me.

I let out a heavy sigh, grabbed my bag and got out of the car. The upside to the hour long drive back to her house was that I was able to collect my thoughts and become the nurse I was. The one who was detached, but caring. The woman who could handle the gore, shout orders and go toe to toe with any doctor or surgeon especially if I knew they were wrong. If Victoria wanted to put on masks, I could too. I would handle her truths like I would looking at someone's chart, only looking for the facts as my heart hid behind the walls to keep it safe.

Walking up the stone path, I saw a white piece of note paper taped to the door.

"Alex. The door is open. I'll be in the den. Please lock it behind you."

I frowned, shaking my head as I snatched the note off the door, crumpling it in my hand. I didn't like how this was already starting off.

Opening the door, I dropped my bag on the floor underneath the coat rack before turning to close and secure the door as instructed. I moved to go into the den, tugging the edges of the long sleeved thermal I threw on in haste, before folding my arms. "Victoria?" I called out tentatively, hoping to mask the burgeoning nerves and anger that were colliding all at once.

"In the den."

Victoria's voice had not a hint of emotion to it. I sighed hard and walked to the den. This was going to be a long night, and not in the way I had imagined it when she showed up at my apartment and started taking my clothes off, groping me in the most amazing ways imaginable. I walked around the corner into the den, looking into the kitchen to see a half empty bottle of bourbon sitting next to a glass smeared with fingerprints, "I locked the door as you asked."

Coming around the corner of the living room, I paused when I turned my head to look into the den. Victoria was standing at the far window across from her desk, looking out it as the night sky was clear enough for the moon and stars to be seen. She had her eyes focused on the sky with her arms folded, still wearing the same clothes she had worn to my apartment, but that wasn't what made me pause. It was the line of items neatly laid out on top of the large wooden desk that drew my full attention.

The shadowbox of her medals sat on the far corner, opened and some of them pulled out to sit on the desktop to the right of the box. Next to that was a thick brown file folder that had the appearance of passing through many hands to get to where it now rested. Underneath the file were a few photographs and patches with dark stains on them and looked to be torn off whatever uniform they had once belonged on.

Taking a step towards the desk, Victoria began to speak, "May 7th was when I was rescued. They never bothered to tell anyone that I had been missing for almost twenty five days. That I was taken hostage since I was the commanding officer and tortured for twenty four of those twenty five days." Victoria peered over her shoulder, nodding at the items on her desk. "Go ahead. It's all there."

I swallowed hard and went for the file, sliding my forefinger under the front page and opening it. I had to hold back the gasp as the first thing I saw were bright color photographs of what I could best describe as the scene of a rescue. I fanned most of the pictures out, grimacing as I caught Victoria's face covered in red splotches. I picked up one that caught my full attention, it was a picture of Victoria sitting outside a building made from stone and mud, smoke billowing around it as she sat on a chunk of broken wall. She was looking off to the side of the photographer, ignoring the person crouched in front of her. Her face was covered in blood. Blood that ran down her face, over her uniform and down to her hands in a morbid abstract painting way. An abstract painting that looked like it fell out of a horror film. I could see large cuts on her forehead, rope burns around her neck and wrists.

There was something in her eyes that upset me deeply, it was the look I had seen far too many times and seeing it in the face of the one I loved with my whole heart, made me want to throw up. I clenched my jaw and looked to the edge of the desk to steady myself, glancing up to look at Victoria now facing me.

Her face was still void of emotion, looking right in my eyes she started speaking again, "It wasn't a citizen refugee rescue envoy I was on. It wasn't a humanitarian mission that went wrong. I was sent in there as an intelligence officer working with the CIA and the NSA in conjunction with the Navy's own intelligence branch. I was to lead a team of six into the small village, town, whatever you want to call it, and interrogate the elders and others. All of us knew that the Iraqi army had folded up and disappeared into the outlying areas of Baghdad hiding with the innocents."

Victoria looked down at her arms, "I wasn't lying to you about my background at the Academy. I just never told you that I had been selected for the intelligence sector because of my test scores and what my instructors saw in me. I wanted to be a Surface Warfare Officer and sail the seas. What I became was an intelligence officer. One who was sent out exactly like you see in the movies. Extract information, but in a gentler way since the states were facing backlash for other techniques they used. So, they picked the top female intel officers and sent us to the desert. I was handpicked by the CIA and the NSA to go into the roughest parts of Baghdad and try to gather intel under a very classified mission that was never to see the light of day. I was twenty-three, young and eager to start my career. Fresh out of the Academy and willing to do my part for the war effort. We were only supposed to gather intel, talk to a few people and send it back. Let the CIA and other agencies do the dirty work." Victoria smirked sarcastically, "But nothing about that was simple. Nothing about war is ever simple, clean and easy."

I stared at the woman, trying hard to hold firm as her voice lacked emotion as she told her story. I turned back down to look at the photographs. "I wouldn't have cared about that, your job in intelligence. I know a lot people who work for the government in jobs that they can't ever really talk about."

I picked up a few aerial photographs, "I just care that you let me in." I kept my voice steady. I wanted to show her that I was listening, but wasn't going to take the usual bullshit reasons Victoria gave for why she couldn't do anything. Couldn't let me touch her, let me love her, let me in.

I felt Victoria move closer to me, "Alex, this is all part of the story of who I am now, who I became." She waved at the photographs, "What's in there is why I can't..."

She let out a soft sigh, "Why I can't be touched." Victoria's voice shook as she spoke, something I had never heard from her. Something was telling me that what she was telling me, was a huge piece of her. A huge piece of her past that had not yet seen the light of day outside of those involved.

I let out my own heavy sigh, closing my eyes, opening my mouth to say something when Victoria filled the awkward pause. "The mission went wrong when our intel was tainted. The insurgents got a hold of it and set my unit up. We never stood a chance as they swarmed us. I was taken first since it was clear I was the commanding officer by the stupid brown bar insignia on my collar. The insurgents had studied our ranking system and I was so young that I hadn't learned the tricks of ripping patches off to hide your identity."

Victoria now stood on the opposite end of the desk. Leaning forward on it, she reached across to the file. Moving the pictures on the top of the stack out of the way, they shifted to images with less dirt and sand filled. The ones at the bottom were cleaner, more sterile looking.

It was pictures of Victoria in a hospital gown sitting on the edge of a bed. Her face was clean, clearly showing the damage done to her face. Her eyes were swollen shut, the gashes and bruises on her forehead and cheeks told me that she had been beaten repeatedly. There were pictures of her hands, swollen and cut in a way that resembled defense wounds. "They beat me. Beat me every day until I passed out hoping I would give up information. They hit harder when they saw I was a woman as my long blonde hair fell free of its ties. Thinking the harder they hit me, the quicker I would give in." She held up the last photograph in front of my face, "I never gave in. Every punch they gave me, I stood back up, ready to take the next one."

She reached around and tapped at the image to draw my attention to it, "Then there's this. This was when their fists stopped having any effect on me. It frustrated them that every time they punched me or slapped me, I would just stare back at them harder in silence or repeat the same bullshit story I'd been fed to use as a cover in case of capture. Recycling old intel that would lead them back to their own pockets of supplies or insurgent hiding places." She picked the photograph up and held it between us so we both could look at it as she continued.

Looking down at the photograph, I had to bite the inside of my cheek to hold back the strangled sound that wanted to come out. It was of Victoria's back. Covered in bruises down to the one spot I knew there was a scar, but instead of puckered and raw skin, there was angry red burns turning yellow at the edges as infection began to set in. There were large puncture holes, three of them. I could easily see they had been reopened over and over, with whatever tool that had caused them, repeatedly. Those wounds were also filled with signs of infection and poor medical treatment.

"They moved to dirty steel rods, sharpened into spikes. Letting a few of them to sit in the fire pit they sat me in front of all day. Forcing me to watch the metal turn a bright molten red color. When the spikes were hot enough, they would pick it up out of the fire and re-ask their questions. Teasing me with the heat and the bright blinding color of the spikes. Thrusting them close enough to my face, I could feel and smell my eyebrows burn."

Victoria tilted her head up to look at the ceiling. "When I wouldn't answer their questions, they would start by driving a clean, cold sharp spike into my back. Tearing through the skin like it was nothing, causing me to almost bleed out. When I was just on the verge of passing out, they would switch to the hot spike to cauterize the wound and stop my bleeding. The extreme pain from the heat and the smell of my own flesh burning would wake me up so they could start the process all over."

Victoria held the photograph up until I took it from her with a shaking hand. My eyes and mind struggling to maintain the nurse in me and not fall apart at what I was looking at. Looking at the one I loved with everything like this. Bloodied, broken.

Victoria straightened up, "I'd endure anywhere from six to fifteen cycles of this particular treatment each day from morning to nightfall. Some days they would beat me after, some days they would leave me after I passed out. All I can remember is the pain and the harsh sounds of men yelling at me in Farsi, Arabic and broken English, asking the same goddamn questions over and over. I would only tell them a few things to keep the others in my team alive. Small useless pieces of intel that was true but would lead them to nothing."

She moved to look back out the window, "For eight days it went on like that, endlessly. Then one day they threw me into a small room and locked me in there with a piece of bread and a cup of dirty water. I was in too much pain to even want to think about eating, so I drank the dirty water and forced myself to stand up. My back and entire body was in unbearable pain, but I couldn't show them that. I knew if I could stand up, they would keep me alive, knowing I was still holding out on them."

I didn't realize I was still holding the photograph of Victoria's back until I glanced down and the jarring image forced me to throw it back down on the desk. I closed the file to remove the images from my sight as I could feel my throat tighten and my eyes well up. All of this was beginning to overwhelm me as I pictured Victoria in a tiny room, fighting for her life, covered in blood and mud. Not knowing if she would live to see another day, another sunrise or sunset. I absently placed my hand over my heart as it began to physically hurt inside of my chest from my imagination running wild.

Victoria had her head down, "When I got to my feet, I suddenly remembered that I had packed a GPS tracker in the front inside pocket of my fatigue pants. The size of a tin of mints, the kidnappers never found it when they roughly searched me and only took my fatigue shirt. I pulled the GPS tracker apart and saw that the tracker chip was still activated and sending out a signal. All I had to do was disconnect and reconnect to send out a SOS signal. It had been at least two or three days since my team was taken, I knew someone would be looking for us."

She let out a slow breath, trying to reign in her emotions that were threatening to spill over like a broken dam, "I did the SOS ten times before I hid the chip in the bottom of my boot, tucking it under a flap of leather and the seam of the sole. I would be able to tap my boot against the wall, or a chair, as I sat. Being interrogated or waiting for the next beating."

I set the file off to the side and moved around the desk to be closer to Victoria. I was so unsure what to do as she poured out all of this information that was making me angrier. Not at her, but at the men who put her in that position and the men who did this to her. Created a woman who was afraid to be touched, loved, held and tell anyone about her past.

Victoria turned her head and saw I was moving closer, she took one step back, "It took thirteen more days after that night I put the chip in my boot, for anyone to find me." She closed her eyes as her lower lip quivered, "But I snapped the day I was rescued. That day I became a monster."

I went to reach for Victoria, shaking my head, "You're not a monster, don't say that." I took another step closer to her.

She held up her hand, "Please don't, Alex." She swallowed hard as I saw her eyes fill up with tears. Something I had never seen from the woman in the entire time I've known her. "Let me finish. You need to hear everything before you decide if you can stay here. Stay in this with me."

I furrowed my brow at her, confused why she dared to think I wouldn't stay with her. I was angry at her for walking away and keeping me out, but there wasn't anything I could think of that would keep me from her. Anger would fade in time, my love for her wouldn't. "Victoria, I don't understand why you think that?"

Victoria suddenly moved around me, grabbing the file she flipped open and walked back over. Shoving the file in my face pointing at what looked to be a psych exam. "This is why." She tapped hard on the middle of the file with her index finger. I frowned, moving to hand it back when she held it firmly, "Read it." She turned away before I could see the lone tear slide down her cheek.

I sucked in a breath and began to gloss over the psychologist's report.

"Lieutenant Bancroft is suffering from severe PTSD and trauma brought on by the endless torture. She is detached, lacks apathy and empathy in most of the tests given. She has no severe head trauma that would link to her change in behavior witnessed that day by the rescue team. Their interviews all have her tied back to what she has told me herself. That she killed her captors without a second thought or care, and did so in such a brutal and semi methodical way, that they would suffer deeply. Their deaths were neither easy nor painless. I cannot, at this time, diagnose Lieutenant Bancroft with anything that could point to what triggered the frenzy she was found in and the current comatose state she appears to be operating in. I will conduct further tests as she heals."

My head shot up from the file to look right into the slate grey eyes of Victoria who was now openly crying, tears running heavily down her face as she bit her bottom lip. "I killed them. I killed them all that day I was rescued. I broke when they came in for the third round of spikes that day. The one who spoke the best English told me that they had killed three of my men. They then showed me the shitty cellphone video of them doing it. Killing one of my men, one that had been a part of my team for the last year. A part of my unit, my family."

Victoria stopped as she swallowed down a sob. She continued a moment later, after slowly exhaling, "My captors told me it was my fault, that I had to give them what they wanted before the last two were killed and I was left to be burned alive."

Victoria closed her eyes as she began to gradually sob, "Something overcame me and the world went black. I only remember head butting him, shattering his nose before I grabbed his knife. He stumbled back, and I when I saw I had the upper hand on him, I went into a frenzy like the reports say. I killed six of my seven captors, torturers, with my bare hands. Slashing, cutting and slicing without a care. Watching them all bleed out as they crumpled to the floor, begging me to stop. When I raced to find the last one, the rescue team broke into the building we were being held in and I collapsed into the arms of one rescuer with green eyes. None of my captors had green eyes."

She sucked in a shaky breath, wiping away the tears. "I was taken outside and that's when a news reporter driving by with an Army unit saw it. Scooping up the story of a lifetime, a female officer being rescued. The CIA and NSA had the story spun into the mess you read on the internet. That's why I was given the medals on the desk. I had saved two of my men, protected precious intel, and done my job by taking out all seven very terrible humans. I did almost die from the infection from my wounds and the damage from starvation and dehydration I faced, but the news and the PR teams all spun it around. Making me a hero who kept her country's secrets intact."

Victoria lifted up her shirt with a shaky hand, just enough to reveal the very large, white puckered scar that started right above her hip and carried up to the middle of her back. It was the width of a tablet screen. I could tell that a plastic surgeon had tried, but there was so much damage done, no one would ever be able to make that part of Victoria disappear. I clenched my own tears back as she looked in my eyes and ran her hands over the scar. "How can I ever ask anyone to live with this, love this? This is who I am, Alex." She dropped the shirt back down and waved her hand over the file and medals on her desk, "That is who I am. That is what I don't want anyone to see and have never let anyone see until you, Alex."

Victoria suddenly stopped and let out a breath, covering her face with her hands as she fell to sit on the edge of the desk, "I was a hero in everyone's eyes, but I'm not. I'm an idiot who followed orders, lost three good people and dragged a handful of others through the mess that came after." She started sobbing so hard, she gasped for breaths, mumbling, "I'm not safe to love, I'm a killer."

I stared at Victoria, slowly absorbing as much as I could of the deluge of information she threw at me. The graphic details of her story matching up to the pictures I had seen, but none of that shook me to my foundation more than looking at the blonde woman sobbing uncontrollably on the edge of her couch.

Victoria never cried.

Never.

Not like this. Not like her entire world had just broken apart in the matter of the time it took her to tell me the shattered bits of pieces of a series of days ten years ago. The way she curled up into herself, her palms pressed against her face as I had seen so many times before in so many others as the doctor delivered the final news, but this was different. This was the woman I loved. Watching her like this hurt to the core.

Out of instinct of from my years of being a nurse, and the fact that this was the woman I loved with all my heart, I rushed over to Victoria, wrapped her up in my arms and held her tightly against my chest. It took a moment for her to unfold her arms, but when she did, she threw them around me. Holding me as tight as she could, making my ribs hurt from the pressure of her strong arms embracing me. Victoria's sobs grew in intensity as she buried her face into the side of my neck and cried for what, I was sure, was the first time in almost ten years.

I held on to the blonde, letting her cry as I bit back my own tears, whispering in her ear, "I will always love you, Victoria. No matter what, I love you. I always have. I'm never going to leave you." After I spoke the words, I realized that Victoria had finally let me in completely. Showing me all of her scars, making me wanted to repel the fear I would walk away like all the others. Wipe out the fear that after everything she told me, I wouldn't want her just like so many who came before me.

She embraced me harder, heaving out another sob, before we let silence fill the air. I continue to hold onto for however long I needed to. For however long it took for Victoria to feel like she could breathe without the weight of all the secrets she had carried for so long.

I held Victoria for an hour, letting her take her time and when I felt her body grow heavier in my arms, I said nothing. I only leaned back, wiped her cheeks and pushed back her hair as she kept her eyes down, focused on whatever it was in front of her. I took her by the arm and wordlessly helped her upstairs to her bed. She collapsed onto the mattress and passed out on top of the blankets. I knew Victoria was beyond emotionally drained from crying as much as she had and letting out buried secrets.

Covering her up with a blanket I found in the closet, I left her and went back downstairs to the den. Slowly starting to pick up the bits and pieces she had laid out, returning the medals to their proper places in the shadowbox. When I was done, I set the shadowbox where it always sat behind her desk, collected the file with the patches and set them in a neat pile next to the shadowbox.

As I turned to walk away, everything Victoria told me, finally struck me and I broke down and fell into the large leather desk chair. I let my own tears and sobs finally come, as they had wanted to halfway through Victoria's story. I covered my face, feeling the tears pool in my palms. The nurse facade had held strong for long enough, I couldn't keep it up anymore after everything I had seen and heard.

I felt guilty for, in some way, forcing her to revisit a time in her life that she should never have to. Forcing her to bring out the old memories of how she survived at the hands of evil and how she felt she became that same evil in order to survive. I finally understood so much about Victoria and why she was so detached. Now I was driven to prove to her that she could have all the things she wanted, or thought she couldn't have. I would be there to love her, hold her up and be the strength she needed to see that she wasn't a killer, a monster, or an idiot. She was human and deserved to be loved regardless of her past.

I sighed, wiping away the tears and stood up from the desk and walked to my bag. I grabbed a few of the articles of clothing I had brought back and changed into them. It was close to five in the morning and I was in no shape to drive home. I also wanted to be here in the morning when Victoria woke up. I wanted her to know that I was still in this with her, now more than ever.

Letting out a shaky, tired breath, I grabbed a blanket from off a chair in the den and headed back to the couch I had slept on the first night I stayed over.

I fell asleep the second my head hit the pillow.

Curled up in a ball in the middle of my bed, I stared at the thick rectangle of light that had sat on the floor in my bedroom, lighting up a perfect square of the hardwood floor. I had been staring at it for an endless amount of time since my eyes flicked open when the alarm went off.

I didn't move. I just laid in the middle of my bed, grasping to the edge of the blanket over my shoulder. I felt like I had that first day I was in the hospital after Dani found me. Numb, empty and afraid.

I couldn't remember much about last night after I lost control and ended up sobbing. I had not cried, or let out any emotion like I did last night, in years. Waking up I felt like I had been hit by a truck and my heart hurt. It hurt because of the look on Alex's face as I drowned her in facts, pictures and hard truths about my scar and that I killed seven men like it was nothing. Like they were nothing, and they were the first of many to come in my life after that day.

It was a look I had seen a handful of times before when my significant other didn't believe the reasons why I had to leave for three or four days, or why I would come home so late smelling like I had just showered when I was supposedly just working late. It was the look of disbelief and goodbye. Alex had that same look even as she held me, and waking up alone, I knew I was now completely alone.

When the rectangle of light moved and became a strange oval shape, I rolled to sit up. I needed to get up and face what was next. Losing Alex would take me a while to get over. Maybe longer because of how much I loved her, but I knew at least I had been able to tell her the truth. And in time if I ever found someone who could compare to Alex, it would be easier to tell them about my scars.

Pushing up from the bed, I ran my hands over my messy hair, collecting it into a ponytail. I needed to shower but would do that after I finished the bottle of bourbon in the kitchen. Then I would call Dani to cancel my vacation and start booking me as many jobs as she could. I shuffled across the floor, my body physically ached from the emotional drain I experienced. My work would be the only way I could find the foundation I needed to stand on as I processed everything. The morbid way it centered me when I failed at being human.

I furrowed my brow as I remembered telling Alex I was a killer, hoping that in a way I could breach that subject slowly. Reveal the full truth that I was still a killer for my country.

Thinking that I could dance around the truth, that yes I had been a killer in a dire circumstance, but it was because of that day that being catalyst and the start of the killer I now had become. Either way, being able to finally admit it and say it aloud, it felt like I had tipped the world off my shoulder for a minute and I could finally breathe easier than I had in years. On a whole, being able to release the pressure of hiding what I was and the true story that the news and the others hid from the world with me, it was freeing. Freeing to a point that I felt like a shell of a human, an empty husk left aimless as to what I was going to do next. It was like I had to learn how to walk all over again.

I glanced at my phone sitting on top of the dresser, there were no missed calls or unread messages. I had to bite the inside of my cheek at the sudden rush of heartbreak. Alex never lied to me, but she couldn't keep doing this with me. I had taken her for granted for a year and only gave her three days of what she deserved, before I burnt us to the ground with one flick of a match. I rubbed my bleary eyes, not wanting to think any more of it. It already hurt too much and I knew the hurt would hover around my heart for a very long time.

Walking down the stairs, I kept my eyes to the floor as I moved to the kitchen. Only looking up to see the bourbon and my glass sitting as I had left them. Opting to stand in the den to try and stay somewhat sober as I showed and told Alex some of who I really was.

Skipping the glass, I picked up the bottle and trudged to the den. I wanted to shove all the memories from a day in May back into its grey plastic bin and shove it further into the closet. Maybe one day I would just burn all the shit and never look back. Looking back hurt not only me but those I loved.

In the den, taking a healthy morning drink from the bottle, my face scrunched up. My desk was clean. My medals were back in their box, placed neatly back against the wall under my diplomas. The file I had shoved in Alex's face sat underneath the Ziploc bag of patches and insignia. I swallowed hard, the bottle hovering by my lips as I felt even sicker, but not from the liquor I was dumping down my throat.

Alex had cleaned up before she left, just like the others before her.

Tipping the bottle back up I heard a familiar raspy morning voice, "French toast goes really well with bourbon."

My head spun around, locking eyes with tired blue ones staring back in mine. "Alex." My voice came forth like a puff of brittle air.

Alex was leaning against the door frame that separated the living room from the den. She was wearing the grey sweatpants and blue SeaBees sweatshirt she had stolen from me, and looked as exhausted as I felt.

She shrugged, "That's my name." Pushing off the door frame, she folded her arms and walked towards the kitchen. "I'll get started on breakfast. How about you put the bottle down and join me."

I didn't move, just followed her with my eyes until she disappeared around the corner. The sounds of pans and bowls being set on the kitchen counter broke my trance of staring. I dropped my hand holding the bottle, looking at it once more before setting it on the desk. I had to be either dreaming or severely hungover. Either way, I knew I should go to the kitchen and confirm which state I was in.

Alex had her head down when I entered the kitchen, dumping random ingredients into a large bowl, reading the side of a bag of powdered sugar as she held a spoon.

"You're still here." It wasn't a question, but a strange request for confirmation that she wasn't a dream or a figment resulting from too much bourbon, too early in the morning.

She raised her eyes from the box, nodding, "I am."

The tension between us was still thick and heavy, I dropped my head down, "Why?" I couldn't help ask it.

Alex set the box down, reaching for the three eggs next to the bowl, "I told you last night, Victoria. I'm never leaving you." Cracking each one, she looked up at me, "I may cry easily, but I don't scare easily. I am far too stubborn." Alex waited a second until she had my full attention, "And I am far too in love with you to be chased away."

I felt my eyes well up, surprising me that I had any tears left to give, "Alex, I..."

She shook her head, turning to wash her hands in the sink before trailing over to where I stood on the other side of the island. Alex faced me, staring deeply in my eyes so I would see she was being honest and genuine with me as she spoke, "I am in love with you Victoria Bancroft. Have been for a very long time." She shrugged, "I won't lie, last night...it was hard, hearing the story behind your scars. It broke my goddamn heart into a million pieces looking at the pictures of you wounded and scared, not being able to do anything about it." Alex continued to hold my eyes, "But I can do something now, I can be here for you now. With one exception, Victoria."

She took a step closer to me. "This, whatever it is in here." Her hand shot out and pressed against my heart, "That is holding you back, let it go. Because I won't stay, I can't stay, if you shut me out. I don't care about the past, because there is nothing I can do to change it." Taking another step closer, Alex placed her other hand on top of the first she placed against my now racing heart, "I can only change the future. I can only promise that as long as you let me in, there will be an us. You will never have to fear whatever it was you once did." Alex stopped, her jaw clenching as her eyes welled up, "Stop being afraid of me. Let me love you, Victoria."

I felt my jaw twitch. I didn't know what to say, there were too many things to be said in this moment. I wanted to tell her I that I loved her just as much, that I wanted us to work, that I was so afraid that she had left like the others, and a million other things. Instead, I covered her hands on my chest pressing them harder against my heart so she could feel exactly what she was doing to me. "No one has ever stayed after I told them anything about my past." I tilted my head up to look in glassy blue eyes, "I honestly don't know what comes next."

Alex dropped her head, moving to pull her hand free from under mine, when I grabbed them both and held them where they lay. Reaching up with my free hand, I pulled her chin up to look at me, "Alex, I mean. What comes next? Do we eat breakfast? Go apple picking? Sit in silence staring at each other?"

I smiled a bit when I saw her roll her eyes in the slightest. The tension in the air started to thin out as she looked back in my eyes, sniffling. "I've never gotten this far."

"I think first we have breakfast, since neither of us has eaten in a day. Then we sit in silence staring at each other." She looked up at the ceiling, "Or we can kiss and make up? Then eat breakfast and talk some more, because clearly there is a lot we still have to talk about." Alex's cute way of joking had been one of her fall backs to cut the tension between us into shreds. It was working now as I felt my heart finally ease up and allow the rest of my body to breathe.

I half smiled, dropping my hand from her chin and grabbing her elbow. "I can do that." I pulled Alex to rest against my body. Bending down, I kissed her delicately, whispering against her mouth, "Thank you for staying."

Alex leaned her forehead against mine, whispering back, "There's nowhere I ever want to be but with you, Victoria." She grinned as a tear slid down her cheek, I caught it with the side of my thumb, wiping it away, I pulled her back into my arms, shifting my hands until my right hand pressed against her back and I could feel her heart race.

Burying my face into her neck, I breathed Alex in deeply, closing my eyes. "There is nowhere else I want you to be, Alex." I pressed a light kiss against her neck and smiled when I felt her grin grow wider against my shoulder.

Chapter 12

Breakfast was mildly awkward. It was inevitable that it would be awkward after the night Alex and I had. I still had very little to say as I watched her make French toast, navigating around my kitchen like it was hers. Alex would look up at me every so often and ask where I kept the griddle and the spatulas. I would point and direct her, sitting down in silence with a hot fresh cup of black coffee to shake out the last of the bourbon I had drunk last night and first thing when I woke up. I watched her, letting it sink in that this was going forward. Alex and I were moving forward. She was staying and I couldn't scare her away, yet.

We ate in silence, staring at each other as we both struggled to find the words to break the ice and pick up whatever normal conversation we had left off at a few days ago. A conversation, I think, was about the simple things in life like planning a boring road trip or going to a farmer's market. I wanted to return to that conversation, but my thoughts were still stuck on last night and all the things I revealed.

Pushing my empty plate to the side, I glanced at Alex sitting next to me at the island, happily shoving the last few bites of her French toast in her mouth. I smiled, "That was really good, thank you." Alex nodded and kept chewing, turning her head to face me as I fidgeted with the napkin in my hands, "Um, so. I, uh, was thinking..."

"I need to go grocery shopping today, and after, I want you to come over to my apartment and look at the brochures I picked up for all those boring things I thought we could do on our time off." Alex said it softly, but with a firm conviction, like she wasn't going to give me an out or allow me to feel nervous.

I chuckled, shaking my head at the bulldog that was the brunette next to me, "I would like that." I stood up, collecting my plate and her now empty one, "I'm buying dinner tonight, deep dish pizza from the sports bar by your place." I raised my eyebrows, "And then I'll tell you about my awkward high school years?"

Alex grinned, wiping her mouth as she gave me a look, "I'm already picturing a nerdy Victoria, wearing big black framed glasses and sitting in the front of the class."

I closed up the dishwasher, walking back over to Alex, "Actually it was more like baggy jeans, Doc Martins and X-files t-shirts, and I hid in the back of the class to avoid teachers and classmates."

I looked down at the brunette, "Before you ask, yes I was an honor student. Straight A's from elementary until I graduated the Academy." I sighed when I saw the way Alex's eyes lit up. I leaned down, kissing her cheek, "I'm going to get cleaned up and changed, then we can head to your place."

Alex snagged my arm as I pulled away, stopping me. "Victoria, I want today to be the first day." She held my eyes for a second before continuing, "Where we hold nothing back from this point on." Her eyebrows raised in silent question if I understood her.

I picked up her hand from my arm, linking our fingers together I kissed her knuckles, "Then today is day one." I smiled as I watched her bite her bottom lip to hold back the massive grin. "I want to tell you everything." I felt my stomach twist when I said it, knowing that I couldn't tell her everything even though I wanted to. There were still a couple secrets I had to hold back for a little longer until I figured out what I wanted to do about Voltaire.

I kissed Alex's knuckles again before releasing her hand, "I smell really bad, like a bourbon soaked hobo." I waved to the guest bathroom off to the left of the laundry room, "There is a shower in the guest bathroom. We can shower at the same time to speed things up, and there are a few more of my shirts in the laundry room you can steal." I turned to look back at Alex to see her still biting her bottom lip, but not in a way that was to hold back a smile, but in a way to hide her thoughts. My throat went dry, realizing the implications of showering at the same time probably put in the woman's head. I felt my own body heat up when the memory of how soft and warm Alex's bare skin felt under my hands the night before. I had been mere inches away from being able to see her in ways I only dreamt about or thought about in between classes.

I took a short step back, hating that my body was starting to react and want to return to last night. It was too soon after everything. I was not ready to take advantage of Alex's kindness and strength in sticking by me, and I wasn't ready to fully show the physical scars I carried. I cleared my throat, waving at the staircase, "I'll go now. Upstairs and, yeah, get ready. If you need anything, holler." I turned quickly, rushing towards the stairs rolling my eyes. Rolling my eyes at how I was my own worst enemy right now, and if I kept it up, I would never get to see Alex naked.

I frowned at the strange inappropriate thought. I was all over the map and needed to rein it in. I was worrying about how to show Alex that I cared about her and that I was taking this third chance she was giving me seriously. I knew I had yet to tell her I loved her, and I probably should have last night when I thought she left me. But I didn't, I couldn't yet. I felt like if I said it now and kept a few more secrets from her, it would be like I was lying to her. Using the power of telling her I loved her to distract her further and keep her away from the other part of my life. The part I was still keeping in the proverbial closet with the black clothing and bag full of tools I used to kill.

I climbed up the stairs, clenching my jaw as I tried hard to shut down my analytical mind and get it to stop picking apart everything. This was how I got into this mess in the first place with Alex, picking apart every little thing and hoping I could control it all. Alex had proven she was far too smart and far too stubborn to let that happen and I was slowly giving in to her. I wanted her, all of her and as a result, I would have to stop thinking so much and just live.

In my bedroom, I let the water run cold as I undressed, hopping into the ice cold water to shock sense back into me before I turned the water to as hot as I could get it to wash out the night and the bourbon from my skin. Leaning my head against the shower wall, I closed my eyes, letting the steam and heat clear out my head so I could focus on the day ahead.

After Victoria left the kitchen, I blew out a hard breath. My body had a quick reaction to her delicate kiss on my cheek, followed by stringing a few words together that had my imagination running wild. Victoria in that shower naked, colliding with spontaneous thoughts of her and I in the shower together and what could possibly come from it. I ended up biting my bottom lip so hard, I flinched and snapped out of my desire filled haze.

I hopped off the stool and rushed to the guest bathroom, finding towels and toiletries under the cabinet, I let the shower heat up as I removed her clothes and folded them neatly on the counter. Climbing in the shower, I let the hot water run over my body and chase away the lingering tension. Last night had been a roller coaster and I wanted nothing more than to wipe the slate clean and start over with Victoria. I wanted to give her the option of having a clean slate to write out her life story to me, with me. Share her past and feel like she could without judgment. Even deep down, I could feel in my gut there was something more to why she kept those pieces of her life hidden from whoever came before me. It felt incredible that I was the one who broke down that final wall and Victoria felt enough trust in me to allow me to climb over the broken pieces of the wall and hear the horrifying truths.

I had noticed that she didn't tell me she loved me back last night. It hurt, but I had to tell myself that Victoria was scarred on so many levels that it would take her a bit longer to let the words out. I knew she loved me, I could tell in the way she looked at me, how she held me and treated me. It was impossible for me to think anything else. Victoria loved me and in time she would say it.

Rinsing the soap and conditioner out of my hair, I shut off the water and stepped out of the shower, wrapping the thick fluffy towel around my body as I moved to the laundry room.

I dug around in the dryer until I found a plain white V-neck t-shirt that was bigger than Victoria's usual fare of Naval related clothing. I scooped it up and hustled to my bag. Grabbing the pair of jeans I wore yesterday, I dressed in the bathroom and looked around in the medicine cabinet for toothpaste, or at least a toothbrush. I could only find toothpaste, "Shit."

I knew Victoria had extra toothbrushes. She told me that she had a serious back stock of travel size toiletries since she traveled all the time. It made me laugh when she handed me a brand new purple toothbrush in the package the last time I stayed over. That's when I remembered I had left it in her bathroom upstairs. I heaved out a sigh and left the bathroom. Rushing up the stairs, I looked down as I gathered my wet hair up in a ponytail, and pushed the bedroom door open without a second thought.

"Victoria is that purple toothbrush still in your bathroom?" I tilted my head up in time to see I had just walked in on Victoria standing next to her dresser, completely topless with just jeans on. My eyes went straight to the curve of her breast and the tiny peek of a nipple, making me gasp as my throat went dry as the Sahara. Then my eyes quickly darted to the scar on her back. "Um, sorry." I had to tear my eyes away from the half-naked woman, force my eyes to the floor and not to return to the scar or those perfect breasts I suddenly had to touch.

"Alex." Victoria's voice was surprised, but deep. Deep in a way that made me shiver.

I turned my back to her, looking for a quick exit as my face was on fire. I was so embarrassed and turned on. "I can brush my teeth when we get to the apartment." I went to walk out of her bedroom, when I felt her body heat come right up on me from behind. Her hands fell on my upper arms, slowly turning me to turn to face her.

"Alex, turn around."

I let out a shaky breath, my nerves going off like fireworks. I closed my eyes and let Victoria turn me around, "I'm sorry, barging in like I own the place."

I heard a soft laugh that sounded almost like a sigh, "Open your eyes." Victoria's hands pressed reassuringly against my arms. "I want you to look."

My knees just about gave out when I heard her say that and I slowly opened my eyes, slowly because I was afraid of my reaction if I popped my eyes open too quickly on a topless Victoria. With eyes finally open, I looked at the woman in front of me. She was now wearing a dark blue bra that made me frown a bit, but I still had a view of Victoria's toned stomach. The sight of that alone, made me bite the inside of my cheek. God, she was perfect, beautiful, sexy, gorgeous and all those other words I would find to describe her.

Lifting my eyes away from the plethora of bare skin in front of me, I met her slate grey eyes looking directly into mine. There was a look of fear and trust in them, and it confused me for a second. I was about to step away and excuse myself, when slender fingers wrapped around the hand down at my side and pulled it up to her side.

Victoria pressed my palm against the skin of her right side. Holding it there for a second, she took in a deep breath and began to move it to her back. My fingers gliding over perfect, warm skin, making my heart and breath quicken. Then my fingertips hit the rough patch I had grazed on my counter top. I went to pull my hand back looking at the silent struggle in Victoria's eyes. She shook her head as tears welled up and kept moving my hand over her scar until my whole hand sat against the scar.

I could feel the ridges and hills that came with skin grafts, the thick lines of her puncture wounds that had too much infection in them and were not cleaned properly for far too long. I bent my head to the side to look at the scar. It wasn't as horrid as I imagined, it was large but it wasn't anything that I would shy away from. Not because I had seen far worse in my nursing career, but because it was a part of the woman I loved. This was a part of her and I would love it and her, no matter what.

I leaned back to watched Victoria close her eyes and drop her hand away, leaving mine where it sat. "Victoria..." My voice betrayed me as it came out harsh and quiet. I wanted to cry looking at how scared she was in this moment, scared because I was the first person she had ever allowed to touch or look at this part of her body.

She opened her eyes, looking in mine she let out a slow breath, bending down, her lips brushed against mine, making me quiver all over. I could feel her warm breath mingle with mine right before she closed the gap and kissed me. Kissed me so deeply, I felt my heart stop. I let out a delicate moan, and it set Victoria off. She grabbed me, pulling me flush against her body. The kiss moving from hard and slow to the one she had unleashed on me on the counter of my apartment. I knew where this was heading, and good lord did I want this. Even more as I felt her hands slide across my waist and dip under the thin V-neck I wore. Her hands met my skin, setting it on fire along with the rest of my body.

I had to grab on to Victoria's other side to hold myself up, my knees and legs had become pure jelly as her tongue moved across my bottom lip before it met mine. She pushed hard against my mouth, her hands moving further up and to the clasp of my bra when my conscience suddenly tapped me on the shoulder, reminding me of the tiniest of secrets I carried. I furrowed my brow, nipping at Victoria's top lip, pulling a deep moan from her. I quickly told my conscience to shut up and go away, that I would be okay.

But it tapped a little harder, reminding me of what Victoria had just poured out in the last twelve or so hours, laid bare her deepest darkest secrets and even though mine was simple and severely embarrassing, Victoria would know.

Right as Victoria's nimble fingers flicked open my bra clasp and went to pull it free, I groaned and cursed, pulling back from her mouth, I tenderly pushed some space between us. "Wait, wait."

Victoria moved forward, trying to kiss me again, "I think we've waited enough, Alex."

I shook my head and took another step back, "Victoria please." I let go of her sides, holding up my hand, "I have to tell you something."

I heard Victoria sigh, the tension in the room turning from an explosive sexual one to that all too familiar one that had hovered around us for a year and a half. "Okay." Victoria looked down at the floor, licking her lips in a way that made me want to tell my conscience to fuck off.

Reaching for her hand, I shook my head, "Don't disappear on me, it's not a big something like I'm married or have four nipples." I half smiled hoping Victoria would take the joke, it fell flat. She just looked up at me with a furrowed brow. I huffed, only way to do this was to rip the band aid off and move past it. I scrunched my face out and let it roll out of my mouth quickly, "Iveneverbeenwithawoman." I mumbled it out in one breath.

Victoria's face turned from furrowed brow to scrunched confusion then to raised eyebrows as she deciphered my words. Her mouth fell open as she looked at me, "Did you just say?" She paused, looking over my beet red face, "You've never been with a woman?" She reached for the shirt she had on top of the dresser when I walked in and started pulling it on.

I squeezed my eyes shut, rubbing my face with my hands, mumbling against the small gap between them. "Yes. I have never been with a woman." I folded my arms tightly against my chest, dropping my head to stare at my bare feet and how they contrasted against the dark hardwood floors, "I didn't want to hide it from you, because if we did this, you'd quickly figure it out. I also didn't think that we'd be um, getting to this point so fast."

I swallowed nervously as the ramble started, "Not that I don't want to with you, oh god do I want to. I mean, I've kissed girls in college and done the whole tops off making out, I mean I was in a sorority for Christ's sake." I shook my head and looked up at Victoria who had a blank face. "I've just never been with a girl, made love to one, or you know."

I frowned, feeling like a teenager all over again when I was faced with this similar issue with my first boyfriend, but Victoria was so much more than a quick teenage romp. I wanted to make love to her and I wanted it to be perfect. "You've let me in so much and I didn't want to..." I rolled my eyes, "I have totally ruined the moment. I'm going to go now, back downstairs and um, yeah. I'll be out at the car when you're ready." I twirled on my heel to run out of the room when Victoria grabbed my elbow, stopping me and tugging me to look at her.

She had a goofy smile on her face and was clearly trying to hold back a laugh, "Alex, it's okay." She smirked, "But yes, you did totally ruin the moment." She tugged my arm when I frowned deeper, asking me to come closer. I sighed and moved back to stand in front of her.

Victoria reached up, placing both of her hands on my cheeks, "We can wait a little longer." She grinned, "When you're ready, I can guide you through it, learn together." Victoria started laughing nervously, shaking her head, "I'm sorry."

I gave her a dirty look, "This is not funny."

Victoria nodded, "It's not, but I can't handle how adorable you are right now." She bent and kissed the tip of my nose, then wrapped me up in a strong embrace. "I'll admit, when you said four nipples, I might have gotten a bit turned on."

I groaned, burying my face in her shoulder as I playfully poked her side, "I'm so embarrassed."

Victoria laughed harder, kissing the top of my head. I poked her again, but secretly I was glad she was laughing. It was one of my favorite things about Victoria. The way she laughed and the way it sounded. I gave up being embarrassed and just held on to Victoria, and mumbled against her, "Well at least all of our secrets are out."

For a split second I swore I felt Victoria tighten up in my arms, before she relaxed, "I guess so."

After picking up her bag and locking the house, I followed Alex out to the old mini cooper. Smiling as I watched her move with her normal ease and confidence, waving at Dale and Mary as they unloaded groceries from the back of their SUV. I waved back at my neighbors, earning a cheery wink from Mary and thumbs up from Dale, making me blush and look down at the faded USNA logo on the right side of my shirt.

I was blushing because my neighbors were happy I had found someone to share my solitary home and life with, and blushing because I knew what they were thinking when they saw Alex wearing my clothes. I let out a slow breath, dropping the keys in to my pocket. I had stopped what was inevitably going to happen in my bedroom, not because I didn't want Alex, but because she had confessed being new to this idea of being with a woman, being with me. It was equally as new to her as it was to me.

I did desperately wanted to consummate the tension of the last year and bring us closer, never mind the fact that my body ached for some sort of release every time Alex was near, especially when we kissed. My body was ready just as much as my heart was, but as Alex revealed her little secret, I had to stop. I didn't want Alex's first time with me, or with a woman be tainted and hurried. I wanted it to be something special. I rolled my eyes at how the phrase sounded in my head, exactly like an after school special.

"Victoria, are you going to stare at me all day or what?"

I blinked, looking up at Alex grinning and holding out a hand to take her overnight bag from me. I shrugged, smiling, "I just might, if it's okay with you?"

Alex giggled, walking over to snatch the bag away from me. "You can stare at me while we are at the grocery store, in my apartment, or wherever and whenever your heart desires it, but we need to get a move on. I'm on vacation and I want to get the errands I have ignored for the last week, done, so all of my undivided attention is yours." She was inches away from me, sighing contently looking over my old shirt, "Maybe we can take you shopping, get you something else to wear that isn't grey, blue or has an angry goat on it."

I rolled my eyes and playfully shoved her back, "It's a fighting goat, Alex. Geez, how many times do I have to tell you?" I followed Alex to the car and got in the passenger side as she dumped her bag in the back.

Alex looked at me, still grinning, "I only say it because it irritates you." She leaned over and kissed me on the cheek, before moving to start the old car. "Oh, I wanted to tell you before I forgot." She looked at me, her grin fading a bit, "You remember that one annoying detective I told you about? The one whi was assigned to my case a year ago? Well, she came to the hospital the other day asking where she could find you."

I looked up at Alex confused, "A police detective?" It was time to pull out all of my acting skills, and keep up appearances while I internally made notes to call Dani and have her dig around in this detective.

Alex nodded, "I think her name is Scarlett or something." She tapped on the steering wheel, "She was asking if I knew you and where she could find you. I guess she has some questions about that night I was attacked." Alex glanced at me, biting her bottom lip, "I told her that you and I really haven't spoken much, or were very close." She shrugged, "Which is the truth since this time last week we were on the verge of being nothing more than memories."

I placed my hand on her arm, "It's okay, Alex. You told her the truth." I smiled a little more, "Why does she want to talk to me?"

Alex shrugged again, "I really don't know. I didn't give her an inch. Told her that you helped me that night and if she wanted to find you, she would have an easier time than I would."

She dug in her purse and pulled out a thin white business card with the corners bent, "She gave me this to give to you, well, more like left another card at the nurse's station after I threw the first one out."

I took the card and scanned over the name in black Times New Roman print.

Detective Jennifer Scarlett. Metropolitan Police Department. District of Columbia.

Tucking the card in my front pocket, I turned back to Alex, "Well, since I am vacation, Detective Scarlett will just have to wait a few more weeks. I really have nothing more I can tell her about that night." I winked at Alex, motioning to the keys in the ignition, "Shall we?"

Alex grinned, starting the car, "We shall."

We both waved to my lovely neighbors as Alex backed out of the driveway and headed out of my subdivision.

Pushing the grocery cart, I was too focused on Alex bending over to pick up a case of water to pay attention to anything she was saying. I had found over the last hour or so since we had almost broke down that final wall, I couldn't stop looking at her and over analyzing how her clothes fit. The way her arms moved, how attractive her hands were and the glimpses of skin I would catch as she reached up for a box of cereal and my shirt rode up.

Alex was beautiful and the longer I looked at her, the harder it was going to be to go slow.

My roaming eyes were pulled away when Alex walked over to the grocery cart and tossed a few items in. "You know, I can feel you staring."

I shrugged, "You said I could."

Alex gave me a half smirk, "I did, but I literally can feel your eyes burning holes in my jeans." She laughed and motioned to the deli counter, "I'll be over there, is there anything I can get you?"

I shook my head, smiling at how utterly domestic this situation was. "I'm all stocked up." I peered around the corner to the bakery section, "But there might be a doughnut or two that needs a good home." I winked at the brunette, "Meet you over there?"

Alex laughed again, "Yes ma'am." She turned on her heel, but spun back around, "Oh, what do you want for dinner? I can make us something or we can order out?"

"I am still voting for a triple cheese deep dish from O'Toole's. We skipped far too many pizza parties and I miss that thick, greasy, gooey pile of a heart attack." I grinned at Alex, "Plus, I want us to have a quiet night together."

She blushed ever so slightly, "Pizza it is then." Alex turned, moving towards the deli counter, throwing an extra bit of swagger in her hips. Knowing I was already staring, I sighed when she threw a mischievous look my way.

I shoved the grocery cart hard, my hands white knuckling it as I headed over to the bakery. Trying to focus on if a dozen or two of doughnuts would be enough to eat away the sexual tension that was building like a wildfire inside of me.

As I filled a bag up with sprinkle doughnuts, my phone vibrated in my pocket. I glanced at the screen, an unrecognized number flashing at me. I never answered unknown callers, leaving it to voicemail to screen those annoying calls out for me. Then the image of the detective's business card flashed in my head, the number on the phone matching the one on the business card.

Taking a deep breath, I answered it, "Commander Victoria Bancroft, how can I help you?" I threw on my best naval officer voice. I knew I would have to be the strong authority figure I once was to get this eager rookie off my ass.

"Hello, Ms. Bancroft, um Commander Bancroft. My name is Detective Jennifer Scarlett with the homicide division over at D.C. Metro police department. Do you have a minute?" Her tone was desperately trying to match mine. I smirked, this could be fun.

"I only have a minute, detective. I'm running a few errands and can't be on the phone for long." I was firm, but polite. I knew in about another thirty seconds I would be able to pick apart the detective and read between the lines of why she was contacting me.

"I won't hold you up then. I was calling because I have been looking for you for a while now. I don't know if you remember assisting a citizen about a year ago? A woman attacked at the metro station near the city hospital?" The detective was smooth. She was being appropriately vague, but I could tell she already had some of the answers to her questions. I glanced over at Alex still standing at the deli counter holding a few packages of cheese and roasted turkey. Of course I would forever remember that night. The night I got involved and ended up falling in love with the defiant woman standing on that platform.

"Vaguely, yes. I had just walked down the station and found an injured woman. I took her to the nearest hospital for further care." I turned back to my overflowing bag of sprinkle doughnuts, "Other than that, I am afraid I have forgotten most of the details of that night you're probably searching for, detective."

The detective blew out a slow breath, "Is there any way we can meet in person Commander Bancroft? I have some pieces of evidence I would like you to look at. Some loose ends that I could use an expert eye on."

I laughed lightly, knowing exactly where she was headed, "I don't think a military history Professor could help with a cold case. Now maybe if you needed to write a paper on Schwarzkopf's attack strategy."

I rolled my eyes, I needed to get off the phone and call Dani. "Anyways, I'm on vacation for the next few weeks and I really need to go. If you would like, I can put you in touch with my secretary and perhaps we can schedule a meeting at my on-campus office, but as I said detective, I fear I may not be much help." I knew what the detective was doing. She was baiting me, hoping that I would slip and say Alex's name when she referred to the woman at the metro station, or slip and give exact details that only I would know since I was there. Since I was the one who killed the four men who attacked Alex, and was the main reason why the detective was searching me out.

"I will do that, Commander Bancroft, and please, if you do remember anything, call me? I want to tie this old case up and make the District Attorney happy." The frustration in the young detective's voice was heavy. It made me smirk, she was smart, but I was smarter. I had played this game far longer than she had, and knew in the end, she would be told to leave the case alone or it would be placed in the hands of a Voltaire asset and forever forgotten. Buried in the basement.

"Of course." I looked up to see Alex staring at me, smiling happily at me, waving in the cutest way imaginable. "Anyway, I must go Detective Scarlett. Please call the Naval Academy admissions office and ask for a Lieutenant Danielle O'Malley. She will get you set up." I issued a quick goodbye and hung up on the detective after I heard her confirm Dani's name.

Alex walked up to me, tossing the deli meats into the cart. "Business call?"

I nodded, palming the phone and setting the doughnuts in the top tray of the cart, "Sort of. That was Detective Scarlett. She wants to meet me and discuss your case." I looked up at Alex to see her tense up. I moved to the end of the cart, picking up her hand, "I directed her to the Academy and my secretary to schedule a meeting when I came back from vacation." I smiled, running my thumb over her knuckles, "It's a shame I actually don't have a secretary, just an in office answering machine that I won't be checking until next month."

Alex gave me a crooked look, "You are sneaky. Why would you do that to the detective?"

I shrugged, "I'm on vacation and unless you're a fugitive on the run, I see no reason for me to meet with the detective. The case was closed a month after it happened, labeled as a bunch of junkies who turned on each other. No reason to drag up the past, Alex, when we have a future ahead of us." I bent forward and kissed her cheek, "You're on cart duty, I am going to go pick some beer while you look for your organic vegetables." I tapped the list in her hand, pointing at her scribbled handwriting. "Kale is disgusting, by the way. Just get some spinach."

She shoved me playfully, "Who is the health care professional here?"

I kissed her again, "If you get spinach, I will make spinach omelets in the morning." I moved to walk over to the liquor section when Alex held onto my hand.

"In the morning? Are you staying over?" She seemed confused by the idea. Confused but excited.

I grinned, "I am. Why do you think I made you drive? I intend to overeat, drink too much beer and maybe get a really cute brunette nurse to give me a physical exam." The words slipped out, and I almost regretted it until I saw Alex bite her bottom lip like she did right before she kissed me.

Winking at her I hustled away from the cart. I wanted to boldly flirt with Alex and get her to relax around me. To make her feel safe in embracing her physical wants and make it easier that if and when we got to that point, she wouldn't be so nervous. She would feel confident that I wanted her just as much as she wanted me. Plus, I loved it when she bit her lip like that.

When I was clear of Alex's line of vision and surrounded by cases of beer, I hit Dani's contact button. Scanning over the various beers as it rang, I rolled my eyes when she answered with a grumble. "It's one o'clock, Professor."

"Yes, it certainly is. Nice to see you can still read a clock." I leaned forward to check out the label of a craft brew I'd never seen before.

"One o'clock is my lunch time. The one hour of the day where I get out of the basement, sit in the air like a normal person and eat hot dogs with the regular folk of the military world. The one hour of the day where I don't have to listen to the plumbers or the old ones." Dani sighed dramatically.

Lifting a case of the craft beer, I cradled the phone in the crook of my shoulder, "You didn't have to answer the phone, Dani."

"I didn't have to, but when I saw it was you calling, I figured I should answer it and see how you were doing after last night. You and nurse blue eyes work it out? Duke it out? Sex it out?"

I huffed, "I love how you wrap your concern for me in sarcasm." Dani had this way about her that was so endearing and amazing, like she was last night as I cried in front of her, then she would turn back to her annoying little sister ways. "Anyway, I am calling you on your precious hot dog hour to ask for you to look into that rookie detective. Detective Jennifer Scarlett."

"Oh that detective. It did pop up that her warrant request from last year was finally granted, even as the case was closed up and shoved away by her boss." Dani hummed, "I wonder why she's poking around dead business affairs?"

I turned to catch Alex coming down the aisle with the cart, "She called me a minute ago, asking to set up a meeting. I directed her to my secretary Lieutenant O'Malley to schedule a meeting." I smirked when I heard Dani groan, "Also, can you run the full boat on her and email me everything you find?"

"You want me to throw her off, or point her in the direction of a good plumber?"

I shook my head, smiling at Alex, "No. I don't want her to disappear. I just want to throw her off my trail, frustrate her to the point she gives up these loose ends she's worried about." I set the case of beer on the bottom of the cart, "Anyway, I have to go, Lieutenant O'Malley. Please forward my office mail to my home address."

"You know that's not my real last name." Dani paused, "Is nurse blue eyes by you? I can hear the stupid grin in your voice."

"You are correct. I will call you when I'm back from vacation. Thanks again." I looked at the pile of spinach Alex had in the cart, along with a few crates of eggs.

"Now you're being annoying, Professor. I will ping you later when I have the details you requested. I'll also dig around in these loose ends and see what I can do there. It'll be much later, though. I have to meet with the old man about Dante. Seems Dante has been given an extended secret recon mission and I need to move around her clients to the other plumbers." I heard Dani stand up, "By the way, I zapped nurse blue eyes house. I wanted to give you at least two places to be yourself, Victoria." She cleared her throat, "You owe me a hot dog."

I genuinely smiled at Dani's last words. "Anything for you." We hung up and I moved to stand next to Alex, leaning into her, "Sorry, another work call. End of the summer semester is usually hectic with closing down the offices and forwarding things." I ran my hand down Alex's shoulder, "Are we done? I'm starving."

"I am all done. Plenty of eggs, cheese and spinach to keep us holed up for days." Alex linked her arm around mine, "We can go, I'll make sandwiches back at my apartment and then we can go find you some shirts sans angry goats."

I shook my head, poking her forearm, "He's not angry..."

"I know, he's a fighting goat." Alex leaned over, kissing me on the cheek as we moved to the checkout.

Lunch was followed by taking Victoria to the mall by my apartment and dragging her to a few clothing stores, where I talked her into buying a few shirts that were not blue, grey or white. She bought a light green one, a pink one and a pale off white one that was my favorite because it was practically see through. After leaving the clothing store, we walked around the mall and looked in stores. I bought a few more random things for my apartment and she bought a few history books.

The whole time I didn't even think about the tension of the night before, I almost couldn't with how normal and perfect it was that Victoria and I were together and acting like a normal couple. Grocery shopping, eating lunch and chatting about the weather, then strolling through the mall. It was a far cry for the heartache and tears of hearing Victoria's story. Hearing the shock in her voice when she saw I was still there in the morning.

I looked up at the blonde, standing in front of a sports store that had Navy apparel in the front window. Her eyes roaming over the t-shirts, scarves and flags that boasted the blue and yellow that encased her life. I wanted to ask her why she loved the Navy so much, especially after what happened to her.

What struck me the most, was how calm and at peace Victoria seemed standing in front of a window. I had never seen her like this in the entire span of our friendship. Gone were the serious and cautious lines around her brow, like she was always thinking carefully what to say and do next. Instead, her face seemed more open and relaxed, and I had seen her smile more in the last few hours than I had in a year. A happy, relaxed Victoria made her a million times more beautiful, sexy and I felt myself sigh just staring at her.

I loved her so much.

The stupid sentence repeated in my head over and over every time I looked at her digging out doughnuts, catching her staring at my ass or just looking at me with a soft smile handing me a package of cheese.

I loved her so much I ached for her. Everywhere.

The ache had been a mild one for the last few days, only growing when we kissed or hugged and I inhaled the smell of her laundry detergent or her shampoo. The smells sending my pheromones to crash into raging hormones, forcing me to control my body and back away from the woman.

Now the ache was growing too unbearable. Notably after I had gotten a full glimpse of what was hiding under those ratty Navy t-shirts and those perfectly tailored uniforms I sometimes saw her in. Barging into her room had been the best mistake I had made in a long time. Then I ruined the moment by spilling the beans about my inexperience.

I grinned at Victoria as she moved away from the window and went into the store. I shook my head and followed after her, knowing she was probably stocking up on more Navy shirts.

Victoria's reaction to my revelation that ladies had not been my forte was amazing and made me fall deeper in love with her. Yes, it was embarrassing and yes, she had laughed at me, but she also made me feel safe as much as she made me feel wanted. Her comments in the grocery store and ogling of my ass, was making it easier for me to get over my fears of being with her, made the ache grow and move further down my body. I was beginning to crave the woman.

Walking into the store, I caught Victoria with a pair of Navy sleep pants and a few shirts in her arms. I grinned, shaking my head, "I can't leave you alone for one minute."

Victoria turned to the sound of my voice, grinning back at me, "These aren't for me." She nodded to the sizes, "They're for you, since you keep stealing mine."

I plucked at the sleep pants and shirt, still grinning when I saw she had specifically picked out ones with the angry goat on the front and side. "Excuses, Commander." I lifted one shirt up and pointed at the tag, "What about this one? It isn't my size."

Victoria's face turned a soft pink color, "Um, I ripped a hole in mine helping Dale fix the fence a week ago."

I laughed at how embarrassed the strong woman was, "Victoria, you don't need to explain it to me. As long as you're happy." I leaned on the counter as she paid for the clothing, "But I do want to know why you love the Navy so much that you practically live and breathe it."

Victoria's smile faded a little as she handed over her credit card to the clerk, "That is a story better left for pizza and beer." She glanced at me, "Just know the Navy is only my second true love."

The way Victoria looked at me, made my heart skip a few beats. I had to look down at the glass display case to hide my own blush. "Fair enough." I looked over my shoulder, afraid to look in her eyes and dug out my phone, searching for O'Toole's number to start ordering the pizza. "Hurry up while I call in the order."

I turned to walk out of the store, sucking in deep breaths. The effect Victoria had on me was profound and I wouldn't have it any other way. I felt the ache inside of me reach between my legs, forcing me to squeeze my eyes shut and curse my conscience. Going slow was going to suck far worse than fumbling through an awkward first time like I could have this morning.

The cheery voice on the other line startled me, asking if I was calling in a carry out or a delivery. I cleared my throat, "Carry out, please."

Two hours later, Victoria and I were elbow deep in beers and pizza. She was in the middle of telling me a story of how the Navy became so ingrained into her life.

"One summer when I was nine, my grandmother took me to the local shipyard and I got to see the biggest aircraft carrier up on dry-docks. They were repainting it and repairing it to send it to Virginia to be sent back out onto the seas. There was something about the sheer size of the ship that captured me as much as it overwhelmed me. Then I saw the sailors walking in and out of the docks. They were just the ship's security, but there was something about that uniform and the way all of the men and woman seemed so happy and proud about the giant ship. It sunk into my young mind."

Victoria looked up at me from the other side of the couch where she sat facing me with her legs crossed, cradling a beer and a plate full of deep dish pizza on her lap, "I became obsessed immediately. I went back to my grandmother's house and pulled out her dusty old encyclopedias to read everything I could about the United States Navy. The history of how it came to be, their uniforms, their influence in all of the wars and I just couldn't get enough."

I smiled softly, twirling my half empty beer in my hands. I was stuffed and falling into a delightful beer buzz, but I was hooked on hearing more about Victoria. "Is that where you also became a history buff?"

Victoria nodded sheepishly, "Sort of. I would ride my bike to the library and pick up all the books I could find on famous Naval officers. Then books written by sailors, soldiers and what not." She sipped her beer, "That lasted until I went to high school and fell into teenage angst mode. Hiding my nerdiness with aloofness and being the science fiction nerd who would read books in the bathroom rather than eat lunch with the others." She picked up her slice of pizza, taking a bite, "I was an honor student and was chosen as valedictorian three months into my senior year. I had maintained a perfect GPA from freshman year on. Nobody knew who I was, though, I always hid in the shadows and studied. I applied to a bunch of universities and was accepted to the best ivy leagues with full scholarships. I was going to get my bachelors and head into the Navy after. Then one day a letter from the Naval Academy fell into my mailbox. Seems my grandmother had sent them my SAT's and ACT's test scores along with my school records. She was the only one who really knew about my obsession with the Navy and wanting to sail the world on one of those big ships."

Victoria began to smile genuinely, picking at the label on her beer, "They offered me anything I wanted. I was a perfect candidate and I signed that day. I graduated a month early so I could start my first semester as a first year and I never looked back. The Navy felt like the home I never had. The way it felt like I had a place in this world." Victoria frowned, her voice softening, "The only other time I felt like that was during the summers I spent with my grandmother. Watching old movies, riding bikes around the town, making crab cakes and chowder. The Navy gave me the same stability and strength my grandmother did." She sighed, taking another drink from her beer, "I will always love the Navy for the life they gave me."

Victoria looked back up at me, "It wasn't their fault I ended up in that desert, it was the fault of others. Singular people who had very singular ideas about how a war should end." She cleared her throat, picking up her pizza to take another bite.

I set my empty down and stood up, pointing to the fridge, "Another?"

Victoria nodded and I grinned, she was starting to get buzzed from the four beers she had polished off. "What about your parents? You never really talk about them, Victoria."

"That's because there is nothing really to talk about." She kept her head down, focused on the beer bottle in her hands. "My grandmother wasn't my maternal grandmother. She was a grandmother in law of sorts and kind of got stuck with me when I was two. My parents were more interested in lord knows what instead of raising a kid." She sighed, "She raised me like I was hers, and in many ways she was my only family."

I could see the sadness in her eyes. Victoria had always been tossed to the side, a second thought to everyone around her, it was no wonder she had trust issues and preferred the solitude of her life. I stared at her, "What was her name?"

Victoria smiled, cocking her head my direction, "Edith. Edith Lamont." She laughed, "A name fit for the old movies she adored." Victoria finished off the rest of her beer, "What about your mom? I know you've talked about her and Bill a little bit."

I continued to take in this version of Victoria, the one I knew was hiding under her cold exterior. I was so happy to finally see it, be a part of it. I smiled, scooping up the beers and the brochures, to walk back over to the couch. "There's very little left to know about mom and Bill. I've probably worn out my welcome nagging about my mom and how protective she can be." I held up the brochures, before setting them on the coffee table, "You can look at these later, but there is one small boring thing that I have to ask you about."

Victoria looked over at the brochures of boring things I had picked out. Museums, rock formations in Georgia, the handful of Civil War battlefields I wanted to visit, and lastly the stupid water park Stacy told me was amazing and worth every penny. "And that boring thing is?"

Handing her another beer, I scrunched up my face, "My mom has cordially invited you to a Sunday dinner with the family. Family meaning Bill, mom, me and the dogs." I sat on the edge of the coffee table closest to her, "I might have told her over the weekend that you and I were working on something more than a friendship. She went into excited mom mode and thinks it's finally time for you to come over and endure a Sunday of meatloaf, gin rummy and walking the dogs as she fills us in on the latest neighborhood gossip."

Victoria looked up at me, her eyes wide with something I couldn't place. Whether it was uncomfortable surprise that I had brought up meeting the parents so soon, or if it was just a look of trying to search out an excuse to get out of it while on a beer buzz. "This coming Sunday?"

I shrugged, "Maybe?" I shook my head, "You don't have to. Things are too new with you and I, and I told mom it might not be a good idea. Family dinner so soon might scare you off."

Victoria's hand fell to my knee, "Can you promise there will be meatloaf?"

Giving her a strange look, raising my eyebrows. "Probably?"

"Then Sunday it is, Alex." She leaned forward, trying to move up to kiss me but stopped mid-way, "I want to do this with you Alex, and I promised that I would be more open, more of what you deserved." She paused, "But only if there is meatloaf."

I laughed, shaking my head, "There will be meatloaf." I squinted my eyes at her, "How tipsy are you? I vaguely remember you offering to tell me about some awkward high school days."

Victoria glanced at her beer, "I might need a few more to break out those stories and how I had a different X-files shirt for everyday of the week and had the biggest crush on a certain redheaded federal agent." She smiled and went to reach for me, tipping the plate of pizza over on her lap. She hopped up as she saw the tomato sauce smear over her shirt, "Shit!"

Before I could help, Victoria was up and running into the bathroom, stripping off her shirt the second she reached the sink. I heard the water run along with vigorous scrubbing sounds. I giggled hearing Victoria curse under her breath as she tried to get the greasy tomato stains out before they set in.

I went to set my beer down and go help her when she rushed out of the bathroom and towards the one large floor lamp I had by my bed, holding up the wet fabric to the light to see if she had gotten all of the grease out. She was still grumbling and mumbling, but I didn't hear one word. I was transfixed by the sight of her without a shirt, the light in the room catching all of her curves and angles in a way that made her glow.

I clutched tightly to the glass beer bottle, hoping the cold condensation would curb some of the rising heat, but it didn't. It only made it worse as I continued to stare. Watching Victoria bend and move, the muscles in her arms and stomach, twist and flex.

"Shit." The curse word blew out in a breath and I bit my bottom lip as my body began to throb, eyes running up and down the blonde standing oblivious to my staring, examining her wet shirt. I sucked in a deep breath, hoping it would help calm me down, but somehow my body saw it as incentive and motivation to stand up and start walking over to the half-naked woman who was now digging in her shopping bags for a clean shirt.

There was only one thought in my head as my liquid courage drove my feet to take step after step. Fuck going slow. I no longer cared if I was a fumbling idiot, I had to touch Victoria. I had to run my hands over those muscles, feel them against me as we made love. I wanted to know how to touch her and turn her into jelly like she did me, and I wanted to know right now.

Slowly walking up behind the distracted blonde ripping off price tags of her brand new shirt, I slid my hands onto her sides, waiting only a second for her to acknowledge and relax as my hands moved further to rest against her warm stomach.

I moved closer until I was fully pressed up against her body, soaking up the warmth that was distinctly Victoria, letting it flood my body with a million sensations and even more courage to follow through.

I placed a light kiss on her shoulder before moving to her neck. Kissing and running the tip of my tongue over the soft skin of her neck. I had no idea what to do, I just knew what I wanted to do. I felt Victoria's breath hitch when my lips moved over her neck and to the back. My fingers running slow circles around her stomach. God her skin was so warm and soft.

I continued to move my kisses down, over her shoulders and then down her spine. Watching the goosebumps rise from where my lips had been, I couldn't get enough, and kept on. I moved my hands from her stomach and back to her sides, holding her steady as I knelt and moved to her lower back. First kissing the unmarred side, before slowly moving to where her scar lay. When I was there, I placed one slow kiss on the ridges and bumps. That's when I heard my name fall from Victoria's mouth in a whisper. I swallowed hard, kissing the scar once more and whispering against her skin, "I want all of you, Victoria."

She turned in my grip, reaching down with both of her hands, Victoria held my face, looking down in my eyes. Hers were glassy, and full of so much emotion like they had been earlier in the morning, it made my heart swell. It was the look of pure love.

Victoria gently motioned me to stand back up, holding on to my face she searched my eyes, her face flush with desire. "Alex, are you sure?" It was a question that had a hint of struggle behind it. I raised my hand up, resting it on the side of her neck, feeling that she was struggling as much as I was. We were one step away from no return.

Bending forward, I brushed my lips against hers, murmuring, "Very sure."

Victoria groaned and closed the gap, kissing me hard. Her hands held my jaw steady as it increased in pressure, her tongue gliding over my bottom lip to ask more from me. I opened my mouth wider to let her in, physically and metaphorically. I dropped my hands to her side, moving to reach for her bra, when she pulled back suddenly, licking her lips and holding my gaze. "Trust me?"

I titled my head, hoping to hell and back that she wasn't going to pull the plug on doing this. Then it struck me, Victoria wanted to do this right. She wanted to show me, take her time. Clearly she had some sort of plan in her head for when the time came, but my beer and hormone soaked brain had blown that plan apart. I smiled, nodding, "With my heart."

Victoria closed her eyes, "Then let me."

I let out a shaky breath as her hands moved to the baggy V-neck I was still wearing. Grabbing the hem and pulled it over my head, then threw it to the floor and pushed me towards the bed until the back of my legs hit it and I fell back.

I went to stand back up when Victoria shook her head no, motioning for me to move further up as she climbed on and hovered over me. She bent down, and as our mouths met in a slow yet feverish pace, she wrapped an arm around my side to pull me and press against her warm skin.

Giving her access to the back of my bra, I felt her hand move quickly and unclasp it. I moaned against her mouth the second I felt her fingertips pull the material forward as she bent back.

Victoria broke off the kiss and held my eyes as she removed my bra, tossing it to the side, she waited a second before looking down at me. She let out a shaky breath, lifting her hand to my collarbone, drawing her fingers slowly down to my bare breasts. "Perfect, absolutely perfect."

I pushed forward, silently giving Victoria permission to do whatever she wanted. I was too far gone to want to stop. I had no idea what I was supposed to do. I just knew I wanted Victoria's hands everywhere and quickly. "Victoria..."

She smirked when she heard the quiet desperation, moving her hand to brush the underside of my left breast. She distracted me by running her thumb over my nipple. I gasped when I felt the delicate roughness and pushed into it, my eyes slamming close as I felt her breath move closer to my neck and back away. Victoria was good at this, the teasing game. It was driving me nuts, she was going so slow.

I went to open my mouth to tell her to hurry up, when I felt the tip of her tongue swirl around my nipple and then cover it completely with her mouth. I blew out a convoluted mixture of curse words, reaching up to run my hand through her hair.

I tangled my fingers into soft blonde hair and held her against me. Biting my lip and pushing into her mouth. Feeling the familiar pressure build between my legs, I knew I was beyond aroused and was close to orgasm. I had to keep biting my lip to hold back, I wanted to make this last.

Victoria's hand left my other breast and trailed down to my stomach to the top of my jeans. When her fingers flicked open the button, she pulled away from my mouth, making me whimper in frustration. I was two seconds away from coming just from feeling her mouth on my breast. I frowned and looked down at Victoria, who was smirking up at me.

"Take off your jeans, Alex."

I gave her a look, forcing out, "If you take off your bra first."

Victoria's smirk grew, as she reached behind and unclasped her bra, pulling it off in one swift motion. I felt my frustration dissipate as I got a full look of what I had only glimpsed this morning. I whimpered uncontrollably and reached for her instinctively. My fingers running along the curve of her breast and over her nipple, I smiled when she gasped and grabbed my hand to stop me. "Jeans, Alex. Take them off."

I looked up in her slate grey eyes only to see them dark with desire. It was a look that told me that I would have plenty of time to touch her and explore her, but for now, Victoria was on a mission. I nodded, pulling my hand free from her, I lifted my hips up to pull my jeans off and kick them away.

Victoria moved over me again. Forcing me to lay back on the bed she laid one hand on my stomach and bent to place delicate kisses on my sternum. Moving up my neck and to my chin she paused, hovering over my lips she looked in my eyes. I went to reach for her head to pull her back down to kiss me, or do something, anything. I was starting to writhe under her, searching out any skin to skin contact that would get me closer to release. "Stop teasing me."

Victoria bent down, brushing her lips over mine whispering as her hand moved to between my legs and covered me, "Let me make love to you, Alex." She pressed her palm against me, groaning out a curse words softly as she felt how incredibly wet I was.

I almost came again hearing those words and feeling her hand, but I forced my body to wait. Wait for what was next, because it would be worth the wait. I held her eyes, nodding once that I understood, trying so hard not to push down on her hand, I let Victoria take over. She smiled, brushing her lips over mine as her fingers pushed the thin cotton of my panties out of the way. Kissing me as her finger ran down the length of me, making me almost pant at how incredible the sensations running through my body were.

I never had a lover be so gentle, so slow nor did I really ever submit to one like I was now with Victoria. That was how I knew I felt safe with her, that I was giving up my body to her and letting her dictate how this first time went. Even if it was painfully slow.

Victoria continued her slow kisses until I nipped her bottom lip, trying to tell her that I needed more, otherwise, I was going to go crazy. She parted from my mouth a millimeter and as I tried to move up to kiss her, I felt her fingers glide into me, sucking all of the air from my lungs at how it felt. My hips bucking up on their own, I knew I had seconds before the strongest orgasm I ever had, hit me. Victoria waited a second for me to adjust before slowly drawing her fingers in and out of me, her mouth hovering inches over mine sharing the same air with me.

I closed my eyes, wrapping my hands in the blankets around me. I couldn't focus, I was so overwhelmed by Victoria's fingers and what they were doing that I could barely breathe. She picked up the pace and when she pushed up, I came hard and fast, catching us both by surprise as a loud strangled moan fell from my mouth.

I literally saw stars and fireworks as my body rode out the wave of pleasure that went all the way down to my toes. I swore I even felt my heart stop for a few moments.

After the wave dissipated, I relaxed my body, shivering when I felt her fingers leave me. I went to open my eyes, feeling her lips against my forehead and on my cheek, before she whispered, "Are you okay?"

I grinned like an idiot and laughed, feeling like a pile of rubber, "Yes." I turned to see Victoria lying next to me, running her fingers through my hair to push it away from my face. She had a look of mild worry on her face, "Yes, I'm okay."

I reached over and pulled her hand down to sit on my heart, so she could feel it thundering in my chest. "That. Wow." I looked in her eyes, seeing the tiny clouds starting to form around the edges. I pushed up and leaned towards her, "Hey, come back."

Victoria looked up at me, "I hope I wasn't too..." she drifted off. It was the same thing she always did when she was afraid she was overstepping whatever imaginary lines she placed between us. I had to cut her off and let her know how wrong she was in this instance.

"Slow? Yes, you were a bit too slow, but aside from that." I bent down and kissed her deeply, "You were. Incredible." I kissed her again, licking my lips, running my eyes over her bare chest and feeling my second wind strike. I looked up in her eyes, smirking, "I have no idea what to do, but I do know those..." I pointed at her jeans, "Need to come off now." I reached down and plucked at the waist of her jeans.

The clouds receded and she cocked an eyebrow at me, "Eager aren't you?"

I nodded, moving to cup her breast, "Eager to taste every inch of you until I get it right." My new found boldness I could blame on post orgasm bliss, but I wouldn't. I wanted Victoria and I knew my instincts would guide me through mapping her body out, even if it took all night.

Victoria moaned and bit her bottom lip, "God, Alex."

I grinned, lunging forward to kiss her. I only had one goal in mind, to find what it took to get her to say that exact same thing as many times as possible.

Chapter 13

Alex's hands were surprisingly strong as she held my hips down against the mattress when I tried to arch up and wriggle free, her head buried between my legs. I kept biting my bottom lip to keep the moans at bay. Alex was definitely a quick study, a very determined quick study. Her tongue moved deftly and intently, replicating what I had done to her, but adding her own flare. With every stroke, she made me gasp harder and wiggle under her grip. I wanted to reach down, tangle my fingers in her hair and touch her, but every time my hands got near, Alex would grab them and push them away. Forcing groans from me at the lack of control I had

I had always been the more dominant one in the bedroom, taking charge for the simple reason I never wanted anyone to touch me or look too closely at my scars. But with Alex, I not only felt completely free with her after letting her in, I felt completely at ease giving her control when she eagerly took it from me.

I went to reach again for the messy brown hair brushing against my inner thighs, when I felt two fingers join her tongue. It only took the sensation of her fingers entering me to give up holding back and I came hard, pushing down on her and feeling her fingertips dig into the flesh of my right hip bone. I let out a soft cry, and a whimper, entangled in Alex's name as my body became overwhelmed and short circuited from the third intense orgasm Alex had unleashed on me since my jeans came off.

As I took in deep breaths, trying to bring air back into my body and allow my heart to settle down, I felt her leave me, trailing soft kisses up my stomach, my sternum and finally to my collarbone as Alex laid her body flat against me. Grinning like an academy award winner, she kissed me quickly, murmuring against my lips, "Third time's the charm?"

I chuckled, wrapping my arm around her as she settled between my legs, slowly pressing us together in a way that made me crave even more from the woman. "You could say that." I reached up, tucking some of her hair back behind her ear, "I feel you have an unfair advantage with your advance anatomical knowledge, nurse." I ran my hand down to her cheek, loving the way her eyes sparkled as they looked down in mine.

She shrugged, running her hand down the middle of my chest to rest underneath my left breast, "I was always a top student in all of my classes, and the most observant in my anatomy classes." Alex kissed me deeply, running her hand over my nipple making me squirm, "Having said that, I think there is a lot more I need to study about your anatomy in particular, Victoria." She watched me react to her touch, grinning as her thumb ran slow circles over my nipple.

I let out a sigh as my body was now ready to go again, it didn't care that we had been exploring each other for almost an hour and a half, it wanted Alex. I wanted Alex. I swallowed hard, slowly moving my hand from her body and between us, "My, my, aren't we a little over confident already?" I winked at her as I pushed my hips up against hers.

Alex rolled her eyes, still grinning, "Maybe, I mean I did get you to cry out my name a handful of times mixed in with cursing the lord." She went to bend and kiss where her thumb had just been.

I took advantage of the moment, sliding my hand up the inside of her thigh, gently sliding two fingers in her, both of us moaning at how wet she was. Alex's eyes slammed shut and she lost all train of thought as I moved in and out of her slowly, watching her cheeks grow flush and hips begin to move with my hand against her will. I stared at her, loving the way she looked in this moment. Perfect, flushed, beautiful and all mine.

I moved us both forward to sit up, wrapping my free arm around Alex to guide her to sit with me. I leaned forward, kissing her on the cheek before I moved down her neck. Alex's hands quickly moved to my shoulders, bracing herself as her hips still acted with a mind of their own. I reached for her one hand, pulling it slowly away from my shoulder and guiding it down to where I needed her.

Alex opened her eyes, staring at me through hazy desire filled blue eyes, silently questioning me. I smiled, nodding for her to trust me and continued to guide her hand to right under my belly button before she took the hint. I let go of her hand as she trailed slow fingers down the crease of my thigh and looked me in the eyes as my hand stilled, waiting for her.

Alex didn't waste time teasing me. She pushed her fingers in smoothly, making my hips jerk at how sensitive I still was. We both waited a moment before I set the rhythm, Alex quickly following me.

The air in the room became filled with nothing but gasps, moans and heavy breathing. I pulled Alex closer against me so I could feel her heart beat against my chest. Burying my face into the curve of her shoulder I bit lightly at the soft skin, feeling her tighten around my fingers. Neither of us was going to last much longer, I picked up the pace and just as I felt, and heard, Alex start to come, I couldn't hold back and let go with her.

As we both recovered, naked, sweaty bodies pressed together, I heard Alex whisper against my ear, "I love you so much."

I closed my eyes to hold back the tears, wishing I could say the same thing to her in that moment, but couldn't. Not yet. Not while I still had one last secret looming around the corner at every corner.

Sneaking out of the bed, I grabbed my ruined t-shirt and the pair of underwear Alex had practically torn off of me. Yanking them on, I turned to see Alex was still passed out. Curled up under her purple blankets and sleeping heavily.

I smiled, walking to the bathroom and grabbing my phone from the kitchen counter. We had worn each other out and eventually had to tap out, falling asleep in each other's arms.

Sneaking to the bathroom, I shook my head at how Alex truly had nothing to worry about. She was quite possibly one of the most dedicated and attentive lovers I ever had. Maybe because it was how we felt for each other and the built up tension that had been hanging around for a year now, either way, I didn't care. All I knew was that I loved Alex more than ever.

I felt my face drop as I walked into the bathroom, looking up in the mirror. I could see the duality in my reflection, the woman who loved the brunette snoring like a muffled weed whacker in the next room, and the woman who couldn't love anyone or anything. The woman who was a killer. I could almost see the faint image of myself wearing all black standing behind me in the mirror. My life was beginning to split apart and I would have to be careful to not let one side bleed into the other.

Turning on the tap, I looked over at my phone. There was one email from Dani, the title reading, "nosy detective." I sighed and pushed the phone to the corner of the bathroom counter, leaning over to wash my face, avoiding another look in the mirror as I dried off and left the bathroom.

I glanced at Alex, still sleeping, but now in the center of the bed on her stomach. The blankets slipping down to give me glimpses of her bare skin. I had to breathe out my rising desire as I walked to the other side of her tiny loft to sit down at the old metal desk pushed near the far set of windows. Sitting down, I opened up the email from Dani.

Professor.

I went digging in the dirt and came up with some interesting things about the rookie detective. Seems she found a pile of hair evidence in the basement while going back over nurse blue eyes case. Ran it on a whim and poof, seems one of your pretty little blonde hairs fell out and was collected by one of Voltaire's insiders. Not that it was a bad thing, except for the fact that the insider forgot to destroy all of the evidence as requested.

But don't you fret! There is nothing else she has on you. I scrubbed the databases and found nothing other than a tiny hair that could be placed there because you rescued the good nurse. I sent in one of my rats to destroy that evidence. I guess the evidence storage room is about to have a sewer line break and flood the area with raw sewage. Particularly in the area where nurse blue eyes case files are being stored.

Also, I've attached pings to Scarlett's phone and work computer, there's something about her I don't like and is all too familiar to me. Her nosy, snoopy ways, that is, reminds me of a certain bald, fat fucker of a Colonel.

Anyway, see attached for the specifics in regards to one Jennifer Scarlett, rookie detective extraordinaire.

I glanced over the picture of the detective from her police identification card, memorizing her face immediately. I saw nothing that piqued my interest and turned to the file Dani had gotten for me, ignoring the closed case file of Alex's attack. I already knew what happened, no need to read it again, or see the pictures of Alex, bruised and bloodied. Looking at the pictures again would sour my euphoria about the night.

Skimming over her school records, there was nothing significant about Scarlett. She had done well in high school and okay in college, opting to go to the police academy as soon as she graduated with her bachelors in criminal justice. Detective Jennifer Scarlett was already proving herself to be a run of the mill rookie detective who wanted to leave her mark in the world.

I swiped through her police record and saw nothing that made her stand out. There were the usual, and boring, commendations for most traffic tickets written in a year and a few marksman ribbons. She had tested and gotten in the homicide division solely based on her score added with the department wanting to add more female blood to the division. She was relatively liked by her commanding officers, but again, she didn't stand out. I now understood why she was like a starving dog with a bone over Alex's case. She wanted to be seen, and noticed.

I yawned lightly, reading nothing that was setting off alarms until I reached some of her case notes on some of the past murder cases she worked. There was something about the way she looked at certain details that made the hair on the back of my neck stand up. I squinted looking at her handwritten notes, realizing that they sounded a lot like the fat Colonel and his way of taking notes during a debriefing. How he always seemed to ignore the obvious in favor of the hidden details of a mission.

I clenched my jaw and fired off an email to Dani.

You're right about the fat bird and the rookie. Can you run a full boat on her family and any job she ever applied for? From fast food places to all law enforcement agencies and beyond.

Can you also poke around using your magical ways, and find out what happened to the fat bird after you and I became a part of Voltaire?

I want to see if she is connected further before I have a heart to heart with her. I know the old lady's been paranoid that the NSA is getting antsy about Voltaire's partnership with the tea drinkers."

I hit send and before I could set the phone down, Dani replied.

A mole hunt, didn't think of that. You are good, Professor.

I went to go over Scarlett's file one more time, leaning over the metal desk turning the phone to its side to expand the file, and yawned again.

"Victoria?" Alex's voice was raspy, low and sleep filled.

I turned to see her awake but still lying on her side, clutching the blankets to her chest, "What are you doing?" She squinted at the digital clock on her bedside table, "It's almost three in the morning."

I smiled at how cute she was with messy hair and a sleepy face, "I had to go to the bathroom and couldn't remember if I turned on the alarm system at home." I held up the phone to show her the alarm company app before waving at the bed, "As soon as I got up, you took over the whole bed."

Alex sighed, smushing her face in my pillow as she held out her hand, waggling her fingers for me to come back. "I'm used to sleeping alone. Come back, I'm cold."

I laughed softly, setting my phone down and stood up to walk over to the bed. I took Alex's hand as soon as it was in reach, laughing harder when she almost yanked me off my feet back into the bed. I was barely in the bed before Alex had her arms wrapped around me, snuggling into my neck and mumbling, "If I wasn't so tired, I'd be upset about you being dressed already."

Kissing the top of her head, I held her firmly against my side, "I'm only wearing a shirt and underwear. I didn't think it appropriate to start walking around your house naked just yet."

Alex tilted her head back to look in my eyes as her hand slid under my shirt to rest flat against my stomach, "I think it is highly appropriate and I think I may have to institute a no clothes policy whenever you're over." She grinned, laying her head back down on my chest, "Matter of fact, if I wake up before you do, I'm hiding all of your clothes."

I chuckled as I felt Alex starting to breathe slower, a sure sign that she was about to pass out on me. "I eagerly wait for the day. You love sleeping in more than you love blueberry bagels."

I glanced down at her to make another comment about how she would never get up before nine on her days off, even if I was standing naked waiting for her, but Alex was out like a light, sleeping heavily with me securely in her arms.

Victoria did indeed wake up before I did and I was okay with it. It allowed me to watch her silently under the guise I was still asleep as she moved quietly to the kitchen to start working on the promised omelets and fresh pot of coffee. I took a quick peek at the clock. It was a quarter after nine in the morning. I stretched my legs out, tilting my head to get a better view of the partially dressed blonde, cursing myself for not waking up sooner and following through on hiding all of her clothes and forcing her to be naked. I smirked as flashes of a naked Victoria filled my head.

I pulled the comforter up higher over my shoulder, resting my head on her pillow, I watched her. Watched how she moved with precision like she always did but there was less tension around her shoulders. She even had a small smile on her face as she rummaged through my disorganized cabinets for pots and pans.

Last night was a first for me, many firsts. My first time with a woman, my first time with someone I deeply loved and the first time I woke up the next morning and felt whole. Whole in a way that Victoria was it for me. She was my one.

I sighed as I worked out the sore kinked muscles in my legs. I was sore everywhere, but I didn't care. I knew why I was sore and just thinking about it made me want to do it all over again. There really had to be nothing better than spending an entire day with Victoria making love in my shitty apartment.

"If you're going to stare, at least come over here and help with the coffee." Victoria looked up at me as she set down mixing bowls and a crate of eggs.

I rolled my eyes, blushing as I pushed the blankets back, catching Victoria's eyes widen when she saw me naked. "I guess I can help with the coffee." I grinned, walking to the dresser to grab a pair of shorts and a t-shirt, feeling Victoria's eyes on me the entire time. I hated putting clothes back on, but I had a weird thing about nudity in the kitchen.

When I was dressed, I walked to the kitchen and started puttering with my coffee maker when I felt her arms slide around my waist, pulling me against her. Victoria's lips brushed over my neck as she murmured, "Good morning you."

I grinned, leaning my head back to receive a proper kiss, "Morning."

"How are you feeling?" Victoria looked down with bright eyes, her eyebrows raised with the mildest concern.

I shrugged, leaning forward to return to the coffee maker, "Happy, tired, sore, hungry." I glanced back at her, "All in all, I feel perfect." I was about to thank her for last night, but I felt it would come off cheesy like it did the morning after my senior prom when I had a similar awkward conversation with my boyfriend at the time. How did you adequately express the mind blowing physical experience I had shared with Victoria? Tell her that it was the best sex I had ever had? That it was the only time in my life I truly felt like I had made love with someone? It all felt too heavy and I didn't want to throw another heavy cloud around us when we just pushed away all of the surrounding storm clouds.

So, instead I opted to play it cheeky, winking at her as she stepped away to move back to the eggs and spinach. I knew Victoria would be concerned, since it was a night of firsts for me. "And how are you feeling?"

She pulled her hair up in a ponytail, "I'm actually borderline exhausted. Someone had me expending a lot of energy that my poor body is not used to." She gave me a look before washing her hands and reaching for a few eggs.

I laughed, hitting the start button on the coffee, "Well if you're lucky, you might be expending a lot more throughout the day."

Victoria blushed, "I think I've created a monster." Cracking an egg, she looked over her shoulder, "I need to run home after we eat. Mary called, said Detective Scarlett knocked on her door this morning, inquiring about me."

I felt my stomach drop at hearing the detective's name. "Okay." I leaned against the counter, folding my arms, "Why is this woman so determined to find you?"

Victoria kept her eyes on the large bowl, "I'm not sure. It's one thing to bother me, but it's another to start knocking on my neighbor's doors." She turned to me, wiping her hands on a towel as she pointed at the frying pan next to me. "I'm going to call her and set up a meeting at the coffee shop by my house. Hopefully, after she meets me and asks her questions, she will piss off for good."

I frowned, running a hand down my neck, feeling the raised lines from tiny bite marks left by Victoria. "Why do I feel like everyone is always trying to burst our bubble? All I had planned for today was breakfast and bed. You, me, no clothes and all the carry out we may need to keep our energy up." I looked at Victoria, catching the smirk on her face. "What's that look for?"

Victoria rolled her eyes, pouring the eggs into the frying pan, "I was going to actually tell you that after I met with the detective, I want to lock us up in my house for the rest of the day." She looked around my apartment, "Not that I don't like it here, I just like it when you're at my house." Her eyes fell on mine, "Having you there finally makes it feel like a home, Alex."

My heart melted at the simple handful of words strung together to create an impactful statement, making me fall even deeper in love with the blonde. "Are you suggesting I should move in?" I narrowed my eyes at her, "Because I don't think I can get my security deposit back until I fix all the hammer holes."

Victoria laughed, grabbing my arm to pull me closer for a quick, but deep kiss. One that made my body wake up fully and want to forgo the delicious breakfast that was assaulting my nose. I wanted to drag Victoria back to bed and try out a few more things I'd thought about. "Let's see how this vacation together goes." She made a face, "But if you did move in, I would at least know where all of my Navy things are hiding."

Releasing me to flip the omelet, I bit my bottom lip, tucking my hands under my arms, "Speaking of Navy things, I kind of always had this fantasy about you in your dress uniform, or any of your uniforms. Do you have one of those big white hats the men wear?" My heart began to race as I pictured Victoria in nothing but her dress uniform shirt, partially buttoned and swaggering into the bedroom.

Victoria kept her focus on the frying pan in front of her, "Funny you should ask, but yes, I do." She then turned and gave me a heated look that made me bite my bottom lip harder in an attempt to funnel out the desire coursing through my veins. "If you're lucky, and you give me back my favorite hoody..."

I pushed off the counter and half ran to my closet, tossing random shirts and scrubs aside I thrust my arm up in the air, a hand wrapped around the worn grey material, "I found it! It's right here!"

I rushed back to where Victoria had her shopping bags from the mall, folding up the cherished hoody and tucking it in her bag, I pointed, "See, all ready to go home with you."

I looked up to see the woman I loved, laughing and shaking her head at me as she plated the omelet, "If I had known that was all it took."

I gave her a dirty look, "You play dirty, Victoria."

She grinned at me, "Yes, I do." She waved me over to grab a plate, "And you will find out how dirty I can play later today."

I groaned, walking towards her. "I really hate this detective."

After breakfast, and a very long shower that started out innocent, but then turned into another teaching lesson about things that can be done in the shower with Victoria, we packed up and drove back to her house.

Holding hands the entire way back, I felt like a giddy idiot. The whole world looked different. The sun seemed brighter and the spring blossoms had a stronger scent as it flooded the mini from the open windows. Even the music on the radio was perfect, the radio stations playing all of my favorite songs as I drove without a thought in my head other than how Victoria's hand felt in mine.

I couldn't stop looking at her at every stop light. I would often catch her staring at me. Grinning and hanging her head down when I caught her. She was a far cry from the guarded, and protective woman I had faced down a few days ago. Replaced by, what I imagine, was the woman she was before the world changed around her and in her.

Right before the exit ramp that would take me to her neighborhood, I had a sudden desire to keep heading south and drive until we found somewhere to stop. Maybe find a nice house on the coast of the Carolina's, move into an old plantation house, leave our lives behind and start a new one where no one knew us. A life that could just be the two of us watching the sun rise and set without a care in the world. No more worrying about double shifts and grading papers.

I rolled my eyes as I hit the on ramp, my hopeless romantic brain getting carried away like it always did. I knew Victoria would never just up and bail on her job at the Academy, and I certainly had too much dedication, and self-created responsibility, to my nursing job to just stop showing up. There was a reality that I had to adapt to now, which was this new beginning with Victoria by my side.

At least I was on vacation, and I could indulge a bit in my fantasies with the woman sitting next to me.

Driving the mini up into her driveway, we both waved to Mary and Dale as they worked on the flowers in the front yard.

Victoria got out immediately and trotted over to Mary, clearly asking about the Detective and what she wanted. The look on the two elderly neighbor's told me that it wasn't anything too disruptive, but as all good neighbors do, they made sure Victoria was told about the snoopy woman and her treading in a territory that was off limits in many ways.

I eased out of the car, reaching for our bags to head in the house when Victoria called out my name and tossed me her house keys, winking at me as I gave her a look. I was still getting used to this open side of Victoria. The ease she now had around me.

I motioned that I would meet her inside and walked to the front door, smiling lightly to myself as I scooped up her mail and took it into the den, dropping the bags on the couch as I went. I sat the few envelopes down on the mahogany desk when one of them caught my eye.

It was a thicker one, a deep blue color and just felt different. The texture of the envelope had a rich feeling like wedding invitations did. I flicked the other envelopes out of the way, reading Victoria's full name and rank in the center in gold ink. I picked it up, looking at the return address.

"Voltaire Clothiers?" I scrunched my face up, recognizing the name of the company from the labels of Stacy's super expensive bras she bought for her second anniversary. I had even gotten a few product catalogs in the mail when I was in New York, tossing them in the recycling after I bought one bra and found it to be an overpriced piece of crap.

I moved to set the envelope back in its spot, trying to remember I had noticed what brand of Victoria's underwear she might own. Smirking as I made it my mission to find out, I set the other mail back on the fancy envelope, barely registering that the return address for the underwear mogul was an address close to the Pentagon.

It disappeared completely when I was swooped up in the strong arms of blonde as I walked out of the den, receiving another kiss that sucked all thoughts from my head.

I left Alex with Dale and Mary in my backyard. The three of them determined to turn the disaster I called a flower garden, into an actual flower garden. Dale taking the lead, digging out the one sad tulip plant I had planted last spring.

I had called Detective Scarlett while Alex was in the laundry room, washing all the new clothes I had bought and a few of her own things she packed. I told the Detective to meet me at the coffee shop around the corner from my house in an hour, giving me enough time to check in with Dani for any last minute things she might have dug up.

As I hung up and went to kiss Alex goodbye, I found myself watching her move around in my laundry room. Setting the washer and adding the right amount of detergent I used, folding up the few towels I had left in the dryer, I suddenly wanted Alex to move in with me. It had been a silly joke at breakfast, a way to distract Alex from lunging at me, but I had meant it when I said she made my house finally feel like a home. She finally made me feel like I had a home and not just a bed where I slept in between jobs.

I frowned looking at my phone as I shoved it in my pocket, I needed to wait longer before I asked her to give up her crappy, drafty apartment and move into this big empty house with me.

I still had to work out how I would navigate my second life with her in it. Another thing that I had to talk to Dani about. An eventual exit strategy and a retirement plan from Voltaire.

In the BMW, I called Dani.

"I was just about to email you, Professor." Dani's tone was less snarky than usual.

"I'm on the way to meet with Scarlett. She was knocking on my neighbor's door this morning." I felt my irritation rise. This meeting was going to be a struggle to keep calm and not resolve to other tactics I knew would work better than polite conversation.

"Yeah, sorry about that, I had gotten a ping from her phone when she made a call out from your address, I missed it. The basement has spotty signal and I was elbow deep in Scarlett secrets."

I gripped the steering wheel tighter as I left my subdivision, "And?"

Dani cleared her throat, "Let me head to the bathroom, I need to pee."

I sighed hard at Dani's code talk. Telling me she had to pee was her way of letting me know she had sensitive information. A minute later Dani cleared her throat again and sounded like she was in a tunnel, "Sorry. I had to zap myself before I continued. I checked on the good detective, and it turns out that nosy Nancy applied to a ton of federal agencies in hopes of becoming a LEO at the highest level. DEA, FBI, ATF, border patrol, and even TSA, all kicked her back since her degree wasn't as diverse as desired these days. So I dug a little deeper and found that she managed to pick up a one year internship with Army Intel."

Dani paused, "A certain fat bird happened to be at a recruiter's office when she went in to try and join up for the cause. He rerouted her to an internship, promising her the same bullshit he promised us."

I felt my jaw clench as I flashed back to the practiced speech I heard sitting in a secured room in the Pentagon, listening to the fat bald fucker talk about how intelligence was the heart and soul of any war effort and that female officers were the future.

If I only had the sense to see it was just a sales speech and he was selling me all the swampland in the world. "Continue."

Dani chuckled, "I knew this would get your whiskers in a twist. Sadly, the good detective was not cut out for the "internship." She was smart, but not smart enough for what the Colonel was looking for. She finished out her internship and was given a thanks, but no thanks, and cycled back down to local police. And that now brings us to the present."

Dani heaved out a sigh, "The thing is, if she got the same training you and I did, she will be able to pick up on certain characteristics about you, Victoria. The same diversion tactics we both rely on in conversation and all the other details she has, will point her in the direction of you being the masked marauder in the metro station that night. This could be why she's super focused on you. Any idiot who knows how to use Google will find pictures of you with the President, the first lady, and the fat fucker grinning like he won the goddamn Super bowl standing next to you. If she's relatively intelligent, she will put A next to B and maybe end up at C. C being that fucking piece of shit Colonel."

She took another slow breath, trying to calm down her own building rage at the man who had a hand in altering both of our lives into this morbid cloak and dagger one. "Now, I double backed and scrubbed your record down to the basics, your navy history and nothing else. I'm currently doing some other digging in places I do not belong to see if Jennifer Scarlett ever met anyone from Voltaire while in the internship."

I groaned, looking up to see a ubiquitous old grey police cruiser pull into the parking lot of the coffee shop, "Shit." I watched the detective exit the car and walk inside the shop. "I'll have to go the teacher route. Put on the same act I do every day for my students." I rubbed my temple, "Any suggestions?"

Dani chuckled, "Aside from throwing Dante on her ass and hacking the police department mainframe to have her fired for evidence tampering, no, Professor, I have nothing. This is a smelly pickle for sure. A pickle who I think has an agenda that might be more than just tying up a cold case. I'm still extracting Voltaire files through the backdoor, but I'm only on the third year you and I were in. I'm nowhere near anything that would suggest if either the patriots, or the tea drinkers, are going rogue and contracting out to root out moles. The old lady has been spazzy lately. Speaking of spazzing, you should have a blue envelope in your mail. I shoved it in your mailbox early this morning, a hand delivery of our yearly face to face review with the old lady and old man after your vacation."

Still rubbing my temple, feeling my head throb harder as I forgot that every spring, Dani and I had to sit in front of our "employers" for a review. I squeezed my eyes shut, "Keep an eye on...everything." I sat up straighter in the seat, "I'll message you after this meeting." I hung up, taking a deep breath to shake away the heavy feeling I now had. I tried to try replace it with the easy going attitude I would need in order to deal with the detective and be the good, professional military Professor who just happened to be a Good Samaritan one night.

Walking towards the coffee shop, I absently smoothed down the brand new, non-Navy, shirt I put on. I didn't want to do this today, or really ever. I wanted to be home, with Alex. That's what was infuriating me the most. That this detective was taking time away from us. It was already bad enough I had wasted so much time over the last year hiding, now I had another new issue to deal with. One that inevitably had me hiding and burying things.

Stepping into the coffee shop, I spotted Scarlett immediately, throwing her a quick wave with a smile as she sat in the furthest corner of the half empty shop. She smiled back, a tight lipped one, but it was a smile. I already didn't like how this was going.

"Afternoon Detective, I apologize for having you come all the way out to my side of town, but it was the most convenient. I'm still on vacation and really won't be back near the city for a few weeks." I set my phone and keys down, waving to the waitress to bring me a drink menu, "Can I get you anything?" I glanced politely at the detective.

She shook her head, "No thank you Commander, I don't drink coffee." She clicked her pen open as she reached for her notepad, "I appreciate you fitting me into your vacation. I had tried to get in touch with your secretary, but I kept getting redirected to an answering machine."

I nodded as I pointed out the coffee I wanted to the cheery waitress, "That does happen. I have put in a request for a new secretary, but I doubt that will ever come to fruition." I smirked, "You know how the government works." I leaned back in the chair, "As for fitting you in, you're welcome. I figured after you went poking around in my nice old neighbor's business, it was time to cut to the chase and sit down with you." I watched as Scarlett's pupils dilated for a second before returning to normal. I was already getting under her skin and it was throwing her off.

"I happened to find your address and tried to knock on your door." She cleared her throat, "Anyway, I just have a couple of questions and then I will leave you be."

I held my tight professional smile, watching the woman fidget and scribble on her notepad. I could clearly see why the Colonel dumped her from his internship. She had too many spontaneous and uncontrollable movements that would give her away under the easiest interrogation.

Scarlett straightened up in her seat, "First off, are you in contact with Ms. Ivers? She mentioned that you had been friends, but were drifting apart."

"We're still friends and working on reconnecting. She had actually called me after you stopped by the hospital and it kind of started a new conversation for us. So, yes, I am in contact with Ms. Ivers and we are friends." I looked her directly in the eye and didn't waver, smiling more as she had to look down from the intensity of my stare.

"Okay. Now, going back to that night Ms. Ivers was attacked. Is there anything you can tell me about that night? When you were on the platform?"

I looked away from the detective, taking the large coffee mug from the waitress, whispering a thank you before I turned to make eye contact once again. "First, I wasn't on the platform during Ms. Ivers' attack. I heard a scuffle from the street as I walked past. It sounded like a moaning, groaning. I peered down the staircase and that's when I saw Ms. Ivers trying to climb up, or rather, drag herself up the stairs. I rushed down to help her and carried her up the stairs. That's how I ended up taking her to the hospital." I picked up the coffee, sipping it. The detective was good, but not as good as I was. She had purposely said when I was on the platform, hoping I would take the bait and lead into how I was on the platform.

Scarlett scribbled, keeping her head down. "You didn't see the whole platform? Or anyone that stuck out of the ordinary around Ms. Ivers?"

I shook my head, "No. As I said, I only went a few steps down to Ms. Ivers, no further."

Scarlett glanced at me, pausing to see if I had anything else to add. She started to tap her pen against the tabletop, a sign that she was trying to think of a new route to take with me. My answers were firm with no hesitation and very direct. Telling her that I was being honest and accurate with my placement on that night. "Can I ask you about your military service? What was your duty station in the Navy?"

I raised my eyebrow, setting the mug down, "I can tell you already know. You probably did a web search of my name?" I smiled pleasantly at the woman.

She nodded, her mouth curving in an embarrassed smile, "I did, yes." She shrugged, "I won't press if it's too difficult to talk about, you survived a lot and I respect your service to the country." Her face flushed a bit, "I just need to know if you possibly had any advance warfare training, tactical training or do any martial arts in your spare time."

I chuckled shaking my head, "No, no. The only physical training I have under my belt is the basics I learned at the Naval Academy. The whole big padded Q-tip fights on a log over a mud pit?" I grinned as the detective laughed with me, "After that, it was only the basics, the yearly training, and nothing more. I was an Intelligence Officer in the Navy, but even there, I was more of an ambassador for refugees and the United States. My commanding officers sent a few female naval officers into some of the villages around Baghdad to help with aid for women and children." I reached for the coffee, "Not to be morbid, but if you read the press about my incident, you'll see that I'm clearly not a fighter, just a survivor."

Scarlett kept her smile as her face grew a deeper red, "I did, and I'm not judging you at all, Commander. Many of us believe you are a hero." She cleared her throat again. I was succeeding in making her feel awkward and throw her off me in every little aspect she thought she had me. "I just had to follow through on a few hunches. Patch up a few ideas I had of who possibly could have murdered Ms. Ivers' attackers."

I faked surprised interest, "I thought that was ruled a junkie on junkie crime? That the men responsible turned on each other due to PCP or meth?" I blinked a few times, "Are you suggesting that I might be responsible?" I chuckled incredulously, "You must have read in my service file that I was medically retired from the Navy due to my injuries, and it took me years to fully heal. Even now, I still have some mobility issues from nerve damage and burn scars."

"I did, yes." Scarlett was now shifting uncomfortably in her chair, "The reason why I needed to meet with you, is one of your hairs was collected as evidence. It was the only clue I had in a year, and you were never formally a part of the investigation, just the woman who helped Ms. Ivers to the hospital." She paused, "Like I said, it was a new clue. A hope you were a witness to something that could help me find some more leads."

I kept my gaze on her, "Well, I can assure you, I was only there to help. I do recall that there was a breeze that night and my hair was down." I sipped from the mug, "But I understand your determination in seeking out proper justice. Junkies or not, murder is murder. All I know, is that I have seen a lifetime of fighting and death overseas, That's why I've become more of a peacekeeper in recent years. I don't even attend the Academy boxing matches or the drill weekends. I choose to teach my students how to survive in a fight based off of my experiences and then fill their heads with boring facts about generals and historic battles."

Scarlett looked in my eyes, watching me for a second as her own gaze softened. The hardened detective looking at a possible suspect had faded into a sympathetic woman sitting across from a weary war hero. "I understand Commander Bancroft." She closed her notebook and set her pen on top of it, "I appreciate you meeting with me."

"Of course." I went to reach in my pocket for a few dollars when Scarlett held up her hand, digging in her suit pocket.

"Let me buy your coffee, it's the least I can do for interrupting your vacation." She smiled genuinely as she set a ten dollar bill on the table before she grabbed her notepad and pen and stood up.

She then extended her hand. I stood up and took it, shaking her hand firmly. "Thank you for the coffee Detective Scarlett, I'm sorry I wasn't more of a help to you."

Releasing my hand, she shook her head, "You have done plenty, I can now cross a few more things off my list and go back to the drawing board." She took a step away, "I hope you enjoy the rest of your vacation, Commander Bancroft."

I whispered a polite thank you, and watched the woman walk out the coffee shop, get into her plain grey police cruiser and drive off. I let out a breath, letting my boring and innocent facade slip away.

Picking up my phone and keys, I dug out another ten dollar bill and laid it on top of Scarlett's. As I walked out of the shop, I dialed Dani, not even waiting for her to say a word, "Scarlett is a dud. I can see why the Colonel dropped her from the internship."

Dani blew out a harsh laugh, "Really? Because her phone just pinged an outgoing call to a number that is attached to a bank of servers in the Pentagon, redirecting her call to a false front."

I stopped in my tracks, "Don't say it."

"Too late, I'm going to say it anyway, a false front that Voltaire uses, particularly one of the Colonel's favorite. Somerset Exports."

"Fuck me." I bit the inside of my mouth to hold back screaming, "What do you think this means Dani?"

"It could mean a few things. Since the police departments are riddled with Voltaire people, one of my contacts could be rerouting her to one of ours. It could mean that she is being played and this is the means to an end for the case of nurse blue eyes." Dani's voice was slightly higher, meaning she was curious about why Scarlett would have a Voltaire front's information. "Big conspiracy theory thought? I need to start hacking deeper into the mainframe, find out if that fucking fat bird is still alive."

I walked quickly to the BMW, "I thought he was a casualty of that embassy explosion in Syria three years ago."

"If dreams could come true, but nothing is as it seems with Voltaire." Dani started clicking rapidly on a keyboard in the background, "Let's play it cool, I'm running pings on everything I have right now. I will make a few calls to my metro boys and I will get back to you. I say if twenty four hours goes by with nothing, we are in the clear. Case closed and you can go back to disrobing your nurse and I can go back to being the reason why the old lady is losing her mind about mainframe hacks."

I hopped into the BMW, starting the car before the door was closed, "Jesus Dani, be careful." I had known for years Dani was internally hacking Voltaire's mainframe since the moment she handed me my unedited mission file from Baghdad. She was on a mission and was peeling apart layer after layer of the secrets Voltaire hid from the world, and the people they worked for.

She laughed, "I will, always am. She trusts me implicitly ever since I exposed Banks three years ago for his own mainframe debacle. Anyway, I need to get to work and you need to get to nurse blue eyes. If you don't hear from me, consider it a good thing. Enjoy your vacation and try not to get her pregnant."

I opened my mouth to curse at her, but was hung up on in the middle of her obnoxious laughter. Throwing my phone into the console, I left the coffee shop and raced home. My gut was all over the map, mainly pointing in the direction that Dani was right. Scarlett was probably being rerouted by one of our inside guys. Trying to clean up the mistakes they made when the evidence didn't disappear with the case file after it was closed a year ago. But deep down, something nagged at me. In particular, the vague connection she had to the Colonel, the internship, and to one of his favorite fronts he had used to recruit Dani and I almost ten years ago.

The only thing that kept me at ease was the fact that I had successfully thrown Scarlett off of me. I could see it in her eyes and the way she felt she needed to buy my coffee. I had succeeded in giving her the impression that I was nothing more than what I presented at that table. Not the killer she was looking for, the woman who eliminated four men without breaking a sweat.

When I arrived back at my house, I couldn't help but smile seeing Alex's car parked at a crooked angle in the driveway. My heart starting to race as I couldn't wait to see her. My excitement grew as I got out of the car and could hear her voice mixed with Mary and Dale's as they laughed, talking about flowers and shrubs.

Inside, I tossed my keys on the side table right inside the door and went for the back patio when I glanced at the den and remembered what Dani had said about the blue envelope. Taking a quick detour, I moved to my desk and snatched the thick blue envelope. I already knew what was inside, the date and the time, things that never changed from year to year. Dani and I would always meet on the same last Thursday in June at exactly one p.m., on the dot, and spend exactly one hour receiving our yearly performance review. I would always receive some sort of pay increase, Dani would be given an action plan and a promise of possible promotion within the next year. Dani and I would then leave the office at exactly two p.m. She would the proceed to gripe and bitch as I took her to lunch at the diner down the street. We would say goodbye before going our separate ways, and not speak unless it was for a new job.

I rolled my eyes as I ran up the stairs to my bedroom, for a black ops organization, Voltaire had some strange issues about consistency and organization. They were far too predictable and it made me wonder how they survived so long in the shadows.

Shoving open my closet doors, I opened the small safe that was bolted to the floor and tossed the blue envelope in with the others. I still had yet to destroy from the last few months. Along with the unopened envelopes, sat stacks of receipt of payments and cashier checks I hadn't bothered to cash. Slamming the safe closed, I stood up, moving my hanging clothes back in their places when I caught the edge of the white dress male officer's cap I had traded with one of my classmates for on graduation day.

I smirked and snatched it off the shelf. After closing the closet doors, I went back downstairs to the kitchen. I could see Alex, Dale, and Mary on their respective sides of the fence. My pitiful tulip garden was now full of small bushes and a few transplants of lilies, daisies and Dale's prize tulips. I grinned looking at the new addition as well as Alex with smudges of dirt on her cheeks, charming the pants off my neighbors.

I bit my bottom lip at how adorable Alex was, standing there in my backyard handing over borrowed flower print gardening gloves. I opened the back door, drawing the attention of the three. Dale winked and saluted me, Mary waved her gloves, and Alex's face lit up like a spotlight. As her eyes landed on mine, I felt the fabled butterflies in my stomach twirl a bit harder.

I went to say something to my landscapers, when Dale placed a hand on his wife's shoulder, "Hey Victoria, you're all set with the yard. Make sure to water it in the morning and it will bloom like wildfire by summer." He motioned to Alex, "Your girl here has a natural green thumb. I told her to come over tomorrow afternoon and I'll show her how to plant seedlings."

Mary shook her head, grabbing his hand, "Never mind him, you two are on vacation, enjoy it." She shooed Dale away, moving to follow him when she called after her shoulder, "But this coming Monday, you girls are invited over for BBQ. Dale and I are heading up to West Virginia to pick up some steaks from his cousin the cattle farmer." She pointed at me with a gloved finger, "You are responsible for dessert."

I grinned, hanging my head down, "Of course. I will make the peach cobbler you love."

Mary smirked at me, "Sounds good, Victoria." She looked at Alex, "Lovely to get to know you Alex."

Alex blushed and smiled, turning to me as my neighbors went inside. She let out a breath and started to take a few steps towards me, "How did the meeting go?"

I shrugged, moving my hand with the hat from behind my back, "It went as expected. I am a boring history Professor, nothing more." I grabbed the hat with both hands holding it up so Alex could see it, "But I did happen to find this in my closet."

I watched as the flush crept up Alex's neck, slowly hitting her cheeks at the same time she bit her bottom lip to hold back from the whimper I knew was on the verge of escaping, "Is that?"

I nodded, "A white Navy dress hat. A man's white Navy dress hat." I placed it on my head on an angle, looking back at Alex as she was now moving quickly towards me, "I think you mentioned something about wanting to see one of these up close?"

Alex gave me a heated look and practically pushed me back from the doorway, slamming the door closed as she attacked me. Grabbing my face as her mouth smashed into mine with an almost guttural growled out yes.

Chapter 14

I kept looking at the intern, the shitheads still standing in the far corner of the station, leering at me. I kept staring forward at the empty tracks. Maybe if ignored them they would leave me alone.

I took in a slow breath, clenching the can of pepper spray tighter, chancing another glance at the intern when I felt a shoulder brush up against mine. I felt my jaw tighten as the overwhelming smell of piss, cigarettes, bad cologne and unbrushed teeth attacked all of my senses, making me want to gag. I took one step closer to the tracks, I willing the train to come bursting out of the tunnel and be my silent rescuer from what I knew was about to happen.

Then it was as if the world fell into slow motion. The touch of a dirty hand to my cheek, his filthy come on hissed through yellowed teeth. The literal knee jerk reaction I had from his touch, thrusting my knee up into his groin.

Then the inevitable, "Fuck her up boys." An order issued out of hurt pride and swollen testicles.

Falling to the ground away from the punches and kicks, I fell through the tile floor and came to land on my feet outside of myself. Watching in confusion as the attacking junkies faded into the shadows, leaving only a blonde stranger standing where I was sure I had fallen after the first fist to the stomach.

This blonde stranger reached out to me with an open hand and I felt a wave of relief replace all of my fear and confusion. This had to be my guardian angel, and as she looked up, I smiled looking in Victoria's slate grey eyes as she moved closer to rescue me.

Suddenly, Victoria's forehead split open with a large gash. Blood pouring forth like a faucet, down over her eyes, covering her cheeks and eventually sliding off her chin in large red drops.

The slate grey eyes that were so clear and determined, clouded over and became devoid of any emotion at all.

She just looked at me with a cold dead stare.

I was locked on those dead eyes and missed the glint of metal, only feeling the knife as it plunged into my stomach as Victoria lunged forward. Sinking the knife in to the hilt just below my sternum.

I shot up in the bed, gasping from the nightmare. I was sweating and could feel the tears on my cheeks. Leaning forward on my knees, I took in deep breaths in the darkness trying to calm my racing heart and shake out the shivers that filled my body. It was a familiar nightmare I had almost every night after the attack. Over time, it would drift away to nothing, but then become more intense when I was extremely tired, or had seen injuries in the ER that made me remember. I knew that having the detective back in my life and poking around in Victoria's, was shoving unresolved issues to the forefront of my mind. But the part with a bloodied and maniac Victoria was different, and it scared the hell out of me.

Blinking a few times, I felt the bed shift, drawing my still very hazy eyes to focus on the body next to me, causing me to almost leap out of the bed until my night vision kicked in, helping me to discern the body next to me was just Victoria lying on her stomach, sleeping undisturbed.

I stared at the shadowed curves of her body as I forced my body, heart and mind to calm down. Finally lying back down on my side when the sweat receded and my heart found its normal rhythm, I held onto the image of Victoria's peaceful face with her arms stretched out under the pillow.

The tank top she threw on an hour ago did very little to keep her covered, and I smiled at the sight, reaching out to run my hand over her shoulder. I suddenly needed to feel she was real after the nightmare left me with a gory, bloodied version of the woman who only murmured at the sensation of my warm hand gliding over her skin. She never opened an eye, even as she moved her arm from under the pillow and wrapped fingers around my bicep.

Moving closer to her warmth, I sighed, cursing my hyperactive imagination. There was no way that the sleeping woman next to me would ever be the monster I had seen in my dreams. She was nothing more than what she told that detective. A boring history Professor who happened to be a war veteran and hero.

I continued to smile as I lifted her hand away from my arm and snuck underneath it, curling up into her completely. Sighing contently when Victoria took the cue and pulled me into her.

The bed was empty when I rolled over twice, desperately searching out the warm body I had grown accustomed to over the last few days. Frowning I peeled my eyes open to see that I was definitely alone in the bed and the morning light was discreetly poking its way through the curtains and blinds of Victoria's bedroom. I sat up in the bed, leaning against the headboard and collecting my wild hair up as I looked around the room.

I frowned deeper when there were no signs of Victoria. I had gotten far too co-dependent, and used to, waking up with her next to me, or at least having her somewhere in the bedroom, that it made me mildly grumpy not having the instant gratification of seeing her the second my eyes opened.

I shook my head, I was definitely smitten and love struck.

Fighting a yawn back, I scooted to the edge of the bed to grab the pair of shorts I might have worn maybe once in the last thirty six hours. My yawn turned into a smirk thinking back over the last thirty six hours.

Victoria and I had not really left the bed, or the house. Only leaving the bedroom to jog down to the kitchen or front door to grab whatever carry out we ordered, then try to eat it over polite conversation or a movie, that would then turn flirty, and that would then turn into dirty banter and take us back to the bedroom. Victoria had shown me a few more things, dominating the bedroom and guiding me as I fumbled a bit here and there. I was not as confident as I had been that first night without any booze to lower my inhibitions. I would try to top her, but found it easier to submit and enjoy the ride, so to speak. I was still able to melt the woman into a pile of blubbering nonsense a few times, but I knew I had a way to go in my education of Ms. Bancroft.

My fingers latched on to the waist of the linen shorts when the smell of fresh coffee swarmed around me.

"It's 8:30 and you're awake. I better document this moment." Victoria's soft morning voice fell to my ears, carried on the ripples of steam from the coffee cups in her hand.

I turned to her, unable to hold back the goofy grin as I looked at the blonde. She was still wearing the loose tank top and a pair of shorts that were cut away from a longer pair of her academy sweatpants. Her hair was loose, and free, looking as if she had just brushed it. Victoria was stunning, glowing and made me shake my head again at how bewitched I was by her. "You probably should." I swiped the shorts up and pulled them on, moving to sit cross legged in the bed. "What day is it?" I furrowed my brow when it struck me that I really had no idea what day it was. Time had just become a haze filled with Chinese takeout, cold French toast leftovers and being naked.

Victoria handed me the battleship coffee mug, scrunching up her face in thought, "I do believe it is Sunday morning." She then moved to the bedside table, setting her angry goat mug down before moving to her closet that sat off to the side of the bathroom. "I had to take a look at the newspapers and mail pile growing at my front door."

I took a sip of the coffee, watching as she disappeared into the closet and I could hear a safe door being opened. The distinctive heavy creak all safe doors made, no matter how big or small, was muffled through the closet wall. "Sunday morning. That means we successfully spent almost two days trapped in bed."

I laughed, "I do believe that is another first for me."

I heard the clang of the safe door being closed and secured, followed by Victoria stepping out with a thin manila envelope tucked under her arm with a couple of the blue envelopes from the underwear company I had picked up the other day with her other mail. She raised her eyebrows, setting the envelope on the dresser, dropping the blue ones in it. "A first?"

I nodded, "I have never spent more than a couple hours in bed with someone, let alone a whole day or two." I scooted back, "I never wanted to, always thought it was wasteful to spend days doing nothing." I shrugged, "Well, doing other things besides nothing." I felt my face turn beet red. How is it that I could spend endless amounts of time with Victoria naked, and yet I couldn't speak it out loud?

Victoria grinned, walking over to the bed with a small rectangular envelope in her hand, "If it makes you feel better, you are the only one I've wanted to spend more than ten minutes in bed together, not sleeping." She sat facing me, "Your mother called your phone an hour ago, and sent a text reminding you about dinner tonight. I thought it was time to get up and take care of a few things that were ignored while we were doing other things besides nothing."

I playfully frowned and poked her, "Don't make fun of me."

She bent forward, kissing me, "Never happen." As she leaned back, Victoria held out the white rectangle envelope, "I know you go back to work on Wednesday, but I was wondering if you could maybe sneak in a sick day the following Saturday."

I set the coffee mug to rest between my legs, taking the envelope from her, "Depends on what for." I glanced at the thick textured envelope that had Victoria's title and rank in black calligraphy on the front. Flipping it over, I lifted the opened flap and tugged out a fancy card that had all of the characteristics of an invitation.

Victoria moved closer to me, looking down at the invitation with me. "The Academy does an end of the year formal ball for faculty, alumni, and a handful of others in the military. It's their prom of sorts, but for adults." She glanced up at me, "Will you be my date?"

I bit my bottom lip, reading over the pomp and circumstance of Victoria and a guest being cordially invited to the alumni formal held at the grand ballroom of the Naval Academy. I looked up at her, "Will you be wearing a dress?"

Victoria tilted her head, "Actually, I'll be wearing my full dress white uniform." Looking directly in my eyes, she added in a low sensual voice, "And my white dress hat."

I bit my lip harder, catching the edge of the white dress hat sitting on top of the one chair. Still sitting as it landed when I ripped it off Victoria's head so I could tangle my fingers in her hair as we set upon another lesson of lovemaking.

I looked back at Victoria, handing her my coffee mug and pointing to my cell phone that set on her side of the bed, "Hand me my phone?"

Victoria nodded, confused as to the strange request instead of answering to her asking me out, "I can wear a dress if you want me to? It's just faculty usually always pull out the full peacock show. It's the only time some of the old men can show off their tarnished medals and talk about the old days."

I laughed, taking the phone from her, grabbing her hand before she went too far. I winked at her, kissing her to shut her up. Three rings and I heard the tired and semi-grumpy voice of my boss. "Edie Rivers, Head Nurse, how can I help you?"

"Edie? Hi, this is Alex Ivers." I wound my fingers into Victoria's, squeezing her hand, "I know my vacation ends this Tuesday, but I was wondering if I could extend that another week?"

I heard Edie shuffle some papers around. "Alex! Are you finally using up your four hundred plus hours of vacation and sick time accrued?" I could almost hear the elation in her voice. I knew if I didn't take a decent amount of my sick time or vacation time every year, the hospital would have to cut a huge check to pay me out.

"I am, yes. I haven't taken a decent vacation in a year and I was just asked to attend some fancy ball this weekend." I smiled as I saw Victoria's eyes light up, "I finally have a reason to avoid work, Edie."

Edie laughed, "I would ask if the Poconos were a success, but I saw that Doctor Dean moping around up in ortho yesterday." I rolled my eyes, good lord was gossip the main topic in that hospital. Everyone knew everyone's business.

I heard a few more papers shuffle, "Your request has been granted. I have two new nurses starting this week and it would be good for Stacy and Deb to brush up on their training." Edie laughed almost maniacally, she knew how much Stacy hated training, "Enjoy your extra week off, and whoever he is, he's one lucky son of a bitch."

My face broke out into a massive grin, "She is definitely one lucky son of a bitch, Edie." Victoria gave me a strange look as I hung up before Edie could prod further into my private business that I knew Stacy was probably already spreading about, or would be, when she went in and saw that I was off for one more week and she was stuck with training new nurses.

I dropped the cell phone on the bed, "I'm all yours, Commander Bancroft, to wine, dine, and dance the night away in a sea of sailors."

Victoria chuckled, raising her eyebrow, "A sea of sailors? Should I be worried about one stealing you away?"

I shook my head, pulling her closer so I could wrap my arms around her, "Never happen, because you are the lucky son of a bitch that is stuck with me forever." I kissed the side of her neck, murmuring under her ear, "I'll find a dress that will keep your eyes only on me." I felt her squeeze me tighter, her hands drifting to the edge of the waistband on my shorts.

"What time is dinner at your moms?" Victoria's voice was heavy with desire, making my body shiver.

I swallowed hard, feeling her slender fingers move lower, "We should leave around two. Bill and mom like to eat early."

I closed my eyes when I heard her whisper, "Plenty of time." Her hands gripping my hips as she lifted me up and laid me down on the bed.

The second her lips met mine, I knew we were going to be late to dinner.

"We should only be a half hour late, mom. The mini wouldn't start." I glared at Victoria as she smirked getting into the driver's seat of her BMW. "Yes, we can stop and grab dessert on the way. I know, Bill likes apple pie." I rolled my eyes at how excited my mother was on the others side of the phone. Rattling on about how she hoped Victoria would like her meatloaf and if there were any special dietary restrictions she needed to pay attention to. I shook my head as Victoria leaned over brushing my thigh when she opened the glove compartment to pull out a phone charger. I gave her another dirty look, knowing what she was up to, "We're hitting the road now, mom. I'll see you when we get there."

I mumbled a few more words of acknowledgment of whatever it was my mother was stuck on, before hanging up and dumping my phone in the cup holder. Leaning back in the seat, I rubbed my temples, "It's your fault we're late, therefore, it's your fault my mom is running around like the president is coming for dinner." I rolled my head to look over at Victoria, sunglasses on as she backed the BMW out of the driveway and onto the street.

She shrugged, smirking, "I actually think it was your fault. I vaguely recall you being the one who was adamant on picking out which shirt I was going to wear tonight, then getting handsy after I took one off."

I tried not to laugh, looking out the windshield, "Maybe." I sighed, reaching over to rest my hand on her forearm as she drove. I had been handsy after our morning session and couldn't resist running my hands over Victoria's skin as I chose the loose blue linen tunic shirt she was now wearing. It seemed Victoria did have an expansive wardrobe outside of navy shirts, but they were hidden in the back of her closet hanging over the floor safe. The same floor safe I'd seen her remove the blue envelopes from earlier.

Squeezing her arm, I asked, "I didn't think you to be a Voltaire Lingerie fan. Their underwear is a bit risqué and see through for a proper, boring history Professor like yourself." I turned to Victoria in time to see her smile flicker for a split second, making me wonder why asking about her underwear would bother her, considering I had seen more than just her underwear over the last few days. "I saw the blue envelope when I picked up the mail the other day, and this morning you had a few more with the piles of mail."

I studied her face, picking up the tiny inflections in her smile and the way her jaw twitched. Something was off. I went for a joke to break up the strange tension creeping into the car, "I used to save their catalogs and mailers to use as fire starters in the fireplace of my old place in Brooklyn. That's all they, and their bras, were good for." I pointed at my chest, "They certainly didn't do these girls any justice. It just felt like I was wearing see through gauze under my scrubs."

Victoria's jaw relaxed as she dropped her hand from the steering wheel to lay it on my thigh, "I don't think there is a bra in the world that could do your chest justice." She grinned at me, "You're quite literally perfect in my eyes, Alex. All of you." My cheeks started to burn as I looked back out the window.

When Victoria did compliment me, it was incredibly sweet and romantic. In a way, that it made me embarrassed anyone could be looking at me that closely. I covered her hand on my thigh, linking our fingers together as she continued, "I kind of have a secret. I'm a stock holder in Voltaire. I bought a ton of stocks when they went public near the end of my time with the navy. All those envelopes you saw are checks from the company." She shrugged, "I don't exactly know what for, I have a stock broker in the city that manages all of that nonsense for me. I get those gaudy blue envelopes in the mail, collect them, wait a month, and then make a massive deposit."

Victoria looked over at me pushing her sunglasses up so I could see her bright grey eyes, "Truth be told, Voltaire Lingerie has paid for this car, my house, and the worry free retirement I will hopefully have in five years. I'll be a giddy, retired forty something year old all because I invested in fancy ladies underwear."

I cleared my throat free of the lingering traces of embarrassment, "At seventy five bucks a pop per bra, I can see it." I paused as she turned back to the road, the tension completely gone from when I initially asked about the stacks of fancy envelopes. Smiling when I saw her easy smile return with every little squeeze of my hand. Letting out a slow breath, I half whispered, "You're perfect too, Victoria."

I frowned and rolled my eyes at how cheesy I sounded in this moment, like a kid with their first elementary school crush.

I held her hand, focusing on the way her fingers fit in mine when I heard, "I'm not perfect Alex, but you make me want to be a better woman. You make me want to pick a life and stick with it. Forget the past and only look to the future." Looking up I saw Victoria's eyes, still straight ahead on the road, welling up, "A future where all I have to worry about is pizza stains, stolen clothes and quiet Saturday night movie marathons." She glanced at me for a second, smiling an almost painful smile, "A future where my past and my present can be forgotten."

I wanted to say something, feeling my stomach wobble at the way she looked at me and the tone of her voice as if in her head she really saw no future until now. But even as she now saw one, it scared her. I wanted to dig deeper when those same clouds met the edge of the tears in her eyes as a strange mysterious feeling thickened between us. The same one that radiated from her in the first few months we had been friends, and recently, when she struggled hiding her scars. I knew Victoria's scars ran deep and thick, but there was more to what she was saying than old buried scars.

Those thoughts never made it to spoken words. Remaining in my head just as curious and concerning thoughts. Victoria distracted me by picking up my hand and kissing the top of it, pulling it over to rest in her lap as she asked about what kind of meatloaf recipe my mother used and that she knew of a small farmer's market near the house where we could stop and get a really nice apple pie.

Even as I held her hand and fell further in love with her, my gut was giving me a dirty look.

The mystery that was Victoria Bancroft was still unsolved, and now had more layers than I really wanted to acknowledge.

I had been to at least one significant others parents' house for dinner. Only one, and it was the most excruciatingly awkward experience of my life. So awkward, it was the eventual nail in the coffin of that particular relationship, sending me towards the option of casual dating and minor relationships at best. Nothing serious where I would have to be put in the position I now was. Standing next to Alex holding a freshly baked apple pie, taking deep breaths as I followed her up to the white front door of her mother's ranch style home in the hills of Sperryville.

It didn't help when Alex brought up the blue envelopes and I had to scramble for a minor lie to cover up the truth. Essentially, yes, I was a stock holder in Voltaire. Dealing and trading in their most precious commodity. Death.

What I didn't expect, was the white lie bringing out the emotions that fell over me like a collapsing brick wall. Each of them hitting me one by one, and stirring up feelings that I had not felt in a very long time, or maybe ever. I'd been brutally honest when I told her she made me a better woman and made me want to pick a life. A life with her where I could be the boring history Professor the world saw, and nothing more.

Those emotions now collided with others. Alex was smart, observant, and paid far more attention to the world around her than most would give her credit for. In time, she would start pushing the questions. Questioning exactly what was inside those blue envelopes, the large sums of money I received from my "stocks", and lastly, when I returned to work. The unexpected trips, the late nights and unusual behavior.

Alex turned to look over her shoulder, reaching back for my hand, "They don't bite, at least mom and Bill won't. Annie and Barney might." She smirked, waiting for me to walk closer.

I shook my head, "Like everything else, it's been a while since I did the whole meet the parents over dinner thing." I shifted the pie plate to my left hand, taking Alex's in my right as she tugged me forward. "This might be silly, but I want to make a good impression." I cocked my eyebrow in a question, the words felt strange as they rolled over my tongue. I'd never cared to make a good impression in my personal life with those that were not close enough to me for me to actually care. I would throw on a happy polite smile, and use all of the manners the Navy, and my grandmother taught me. Steering through any kind of dinner, or cocktail conversation, in a way that left many impressed but curious.

That was not the case with Alex. With Alex, I wanted to do everything right. I wanted to impress her family in a way that I could continue to look at a future with the brunette. Give me the strength, and hope, I would need as I worked towards an exit from Voltaire and hopefully bury the black hooded figure who constantly stood one step behind me.

I would need to find that exit because I had to. There was no more room in the closet for my uniforms, my t-shirts, and the safe at the bottom. There was no room in my life for the killer, especially when I wanted nothing more than to keep what Alex had brought into it over the last few days.

I hated the way this all felt. It scared me more than any of those days I spent in that dusty hole staring at the bright molten red spike tips. It scared me because Alex made me feel human, and want to continue to feel human.

"Trust me, Victoria, you will win them over the second you hand over the pie and say hello." Alex curled her fingers into mine. "I've never brought anyone home to meet the dogs, they might take some time to get used to you." Alex grinned at me, nudging my shoulder, "You'll be fine. I'll be right next to you the whole time and I'm open to faking an illness if it becomes too much for you."

I smiled softly, looking down in those blue eyes that had hooked me from the first second she peered over at me on the metro station platform. "I think you would fake an illness just to con me into taking care of you in bed for a day or two."

Alex shrugged, "Maybe." She turned to the wooden white door, lifted up the black wrought iron knocker and knocked three times. She gave me one more look, squeezing my hand, "You'll be okay, Victoria. It's just mom and Bill."

Before I could protest, the white door swung open revealing a grinning older woman who looked like she could've been Alex's older sister. "Alexandra Ava!" She held her arms out in the same exact manner Alex did when she was handing out her rib crushing hugs.

Alex dropped my hand to walk into the wide outstretched arms, "Hi Mom."

I smiled softly, filling my now empty hand with the other edge of the pie plate, taking a good look at Alex's mother as she squished the air from her daughter's lungs. For a moment, I felt the heavy sadness that came when I thought about how I had no family and had not been party to such hearty greetings by a mother, a father, or anyone really, for most of my adult life. I turned away from the mother daughter embrace to stare at a red, blue, and yellow garden gnome holding up a porcelain basket of daisies.

I was lost in the curves and sharp edges of the peeling red paint on his pointy hat that I didn't hear my name being called. I shot my eyes up when a hand on my shoulder connected my brain to the fact my name was being called, "Victoria?" Alex gave me a look, silently asking if I was okay.

I nodded and put on my social gathering smile, "Sorry, I was staring at the gnome." I motioned to it as I looked between Alex and her mother. I cleared my throat, shifting the pie's weight to one hand. "Hello Mrs. Ivers, Victoria Bancroft."

Alex's mom grinned, shaking her head and flicking a dismissive hand at me. "Please call me Katherine." Her grin grew a little bigger, "It's great to finally meet you Victoria."

I had to urge to tilt my head back to the gnome, feeling awkward from the tone in her voice. It held appreciation for saving her daughter that night, being her closest friend and now as I glanced back at her eyes, the tone of finally meeting the one person that had stolen her only child's heart.

I held out the pie, trying to redirect the awkwardness, "Alex said you liked apple pie?"

Katherine laughed, "Bill loves it, I like it." She took the heavy pie from my hands, "Please come inside, girls. Bill should be just about done setting the table."

I let out a slow sigh as Katherine walked back into the house, telling Alex over her shoulder to make sure the screen door was locked since Barney was a bit of an escape artist. I chanced another glance at the gnome, suddenly wishing he and I could trade places.

"Victoria, you'll be okay." Alex appeared on my right side, linking her hand in mine, staring up at me with the same bright blue eyes her mother had, "Don't be nervous."

Nodding, I squeezed her hand, "I'll try." I smiled for Alex's benefit, "I've just not had much practice in being around regular people who I didn't have to salute or put on a mask for." I bit back the last couple of words. My subconscious was pushing through the surface any chance it got, wanting me to just release all of the secrets I kept hidden to Alex and free myself of the perpetual game of hide and seek I played. Alex nudged my shoulder as she led me into the house, "My mom already loves you." The second step inside the warm and quaint house, I could hear the soft thundering of paws across wooden floors followed by yips and half barks. Alex started to giggle as two black heads of a pair of Scotties came rushing at us, determined to attack whomever was breaching into their territory. "Now, these two...that will be the true test."

The smaller of the two hopped up on two legs, placing tiny black paws on my knees, wagging a tail and barking excitedly at me. I knelt down as Alex introduced me, "That's Annie, she loves everyone." I reached out, scratching the top of Annie's head as she pushed harder against my hands. "Hello Annie." I smiled when she yipped at me.

The second Scottie, larger and definitely a boy by how broad his little dog body was, eyed me suspiciously. Sniffing the ground around my feet, moving in a circle. Alex crouched down with me, receiving a few licks on the arm from Annie, "That's old Barney. He's the guard of the house. He only really likes my mom, me, and Bill." She motioned to him circling me. "He'll sniff you then ignore you for the rest of the time you're in his house, so don't be offended if he walks away in a second."

I nodded, watching the old man finish his circle. "It's okay, I can understand where he's coming from." Annie hopped from my knees to lavish Alex with attention. Leaving me to stand up and brush my jeans off, when Barney slowly climbed to rest his paws on my knees and gave me a soft look hooded by fluffy eyebrows. I looked at him, smiling, "Hello there,"

Alex turned to look at me, confused and about to shove Barney down thinking he was going to bite me or bark, when I shook my head. Barney and I stared at each other for a moment and it was as if he could read me. Understanding that deep down I was the bigger protector in the house. Someone he could relax around and know his family would be safe. He saw through my facade and saw everything I hid from the humans around him. That I was just as much harmless in his home, around Alex and her family, as I was dangerous.

I watched as his tail began to wag excitedly. Leaning forward, Barney licked the top of my hand, nuzzling his nose under it to signify that he wanted to be pet.

I obliged him, running my hand over his coarser fur and scratching behind his ears. I glanced at Alex, a crooked grin on her face as she watched Barney and I bond. "That settles it, welcome to the family Victoria."

She stood up, Annie scattering off into the kitchen with Barney quickly following. I stood up with her, shrugging, "I probably smell like bacon from breakfast."

Alex folded her arms across her chest, "I doubt it. I was there for the very lengthy shower we both took after breakfast." She giggled when I blushed, "Come on, I'll introduce you to Bill. He'll probably chew your ear off about history, the Navy, or anything he can think of." She started walking towards the kitchen as I followed quickly behind, sighing as I saw an older man built like a brick wall with salt and pepper hair cut in a conservative way, standing next to Katherine, finishing up setting the table.

When Alex entered, his eyes focused on mine and a huge grin appeared on his face. Bill hustled around the table, hand extended out in greeting, "Hi, you must be Victoria, Alex's lady friend. I'm Bill Augustine. Katherine's boyfriend and Alex's..." He paused, suddenly searching for an appropriate term.

"He's my dad, Victoria. Bill's my dad." She grinned happily, leaning against her mom as I took Bill's meaty hand. Watching as he turned very shy and nodded slightly. "Victoria, these are my parents." Katherine and Bill continued to grin. I soon realized that this was the first time Alex was introducing anyone to her parents, and her parents to a significant other as her parents. Telling the three of us, that I was something more, someone more than a friend. I was the woman she clearly loved deeply.

It was in that moment I knew I was definitely stuck with Alex forever and didn't mind it one bit. I was changing her life as much as she had changed mine.

Dinner was a smattering of casual conversation mixed in among happy bites of food. Alex's mom made one hell of a meatloaf and was more than happy to keep my plate full of it. The conversation hovered around how Alex was doing at work, how her apartment was coming along with the ever ongoing repairs and what she had planned for the rest of her vacation. I smiled to myself when Alex's mom kept calling her by her middle name, turning the stubborn nurse into a sheepish mumbling little girl, politely asking her mom to not call her Ava in front of everyone.

Not once, did the usual dinner with the parents questions come my way, allowing me to breathe easier and eat meatloaf happily. But as the pie was served up, Katherine slid a cup of coffee in front of me, "Victoria, I want to thank you for helping Alex. That night and over the last year." She paused her words, sitting down in her chair next to Bill and hearing Alex quietly protest where the conversation was heading.

Katherine waved her napkin at her daughter, "It's okay. This is the first time I meet the stranger who has made my little Ava smile more than she has since I first took her to the movies." She turned back to me, sighing, "Thank you, Victoria. Thank you for bringing the sun back into the world for my daughter. I can see she really thinks you created the world and all the stars in the sky."

She smirked as I blushed. "Oh dear, don't get embarrassed. It's a good thing, and for once in my life, I give my blessing to this." She waved her hands at Alex and I. "I never liked any of the others Alex dated or brought over. I felt they were beneath her, not her equal." Katherine leaned against Bill's shoulder, smiling at the man in the same way Alex smiled at me first thing in the morning.

Poking at the leftover crust of apple pie, I held my head down, "You don't need to thank me, Katherine. I did what I thought I was right." I turned to look at Alex, "From that day and every day after. I have always tried to do the right thing by Alex." I smiled when Alex laid her hand on my arm, whispering my name. Covering her hand with mine, I met her mother's eyes, "To be honest, I often look back and realize I never looked at the sun or appreciated the good days as much as I do now. All because of your tenacious and incredible daughter." I felt Alex's hand squeeze my arm, "Little Ava here has changed my life in ways I never thought was imaginable."

Katherine and Bill both stared at me with sappy grins. I cleared my throat, feeling in the spotlight, and picked up my empty plate, making a motion to grab the others when Bill spoke up, "Leave it Victoria. I can get it." He stood up, kissing the top of Katherine's head, "I have to say, I'm impressed, astonished, and grateful that Alex here has you. I always wanted the best for her and I can see you are the best. Hell, I am a bit envious that she snagged you." He chuckled, winking at me as Katherine playfully smacked his arm.

Alex groaned, hiding her face in my shoulder, "Oh Bill."

Katherine started laughing, standing to help Bill with other dishes, "You two have nothing to be shy or coy about. Love is a grandiose thing and it should be embraced, not hidden." She moved over to Alex, kissing the top of her head, "Now Ava, go get the kids ready for their walk."

Alex groaned again, shuffling to stand up and it made me smile, catching a tiny glimpse of what Alex probably was like as a teenager. Shy, cute, semi defiant, and equally as loving as she was now looking up at me with big blue eyes, her chin perched on my shoulder. "You want to help me with the kids? Now that you and Barney are best friends forever?"

I laughed, nodding, running my hand down her cheek, "Of course I will, Ava."

Alex rolled her eyes and groaned, "Not you too."

I couldn't help but laugh harder, following her shuffle to the back door where I saw red leashes and harnesses neatly hung up by the door, "Oh yes, me too."

She gave me a pout, shoving a leash and harness in my hand calling for Barney and Annie. Alex tried hard to give me the evil eye until the two black dogs came rushing at us yipping and barking with excitement.

She gave in when she saw Barney run right for me and climb into his harness without a fuss, shaking her head and giggling at how the old dog was licking my hand, wagging his tail. "Should I be worried or jealous of you two?"

I winked at her, "Maybe. He probably wouldn't smother me in bed or steal my pillows." Standing up, I held out my hand to the pouting brunette, pulling her towards me when her hand fell into mine. I kissed her softly on the lips, murmuring, "I'm kidding, no one could ever replace you, Ava."

Alex sighed contently, poking me in the ribs with her leash covered hand, "Good." She tried to kiss me again, but was yanked away by the hyper Annie who saw a bird out the screen door and was determined to either kill it, or make friends with it. "I'll get you back later, Victoria."

I raised my eyebrows at the seductive, yet revengeful, tone in her face. I shrugged looking down at Barney waiting to take the lead, "Your big sister is a bit of a naughty one."

Barney barked in what I imagined to be him agreeing with me, his tail wagging in circles waiting for me to take the first step. I stared at the dog until I heard Alex shove the screen door open and holler back for me to hurry up. I sighed, motioning for Barney to go ahead. His sturdy legs taking off in a dedicated cadence, showing me that he was very serious about his afternoon walks.

I grinned, following him out and towards Alex who was desperately trying to untangle the leash wrapped around her legs.

I could get used to these kind of days.

Victoria walked ahead of my mom and I. Bill next to her taking over leash duties for Barney as we all walked around the neighborhood on the sunny late afternoon. I could tell Bill was off on one of his diatribes, more than likely about the Naval Academy from the snippets of conversation that floating back to me.

Mom and I were discussing her book club and the new romance adventure novel they started. I still had control of Annie and was constantly looking down and stepping over her leash as she ran in hyper semi circles chasing leaves, birds, squirrels, her own shadow.

"I like Victoria a lot." My mom's voice had taken on that subtle tone of judgment it often did when she was appraising my life choices. She looked over at me, eyebrow raised with a curious smile, "She's very beautiful."

I tugged on Annie's leash, trying to get her to settle down, "You say that as if you're surprised it's a she and not a he?" I kept my eyes on the black blur of a tail. I hated when my mom had these kind of heart to hearts with me. It usually ended up in her talking my ear off about making my life into something more in one avenue or another. Whether it was work, upgrading my nursing skills to get out of the trauma ward, or finding marriage material, she had a way about her that made me question if I was doing the right thing. She did it in a loving way, but it still made me irritated that she still couldn't let go of me even as my thirty first birthday was just a few months away. I was forever her little girl, her only little girl.

My mom linked her arm into mine, "Oh Alex, not at all. Love is blind on many levels. Who am I to question where anyone, especially my daughter, finds it." She patted my wrist, "I like her, I mean it. She's polite, intelligent, stunning, charismatic, funny, and seems to really like you."

I shrugged, fighting the involuntary grin that wanted to cross my face, "I really like her too, Mom."

"Do you love her?" My mom asked the question as if she already knew the answer.

I looked at my mom, waiting until she made eye contact with me. Looking in the dark blue eyes I had inherited, I nodded, "With my whole being." I smiled, turning back to look at Bill and Victoria walking ahead of us. "I love Victoria. I think I finally understand what you've been telling me all these years about finding the one." I sighed, "She makes me want to slow down in life and enjoy the day and not rush through it in the name of getting things done. I still have so much to learn about her, and for once, I actually have the patience to sit and wait for her to tell me everything."

I bit the inside of my mouth, remembering the night Victoria poured her heart out about her scars. It broke my heart and I had a strange feeling there was still more about the blonde that would be hard to absorb. She carried a wealth of secrets, the thunderclouds that fell across her eyes in the car told me there would be things I wished I never asked about, but would because I loved her so deeply.

"The girl does remind me of Gary Cooper in the Fountainhead, there's a mystery about her." My Mom winked at me, "Adds to her charisma." I rolled my eyes, giving Annie a dirty look as she wrapped around my legs for the hundredth time, my Mom laughing as she continued, "You said the other night that she was in the war and a hero? Is that how she got the teaching job and the fancy car? It's nice that the Navy helped her after all that mess."

I nodded, my head looking up from Annie just in time to catch Victoria looking back, her eyes meeting mine, making us both grin stupidly, "She was, Mom, and the Navy did help her. As for the fancy car, she is a stock holder in that fancy underwear company Voltaire, the one that sells bras for the price of my car payment." I leaned into her arm, hoping she would stop the impromptu interrogation of my new relationship. "Victoria gets checks at least once a month from the stocks and has been saving up for the last few years."

I furrowed my brow when a quick flash of the address on the upper corner of the blue envelopes struck me. The address on that one and a few others in Victoria's hands this morning had a D.C. address near the Pentagon. I vaguely recalled seeing a New York address a million and a half times on the stupid catalogs I recycled. Even once writing it down on a hare brained idea to walk over to their office when I lived in Manhattan to dump the huge box of glossy ads I had collected in a three month period, and tell them to shove their pricey, crappy lingerie up their bum and take me off the mailing list.

"Smart and thrifty. She's a keeper Ava." My Mom laughed, reaching to take over the reins on Annie while I stared at the sidewalk, my mind stitching odds and ends together about those damn blue envelopes.

I nodded, "Yeah, she really is." I smiled as my Mom took Annie and caught up to Bill and Victoria, sidling her way into their conversation as the weird feeling I had in the car when Victoria told me about her stocks, returned. There was a new mystery hiding in plain sight, written in gold print on blue envelopes. A mystery that I knew was better left alone, but knowing my inquisitive nature and that I wanted to know everything I could about Victoria, I would find a way to poke around and get my gut to relax with its constant red flag waving.

Bill calling my name roped my attention back into the present, waving me over to join the other three as we rounded the last corner of the walk. I waved back and jogged to catch up, grabbing Victoria's offered hand. Telling my gut as our fingers intertwined to leave it alone, all I wanted was to be in love and happy. Not embarking on a miniature investigation about my lover's financial business dealings.

After the afternoon walk with Alex's parents and dogs, there was a cup of coffee and the usual parental questions of what were my intentions with Alex. Barney even joined in by climbing up and lying down in my lap for a healthy nap as I stroked his back. Alex tried to protest the awkward questioning and get her parents off the topic, but I allowed it to happen. I had grown very fond of her parents over dinner and during the walk. Finding both of them to be kindhearted people who raised Alex to be the incredible woman she was now. I wanted to be open to her family and in turn her.

So, I answered their questions, honestly. For the first time in a long time, I didn't avoid the truth. I let my heart have the floor and spoke from it, seeing the happiness in Alex's eyes as I promised to do my best by her and do whatever I had to as we continued to move forward.

After winning her parents over and prying Barney off my lap, Alex and I said our goodbyes with a promise to come back next week for dinner. Her mother and Bill hugged me, whispering quiet thank you's, before sending us on our way with leftover meatloaf.

I couldn't wipe away the grin on my face during the early evening drive back to my house. Alex passed out the second we hit the highway, holding my hand on her lap as she slept. It all felt so surreal to me. The dinner felt unreal in a good way, the way her parents silently approved of their daughter being with me was something new to me. I had been in more than one relationship where the conservative parents couldn't wrap their head around the fact I was a woman in the military dating other women. It was nice and made it easier to relax and open up more and more to Alex, seeing that her and her family welcomed me with wide open arms.

Pulling into my neighborhood, I glanced at the sleeping brunette. Her face was peaceful as she breathed in and out heavily. Catching Alex asleep was my favorite thing, she was so stunning and beautiful when she was at rest, lost in whatever dreams she was having. It was the only time that I felt the world I knew didn't exist.

I grinned, squeezing her hand when we got closer to my house. I went to wake her up when I looked up and saw Dani parked behind Alex's mini, sitting on the trunk of the black sedan in her uniform, playing on her phone. My heart dropped into my stomach and my grin morphed into a heavy frown.

Letting go of Alex's hand, I pulled the BMW into the driveway and glared at the redhead. She glared back with a smirk and a shrug of her shoulders. Blowing out a heavy sigh I reached for Alex, gently shaking her awake. "Alex? We're home."

Alex snorted softly and opened her eyes, blinking and pushing the hair out of her face, "Did I pass out?" She looked at me and the small smile on my face, "I passed out." She scrunched up her nose, "Sorry, Mom's meatloaf makes me sleepy." She turned to look out the passenger side window, catching Dani now standing next to the black sedan. "Who is that?"

I sighed, shutting off the car and yanking out the keys, "That is my co-worker who apparently doesn't understand what I'm on vacation means." I pushed my door open, reaching for the bag of leftovers in the backseat, "I'll introduce you two before I tell her to piss off."

Alex chuckled, giving me a look, "Let me guess, is she the shitty secretary that calls and texts you? Turning you into grumpy Victoria?"

I nodded, "She is indeed a shitty secretary." I climbed out of the car and walked around to the back, making eye contact with Dani.

She smirked at me, "Evening Professor."

I glared at her, noticing the grey laptop bag next to her on the trunk with the large manila envelope sitting on top, "Lieutenant."

Dani raised an eyebrow at me, then turned to see Alex exit the passenger side and walk towards us. "I apologize for interrupting, didn't expect you to have company." Dani met my eyes, I could tell in that one look, my vacation was about to be put on hold.

Holding out the bag of food to Alex, I waved her over, "Alex, I would like you to meet Lieutenant Danielle O'Malley, my secretary at the Academy." I smirked at the sight of Dani grimacing when I referred to her as my secretary, "Lieutenant, I would like you to meet Alex Ivers, my girlfriend."

Alex grinned wider when she heard the formal title, extending her hand out to Dani, "Hi, it's nice to finally meet one of Victoria's co-workers." Alex leaned into me, wrapping an arm around my waist, "I hope you're not here to throw some work her way. We're on vacation."

I could see Dani fighting the urge to roll her eyes at the public display. She folded her arms across her chest, sighing dramatically, "Actually, I'm here to do just that." She frowned playfully at Alex, "School's out but the Navy never stops for the summer." She then made eye contact with me, "Alex, do you mind if the good Professor Bancroft and I have a minute to talk?"

Alex nodded, "Sure." She then grabbed the bag and squeezed my side, "I'll be in the living room, checking to see if your dragon show recorded." She then smiled at Dani, "Nice to meet you Lieutenant O'Malley."

Dani nodded, "Likewise." We both watched Alex walk into the house and close the door. "Your girlfriend is adorable, Professor." There was an edge to girlfriend when she spoke the word. "Can we take this inside?"

I clenched my jaw, pointing towards the garage, "In there."

Dani scooped up the laptop and manila envelope, walking towards the side door entrance to the garage, "You know O'Malley is not my real last name."

I closed the door behind us, "Even though I trust Alex, I would never reveal your true last name to anyone who didn't need to know it, Dani." I leaned against the small workbench Dale had built for me a few months after I moved in, "Get it over with."

Dani chuckled, setting the laptop bag down next to me, "Okay Professor grump." She unclicked the bag latches and removed a brand new, thinner black laptop, "I've heard tonight's episode of your dragon show is quite the killer." Dani pushed the laptop closer, "Speaking of killer episodes."

I felt my jaw twitch, "I'm on vacation." I then motioned to the laptop, "Why the new equipment?"

Dani hopped up on to the workbench, letting her khaki clad legs swing freely, "First, the old lady has issued new laptops to the plumbers. I was sent to hand deliver yours. Her paranoia is reaching epic levels, so she had the nerd herd build all new ones and then sent them all over to me to install heavy duty firewalls with heavy encryption." Dani winked at me, grinning, "That alone made my day. The old lady literally handed me the keys to the head office and said, be free little one! Be free!"

Frowning I stared at the dust covered Navy flag hanging on the opposite wall, "Dani, don't get too big for your britches."

"Yes pa, I'll try not to." Dani rolled her eyes, "If they haven't noticed now, they never will. Three years and I'm one of the master hackers out there. I have white hat hackers, black hat hackers and most of the deep web knocking on my door for tips."

She reached for the manila envelope, tossing it towards me, "Back to the real reason I'm here. Aside from dropping off the new laptop, the old man wants you to do a job." She held up her hand as I began to say something, "He knows you're on vacation, but wanted me to tell you that he only trusts you to do this one. Not even the old lady knows about is job. You're the old man's favorite and he requested you do this job clean and quick. No huge mess."

Picking up the envelope I held it in both of my hands, "I can't."

"You can, because you have to." Dani shrugged, "Voltaire doesn't negotiate, even inside their own walls." She pointed at the envelope, "It's a one day job, up in Manhattan. A British trillionaire oil magnate has started to lose his mind and is going rogue, selling off his international oil fields to terrorist groups in the middle east with one hand and using the profits to fund North Korea's burgeoning new nuclear weapon program. He's truly misbehaving and the old man wants him put to bed. Stop the funneling of millions to groups who could shatter the free world with a sneeze."

I closed my eyes, crumpling up the edges of the envelope, "I'm on vacation, and Alex."

Dani slid off the workbench, moving to stand in front of me, her hands settling on my upper arms, "Victoria, I know. Trust me I know. I know what it's like to feel like a normal human enjoying a Sunday funday, then have the boogey man knock on my door and shove the ugly reality in." Dani waited until I looked in her eyes, "I was able to get the old man to give you four times the usual since you are on vacation."

I shook my head, my stomach beginning to turn. "It's not just that Dani." I met her eyes again, "I want to stop doing this shit. I want the life I never got a chance to have." I paused, weighing the words before I spoke them, knowing when I did, it would set things in motion. I sucked in a breath, "I want out."

Dani's eyes flickered a second, she let me go of my arms and stepped back, "Do you really want out?" Her voice was soft, genuine.

"Yes." I dropped the envelope on the workbench, looking over to the door that led into the house, "I can't do this double life, not with Alex. Anyone else yes, I could and did do it, but not her. She deserves a life that isn't partially in the shadows, and a girlfriend who hides in those same shadows killing and disposing of bodies in the name of God and country."

Dani began to chew on her bottom lip, "You know what will happen if they hear of this?"

"I do." I gripped on the edge of the stone edge of the workbench, "But I also remember a conversation we had while I was in Uganda. The night I got caught dismembering that drug chieftain and ended up killing seven Ugandan rebels, the same night I had to get fifteen stitches to close up the split on the back of my head from the butt of a AK-47."

Dani held up her hand to stop me, "I do, Victoria, I remember that night and every goddamn night of every goddamn job you've gone on. The good ones, the bad ones, the bloody ones, all of them." She peered up at me, her green eyes searching mine as silence dropped in the garage.

After a few minutes, she let out a slow breath, "Can you give me a few months? I am so close Victoria, so fucking close." She turned to the garage door, her mind clearly working a thousand miles an hour like it always did when she was hatching a plan, "I will need a few months to get you out. To create the perfect exit strategy that will keep you alive and nurse blue eyes out of the hands of Voltaire." She gave me a sideways look, "You think you can wait a few months?"

I gripped on the edge of the workbench harder, feeling the stone dig into my palms and sting, "I think I have to." I let out a shaky breath, "Please, Dani, I mean it this time. I can't keep living these fucked up lives the Colonel handed us. I hate to sound cliché, but I have found the light at the end of the tunnel and she has brown hair, blue eyes and a heart that I don't dare break." I felt my eyes well up at the simple thought of ever breaking Alex's heart.

Dani huffed, "You are a walking cliché, Professor, but I'm also a closet romantic." She turned to face me, dropping her arms down, her hands smoothing out her uniform shirt, "I'll make it happen. But we have to keep this to ourselves, not let them see anything but happy happy Voltaire employees at our early evaluation. The old man is a genius at reading body language, he will notice something is up if we don't drink the Kool-Aid and stick to it."

I nodded, pushing away from the workbench, "I know." I picked up the envelope and shoved it in the bag with the new laptop, zipping it closed. "You can tell him that I'll take this job. I'll tell Alex I have to fly out to Rhode Island again to assist in the OCS intake process." I lifted the laptop and tucked it under my arm, looking dead at a pair of green eyes, I spoke, "Promise me..."

"Don't. We don't make promises, Victoria. Last time we did." Dani shrugged, "We ended up here." She half saluted me, walking to the side door, pausing as she pulled it open, "For what it's worth, I can tell in the way you two look at each other that she, this love, is worth the risk of bailing on Voltaire." She smiled tightly, "Just try to be patient and I will get you out."

I said nothing in return, leaving Dani to close the garage door behind her.

When she was gone and I could hear her car drive off in the distance, I continued to stand in the middle of the cold, dark garage. Holding onto the laptop with one hand and looking at the door that would take me back to Alex and the new life I wanted, I could feel my being start to split. The small cracks that formed the day Alex stood in my office, shoving my two lives apart, were growing. Splitting into massive cracks that in time, I feared I'd shatter under if I didn't get out of Voltaire.

I took a few more minutes to settle down and regain my composure, I didn't want Alex to notice that I was upset or was about to lie to her. I wanted to walk in to the house, dump the laptop in my desk drawer and forget about it for a few more hours.

Chapter 15

The cold spot on the bed had my eyes peeling open against my will. The bed, and the room, was very empty. The sparse moonlight was my only companion, and it made me frown. I rubbed away the sleep, staring at the clock blinking three fifteen at me.

I sighed, dropping my head back on to the pillow. It was clear Victoria had been gone for longer than a trip to the bathroom, or to grab a late night snack. The coolness of her side of the bed and pillow told me such. Rolling to sit up, I grabbed my shorts from the chair and wrapped up in the afghan lying next to it, and went to find Victoria.

She'd acted strange for the rest of the night as we watched television and ate popcorn. Then she was a bit distant when I tried to get her naked and into bed, settling for an intense make out session that led us to nowhere but breathless, snuggling on top of the covers. I was starting to think that taking her to my parents' house had been too much, and now Victoria was digesting the day, trying to process the ubiquitous parental questioning she endured.

Tucking my arms under the afghan, I had wanted to ask Victoria what was wrong the moment she curled up in my arms in bed, murmuring out a thank you for the day, and telling me how tired she was. I decided when I found her, I would ask her what was wrong and hope she would talk to me.

Shuffling down the stairs, I saw the desk light on in the den, casting a soft yellow glow out into the kitchen. Walking into the kitchen, I saw a bottle of bourbon sitting next to the coffee maker with a glass that had a splash of the dark amber liquor lingering in the bottom. I frowned, moving to the edge of the doorway leading into Victoria's den and peeked around the corner.

Victoria was sitting at her desk, leaning over a thin, sleek looking black laptop, touching the screen and moving images around. I could see the edge of her jaw clench and release as she quickly typed in a chat window. Squinting in the ambient light, I was able to make out what appeared to be a driver's license photograph of an older man I vaguely recognized as the one oil baron who was everywhere in the news lately, defending the rising oil prices.

Before I could confirm it was him, I saw a unique logo with a lion and a unicorn cradling a crown, with their respective hoofs, and the words secret intelligence service underneath it followed by a bright blocky classified stamp at the top of a memo.

I bent my head down at the floor, knowing that I should just turn around and go back upstairs to bed, or at least take a few steps back and loudly call for Victoria. Give her the opportunity to prepare for my sudden appearance in her den in the middle of the night.

But I didn't. I returned to the laptop screen, not moving so I wouldn't disturb Victoria and risk getting caught snooping like I was. I couldn't see much from where I stood, only catching the bold lettering of a few words. Words like termination, national security, and classified, operative code named Chimera assigned, and SIS eyes only, fluttered across the screen Making me swallow hard as my gut chirped at me to pay attention to everything I'd been ignoring.

I was entranced by the veritable spy novel buffet in front of me, squinting as hard as I could to read more when Victoria shifted in her seat, looking over her shoulder for a second. Her face was quickly illuminated by the desk lamp light, casting hard shadows across her face, giving her sharp angles that gave the woman a frightening appearance. This image before me, echoed the same images she showed me of her covered in blood the day she was rescued.

I gasped at the sight, covering my mouth and escaping back into the shadows of the kitchen before she spotted me standing in the doorway. I waited a second, holding my breath, pressing my hand harder against my mouth, listening for Victoria.

I let out my breath when I heard the quick rapid clicking of the keyboard, signaling that Victoria had not seen me. Dropping my hand away from my mouth, I rushed back upstairs and sat on the edge of the bed. My heart beating furiously at the look in her eyes. The distant, dead look in her eyes. A look that I'd seen a thousand times as a nurse, but never shook down to the depths of my heart like hers just did.

My body shivered from the chill in the room, the chill running down my spine and down to my fingertips. I tucked my limbs and chin deeper into the afghan, sitting on the bed. I debated if I should try and go back to sleep, if I should wait for Victoria to come back to bed, or go to her and ask her why she was up so late.

As I moved to return downstairs, opting to go confront her, the bedroom door opened, Victoria walked in, smiling when she saw me, "Hey, did I wake you up?" She closed the door behind her, reaching for my hand.

I snaked it from under the afghan, sighing when I felt her warm hand in mine and how perfect it always felt, helping to chase away the shivers. "I woke up to go to the bathroom and you were missing. I've been debating for the last five minutes whether or not to go back to bed or eat the rest of mom's meatloaf." I smiled, looking up in her eyes and saw no trace of what I had in the den. The darkness in her eyes that frightened me.

Victoria sat next to me, "I ate the rest of it with the bourbon." She frowned playfully, "I couldn't sleep and the bourbon wasn't working so I started working on boring myself to sleep with some of the intake forms for my trip. I got hungry and made a meatloaf sandwich." She kissed the side of my head. "Sorry, I'll make it up to you at breakfast."

I leaned against her, shutting my eyes as the sting of her white lie hit. "You better be making waffles to make up for it."

Victoria laughed, standing up, my hand still in hers, "For you, anything." She motioned to the empty bed with the blankets tossed around, "Let's get some sleep, I'm already dreading spending a night away from you."

I swallowed hard, my heart fluttering in my chest at her words, her touch, and how Victoria in general made my heart so full and happy. Overcoming the sick feeling my gut was stirring up from the white lie and what I saw on her laptop. I dropped her hand, crawling to my side of the bed and throwing the afghan to the edge of the bed as I settled against a pillow, waiting for her to get in. As she slid into the bed, Victoria immediately reached for me, lying her head on my chest and pulling the blankets over us, "I'm sorry about tonight."

I glanced down at her, giving her a confused look, "Sorry for what?"

"For disappearing on you after my secretary stopped by." Victoria looked up at me, "I couldn't help it. My job has always been the one constant in my life for a very long time. I sometimes let it control my mood." She ran her hand over my stomach, "That's why I am apologizing, Alex, I want you to know that it isn't your fault when I become the grumpy gus."

I shrugged, choosing to use humor to ease the tension. "If I had a shitty secretary like yours, I would probably be grumpy every day." I brushed some hair from her face, "How did you know I noticed you were disappearing after your secretary left?" My gut wanted me to ask her about Dani and the things I saw on the laptop, but I lacked the courage. I was so stupidly in love that I was afraid to upset the balance Victoria and I had finally found.

Victoria smiled, squeezing my side, "You eat excessively when you're nervous. You devoured the entire bowl of popcorn before I had two handfuls. You also stare at me biting your lip in that way you want to ask me something, but don't know how to." She kissed the corner of my mouth, "After this vacation I'm going to work on next semester being my last at the academy."

I shot Victoria a look, "Really?" I was shocked and confused, "You love teaching and the Navy, why would want to leave?"

Victoria laid her head back on my chest, "Because I have finally found a reason to live freely, a reason to want to."

Before I could say anything, I felt her press her body deeper into mine while I blinked back tears. I was speechless at her confession, vague as it was, I knew I was the reason she was about to give up the one thing I was sure she loved more than me. I looked down at the woman, her eyes now closed and sleeping, I let out a slow breath.

My gut still twisted into knots, wanting me to explore the secrets Victoria kept. While my heart begged me to get Victoria to finally tell me that she loved me instead of tip toeing around it with grand comments that swept me off my feet.

"You can stay here, I don't mind." I looked at Alex sitting in the chair next to the bed, holding a cup of coffee wearing my sweatshirt. I'd just come upstairs from loading my bags into the back of the BMW in preparation of leaving for New York in a handful of minutes. The day had gone by faster than expected and now I was milling around the room, dreading having to say goodbye and return to my work.

Alex smiled over the rim of the coffee cup, "I would feel weird being here without you."

"Why?" I leaned against the dresser, "I've hidden most of my porn and with one phone call, I can have the nicest and snoopiest neighbor's at my house in three seconds." I cocked an eyebrow, "Dale and Mary do a have a key."

Alex giggled, setting the cup down to reach for me, "I have my own porn." She took my hand, dragging me over to sit on the edge of the chair. "I feel weird being here without you. Like I might spill something on the couch, fall asleep with all the lights on, or that a stray spider may encourage a drastic reaction from me." She looked at me with a soft smile. "I can live without being around you for a day. I have a fully stocked fridge and pantry that will allow me to eat away my emotions from missing you."

I laughed, bending down to kiss her, "Fine, but if you change your mind, there's a spare key in the light over the front door." Turning away from her, I caught the clock telling me that I needed to leave in five minutes to get to the private airport and meet up with the clean-up crew. Groaning, I stood up reluctantly, "I need to get going. My flight leaves in three hours."

Alex frowned, holding tightly onto my hand until releasing it to stand up with me. "When will you back?"

"Late Tuesday night if the flights are on time, latest, Wednesday morning by the time you wake up." I dropped her hand, picking up my briefcase. "And I'm hoping that when I come home, there will be a warm, sleepy brunette hogging the entire width of that bed."

Alex moved into my personal space, wrapping her arms around my waist, "Are you suggesting something?"

I nodded, glancing at the bed, "I might be, and if this brunette is in that bed when I come home, I will make it worth her time." I smirked, bending forward and brushing my lips over hers. Feeling Alex shiver and gasp before I kissed her hard. Breaking away from her, I latched onto her arm to take her downstairs before I made myself late for the flight.

Shutting the back hatch of the BMW, I turned to Alex leaning against the driver's door of her mini. "I'll call you when I land and text you throughout the day when I can." I rolled my eyes, "You know the usual."

Alex smiled, "You better." She pushed off from the car, "Why does this feel weird? You've gone on a million trips and it felt like nothing."

I shrugged, "I blame the bubble."

"The bubble?" Alex gave me a look.

"Yes, the bubble. The bubble we created where it's nothing but you and I." I smirked, "Without clothing." I reached out, running my hands down her arms, "It's weird because after wasting a year, I think neither of us want to waste any more time." I felt my face fall, "Alex, when I get home, I want us to talk about the future." I peered at the blue eyes that were driving me to change ten years of stoic routine.

Alex bit her bottom lip, "The future." Her cheeks were flushed, "Yes, let's talk about the future." She bent her head down when the grin finally took over, shoving me playfully, "You better go before I trap you in the bubble and call your secretary to tell her you have the bubonic plague."

I laughed, opening my arms to welcome one of her rib crushing hugs. "Bring it in Ivers."

Alex fell into my open arms, squeezing me until I grunted softly, leaning back after a moment, she kissed me softly. Murmuring against my lips, "Be safe and come home soon, Victoria. I love you."

I fought the clench in my jaw, kissing her back and whispering, "I will." before untangling from her arms and walking to the driver's side. I didn't want to look at Alex's face. I knew she was waiting for the moment when I finally returned those three little words to her, and I knew that time had to come soon.

I just needed to get the exit plan with Dani started before I could tell Alex I loved her without feeling like it was a fruitless lie.

I backed the BMW out of the driveway, waving at Alex as she climbed into her mini, going to the right as I went to the left. A strange metaphor of how our lives connected in the middle but still divided at the ends.

I distracted my heavy thoughts and heart by calling Dani to tell her I was on my way.

I couldn't sleep as night fell when I was finally back in my apartment. Being alone in my apartment made it feel cold and empty. My bed felt too big, and no matter how many times I rolled over, hoping to collide into a warm body, I just found the cold corners of the bed. Victoria had called and texted as she promised, but it did little to fill the void curating in my heart and body.

Finally, around three in the morning I gave in. I turned on the television and surfing through late night infomercials and reruns, flipping around channels without a purpose. When that did nothing to put me to sleep, I picked up my laptop to play one of the annoying computer games Stacy had downloaded after my incident. A year later, I figured it was good time to check on my simulated family and hope they were still alive.

After confirming that the simulated family was still alive and that I lacked any of the patience needed to take care of them, I closed out of the game and went back online, reading the news. Five minutes into an article about the upcoming elections and which candidates where best for me, I leaned against the headboard and closed my eyes. Willing my body to go to sleep and stay asleep.

Instead, my mind started back up. Thinking about the laundry I still had to do, that I should clean out the fridge, or maybe I should just go back to Victoria's house where the fridge was clean and didn't smell like old plastic Tupperware and baking soda. That's when my mind drifted to the things I'd seen on her laptop late last night. The strange terms and images that looked like they belonged in a James Bond movie and not on my girlfriend's computer.

Hesitating for a few minutes, I folded to my gut and my curiosity and started searching the terms and images I could remember.

The search results were fruitless, leading me to Greek mythology sites and spy novel suggestions. All of it easing my suspicions until I typed in SIS along with the lion, crown, unicorn image I saw on Victoria's laptop.

Those two brought up the homepage for the British intelligence service, particularly MI6. I paused, staring at the fridge from my bed, maybe Victoria was a secret James Bond fan, or she was writing a spy novel in her very spare time. Then I remembered the picture of that old oil baron who flashed on the screen. I searched for all the British oil companies and was able to find the man after clicking through three different websites.

Bertram Spencer was the richest oil baron in the world, turning his company from one oil well in a desert to an endless empire that fed most of the world's petrol needs. Clicking on his name, the laptop screen became littered with news reports from every media outlet. All of them discussing how Bertram was suspected of gouging his buyers and using the profits to finance terrorism.

I scrolled, reading article after article about Bertram. His eccentric ways and outspoken thoughts on how the world fared better when the eastern block was under full communistic control. The United States had him barred from entering the country due to his suspect collaboration with America's enemies, and now his own country was seeking out charges for plotting and treason. In particular, MI6.

I looked away from the screen, this wasn't a spy novel or a spy movie, this was real life. There was something more to why this man and the strange key phrases lit up Victoria's screen last night. Leaving me with the sinking feeling that it all went far beyond anything simple.

I woke up a few hours after shutting off my laptop and laying down in the dark. My mind in hyper drive as it went through the possible reasons why Victoria would have sensitive information on her computer. She was a retired intelligence officer, she worked for the Navy in some capacity, and maybe she was helping them out. Maybe she was writing a lesson plan for next semester around current events that would become military history.

Maybe I was crazy and reading far more into everything than was necessary.

When I woke up in the morning, grumbling at how tired I was, I went about taking care of the laundry and ignoring cleaning the fridge. I'd decided that I would meet Stacy for lunch after I picked up Victoria's mail, then head back to her house for the night. Make dinner and maybe hang out with her neighbors.

Victoria had sent me a few texts, a good morning one and a few about how boring the meetings were and that she was still on schedule for being home on the last late flight out of Rhode Island. I smiled, sighing like a lovesick idiot whenever I read her texts. Feeling the stupid swirl of butterflies in my stomach when I thought about seeing her again and sleeping next to her. I sent back a few texts and headed out the door, calling Stacey and asking her to meet me in a couple of hours.

When I pulled the old mini into Victoria's driveway, waving at Dale sweeping his driveway, I opened the car door to find a black sedan pulling up behind me. The familiar redhead dressed in the same uniform from the other day, hopped out of the car a second later, dragging a tailor's suit bag with her.

Dani smiled at me, "Hi Alex, how are you?"

I smiled politely, "Good. Victoria's not here, she's up in Rhode Island." I shifted my bag on my shoulder, the weird feelings coming back from the last time I saw Dani and from last night when I was doing my late night searches. I was also a bit suspicious as to why Dani was at the house when she would know better than anyone else where Victoria was.

Dani nodded, "Oh I know, she is knee deep in OCS candidate intake forms." She motioned to the suit bag in her hand, "I wanted to drop off her dress uniform for Saturday's event, we use the same tailor and she asked me to drop hers off when I picked up mine." She continued to smile, noticing the wary look I was giving her, "The spare key is above the front door light, the neighbors and I trade off on keeping an eye on Casa De Commander since she moved in five years ago."

I frowned lightly, "Okay." I was starting to really not like, or trust, the redhead. "I guess I'll grab the mail while you unlock the door?"

Dani winked at me. "Sounds like a plan." She took a few steps past me, looking over her shoulder. "I'll make a pot of coffee. I can see you have a few questions for me, Alex."

I stared back at the redhead, watching her reach up and grab the spare key like it was something she did every day. I glanced over at Dale, still sweeping his driveway like it was nothing. At least that gave me some comfort. If Dani wasn't a trusted visitor, Dale and Mary would be glaring over the fence waiting for me to give them the signal to either attack, or call the police.

Grabbing the mail, I walked into the house, spotting Dani in the kitchen fiddling with the coffee maker. I set the mail down on the island, "How exactly do you know Victoria?" This woman had my defenses up. My instincts were in over drive and my gut sat up on my shoulder. Leering at the redhead in her perfectly pressed khaki Navy uniform that had just as many ribbons over her chest as Victoria did when she wore hers.

Dani didn't look at me, focusing her energy on making coffee. "She calls me her shitty, inept secretary, but in reality it's an exaggeration of the truth."

She turned to face me, leaning against the counter top, smiling my way. "I'm more of an administrative assistant, a term that allows me to come and go in the halls of the Academy without too much guff from the eager Ensigns who actually are secretaries."

I frowned, folding my arms across my chest. "You're in all of the pictures with Victoria from the news after she was rescued, and from when you met the president, and all those other medal ceremonies she had to go to. You're even in the pictures Victoria showed me when she told me what happened." I stumbled over the last bit. I wasn't sure how much Dani knew and if she was to be trusted in the slightest.

Dani sucked in a breath through her nose, nodding slowly. "You are a smart one, nurse, smarter than I think a lot of people give you credit for." She held up her hand to stop me when I threw a dirty look her way. "It's not an insult, it's a compliment, and to answer your questions, yes, I am in those pictures with Victoria, and yes I know Victoria on more than just a secretarial level."

I stared at the redhead, clenching my fists to prevent from hitting her or yelling at her. She was pissing me off with her flippant tone.

Dani moved closer to the island, "I know Victoria told you everything that happened in the war. I know she showed you the file, the same file I have seen a thousand times before, scrubbing over it trying to figure out what I could've done to find her a day, or two, sooner."

Dani's snarky smile faded away, her green eyes clouding over like Victoria's often did. "I know Victoria because I'm the intelligence officer who found her in that mud hut of hell. I was the first person to find her and draw her out of her confused state." The redhead paused. "She also saved my life."

My hands relaxed and I moved to sit on the stool in front of the island, feeling a bit shitty for wanting to hit her. I should have known that Dani was an integral part in Victoria's rescue. "I thought Victoria was alone when the rescue team found her?"

Dani shrugged, "We all thought that, but one of the hostage takers had squirreled away and snuck up behind me. I was sixty seconds away from being another casualty of that hole, when Victoria eliminated him." Dani carefully pronounced the one word. Her distaste in the word was evident. "So, I saved her and she saved me. We were both heralded as American heroes, but neither of us felt like it. We both carry some sort of regret or guilt that we didn't do as much as we could have that day, or in the days following up to that one day. I owe her my life and I have a lot of mistakes I need to amend for."

Dani's face fell as her eyes completely clouded over, looking past me, lost in terrible memories. The way she spoke in very little detail and got right to the point, suggested that Dani was only willing to tell me the key points of her and Victoria's relationship. Suggesting that if I poked any deeper, I would be shut out. I had learned over the years, that most war veterans only spoke about the war when they felt comfortable.

They would only speak of the details if their guard was completely down and trusted you. Victoria had been like that from the first day we met until a week ago when she let all the walls down. Dani was the same type of woman and veteran who would only give me the large chunks I needed to know, nothing more, at least until I had earned all of her trust. It was something I would have to respect, and would, like I had with Victoria.

I glanced at the granite counter top, "Dani, you don't have to tell me, if it's difficult to talk about." I suddenly felt terrible this woman was reopening old wounds to put me at ease. "I just can tell the difference between a real secretary and a pretend one." I looked up into her green eyes, "You and Victoria have a connection that goes beyond that." My irritation edged away, thinking back on the file I read and the pictures in it. The horror show it all was, imagining that Dani's memories were probably a thousand times more vivid and harder to shake away.

Dani laughed, "Do we? I'm pretty sure we have a connection that makes us want to slap each other any chance we get. It's like a step sibling love hate relationship, but I do what I can for her." She waved to the suit bag hanging by the laundry room, "Like picking up her dry cleaning, gathering her mail, and watering her fake plants when she's out recruiting fresh faces to fill the boats of the Navy."

I smiled, shaking my head, "I suspect that you can't tell me the true nature of your business relationship, you both being intelligence officers, retired and not retired."

Dani made a face, "Some of it no, I can't tell you." She gave me a smirk, "Because if I did, I would have to kill you and yadda yadda. Keep the government secrets, secret, and protect the homeland clauses."

Dani waited a second, "What I can tell you is this, Victoria saved my ass more times than I count. After her incident, we worked together in the intelligence unit back in the states, sitting and reading over boring information trying to put together the puzzle with the tiniest pieces. She eventually called it quits and retired to become an even more boring Professor. I stayed on, hoping to at least make a higher rank to retire off of."

Dani smiled gently, "Even though she is retired and I'm far from it, she is still one of the most brilliant intelligence officers the Navy has ever seen. I sometimes call upon her to help me sift through intel and read between the lines when I am missing things. Connect the dots I may have missed."

I let out a slow breath, nodding, "The other night makes sense now." I glanced back up at the redhead, her green eyes returning to bright intense ones, "I guess I'm still learning about Victoria."

Dani winked at me, grabbing the coffee pot from the maker and filling up a metal travel mug she removed from a cabinet, "Aren't we all, Alex? The good Professor is an enigma that still surprises me after working with her for almost ten years."

Screwing the top on the metal mug, Dani leaned back over the island, "I can tell you one thing, that Professor really likes you and you have nothing to worry about, Alex. Ever." Dani moved around the island, heading back towards the front door, "When you talk to Victoria later, tell her that I was able to get all new medals for her dress uniform and that it should fit her like a glove."

She reached for the door knob, "And Alex, don't tell Victoria we had this air clearing conversation. She would hate to think that the Navy might be getting in the way of her relationship with you."

I slid off the stool and followed the redhead to the front door, "Dani, I appreciate you talking to me. I knew I was being a little crazy about a few things, my mind running rampant thinking Victoria was a spy or hired killer." I smiled, chuckling, "I couldn't see her hurting a fly let alone another human."

Dani stepped out onto the porch, turning to face me as she pushed sunglasses on her face, "No, no, the good Professor only does her damage with red pens on terrible essays." She raised the thermos, "I'll bring this back eventually, enjoy the rest of your day Alex. Tell Victoria I said hello."

I smiled, "I will." I glanced out into the front yard, "Maybe I'll ask her to share her stock investing tips in Voltaire Lingerie with you. Help speed up your retirement a bit."

Dani paused, turning back to me, "What was that?"

"Victoria's investments, she's a stock holder in that fancy underwear company, Voltaire? Has been since around the time she retired. She gets these fancy blue envelopes with checks in them every other week or so." I waved at the house, "It afforded her this house and clearly her early retirement."

Dani's face pulled up into a forced smile, "Hmm, Voltaire Lingerie. I will definitely have to inquire about that." She held up her hand, "I should look into retiring early. I get a little jealous when the professor talks about boring summers spent doing nothing." The redhead smiled and waved, "Thanks again Alex and please try not to tell Victoria we had a heart to heart."

"I promise." I folded my arms, leaning against the white pillar at the edge of the front porch, "Dani, um, thank you for saving Victoria's life." I blushed, unsure why I was compelled to say it to her. "Being there for her." I cleared my throat, my mind wandering to the what if's.

"I should thank you, Alex." Dani looked over the top of her sunglasses, "You've brought back the beautiful human that has been trapped in the Professor for as long as I have known her. Not that I'm interested in her romantically, it's just good to see my friend, my best friend, smile and mean it." She paused, swallowing thickly, pushing up her sunglasses to cover her glassy eyes.

Dani turned after throwing a quick wave goodbye to me, and walked off the porch to her car, driving off with another short wave to Dale and I. Leaving me in alone Victoria's house and feeling a thousand times lighter as I moved back to the kitchen to get started on dinner for my girlfriends return.

Chapter 16

Manhattan always left me with a strange taste in my mouth. It wasn't that I disliked the city. I liked it just the same as the others I had been in across the world. But Manhattan, it pushed my all of my buttons. Too many people, too many cars, and too many buildings stacked on top of each other.

Maybe I hated it because it was a city where I had killed the most and the most often. The only reason why I would ever be here, was to do that exact thing. It certainly wasn't to see the sights.

Standing in the middle of the massive open living room, surrounded by tinted windows, I started to prepare for the job I was sent here to do. Eliminate a puffy, rich old man who had pissed someone off in one of the controlling governments with his ideals of turning back the clock and allowing the heathens to run the modern world.

I was waiting for Dani to call and get the job started, wanting to get it over with so I could go home and forget for a few more weeks who I was. I had spoken to Alex an hour ago, sharing a short phone call with a couple of texts after. Nothing earth shattering, but it still made me despise this job and the lies that came with it.

Walking from the windows, I headed to the bedroom where I had laid out the all black clothing I called my uniform, to get dressed and ready for my mark. I had reviewed the case file of Bertram Spencer a hundred times, memorizing his face, his apartment layout, and his very strict routine within that apartment. If it was up to me, I would have already done the job the moment I landed in the city and been on the verge of pulling back into my driveway in Annapolis.

But, Dani didn't operate that way. Voltaire didn't operate that way and I was stuck stewing in my own thoughts and building anger of wanting to be out of this life. I wanted out of Voltaire so badly, that I was willing to walk away, burn myself, and deal with the consequences as they came.

Breathing through my nose to settle the angry nerves and my head, I pulled the black running tights on along with the thin long sleeve running top, and went for my phone just as Dani's ringtone filled the living room.

I answered the phone while setting the earpiece into my ear. "Can we get this started? It's already close to seven and I want to be home by at least midnight."

"Good evening to you too, and yes, we can get started. Hence, why I'm calling you. It's certainly not to talk about your muffin recipe, and how you get them so moist." Dani had an extra bite to her as she continued on, "Okay, I have the full green light to go ahead with Bert."

I rolled my eyes, walking back in to the bedroom for the duffel bag, "Where do I have to go, and what are my options?"

"Your only option, selected by our bosses, is strangulation by garrote. It's a known method of the militant group he's been dirty dealing with. The clean-up crew has given you a nice selection in your lovely overnight bag." Dani paused, the ever present sound of her keyboard clicking away in the background, "As for where you are to go, that's the easy part. Bert is in the apartment right below you. Seems Voltaire and Bertram have similar tastes in real estate."

I blew out a hard breath, sitting on the edge of the bed to dig around in the duffel bag, "Why didn't you tell me that in the initial briefing?" I didn't like shitting so close to where I ate.

"Because I didn't know until three minutes before I hit Professor asshat on my contact list." She snapped at me, "Let's focus and have the pissing match after." She huffed, the clicks becoming harder as she punched the keyboard. "In the back pantry of the kitchen. There is a dumb waiter, a modern dumb waiter. You are to take that down to the floor below you and sneak out into Bert's pantry. He should be in the main dining room facing the eastern most set of windows, sipping on a million dollar glass of wine and ruminating about world domination."

"Dani, can we keep the color commentary to a minimum?" I was getting irritated by her off handed way, something was wrong and it was clear in the way Dani was being snarky.

"You can, but I won't. I've had an interesting day, an interesting day that I will be happy to tell you about when we are done and I've sent the cleanup crew in." Dani sent a text to the phone in my hand, "I just sent you the schematics of his apartment, its set up exactly like the one you are in, so it shouldn't be too hard to move around. You have an hour to get in, dispose of petrol pants and then escape. I'll be sitting on your shoulder like always, fudging the security system and watching your back."

I scrolled through the schematics, memorizing the layout in an instant, "I'll be done in twenty minutes, can you have a flight waiting for me?"

"I can, but I think it's high time you meet me at the bar and we have that birthday drink you promised me."

I froze hearing Dani's words, another code phrase we had not used since our early days of working together at Voltaire, and I would actually have to meet face to face with Dani for briefing and de-briefing. If she was slinging out code phrases, it could mean many things. Many of them not good things. "Of course, I forgot." I stood up, dropping the phone on the bed, switching on the blue tooth. I didn't need the phone with me if I was going one floor below, the signal would be strong enough. "I'm going to the pantry now."

"Roger that. Bert is currently walking out of his wine cellar, you are good to go." Dani's tone shifted down a notch, "Be careful Victoria."

I nodded to the empty room and hit mute on the ear piece as I moved towards the kitchen.

The dumbwaiter was larger than I thought. I could fit in it comfortably, and thankfully, it was on a hydraulic system that moved silently with the push of a button. Sliding open the steel door, I was struck by loud forties music pouring out of the living room and into the kitchen as if I was standing next to the radio. I winced at how loud the music was, even though it was an added bonus for covering my movements through the apartment.

"He's on the couch facing the east windows. Smoking a cigar while he waits for the vintage red to breathe." Dani's voice cut through the heavy horns and piano of the music. I nodded, knowing she could see me and climbed out of the dumb waiter. I walked normally, but quickly, through the kitchen and out into the living room. I didn't want to waste time with stealth, nor did I want to spend any more time than I had to on this job.

Unwinding the steel garrote in my right hand, I took up the slack with my left, raising the wire up to rest level with Bertram's neck. Without a second blink, I dropped the garrote, yanking hard on the wire around his neck. Twisting as hard as I could at the base of his neck.

I caught him by surprise, but it didn't give me the upper hand. He stood straight up, fingers slapping around at his neck, trying to grab at the steel wire cutting in to his fat flesh.

I tried to drop my weight down, using the edge of the couch as a bracing point to drag Bertram down to his death quicker. But he fought back and he was far larger in person versus the description and measurements included in his case file.

He suddenly lifted his body forward, flinging me with him. I tumbled over the back of the couch, losing some of my grip on the garrote, giving Bertram a gasp of air and a boost of adrenaline. The quick gasp of air allowed him to drag me over the couch as he rushed forward to a window.

Bertram was in a full blown panic, clawing at his neck as I stepped on the couch cushions tightening the garrote, trying to get a better grip and pull him back into my control. He was gurgling, gasping, wheezing and running towards the wall where a fireplace stood. I clenched my jaw, finding my footing again and finding the leverage to yank Bertram back, but I was two seconds too slow.

Bertram turned quickly, throwing him and I into the sold brick wall that edged the fireplace. I cringed, feeling my ribs crack from the force of impact.

I hissed, my anger rising. This was taking too long and it irritated me. I wrapped my legs around his waist, locking my ankles together I squeezed both my legs and the garrote. The gargling man continued to slam his body against the brick wall even as I squeezed the life out of him.

I continued twisting, finally getting the man to fall to his knees in a desperate attempt to get a breath of air or crawl away from me, thinking I would just let go when he fell to his knees.

As the flats of my feet found solid ground, I stood up quickly, yanking up with the garrote with all of my strength. Hearing the gurgle scream one makes as the last breath of life is leaving them, I looked down to see Bertram go completely limp, his hands dropping like wet noodles as a thin line of blood droplets fell to the floor.

"Fucking hell." I released one side of garrote, kicking Bertram to the floor and away from me. I winced when I lifted my arm on the side Bertram slammed against the wall. The ribs were definitely fractured, if not broken.

I tapped the mute button on the earpiece. "Dani...."

"You don't have to say it, I saw everything. The clean-up crew is on their way up now. You're free to head back upstairs." Her tone was serious, shaken, but serious.

I winced when I turned to head back into the kitchen to the dumbwaiter, "Tell them to scrub it for everything, it's bad enough I already have one lie I need to make up." I held on to my side, trying not to yelp from the immense pain from folding myself back up into a steel square box.

Closing the dumbwaiter door, Dani popped back into my ear. "Clean up in the apartment. Burn everything, shower and then leave normally. I'll meet you at the White Horse for that drink."

I closed my eyes, trying to fight the pain and the hindering feeling that this drink had no good news behind it. "I understand Dani."

"Good. Meet me in the back room and I'll take a look at your ribs." Dani took a breath as if she was about to say one more thing, but didn't. She ended the connection and left me in a nervous silence. A type of silence I hadn't experienced from her since we both sat next to each on a transport plane back to the states.

Thirty minutes later I was gingerly pushing through a pre-dinner drinks crowd. Laughing and smiling with large beers and cocktails that were making my mouth water at the sight. I needed something to take the edge off of the pain in my side and the rising anxiety of meeting Dani in public.

I found Dani sitting in a booth in the far back, dressed down in a plain t-shirt and blue pullover. Her red hair was out of the traditional high and tight bun, gathered up into a loose ponytail. She looked up when I sat down, holding on to angry ribs. "I ordered you a shot and a beer, Victoria."

I rolled my eyes. "Thanks."

She scooted closer to me, pointing at the oversized shirt I found to wear over the bandage I wrapped around the growing bruise. "How are you feeling?"

"Like I was slammed into a wall by an oversized asshole." I leaned back in the booth, blowing out a slow breath. It hurt to sit, to breathe, to move, to basically do anything. I swallowed down a wince of pain. "Why am I here?"

Dani smiled at me and the cute bar girl who brought two giant beers and two shots of whiskey, waiting until the girl disappeared back into the crowd before shoving the drinks my way, "You're here because I need to talk to you before you go home and return to the life you want."

Dani slammed the shot, sucking air in between her teeth from the harsh sting of the alcohol and reached for the giant beer, "Your girlfriend's laptop went hot like the fourth of July in a redneck's backyard. Internet searches for SIS, Chimera, Bert, and a few other key words that fell across my alerts in the middle of the night while I was sleeping and trying to dream of a boathouse in Vancouver."

I closed my eyes, blindly reaching for the shot and downing it just as fast, "And?" I had a strange sensation that there was someone watching me the other night while I was reviewing the case, but it was too dark and I felt paranoid for no reason. I was positive I had left Alex dead to the world in bed that night, and picked up on nothing when I went back upstairs. Obviously she had seen something that caused her to search those very unique words, one of them being my operative code name. Chimera.

Dani sighed, leaning back in the booth, "I went to go see her, at your house of course. Made up an excuse of dropping off your outfit for Saturday." She paused, drawing a finger down the condensation of the beer glass, "Your nurse is smart, smarter than I thought she would be." She peered up at me, smirking, "Not that you would ever date a bimbo or give up this glorious life for a dipshit, but I have to say it like this, Victoria, she might be too smart for her own good."

I scowled, moving the beer up to my lips, "Dani, get to the goddamn point. You and I never have drinks, so why am I having drinks with you."

Dani chuckled. "We used to have drinks, back in the day when we were just war heroes trying to find a life outside of sand and blood, but, yes, we never have drinks and my goddamn point is this."

She sat back up, resting her arms on the edge of the decrepit wood table with initials carved over every inch, "You need to be careful. You need to make sure Alex isn't sticking her nose in places that could get her throat cut. It's bad enough that you're going to have to lie about Bert's actions, which I apologize for. I had no idea he would become the incredible hulk at the last minute. He seemed puffy and slow in all of the recon."

Rubbing at my temples, I closed my eyes. "Dani, what did you tell Alex?"

"I know you're mad." She sighed, "I talked to her. She confronted me about our relationship and I told her the clean truth. That you had saved my life and I have been trying to repay you ever since and make up for the stupid mistake I made of getting you into Voltaire in the first place." Her eyes fell to the edge of the glass, "I should have known about the Colonel, I should have known he was full of shit."

I opened my eyes, shifting to rest on my uninjured side. "Dani, you gave me the choice, and I took the wrong one. You're not to blame for me getting locked into Voltaire and becoming this." I took another long sip of the beer. "Did Alex think you and I were sleeping together?" I had the sinking feeling that Alex would pick up on the strange closeness Dani and I shared.

Dani's eyebrow rose, "I think she might have thought that way, but I told her that as much as I love you, I couldn't stand to touch you with a ten-foot pole." She grinned at the dirty look I gave her, "I told her that I wasn't your inept secretary, but that you worked with me. I threw myself under the bus and revealed that I'm an intelligence officer and I often call upon your brilliance to help me look over cases or intel to find the pieces I would need to save the world."

Dani paused again, her grin fading, "Like I said, Alex is smart, she has a hunch about you that is dead on and I don't know how many more lies and covering make up is going to keep her away from finding the eventual truth."

I groaned, covering my face, feeling the tears build, "I hate lying to her. I know she is smart, I know she is picking up on my odd behavior and it's getting harder to lie when I am no longer interested in lying anymore." I bit my bottom lip, looking up at Dani, "Are you any closer to what we discussed?"

Dani shook her head, "I need a few more months. I was able to move some of your jobs around, claiming that it was time the other newer plumbers got a chance to spread the wealth. The old lady bought it. The old man, I don't know about him yet, he keeps talking about brining Dante on board to work with me. I can't get much of a read when he switches into work talk." Dani paused, sighing quietly, "When we have our yearly with the two, I can go from there."

I nodded slowly, draining the rest of the beer, "Can she be protected?"

Dani nodded quickly, "She can, and she will be. I have taken it upon myself to keep Alex off the radar. I've encrypted her phone and laptop, her activity there will just bounce around in cyberspace until it fades off. Her apartment was zapped a while ago and I keep tabs on her from afar whenever she isn't with you." She shrugged, "It's creepy stalkerish, but if Voltaire sees an innocent idiot, they'll leave her alone."

I swallowed hard, whispering, "Thank you Dani."

"No problem Professor, like I said, I owe you." Dani waved at the bar girl, asking for another beer and shot. "One more thing, stop talking about Voltaire with her."

I raised my head up, my eyes locking on Dani's. "What?" My heart pounded on its quick descent to my stomach.

Dani glared at me. "She told me I should talk to you about investing in Voltaire to help with my retirement goals. She said you're a stock holder, and that you told her about how it helped buy your house and set you up for a worry free future after you've hung up your books and lesson plans."

She held the intense stare. "Stop talking about it, stop hoarding the envelopes and don't bring it up again. I will find another way to get you the payments while the old lady is being a spaz and avoiding electronic transfers or deposits. If Alex asks again, tell her your broker sold off all the stocks and you've reinvested in a cable TV network, or something."

The intensity in Dani's tone told me I was getting too close to the invisible line Voltaire drew in the proverbial sand. Drawing attention to it through Alex, would put Alex and I in danger.

Dani and I sat, staring at each other as the girl brought the next round. Dani broke the silent stare after slamming the second shot, pointing at my ribs with the empty shot glass. "So, I was thinking that we tell her I hit you with the car door when I picked you up from the airport?"

I shook my head, sighing hard. "I don't think she will believe that, even if it was true." I spun the shot of whiskey, "I can tell her I tripped in the bulkhead and fell on the edge of a porthole." I cringed at the memory of the first time I had actually done that on the boat over to the desert. I cracked two of my ribs and couldn't breathe deeply for a week.

Dani chuckled. "I remember when you did that on the boat back to Germany. Lucky for you, I was there to catch you." She met my eyes, hearing the true sentiment in her final words. Dani had been there to catch me a handful of times and was doing it again by protecting the woman I loved while I sought out my freedom.

"Yes you have, Dani." I picked up the shot. "The next round is on me then I have to go home."

Dani smiled. "Are we actually going to have a drink like old times? Not a coded drink where I tell you secrets and lies?"

I half smiled. "I think it's time we both start looking for the reality we both want and need in all of our code talk." I motioned to her beer, "Non sibi sed patriae."

She grinned, shaking her head and raised the beer glass, "Non sibi sed patriae."

I took the shot and asked Dani about the farmhouse she was restoring in Maryland, letting go of the world her and I lived in for a minute. Try to reconnect as the friends we started out as so many years ago, before the Colonel and Voltaire tore apart our lives and rebuilt them as they saw fit.

Standing in the doorway to my bedroom, I stared at the lump in my bed, snoring lightly as she took up the full expanse of the queen sized bed. I had a lingering buzz from a few more rounds with Dani, relaxing me and edging back the pain from the bruised ribs the in-flight nurse diagnosed me with. I had no cracks or fractures, just a healthy bruise on both the muscle and ribs, which I was thankful for. It would be easier to explain away a bruise than a full set of cracked ribs to the nurse in front of me.

I had ended up on the very last flight back home, but was grateful to have the real moments with Dani and a chance to unwind with her rather than drag it back home. Back home where I would stand in front of the fireplace as my routine demanded and fall deeper into my head, sorting out the fact I had just killed again and felt little to nothing about it.

I continued to stare at Alex in the bed. Huddled up in blankets with the moonlight casting stripes of light over her and accentuating my favorite curves on her.

I loved her more than I thought and had told Dani around the fourth shot that I loved Alex so much, I would sacrifice my life for her if I had to. Dani commented that she could tell the minute I asked for her to find Alex the day after the metro station incident, that I was a goner. I tried to counter that it was the day Alex showed up at my office, but it was a moot point. I was in love with her and now had the overwhelming need to tell her as soon as I could.

Shoving away from the doorframe, I removed my jeans and threw them into the closet. I wanted to undress fully and sneak into the bed, but I didn't want to risk raising the arm on my bad side, nor did I want Alex to see the ugly black and purple bruise just yet.

I moved the blankets back and slipped into the bed as quietly as I could. I didn't want to disturb the sleeping brunette as she looked so adorable with messy hair and the flushed cheeks that came with sleeping hard.

Alex murmured, mashing her face deeper into the pillow. I smiled as I settled down into the fluffy pillow on my good side facing Alex, reaching up to brush the back of my hand over her cheek. The contact of my hand on her warm cheeks, popped Alex's eyes open a sliver. "Victoria..."

I grinned. "I see you found the spare key."

She tried to smile, but yawned half through it. "And your secret porn stash." She grabbed my hand, pulling it up to kiss the palm. "I made dinner, but you were late." Alex closed her eyes, her fingers finding their place in mine. I could tell she was still half asleep and nowhere near coherent enough to have a lengthy conversation at this late hour.

I stared at the woman, absorbing every little detail of her face the moonlight offered up. "I know." I leaned forward, kissing her forehead. "I missed you."

Alex smiled, mumbling. "Miss you." She let out a heavy breath, moving her body to rest against mine and promptly fell back asleep in my arms.

I held her tightly, whispering against her forehead. "I love you."

I woke up excited, vaguely having a very real dream about Victoria coming home and sneaking into the bed, smothering me in her arms as I slept like a rock. Then finding the bed empty chased all of the excitement away. I was alone and there was no sign of Victoria.

Rolling over, I checked my phone to find nothing new from her. I yawned and hit her contact button, rubbing the sleep from my eyes as it rang twice before she answered, "Good morning."

My heart fluttered at the sound of her voice, turning my frown into a sheepish grin, "Where are you? I have been waiting in this bed all night like you suggested and now I feel like a squatter."

"Do you now? I did give you a spare key, so technically you're a welcomed squatter." Victoria's voice sounded worn down, as if she had just woken up.

"Are you still in Rhode Island?" I tried not to sound desperate, but I missed her so much, and I was failing miserably at hiding it. I looked at her side of the bed, running my hand over her pillow. "When will you be home?"

"Did you water the tulips this morning like Dale told us we should in order for them to bloom?"

I rolled my eyes, "Victoria, you're evading the question. I won't be mad if you missed your flight or if you have to stay another day. I can continue on with my binge watching and eating cookies in your bed."

"You should probably go outside and water the tulips, and you better not be eating cookies in that bed. I hate sleeping on crumbs." Victoria wasn't giving me an inch, "Go outside and I will talk to you as you water the tulips."

I groaned, getting out of the bed and sliding my flip flops on. "Well, I hate sleeping in any bed without you, Victoria." I ran down the stairs, towards the back patio doors. "I'm on my way out to water the stupid tulips, so will you tell me when you will be home?" I was getting angry and frustrated. This was shaping up to be our first fight.

Shoving the back patio door open, I squinted at the bright morning sunlight, huffing. "Where is the hose?"

"It's right next to you on the wall, right by your left hand." Victoria's voice crept up from behind me at the same moment her end of the phone call went dead.

I spun around to see Victoria sitting in a patio chair in a Navy shirt and long shorts baring my favorite parts of her legs, as they sat, propped up on a small wooden bench, holding a cup of coffee with both hands. She grinned at me, her eyes dropping to my lower half, "You should probably wear shorts or pants. Dale gets up pretty early and I would hate for you to give him a heart attack." She waved a hand over the lack of anything covering my dark blue bikini underwear. "Oh and I got home late last night, early this morning, found a sleeping brunette bear in my bed. She growled at me then wrapped me up in a bear hug before she passed out on my shoulder, drooling all over the pillows."

I felt my face turn a bright red but I didn't care. I grinned and rushed towards Victoria, grabbing her face and kissing her. My cheeks were on fire from embarrassment and the kiss, Victoria pushing back just as hard against my mouth. I sighed contently as I parted from her. "So it wasn't a dream?"

Victoria ran a hand down my cheek, "It wasn't. You really did growl at me and I had no idea you were such a drooler."

I shook my head, kissing her once more, "Har Har." I then looked up in her eyes, seeing them bright and clear, but very tired. "Hi."

She grinned, "Hi." Victoria motioned to the kitchen, "Are you hungry? I was thinking eggs and bacon?"

I nodded, even though I had other things on my mind, I was starving. I stood up, reaching for Victoria's hand "I made pork chops last night, we can eat them with some eggs."

Victoria took my hand and tried to stand up, wincing and grabbing her right side when I yanked her up too quickly. I let go, the nurse in me kicking in, "Are you hurt?"

She squinted, clearly in visible pain. "I bruised some ribs. I tripped in the bulkhead of the training ship showing the new candidates around. I landed on my side in the porthole." She let out a slow breath, "I've done it a few times when I was in the Navy, I always forget to step up and over while I'm talking."

I frowned, reaching for the edge of her shirt and pulling it up to reveal an angry black and purple bruise. "Jesus Victoria." I ran my fingers over it, causing Victoria to flinch away. I glared at her, "Inside now and take off your shirt."

Victoria tried to smirk, "I was thinking we could do that after breakfast."

I gave her my best pissed off nurse look, "Inside and take off your shirt so I can look it over." I folded my arms, motioning for her to go in the house. "Why isn't it wrapped up?"

She walked slowly into the house, stopping at the island to remove her shirt. "They were, but I took it off when I woke up. I was having a hell of a time breathing with the bandage wrapped around me."

I helped her with taking off the shirt, not looking anywhere but the large bruise on her right side. "Jesus Victoria, it looks like a car hit you." I ran my hand over the angry skin, Victoria gasping when a finger brushed a very sore spot. Looking at her, "How did you do this again?"

She closed her eyes while I poked and prodded, making sure there were no breaks or fractures. "I fell in the ship, tripped and landed hard on the steel floor." She blew out a slow breath, "Can you not push on it? I had the base nurse do that and she didn't have the gentle hand you do."

I shook my head, walking to my bag where I kept some supplies out of habit, "I would feel better if you had x-rays." Picking up a large roll of ace bandage and a white bottle of extra strength ibuprofen, I walked back to the half-naked woman sitting still on the stool. Her head was down, playing with the shirt in her hands. I had a gut feeling the bruise on her side was not from a clumsy mishap of talking while walking. Even my nurse instinct shouted at me this was the kind of bruise that came from a strong impact, like a car hitting her or someone throwing the woman into a wall.

The old scar on her back was covered in blacks, purples and yellows, giving it a morbid mural effect done by an abstract painter. It forced a heavy sigh from me at the sight. Victoria was my world and I hated seeing her hurt, but there was nothing I could do if she kept blurring the truth.

"Alex, I will be fine. I just need to take it easy for a few days and rest." Victoria kept her back to me as she spoke. "I don't need to waste the time of doctors and nurses who have people who need real help."

I walked to stand right behind her, placing my hand on the bare space between her shoulders, feeling her react then relax from the warmth of my palm. "I know, but I hate seeing you in pain." I bent forward, unable to resist kissing her shoulder, "I really missed you."

Victoria leaned back, looking down at me as I propped my chin on her shoulder, "I really missed you and I had a few things planned for when I got home." She kissed the side of my head, "Then my clumsy ways ruined that."

I smiled softly, "Upside is I get to take care of you, keep you in bed all day if I need to." I backed away, trailing fingers down her skin. "Turn around and put your hands on the counter so I can wrap your side up." I pushed the white bottle towards her. "Take two of these, it should reduce the pain and swelling."

"Yes ma'am." Victoria croaked the words out, flinching when I held the one end of the bandage against her side. I could feel her heart race every time I had to brush against her when I ran the bandage around her body. I had not only missed her, but I missed her touch and after less than two days without having that intimate contact, it was driving me insane and now extremely frustrated.

"Victoria, I am not going to take advantage of an injured woman." I saw her give me a sad look, making me smile. "You need rest and low physical activity." I kissed her cheek finishing up, "And we both know that is not in our vocabulary when we are naked." Sliding my arms around her waist, I hugged her gently. "Maybe you will remember that the next time you are rambling and walking at the same time, Professor."

Victoria pressed her hands on top of mine as they rest on her stomach, "I need to take it easy, but my hands are very much unharmed." She bent her head back, finding my lips to kiss me deeply, whispering against them, "You might not take advantage of me, but I am going to do my best to take advantage of you any chance I get, Alex."

My knees buckled from the tone in her voice and the look in her eyes, I swallowed thickly. "Breakfast. We need to eat breakfast and you need to take the ibuprofen." I backed away from Victoria, if I stayed in her arms I would break the nurse's oath of putting the care of a patient first. I let out a slow breath, reaching for her shirt and handing it over to the smirking blonde. I shook my head, blushing, "You are nothing but trouble."

I opened the fridge to remove the pork chops and eggs, trying so hard to focus on the task of feeding Victoria before I forced her to lie down and rest when all I wanted was to take her to bed and make love to her.

"Yes, but you love me." Victoria's voice had a slight questioning tone behind it, as if to ask if I really did love her for everything she was.

Setting the plate down on the counter, I looked up at Victoria, tugging on the shirt with some difficulty. "Victoria, I love you with everything I am, and will be." I shrugged, "Even though you are a stubborn clumsy fool, I will always love you." I paused, deciding to continue. "No matter who you are or what you think you are, I love you."

Victoria smiled painfully, her eyes welling up to the point I knew I had hit a deep buried part of her that I was still desperate to dig out. There was a truth inside of her that was still waiting to be discovered. A truth Dani had hinted at the other day. I could see it now even through the paper thin excuses of falling in ships.

I stared at Victoria for a second, my gut wanting to pick now as the time that I dug deeper, but my heart saw the look in her eyes as she picked up the white bottle of pills pretending to read the label, and decided now wasn't the right time. Victoria needed me right now, not the inquisition I was so very close to embarking on. Dani's comments about Victoria being an enigma even to her, told me it would take more time for Victoria to open up.

I smiled tightly, returning to pulling the saran wrap off the pork chops, maybe one day when Victoria finally returned the sentiment of love, I would pick at the remaining secrets. Until then I would continue to wait.

Chapter 17

Victoria was asleep, passed out to the world, leaning on my shoulder with her half eaten plate of eggs and pork chops balanced on her lap. She had fallen asleep while we, well I, sat watching Summertime with Katharine Hepburn. Victoria was zonked out from the extra strength ibuprofen doing its job in easing the pain in her side. It was enough for her to get the sleep she desperately needed for the healing process to start.

I pressed my hand against her forehead to check if a fever was setting in, along with any other signs that her body was hiding more than just tender, bruised ribs. Victoria's forehead was warm and she stirred awake from my touch. She blinked heavy eyelids. "Alex, I'm okay. Stop worrying."

I rolled my eyes, "I can't help it, I'm a nurse." I reached down, lifting her plate as I stood up, "We need to get you to bed and lie down for a while. This couch and odd angle you're in isn't good for the ribs. I don't want your lungs to get congested." I set her plate on top of my empty one, holding out a hand for her to take, "Let's go."

Victoria offered up a dirty look at the tone of my voice. I sighed harder, "Up! You're going to bed. No if's, ands, or buts." I glared in groggy grey eyes, "You passed out on your pork chops. A distinct sign that it's time for you to rest and not object."

She frowned at me, "What if I told you I didn't like pork chops?"

I folded my arms, "I would say you're full of shit, Victoria. You love my pork chops." I shook my head, "Why are you being stubborn? You have a personal nurse standing in front of you, offering to take care of you and maybe even give you a sponge bath."

"Sponge bath?" Victoria's eyes perked up as she reached for the arm of the couch, "You should have said that first." She pushed up, wincing tightly when sore muscles fought back.

After helping Victoria upstairs and to the edge of the bed, I went about drawing a hot bath for her. "Do you have Epsom salts anywhere?" I called out from the depths of the bathroom cabinet.

"Linen closet, bottom shelf, there should be a few bags."

Walking to the linen closet, I found a nice stash of Epsom salt bags all neatly lined up along the bottom, making me curious as to why Victoria had a healthy supply.

I sighed, picking up the closest one and dumping a few scoops into the hot water. "I want you to soak for at least an hour then go to bed. We need to get the inflammation down and reduce the tightness to ease your breathing." I grabbed a thick fluffy towel, setting it on the edge of the tub before walking back out to the tired woman. "Do you want help with your clothes?"

Victoria smirked, nodding, "I might need you to wash my back too."

I rolled my eyes, Victoria was being overly cheeky and as much as I was still miffed at her, it was adorable. "I will get in the bath with you, but no funny business." I walked over, waving my hands to get her to lift her arms up. "If you behave, I will give you ice cream in bed."

Victoria smiled through the grimace as her arms tugged and pulled on her side, "If I behave? Am I on punishment, Alex?"

I shook my head, tossing her shirt to the floor and moving to unwrap her bandages "I'm a little angry at you for getting hurt and not telling me." I sighed, noting how clingy and bossy I suddenly sounded, "It's silly, but..." My feelings were all over the map. My gut telling me one thing, while my heart kept telling me to keep Victoria close and protect her.

Victoria grabbed my hand, "It's not silly. I'm just not used to someone worrying about me. Caring when I take a clumsy tumble and bash my body up." She looked down at our hands, "Dani told me she dropped by."

I smiled, letting go of her hand as jealousy flicked its way into my body, "She brought by your uniform for Saturday." I moved back towards the bathroom to check on the bath. I wanted to ask the questions that had been rattling around my thoughts since Dani stopped by. Who was she to Victoria? Why was she so interested in our relationship? How did she tie into Victoria's past? There was something more to Dani and Victoria that gave off the feeling there was so much more to the redhead's impromptu visit.

Shutting off the water, I ran my hand in the tub, swirling the hot water and salt together. Straightening back up, I felt the sudden need to be away from Victoria before I asked the questions I wanted, adding more tension to the room. "Victoria, I think I'm going to run out and get that ice cream while you soak."

I turned to come face to face with the woman standing right behind me, the ace bandage rolled up her in hand and wearing nothing but a bra, "Alex." I swallowed hard glancing at the gruesome bruise on her perfect skin. Skin I really wanted to see more of. "Alex, Dani is no one you should be jealous of."

I furrowed my brow, folding my arms over my chest, "I'm not jealous." I mumbled the words, hoping my tone wouldn't betray the lie.

Victoria chuckled, moving closer as she set the roll of bandage down on the counter, "You are jealous. You're also pissed off, grumpy, and wound up." I felt her hand fall to my neck, "Don't tell me you're not. I've always been able to read your emotions since the first day we met. You won't look at me for long when you're jealous. Your jaw twitches under the fake smile you give me when you're pissed. Lastly, you sigh heavily and avoid touching me when you're grumpy and wound up."

I frowned deeper, glaring at her, hating that she was exactly dead on. "I am none of those things." I looked over my shoulder at the bath. "You should get in before the water cools."

It was Victoria's turn to sigh, "Alex, Dani isn't an ex-girlfriend, an ex-lover, a one night stand, or anything that would link us romantically or physically. The only time her and I have been physical is when she broke my nose one drunken night in Italy." I glanced up to see Victoria grinning, "I kind of broke one of her ribs with a sucker punch. It's a long, terrible story that I'll save for ice cream."

She moved closer, gently grabbing both sides of my face, "Dani told me she came by and told you bits and pieces of how I still help her with intelligence work. How she led the rescue team to save me and how we ended up being stuck together as we became media darlings."

Victoria paused, waiting for me to look up in her eyes, "Dani is the sister I never wanted. She is my dearest friend and old Navy buddy, but that's where it stops." She let out a slow breath, "She's also helping me with a few things to speed up my retirement from the Academy so I can be a lazy slob watering the tulips in the morning over a glass of bourbon."

I bit my bottom lip, hating the way she looked at me, melting my heart into goo. I also felt stupid seeing the pure honesty in her eyes. There was nothing to worry about other than the stupid fears from my past creeping up. It still stung that I had yet to hear the three little words come from her mouth. Three stupid little words that seemed to hold so much weight in our relationship. "I didn't like the way she looked at you the other day. I thought maybe you and her have, had, a past that I couldn't compete with."

I huffed, "I'm mad that you hurt yourself and didn't tell me. I think it's left over from my incident on the metro station. I'm always looking over my shoulder and nervous when night falls. Then I'm always afraid you're going to get hurt and there's nothing I can do to help it, but I'm also always worried in general because you mean so much to me." I unfolded my arms, reaching up to delicately run my fingers over her uninjured skin. "Yes, to grumpy and being wound up. I've never felt like this for anyone and I didn't think I would crave to be around someone so much that it ached." I frowned. "Now I sound super clingy and co-dependent."

Victoria held my eyes, "Alex, you have nothing to worry about. I promise, and no, you don't sound like either of those. I understand that us, this relationship of ours, was born out of the fire so to speak. A tragic circumstance provoked by four men who should have known better, but got exactly what they deserved." She gently tugged me into a hug, holding me as tight as possible without mashing her side. "I will always be here to protect you."

I sighed against her shoulder, her words came out with a tone that told me she was one hundred percent honest, but there was more to that tone that sent shivers down my spine. Recanting memories of how I once looked at this woman and felt she could be very dangerous if provoked.

I left Victoria in the bedroom to get settled into bed after her bath. A bath she swindled me into joining her in and then followed through on her promise of taking advantage of me with her very capable hands. Not that I was that upset with her for breaking nurse's orders. I just hated that she already knew my weak points and how to touch me in just the right spot to pull all words from my mouth. Whittling me down to a gasping mess in her arms.

Even though it was early afternoon, I wanted Victoria to take it easy and talked her back into lying in bed. Promising to watch movies together as we ate fancy roast beef sandwiches, bowls of ice cream and more ibuprofen to ease her pain. I scooted into the kitchen, moving to gather up the goods I would need when I spotted my phone next to the coffee pot as I had left it when Victoria showed me her side.

I scooped it up, checking missed messages and calls when one caught my eye. Biting my bottom lip, debating whether or not to return the call. My head was full of crazy ideas after Dani came over and threw the book of Victoria Bond my way. I believed most of it, but there were a few things I wanted to double check before I finally shoved my gut to the side and lived in half-truths or ignorance.

I shook my head, my gut winning out again and called upstairs. "Victoria? I'll be a few minutes. I have to call my mom back. She wants to know if I can watch the dogs this weekend." When I heard her mumble a sleepy okay, I walked out the back patio doors and out to the middle of the yard.

Hitting the missed call, I chewed on my thumb listening to the rings.

"Sergeant James Hewlett NYPD Internet Crimes Division, how can I help you?"

I shook my head at his cocky tone. "James, you have caller ID, you know it's me."

He chuckled. "Of course I do Alex, but I love answering the phone with Sergeant Hewlett."

"Congratulations on your promotion by the way. Petey told me last night when I called the desk." I cleared my throat. My ex and I were on good terms even with the past we had, and James was someone I could trust.

"Yeah, fancy hearing that I had a message from you waiting at my desk. You left New York almost two years ago. I didn't expect you to come a calling on your NYPD ex." James blew out a breath, "Before I get to what you called me about last night, how are you, Alex? I meant to call after I heard about the incident, but I wasn't sure you wanted to hear from me."

I tucked a hand under my arm, staring out at the blooming tulip plant. "It's okay James, we needed the time. I'm doing good, really good." I paused, trying to find a balance in the awkwardness of wanting to share how happy I was without making James feel like crap. "It wasn't your fault, James. Looking back, I truly think we weren't meant to be."

"Yeah, can't put two bulls in a room and expect anyone to come out unscathed." He let out a slow breath, "I looked into that address you sent me and I don't even want to ask why you sent it from a random email account, but I understand. That address does trace back to Voltaire Industries, the mother company for Voltaire Lingerie. Now the address you found on the envelope, it's a building in the federal hub of the capital, right by the Pentagon. I went deeper, and something is hinky, Alex. There are no stockholders in Voltaire Lingerie. It's all privately owned and not anywhere near the stock market as a public IPO."

I felt my stomach turn, "Did you find anything else that was strange?" I began to gnaw on my thumb, why was I doing this? Digging into things I knew I shouldn't.

"Not really, I have one of my hacker hookups looking for more. If anything, it looks like Voltaire is one of those giant conglomerate companies that deals in everything from underwear to oil drilling. I want to keep looking into them. The address you gave me popped up in our database linked to an old cold murder case. Some sort of dipshit drug dealer in the Bronx was found dead from an overdose, but had an envelope with that address on it tucked in his safe with a huge wad of cash." James sighed. "Alex, is there anything I need to know about this? You said it was your friend who was getting taken down the river in the stock market by this company. Should I call the SEC and get them involved?"

I shook my head furiously, turning to catch Dale coming out with a bag of trash, "No, James, it's like I said, a friend of mine has been getting weird stock tip letters from that address I gave you. I told her I knew a boy in blue that loved to be a bloodhound when it came to this kind of detective work."

I waved at Dale. "It's no big deal, if you find anything call me or just ignore it."

I sighed, trying to reel in my building nerves. "I need to go, James. It was good to hear from you and maybe the next time I'm in New York we can get a drink and get caught up."

James chuckled, "Sounds good, but make sure your girlfriend is okay with it."

I almost choked on my own spit, "What?

"It's okay, I called the hospital this morning to get ahold of you. I ended up talking to a nurse named Stacy for about twenty minutes. She told me you have a wonderful girlfriend that could kick my ass. Seems you told her all about my bad characteristics?"

I covered my face with a hand. "James, I…"

He interrupted me, "Alex, no worries. I was a shit to you and lost a damn good girl because of it. I hope she treats you like gold and regardless of our past, you'll always have a boy in blue in your back pocket." He coughed lightly, "I'll call you later if I find more, Alex. Take care of yourself."

I whispered out a goodbye, hung up and stared back at the house. What the hell was I doing? I had found one of Victoria's blue envelopes tucked in her DVD's when I went looking for a movie to watch while she was still in Rhode Island. The envelope was empty and the postmark was from a few years back, but it had the same address as the first blue envelope I saw in her mail. I took a picture of it and let it sit in the back of my head for hours until my gut poked harder and harder, forcing me to pop into the library and use their computers.

I quickly set up a random email account and sent it to James, hoping his vast connections in the NYPD could help me put fears to rest. After Dani's visit, I couldn't stop thinking about Victoria and her past in the military. How it was the perfect foundation for a perfect spy novel.

I sighed, moving back towards the house. If Voltaire was a giant conglomerate company, it would make sense if Victoria was working for them through a government contract. Or maybe she did have an inside stock tip from a CEO who worked there and she was getting paid out. There were a lot of what ifs and maybes, none of them put me at ease and James' information of the address being close to the Pentagon, had my gut twirling.

Pulling open the back door, I couldn't shake the idea that my girlfriend was more super spy than teacher.

I woke up from a lengthy nap to find the television on and the room empty, a note on the bedside table from Alex.

-Went out to get groceries and to pick up my dress for Saturday. Stay in bed, rest and I'll be home with Thai food. Love you, A –

I smiled, rolling to sit up and get out of bed. My side was faring much better after the long hot bath and nap. I could move without having to catch my breath and stop every time I lifted my arm up.

Getting out of the bed, I shuffled to the closet to where my dress uniform hung up in its black bag. I didn't have to unzip it to know what it looked like, it was the same silly uniform I had worn for a week straight during the media blitz of being the hero for a minute.

I closed my eyes, pressing a hand against the rough black plastic bag. The crisp white lines of the sleeves would trail down into the gold cord at the cuffs. The left side would be nothing but a block of ribbons from the top of my shoulder down to the second button of the jacket. Dani would have already gone through the trouble of placing my rank perfectly on the collar, the name tag on the right side perfectly centered and all the other stupid bells and whistles that I once wore with chest puffing pride, would all be perfect and spotless.

Something I certainly was not.

Dragging my hand down and away from the bag, I turned to head back out and down to the kitchen for something to drink.

Seeing Alex and how upset she was with my injuries made me sick to my stomach, and I tried to play it off with flirting and stupid jokes. I was telling her the truth when I told her I wasn't used to anyone taking care of me, or caring if I came home broken or bloodied. Everyone in my life would accept the stories of clumsy accidents on ships or falling during a run. The ones I had relationships with before Alex, cared very little to look past the mask I wore since I never let them in any deeper than just below the surface.

The biggest problem was, that I now cared. I cared for and loved Alex so much that I was tired of having to lie to her. Opting for silence instead of truths, or kissing her to distract her gentle interrogations. It wouldn't last long, as Dani said. Alex was smart and would begin to press harder.

She did just that in the kitchen when I sheepishly asked if she loved me, and she replied with always loving me regardless of who I was or what I thought I was. That alone, told me she was starting to see the cracks in my mask. Catching glimpses of the black hooded figure hiding just under the thin layer of humanity I used to trick the world.

Yanking open the fridge I grabbed the large bottle of her green tea, smiling at how the fridge was now fuller with the addition of her weird healthy foods sitting next to my beers and deli meats. I bit the inside of my cheek, closing the fridge door to stare at a printed out picture of Alex and I from her parents house the other day, holding hands walking the dogs. Barney and Annie walking happily under our joined hands.

I bit harder, fighting the tears back and making the decision that on Saturday, after the formal, I would ask her to move in. Then at the yearly meeting with the old man and old lady I would ask to apply for my retirement. I was five years away under Voltaire's strange standards, but I knew I was the best and could at least appeal to the old man. He was the one half of my bosses who always had a special soft spot for me since that day I met him in the back room of the oval office with the Colonel. He was the one who asked me three times if I was sure I wanted to join the cause the Colonel kept feeding me. I was so lost in the depths of PTSD and hatred, I didn't hear him, only nodded my head and signed the offered contract.

It took me ten years and a brunette with the biggest heart for me to realize I should have taken the out when he offered it to me.

Maybe then, I would still feel like I could be human.

Pouring green tea in a large pint glass emblazoned with the Academy logo, I decided that I had to tell Alex I was in love with her the first chance I could. I had to start finding the last thread of humanity hiding in me and work on it more. I would ask Alex to move in with me, then I would ask for my retirement from Voltaire. After securing a promised retirement, I would tell Alex exactly how I felt about her and start breathing and finally living.

I grabbed the glass, if I had to, I would use all of the money I tucked away from Voltaire and start a brand new life with Alex somewhere far away from here.

I let out a slow breath when I heard my phone ring from inside the den, it was Dani. I groaned, wobbling over to the den, hoping to hell it wasn't a last minute job or something that would interrupt the rest of my vacation.

Scooping up the phone from the desk, replacing it with the glass of tea in my hand, I answered it, "What?"

"Did you know that nurse blue eyes has an ex-boyfriend who is a cop? One of New York's finest?" Dani's tone was one that told me she was not in the mood for our usual bickering banter.

"She mentioned having an ex who was a cop when she lived in New York." I ran my fingers along the edge of the glass, "I honestly don't care about her exes and you shouldn't be digging in her past."

Dani huffed, "I would very much like to not be digging in her past relationships. But when I get an email notification from the New York office asking me to go digging in the personnel files of a James Hewlett, Sergeant for the NYPD's internet crime unit, who is poking his nose into the cold case murder of one Martines Rodriguez in 2010 and kicking up dust. I go digging."

My fingers stopped their slow movements, "Martines? Wasn't he the Manhattan plumber Voltaire had removed for going rogue on his contracts, deciding he could double dip and be a plumber for both Voltaire and the Colombians?"

"Yup, that Martines. He was handing off Voltaire's classified information to the Colombians, and they would pay him twice as much to eliminate Voltaire operatives. Luckily he was stopped after one hit. The old lady lost her shit when she found out his devious ways and did the hit herself." Dani let out a slow breath, "That is a mess I wish I could erase from my memory."

I closed my eyes, rubbing at the side of my head remembering the fallout from that whole disaster. I was sent to England for a few months to work with the old man in his home office, keeping me out of that dust storm. The old lady had wanted me to be her personal housecleaner when she went on a tirade and started vetting all of the plumbers she was suspicious of after Martines. The old man pulled me away, fearing if I started killing my own, I would never be the same. "Dani, why are you calling me and bringing up the past?"

"Normally I wouldn't. Some random cop trying to earn his stripes or bars is nothing to me. It doesn't even matter that he and nurse blue eyes dated for a couple of years and were on the verge of marriage, babies, and puppies in a house on Staten Island. It matters to me when this random cop just called the woman you want babies and puppies with a couple of hours ago. They talked for about five minutes and when that call ended, his computer started lighting up with Martines name, Voltaire's Pentagon address and a few interesting facts that have Sergeant James Hewlett on the short list to having a strange accident one late night in the big apple."

Dani's rapid fire speech told me she was doing her best to keep Alex out of the line of fire. "I told you to stop talking about...."

"I haven't said a goddamn thing, Dani. So fucking stop before you even get started." I spun away from my desk to lock eyes on all of the medals in the box behind the desk. "We don't even know what they talked about. We don't know if he suddenly missed her and called her out of the blue, and it could be that since he is a newly promoted sergeant, he's trying to prove his worth by digging in cold cases."

I clenched my jaw to reign in my building rage, "Martines was a fuck up, a giant fuck up and left a giant fucking mess for everyone to clean up. I wouldn't be surprised if the old lady fucked up and left a mess when she killed him. Regardless, I don't need to hear about Alex's past lover or almost whatever. I can't, because I don't want to slip back into who I was then when I am trying so hard to be..." I swallowed hard, choking on a half sob as the emotions all swung home, hard. "Human."

There was an awkward silence on the phone before Dani broke it, "I know Victoria, but I made a fucking promise to you, years ago, and I don't break any of my fucking promises. I'm only telling you so that you know what I am doing. I am going to write in my formal report to the Manhattan office to monitor this Hewlett from a distance, and let him root around in his cold case. I will also write up that all of his phone calls, internet activity, and whatever, is nothing to be concerned with. Just phone calls to family, friends, co-workers and the like. I may have already deleted his phone call to Alex." She let out a slow breath, "But you might want to talk to her. Like I said, she's smarter than we think."

I clenched my jaw harder, "If I talk to her, it might lead to a conversation that I have no idea how to have. It may lead to me having to tell her things that I can't, or won't, hide anymore."

I picked up the box of medals, squeezing the frame so hard, I heard the wood creak, "Dani, how the hell do I tell her I'm a killer? I can barely tell her that I love her when she's awake." I sucked in an angry breath, "How the fuck do I tell her anything that isn't a lie and have her stay or stay alive? How can I have anything?" I didn't realize I was yelling into the phone until Dani snapped back.

"Shut it down, Victoria! Stop yelling at me before I drive up there and break your nose again!" She blew out a breath, "I understand everything you're going through, trust me, this is why I live in a big empty house with computers and secrets. I lost the ability to tell anyone anything but the truth a long time ago, so don't lay the pity party on me. I fully understand, Victoria, and I'm trying to help you and help myself as we both struggle to find the human in the human suits we put on every day."

Slamming the medal box back down on the bookshelf behind the desk, I rubbed my face, wiping away the angry tears, "I'm tired, Dani." I paused, hearing Alex's mini cooper pull into the driveway. "I have to go, Alex is home."

"Talk to her Victoria, tell her that you love her. That you want her forever and then worry about the now with her while I worry about the rest. I will get you out of this, somehow, but in the meantime, talk to her. Leave all the masks in the garage in that shitty duffle bag and put your Victoria face on, the one that I love dearly even though it's the biggest pain in my ass, and live. Live the life you want and in the end you will have it." Dani suddenly sniffled, "I'll talk to you later, fuck this world."

She hung up before I could say another word, I tucked the phone away in my desk and wiped my face. Trying to rub it so it looked like I just woke up and wasn't crying as I heard Alex's key jingle in the front door.

I wasn't jealous of Alex and her past, I didn't have it in me to feel jealousy when I could look in her eyes and just read her emotions and love for me like they were a bright neon sign.

I was angry. Angry at Voltaire for always being a part of my life and not being able to do anything about it.

I took a steadying breath as Alex entered the kitchen, setting a few paper bags on the counter with grease spots, before spinning around with a white plastic dress bag in her hands. She caught me leaning against the doorframe of the den, grinning as she blushed, "You're supposed to be resting."

I shrugged, "I never listen to orders." I smiled softly, taking her in as it made my heart ache to know that Alex was too special to keep in the dark and I needed to listen to Dani. I needed to put my real face on and let this incredible woman in as far as I could before I introduced her to the hooded figure, if I ever did. I nodded at the bag hanging from her hand. "Can I see the dress?"

Alex shook her head, "Nope." She walked to the laundry room to hang it up, "You can see it on Saturday, I want to surprise you." She moved to the counter, removing white paper containers full of delicious smells. "How are you feeling?"

"Better." I looked down at the floor, "Alex, when is the lease up at your apartment?"

She sighed, reaching for plates, "Not for another six months, I just signed on for a six-month extension when we kind of stopped talking. I was going to ride it out here for a while, then thought about moving back to New York or to San Diego." Alex looked at me, "My security deposit was so ridiculous that I'm stuck with it until Christmas." She squinted at me, "Why do you ask?"

I smiled, shaking my head. I already planned a visit to her landlord in a few days to make sure she got out of her lease and all of her money back before I asked her to move in with me Saturday night. "No reason."

I pushed away from the doorframe, walking over to the woman who was changing my life every minute she was in it. "Did I ever tell you about my sixth birthday party? Where Grandma Edith took me to a Judy Garland drag show?"

Alex giggled, looking sideways at me, "Why Ms. Bancroft are you about to tell me a story about your childhood?" She covered her heart in mock surprise, winking at me, "Please do go on."

I sat gingerly on the counter, watching Alex fill plates up with fragrant Thai food. I told her about what it was like for a six-year-old to eat birthday cake sitting on a bar stool and being sung happy birthday by a Tina Turner impersonator while my grandma slipped me some of her Manhattan. I watched Alex's face light up with joy as I shared more and more about myself. Taking the first step in listening to Dani's advice.

Start living the life I wanted and not the one the Colonel and Voltaire gave me.

Chapter 18

~Saturday~

The white dinner jacket hung on the back of my desk chair. The evening sunlight pushing and finding its way to the gold and silver edges of my Navy flair, casting back stray lines of light across the old desk. I stood next to the chair, looking out the window, nursing a glass of Jack Daniels while Alex finished getting ready. We had parted ways a couple of hours ago to get ready for the formal simultaneously. Knowing that eager hands and libidos would delay getting dressed, making us very fashionably late.

Alex and I had fallen back into our blissful bubble over the last couple of days. Sleeping in late, watching movies and her silly dragon show, having a few barbecue lunches with Dale and Mary, and fooling around as much as my body would let me. I smirked at the memory of the night after Thai food. I couldn't resist not touching Alex and trying to initiate something on the couch while we watched one of her saved episodes.

I may have pissed Alex off when I distracted her during an important plot twist, but the payback was definitely worth it. Worth the pain of arching my back off the couch as the angry, but determined, woman kept a death grip on my thighs. Showing me that I would soon have a hell of a time remaining the teacher to Alex's student.

The smirk remained as I turned to set the watered down drink on the desk. Glancing at the white jacket, I sighed looking at all of the medals, ribbons, gold and everything that told my story in one look. This formal would be full of my fellow faculty members, and not all knew my military history since I often left certain ribbons off and tucked away in a desk drawer.

I titled my head up to look at the stairs, hearing the bedroom bathroom drawers open and close. Alex should be ready soon. She was taking longer than I had, since she had far more to do than I. I just had to adhere to existing military standards for hair, makeup and jewelry.

The fit of my very tailored uniform was the only deviation. Tailored to fit all of my curves perfectly. If I couldn't wear a dress of my choice, I wanted to look impeccable at this event. Deep down I tailored the uniform for Alex, knowing she had a thing for me in uniform.

Hearing the creak of the stairs, I turned to look in the kitchen, reaching for the white jacket, "Alex, I hope you're ready, I would like to leave soon. Dani is expecting to meet us in front of the hall. She said something about not wanting to go in alone." I shook my head, Dani was a tough, dangerous Naval officer, but balked like a small child at any, and all, social gatherings, never wanting to be alone for too long.

"Yes, I'm ready." Alex's voice echoed what I was sure, was a smile on her face, drawing my eyes from the collar of the jacket to her.

Alex stood in front of me, grinning as predicted, watching my eyes widen at the pure beauty on display in front of me.

The dress she wore was a lavender grey color, floor length with a sweetheart neckline that accentuated the woman's elegance. The dress fell to gather up in the middle, a crystal brooch in the center resting on the top of a slit in the dress that made my mouth water when it offered a glimpse of her thigh. The garment was elegant, beautiful, and sexy as hell in the way it wrapped around her. Her hair was down, falling over her shoulder in soft layers, and her makeup was minimal but highlighted her natural beauty. Alex rarely ever needed much makeup, in my opinion. She often looked stunning with plain old lip gloss on.

I stood dumbfounded at the sight of the gorgeous woman before me. I knew Alex was beautiful, but this dress took her above and beyond that. Alex looked like a princess waiting for her prince charming, with a big grin and cocked eyebrow.

"Victoria? Are you okay? You seem stuck." Alex's grin morphed into her infamous smirk. The same one she always tossed my way the moment before I had my clothing attacked in a brunette's fury to remove them as quickly as possible.

I blinked a few times, trying to unstick my brain that had short fused on first sight. "Um, you...stunning, Alex."

She blushed, tipping her head down to look at the floor. "I've managed to reduce a brilliant Professor down to caveman speech." She peered up through her eyelashes, "I guess the dress is a hit?"

I nodded, swallowing as I took two long steps towards her. Reaching out, I grabbed the side of Alex's neck and pulled her closer, kissing her as hard as I could politely without turning this moment into ripping apart her dress and forgoing the entire formal. Feeling her moan against my lips, I broke off the kiss, leaning back enough to look in her blue eyes and still share the same breath with her, "I've always thought you to be beautiful even though I've only seen you in scrubs, t-shirts, jeans, and my stolen clothing, but this." I held out my hand for her to take, smiling as it fell into mine without hesitation. "Is something I will remember for a very long time."

I took a step back, lifting her hand to my lips, kissing it gently. "You will steal the show."

Alex's face turned a deeper shade of crimson, her eyes roaming over my very bland and traditional outfit. "You look beautiful too, Victoria."

I shook my head, laughing, "I look like a prudish school marm." I waved at the white jacket, "Trust me, I will pale in comparison to you." Tugging her hand, I lifted the jacket from the counter. "You ready to mingle with old crotchey military Professors?"

Alex's hand slid to the crook of my elbow, "Am I ever."

I covered her hand with mine and walked us out the front door, laughing again when Alex gave me look as I stopped to put on the boxy white hat, "Tradition runs deep, even if I look like a modern ice cream truck driver."

Alex raised her eyebrow. "Oh I have other things running through my head, some of them involve ice cream and that hat." She winked at me before sauntering off to the BMW.

I shook my head, calling after her, "And to think there was a time you were embarrassed to tell me that you had never been with a woman."

Alex's cheeks pinked up, but she stayed confident, "Like I said, I'm a fast learner and you make me want to study as much as possible."

I moved to her side of the car, opening it for her to climb in, "Then I guess it's time to move on to the advanced classes." I dropped my voice low, adding a heavy dose of sensuality, knowing it would throw Alex off her game.

Alex shot me a look, I winked back and shut the door, opting to let her simmer and stew in what I insinuated.

She was silent and staring at me when I got in the car, setting my hat and jacket in the backseat, "Victoria, what did you mean?" Her voice had a hint of anxious excitement, making me laugh at all the insane ideas roaming through her head.

I grinned, looking back to watch the driveway as I backed the car out, "Oh nothing, Alex."

She sat in silence, glaring at me for a few minutes until I picked up her hand, kissing her knuckles before asking her if she knew how to dance.

Victoria looked delectable as she climbed out of the BMW, slipping her arms into the fancy white jacket that fit like a glove around her body. The knee length black skirt, the gold cummerbund with the silly white tuxedo shirt and the black curved tie all came together to paint a picture of Victoria that I knew I would call upon on during long nights in the hospital. She looked incredible, graceful, and was reaching depths of my fantasies I never knew I had until she came around the front of the car to escort me out.

Even the medals hanging on her chest made me sigh like a teenage girl in New York City during fleet week. A woman in uniform, particularly this woman in uniform, made me feel like I was in the thick of a fairy tale written just for me.

I loved her with my entire being and no matter how many times I looked at her, the first thought that would always pop in my head was how much I loved the woman smiling at me and offering her hand for me to take.

Grinning as I took her hand, I let out a gentle sigh, feeling my nerves edge up looking at the masses of uniforms, tuxedos and ball gowns filtering past us in the parking lot. This was an event that I knew I would have to put on my best manners and keep them on throughout the night. I didn't want to embarrass Victoria and I knew it would be a feat to maintain conversation with old military veterans steeped deeply in the tradition centuries old military branches had to offer.

"Alex, relax. They may look older than dirt, but they are all kind and will adore you." Victoria's breath tickled my ear, calming me down immediately. "This is nothing compared to what I put you through when we first met in my office." I glanced up at her, catching half a smirk on her face and something else in her eyes. She turned away before I asked what she really meant. "There's Dani." Victoria waved her free hand towards the front doors of the hall.

My eyes settled on the redhead, and I let out a small breath, taking in how utterly stunning Dani looked standing of to the side in the exact same uniform Victoria wore, but with less medals and gold flair. She was nodding and smiling at Naval officers she knew as they passed by into the hall. "Wow, she looks different."

Victoria laughed, "She cleans up very well, but is still the agitating ass under the spit polish on her shoes."

I laughed at the comment, shaking my head, "Are you sure you two are friends?"

Victoria shrugged. "Sadly yes, I trust her with my life and yours."

The tone in her voice told me a thousand different things, but again, before I could confront it, Victoria stepped away from me to greet Dani while still holding on to my fingers.

Dani smirked at Victoria. "I see why you had this thing tailored, you look like you belong in the Navy."

She then looked my way after earning a grumbled huff from Victoria, her eyes lighting up as she took in my dress. "Wow, you look incredible Alex. It's strange to see you something other than scrubs or sweats." She smiled genuinely at me, "And I mean that as a simple compliment." She threw a side glare towards an irritated blonde, "No need to gut punch me, Professor."

"Dani, get the door for Alex and I, and try to keep the snark at a minimum tonight? If that is even possible for you." Victoria tugged my hand, silently asking me to return to stand next to her.

Dani shrugged, rolling her eyes, "I make no promises. I'm only here because I'm alumni and it's a free dinner that I don't have to take out of a box." She turned, opening the wide wooden door for us, bending at the waist slightly. "Ladies, after you."

I barely issued a thank you when I was enraptured by the sight of the old granite pillars sweeping up into ornate open ceilings with decorations that transported me back to what I imagine all buildings looked like in the mid 1900's. The floors were black and pale red granite, all laid out to form an incredible design I had a difficult time discerning what it was by standing right on top of it. The hall was incredible and made me feel very out of place. I had gone to many fancy events in my life, some of the best restaurants in New York City on James arm when he felt it necessary to spend a little more on date night.

But nothing compared to the grand elegance of this hall, a room that made me feel like I was back in time and that I should be wearing some sort of uniform.

"This is Bancroft Hall. They have the cocktail mixer here first. Gives us old veterans an opportunity to show off our history and puff out our chests over gin and tonics." Victoria looked down at me, her hat now tucked under the other arm, "The dinner will be down the hallway in one of the smaller, more modern rooms." She grinned as I looked at her with wide eyes, "Can I get you a drink, Alex?"

"Um, yes please, a vodka and cranberry?" I scanned around the massive hall, "I feel like I'm on the titanic." I half whispered it, hoping no one would hear me, including Victoria. I then glanced at her, "Wait, Bancroft Hall? Are you related to this marble, granite behemoth?" I bit my bottom lip as I tried not to giggle.

"The titanic would be envious of this hall." Victoria winked, "And no. I'm not related to the hall or the Bancroft's who built it. It's just a happy accident we both share a rather amazing last name." She patted my hand once more, before moving towards the wooden bar top in the rear of the room near an ornate staircase.

I quickly folded my hands in front of me, clutching the small purse I brought as a last minute idea. I swallowed a few times, my stomach fluttering with nerves as to what I would say if any of these esteemed co-workers of Victoria's would come my way for conversation.

Fidgeting with the clasp on the bag, I moved to a corner where I saw Dani swirling a straw in a glass. I wasn't fond of the woman, but she was a veritable life boat in this sea of uniforms. She looked up when I stepped closer, smirking at me with bright green eyes that were accentuated by her flame red hair. Dani was attractive, sending another hit of jealousy through my system at the closeness she shared with my girlfriend. "Stuffy as hell, right?" Dani took a healthy swig of her drink, "By the way, you'll hear a ton of corny jokes about the professor and the hall having the same name. It gets annoying real fast." She rolled her eyes and blew out an exasperated sigh.

I shrugged, "I don't know, I've only been here for five minutes?" I looked around the room, catching a few stares in my direction. "I hope no one asks if she's my girlfriend." I cringed when I smelled the pure, straight up vodka in her glass.

Dani chuckled, "Alex, no one gives two shits about the Professor's personal life. They all respect her for who she is, what she has done, and what she continues to do. Plus, I don't know if you read the news, but don't ask don't tell went down the drain along with Britney's last hit album. So, no need to fret."

She waved her glass of vodka around. "All these old men and woman are the best the Navy has to offer. All future forward thinkers who have reshaped the Academy over the last few years. Victoria's personal life was laid out for everyone to see long before she picked up her ruler and chalk to teach young minds."

I half glared at Dani, "You and Victoria confuse me."

Dani cocked an eyebrow as she sipped more of the clear liquid, "And how do we confuse you?"

I frowned, hating my jealousy right now, pushing words out of my mouth faster than I wanted. It was ramping up based off the fact I was still waiting to hear Victoria tell me what she felt for me, instead of playing the constant guessing game. "It's like you two have this caustic relationship with an intense chemistry I've never seen before." I sighed heavily, "Whatever, maybe it's because you know all of her buttons and which ones to push." I tilted my head up to silently change the subject and spotted Victoria standing at the bar, drinks in hand and chatting with a white haired man that had so many stars on his collar, he had to be an admiral.

A moment of silence passed between Dani and I, suggesting that I should probably move on before I said something else stupid.

"She still hasn't told you she loves you, has she Alex?" Dani's tone was completely void of snark, sass, irritation and all the other bits of her personality that rubbed everyone the wrong way. I turned to look in her eyes, seeing the softness as she spoke again, "Victoria hasn't told you anything about what she thinks of you or feels about you?"

I groaned, not wanting to have a heart to heart with this woman, but maybe she could give me insight on how to get Victoria to say those daunting three words that I seemed to hold so much weight in. "No, she hasn't. She tells me I'm beautiful, smart, sexy, funny and that she would do anything to protect me. Which I know anyone would be grateful to hear from their significant other, but." I paused, catching Victoria look at me and grin, holding up a finger to tell me she would be right over. "But."

"But sometimes all the heart wants, is the truth." Dani sighed, placing a warm hand on my shoulder. "I wish I could get the stubborn Professor to say it, but after being by her side for ten years and knowing her as well as I do, it will take time. No matter how many times I tell her to let go and just say it, she won't."

Dani looked down at me, "The only thing I can say is that in all of the years we've gone to this formal, this is the first time she's brought someone as her date. It's always been her and I, sitting for an hour then blowing this place and drinking away the bad memories that come with these stupid uniforms in the shitty midshipmen's bar three blocks down." She let out a slow breath, "You've gotten more of her than any of us ever will. You've brought more of her back to the world. Pieces of her I saw before everything went to shit and hoped every day would come back."

Dani smiled crookedly, her eyes glassing over, "I promise you Alex, you will hear it and pay attention when it happens. Knowing her, she will slip it out while asking you to pass the salt."

I held the woman's gaze, that sinking feeling from all the nights I sat thinking about Victoria's computer, Voltaire Lingerie and what James told me, all started to feel like a heavy rock sitting the bottom of my gut. Dani's genuine speech told me there was far more to the incident in the desert that scarred Victoria, far more that went past just her helping Dani out in intelligence work. It was if Victoria had a terminal disease and everyone but I, knew it.

I squinted at Dani. "What really happened that day you saved Victoria?"

She smirked, lifting the vodka to her lips, "You are a smart one, nurse blue eyes, you read between the lines better than anyone I've ever met. That's saying a lot since all I do is work with idiots whose sole mission in life is to read between the lines." She took a long sip, licking her lips before looking at me, "A big fat fuck happened that day I saved Victoria, and I've spent my life since trying to right that asshole's wrongs." She shrugged, "All I can say is this Alex, some mysteries are better left as cold cases. All of them."

Dani gave me a hard look before another smirk broke out, "You want to hear the story of how I broke her nose in Italy? Her left side is her weak side, in case you two ever get into a fight."

I smiled tightly, nodding for Dani to embark on her story as Victoria slowly returned to us.

My smile was fake. My gut was stirring up a hurricane sized storm when I heard cold cases. Leading me to fear that I had not been careful enough when I contacted James to look into that strange address for Voltaire near the Pentagon.

Taking a quick inventory, I saw Dani was on her way to getting drunk. The empty glass behind her with her traditional chewed up red straw plus the one in her hand with a half inch of clear vodka in it, told me that in the ten minutes we had been in the hall, Dani had downed two drinks like they were water.

She was holding true to her own tradition, taking full advantage of the free booze and food.

After handing Alex her drink, I reached over and plucked the glass from Dani's, "Slow it down Lieutenant O'Malley." Dani frowned at me, hating I was using her fake last name and had taken away her drink. The look on Alex's face told me Dani not only started on the path of being blitzed, but she left the filter on her mouth at home. "Admiral Odell was asking about you, he's near the back by the h'ordeves table." I gave her a hard glare, silently telling her to go away, eat something and knock whatever she was already starting, off.

Dani rolled her eyes, flicking her hand at me, "Yes Commander Bancroft." She sauntered off towards a group of admirals mingling together with their wives.

I sighed. "Never fails, every damn year she does this." I turned to Alex, smiling, "Dinner should be in twenty minutes, but if you're hungry we can pick at some cocktail wieners."

Alex smiled tightly, shaking her head, "I'm fine with the drink. Thank you."

I knew that tight smile of Alex's, it was the same one I had seen a hundred times while we were friends. It was the same one she had when I popped in on her at the hospital and met Doctor Dean. It was her worst fake, I'm okay, smile.

Cursing Dani for the millionth time, I moved closer to Alex, running my hand over her arm. "What did Dani say to you?"

Alex shrugged, fake smile still holding strong, "Nothing important, she was telling me about Italy and the fight you two had." She barely looked in my eyes as she sipped the vodka cranberry, "I told her that I'm still trying to understand your odd sibling like relationship."

I blew out a calming breath through my nose. Dani had said more. Dani had said things that got right into all of Alex's cracks and sat on top of whatever it was that caused her jealousy to show up. Dani had done something to push Alex into her fake smile and take away the excited glint in her eyes I saw when we walked into the marbled hall.

Nodding I held on to her wrist. "Alex, Dani is an asshole. An asshole with a heart of gold that is currently being drowned in pure vodka. She'll get worse before the night ends, but she has our best intentions in that heart of hers." I paused, waiting for Alex to finally look at me, "What did she say? I know she probably told you her version of the Italy fight and not the accurate version."

Alex softened, closing her eyes, "She said something that got under my skin, maybe it's a forgotten trigger from my incident, but she said that some mysteries are better left cold cases." She opened her eyes, "It reminded me that my case is still open and somewhere Detective Scarlett is going to pop out of the woodwork to ruin my day." Alex moved her hand, grabbing a few of my fingers, "Dani also told me you instigated the fight in Italy, you both were hammered and she stuck you with the tab."

I raised my eyebrows, trying to cover up that I knew exactly what Dani's loose lips was hinting at. In her drunken stupidity, Dani was trying to warn Alex about her ex. The redhead's shitty attempt at telling Alex to keep her nose out of the dark corners kept by Voltaire. "She was hammered, I was buzzed. It wasn't the enormous bar tab she stuck me with, it was the screaming Italian bar owner who threw a broom at me when Dani started calling him unpleasant names in Italian."

I smiled, watching Alex's face ease away from tense and back to the excited woman I was eager to spend the night with. "Her and I got into a screaming match and since we both were still a little battle weary, tensions overtook us and she hit first. Popping me in the nose with a right hook, breaking it. I returned the favor, cracking three of her ribs and shoving her into the canal right outside. Leaving her to the fishes."

Alex laughed, shaking her head, "I don't think I'll ever get you two, I know I've said it a million times." She sighed gently, "Must be a Navy thing."

I rolled my eyes, "It's a Dani is a pain in my ass thing." I smiled at the big blue eyes in front of me, lifting her hand to my lips to kiss warm fingers that would always make my stomach flop when I touched them. "Thank you for being here with me."

Alex grinned, squeezing my hand, "You did ask me to be your date, Victoria."

I nodded. "But you didn't have to accept, Alex."

She opened her mouth to issue witty, sassy retort when I felt a strong hand clasp onto my shoulder.

"Commander Bancroft, you must introduce me to this enchanting woman on your arm."

The sound of the deep voice, immediately relaxed me the second I recognized it. I turned to grin in response to the massive grin on the face of Vice Admiral Ward Atlas. "Admiral Atlas, it would my pleasure." Letting go of Alex's hand, I moved to stand at her side. "Sir, this is Alexandra Ivers, but she prefers to be called Alex and she is my date for the evening." I glanced down, "Alex, this is my second favorite Admiral in the entire Navy, Ward Atlas."

The Admiral laughed heartily, shaking his head, holding his hand out towards Alex, "You should ask her who her first favorite is." He winked at me, offering his polite greetings to a suddenly very shy Alex, "And please, call me Ward." He nodded towards me, "This one won't tell anyone who her favorite is in polite company while in these outfits, well maybe after a few more drinks she might let it slip."

Alex chuckled, offering up her own polite greetings. Ward was a man in his late fifties and lived and breathed the Navy deeper than I did and ever would. He had a head of silver hair that was longer than the usual buzz cuts around us, bright mischievous blue eyes and a white shining grin that I knew melted hearts when he was a young Ensign back in the day. I adored Ward and the joke about being my second favorite admiral was an inside joke between us that had been going on for the last five years.

The man knew exactly where he sat in on my list of people I trusted and cared for. He had been the Rear Admiral on the ship taking me home after my rescue. The only man and person other than Dani that I would actually respond to when I was deeply imbedded in the shock of having survived what I did. He was the one who took it upon himself to take care of everything I couldn't, my hospital care, the therapy sessions and finally a job at the academy when I was discharged but had no idea what to with my life when I was left with Voltaire as the only job option.

Ward had been one of the sole people that kept me hanging on to the tiny pieces of my humanity. Pieces I had been so close to shedding in favor of the monster born that day in the sand and the one Voltaire was cultivating.

I tipped my head down, placing my hand at the small of Alex's back. "My first favorite Admiral will always be M." I felt the heat run around my cheeks, "I should have never told you that, every time you bring it up, I feel nerdy, sir."

Ward guffawed. "My dear Victoria, as a history Professor, you are already classified as a nerd." He nudged my shoulder, returning his attention back to Alex, "I gave Victoria her first James Bond book on the boat years ago, it was my personal copy of Casino Royale." He paused, looking at me softly with those piercing blue eyes, "It opened up a conversation between us." Ward winked my way, "So Alex, tell me about yourself and how you manage to capture this brilliant woman's attention?"

"I caught it with a club sandwich the size of a small car and pure persistence. Victoria wasn't easy to tie down, she offered a challenge or two before I won." Alex's confident tone had Ward grinning brighter.

"The way I see it, Victoria has won." Ward gave me a knowing look before asking Alex to continue on discussing the finer details of her work as a nurse, and if she was enjoying herself at the formal so far.

I sat back, watching Alex charm the stars right off the Admirals collar, winning him over in a few minutes. She was perfect, incredible and could hold her own with Ward's witty sense of humor. I was soon forgotten as the two discussed Alex possibly taking a tour with the Admiral over at the naval hospital. Alex eagerly discussing the idea of working in a hospital that was slower, but did far more good in the long run for the patients it served.

I drifted off, looking around the room at the other attendees, smiling and nodding at a few of my co-workers and a few others that I had spent time with on a ship throughout the years. I was at ease, comfortable and enjoying myself at the formal. Smiling I shook my head, I had never enjoyed this tepid mandatory event, always dreading it year after year. Feeling Alex lean into me as she laughed at one of Ward's dumb jokes, I felt the warmth of her soak into my uniform jacket and soar right to my heart. I swallowed hard looking over at the woman charming the pants off one of the most revered Admirals in this day's Navy, tonight was the night.

Tonight I would tell her what she meant to me and finally release the last ten years of my life, letting her be the wind that carried me home. Home with her.

"Victoria, you're staring and Ward asked you a question." Alex looked up at me, her eyes smirking at how dreamy I must have looked while staring at her, lost in my thoughts.

"I don't blame her, Alex. I remember what it's like to see the world in the one person who holds yours." Ward patted my shoulder, "I was asking if you had intentions of hanging around for dessert? We do the yearly presentations of faculty awards and I have something special for you, Victoria."

I cleared my throat, trying to recover from sounding embarrassed that I had been caught staring, "Yes, I think we can manage to stay for dessert." I felt Alex's hand fall into mine. "As long as it isn't a teacher of the year award."

Ward chuckled, "Sadly Captain Pegg has that one in the bag, has for the last five years." He shrugged, "The man lives and breathes shaping midshipmen while the rest of us just live and breathe." Ward nodded in my direction, "I should check on my wife, Commander Albus seemed taken with her when we walked in." He smiled at Alex, "Fantastic to meet you, Alex. please call me on Monday and I will set up that tour."

"I certainly will, and thank you." Alex turned to look at me as Ward moved back into the crowd, "He's very fond of you."

I shrugged, "Can you blame him?" I grinned at her, tugging her hand before she could give me a dirty look, "Let's go find our table for dinner, be warned, I think Dani is sitting with us."

Alex blew out a slow breath, looking over my shoulder, "Speak of the devil."

Dani stopped in front of us, another full glass of vodka in her hands, her face looked as if she had seen a ghost or her worse enemy, "Professor, I am bailing on this shit show."

I frowned, "Why? Did they run out of vodka or cut you off?" I could see the booze taking hold in the way her eyes were clouding over.

She shook her head curtly, "No, I was just invited to tea by a mutual friend in the corner. Seems they happened to be in the area and stopped by to say hello to the Academy Superintendent." She pulled out a small matchbook from her inside pocket, reaching over to jam it into mine. "They wanted me to give you this."

My jaw was clenched tightly, along with my free hand hearing Dani's code phrase for the old man, "Did they say if they were staying? Maybe I could catch them before dinner."

Dani shook her head, smiling painfully, "Nope, rushed out on a phone call. Also had a copy of Dante's Inferno in their pocket." She held my eyes, silently communicating that she wanted to get the hell out of here now that the old man had made a surprise appearance with my least favorite plumber, Dante. I scanned the room, looking for either the old man or Dante's smug face peering out from a shadow. I didn't like that the old man and Dante were growing closer, it meant many things. One of them being that my time frame to ask for retirement was growing smaller.

I saw the impromptu appearance of the old man and Dante rattled Dani as much as it enraged me. "This place is too stuffy for me and Lieutenant Cable keeps hitting on me. I'm about to slug him." Dani smirked, rolling her eyes for Alex's benefit, "You think these uniforms would come with manners, but they clearly don't."

I knew in the tone of Dani's voice, the old man had seen Alex with me, picked up on our interactions. The note on the matchbook would be a code phrase that would lead to an interesting conversation at Voltaire's evaluation Dani and I were two weeks out from. I could deal with the old man then, I just had to figure out how Dante fit into the picture.

"Anyway, I'm heading to Goaties over by the rower's quad to be amongst normal pigs." She looked at Alex, throwing on a genuine smile, "Alex, you look stunning and forgive my loose boozy lips. I seem to forget my manners regardless of the fact that I look like a butler in this outfit." She motioned over her dress uniform, "Take care of the Professor here." She then looked at me, her green eyes always telling me a thousand things in one glance. "Professor, enjoy the rest of your night."

I nodded, "Thank you, Dani." As she took a step away, I grabbed her arm, "Take it easy at Goaties and call a cab."

Dani laughed, patting my hand, "I will." She glanced at Alex, before whispering so only the two of us could hear, "I will work faster on getting you out and why the fuck Dante is suddenly in the family picture." Dani turned and walked out of my grasp.

"She's very aggressive and uptight, two things that I never thought I would see in one person at the same time." Alex's voice drew me back into the present reality. I faced her, she had a soft smile on her face, shaking her head at Dani's departure like a confused parent of a teenager.

I sighed, drawing a calming breath in, "The military does that to a person, plus she was already uptight when the Navy trained her to be aggressive." I slid my hand up to the crook of Alex's elbow, "Shall we go to our table? I see Ward waving us over."

Alex nodded, taking my lead and with every step we took to the dining room, I took one more calming breath in. Desperate to calm my rushing blood and pounding heart down.

If the old man had seen what I know he did, Alex was now exactly where I never wanted her to be.

On Voltaire's radar.

I chalked it up to Victoria being worried about Dani, the quick change in her demeanor when the semi-drunk redhead strutted over to us, rambling about a mutual friend stopping by. I would have asked more about it, but Victoria's eyes told me it was nothing more than her annoying Navy buddy being annoying and she returned to the attentive woman I began the night with.

Plus, I wasn't going to let Dani and her weirdness ruin this amazing night. I was truly enjoying being around all of Victoria's fellow officers, especially Ward who was sitting next to me. He was a witty, intelligent and kind man that engaged me in conversation, making me feel like an equal in the room full of gold bars and stiff uniforms.

He seemed to bring out a side of Victoria that was one I only saw in the bedroom first thing in the morning when she woke up and had little time to fall into her head, or whatever thoughts that had her often creasing her brow as the clouds filled those beautiful eyes of hers.

I could see Ward was a father figure to Victoria and it made me happy to see another side of her that didn't only exist in the walls of her home.

Throughout the dinner, she laughed, cracked jokes and never let her hand leave me unless it was to grab salt or to refill my water glass. It all made me smile and my heart swell to the size of Texas of how much I loved her and loved every single side I was slowly getting to see of the blonde.

Then dessert came and Victoria went into her jacket pocket to grab my lipstick I had asked her to carry when I ran out of room in my tiny purse, filling it with Ward's business card and a handful of mints I took from the bathroom. Along with the lipstick, Victoria also pulled out the matchbook Dani shoved in there. I caught a glimpse of her reading the inside flap of it while handing me the lipstick.

Her face changed, her jaw twitched and the clouds swarmed in like a quick squall. I leaned over, whispering to her over Ward speaking up at the front of the room announcing it was that time of the evening to hand out this year's faculty awards, "Are you okay?"

Victoria smiled tightly, shoving the matchbook back in her pocket. "Of course." She turned her attention to Ward.

I knew what was happening, she was retreating. Whatever was written on that matchbook had disturbed her happiness and brought out the cold, careful woman I had spent a year trying to break through to.

Placing a hand on her leg, I squeezed. "What's wrong? I know something is up. What did Dani write on that matchbook?"

Victoria shook her head, eyes still forward, "It's nothing, Alex." She motioned to the half-eaten cheesecake in front of me. "You should eat the rest, it's the best in Maryland."

I sighed hard, "Victoria, don't do this."

She faced me, "I'm not doing anything." She tried to smile around the dark clouds swallowing up her irises, "I just find this part of the evening boring." She then patted my hand on her leg, turning back to listen to Ward's speech.

I slid my hand from her leg, I was irritated now. Pissed off. She was falling back into her old habits, the ones that almost tore us apart and I didn't want to make a scene, but I wasn't going to put up with it.

I looked at her, deciding to ask her to go to the bathroom with me so we could talk without so many ears around us, when the sound of her name coming from the front of the room caught my attention.

"As you all know, Commander Victoria Bancroft has been the academy's military history and tactics Professor for the last few years now. She has managed to keep the midshipmen entertained, as well as, bringing up the overall class scores in that program curriculum that has us all astounded. I remember how utterly bored I was in that class as a midshipmen and having to struggle to stay awake and not drool on my desk." Ward chuckled with the room, "Aside from her magical gift of keeping students awake, she is alumni, she is a hero, a veteran and my friend. Now, this is normally where I close up the awards portion of the evening and call upon us all to head to the dance floor with full drinks, but tonight I have one last thing before we dance the night away."

He cleared his throat. "I spent a lot of time with the Commander on a boat, taking her back home from the desert. I learned a million things about her, her incredible brilliant mind for detail, her quiet kindness and fierce courage that saved many lives over a few days in May." Ward paused, his eyes turning glassy, "I also learned that her biggest regret was missing her graduation ring ceremony because she had chosen to take an immediate duty station the day after graduation. Hence never receiving her class ring."

I turned to look at Victoria, wiping a tear from moving further down her cheek. I watched as she hung her head down, lost in memories that weren't good memories. I was still irritated with her, but it was fading fast as I watched the woman struggle silently. I reached for her hand when Ward called for her to come up, "Victoria, if you would join me up here, I have something I want to give you."

Victoria moved to stand from her seat, when she looked right at me, her face softening ever so slightly, but the storm in her eyes was still present and starting to frighten me.

Before I could say anything, Victoria suddenly leaned over, kissing me on the cheek and whispered right under my ear, "I love you, Alex."

She looked away from me, leaving the table and me completely dumbfounded at what she just said. I knew I should have been feeling ecstatic that Victoria finally said it, but instead I was angry. Angry that it literally fell out of her mouth like Dani said it would. Falling out of her mouth like she was asking me to pass her the salt and it felt like she had to say it, not because she wanted to.

Chapter 19

I was overwhelmed. Lost in my head trying to sort out why the hell the old man would be here, while trying not to fall apart at the gesture Ward had presented me with. My head was jumbled and a twisted ball of emotions and I barely heard the applause or acknowledged Ward handing me the class ring. All I could do was stand there, smile and bite the inside of my cheek to hold back from crying.

I held it together as Ward and I took the photographs, and when he shook my hand and hugged me. I kept my composure shaking hands with most of the faculty and other esteemed guests. By the time I returned to the table, I had almost recovered to continue showing no emotion other than what I wanted others to see.

Then I looked up, my view falling right on Alex sitting at the table, holding her water glass and talking to Ward's wife next to her. She glanced at me, and I saw the fire in her eyes. It wasn't the bright fire, born of love and lust. It was one that telegraphed implicitly that she was angry, very angry.

I reached the table as the others stood up to make their way to the dance floor and the bar, patting my back with smiles as they passed. I went to sit down, clutching the burgundy ring box in my palm. "Alex, would you like to dance?" I swallowed hard, noticing the waver in my voice. I was struggling with keeping it together and it was difficult to hold up the steel walls with her.

She shook her head, smiling tightly, "I'm okay. I think I'm going to step outside for some fresh air, it's warm in here." Pushing the chair back before I could get it for her, she wouldn't look at me, "I'll be back inside in a few minutes. You should go and mingle with the others."

I bent my head down, confused at the sudden change in Alex. "Alex? What's wrong?" I looked over my shoulder at the flood of white and black moving out of the room, "I had no idea Ward was going to do this, it caught me off guard." I took in a deep breath, thinking about Ward's gesture and how the old man crashed the party.

Alex shook her head. "I just need a minute or two to clear my head from the cocktails." She walked away before I could stop her, heading towards the double doors that led to the front courtyard.

I was completely confused now. I knew I had shut down after reading the old man's note. Opting to burrow deep into my internal cave and reel in the ultimate desire to destroy Voltaire before the night was over.

I knew Alex was worried when I slipped a step, keeping her at bay for a second. Then when I looked at her as Ward called me up, I felt all of the fear of losing her rush over me like an avalanche and I let go, telling her I loved her. Doing so cemented so much inside of me, it cemented the fight I was now in and the one that was still coming for us.

I pushed through the double doors, looking at Alex standing in the middle of the courtyard. The night breeze twirling her skirt and hair around, making her look like an image right out of any romantic movie. I reached into the jacket pocket, opening the matchbook and removing a match, I read the note one last time before lighting the thing on fire and dropping it in an ashtray.

-We need to have a conversation, Chimera. OM-

I clenched my jaw, holding the matchbook as long as I could. Watching the flames eat away the black ink and the entire message, before the heat licked at my fingers. I flicked the burning paper away and took a deep breath. "Alex, we can go home if you would like."

She kept her back to me, "Is that what you want?"

I stopped to stand a step or two behind Alex. She was upset and I knew I was the culprit. "I want you to have a good time tonight. Enjoy yourself, feel special and maybe dance with me."

Alex's head tilted up to the night sky, "Why does this always happen? We find a good place, and I mean a really good place to be and I think to myself, this is perfect. Then something or someone tugs on those mysterious parts of you and it all falls to shit." She half turned to look over her shoulder, "Can you answer that, Victoria? The why's?"

I looked down at the white pea gravel of the courtyard, "I don't understand, Alex."

She spun around, glaring at me, "Yes, you do understand. There isn't anything you don't understand, Victoria." She folded her arms over her chest, turning to look down the length of the courtyard. "You understand that Dani got under my skin tonight, casting a new set of doubts about her place in your life. You understand that I wanted this night to be about us, opening up a new chapter for us to continue writing our story in."

She paused, her jaw twitching, "You understand how much I love you and how long I have been patiently waiting for the day to hear you say it back to me." She bit her bottom lip, her eyes shining as the moonlight sunk into the tears brimming. "Dani was right, she seems to always be right about you. You say it like it's nothing, just a few words strung together."

I cringed hearing the last bit. "Alex, I meant what I said." I licked my lips, "Dani isn't right about me, she doesn't know or understand the why's I carry with me."

I took one step closer, feeling my irritation compound as I was about to open up more to this woman in front of me, knowing that it would be painful and bring her deeper into a world I was scared to live in alone, let alone bring Alex into it.

Alex shook her head, "Leave it Victoria. I will be fine in a few minutes and we can go back inside and pretend for however longer you need to."

I grit my teeth, "I've pretended for ten years. You're the first person I have shed my thick skin for." I felt my anger spiraling up, "Alex, look at me."

She sighed heavily, "Victoria, please. I want to be alone before I say something I regret."

I felt my temper flicker, her pissy attitude combined with everything else, pushed my last button. "What are you going to say, Alex? Say it, look me in the goddamn eyes and say it. I never want you to think I can't handle the truth." I half shouted it at her, startling the brunette to turn and face me. I chuckled, "I understand you're pissed off at me, pissed off that my only friend in this world, the annoying redhead is shoving me into humanity kicking and screaming. Seeing that the woman I love is the only person I have ever loved, and she is doing everything she can to make me see it and make you see that."

I looked up at the sky. "Are you pissed that I finally told you I loved you in the way I did? That it fell out of my mouth like a yawn or a spontaneous utterance? Because guess what Alex, I didn't know how to tell you that I love you and it fell out of my mouth in that moment, because looking over at you, you were the one thing in that entire room that grounded me."

I closed my eyes, "God do I love you, Alex, have from the first moment your big blue eyes looked in mine." I bit the inside of my cheek, "But through my entire life, love has been a casual idea. I don't have a good foundation of family love to stand on, just my alcoholic grandmother who isn't really mine. I never learned how to love like people wanted me to love them. The desert and the war took that away from me."

I could feel the tears streaming down my cheeks, I opened the emotional dams that had been sealed for a decade. "I never thought that stupid word would ever apply to my life, I never cared about anyone to the point that I wanted to use the word until you. But then my life, my life is a complicated pile of shit at times that I am scared to love knowing I can, and probably will lose everything and everyone I love."

I glanced at Alex, staring at me with a hard look, "I struggle every goddamn day, and I know I have told you that I'm not good at expressing normal things like a normal person should. I could blame the PTSD or a thousand other things, but the thing is I struggle, and I know you see it the instant it starts, but I can't stop it. I struggle when we are outside of our bubble and I have to interact with the world I live in and not show anyone that you are the most important piece of my heart, my soul, my reason to change everything I am."

I swallowed hard, the old man's message burned in my mind, "If the world finds out how much I love you and how completely weak and human you make me, I will lose you." I half smiled, feeling the waves of exhaustion roll over me, "It's not the PTSD, it's not Dani whispering snarky comments in your ear, it's not the lifetime of lies I have told myself and the world. It's the double life I live and the fact that I have never loved anyone like I love you, Alex, and I struggle with the fear that my love might not ever be enough to keep you safe." My voice hung in the stillness of the night. I didn't realize I had been half yelling throughout the whole diatribe.

I rubbed at my forehead nervously. The truth still lingered, the full truth was right on the edge of my tongue, ready to spill out onto the courtyard. Throw the black hooded figure in between us and point at it, revealing to Alex that I was a killer. I was a killer who had killed hundreds over the years and killed for her.

I clenched my jaw to hold back the words, looking up at Alex. She stood facing me with tears covering her cheeks, but she wasn't flinching or reacting to any of what I said. I had finally broken the woman, shattered her.

I shook my head, digging into my pocket for the car keys. I moved closer, picking up her hand to place the car keys in her palm. "I'm going to walk to for a while, I don't want to be here anymore." I smiled tightly, turning to walk away. "I don't know what else to say, or do, to get you to understand Alex. I'm not asking you to blindly accept my faults, or the bullshit I carry on my back. I couldn't do that to you, punish you with the life I had before you changed it all. There are things I have yet to tell you, and I pray to hell and back I will find the courage to do that."

I took one step away, squinting in the direction of Goaties, my instinct suggesting I meet up with Dani and indulge in old traditions. "Tell Ward I'll talk to him on Monday." I turned back to the still expressionless Alex. With a weak smile, I nodded, "The only thing in the world that I know is real, is how much I fucking love you, Alexandra Ava Ivers."

Sniffling I turned, tucking shaking arms close to my chest I started the wobbly walk to Goaties, shaking my head as grandma Edith's wise words filled my head. "Love will kick you in the tits any chance it can. That's the torrid affair called life, kid."

I frowned, I was starting to hate myself for every choice I had made in this torrid affair I called my life.

I watched her walk two steps away from me before I reacted. Clenching the car keys in my right hand, I shook my head before pulling my arm back and launching the keys at Victoria's back.

The black key fob glanced off her shoulder before falling into the gravel right in front of her, effectively stunning the blonde. She stumbled, looking down at the keys cradled in the white pea gravel. She turned to look over her shoulder, a confused look adding to her flushed cheeks.

I took in a steady breath, "You're taking me home, Victoria. You brought me here and you're going to take me home. That's how dates work." I tried desperately to keep my voice even and strong, but it wouldn't last long. I was completely taken aback by Victoria's strange, yet incredible outburst.

She had made up for telling me she loved me like she was reading off a grocery list by expressing almost everything I had been waiting to hear for a year, but then there were the undertones of fear, apprehension, and double meanings tucked away in her words.

I was still angry at her, but there was no chance in hell was I going to let her walk away from me like she had in the past. I needed her to stay, face me, face us and face whatever demons sitting on her shoulder. Rubbing my arms to warm them, I stared at Victoria. "I'm waiting. It's getting chilly out so you should probably hurry."

Victoria's face softened, "Alex, I thought…."

"You thought what? That you had succeeded in scaring me off for the third time? Laying out more pieces of you that you think will scare me?" I blew out an irritated sigh, "I mean, I never heard you say fuck before, that part was rather different. The rest?"

I waved my hand in the air, "I've had three serious relationships in my life. My college boyfriend who turned into a shit after I thought he was the one. Then there was the X-ray tech in New York that I really wanted to be the one, and I told him I was in love with him and he proceeded to tell me he was in love with the Pediatric surgeon I worked with. They were just married last fall. Then there was the cop, James."

I sniffled, the cold air getting to me. "James was my everything. I dated him for a couple of years before it became a roommate situation. I told him I loved him and goddamn did I mean it. I had started picking out dresses and flower arrangements. Dreaming about an upstate ranch where kids and dogs could run free from the city. Then he and I came to an agreement, it wasn't love we were in. It was a fear of trying to live life to the fullest since our jobs were so unpredictable."

I paused, looking up into the stormy slate grey eyes. "Then I met you and I fought it. I fought the warm feeling you brought whenever you were near me. The crazy tingles you gave me when our hands touched, or from when you grabbed me from walking out into traffic because I'm a ditz. I was scared for a very long time of the feeling choking my heart and soul. And like you, I had a string of shit in my life that lead me to believe love was only for the movies and greeting cards."

I bit my bottom lip, "Then I gave up fighting and I chose to live, fear or no fear and I fell in love with you. I fell in love so deep and hard that I put blinders on to look past the little things my gut tells me to pay attention to. Yes, it's only been two weeks at best in this relationship, but it's one will be last one I ever want to be in. I want a future with you. A house of our own with a hopeless garden in the backyard, a dog or two that likes me but loves you, and I want to grow old sitting next to you on a porch swing looking back at the good old days." I sighed, "I don't care if this is overwhelming, my love for you has been overwhelming and new, so I understand your struggle. I really do, Victoria, because fuck, sometimes it's so hard to get through to you unless it in a situation like this. I hate confrontation, especially when it's with you."

I took a step towards Victoria. "I've waited patiently for you to tell me how you felt about me. It was like waiting for Christmas day and unwrapping the pony I always wanted, and when you finally say it, it's in passing like you're pointing me in the direction of the bathroom. So yes, I am pissed at you for that. We have been friends for a year and a half, I trust you implicitly and would hope you'd trust me as much to not profess your love like you just did in that room full of people."

I blew out another breath, I was on a roll and didn't want to slow down, "Then I'm pissed off at you that, for whatever reason trapped in your beautiful mind, you think that loving me will start the next great apocalypse. Well, you know what? So be it, Victoria. Let you being in love with me be the end of the world as we know it. Because at least at the end, while we watch the sky burn, we will know we both followed our hearts and loved truly, deeply and with reckless abandon."

I pointed at the keys now in her hand. "I'm not letting you walk away. I am not letting you take the easy, moody way out. I am here, you are stuck with me so man up and deal with it. Because guess what, Victoria, god, I don't even know your middle name, Bancroft? I fucking love you." I tucked my arms back against my body, "I am in this with my whole life and I will risk my life to be with you, but do me one favor, cut the weird cloak and dagger spy talk out. I feel like I'm trapped in a stupid action movie from the eighties. Last I checked, we weren't at war with the Russians."

Victoria looked at the keys in her hand, twirling them as silence fell. I shook my head, grumbling, "Victoria, it's getting cold."

"The Russians are still iffy, but yes, we are no longer at war with them." Victoria's voice trembled as she held up the car keys. "Did you really just throw car keys at me?"

I shrugged, "Yes I did, what are you going to do about it?" I placed my hands on my hips in a challenging manner. "At least it wasn't the mini keys, they weigh a ton and have sharp edges that could take an eye out."

I saw the beginnings of a smirk grace the edge of her mouth, "I should take you home, shouldn't I?"

"That might be in your best interest right now." I spun on my heel, starting to head back to the side lot where we parked, "We're stopping to get cheesecake on the way home."

When my back was turned, my entire body began shaking as I heard her steps crunch on the gravel. I closed my eyes, hoping I could hold onto the courage until I was able to climb into bed and sleep away this unusual night.

Three steps away, a warm hand clasped around my elbow, stilling me. I glanced to the right, Victoria was standing next to me, shrugging off her pristine white jacket before placing it over my shoulders, smiling softly as she pulled me closer to her warmth. The same warmth that I had grown horribly addicted to over the last week or two. I groaned internally when my body betrayed my mind, leaning against her when she wrapped an arm around my waist.

We walked a few more feet, when I heard, "I've always wanted a dog."

I looked at her, my brow scrunched up, "Excuse me?"

Victoria was looking straight ahead, smiling softly. "Nothing, Alex." She tilted her head down, catching my eyes, "I love you, Alex."

I shivered again, and not from the cold, but from the genuine and intense sincerity Victoria spoke those words. "I love you, Victoria."

"My middle name is Eleanor. Victoria Eleanor Bancroft." Victoria pulled me deeper into her side.

I bit the inside of my mouth, trying not to smile at the very vintage middle name, "Well, then. I love you Victoria Eleanor Bancroft." I paused, "I thought it was Victoria C. Bancroft?"

She laughed lightly, shaking her head, "That was a misprint I never bothered to have revised, gave me a little more privacy." She then looked down at me, "I'm never going to get rid of you, am I?"

"Nope." I tugged the jacket over my arms, "Not even the Russians could pry me away."

"Alex..." I could feel her eyes rolling in the way she said my name.

We walked back to the car in silence. Tonight wasn't the final solution to everything that was a flawed work in progress, but it was a start, and that was good enough for me to keep fighting. Victoria was worth it, even if all the weird cloak and dagger crap was real and she was spy. She was worth it. She was my heart.

Awkward silence.

It was becoming Alex and I's song, awkward silence.

It seemed to follow us every time we had a heart to heart of explosive emotions.

The silence was heavy in the car as I drove us home. Alex was huddled up in my white jacket, staring out her window with a boxed cheesecake on her lap. I knew that it was going to take more than a silent drive home to seal up the rift created in the courtyard. I was almost worried what would happen when we got home, I didn't want to ignore or disregard what we hashed out, but at the same time it unnerved me. We ended the heart to heart with smiles and hugs, but as soon as we got into the car and broke off physical contact, the awkward silence found its opportunity and swallowed us whole.

The cloak and dagger crap Alex mentioned, unnerved me. She hit the nail on the head and proved Dani was dead on about Alex. She was smarter than all of the others. Which was probably why the redhead brought it up every chance she could, when discussing the brunette. Hearing her spew out her emotions about us, she was closer to figuring out my secret life. She was getting closer to Voltaire and both were slow burning fuses.

Granted, I didn't help with my verbal vomiting of how my double life would eventually put her in jeopardy, but like they say, in the heat of the moment, truths are spilled.

Looking over at her, the truths were spilled, all of them. I loved Alex so much that it was ridiculous what I would do for her. What I was going to do for her. Especially after she threw the growing old together comment on the ground as a challenge. I had no idea I wanted that until it was there barreling my way, spewed from her mouth to hopefully hit my ears and talk some sense into my heart. Regardless of how much we loved each other, in the end I knew I was going to lose Alex, and she was right, if the world was going to end tomorrow, I would want it to end with her in my arms.

Turning back to focus on catching the last turn into the driveway, I decided to break the silence, "I'll take the cheesecake while you head upstairs to change. I made room in the closet for your dress." I cringed at myself, I was being incredibly awkward.

Alex sighed with a smile, "It's still early, I might make some popcorn and close out this Saturday night with a cheesy movie." She glanced at me, her eyes filled with a thousand more things she wanted to ask.

Nodding, I put the car in park, hustling to get out and move to her side to open the door and help her out. I might have fucked up most of the night, but I still had manners. Holding out my hand, I swallowed hard when hers took mine. Alex was always so warm, one of the million things I adored about her. "I think there is some leftover beer in the garage fridge, I can grab it if you want?"

Alex smiled, pulling my jacket tighter over her shoulder, handing the cheesecake over. "Thank you."

She stepped away while I closed and locked the car, turning to stare at her while she unlocked the front door and disappeared inside. When she was out of sight, I felt my shoulders sag, I really ruined this night for her. My whole plan to tell her I loved her as we walked along the back tree line near my office, under the moonlight, failed. I had wanted to ask her to move in with me as soon as Monday morning rolled around. I would then call her landlord and convince him it was a really good idea to give Alex back the deposit, and then spend the rest of her vacation making room for her in my home, and move her in.

I had to make it up to her, somehow.

After locking the front door, I shuffled to the kitchen, dropping the cheesecake in the fridge and then grabbed the popcorn and red bowl Alex had designated as her popcorn bowl. Setting them to the side, I ran my hands down the stiff polyester skirt, looking up at the sound of Alex's heels scraping across the wooden floors. I suddenly wanted to be out of this uniform. The uniform that always brought me trouble and heartache.

Groaning, I yanked the black tie apart and headed upstairs. I was going to shove this god awful outfit back into the black bag. Tuck it into the depths of my closet to never find my sight until next year's formal. I wanted to grab all of my uniforms and take them to the basement and shove them into a plastic bin. I didn't want that life anymore. I wasn't happy being complacent with the life the uniforms held like I had been for the last few years.

I pushed the bedroom door open, finding Alex sitting on the edge of the bed, still wearing her dress. Her head was bent down, staring at her hands. I paused, "Alex?"

She looked up at me, her eyes very tired and glassy, "Hmm?"

I stepped closer, "Are you okay?"

She nodded slowly, running her hands over the fabric of her skirt. "Yeah, I was just thinking about a few things."

I dropped my hands to my hips, fearing what those things were, "Hopefully they are good things?" I spotted the dinner jacket sitting next to her, I reached for it, "I should hang that up." Picking the white fabric up, I squeezed the ring box in the front pocket. Removing it, I set it down on the side table.

"They are for the most part." Alex half smiled as I looked over my shoulder from the closet, shoving the jacket on a hanger. I raised an eyebrow in question, she shrugged, "My thoughts, they're good things." Her voice trembled slightly, worrying me.

Moving from the closet to stand in front of her, I waited for her to look in my eyes, "Alex, what is it? I can tell something is rattling around in your head."

Alex continued to pick at her skirt, sitting in silence. I finally looked away, the night was over and I didn't want to keep poking Alex. "I'm going to take a shower then go downstairs to the office to put a few things away." I wanted to call Dani or email her. Tear her a new one for inspiring Alex to speak her mind and for mentioning knowing about Alex's ex-boyfriend digging into Voltaire.

Dropping my hands from my waist, I turned towards the bathroom, when Alex's fingers wrapped around my wrist tightly. Startling me.

Alex stood up slowly, holding on, "There is something rattling around my head, something that seems to be heavier than everything else spoken tonight." She stepped closer, "You might be a spy for the Navy, a modern day Jane Bond. You could be someone completely broken and I have yet to find all of the piece's others chipped out of you along the road. Things that I can deal with, work with, we can work through."

She sighed slowly, her hand moving from my wrist, and up the stiff white fabric of the dress shirt. "Sitting in the car waiting for you to fulfill my stupid request for a raspberry cheesecake, I fell even more in love with you. Then that's when the anvil dropped, a silly thing popped into my head, and the more I thought about it during the ride back. The more it spoke volumes in my heart and body." Her hands moved to the top button of my shirt, pulling away the loose black tie, looking deep into my eyes. "I've never made love to anyone before."

I tilted my head down, moving to reach and cover her hands with mine, "Alex, we've...."

She shook her head, "You have. That first night, you made love to me and what followed was an incredible discovery of a million things within myself."

Alex dropped the tie to the floor, moving for the buttons, slowly undoing each one and letting cool air float in, making me shiver from it and what Alex was sharing with me. "I've never made love to anyone who I was beyond hopelessly in love with. I've never had the chance to or wanted to."

She tugged the shirt free from the top of my skirt, letting it hang open as her hands glide across my stomach and up my sides. "I had romantic high hopes about tonight, most of those hopes came true, but when I sat in the car after our fight, I was worried I blew it."

I closed my eyes at the way her hands moved over my body. Her fingertips grazing my scar and still healing bruise, before moving on to my side, "Alex, you didn't do anything wrong." I opened my eyes to look in determined blue ones, asking me as much as they were telling me what Alex wanted. I swallowed hard, nerves edging in with the slow arousal her hands were building. Sliding my hands over the sides of her face, I bent down and kissed Alex.

Pushing hard against her mouth when I felt fingertips dig into the thin bandage I wore to cover up the ugly yellowing bruise on my side. Her mouth opened wider, our tongues meeting to tease and ask for more. Feeling her teeth graze the tip of my tongue before she nipped at my bottom lip, I parted for air. Holding her face in my hands, I whispered, "I've never done this either." It was the truth, I had never loved anyone like this woman and been in a moment like this. It was truly my first time.

Alex looked up, her eyes wide with her own brand of nerves. "Victoria..."

I shook my head, kissing her softly once more. "Do what you wish to me, I love you, Alex. I trust you." I ran my hand over her shoulders, finding the zipper to her dress, and pulled it down to loosen the garment before stepping back to remove my shirt and work on the wrap.

Alex took the hint and quickly slipped out of her dress, picking it up and tossing it on the chair by the bed. She did the same with her shoes before she came for me. Grabbing my hands to stop them from finishing the removal of my bra, the bandage floating to the floor. She stood before me completely naked, making my very analytical mind focus on the small detail that Alex had not worn any undergarments throughout the night, sending my desire for the woman into overdrive.

Her warm hands discarded my bra with a sense of expertise, then ran down my collarbone, the middle of my chest before she palmed my breasts, "Say it again." Alex pressed against me as she nuzzled into my neck, pressing kisses and small bites along the skin. I barely registered her unzipping my skirt until I felt it drift to the floor to rest at my ankles. Deft and stealthy hands soon removed my panties like she was a professional pickpocket.

"I love you." The words fumbled out, I was losing all thought from the sensations from her hands and lips brushing across my skin. I felt Alex smile against my skin, her hands gently squeezing my breasts before moving down to my hips. I was pulled towards the bed, turned and delicately nudged to lie down. Alex followed, lying her body flush against mine, kissing me intensely as she settled between my legs. There was a slow, purposeful way about her kisses, her hands and the way she looked at me.

Reaching up, I brushed her hair back, "I love you, Alex." Watching the shy grin cover her face, made me want to say the words in every breath I took around her. She bent her head down, kissing the bare skin in front of her, moving slowly down with her hands mapping out the next stop. My heart raced, my breath quickened when firm fingers trailed down my stomach and over the crease of my thighs, teasing where I ached for Alex.

I could feel her watching me with every teasing brush of those determined fingertips. "Victoria, look at me." I glanced up, finding Alex as she hovered over me, her fingers slowly sliding into me as she whispered, "I love you, Victoria."

I couldn't speak, the slow torture of her fingers made it difficult, my hips moving in cadence with Alex was the only way I could communicate. She smirked, picking up the pace, pressing her body against me. With her other hands, she pulled my chin towards her, brushing her lips over mine as we shared the same air. I swallowed hard, trying to make this last but with every movement of Alex's fingers and thumb caressing me, I was seconds away from a powerful orgasm. Every one of her touches, kisses, thrusts and looks were founded in love, in purpose, and asking me to finally submit to the fact I was in love and there was no turning back. I had finally given everything I had, and was, to this brunette hovering over me, taking my breath away with every slow movement she made.

Lifting my chin to kiss her, Alex's lips met mine at the same time she thrusted deep inside of me, her thumb pressing down on the swollen nub, sending an electrical storm through my body as I came hard. Crying out her name, clutching on to her shoulders to steady me as I drifted off into a sea of blackness that only came from being swallowed whole by intense pleasure.

The sound of my own pants drew me back to the light and the image of Alex looking at me with worried eyes, brushing some of the hair that freed itself from the forgotten bun I still had my hair in, "Are you okay? Did I…was it too much?" She looked down at my bruise, running trembling fingers over it. "I forgot about this."

I shook my head, grabbing her hand to roll her over so I could be on top. I held her arms over her head, scanning over the beauty beneath me, "I did too." I bent, brushing over her lips, "It's my turn to make you forget." I kissed her intensely, "Forget that there was a day you ever thought I didn't love you."

I heard Alex gasp slightly, her eyes turning glassy before I shook my head, kissing her once more before moving to kiss down her body. Settling in between her legs, I saw how much Alex needed me, wanted me. I didn't waste another moment, covering her with my mouth I held onto her hips with my hands as she jutted up from the bed. I smiled as my tongue moved against her, showing Alex that I was still the teacher and she still the student. I lost myself in the sounds of her moans, gasps, her fingers digging into my hair and yanking out the bun in attempts to pull me deeper into her. I only let go of her hip to glide my fingers where my tongue had been, watching her come instantly from the simple sensation. Her entire body flushing a soft pink as pleasure overwhelmed her. Alex was so beautiful even in a moment like this. Sweaty, gasping, cursing and breathing like she had ran back to back marathons.

After letting her recover, I crawled up to lie against her. Loving the way it felt to have her heart pound against my chest, I kissed the corner of her mouth, whispering, "Did it work?"

Alex smiled sheepishly, licking her lips. "I don't even know my name right now." She pressed a hand against my face, "But I still love you, Victoria, that I haven't forgotten."

I blushed, nodding, "Good, I don't ever want you to forget."

Alex smiled, tugging me to snuggle up into her arms, her face buried in my shoulder, "Never happen."

Morning came far too quickly. Normally I would have welcomed the bright rays filtering through the blinds in Victoria's bedroom, but today, I wanted them to go away and leave me alone. Leave me in this moment forever. I was happily wrapped up in Victoria's arms, naked, half asleep and deeper in love than I could ever imagine.

I glanced up at the sleeping blonde, hair tousled about with a few hair pins still sticking out here and there. Formalities of removing those in the heat of the moment never happened, it was mentioned she should take them out, but Victoria passed out on me before we got that far. She slept heavily, not even budging when I couldn't resist running a hand along her neck and over the small red marks I had left.

I grinned, pushing my head deeper into the pillow, I had made love to Victoria last night, all night and it was incredible.

It was incredible to have someone give themselves to me like she did, trust me and love me like she did, does. I had felt silly and stupid for being tentative in telling her, but then I saw the sadness in her eyes as she asked me what was wrong. I didn't want her to drift away from me when we had covered so much ground.

In this moment, the morning light catching pieces of her hair and making them glow, I honestly didn't care if she was a Jane Bond. A cloak wearing, dagger carrying denizen of the government, or god knows whatever else. I loved her and she was my whole world, last night proved that. I was in this far too deep to walk away no matter what.

I sat up, kissing her softly on the forehead before sneaking out from under the covers, cursing the bright Sunday morning sun as I wobbled to the bathroom. I was hungover, sleepy, and starving. My body burning through the small amount of food I ate last night, but not the large amounts of alcohol I drank.

Washing my hands, I grabbed Victoria's shorts and shirt from the bottom shelf of her linen shelves. Throwing them on, I crept out of the bedroom to head down to the kitchen and raid the stupid cheesecake I requested, because it was the only thing I could think of to break up the tension.

Crawling up on the counter, I didn't bother cutting a slice of cheesecake to plate it. I just dug into it with a fork as the box sat on my lap. My legs swung freely as I faced the patio doors, catching Dale walk outside to water his tulips. I groaned in delight at how tasty the raspberry cheesecake was, not caring that it was probably too decadent for an empty stomach.

Whatever, I was on vacation and in love.

Setting the box down after a few bites, I opted to make a pot of coffee and maybe a pile of eggs and bacon. Stretching sore arms over my head, I grinned again at why they were sore, and sighed out loud with content.

"You know cheesecake is going to give you a stomach ache?" Victoria's raspy voice made me grin wider and blush, "Especially an empty one like yours." She moved to the coffee pot, winking at me as I turned to look at her over my shoulder.

"I was hungry and too tired to think about making real food. Figured the sugar boost would motivate me." I waved my hand over her outfit, one of my scrub tops and her ratty Navy shorts. "Stealing from me now?"

Victoria grinned, shaking her head, "All's fair." She set up the coffee pot, filling the kitchen with the delicious smells of hot fresh coffee, before walking over and kissing me. "Good morning."

I bit my bottom lip, savoring the way her lips always tasted like vanilla, "Morning." I ran a hand over her arm as she reached for a frying pan, "I can make breakfast since I'm up before you. Which should be documented in our history book."

Victoria laughed. "I will make a notation first thing after breakfast." She set the frying pan on the stove, motioning for me to grab eggs and bacon from the fridge, "I was wondering about two things Alex."

Sliding off the counter, I raised an eyebrow. "And those are?" I yanked open the fridge, grabbing eggs and bacon. Holding them over to Victoria as I waited for her to tell me.

She took the food from me, dug into the pocket of her baggy sweat shorts, removing the burgundy ring box from last night. "It's a tradition in the Navy, well the Academy, that when alumni are dating someone they really like, they give them their class ring and ask them to go steady." She flipped open the lid, pulling out the shiny class ring with a dark blue gemstone in the center. Victoria reached for my right hand, "I don't think this will fit your ring finger since mine are bony and big, but." She looked up at me with a silly smirk, "Will you go steady with me, Alexandra Ivers?"

I shook my head, grinning like an idiot as she slowly placed the ring on my middle finger, "I think you already know the answer, but yes, Victoria Bancroft, I will be your girlfriend." When she was done, I wrapped my fingers in hers, pulling her hand up to kiss, "And for the record, your fingers are absolutely perfect, trust me." I winked at her, "So what's the second thing you wondering about?"

Victoria kissed my cheek, moving to turn on the stove. "When do you go back to work?"

I frowned, hating that reality was right around the corner. "Sadly, this Thursday is my first double. I will have Sunday and Mondays off, but it's back to my old schedule of endless twelve hour shifts with Stacy." I couldn't stop looking at the silver and blue ring on my finger, my mind slowly drifting to a future with a different ring on a different finger. "I can take more vacation days in a couple of months."

Victoria nodded, cracking a few eggs. "How long do you think it would take you to pack up your apartment? If I helped and maybe Dale and Mary?"

I tore my eyes away from the ring, my brow furrowing, "Um, why?"

Victoria stood off to the side of the frying pan. "Move in with me, tomorrow, Alex." She sighed with a soft smile, "You practically live here and I don't like it when you aren't here, plus that apartment is a giant shithole that you pay too much for." She waved the spatula around, "I have plenty of room here and I know it will be further from work...."

I cut her off, jumping into her open arms, kissing her. "I can be packed up in a day. I never really fully unpacked from a year ago." I couldn't hold back the giant grin, "Are you sure?" I couldn't believe that in the last handful of hours I had gone from thinking I was about to live in silence, hoping Victoria would open up, to having everything and more.

Victoria nodded, squeezing my side. "I am. I've never been more sure about anything in my entire life. I want you, Alex. I want to come home to you, wake up to you, catch you stealing my shirts and leaving dirty plates or popcorn bowls in the living room. I want to come home from a trip to you watering tulips in your underwear trying to give Dale a heart attack." She ran a hand down my hair, "You are my home, Alex."

I shook my head, my eyes filling with happy tears. "Tomorrow it is then." I kissed her once more before squinting playfully at her, "This isn't a ruse to get me to give you back all the clothes I've stolen from you?"

Victoria chuckled, "Maybe, I know you took my favorite sweatshirt again. Stacy sent me a picture."

I frowned, "That's it, no more bagel Thursdays for her." I sighed, moving to hug Victoria again, "We're really going to do this?"

I felt her nod, embracing me tighter, "I am, we are, yes. I'm tired of wasting time." She sighed in my arms.

I sniffled, opening my eyes to see the eggs starting to burn. I poked Victoria in the side, "We're about to waste some eggs."

She spun around, whispering a curse word before scraping at the eggs.

I laughed, shaking my head, "I don't think I'll ever get used to you saying fuck."

She peered over her shoulder, the devilish twinkle in her eye that popped in right before she had me crying out her name under her body, "In time you will, trust me." She turned back to the frying pan, "Can you water the tulips? And ask Dale if he'll help us move tomorrow while I finish breakfast?"

I could only nod at her back, my heart and body throbbing suddenly at the promise of what was to come in time.

Pushing open the patio door, I waved at Dale greeting me with a hearty hello. I proceeded to unwind the hose as I asked my new neighbor if he and his wife could be swindled into helping me move.

Chapter 20

I should have been moving the boxes stacked up in front of me, but I was too busy staring. Staring at Victoria as she unloaded boxes from the back of her BMW. Sweaty, flush faced and her muscles moving in ways that made my heart race.

I had tried my best to get her to take the light stuff since her side was still healing, but she refused. Taking over the heavy lifting for me and Dale as we moved me out of my crappy apartment. I didn't really have much of anything, just books, clothes, linens and my extensive movie collection. Most of my furniture was junky and cheap and would stick out in Victoria's home, so we donated a lot of it, but I did keep the metal desk I rescued many years ago. That desk was sitting in her basement moved into a spot that Victoria was going to dedicate as my area where I could go to work on whatever while she sat on the couch.

I grinned, biting my bottom lip. Victoria had made a lot of room in her home for me. Spending all day yesterday moving things out of her closet to make more room my clothes to hang. She even thinned out her book collection to give mine a place on the shelves, and she did it all with a strange giddiness I thought I would never see in the woman.

"If Victoria was getting paid in stares, she would be a rich woman."

I broke away from my girlfriend, turning to blush at Mary coming out of the house to pick up another box. "Mary…I."

She patted my back, "Don't worry, I remember what it was like." She reached for my right hand, holding it up to look at the academy ring on my middle finger, "I remember when Dale gave me his. It was more exciting than when he proposed to me right before he left for the war." Mary grinned, letting my hand go, "A little bit of advice, being with a Navy officer is tough at times. They always have an intense sense of duty that we normal folk can't understand." She bent down, picking up a box of my shirts. "If you ever want to talk or what have you, I'm right next door, Alex."

I reached down, grabbing another box, still embarrassed at being caught by my neighbor. "Thanks Mary, I might do that. When Victoria goes back to work, she is usually in and out of town and when we do talk, I don't understand half of the words she uses. Bow and stern, port head, and other gibberish." I shifted the box, following Mary into the den. "How long have you and Dale been together? And was it really better than getting engaged when he gave you his class ring?"

Mary grinned, setting the box next to the others labeled clothes, "We have been together almost forty-three years and yes, it was far better than when he popped the question." She turned to face me, "Because when a Navy man or woman, gives you their ring, it's their way of telling you that you are their forever." She chuckled, "For the single reason that none of them want to tarnish their pride by asking for it back if you're not the one." Mary dug under her shirt, pulling out a necklace with a similar ring like mine looped around a chain, "I've worn this for almost a half century and every time I look at it, I fall in love with that old coot all over again."

I glanced at my hand, twisting the ring and wanting to change the subject. The idea of marrying Victoria was exciting, but frightening. There were still a few secrets I had to uncover before we got to that point. Either way, I knew Victoria was my forever. "Thanks for helping us today, Mary. I really appreciate it." I smiled at the older woman, "This was definitely last minute."

"Don't even think about it, Alex. Dale and I were happy to hear that our lovely neighbor finally decided to live a little." She moved to stand in front of me, both of us looking toward the open front door, hearing Dale and Victoria laughing. "Victoria is like one of our kids. We keep an eye on her and over the years have grown attached to her. We were excited to see her face and eyes light up whenever she mentioned her nurse friend." She winked at me as I blushed again, "Welcome to the neighborhood, let's go help them before Dale tweaks his back and Victoria pulls her side."

I sighed, "I told them both I could handle it."

Mary laughed, "Lesson one about being with the Navy, they don't listen and will try to save the world." She patted my back, "By the way, my husband might chew your ear off about restoring your car. He's been eyeballing it every morning, trying to figure out a way to ask you."

I shook my head laughing, my grin growing as Victoria and I made eye contact, "He can have it, that car has been nothing but problems since I first bought it." I swallowed hard as Victoria lifted her shirt to wipe sweat from her forehead, giving me views of her skin that had me shoving my hands in my pocket, "The only good thing it did was break down and lead me to her."

I heard Mary issue a soft aw, before hollering at her husband trying to lift a very full box of books, leading me to holler at Victoria for trying to lift the same box.

"I still can't believe my landlord gave me back my security deposit and next month's prepaid rent. I signed a contract giving him free will to screw me over." I stood in the closet, trying to arrange my clothes to fit in neatly with Victoria's uniforms and suits, the box I was emptying sitting on top of the small floor safe.

The day had gone quickly and with the help of Dale and Mary, I was completely moved in by dinner time. Victoria and I took over unpacking as our neighbors headed in for the night with promises they would come over tomorrow for steaks as our way of thanking the kind couple for their help.

We were almost done unpacking my meager belongings, all that was left was my clothes and finding space in drawers full of Victoria's endless Navy shirts.

"I guess he was feeling generous?" Victoria stood near the bed with a strange smirk on her face, folding up the last empty box that held my clothes. "Plus he was screwing you and all the other tenants over. Charging you that much to live in a building full of code violations and never fixing that terrible shower of yours,"

I poked my head around the corner, grinning at the blonde standing in her still sweaty Navy football shirt and jeans, looking around the room trying to make sure everything was in order. "I can recall once or twice you loved that shower."

Victoria looked at me, "Only because you were in it with me, showing off your anatomy skills." She bent her head down, reaching for another small box, "Everything is put away, I just need to move the safe into the basement so you have more room in the closet." She paused, her face furrowing as if she remembered something. "Alex, um."

I stepped out of the closet, "What is it? Already having regrets about this?" I tried to keep my tone light, suddenly nervous.

Victoria shook her head, "Never happen. I forgot to show you a few things." She set the empty boxes outside the door and waved me over to the bedside table, "I want to show you this for when I have to go out of town and you're home alone." Sitting on the edge of the bed, she pulled the drawer open and lifted the bottom up, revealing a black gun in a holster. Victoria glanced at me, "This is a .40 caliber Smith and Wesson. It holds fifteen rounds and there's an extra magazine in the drawer." She paused, waiting for a reaction from me.

I shrugged, "I'm used to Glocks, so you will have to show me how to load this one." I looked up at Victoria, her eyes curious at my comment. I smiled, "I dated a cop, remember? James taught me how to use a gun years ago. Took me to the range and showed me how to shoot, I just opted to never carry one. I've seen the damage they do in the emergency room to want to have the responsibility of ever having to be one the to cause it." Moving to sit next to her, "He always kept his tucked between the mattress and the bed frame."

Victoria tilted her head down, covering the gun back up and closing the drawer, "There is one in my desk, and down in the basement tucked under the first set of couch cushions." She half looked at me, her eyes turning cloudy, "It took me a long time to feel safe, normal and...."

I grabbed her hand, shaking my head, "You don't need to tell me, I get it." I kissed her shoulder, standing up from the bed to return to the closet, "But please show me how to set the alarm. I'd rather have that as the first defense." I smiled, digging back into the box for the last few shirts to hang up. "How about you order pizza while I run a bath and we can both soak away the day?" I tilted my head back towards Victoria, her eyes back to clear.

"Double cheese?"

"Of course, and can you grab the bottle of wine I set in the fridge?" I held a shirt in my hand, staring at the hanger.

"Yes ma'am." Victoria appeared around the corner of the closet, grinning at me as she brushed a few strands from my face. I met her eyes, smiling as she bent forward and kissed me, whispering against my lips, "I love you." Before skittering out of the room and down to the kitchen.

When she was gone, I set down the hanger, blowing out a slow breath. I was honest in telling her that guns didn't bother me. I had lived with James and there was always some sort of firearm around the apartment. What did bother me was that my very bland Professor of a girlfriend had a high grade military issued firearm in her bedside table with hollow point ammunition.

All small details James had blithered my way in his version of dinner conversation. Details that told me a retired Naval Professor should not have such things readily at hand.

Details that kept pulling my gut in the same direction it was heading on Saturday.

"I don't think this tub was meant for two." I stretched my leg around Alex, sloshing more bubble water over the side. "And I'm seriously rethinking about eating in the bathroom." I felt her laugh as she laid against my chest, wine glass in hand and a piece of pizza in the other. Shaking my head, I ran my hand along her side, pinching lightly. "I'm serious. I keep looking at the toilet and the pizza. It's killing my appetite." Even though I loved the idea of taking a bath together, I was rethinking eating in the bath together.

"The toilet and this entire bathroom is spotless, cleaner than an operating room." She tilted her head back, offering me a bite of her pizza, "Why in the world are you thinking about germs when you're sharing bath water with me?"

I looked past the pizza at her naked chest with bubbles barely covering anything, "I honestly have no idea." Kissing her cheek, I took a bite, moving my hand from her side to her stomach, pressing her closer against me. "But I think I will look into getting a new tub, a bigger one."

Alex sighed happily against me, snuggling deeper into my arms, "I'll help you pay for it." Lying her head on my shoulder, she looked up at me, "We should figure out how to split the bills, groceries and other things."

I shook my head, turning away from the half of pizza sitting on the counter torturing me since I was starving, but utterly grossed out. "Don't worry about anything Alex, I have it covered." I glanced at her, seeing Alex's brow scrunch up in that way it did when she was peeved, "Just don't buy too much kale when you do the grocery shopping, I hate that stuff."

Alex suddenly scooted away from me, sloshing water around and bringing a chill to my skin. Turning around to face me, she set her wine glass down, "Victoria, I have a good job and can contribute to the household. I didn't move in to be a pampered woman." She folded her arms across her chest, covering up and making me frown internally.

I set my own wine down, moving closer to the brunette who looked stunning with her wet hair piled on top of her head, pink cheeks with the cutest pout. "Alex, I asked you to move in for completely selfish reasons. Sharing bills and the other boring things in life never entered my head when I asked you."

I pushed her legs open so I could wrap them around my waist, smiling as I saw it melting her stubbornness when our skin touched. "I wasn't lying when I said I wanted to come home to you, wake up to you and spend every minute I can with you. My request, if anything, was born out of pure selfishness." I ran my hand up her arm, "I want you to be happy as you make me." My fingers glided over her collarbone, "So, if it makes you happy, you can pay the cable bill and every other week of groceries."

I felt her sigh under my touch, her legs pulling me in further. She finally looked in my eyes, a small smile playing at the corners of her mouth. I settled my hand against her neck, right over a racing pulse, "Alex, I love you and there isn't a thing I wouldn't do for you if you asked me." I rolled my eyes, "Well, I still won't ever eat kale, but you get the point." I looked back down at the grinning brunette, her hands running up and down my sides.

"I've always been independent, Victoria, never relied on anyone and I don't want you to think that I'm ever taking advantage of you. I trust you and I want you to trust me." She searched my eyes in a way that told me she was asking more of me than sharing bills. "For the record, you make me happier than I have ever been, just by the little cheesy romantic things you say. It's one of the reasons why I love you." She bent forward kissing the tip of my nose, leaning back to meet my eyes again she smiled lightly, "Can you turn on the hot water? The water's getting cold."

I grinned, watching her gaze shift behind me where the taps were. "I have an idea, how about we get out of the tub, reorder another pizza, eat it downstairs while watching a movie in the living room. Celebrate out first night in this house together." She was barely paying attention to my other hand moving slowly between us.

Alex nodded, still smiling, "Can't shake the gross out factor, can you?" She went to reach for the taps and the drain.

I bent forward, meeting her halfway and kissing her hard, pulling away enough to murmur, "Not yet, I want to warm you up the old fashioned way and christen this tub before we replace it."

Alex went to make a comment, when nothing but a gasp came out as my fingers moved easily into her. Her skin flushed instantly, her eyes closing as she took a deep breath, "Victoria...."

I grinned, kissing her again while my fingers moved, shutting down all of her thoughts and reducing the woman to gasps and soft moans followed by her hands gripping on to mine to prevent from slipping under the water. I continued moving in and out of her, watching the woman unravel in the most beautiful way under my touch. It was another thing I had grown selfishly addicted to, and would do as often as I could now that Alex was living with me. I loved her, I trusted her and I would show her every chance I could.

There truly wasn't a damn thing I wouldn't do for Alex if she asked me, and I knew that promise included telling her everything when the time came, and it was coming soon.

~Saturday ~

Alex had gone back to work on Thursday, and even though it had been barely a week since she moved in, it felt like she had always belonged in the house. She still slept in as much as possible, growling like a hibernating bear when I tried to wake her up for breakfast. Learning that she would wake up on her own and find me on the back patio for coffee before we decided on what to eat.

I would pack her lunch and send her off with kisses, handing over the keys to my BMW with the adamant instructions that she was to drive my car instead of that old mini for her safety. Dale had taken on the task of rebuilding the entire engine on the car and embarked on a restoration project with Alex's help on her days off. I didn't need the car. I never had to leave the house unless it was for work or grocery shopping. She fought me for a day until I forced her, then she found that the car had satellite radio and consistent working air conditioning. Now I knew I would rarely ever drive that car again and should start looking for a new one.

While she was at work, Alex would text me, call me and ask me what I was doing. Stacy was on a week off and she was left with the new nurses to talk to. She had been on back to back doubles since going back and I hated it. I missed her as much as she missed me, and I couldn't fall asleep until I heard her keys in the front door. Hear her tossing her bag in the laundry room, then raid the fridge before trudging up the stairs to crawl on the bed and wake me up by asking, "Are you asleep?" I would tell her no, open my arms and let her crawl in them. We would then talk about her day while she ate cookies in her scrubs and whatever sweatshirt of mine she had stolen for the day.

Everything was perfect until Friday night when Dani sent me a reminder.

-Hate to burst the happy frappy bubble fun, but tomorrow at one p.m. yearly eval fun.–

And now I stood in the bathroom, fixing the last button on my khaki uniform, staring back at myself, wishing I could take all of my six hundred hours of vacation and look for a new job.

Alex was running around the bedroom, trying to find her clean scrubs. "Are you sure I washed them after unpacking?"

I nodded, smoothing a few strands of hair back into the tight bun, looking away as the black hooded figure appeared behind me, reminding me. I looked away, putting away the hair brush, "You did, then I folded them last night and put them in the dresser. Third drawer next to my sweatpants."

Walking out of the bathroom, I spotted a pantless Alex rummaging through the drawer, pulling out a pair of dark purple scrubs. "You are amazing." She turned to look at me, clutching the scrub pants to her chest, "And you look amazing. I don't think I'll ever get tired of the way you look in uniform." She winked at me before sitting on the bed to cover up legs I dreamt about. "How long is your meeting?"

I tore my eyes away the second they were covered, "About two hours, it's the yearly teacher evaluation and then they go over the new class of incoming midshipmen." I moved to the dresser, grabbing my watch and wallet, "I might stop by the hospital when I'm done, bring you lunch if that's okay?"

Alex grinned, "It's always okay, but be warned, Stacy is back today and she might interrogate you." She stood up, gathering her hair in a ponytail, "I asked Dale this morning if I could borrow his truck, since my mini is in pieces in his garage."

"You can take the BMW. Dani is picking me up." I ran my hands down the front of my shirt, "She's meeting with Ward. He wants to bring her on next semester as a student advisor." I smiled, catching the ring on Alex's finger and that she had no negative reaction to hearing Dani's name. It seemed that after the formal and concreting my feelings for Alex in words and actions, she was no longer super suspicious and jealous of the redhead.

"Are you sure? I can always take a cab or the metro." Alex was hustling around, picking up clothes and straightening the bed.

I felt my stomach twist in knots when I heard the metro. The faces of those four men flickering through like a cheap movie reel, "Take the car, I'm sure." I let out a slow breath, trying to calm my rolling stomach. "On Monday can we stop by the dealership before we grocery shop? I want to look at a few new cars, find something for you while Dale works on your car."

Alex gave me a look, stuffing random things in her bag. "Okay, but I can only afford…"

"Just a rental, Alex. I don't want you to ever take the metro, a cab or anything again. You work too late to not have something reliable." I swallowed, or put me in a position where I have to kill shitheads with the audacity to think about harming her, glancing at the clock, "You should probably get going or you'll get stuck in traffic and Dani should be here in five minutes."

Alex sighed, picking up her bag, "I know." She walked over to me, lifting her hands to the sides of my face. "I'll be home at two. Will you have cookies and cuddles ready?"

I couldn't help but grin and wrap my arms around her, "Don't I always?" I bent down to kiss her, absorbing and memorizing the way Alex felt in my arms and in my heart.

"Yes you do, but we're running out of cookies." Alex kissed me once more before sighing and moving out my arms. We both hated having to leave the warm bubble we had created in this house over the last few weeks. I hated it more knowing what my outside held.

I walked down with Alex, grabbing her lunch and walking her out to the car. Kissing her once more with a rib crushing hug and promises of stopping by after my meeting.

As Alex turned down the last curve out of my subdivision, Dani pulled into the driveway in a black sedan. Stepping out and smoothing down her identical khaki uniform.

"Afternoon Professor, you ready for this bullshit?" She squinted at me, leaning on the top of the sedan.

"Nope." I turned to her, "Are you any further with…things?" I looked down, idly noting I needed to cut the lawn.

"Two steps further than I was, but still a thousand steps away from the end." She sighed, "But I'm getting closer." She cleared her throat, "Where's nurse blue eyes? I haven't seen her since the formal. I see you two shacked up."

Before I could give her a dirty look she pointed at the mini up on a ramp next door, "Her car is in pieces next door and your beamer is missing. More importantly, you have forgotten that I've been monitoring her. She filed her change of address at the post office online yesterday from the hospital, which I conveniently buried away from prying eyes."

I furrowed my brow, "You are prying eyes." I let out a breath, "Let me get my briefcase and then we can go. I might need you to stop by the hospital afterwards, I promised to get Alex lunch."

Dani chuckled, "You are whipped like whipped cream, Professor." She winked at me, "It's the most beautiful thing I have seen in a long time." She tapped the top of the car, "Hurry it up, I want coffee before we visit the old ones. The old lady bores me to tears."

I glared at her one more time, turning back the way Alex had driven. Wishing I could follow her and never look back.

Voltaire's main headquarters was near the Pentagon and the NSA building, disguised as a typical federal government building. Tall, wide and covered in black glass, it looked like any other building with people in suits and military uniforms walking in and around the halls.

I felt my entire being shift the second we entered, like the black hooded figure and I merged back into the same person, not the split personalities I had been carrying for the last few weeks while I started a life with Alex. I was beginning to struggle maintaining a dual identity, widening the cracks that started to the form the day Alex stood in my office almost a year ago.

"You ready?" Dani glanced at me, sticking her palm in a biometric scanner next to the one bank of elevators.

I sighed, sticking my hand in, letting the scanner read my hand. My stoic face popped up on the small screen with a green light, opening the elevator doors. "Not really, but the sooner I get this done, the sooner I can go home."

Dani and I stepped into the elevator, "Don't forget, the old man wants to see you after. He also wants to see me after he sees you." I turned to look at Dani, she was clenching her jaw and picking at the ribbons on her chest, "I hate the one on ones."

I felt my fear rise, "Do you think he knows?"

Dani waved her hand at me, smirking, "No, trust me. I'm the best for a reason." She looked up at me with wide green eyes, "I hate the one on ones because it usually leads to a big job for the both of us." Her smirk faded into a tight lipped smile. I nodded, turning back to the floor counter.

She was right, anytime she had a one on one with the old man or the old lady, she and I would be shipped off to the ass end corners of the world for two or three weeks on an endless run of jobs. Sniper hits, interrogations, close up work. All were messy and physical, and I would return home with a few more stitches and bruises. I clenched my jaw, I couldn't do it this time. I couldn't leave Alex and come home with bruises and stitches, if I did, she would push harder for the truth.

And I would lose her.

The elevator doors opened up the same time Dani laid a hand on my back, drawing my thoughts back into the present. "Victoria, I promised you I would find the way out." She looked at me with intense green eyes, "And I will, but pull it together and put your Professor face on. The old man will read through you like a cheap newspaper." She smiled, patting me, "Think about nurse blue eyes in scrubs, waiting for you to bring her lunch. Everything else, zone out like I do until they say your name."

I rolled my eyes, smiling, "You are so very strange."

Dani shrugged, walking out the elevator, "And you are so very stiff, quite the pair we make." She motioned towards the large oak doors to the right, "Let's get this bullshit over with."

As we both turned to put on our tight game faces, Dante strolled around the corner in her crisp Marine uniform. "Ladies." She smirked, folding her arms. "It's always a pleasure to see the dream team together."

I felt my jaw twitch, "Dante." The woman was what my grandmother would call a beautiful devil. Stunning in her looks, her Argentinean roots giving her a sensuality that had more than all of us looking twice at the woman, but the devil side of her was what kept me back. Dante was sneaky, slimy and killed without a thought other than how quickly she could get paid and on onto the next job. This was why she was the old lady's favorite, confusing me why she was seen with the old man as of late.

Dani rolled her eyes, "Why are you here you? Aren't you still on secret old man duty? Wiping his ass everywhere he goes?" The redhead faced the taller woman. "I saw you at the formal. I didn't know they let in noncommissioned officers in there."

Dante rolled her eyes and laughed, brushing her hand over a brand new set of silver lieutenant bars on her collar. "I've been a good girl, moved up in the world."

She then looked up at me, "How's that gorgeous girlfriend of yours? The one I saw draped on your arm. Old man tells me she's a nurse downtown." Her smirk grew into a grin when she saw my slight reaction. "I should go visit her, see what she knows about Voltaire and maybe persuade her that you're not who she thinks you are."

I spun my head to glare at the woman, "I will kill you, if you…"

Dani shoved me back, "Dante, get the fuck out of here, before I show the old man your Moscow mission notes. You know the one." Dani smiled as Dante's face fell.

Dante rolled her eyes again and dropped her arms, "Whatever. Your glorious run is coming to an end Chimera. It's time to let the kids have their fun." She winked at me, "Tell your nurse I said hello."

Dante spun and laughed as I lunged at her. Dani grabbing my arms to hold me back, "Yo, Vic the Dick. Settle down. We're on sacred ground where blood stays in our bodies and not on the floor." She tilted her head until I met her eyes. "You're good. Dante is just a shitty bitch that has some serious jealousy issues. I'll put a bug on her and figure out why the old man has such a boner for her."

I closed my eyes, "Find out how she knows about Alex and if she's been poking around where she doesn't belong. Give me a reason not to kill her." I slowly opened my eyes.

Dani nodded, "You got it." She reached up and smoothed out my lapel. "You ready to get this over with?" I took a long breath in and nodded.

I sucked in another deep gasp of air to calm down, before walking out and past the large oak door Dani held open for me.

I did think about Alex as I sat in the leather chair facing the large wooden desk waiting for the old lady and old man to enter. Dani was sitting next to me, eating from the bowl of nuts that was set out for decoration and not consumption. I gave her a dirty look, she only shrugged, popping another handful in her mouth.

I went to reach and slide the bowl away when the doors behind the table opened up. First to enter the room was a tall slender man in his fifties with grey hair in a neat politician hairstyle. He wore a dark blue pinstripe suit with a red tie. He kept his head down, buried in the stack of files in his hands.

Next to enter was an older woman, also in her late fifties with silver hair cut in a very clean, stylish, modern haircut. She was tall, slender and commanded attention with her bright blue eyes and dark grey pantsuit. The woman was very attractive and carried herself with grace, something I admired about her. She smiled gently at me, setting a large stack of files down in front of her seat.

I stood up at attention as my bosses entered the room.

The man was Joseph Arthur, head of the CIA branch of Voltaire, codenamed old lady. The woman, Margaret Gaines, head of the MI6 branch of Voltaire, codenamed the old man and affectionately nicknamed the Iron Hammer since she often resembled Margaret Thatcher in her cold, calculating way of hammering down orders.

Arthur never looked up, only moving to the intercom on the table. "Where is my coffee? I asked for it to be waiting for me ten minutes ago." He clicked off with a huff and sat down, even his voice was agitating in the high pitched, almost whining tone he had.

Dani looked at me, whispering, "Every time I think their code names are weird. He acts like a pissy bitch, and then it makes perfect sense why he got old lady. Cranky old lady."

I bit the inside of my mouth to prevent from laughing. Dani was right, I had always thought the code names were strange for the two, an old distraction technique leftover from world war two, but when I met the two, it was appropriate. Gaines wore the pants and controlled the show with professionalism, tact and a steady hand. Arthur was brash, childish and a pissy bitch. I also hated him more for the fact he and the Colonel were the two who latched onto me like leeches after I was rescued. Preying on my shocked state to pull me into Voltaire.

"Ladies, you may be seated." Gaines waved at our seats, her English accented voice was smooth and oddly comforting, waiting for us to sit before she took her own seat. "Commander Bancroft, Lieutenant Beckham, thank you for meeting us today. We will be quick." She glared at Arthur, the two had a semi volatile relationship as one does if they are on opposite sides of the fence.

I tried to avoid making eye contact with the woman, knowing she could read me like the expert she was. Instead I focused on Arthur flipping through my file like a manic child.

He cleared his throat, "Commander, you have done exceptionally well for us this year. Your work has been clean, precise and punctual. Something that does not go unnoticed here at Voltaire." He flipped a few pages, "Your cleanup is immaculate and perfect, and we've had extensive compliments on your work from our clients." He looked up at me with a smarmy brown eyes, "You've done us proud, just like I knew you would when I found you." He winked at me and I almost gagged, but instead I smiled tightly and nodded a thank you.

Gaines sighed heavily, glaring at her coworker, "Yes, Commander Bancroft. Your work has been impressive this year. One of your smoothest by far, it's apparent you have found a calmer way of approaching your work."

She waited until I met her eyes, reading them quickly with a smile, "As for your evaluation, I took on most of it since your jobs fell on my side of the table this year. We are giving you a thirty percent increase in your payments and moving you to a level three operative. You will still hold Chimera as your operative name, but you will now be handed the level three classified clients." She paused, waiting for me again to look at her, "Level three brings less travel, but when you do travel it will be longer than the one day trips you've been used to."

I nodded, clenching my jaw, this was exactly what I didn't want. Having to craft excuses why I was taking longer trips during the summer. "Thank you, ma'am."

She continued to look at me, "You're welcome, Commander Bancroft. You've seem to have found something in your life to calm you, and it has shown in your work. You're far more careful than you used to be."

My jaw twitched as I nodded once more. My anger was beginning to boil up, I wanted to get to the after meeting with Gaines and find out what she knew about Alex.

Gaines closed my file and set it to the side, looking at Arthur who was too busy hitting on the secretary who brought his coffee in. She rolled her eyes, "Lieutenant Beckham, looking over your files and reports, you've improved as well." I smiled hearing Dani's real name and how much she hated it, only for the reason people asked if she was related to that soccer player.

I could see Dani try with all of her might not to roll her eyes. "Thank you, ma'am."

Arthur finally spoke up, scattering the files in front of him until he found Dani's, "Yes, you have been incredible with the mainframe breaches and keeping our favorite, Chimera here, in check." He smiled and winked at me like a cheesy car salesman. I bit the inside of my mouth, Arthur would always refer to me by my operative name and I hated it, it made me feel like an object and not a person. "Because of this, we are promoting you to the rank of Lieutenant Commander, effective immediately."

Dani coughed, looking at me with confused eyes, "Um, thank you, sir?" Even I was confused. Dani had been stuck at Lieutenant for the last ten years, always being told that she had this or that to work on. That she needed to be a little more dedicated to the mission statement of Voltaire.

Arthur winked at Dani in an equally disgusting way, "You have saved my ass a time or two with these breaches and helping us develop more secure way to communicate and compensate the operatives."

Gaines cut in, "It was my suggestion that we finally move you up." She looked at me, "With this promotion, you will remain as Commander Bancroft's handler alone. You will also be granted a level three clearance to continue the work on the mainframe breaches."

She paused, boring into my eyes in a way that had me fearful she knew everything Dani and I were trying to work on. She finally moved back to a shocked Dani, sliding a white card with her new insignia on it across to her, "We will discuss details further after the meeting."

Dani nodded, taking the gold oak leaves, still in shock. "Thank you, ma'am, sir."

Gaines smiled genuinely while Arthur leered at us with that stupid smile of his. Picking up his coffee, he slapped our files closed, "With that, I have a lunch meeting with the NSA director." He stood up, "You ladies keep up the good work. I should have something on tap for you two by the end of the week."

Dani and I stood up at attention, watching Arthur issue Gaines a fake smile before exiting the room. Gaines took her time in standing up, "Commander, will you walk me to my office?"

I gave Dani a look, "Yes ma'am." Dani shrugged in a comforting way.

Gaines walked around the table, looking over at Dani, "Lieutenant Commander Beckham, meet me in my office in ten minutes."

Dani nodded, issuing her own yes ma'am as I went to open the door for Gaines.

Closing the door behind us Gaines, looked at me with her intense blue eyes, "Shall we take the stairs?"

I smiled lightly, "I could use the exercise." I knew that the staircase was nothing but pure, eight inch thick concrete that any listening device would struggle to cut through. It was old fashioned of Voltaire, but it made sense, sometimes the ones breaching the world's privacy needed their own.

Inside the stairwell, Gaines wasted no time, "That lovely elegant woman on your arm at the formal, is she the calm you've found?" She caught my reaction, "Relax, I honestly was there to meet with the Superintendent. Spotted you glowing from a mile away, and I must admit, it was refreshing to see you at ease."

I swallowed hard, clenching my fists, knowing it was useless to lie to the Iron Hammer, "Yes ma'am, she is." I kept my tone clipped, not giving the woman more to read and expand on. She was already well past my stiff façade that worked on Arthur, but again, Maggie was the best the MI6 had, hence why she was in the position she was now.

Gaines stopped on a landing one floor up from the meeting room, "Victoria, leave the formalities for that shitbird Arthur. You and I have always had a different relationship." She smiled gently. She was right, her and I had a different relationship. One that I didn't understand in the early years when the Colonel and Arthur were taking advantage of my PTSD and underlying fury kicked off by my torturers.

In the last few years, I came to see she was treating me like a human and had all along the way, but I never saw it until it was too late and I thought I was lost to the world, then I met Alex and found my world.

"I'm sorry, Maggie." I folded my arms across my chest, looking at my perfectly shined black shoes. "Is she the conversation we need to have?" I grimaced, remembering the matchbook delivered to me by a drunk Dani.

She laughed, grabbing my elbow, "Part of it, yes. Relax Victoria, I can assure you, I already know what Dani is doing. That she is the reason why Arthur is slowly losing his mind. Those mainframe hacks my tech unit back at MI6 traced to the North Koreans, but they also found a unique signature when those hacks were stitched up."

I could feel the blood drain out of my face, "I don't…"

Maggie cut me off, shifting away from Dani's devious activities in the basement, "Do you want out of Voltaire?" Her face was void of any negative emotion, her eyes pure with concern and expecting honesty. "I've known you for ten years, watched you grow from a despondent zombie following orders, to a heart beating inside of a human shell, struggling to understand how to live, to the bright shining woman I saw with that brunette on Saturday." She let go of my elbow, stepping back to lean against the concrete wall, "Victoria, you and I are very similar in how we fell into this work. I won't try to say I understand, but in some ways I do." She looked at me, "That is why I asked you over and over that day in the oval office if you were sure. If you were sure you wanted what the old lady and the Colonel was asking of you."

I clenched my jaw harder, trying to hold back my tears. "I can't retire, it's been made clear that I have another ten years and that plumbers never get to retire alive." I gave Maggie a hard look, "But to answer your question, because I have always been honest with you since you are the only one who has ever treated me like a person in this stupid job, yes I want out. Yes, it's because of that woman you saw on my arm." I curled my hands into tight fists, "I don't know how to do the double life like the rest of you."

Maggie laughed softly, "None of us do, my dear girl, we all just play it by ear and pray no one notices we suffer in silence with plastic smiles on our face." She blew out a breath, shifting the files in her arms. "To the point of why I ask if you want out. I think I might be able to help." She pushed away from the wall to stand in front of me, "As you know the old lady, Arthur, has been acting like a petulant trophy wife. Losing his mind in paranoia and picking strange bedfellows as our new clients." Maggie sighed, "He's drawing too much attention and this is not why Voltaire was created. We were created to bring two interests together and take care of mutual problems. He has begun to make it personal and become the housekeeping services for the world's trash. I don't agree with his ways, and there are others with me that also don't agree and want to do something about it."

I sighed, "The Russians and the others, the drug dealers and traffickers?" I could clearly see the scum I had killed against my own moral compass, killing shit to help shit.

Maggie nodded, "Yes, it's coming back to bite us in the ass." She turned towards the staircase door, hearing footsteps, "I'm going to discuss this with Dani in a moment, I have a side project in the works that may benefit you, I just needed to know if you wanted out of this organization to finally live like you should have long before the Colonel and the old lady chose the life they did for you." She turned back to me, removing a small envelope from the files in her hand, "I have heard there is a Detective Scarlett bothering you?"

I knew my wide look betrayed any lie I could make up. Maggie smirked, "You've forgotten that I know everything, I just don't always speak about the things I know." She held up the envelope, "You might find this interesting and it might inspire you to take me up on a future offer I will have for you." She caught my weary look, "Victoria, I would never hurt you, you're too valuable and important to this world."

I slowly took the envelope, folding it in half and jamming it into my pocket, "Why are you doing this? It could get us both killed, Voltaire…"

"I know. Voltaire doesn't play well with the secret sharing." She patted my shoulder, "I helped create this organization with the old CIA liaison before Arthur made a deal with the devil and took that seat. Victoria, I hold the keys to the front door of this place, I can burn it down in a second if I so choose." Maggie turned to the door, her hand falling on the handle. "Alex is safe, she will always be safe, Victoria." She looked in my eyes, "I promise you, not one hair on her head will ever be harmed." The way she said it, I easily felt the genuine promise that Alex would be safe under Maggie's watch. For the ten years I worked for the woman, she never betrayed a promise made. Arthur on the other hand, could not be trusted.

She opened the door a crack, "Maggie, why are you doing this?" I asked again, feeling tears well up as my stomach turned with anger, rage and hatred that this was my life and Alex was very much a part of it.

I watched her tilt her head down, "You will learn, soon, that I have things I need to amend for and the only way I can is by letting go." She smiled tightly without looking at me. "Have a good afternoon, Victoria. I will send Dani to meet you in the lobby." And with that, she walked out the doorway, leaving me in the cool concrete staircase to read between the lines of everything she had just said and offered me.

My mind went blank for a lengthy amount of time, my feet moved on their own as I ran down the last few flights of stairs and out the lobby. I hailed a cab as I ran to the curb and half startled the poor driver as I barked out the hospital address, texting Dani that I didn't need a ride and that we would talk later about our conversations with Maggie.

I had to sit on shaking hands and fight tears as I rode to the hospital, I couldn't think, I couldn't focus on anything that was thrown my way. Things that were confusing, dangerous and frightening how Maggie seemed to literally know everything that had happened over the last few weeks.

All I knew, all I wanted, was to see Alex. Wrap her up in my arms and hold her until the world stopped spinning and I could make sense of it.

Chapter 21

"Please, I'm begging you, never leave me with new nurses ever again, Alex." Stacy had snatched me up in a crushing embrace the moment she came back to the nurses' station and saw me digging through the day's charts. "If I had a quarter for every IV had I to reset after watching the little blonde one dig in arms like she was a miner, I'd be able to retire to the Bahamas tomorrow."

I laughed, patting her back, "I was only gone a week and a half." I shook my head, stepping out of the aggressive hug, had it only been a week and a half? So much had changed in such a short period of time. It felt like months, or years living in the bliss of my new relationship with Victoria. It had been quite the rollercoaster.

"I know, that's why I had to take a long weekend. Get away from this place before I lost my mind and went back to hairdressing." Stacy sighed dramatically, moving to her spot on the desk and picking up her jug of coffee. "So, how was your vacation? How's the lady friend? You two do anything?" She smirked, wiggling her eyebrows in a deviant way.

Rolling my eyes, I started pulling charts, "We had dinner at my mom's house, did some shopping and went to this fancy formal for the Naval Academy." I smiled to myself, looking at Victoria's class ring on my finger, "Nothing exciting. It was a staycation."

Stacy hummed out a mmhmm, "I bet. Stayed in bed all day and all night, learning the ins and outs of one mysterious lady in white?" She winked at me, "What's it like? She looks like she knows her way around a ship let alone a hot body like yours." Stacy sipped at her coffee, looking up at the tiled ceiling, "I mean I have an idea. I had a crazy moment back in my punk rocker days. There was this girl drummer from this one band. Damn, could she do things with her hands."

I shook my head, letting Stacy ramble on as I flipped through the day's patients when I heard, "What is that on your finger?! Is that, a promise ring? A be my girl ring?" She slid off the desk and hopped over to me, grabbing my right hand and sucking in a dramatic breath, "Oh my god, she gave you her class ring! You two are so going to get married." She grinned at me as I blushed, "We should go on a double date, have dinner and drinks at your apartment. I can bring my boyfriend."

I gently removed my hand, "We can do dinner and drinks, but not at my apartment. I, uh, moved in with Victoria on Monday." I bent my head down, scribbling notes in a chart.

Stacy's eyes grew to the size of dinner plates, "What!? You moved in? You two are shacking up?" She bent her head down to catch my eyes, "Shut up Alex Ivers, you never doing anything on a whim."

I sighed, looking at my friend, "We've been friends for almost two years and it made sense when she asked me." I leaned against the side of the desk, "It hasn't been all roses and butterflies, it's been a hard road that I think is finally smoothing out." I bit my lip, "There are some things about Victoria I'm still learning about, but overall, I am stupidly in love with her and I think we both want this. This relationship." I twisted the ring on my finger, "I'm happy."

"But? There's a but hanging in the air at the end of that statement." Stacy placed a hand on my arm, "What is it Alex?"

I shrugged, picking up the charts, "Walk with me? I want to get a jump start on rounds. Victoria might be stopping by after her meeting for lunch."

Stacy and I did rounds while I filled her on everything, the fights, the makeups, the trip to my mom's house, the nights we made love sans explicit details, and then finally, the strange things about Victoria that bothered me. The weirdness, the way she seemed to move in the shadows, and the few things she spilled at the formal.

"Basically your girlfriend might be an international woman of mystery? Working for the government." Stacy held rolls of gauze as I changed a sleeping patient's leg bandage. "Aside from that, she sounds pretty damn perfect. Why are you focusing on the little things that to me, seem not to be such a big deal? She works for the Navy, and judging by her history with them, they'd be dumb to let her go off into the sunset and retire without tapping into her here and there to help." Stacy handed me scissors, "Maybe it is leftover PTSD. Sounds like she survived hell and there might always be those pockets of darkness that won't shake away. I heard one vet say, once you let the darkness in, it never leaves."

Stacy suddenly let out a groan as she looked out the open door to the room "Fuck. It's that creeper EMT. Diablo. She's been really annoying the week you've been gone. I think she has a serious boner for you, always asking where you are, if you're single and if I've ever seen the person you're dating. She's super creepy. I caught her digging in your locker the other night. She played it off as a mistake, but I swear I saw her pocket a picture of you and the hot professor." Stacy glared at the woman who gave me a smirk with a wink and disappeared around the corner. I shivered slightly when she looked at me, but shrugged it off.

I sighed, tugging on the stethoscope around my neck. "I'll head down to security later. Report her to them and leave it. She's just a typical EMT with a god complex." I glanced up to see Diablo walking out of view.

Stacy rolled her eyes, "You mean a stalker complex. I'm telling you Alex, she's a creeper king." She shook her head, "Maybe Victoria can have a chat with her during lunch. And by lunch, I mean punch her face in."

I laughed, shaking my head, "Victoria isn't one for violence, if anything she would give her a hearty lecture." I frowned a little. Victoria and violence didn't really go together but there was that mysterious air about her. I sucked in a slow breath and returned to what Stacy and I had been discussing in regards to my girlfriend. "I don't know. There are these weird bits and pieces about Victoria that keep my gut tugging at my heart to listen and pay more attention."

I held out my hand for tape, frowning at the analogy Stacy used in describing letting the darkness in. I knew she was possibly right about the darkness lingering from Victoria's incident in the war. "Then I see how much she loves me and I forget the world and my name. She's incredible, Stacy. I've never been with anyone like her before." I finished the bandage and stood up, peeling of my gloves, "But there's that but. There's something she's hiding from me and I'm scared to find out what it is."

"So what if she is still doing intelligence work? It's kind of hot in my opinion." Stacy cleaned up the trash, grabbed the chart and walked back with me to the station. "You should ask her to dress up in a tuxedo one night and make you martini's."

I rolled my eyes, "There's something in her eyes that goes beyond boring intelligence work. It's something darker and it's like she shifts into a whole different person." I sighed, "I don't know, maybe I'm making a big deal out of nothing." I slid the chart in a slot. "Everything is so perfect. I have everything I've ever wanted or dreamt of. She is the knight in shining armor I always dreamt of. I should focus on that, not digging in the dusty corners hoping to find things I really don't want to find."

"If it bothers you so much, Alex, why don't you ask her upfront one night after blowing her mind in bed. That's usually how I get my boyfriend to agree to going to chick flicks with me." Stacy giggled when I slapped her arm, her eyes drifting up to the elevator door dinging open. "Speaking of your knight in an over starched khaki uniform." Stacy poked my shoulder, drawing my attention to Victoria walking out of the elevator with grease spotted brown bags, "Looks like lunch is served."

The grin was uncontrollable like always when I saw her, she grinned back, looking at the floor to hide the blush. I could feel my heart race the closer she got, and for a moment I wondered if it would always be like this. A few weeks or a few years down the road, would she always make my heart thunder in my chest like a speeding train?

"You two are so disgusting, go back to whatever cheesy romantic movie you fell out of." Stacy rolled her eyes with a smile on her face, then leaned closer to me, "But she is stupid hot in that uniform."

I nudged her in the side with an elbow, "Shut it and behave." I turned back to Victoria setting the bags on the high edge of the station.

"I stopped at Monument Meats on the way, picked up the Reagan club and the Washington cherry chicken salad." She focused on digging around the bags with a serious look on her face, "Stacy, I grabbed you the Clinton fried chicken with sweet potato fries."

Stacy practically shoved me out of the way to take the offered bag of food, "Will you marry me? Please?" She sniffed the bag with an exaggerated sniff, "I have missed you Victoria."

Victoria laughed, folding her arms across her chest, "You've missed the food I bring." She glanced at me, smiling even as it looked like she was about to cry, the heavy clouds were swirling in her eyes. "Can I snag Alex for a few minutes to have lunch?"

Stacy was already two giant bites into her sandwich, waving us off, "Go, go, the on call room is empty and I changed the sheets this morning. Make sure you lock the door if you're going to indulge in some physical dessert. The new girl is still learning how to knock before entering. Caught Mr. Johnson in his eighty year old birthday suit and a full catheter bag last night. Needless to say, they scared the piss out of each other." She looked up to both Victoria and I scowling at her like embarrassed parents, she waved us off, "I got you covered Alex, I'll get you if I need you."

I could only shake my head, grab the other two bags and motion Victoria to follow me, "I'm sorry." I suddenly felt bashful that I had told Stacy everything without asking Victoria if it was okay to tell anyone what had happened over the last few weeks. "I got carried away catching up with her."

I held open the door to the on call room, letting Victoria walk in first, "How was your meeting?" I wanted to shift subjects, distract both of us from the fact I had been basically gossiping about our relationship for the last three hours.

I barely set the food down on the tiny round table in the room when I was scooped up in Victoria's arms in an all-consuming hug. It startled me, but I soon relaxed into her warmth, hugging her back. "Hi?"

I could feel and hear her heart pound, "Victoria? Are you okay?" She was holding on to me like she hadn't seen me in years. Like I was going to run away and never look back.

She sighed heavily, tucking her head into my shoulder, "Yes, I just missed you. The meeting was very drab and the same garbage it is every year." She squeezed me once more before stepping away and sitting down at the table, reaching for a bag. "Dani was finally promoted. They gave me a raise, but it comes with upgrading my involvement in the Academy recruitment." Victoria was keeping her eyes on the food, not bothering to look at me as she spoke.

"That's a good thing right?" I sat across from her, "Oh shoot, what did you want to drink?" I stood up, moving to the small vending machine tucked in the corner. I furrowed my brow, curious as to why Dani's meeting with a faculty advisor would result in her being promoted. I had remembered when James was promoted to detective. He had to sit in on numerous meetings with supervisors, command staff and eventually the precinct captain. It was strange, but I didn't care too much about Dani to question it.

"A coke is fine." Victoria still wasn't looking at me, "I guess it's a good thing. I'll travel less, but when I do it will be a longer period of time." She continued unwrapping her sandwich, picking up her pickle and setting on my sandwich, making me smile at how cute she was with her hatred of pickles.

I glanced at Victoria, I could feel she wasn't happy with the good news of her evaluation, "I'm used to you traveling. It's not a big deal especially if you're going to do less of it." I set down a can of coke in front of her before sitting back down. "I can always pick up double shifts when you're gone. Helps make the time go quicker." I smiled at the blonde, biting into the pickle.

Victoria shrugged, slowly eating her chips, "Maybe I've grown so used to being lazy with nothing to do, that it doesn't excite me anymore to go back to work or travel for recruitment fairs." She sighed, opening her coke. "My retirement was discussed."

I nodded and spoke around a huge mouthful of food, "That's great! Are they going to let you retire?" I suddenly got excited about the idea of Victoria being home all the time. Puttering around in the backyard getting dirty and sweaty, or coming to see me on long days at the hospital bringing me lunch, then sneaking away to linen closets to make out. Those thoughts drifted to long term ideas, dogs, long romantic trips, marriage. I swallowed the food down, marriage. Slow it down Alex, you two have only been official for two weeks. I sipped my diet coke trying to refocus on Victoria and not my rampant romantic ideas.

She nodded slowly, "We are going to work on it, no guarantees yet." She smiled tightly before taking a large bite of her food.

There was definitely something bothering Victoria, I hadn't seen her this closed off and distant since the first few months of our friendship when I felt like she was so very tentative and afraid to share. She also looked defeated, like she had fought fifteen rounds gallantly and just gave up in the last few seconds. Letting her opponent beat her down. Before I could ask, she looked up, "So, what did you tell Stacy about us?" She said it with a gentle smirk.

I took the offered change in subject, taking part one of Stacy's advice and not focus on the little things right now. Maybe I would wait until later when I came home and had Victoria under me, writhing and moaning out my name. Then ask questions when her mind was void of much coherent thought to lie to me.

I proceeded to tell her about my gossiping, injecting the dinner date idea Stacy presented and with every word, I saw Victoria relax as she stared at me. Stared at me in a way that she was memorizing this moment. I could see the clouds move away and replaced by the grey eyes filled with more love than I ever thought conceivable.

I loved her so much and deep down I wished the mystery hanging over her like a dark thunderstorm cloud would just piss off and let me live in the bliss with her. But I knew it wasn't going to be possible, I was too smart to let myself be that stupid.

Watching Alex eat and go on about Stacy and her day, melted much of the stress from my conversation with the old man. The way she told nurse jokes that weren't that funny, but made me smile. The way she devoured the pound of food in front of her with elegance, and lastly just the way she looked at me. It slowly brought my world back to a calm and normal rotation.

I almost forgot we were still in the hospital when Stacy popped her head in, "Alex, we're needed down in the emergency room. Traffic accident on the highway and we are about to get slammed." She smiled softly in my direction to apologize for the intrusion.

Alex snapped into nurse mode, standing up, "I'll be right behind you." She turned to me, reaching for the garbage, "Sorry Victoria."

I shook my head, standing up and holding up a hand to tell her I would clean up, "It's fine, go help some people." I grinned when she grabbed my face for a quick intense kissing, whispering how much she loved me against my lips before running out of the room.

Picking up the remnants of her demolished lunch, I shoved it in the trash can before carefully packing up the half sandwich I had left. Writing her name on it and tucking it in the fridge for her to have later. I scanned the room to make sure it was left exactly as we found it, when my phone rang.

I frowned looking at Dani's name blazing on the screen. Tapping the screen, I closed my eyes, "Don't even say it, I took a cab."

"I wasn't going to say shit, Professor. I don't blame you for bolting out as soon as you could. I ran into the old lady after meeting with the old man. I will never get used to Arthur's nasty way of flirting."

Dani blew out an irritated sigh, "Anyway, where are you? We need to talk." I quickly heard two clicks signifying Dani had secured our line, giving us freedom to speak candidly.

I rubbed the sides of my head, "I'm at the hospital." I paused, "I'm assuming Gaines spoke to you about a few things?"

Dani chuckled, "Boy did she ever! I 'm impressed by her tech unit out in jolly old England and should have known they'd have a few of my fellow white hat hackers working for them."

"Are you in trouble?" Even though I wanted to run Dani over with my car, I still cared about her and sadly needed her to stay on as my handler until I was out.

"Nope. My shenanigans were the main reason I finally moved up in rank." Dani huffed, "Downside, she presented me with a unique proposition that coincides with your eventual retirement."

I chewed the inside of my lip, "And?"

"We are working on something, something that will move up our timeframe. If this works out, you'll be collecting a pension by the new year." She paused, sucking in a breath, "But it won't be easy, and it certainly won't be pretty. The old man wants to cut ties with the old lady. She has the backing of the tea drinkers and is working on the patriots. Her and I only worked out the information gathering details of this endeavor of hers. I don't know any more than the promises that there will be an exit for you and for me, soon."

Furrowing my brow, I stood up straighter, "I don't like the sound of any of this." I jammed my hand in my pocket, poking my fingers on the envelope from Gaines. I yanked it out looking at it, debating on throwing it out or opening it up and finding out what she had on Scarlett that would chase the detective off my tail permanently.

"The colonel is alive. She showed me photographs of him in Chile' last week." Dani threw the words up like a drunk in an alley. "He's been working with the old lady. That's why your jobs have begun to get more and more tasteless. Vague rumors have it that the two are back in black trying to create their own Voltaire. One that works for the good guys and the bad guys."

The rage spilled over like a popped champagne cork, "No, he died in that explosion…." I began to pace, looking for something to ram my fist through to take the edge off.

"Smoke and mirrors, Victoria. A magic trick he crafted." Dani's voice changed to one that was trying to be comforting. She knew how much I hated that fat man with every bone in my body. "The old man gave me the level one access code to go sniffing about in Voltaire's mainframe."

My fists clenched on their own, the knuckles a pure white as I crumpled the envelope, "I will…kill him."

"Victoria, relax. I'm outside the hospital. Get in the car and I'll take you home." Dani was speaking slower, trying to calm the blurring rage she knew was washing over me. "Leave now before Alex sees you."

I flinched hearing her name, "Fine." I hung up on Dani and left the on call room, rushing past nurses and taking the stairwell down to the lobby. I knew if I spotted Alex in the emergency room I would either grab her and beg her to run away with me or walk away. Tell her to run from me as my past was colliding with my present and the black hooded figure was seeping back in. The killer was sparking back to life in a long forgotten promise I made to myself and Dani when I found out the truth about the Colonel. To kill that fat bastard with my bare hands and make him suffer.

Outside I squinted at the bright sun, heading to the black sedan and getting in without a word. Dani looked at me, pulling the sedan out of the fire lane, "Are you okay?"

I huffed, "I wish people would stop asking me that, including you." I glared at her, holding up the wrinkled envelope, "The old man gave me this at the end of our meeting. She mentioned it would help chase Scarlett off my ass."

Dani glanced at it, "Open it. The car is secure and we can make a side trip to Metro for a quick face to face with Scarlett if need be."

I closed my eyes, tearing open the envelope, "I just want to be free, live a quiet boring life and not this fucked up one. Alex knew something was wrong with me at lunch, but didn't press. I hate lying or avoiding conversation with her." I ripped the two sheets of paper out, unfolding them before opening my eyes to read what the old man had done.

The first page was written in Gaine's delicate hand.

"Chimera,

This floated across my desk last week along with my tech report for Beckham's activities. I know about the metro station incident. Those men got exactly what they deserved and that case was closed properly by our Metro assets. Case closed as a drug deal gone wrong. Then Jennifer Scarlett's face passed across my desk and I vaguely remembered her.

She was a failed operative candidate of Voltaire's four years ago, never made it through the operative training. She had poor scoring and seemed a bit too adept in adhering to every word and whim of Arthur. When I had her disavowed, Arthur was upset, but easily agreed. I assumed the problem was taken care of.

Until I saw she was a homicide detective without ever passing the necessary tests required.

The woman's real name and personnel file is included. She was an asset of Arthur's and you were her target, a morbid way to expose our operatives to the world in hopes of dissolving Voltaire for Arthur's gain.

Yes, I did write was. She had a terrible accident, a skiing accident, on vacation up in Colorado last week.

She will not bother you again and the metro station case has been reclosed due to the new evidence leading to the same outcome as the original case.

Burn this letter, Chimera and continue as you have. I will contact you when the time is right and we will move forth with the exit plan I spoke of.

-OM"

I shook my head, "What the fuck is going on?" I handed Dani the letter from Gaines, looking down at the single piece of paper that held Scarlett's face and her dossier from Voltaire. "Kelsey Stanton, United States Marines. Former Voltaire operative candidate, handpicked by that fat fucking bird and the old lady five years ago. Now she's conveniently dead in a skiing accident, courtesy of Voltaire."

I lifted my head up, tossing the page on the console for Dani to snatch up, "Why does it suddenly feel the entire world is falling apart around us?" I rubbed my face with both hands, "I'm losing my goddamn mind with all this shit."

Dani read while she drove, muttering curse words as she navigated traffic and the facts in front of her, "Fucking fuck. I knew that detective was shady as hell. I should have known her file I pulled was creative writing. I've written a million fake identities to know how to spot one." She threw the pages back down, revving the car up to get us out of traffic. "The world is falling apart, our carefully crafted world of shit. It's falling apart, you're right Victoria, but it might be the best thing." She looked over at me, "I know it's the one thing I have been dreaming about for years, Voltaire imploding into a pile of ashes while I stand, point and laugh." She reached over, grabbing my shoulder, "The old man is giving us the heads up, giving us the ability to stand outside and seek the justice and peace we've deserved."

I shot a look at her, confused why she would be excited about this, "Did you drink the Kool Aid she offered you? This isn't going to be good, this isn't going to end up with any of us riding off in the sunset, and you know that."

Dani chuckled, "I've never expected to live to sit in a motorized scooter stealing the neighbor kids balls when it lands on my lawn. I accepted that I have an expiration date since the day we stood in the oval office, signing on the dotted line." She turned to me, "I don't care about my life, Victoria, never really have. The only thing I have cared about is staying alive to make sure I kept you alive."

She cleared her throat, the emotion rising up, "I will make sure you make it out, even if I have to sell my soul a third time to the devil." She smirked, sniffling, "Just make sure at the wedding you and nurse blue eyes have a toast in my name."

I turned away from the redhead, clenching my hands into fists to fight back tears, "Dani…"

"Shut up, I know." She drove the sedan up into my driveway, waving to my neighbors, muttering as we both looked out the window. "I would give my life to save yours, Victoria, so you can walk off into the sunset with Alex and forget. Forget that we ever did any of the things we have." She hit the unlock button, "Now get the fuck out of my car and enjoy the rest of your vacation. I'm going home to drink a bottle of vodka and have some late night fun with my level one code."

I swallowed hard, "Dani...I."

She shook her head, shoving me against the door, with tears in her eyes, "Get out of the damn car before you see me cry."

I nodded, shoving the car door open and stepping out, sucking in deep breaths of air to calm my stomach and heart down. I didn't turn around when Dani backed out of the driveway and tore off in a rush. I just walked to my mailbox, collected the mail and myself before I turned to Dale waving at me as he stood in front of Alex's mini cooper with oil stains on his shirt.

I kept a tight smile until I walked into the house, down to the basement where I grabbed a bottle of bourbon and began sipping it straight out of the bottle. Still gripping on to the two pages about Scarlett, I picked up a large ashtray a book of matches Dani stole from a hotel in Paris as my birthday gift three years ago.

Dropping the pages in the middle, I lit a match. I stared at the flame as it reflected off the amber liquid in the liquor bottle, then I lit the edges of the pages on fire. Watching the flames consume the pages like nothing, I took a larger drink from the bottle.

This was the beginning. These two pages burning was the catalyst of the world around me eventually burning to the ground.

~Six months later – Columbia~

"I'll be home in the morning, Alex, before your shift is over." I paced around the safe house, watching my clothes burn in the fireplace in between looking out the window on to the picturesque view of the hills of Bogota rolling before me.

Pressing my hand against the glass, cringing at the purple bruise growing around my knuckles from the hard nose I broke a half hour ago. "I miss you too, this should be the last trip for a month or so. The recruitment fairs usually taper off during the holiday months for breaks." I closed my eyes, listening to Alex's voice with the calming background noises of the hospital.

I had just finished a job interrogating and killing the head of a narcotics ring, delivering cocaine for a known terrorist group to fund their activities. This job, like all of my others in the last six months since my meeting with the old man, was sent down by the old man and it was a clean job. Well, clean in the purpose behind it. I ended up covered in blood after getting into a fist fight with the big Colombian after the first injection I gave him only amplified the PCP he took. He had to be put down by slicing his throat open after I gouged both his eyes out with my thumbs to throw him out his PCP rage.

I had met the clean-up crew in blood soaked clothes and a desperate need to hear Alex's voice.

I had managed to live a dual life with her with some success. It did help that my jobs were longer in time away but shorter in how many I had to do. Gone were the weekly jobs. I was now traveling once a month at best, but doing two or three jobs in that time period. I would make sure I came home before her shifts were done so I had enough time to relax and switch the masks I wore. Once or twice, I had slipped after a particularly hard job that got too close like the job in Ireland had, and Alex would call me out on it. I would try to lie, without success, and we fought.

The last time was because she was home before I was and I wouldn't let her touch me until I took a scalding shower to wash away the hidden filth I felt of strangling a black arms dealer with my bare hands. The smell of his sweat, fear and vomit lingering in my nose and my pores.

Alex demanded me to tell her why I wouldn't let her touch me, why I flinched when she tried to hug me. I almost broke down then, pouring out the full truth in hopes she would walk away. Instead I made up a lie I was coming down with a cold and my body ached.

She saw through my bullshit and we fought some more until she left the house in anger and came back three hours later. Her hands filled with bags of Thai food, a case of beer and a stuffed Navy goat in her arms. She looked at me, hurt radiating from her eyes and making my heart break at the sight, "This is the last time I play the mysterious secret game with you. If you don't want to tell me, I can't make you. I love you Victoria Bancroft, and the next time you refuse to let me touch you, or hug you, will be the last time."

She held my eyes, "Trust me, Victoria. Whatever it is, it can't be so horrible that you hide from the one person who loves you more than her own life." She looked at the beer, "One day you will have to tell me, and no matter what, I will listen to it all."

She then shoved the stuffed goat my way, "I went to the mall to shop away being pissed off, saw this and I couldn't stop thinking about you. It reminds me of you, the angry goat."

The fear of her actually walking away from me scared me more than having her see the killer in me. I made a promise that day that I would never hurt Alex like I did. I only had a few more months to go and I would be free. Dani was getting closer with the old man on getting me out, it was just a matter of when the plan would be set in motion.

Other than trying to hide my double life, life with Alex was perfect. Living with her was what I had imagined being complete was. We would spend our days off doing domestic things like grocery shop, garden, shop for a bigger bathtub, and lie around for hours on Sunday morning's making love or watching movies while we ate breakfast in bed. I was very much in love with Alex and it amplified my desire to leave Voltaire and find the normalcy I needed and craved.

I had zoned out, staring out the window, barely hearing Alex ask me about my birthday. "What was that?" I cleared my throat, "I was distracted by this high schooler with blue hair and barely there jean shorts."

Alex laughed, "I could remember making fun of the girls who let everything hang out in high school." She sighed, "How is Minnesota? Is it snowing there yet?"

I frowned, looking at very green hills standing over an air conditioner that was doing its best to chase out the ninety-degree humid heat of Columbia and the fireplace roaring behind me, "Not yet. "It's cold here and the clouds look like they are threatening to dump a foot down on us. The weather report said by this weekend it will hit, thank god my flight leaves in a couple hours." I glanced at my hand, "By the way, one of the kids kicked open a door not knowing I was behind it. My right hand took the brunt of the handle. It's a purple swollen mess and is hard to move." I stared at the knuckles. The lie I just told would be sufficient enough to cover up the fact I had pounded a face in, not caught a door handle.

"Make sure you ice it and I'll look at it when you get home. Maybe kiss it and make it better. I'm happy you booked the early flight home I've missed cookies and cuddles this week." She sighed tiredly, "Your birthday is tomorrow, is there anything you want to do? I took the rest of the week off to be with you."

I grinned, "Besides you? I can't think of anything." I dropped my hand away from the glass, turning back to the fireplace and the smoldering remnants of clothes. "Maybe we can go to a cider mill? Or talk your mom into making a meatloaf. I've missed her meatloaf and the dogs."

Alex laughed, "I can make that happen, all of it. I've missed you, a lot. Stacy and I were reading an article in one of her silly woman's magazine about how to teach your man new bedroom tricks. It led to us researching a few new things I have in mind for you."

I felt my skin flush at the implications, "Birthday sex? I don't think I've ever had birthday sex." I scrunched my face up, realizing that I had never been with anyone who actually knew what day my real birthday was, or stayed with me long enough to share a birthday. "I feel bad, I missed yours this year. We were in our weird place and you were with that doctor dean."

Alex chuckled, "You can make up for it at Christmas and my birthday next year." I heard Stacy in the background cat call me, "Stacy says hey, and I have to go. Mrs. Simon pulled her catheter out again." Alex groaned, "I'll call mom and get the birthday meatloaf request in. Hurry home, fly safe and I'll wake you up when I get home?"

"As long as it's with kisses and not your grumpy growls. I'll stop for cookies on the way home." I looked up at the ceiling, "I love you, Alex."

I could hear her grin through the phone, "I love you, Victoria. Hurry up and get here." She hung up leaving me with a sad smile on my face.

Tucking the phone back into my bag, I finished getting dressed and met the clean-up crew outside. We drove to the airport in silence, my only thoughts were that I couldn't really remember how old I was off the top of my head. I had to look at my license to double check, which lead me to think about the last birthday I celebrated. I was eighteen with grandma Edith dropping me off at the front gate of the Academy, handing me a cupcake with a cigarette hanging out of her mouth while she wished me luck in taking the world by the balls.

"Stacy did you get it?" I rushed out of the hospital after meeting Stacy in the lobby. She had left four hours before me, and I conned her into picking up Victoria's birthday gift so I could give it to her when I got home. The place closed at nine and I wasn't off until midnight with another half hour drive to get her gift. I was grateful when Stacy agreed to helping me out after I told her the surprise I had planned.

"Yes, but I want to keep it." She smirked at me as we walked to where I had parked Victoria's BMW. I always drove her car when she was out of town, leaving the boring sedan I picked out as my temporary car months ago. Victoria was set on buying me a BMW but I opted for leasing the fuel efficient sedan, thinking it would be a better choice. It was, but I still drove her car when she was gone because it was my weird way of having her close. I was excited that Dale was almost done with my mini. All he had to do was paint it and I could have the old girl back.

"You can't. I spent weeks finding it and half of this month's salary on it." We stopped at the back of her car, I could see the silly wrapping paper on the medium sized box, "Is that SpongeBob wrapping paper?"

Stacy giggled, nodding, "You asked me to make it birthday like! All I had was this leftover paper from my nephew's birthday. Victoria will get a kick out of it." She opened the hatch and lifted the box out, both of us looking inside and smiling. "I'll put it in the front seat for you."

I nodded, grinning with excitement, "It's perfect, but I hope she likes it." I rushed to the BMW, opening the passenger side for Stacy, "I think I'm going to get her out for drinks on Saturday to celebrate her birthday. You're more than welcome to join us. I think she has grown attached to you."

Stacy set the box down on the floor, looking once more in the box, "I agree. The woman knows all of my favorite menu items from all my favorite places, and she makes my coffee better than I could on bagel Thursdays." She reluctantly closed the door, "If you don't marry her, I will." She winked my way, shoving me, "Get to gettin'. Her flight landed thirty minutes ago. I checked online when I picked up the gift. Your surprise will go off perfectly."

I grinned again, hugging my friend, "I owe you."

Stacy patted my back, "You do. So when you come back from your little birthday vacation, you get poop bag duties for a week."

I frowned, "Whatever." I sighed, feeling nervous out of nowhere, "Okay, I'm going to go. I'll call you tomorrow let you know how it went."

Stacy winked at me, "I'll be waiting. Night Alex, tell Victoria happy birthday from me."

I grinned as Stacy head over to her car before closing the passenger door, double checking that the box was secure enough to make it home. I went to put my bag in the backseat, trying to calm down my own excitement when I saw something out of the corner of my eye.

I gripped the car keys in my palm and looked over my shoulder. I groaned softly when I saw Diablo swaggering over. She grinned and threw up a small wave, "Good evening Alex."

I smiled tightly and threw my bag into the backseat, "Hey." I tucked my head down and went to the driver's side. I hoped being distant and curt with the woman, she would slowly get the hint before I did actually go and file a report with hospital security. The cocky EMT was everywhere I turned lately. Peering in as I did rounds, poking her nose in things at the nurses' station, and I tried to be polite when she asked very personal questions about me and Victoria. Stacy begged me to take care of it and get the woman fired, but there was something about Diablo that made me nervous. Nervous in the way Victoria did when I first met her

"I thought Stacy got off a couple of hours ago? You guys going out for drinks?" Diablo motioned in the direction Stacy had gone. She then looked at me, that odd smirk covering her face, "You two looked excited with that big birthday gift. Is it Victoria's birthday today?"

I felt my jaw tighten as I glared at the woman. She had stepped over a line. "Why do you keep following me? Harassing me and digging around in my life?" I folded my arms across my chest, "I'm in a relationship and I am never going out with you. So, please. Leave me alone before I have to file a report against you."

Diablo laughed shaking her head as she moved closer. "They always say you're smarter than you look." She rolled her eyes, "My jury is still out on that fact, Alex." She sucked in a slow breath, "I'm not interested in you, romantically. I'm just very curious about you on a whole."

I felt a slow shiver run down my spine. The way her voice lowered gave off a very predatory feel. "Well, I suggest you find someone else to be curious about." I swung the car keys out of my palm. "Please don't bother me or ask about me anymore."

I heard her laugh again, "I wish I could, but there are bigger things in play here. Not just some silly imagined crush on a lovely nurse." She sighed softly, "I won't hurt you, I just need to understand why. Why Chimera is doing any of this." Diablo waved me off, "Goodnight nurse Ivers. Drive safe."

With that, the woman turned back around and disappeared into the mottled shadows of the parking structure. I had a wave of nervous fear wash over me, but shook it off. Diablo was a weird one, Stacy had told me a few stories about her while I was on vacation. I half shrugged off her weirdness as a side effect of her own form of PTSD of being a EMT in a dangerous city.

I climbed into the driver's seat and locked myself inside. In the morning I would call and report Diablo.

Sneaking into the house, I set the alarm, tossed my bag in the laundry room before grabbing the box and heading up stairs to our bedroom. I set the box outside the door, and crept in. Seeing Victoria curled up in blankets, clutching my pillow, I felt my excitement soar. I crawled onto the bed, poking her leg and her shoulder like I did every night, whispering, "Are you asleep?"

Victoria mumbled, mushing her face into my pillow. I bit my bottom lip, leaning over to kiss the edge of her jaw, moving to her ear, "You are so asleep right now. Guess I'll go sleep on the couch." I leaned back to roll off the bed, when a strong hand wrapped around my arm, pulling me back down to sleepy grey eyes.

"I'll throw that damn couch out before that happens." Victoria pulled me down, meeting me half way in a deep, hard kiss.

Her tongue gliding over my bottom lip and melting my will, as I opened my mouth wider and laid on top of her. No matter how much I had her every day she was home, a few days away felt like I was stranded in a desert and she was my oasis. I nipped at her lip, her hands moving up under my long sleeved thermal. Her warm hands sending goosebumps up my back. I was about to lose all of my sense and give in when I heard a faint scratching noise outside the door.

Grinning I pulled back, hearing Victoria moan in protest. I looked down at her, running my thumb over her mouth, "Happy birthday."

She rolled her eyes, "It's not my birthday yet." She tugged at my arm, "Come back down here."

I chuckled, "You are tired." I pushed up from her grip, "It's two in the morning, your birthday started two hours ago." I managed to escape her grabby hands.

"I was born at eleven in the morning, so technically...." Victoria's raspy voice was doing little in calming my libido down from those kisses I wanted more of, but I had a mission.

"Technically, you need to shush up and let me give you your gift." I rolled off the bed, kicking off my shoes.

"Come back and I'll unwrap you." Victoria sat up, turning on the bedside lamp, "It's been a long five days without you next to me."

I blushed at the tone in her voice, moving to the box I picked it up and walked back in, "The wrapping wasn't my idea, but." I reached in the box watching a confused Victoria stare at the happy images of SpongeBob covering the sides. "You remember what you said at the formal?"

Victoria sighed, picking at the fading Navy logo on her shirt, "I said a lot of things, then you threw car keys at me." She raised an eyebrow, "I do remember what happened after....and..."

I rolled my eyes, "Can you go with it for a minute? Then I promise I'll get naked and you can have your other gift." I grinned as I wrapped gentle hands around the tiny fluffy black blob looking up at me in the box. "You said you always wanted a dog that night, and since we've been living together for the last six months, I thought it was time to take the next step."

I lifted the Scottie puppy up, cradling her to my chest, I looked up at Victoria as I walked back over and sat next to her. "I figured since you love Annie and Barney and I've always had Scotties, well, happy birthday Victoria."

I set the puppy down on the bed and watched it sniff the bed as she crawled over to Victoria, sniffing her hand before licking it and crawling up further to stand on Victoria's chest. Victoria looked down at the small puppy, "You got me a dog?"

I nodded, reaching over to pet the tiny little thing. "I did. You clearly love mom's dogs, you practically tried to steal Annie last month when we watched them." I shrugged, "And I can see how your eyes are lighting up right now looking at her." I bit my lip, "I love you Victoria and I love seeing you happy like this."

Victoria had the dopiest grin on her face as she picked up the puppy, holding it against her chest and petting her head as the puppy licked her hand, "Alex, I…" She buried her nose in the top of the puppy's head, "No one has ever…paid attention. My parents, grandma Edith, I told them all every year I wanted a dog, because I thought at least I would have someone who loved me and they could be my family where my real family fell vacant." Victoria sniffled, smiling as tears fell.

I felt my heart swell, I leaned forward, kissing her forehead, "You're my family, Victoria. You are everything I want and this is the first step in building our own family." I ran my hand down her face, holding it against her cheek as she grabbed it and pressed into it. I half expected her eyes to cloud over when I said what I did, instead, her eyes lit up brighter. "And maybe we won't both be so lonely when I'm at work, or you're on one of your trips."

Victoria sniffled again, smiling as the puppy yipped in her hand, asking for more pets, "I love you so much Alex, thank you. For everything." She bent forward, kissing me softly on the lips before tugging me to lay next to her and the puppy. She started laughing when a small black nose began sniffing inside her shirt, "What do we name her?"

I laughed, leaning on Victoria's shoulder, "Goat? USS Scottie? Or something Navy related, knowing you." I giggled when Victoria playfully scowled at me, lifting a nosy Scottie out of her baggy shirt.

"Alex, I'm serious. We should name her together." She kissed the side of my head, "What about pancake? Or Annie junior?"

I snuggled deeper into my girlfriend, reaching a hand out to the little black nose, letting it sniff me. "You're not very creative when you're sleepy." I squinted for a second, "Holly."

Victoria grinned, lifting the puppy up, "Holly for Holly Golightly. The first movie we watched together at your apartment." The puppy started barking tiny little barks, not out of fear but cute little demands that we put her back down to let her continue sniffing around.

I nodded, blushing that Victoria remembered that first movie night, "Exactly. She's quite independent and sassy."

Victoria laughed, setting the puppy back down on her chest, laughing harder as she immediately went back to digging in the oversized shirt. "Holly it is." She turned, "She's perfect, just like you Alex." Victoria kissed me again, longer than the last kiss, making me moan as she pulled away, "I love you."

I sighed happily, nuzzling Victoria's shoulder. Every time she told me she loved me, I felt like I could fight the world singlehandedly, that there was literally nothing that would stop me from being by her side. I looked up in her happy slate grey eyes, laughing as she held up the bottom of her shirt for Holly to crawl out of.

"I love you, Victoria and will forever." I sat up, crawling over and Holly, "I'm going to take a shower." I yanked off my long sleeve thermal as I stood up from the bed, looking over my shoulder at my two girls. "If you want, another of your many gifts will be waiting for you in the shower." I hooked my fingers in the side of my scrub pants, pulling them down with my underwear as I stepped out. Giving Victoria a quick glimpse of my naked rear before walking into the bathroom.

Closing the door, I chuckled to myself, hearing Victoria whisper to Holly that she would be right back, and set the barking puppy back in her box before half running and half stumbling to meet me in the bathroom.

Chapter 22

I sat cross legged in the grass, a cup of coffee next to me, laughing and watching Holly explore the backyard. Biting grass, chasing bugs and barking at the lone tulip plant under the tree. I had taken the puppy outside to play while Alex slept like a dead rock in the middle of the bed. Once again claiming it as her own as soon as I left it. I almost felt bad wearing the woman down to complete exhaustion, but my birthday gift in the shower was too tempting not to exploit to its fullest. I had missed Alex to a painful point over the last few days, and having her stand in front of me, that happy half grin on her face as she began running her hands over my skin under the water, all I wanted was to ease away the ache in my heart.

I stretched out my bruised hand, trying to work out the growing stiffness lingering around the purple and yellow mess of knuckles. Alex would give me hell when she woke up and got a real glimpse at it. I sighed. I hated hiding and lying, and I had done a decent job avoiding it, but this last job required a stronger approach. I frowned, cringing at the soreness deciding to call Dani later and prod her for an update on my retirement plan.

Hearing a quick yip, I looked up to see Holly jump over a tall patch of grass, then hop over to me. Her tail wagging like it was motorized. I grinned, opening my hands to encourage her to come closer, and she did. Running as fast as her tiny legs could and smashing her equally as tiny body into my hands. Lifting her up, I cradled her to my chest, laughing as she wiggled about trying to lick me to death.

"I thought I heard a creature out here." Mary appeared at the top of the fence, smiling and nodding at the puppy in my arms.

I nodded and moved to stand up, "This is Holly, the newest resident of this house." I held Holly tightly as she kept wiggling and squirming. "Holly, this is Mary."

I stopped at the fence, letting Mary hold her hand out for the puppy to sniff before licking it and barking happily at her, asking to be held. Mary chuckled, taking her, "She's sickeningly adorable."

I smiled, "She is. Eight weeks old and already full of piss and vinegar." I leaned on the fence, "She's my birthday present from Alex." I grinned halfway through the sentence, loving the way every syllable felt saying it.

Mary grinned back, "I know. Alex was asking for my advice and I guess, our permission? A few days ago while you were out of town." She met my eyes, "That girl is a keeper, you know that right?"

I looked down at my bare feet, whispering, "I do. At the same time, I don't know what I did to deserve her."

"You love her with the truest form of yourself, Victoria." Mary raised an eyebrow, "That's how. It's the same thing I did to win Dale over when we started dating when the dinosaurs still roamed the earth." She laughed, handing Holly back to me, "She mentioned you might be hanging up your teacher's hat soon? I thought you were like my husband, Navy till the day you die and maybe a few more days after that."

I swallowed hard, laughing to cover up that there was something in what Mary said that had my intuition tingling. "I'm working on it. I love the Navy, but I think it's been my mistress and first love long enough. I want a family and not worry about midterms, recruitment fairs and grooming the future leaders of our world." I bent down, setting the wiggly puppy back into the grass, watching her pounce on a leaf. "After a decade, it's time to live."

"I agree, Victoria, I've only known you as the nice girl next door who shovels our driveway, drags our trash cans up and helps my stubborn old man plant trees, but in the last few months, I've seen a beautiful young woman find her place in this world, and I'm happy to call you neighbor and friend." Mary reached over, squeezing my shoulder, "Not to sound like the old wise neighbor, but I understand Victoria. You remind me a lot of what I was like when I was younger than you. Trying to make sense of the world I was in. It was hard when Dale was in Vietnam, I always felt like I had to hide things from him to keep him safe."

I stared at the older woman for a second, her eyes glinting in a way that had my gut and training reacting. There was something in between the lines of her words. I smiled tightly, turning to the house when my eye caught the bedroom blinds being opened, Alex squinting at the bright sun pouring in, frowning then closing the blinds again.

I chuckled, shaking my head, "I should go see if the bear is awake and ready for breakfast." I glanced at Mary, "Thank you, for your kind words. I have grown fond of you and Dale, and if there is anything I or Alex can do for you two, please don't hesitate to ask." I was pouring on the manners, trying to work around the fact I was beyond curious about what she was trying to tell me.

Mary looked at me for a second more before drawing her eyes to Holly batting at the leaf, "I should see if Dale is up and ready to go for the day." She glanced at me, "Its grocery day, his least favorite day of the week, he gets grumpy when I find all of the junk food he hides under the vegetables." We both laughed, Mary patted my shoulder once more, "Happy Birthday to you and if you need a dog sitter." She winked at me, "Tell Alex I said hello and if you girls need anything while we're out, call."

I whispered a thank you and parted from the fence, walking over to Holly chewing on the leaf. I bent down to her, smiling as she rushed over to me pawing at my legs to be picked up. "You want to go see if Alex is awake?" Holly barked twice, trying to climb up on my knees before I caved and scooped her up, kissing the top of her head. "Hopefully she doesn't growl at you if she's still cranky." Holly barked at me confidently. Her bright brown eyes saying, bring on that bear, I'll out growl her. I shook my head, "Piss and vinegar."

I found Alex in the kitchen, sitting and yawning as she stared at the coffee machine. Holly began barking with excitement when she spotted Alex, making the sleepy woman turn and smile at us, "Good morning birthday girl."

I smiled back, leaning over the island to hand her Holly before kissing her forehead, "Would you like some coffee or are you enjoying the staring contest with an inanimate object?"

Alex gave me a playful dirty look, sighing as she struggled containing Holly. "I do, desperately, and was hoping I could use mind power to bring it to me." She met my eyes, "I'm more tired than I thought I would be."

I glanced at her, filling up the goat mug that had become Alex's mug over the last few months, "I should apologize."

"No, you don't. Never apologize for making me tired, Victoria." The look she gave me was nothing but pure love, and it made my entire soul quiver. "I missed you just as much. The hospital was oddly busier than usual and I ran my wheels off." She bent down, setting Holly down to scamper around the tile floor, barking at her stuffed bone toy that was in her box. "Do you have class Monday?"

I nodded, focusing back on pouring the exact amount of cream and sugar in Alex's mug, "I do. Captain Pegg filled in for me this trip, but is happily handing it back to me just in time for finals." I frowned, "Which I have to write sometime this weekend." I set her mug in front of her, smiling as she quickly wrapped her hands around it, "I might do that later tonight after you're in a meatloaf coma. By the way, I was thinking of maybe having your mom and Bill come here instead? I can get a meatloaf recipe from Mary." I reached for a napkin, catching a glimpse of my injured hand. I quickly went to shove it in my short pockets, when Alex grabbed it, lifting it gently and squinting at the nasty bruise.

"Victoria, did you get this looked at?"

I nodded slowly, "I did. The school nurse was first to examine it, she gave me an ice pack until I was able to get to an urgent care for X-rays. It's just a horrible bruise and a nasty strain where the handle smacked the tendons. Ice, rest and Motrin."

I smiled, at least I was telling the truth. I had gone to a Voltaire doctor near the airport. He signed off on the diagnosis and instructions I repeated to Alex, but he prescribed me Vicodin, which I threw away the second I walked out of his office.

Alex ran delicate fingers over the purple edges, "I should track that kid down and give him a piece of my mind."

I laughed, catching her hands so I could link our fingers together, "It was an accident. A hyper kid jacked up on mountain dew. He didn't mean it." I bit the inside of my cheek to hold the smile. The big Colombian did deserve it. He did mean to kill me if I hadn't shattered his nose into shards. I cleared my throat, clearing away the sounds of his bones breaking and the smell of fresh blood that poured out of his nose. I gave Alex a playful smirk "If you did find him, were you going to mean mug him to death?" She frowned at me, I shook my head, squeezing her hand.

"To be honest, Victoria, I'd probably kick his ass if I was there and saw it." Alex winked at me, "I'm very protective of my seemingly clumsy girlfriend and I hate when you get hurt, especially when it's these beautiful hands." She pulled my hand closer, pressing a gentle kiss at the edge of the bruise.

I cocked an eyebrow, "But you're a nurse, you took an oath."

"Oath schmoath." She stood up, moving to stand next to me, sliding her arms around my waist, "You're my everything and I love you. Therefore, all's fair, even kicking a teenager's ass." She chuckled when I gave her another dirty look, "I'm kidding." A soft kiss landed on my cheek, followed by small paws batting my ankles.

We both looked down at a pair of shiny brown eyes, Alex shaking her head, "She already loves you more than me."

I laughed, tugging Alex closer, "Maybe, but I love you more." I sighed, letting her warmth ease me back into the real me completely. Allowing the black hooded figure that had been lingering in the edges of my vision all last night when I got home and this morning, fade away.

I could feel Alex smile against my chest, "I called my mom while you were in the backyard and rescheduled dinner with them for tomorrow. In the meantime, I'm going to make you a birthday breakfast while you open the rest of the presents I got you. I was too tired to try and get ready to go to their house, and Stacy wants us to meet her and her boyfriend at the bar tonight for birthday drinks. You can invite Dani and maybe Ward." She smirked, "I kind of want to get you liquored up and have my way with you."

I leaned back to look at the woman, "You do realize I learned how to drink in the Navy? I have the alcohol tolerance of a moose, Dani too, but I'll call her after we eat."

I then sighed, searching her eyes, "Alex, Holly is plenty." I smirked, "And the shower, that was, well all I can say is this has been the best birthday I've had in a long time."

Alex shrugged, looking in my eyes, "And you're the best thing to happen to me in a very long time and I want to spoil you." The words came out soft and heavy with so much emotion it made my heart skip. I loved and hated when Alex said things like that. Only because I was still hiding from her a large part of my life and I didn't know how much longer I could avoid it. I needed to get out of Voltaire and I needed it to happen yesterday.

Alex's face broke out in a huge grin, looking away from me and down at the spastic dog now whining that she was being ignored. "I'll make breakfast while you play with our fur baby."

She stepped out of my arms, ignoring my silent protest that she stays with me, "But I want you to play with me." I pouted as Holly was shoved gently into my hands.

Alex raised her eyebrows, moving to the fridge, "There's plenty of time for that later, but we are going to have to make room in our lives for that one." She laughed, "It's good practice for when we have kids."

The second the words fell out, I could see her turn red and stumble to retract the slip, "I mean more dogs or something, fish?" She sighed nervously, sticking her face in the fridge, "Did you drink all of the orange juice last night?"

I swallowed down a very dry throat, letting her slipped words sink into my mind and my heart. Kids. Kids meant marriage, marriage meant forever, forever with Alex. The panic was immediate and was quick to spur a thousand other things. I bent down to look at Holly, hoping she was doing something that I could comment on and ease the iceberg sized tension that blew into the kitchen, but Holly was completely passed out. Breathing heavily with her face smashed into the crook of my elbow. I winced at the little girl, way to bail on me when I needed you the most. I sucked in a breath and moved closer to Alex still rummaging around in the fridge for juice and a reprieve from the awkwardness she threw down.

"Alex, do you want to have kids?" I frowned at the way my voice sounded so meek and unsteady.

Alex straightened up, clutching a bottle of cranberry juice like it was her lifeline as she turned to face me. Her eyes wide with worry, "I didn't mean to, it slipped out." She moved her eyes to the plastic bottle cap, "We've barely been in a relationship for a year, I don't want you to think I'm trying to rush things." She peered at the sleeping black fluff in my arm, "I didn't get Holly as a test. I just remember you saying you wanted a dog and I couldn't resist and I don't know, I'm rambling." She turned to set the bottle on the counter, "I'll make French toast."

Alex was rambling, it was her go to when she felt she had shit the bed in terms of the delicate balance we still held in aspects of our relationship. I moved closer, grabbing her upper arm, "Alex, do you want to have kids? And all that comes with it?" I was now asking because I wanted to know her honest answer, not an answer she would give to appease me.

Alex face me, her face covered in a sheepish look as she nodded slowly, "I do. I want kids, dogs, a house, and a quiet wedding." She bit her bottom lip, whispering, "All with you."

I could feel my stomach turn in knots, twisting one way that made me giddy then another way that made me want to vomit. The look in Alex's eyes told me that she was telling me the purest of truths she could. Truthfully, I also wanted all of those things and with her. I just didn't realize it until a few seconds ago. My small silence, as usual, made Alex's panic creep up. She went to turn back to the stove, "It's your birthday. We should be talking about that and what you want to do today, not the silly things in my head."

I stared at her back, my two lives coming together and dueling it out, my black hooded figure twin suddenly appearing next to her with my own eyes staring back at me. The head cocked asking me in silence what did I really want versus what the reality of what I could have, be.

Glaring hard at my twin, I spoke, "I want that all too, Alex. With you and only you." I swallowed hard as my twin nodded and slowly faded away as I spoke the last few words, "I never knew I wanted it until this moment."

Alex spun around, her eyes wide and glassy, a smile tugging at her lips. "Really? You're not saying this to make me happy or to shut me up for a minute?"

I shook my head, leaning over to kiss her softly, murmuring against her lips, "Never, especially since I have other ways to shut you up for more than a minute." I leaned back to look in her eyes, "I want all of this, I want a forever with you Alex."

Alex's grin could have provided all of the electricity in New York city for a year, it was so bright. She grabbed my face, kissing me hard. "Then forever it will be, but after you retire. I want you all to myself, free from the Navy." She smiled when she saw the strange look on my face, "Victoria, I can wait. I want to wait." She stepped back, "I called Ward while you were gone. He and I are working on getting me into Bethesda Naval hospital with the mental health administrator. I decided I want to go back to school and get my masters in therapy so I can heal not only broken bodies, but broken minds." The tension had shifted like I flicked a light switch. Alex was now rambling excitedly like she did when she woke me up in the middle of the night to tell me how she saved a life, or pumped someone's heart with her bare hands.

I shifted the still passed out Holly to my other arm, "When did you make this decision?" I wasn't mad, I was just very surprised. Alex loved being a nurse and I would hate it if I was the reason she was changing her life.

"Stacy and I were talking about it while reinserting Mrs. Crowley's catheter. Stacy was the one who started it. Talking about how she signed up for online classes to move towards her nurse practitioner degree. It got me thinking about the wish list I had when I moved to New York. Get my master's and move into doing more with patients than issuing band aids."

She turned back to the cabinets, grabbing a pan, "After mapping it out during our break, it's very doable within the next year. My credits will transfer to Georgetown and Ward is willing to help me get the intern hours I need. Really, more than anything, I'm tired of these damn double triple shifts were I only get to see you in the morning when you wake me up before you go teach. I want a nine to five and come home to you for dinner, not late night cookies and cuddles." She shrugged, "And I'll be making more money for whatever future we decide on." Alex smiled, "The biggest reason is, I miss you and want to spend more time with you, living this life."

I sat down on the stool, setting Holly on my lap, "I do love late night cookies and cuddles." I rolled my eyes, "But, I also don't like the grumpy, growly Alex bear in my bed when I wake you up well before you're ready."

Alex frowned, playfully swatting me with the spatula. "Rude."

I laughed, shaking my head at how light and fun this tense moment had become, a sure small sign that Alex might be able to handle the whole truth of what I was when the time came. I pushed that thought out before it took hold, and ruined the mood.

Alex skipped over to me, kissing me quickly. She motioned to the sleeping puppy in my arms, "If you keep holding her while she sleeps, she'll never want to sleep anywhere else."

I shrugged, "Perhaps, but she'll probably learn it by watching you every night." I stood up, moving out of the way of another impending spatula to the arm, "I'll take her upstairs, lay her down and come back down for you."

Alex shook her head, still grinning like it was her birthday and Christmas rolled in one, and it made my heart swell knowing I placed that grin on her face. A grin that I would memorize and tuck in the recesses of my mind to pull onto chase away the black hooded figure when she wanted to creep in and remind me of far too many things.

I paused at the bottom of the steps, staring back at Alex. "Alex, I love you. Never forget that. You will always be the life I want."

Alex's eyes met mine, her grin growing wider, "I love you, Victoria." She flicked her hand at me, "Get out of here and let me cook birthday girl."

I grinned catching the edges of her cheeks pink up before I went upstairs to put Holly in her box.

Chapter 23

"Are you sure she'll be okay?" Victoria was bent down, looking over the kiddie gate we had placed at the bathroom door to encase Holly in.

I chuckled, bending down next to her, my hand on her back, "Yes. She has her brand new bone patterned bed, her bone toy, her Navy blanket and the floor is covered in pee pads." I shook my head laughing at the shopping extravaganza Victoria went on after breakfast. Carting Holly around in her sweatshirt as we trolled up and down the aisles at the pet store, buying the little dog anything she sniffed or looked at. I pointed at the stuffed goat Holly was currently pawing at, "I even gave her that, since it smells like you." I stood up, plucking at Victoria, "She has water and I have Mary on speed dial if you panic."

Victoria sighed, reaching down to pet the puppy one more time before standing up, "I hate leaving her, it's only been a day." She looked at me with her own big grey puppy dog eyes.

I frowned playfully, whispering an awe and bending down to kiss her, "We will be back in a few hours, she'll survive. She survived two hours in a car with Stacy." I yanked on Victoria's arm, hearing my phone ring, "Oh, that's probably Stacy. She was going to head to the restaurant and grab a table." I let go of her arm, walking to the bed to open the text from Stacy. "Yep, she's there and says it's busy as fucking fuck." I rolled my eyes, reaching for my leather jacket.

"Can we stay home? Rent a movie and snuggle on the couch? All three of us?" Victoria stood up fully from Holly, smoothing out her tight dark blue blouse that met very tight dark blue jeans that had my mouth watering and eager to regift her first birthday gift.

I shook my head, swallowing hard, "Nope. This is your birthday and it would be good for us to get out of the house and mingle with our friends. Dani is on her way, she messaged me while you were telling Holly we weren't leaving her forever. Stacy is there without her boyfriend, meaning they had a fight and she will want to get toasted." I shrugged my jacket on, walking back over, "And I want to go out on the town with this gorgeous woman on my arm and have every man, woman, and animal jealous of me."

Victoria rolled her eyes, reaching for me, "Alex."

"Don't Alex me, I mean it." I winked at her, winding my fingers in her uninjured hand, "Let me take you out and let loose. Be crazy and silly for your birthday." I looked over her shoulder at Holly dragging the stuffed goat into her bed, curl up with it and pass out in two breaths. "See, even Holly wants you to go out."

Victoria looked over, smiling at how ridiculously cute the puppy was, "Fine. But can we be home before two? I don't want to sleep away tomorrow before we go to your moms."

I nodded, kissing her cheek before rushing over to the end of the bed where I had set the small purple bag with the rest of her gifts in it, "Deal." I also snagged the car keys from the dresser, "I'm designated driver tonight. I already told Dani that too. So you two can indulge in your weird sailor drinking games."

Grabbing the bag and my purse, I shook my head one more time glancing at Victoria whispering to Holly that we would be back and not to worry. My girlfriend was a giant soft hearted mush.

I moved downstairs to the kitchen, setting the gift bag and my purse on the island counter so I could dig around making sure I had everything, when I felt two arms slide over my waist and pull me into her body.

A small kiss landed on my neck, "Thank you, Alex."

I sighed, leaning back against Victoria, "You don't have to keep thanking me. It's your day." I grinned, motioning to the gift bag, "You still have a couple more to open and knowing mom, she'll have something for you."

Victoria kissed me again, "I want to thank you. Today has been amazing. Everything you've done today, has made me happy and excited that it's actually my birthday." She leaned away, "Makes it easier to take turning thirty-two."

I glanced over my shoulder, "Thirty-two? My, aren't you an old lady."

Victoria rolled her eyes, "I had to look at my license and make sure. My memory isn't what it used to be, plus you're right behind me in years." She winked at me, reaching around to grab the gift bag. "Can we leave this here? Open it later?" She lifted the bag.

I sighed heavily, folding my arms and giving the blonde a look, "You can open it now." I smiled lightly, "I did have second thoughts about taking it to the bar. Knowing how much Dani drinks, she'd probably spill something on it."

Victoria gave me a knowing look, "Yes she would." She dug in to the bag, "Alex, you didn't have to get me more. Holly and the shower gift was plenty." She smirked at me, lifting the tissue wrapped gift out of the bag. "And then there was the unexpected lunchtime gift in the living room."

I felt my cheeks heat up, "I couldn't resist. You know how much I love those ripped jeans of yours. Giving me sneak peeks, begging me to do something about it." I ran a hand over my hair, feeling very shy at how much I always wanted to touch her, no matter what she was wearing.

Victoria laughed, unwrapping the light lavender colored tissue, "Remind me to wear those jeans every day, even to the office when school starts." She turned back to the gift, her smile fading as more was revealed to her. "Alex...I."

I moved to stand next to her. "Ward helped me with this. I called him about the hospital tour and we got to talking. I rambled about how your birthday was coming and what to get the woman who has everything Navy related in the world." Leaning against her, "He gave me a few ideas and helped me track this down."

Victoria delicately lifted the old book up, running her hands over the thick cover, "Alex, this must have cost a fortune." She looked at me with glassy eyes, "I...don't..."

I placed my hand on her back, "You don't have to say anything. Ward pulled a few strings and called in a few favors. Found the book in an old shop in Scotland run by one of his old Royal Navy buddies." I smiled, kissing her cheek, "I owe Ward my first born, but he and I both agreed this was the perfect gift for you."

Victoria smiled, shaking her head, "It's incredible. A first edition of Casino Royale, in hardcover." She ran her eyes over the blue grey jacket, the red hearts only mildly faded as they bordered the yellow wreath. Victoria grinned, "A whisper of love, a whisper of hate." She titled her head down, "Words that stuck with me from the first day I read this book and still carries with me now." She looked up at me. Her eyes happy, bright and teary. "It also reminds me of how we met."

I took one step closer, my eyes searching hers, "In your office?"

She shook her head, turning back to the book, "No, in the metro station." She paused, her face falling for a second, "A whisper of hate led me a whisper of love." Victoria sniffled, setting the book down on the tissue, "Until that point, I only heard the whispers of hate." She half murmured the words out, gently wrapping the book back in the paper. She cleared her voice and took one step away from me, "We should get going before Dani starts calling every three seconds."

I nodded, "Okay." I watched her smile, her eyes meeting mine for a split second, the clouds bearing heavy around her irises before she turned away, moving into the den where I heard her set the book down on the desk and slip out what sounded like a muffled sob.

My instinct was to run to the den and ask if she was okay, if I had stepped across a line by asking Ward, or what she really meant about that night in the metro station. The way she looked at me and spoke the words from the book, told me there was something more to her memories of that night versus what we both accepted as the truth.

I felt my jaw twitch, my gut twist and all of the strange wary feelings I had shoved away since the Navy formal and Victoria's weirdness from months ago, came back. All rolling into a tidal wave that woke me up to the fact I shouldn't be so blind for the sake of love.

Victoria appeared around the corner, her face back to the light happy one from before, "Are you ready?" She held up her phone, "Dani is already there. It seems her and Stacy have birthday shots lined up and waiting."

I forced a smile, turning to my purse for the car keys, "Then we better get going, Stacy left alone with shots for too long means I will be hooking her up to an IV as she barfs into a plastic bag." I rolled my eyes, trying to chase away the strange feeling. I took two steps to the door, Victoria's hand falling into mine like normal as we left the house. She squeezed my hand, holding the door open for me to go out first. I glanced at her, whispering a thank you and catching the look in her eyes. One of love and fear, a look I had not seen in a very long time.

I sucked in huge breath of the cold night air, and walked to the car, smiling to Victoria talk about the first time she got really drunk at eighteen with grandma Edith at a boozy bingo party.

I listened, wishing that I could stay blind forever, but I couldn't and it was getting harder to when Victoria was showing more and more that she was hiding something from me.

The bar was packed for a Saturday night, filled with couples trying to keep the romance alive, groups of sports fans hooting and hollering over the football game on large TV screens lining the walls. Then there was the occasional single and wanting to mingle, weaving their way through the bar, smiling and winking at everything with a heartbeat.

I laughed to myself when a few gentleman eyes fell my way, urging Victoria on to scowl at them and pull me closer. Staking her claim on me and earning a few soft sighs from a lady or two, wishing their man or woman was so chivalrous or as hot as Victoria. I held tightly on to her hand, leading us to the back of the bar where it was a quieter and less crowded. Spotting Stacy right away, I waved at her, she waved back excitedly while still drinking from the giant beer glass in her hand. Dani was across from her, a small army of empty shot glasses lined up in front of her.

She grinned and waved back as she spotted us, shifting out of the booth to take a few steps towards us. "Well I'll be damned to hell and back, the Professor left the house. I had my money on her talking you out of coming out tonight. Choosing instead to stay in with a bottle of bourbon and pajamas."

Dani opened her arms for a hug, I shook my head laughing as I quickly hugged the redhead. The last few months, Dani and I came to a strange, tentative friendship that was weird but worked. Smelling the whiskey on her, I realized she was on her way to getting hammered. "It took some work. She did almost talk me into a pajama party." I backed out of her arms, watching her rush to Victoria and bear hug her. I laughed shaking my head as Stacy appeared next to me, poking my shoulder.

"That sailor can drink. There's no way in hell I'll be able to keep up with her." She grinned at me, "Victoria is going to get wasted tonight, you know that, right?"

I sighed, setting my purse down in the booth, nodding, "I do, but it's her birthday and she's earned her right to get wasted and relax." I smiled, watching Dani and Victoria laugh and smile like I had never seen the two do before, "I like seeing her like this, it's rare to see her so free and happy outside of our bubble."

Stacy took a large sip of beer, "Did she like the fur baby?"

"She did, loved it. Victoria wanted to cancel tonight for fear of leaving Holly at home alone." I glanced at Stacy, "She hasn't had the dog a whole day yet and she's already spoiled her and become the overprotective parent."

Stacy giggled, nudging me, "And here we thought you would be the overbearing mom. I can only imagine what will happen when you two start pushing out babies." She raised an eyebrow, "If you two decide to do that. I know it's only been a few months."

I patted my friend on the back, "Good thing Victoria and I had a hearty life talk this morning." I glanced at the ring on my right hand, running my thumb over it, "The only thing I have to worry about is making you godmother to one of our little ones."

I looked up at Stacy, grinning at me like she had won the lottery, "About fucking time." She tilted her head towards Victoria and Dani rushing off to the bar, "Just don't make me maid of honor, I'm not spending your wedding day following you around and helping you pee in whatever fluffy ruffly dress you wear." She shook her head and picked up the shot in front of her. "And so it begins." She then turned to me, "Can you call a cab for me later? The boyfriend bailed on me. I intend to get tipsy and ignore him for the weekend."

I chuckled, moving to sit in the booth, "I can." I waved down a waitress for a large pitcher of water, catching Victoria and Dani slam down shots that had them both cringing and gagging. I blew out a breath, "Even if I end up regretting tonight."

One hour into being at the bar and Victoria and Dani were hammered, Stacy was buzzed and I was entranced at the three lady debacle in front of me. Stacy was leaning on Dani, sipping on a long island ice tea, as Dani told another story about Victoria and her stealing ashtrays from the White House.

Dani squinted at me, holding up a glass with a fingers worth of whiskey in it, "So, I tell the uppity Professor here, hey! Let's steal some shit from Lincoln's bedroom." She giggled, poking Victoria in the arm, "She protested, as she normally does with every fun idea I have."

Victoria frowned, sipping down what had to be her third Manhattan aside from the handful of shots that would have laid out any normal human. "You have really, really, really bad ideas that aren't fun. Nope." She shook her head, making me giggle when she made herself dizzy.

Dani scowled, "Shush it. It was a good idea. I got us those super sweet ashtrays and that coffee mug you hide in the back of your cabinet in fear that if you use it, the secret service will raid your house." She laughed, slurring her words trying to say secret service, only to have it come out sounding like shecret shervise.

I laughed as Victoria shoved Dani into Stacy, making Stacy spill some of her long island iced tea down her shirt. "You sailors are sloppy ass sailors!" Stacy wiped at her shirt, moving to stand up, "I gotta pee, move it you boat queens!"

Victoria and Dani stumbled out of the booth, freeing Stacy to stumble to her feet before weaving and wobbling to the bathroom. The two very drunk women flopped back into the booth, Dani slapping Victoria's bruised hand and shouting, "Shots! More shots!"

Victoria yelped from the pain and shoved Dani back, "Sit down you cow." She frowned, her eyes heavy with alcohol, "You know what was another bad idea of yours? Colombia." She held up her purple hand, "You could have chimed in when that giant fucker popped out of the bedroom. I had to hit him five times before he dropped, five more after I broke his junkie nose to keep him down." Victoria closed her eyes, shaking her head, mumbling, "I hate Colombia. It's so goddamn hot there."

I felt my smile fade as I leaned closer, staring at Victoria as she mumbled, "Even the Colombian doctors are junkies, trying to give me Vicodin for this hand." She slid down the booth, reaching for her glass when Dani grabbed her under the arm, lifting her up. "I should've taken them all out."

I glanced at Dani and caught a look in her eyes that betrayed her drunkenness, "Up Professor, no passing out. We still have shots to do." She struggled getting Victoria up, waving the waitress over for more shots. "It's your favorite, Irish car bombs."

Victoria groaned, "Fuck Ireland too. That stupid bitch and her stupid bathtub, getting in my brain before I got hers all over my hands."

I felt my stomach twist into knots, Victoria's mumblings were drunken, yes, but there was a harsh truth behind what she was saying. From my years as a nurse and being a college lush, I knew that alcohol was the greatest truth serum in the world. Loose lips always sunk ships.

I went for Victoria, glaring at Dani, "I think she's had enough."

Dani chuckled, smirking at me, "She hasn't had enough until she's forgotten, until we both have forgotten." She waved me back, "It's our brand of medicine." She tapped at her head messily, with a sad look on her face, "There's so much that needs to be forgotten." She shook her head, reaching for the shots the waitress set down. "I wish I could tell you, Alex, but then there wouldn't be enough whiskey in the world to repent for our sins."

She nudged Victoria, who was starting to pass out, handing her the full pint glass of Guinness and the small shot of whiskey, "Up Commander! Up to the bow of the ship! Full steam ahead!" Dani then boomed out, "Non sibi sed patriae!"

Victoria's eyes shot open, her body sitting up straight as she tried to focus hazy, drunken eyes on the world spinning around her, "Non sibi sed patriae!" She then dropped the shot in to the pint glass, and chugged as much of it back as she could before gagging and slamming the glass back on the counter. She wiped her mouth with the back of her hand and promptly passed out. Her head dropping to her chest as she slumped back into the booth.

I sighed hard, getting up to start the process of removing my dead drunk girlfriend. "Victoria, we need to get you home."

Victoria mumbled, still passed out. I looked over at Dani, laughing and shaking her head, "Hard to fathom I once watched her outdrink a group of marines in a bar in Tunisia." She then sucked in a breath, looking right in my eyes, with glossy foggy green ones, "Dear God, I hope I can save you both." She then smiled weakly and laid her head on the table, passing out in two ragged breaths.

"Fuck." I groaned, I now had two piss drunk women to wrangle into the car. I also was incredibly frustrated about what both of them said. The stupid cloak and dagger dialogue weaseling its way back into my life. I went to flag down one of the bouncers when Stacy popped around the corner, she looked far better than she did when she went to the bathroom, telling me she probably threw up most of what she drank.

"Did I miss something?"

I groaned, grabbing her, "Help me with these two." I shook my head, lifting up the dead log that was Victoria, "These two sailors have drunk themselves to the point of blacking out." I threw her arm over my shoulder and was able to lift her to her feet. Victoria stirred a bit, finding her feet while mumbling. At least she was on her feet, leaning against me and helping me move her from the booth. "Can you grab Dani?"

Stacy gave me a look until I scowled, "Okay! Okay!" She moved over to Dani, slapping her on the face lightly, "Hey, drunky crow. Get up." Dani frowned, slapping Stacy's hand away until Stacy just grabbed her and yanked her out of the booth, catching her in an awkward embrace. "Whoa there red! I have a boyfriend."

Dani mumbled as Stacy shifted her to the same position I had Victoria in. "What the hell happened while I was peeing and barfing?"

I shook my head, hoisting Victoria up more to walk her out of the bar. "They got out of hand and I was stupid enough to let them." I smiled at a few people on the way, shaking my head no when the one bouncer asked if I needed help. I clenched my jaw, throwing the keys to the valet, and looked at Stacy, trying to keep her face away from Dani who was making a strange gurgling snoring noise. "You look more pissed off than one would be when their girlfriend gets shitfaced at a bar. What really happened, Alex?"

I sighed, looking up at the night sky, "I think Victoria lied to me about her trip this week."

Stacy chuckled, "Who would lie about going to Minnesota for a boring ass teachers conference? I mean it's not glamorous, it's a state made for boring things and football."

I closed my eyes, feeling my anger build as my gut started to race to put pieces together. Opening them, I glanced at Victoria's hand around my shoulder, the purple bruise spurring me on. "She started talking about Colombia and beating the hell out of some guy's face." I scanned the edges of her knuckles, seeing all of the signs that the bruise was created by doing that exact thing. The small lacerations, the scrapes, the way the bruise had a distinct impact area, all lead my medical knowledge to tell me the truth. I had seen a million hand injuries like this in my nursing career, all of them from fights or smashing the hand into something while curled into a fist. "I think she lied to me, I think she's been lying to me." I turned to Dani slung over Stacy's arm, "They both have been."

Stacy stared at me wide eyed and blinking, "Why the fuck would Victoria be in Colombia?" She blinked a few more times, her mouth shifting open, "Wait, do you think her and red are drug dealers?" She glanced at Dani drooling on her shoulder, "Like smuggling cocaine up their butt?"

"Stacy, shut up." I glared at her as the BMW was pulled to the curb, "Victoria is not a drug dealer." I shifted the passed out blonde again, moving to the BMW, "But she is something and I think it's time I try to find out."

I heard Stacy whistle under her breath, "Someone's pissed."

I frowned, shoving Victoria into the passenger seat and buckling her in, "I'm not pissed, Stacy. I'm just tired of feeling like I'm on the outside looking in. That there's a part of Victoria she thinks she has to hide from me." I looked over the top of the headrest at Stacy shoving Dani, less than delicately into the back seat, "She said something tonight that scared me." I straightened up, looking down at Victoria. Her cheeks were a bright red as she slept heavily.

"Did she finally tell you that her and Victoria did indeed dibble dabbled in the Navy?" Stacy slammed the back door close, throwing herself off balance before I grabbed her from falling to the curb. "Shit, I need to call a cab and get some water."

"You do." I steadied her while she pulled out her phone, "Dani said that she hoped to god she could save both Victoria and I." I turned to look at Victoria with her head pressed against the glass.

Stacy blew out a breath, "Red is a weird one. She was telling me some fucked up stories about the war while we waited for you two. Kept talking about a bird who took away her life and turned her best friend into a machine. A cold machine without feelings." Stacy shrugged, "She was at least four shots and two straight vodkas in by then. She kept calling me Casey."

I chewed on my lip, remembering a few things Dani told me about at the formal, a Colonel she and Victoria knew. I also remembered Bill telling me that the military nickname for a Colonel was bird. I swallowed hard, more pieces falling into my lap, begging me to be placed in the overall puzzle I had been trying to sort out for as long as I knew Victoria.

I stared at Stacy until her taxi cab pulled up on the curb, she shook her head, rushing to hug me. "Call me when you get home, so I know you made it in." She winked at me, "If I were you, I'd leave red in the car to sleep it off."

I smiled, "I just might." I shoved her away, "Text me when you get home and thanks for coming out."

Stacy nodded and half ran to the cab, "Tell Victoria I said happy birthday and a bloody Mary is the best morning after cure!" She waved at me, hopping in to the cab.

I waited until the cab was around the corner before climbing into the BMW. Dani was snoring loudly on her side in the back seat and Victoria was still pressed against the window, her face scrunched up, cheeks flushed as her body started its goal of processing the alcohol out of her system as quickly as possible.

I couldn't resist running my hand down her cheek, pushing some of the hair away from her face, "I love you so much, Victoria." I whispered it, "Please don't lie to me." I frowned, starting the car and pulling away from the bar.

The ride home, I began crafting the speech I would give her when she woke up. Ask her for the truth and prepare myself, I would have to ensure that Victoria knew, no matter how bad she thought it was, no secret of hers would chase me away. I loved her with everything I had and if she was hiding something that scared Dani, I needed to know. So I could do my best to protect Victoria.

The thick tomato and pepper smell made my stomach turn, I went to open my eyes to swat away the offending scent, only to see Dani sitting across from me holding out a large full glass of bloody Mary. I swallowed down a few times, coaxing my stomach to settle down and not launch its entire contents everywhere. Closing my eyes, I covered my nose with the pillow in hopes of blocking out the smell, "You're in my bedroom."

"You've always been known for your keen observation skills." Dani's voice was rough and raspy, "It's a nice room, looks better with the addition of another human sharing it with you."

I peeled my eyes open once more, trying to get them to focus on the redhead sitting across from me, "Why are you in my bedroom?"

Dani smiled softly, "I've taken on the task of getting your ass out of bed and on the road to recovery." She set the full glass down on the table next to me, "Hair of the dog, my own special recipe." She leaned back in the chair, folding her arms over her stomach. "I suggest you drink it before you get up or you'll be cradling the toilet."

I frowned, trying to move in the bed, feeling my head pound like a tank battalion was rolling through it, I stopped for a minute. "How did I? Where's Alex?"

"Alex is outside with your fur covered daughter. Has been all morning. She was a little pissed off this morning when I woke up to defile the laundry sink with Irish car bombs." Dani frowned painfully, "We, I, got us out of hand last night. We drank a paycheck's worth last night." She rubbed her forehead, "Good thing I set the tab up while I was sober. Closed it out while I was making the hangover cure."

I scooted to sit up, clutching my head at the sudden movement, "Dammit." I gave in, grabbing the glass and chugged the sludgy cocktail, trying hard not to taste it or smell it before it was gone. Setting the glass back down, I looked around the room. The blinds were still drawn tight and the only light in the room was coming from the small bedside lamp on Alex's side. I looked down and saw I was still in my outfit from last night and that Alex had not shared the bed with me. I leaned forward, cradling my head, "What did we do?"

Dani sighed, sitting forward with her elbows on her knees, "We drank a lot." She paused, looking up in my eyes, "And we said a lot."

I turned to look at her slowly, "We said a lot?"

She nodded slowly, fidgeting nervously with her hands. "When I woke up and after I gave the laundry sink a live performance of the exorcist, I went to find Alex. Thank her for letting me stay here and taking care of me." She laughed lightly, "Shit, she even left a bottle of water and a puke bucket after tucking me in. She's a keeper."

I groaned, swallowing down a tomato juice covered throat, "Dani…"

Dani nodded, standing up and walking to the bathroom to get a glass of water, "I know." She came back to the chair, handing me the glass, "After a bit of polite conversation and an offer to make greasy eggs, Alex flat out asked me why you were in Columbia and not Minnesota last week."

I clutched the glass tightly, my heart starting to race, "Why would, how?"

Dani blew out a slow breath, looking up at me with a soft look, "We fucked up, I fucked up. I got you hammered and god knows why I did, knowing how we talk with our guard down." She bit her bottom lip, "Alex pressed harder, in her polite way, asking why you were in Colombia and why did you have to beat someone up." Dani sucked in a breath, "It seems you rambled about beating the shit out of the drug lord and placing the blame my way for not chiming in when I saw him rush out of the bedroom at you."

I stared at the water in my hand, the water rippling as my hand shook, I asked softly, "What did you tell her?"

Dani scrunched up her face, "I went to lie when Alex asked me what I meant when I prayed to God I could save you both." I saw her jaw twitch as her eyes turned glassy, "I don't remember any of this, Victoria, I slipped up. Getting so drunk because it's the only time that my brain and the memories slow down. That I can feel what I used to feel like before all of this started." She sniffled, "I'm so sorry Victoria."

I could hear in her voice the desperation, the sadness and the panic, I looked at her, my voice wavering, "Did you tell her the truth?"

Dani shook her head furiously. "I couldn't, I wanted to, but I couldn't." She tucked her arms tightly against her chest, "I lied, I made up a lie on the spot like I only know how to do. I told Alex you were in Colombia with me on an intelligence gathering operation for the Navy. That we issued you the cover story of going to Minnesota to keep the listeners off your trail. I told her that you didn't want to go, but I talked you into it and it was a joint operation with the Navy and the Colombian government to stop drug smugglers from using human traffickers." Dani laughed shaking her head, "Sadly that's the truth, but I left out the part where I sent you in to kill that giant junkie with your bare hands."

I looked at my hand before shoving it under the blankets to hide it. "My hand, she asked how I hurt my hand, didn't she?"

Dani shook her head, "She didn't. I was waiting for her to ask me about that, but she never did. Alex just stared at me, watching me eat the pile of eggs and bacon she made, holding Holly and smiling in a way that unnerved me." She covered her face with her hands, "Victoria, she's going to ask you for the truth and I don't think she's going to walk away without hearing all of it. And I do mean all of it."

I closed my eyes, feeling my heart crack and separate, the black hooded figure appearing in my mind shaking her head no, telling me there was no way for that part of me to be revealed and have all the things I had now or wanted in the future. I squeezed my eyes tighter, "How quickly can you and the old man initiate the plan you showed me last week?"

Dani's head shot up, "Victoria, we're at least another month away from even getting the equipment we need for that. It all has to be done discreetly." She searched my eyes, "It's a loose plan, a crazy plan that needs refinement."

I turned to look at Dani, the black hooded figure standing behind her. I glanced at it before returning to Dani, "How quickly can you make it a solid plan without the equipment?"

Dani held my gaze, the realization of what I was asking falling in quickly to a point of no negotiation. "Two weeks. I can pull something together in two weeks, but you will still have to go to New York City to the Voltaire safe house for it to work right. The old man offered up her secret residence as the extraction point."

I nodded slowly, "Can we get Alex out in two weeks?"

"I can, she will be easier than you. Less ties to break, but yes, I can get her out and safe in two weeks. I have a plan to take her to England for a few days while you bounce around and fall off Voltaire's radar, and I'll explain all of that to her." Dani sighed, "Shit, Victoria, you really are going to tell her everything, even the metro station incident, aren't you?"

I swung my legs free from the bed, grabbing onto the edge of the mattress, I steadied my swirling head. "I am, yes. And if she rejects me for the monster I am…" I paused looking up at the black figure still shaking her head at me behind Dani. I looked away without finishing my thought and frowned as my voice rasped out, "Please keep her safe, Dani. Keep Voltaire's interest away from her." I stood up slowly, Dani standing with me, "You have everything I gave you last month?"

She nodded, "It's locked up in the safe at the lake house in Maine."

I smiled, "Good." I shuffled to the bathroom, eager to wash the stink off booze, fear and determination of what I was about to do away. Hoping I would come to my senses or at least come up with a sturdy lie when the truth was too frightening to speak. I would lose Alex when I told her everything, but I knew I would lose her if I continued to lie. "I'll be down in a minute."

Dani stared at me, "Victoria, when are you going to tell her?"

I paused at the doorway to the bathroom, "Tonight, when she finally asks me. She won't before, she'll want to make sure I'm okay before we go to her parent's house for my birthday dinner. Alex will put on a brave face and ignore the need to hear the truth for a little longer."

"How do you know that? She was pretty ballsy and bold with me." Dani folded her arms.

I shrugged, "She isn't in love with you, Dani. The one thing I have learned about Alex over the last year and a half is that she will always put love before anything else. She will let it blind her from the truth willingly, because like me, she's never had a love like this. A love that begs to catered to no matter the consequences."

I sighed, looking down at the wood floor. "But I'm tired of letting the whispers of hate cancel out the whispers of love. I want to be free, free with her and I no longer care about the consequences. Alex needs to hear the truth and I need to know if she can stay with me after I tell her everything." I felt my eyes well up as my heart tightened, "I'm tired of letting the Colonel win with every breath I take."

Dani stared at me, letting silence fill the room. She tilted her head towards the door, "Two weeks, Victoria, two weeks and you and her can be free." Dani turned to walk out of the door, "I will figure this out and save you both." She threw me a tight smile before leaving the room.

When she was gone, I let out a shuddering breath, clutching on to the edge of the shower door as I began to shake. Shake not from the lingering hangover that was cursing me, but from the fear of what I was about to do. I breathed in and out heavily a few times to calm down, moving to the small window over the toilet, I looked out on the backyard.

Alex was laying in the middle of the yard, her hair splayed out like a splatter of chocolate paint on a green canvas. She was laughing, grinning as Holly ran around her, barking at the leaves Alex held in her hand. She wore my Academy sweatshirt and a pair of jeans with no shoes. She looked happy, perfect and at peace. Grabbing at the excited puppy anytime she tried to attack her faces with kisses. Alex would laugh genuinely and snuggle the puppy to her chest until Holly broke free to chase whatever caught her fancy.

I watched Alex, watching and memorizing everything I saw. I loved Alex with every broken and whole part of myself and it was time she got all of me. The good, the bad, the ugly and the killer that I could feel standing next to me, looking out the window with me.

It was time. It was time that I gave her that last piece of my life and prayed to gods I no longer believed in, that Alex would somehow accept it and stay with me.

I moved away from the window, my eyes full of tears, and started the shower.

Who was I kidding? When she heard the truth, Alex would be gone the second I finished telling her everything.

Chapter 24

"Come Holly, let's go see if your mom is up." I grinned at the black ball of furry energy as she rushed towards me, a stick in her mouth, barking around it excitedly. I couldn't help but laugh and shake my head at the little girl, so full of excitement over a piece of wood.

Opening the back door, I grabbed the stick from her before she dragged it into the house. Holly barked, giving me a strange look for taking it away from her. I bent down, scratching her head. "No sticks in the house, now go find Victoria."

Holly barked, hopping on her feet before skittering across the floor to run and find her person. I closed the back door, sighing as I looked at the clock and saw it was almost noon. Victoria had been passed out with no signs of getting up when I checked on her after my shower. She was still in the same curled up ball position I had left her in, after I opted to sleep in the spare room next to us. I was mad at her, but it wasn't why I chose the spare room. Victoria was super drunk and would roll all over the bed and probably throw up on me if I slept next to her. Plus, it allowed me time to think about the things that slipped out of her boozed soaked mouth.

Moving through the kitchen, I spotted a note under the Navy football mug I poured Dani's coffee in.

"Alex,

Thanks for breakfast, the ride, the puke bucket, and making sure I survived last night.

Talk to her, she's ready for you to ask.

Dani."

I frowned, crumpling the note up and throwing it in the trash under the sink. My frown softened when I noticed Dani had washed all of the dishes from breakfast and packed up the leftovers in a neat stack of containers. I shook my head, there were moments that Dani made it veritably impossible to hate her for very long.

Lifting the stack, I moved to the fridge to put them away before I tried to rouse the blonde upstairs, when I heard a small yip and a very tired, raspy voice telling Holly she was a good girl.

My stomach dropped as I caught a glimpse of Victoria walking in the kitchen. Her hair still wet from the shower, she looked better than when I dumped her in bed.

"Hi." Her voice was very raspy, her eyes were tired and tinged with a strange sadness. "Sorry about oversleeping and for last night." She cradled the dog in her arms, moving to sit down at the island. "I'm still up for dinner with your mom."

Victoria said it in a half questioning way, clearly testing the waters with me. I sighed, grabbing the containers to take them to the fridge. I didn't want to look at her, I was afraid to look at her. I was afraid that with one look, I would falter in one way or another. "Mom called this morning. I told her you had a rough night and I would check with you when you got up."

"I could use some meatloaf. I hear it's a great hangover cure." I could hear the smirk in her voice.

Nodding with my back still turned, "We can leave in a couple hours, take Holly to meet Annie and Barney." I bent down, moving things absently mindedly around in the fridge.

A heavy silence fell between us. Just when I had thought we were past the awkward heavy silences, they would sneak in like a lead weight dropped into a pool.

"Alex." Victoria's voice was painfully soft, silently asking me the one question I didn't want her to ask.

I straightened up, turning around to face her as I closed the fridge door, "We will go to dinner, enjoy this Sunday after your birthday. You'll have the meatloaf you love, play with the dogs you love and then after." I sucked in a slow breath, "We'll talk." I raised my eyes up to meet hers, my heart squeezing tightly to hold it together.

Victoria and I stared at each other before she nodded slowly, whispering, "Okay."

Another quick beat of silence, "Victoria, I love you." The overwhelming sense to say the words hit me like a proverbial ton of bricks. I loved her, completely, wholly and to the point I would cripple my emotions to keep her in my heart. Maybe I could live in the darkness of secrets for the rest of my life.

She nodded, her face contorting a bit, "I love you." She sniffled, burying her nose in the top of Holly's head, clearing her throat, "Holly figured out how to jump on the bed."

Holly turned my way, her pink tongue hanging out when she yipped as if to confirm what Victoria told me. I smiled, shaking my head and moving to my two girls, "Did she now?" I ran a hand over her soft fur, leaning against Victoria's side, feeling her lean back into me.

Dear god, my will to talk to her was slowly melting away. Ignorance was bliss and I began to cling to that idea.

"Does this mean there's grandchildren on the horizon?" My mom nudged me as I handed her still warm plates from the dishwasher.

"Mom, it's just a puppy. Not a child." I rolled my eyes, reaching down for another plate, "Victoria always wanted a dog and I miss having one around. It made sense." I shook my head. My mom had been bothering me from the moment she met Holly about future grandchildren, marriage, and when would either Victoria or I were going to pop the question.

She looked over her shoulder out into the living room at Victoria sitting with Bill on the couch, watching the football game. Victoria was covered in dogs, all three of them sleeping contently on my girlfriend. Annie and Barney had taken a quick liking to Holly within a few sniffs and all three adored Victoria. Curling up on any available lap space they could search out. "That girl is a dog whisperer, imagine her with a baby or two."

I groaned, "Mom, please not now." I glanced at the couch, smiling painfully at the sight that warmed my heart but also made it hurt. The impending talk later might taint these moments.

"Uh oh, the honeymoon over?" My mom returned to the dishes, "I know that tone, irritated Ava."

I clenched my jaw. "The honeymoon isn't over." I hesitated, "Victoria and I need to talk about a few things that happened last night and I'm not sure if it's something I want to do."

"Oh honey, you're going to have your fights, it's a part of relationships. By the look of things, it can't be anything too bad. That girl still looks at you like you invented the world just for her." My mom grinned, "I really hope one of you shits or gets off the pot and propose. I've never seen a love like you two have. It kind of makes me jealous." She chuckled.

I huffed, standing up from the dishwasher, "There's more to it that I really don't want to get into. Victoria got hammered last night and said some things that bothered me. I'm being nice and ignoring it in the name of her birthday." I turned around, keeping my head down, "I love her so much, mom."

My mom stopped what she was doing, looked at me as she placed a warm hand on my arm, "Then you'll get through this. I can't tell you how many times Bill and I had rough spats that hurt, but we always got over it. Worked through it and our relationship has never been stronger." She bent down until she caught my eyes, "Ava, no matter what, I know you two will always come back to each other."

I nodded, looking in the same blue eyes I had, "I know." I then drew my eyes to Victoria, smiling and laughing with Bill. "She is the other half of my heart and my life. I know that and always will."

I let out a quick breath, turning back around, "Let's get the cake out and embarrass my girlfriend."

My mom patted my back, rushing to get the cheesy candles I brought over while I grabbed a few more plates. She was right. I knew deep down in the pit of my stomach that whatever life threw at Victoria and I, whatever secrets she held, it would shake us but never break us. I would always come back to her, no matter what.

Dinner at Alex's parents had gone far better than I expected. There had been a strange tense moment or two when I caught Alex staring at me with a pained look, but she would smile and shake it off. I hated the hovering weight of what was coming, but I understood why Alex insisted on going through with dinner. It would ease the smothering tension that was there the second I woke up to the sick smell of Dani's bloody Mary.

I was glad, for selfish reasons, that Alex gently forced this day. It would give me something to fall back on when the truth came out. I adored Bill and her mother. They embraced me like I was family and I knew the way her mom looked at me, she was expecting an engagement in the coming months. I hoped that I could give that to them in the near future.

The drive back had been quiet, Alex passing out like she always did with Holly in her lap, sleeping or keeping watch as I drove us back home. Pulling into the driveway my stomach began to roll. Alex silently exited the car, handing Holly over to me so she could put away the leftovers her mom sent home with us.

"I'm going to put my pajamas on. I'll be down in a minute." She smiled tightly, barely looking at me as she hit the stairs to go to the bedroom.

I could only nod and hold Holly closer to me, "I'll be in the den." The air was already incredibly thick with tension. This wasn't going to be an easy night. Alex gave a curt nod before disappearing up the stairs, leaving me to sigh heavily and head to the den.

An hour later and one glass of bourbon later, Alex shuffled into the den, wearing the Navy sweatpants and hoody I had bought her at the start of our relationship. I glanced at her, my legs up on my desk with Holly sleeping on my chest, zipped up in my own grey academy hoody. I was feeling the warmth from the bourbon wash over me slowly, easing the nerves and the fear still bubbling in my stomach.

Alex leaned against the doorframe, staring at the puppy sleeping blissfully in the hoody, "I don't think I ever stood a chance."

I raised an eyebrow, moving to set the last sip of bourbon on the desk. "What do you mean?"

She smiled, motioning to the puppy, "Holly, I think she took one look at you and it was a done deal." She then moved her eyes to meet mine, "Unconditional love at first sight."

Swallowing hard at her words, I looked down at the puppy. "She loves you just as much, Alex." I dropped my legs down from the desk, standing up carefully not to disturb the little girl, "Let me put her down in her bed and then, then we can talk." The words caught in my throat, I'd rather be anywhere but here, starting this conversation that I knew would change the life I had grown to love and cherish.

Upstairs I set the sleeping puppy in her bed and watched her for a second, watching her snuggle into a blanket and let out a hearty sigh of content. Holly was happy, I was happy, and Alex was happy. Why was I going to destroy all of it? I didn't have to, I could craft a creative story on the spot and call Dani to help me find a different way to keep Alex safe.

I closed my eyes, standing up slowly. There was no way I could get out of this without telling the bold face truth. I was happy, but I was tired of lying and watching every one of those lies hurt Alex. I moved to the closet and bent down to the safe. Punching in the code I opened the door quietly and removed the black laptop and the thin stack of papers that was my second life. Proof Alex would need when I started telling the fantastical truth that was my employment with Voltaire.

Lifting the laptop, I pressed it against my stomach and took a look around the bedroom. Off in the corner next to Alex's side of the bed was the black hooded figure, staring back at me as she pushed the hood back. Revealing my own face with dark lifeless eyes staring back, she tilted her head in silent question. I closed my eyes, whispering, "I have to do this." When I opened them again, the hooded figure nodded and walked towards me as I turned to walk out the door.

At the top of the steps, the hooded figure and I became one.

I sat in the leather chair across from the desk, legs curled up underneath me, the anxiety started to grow. I wasn't sure if I wanted to do this, if I wanted to know the truth Victoria clearly was about to tell me. I could end this, tell her that whatever it was, I didn't need to know.

I shook my head, staring at the glass on the desk. I had to do this, it would forever eat at my gut if I played stupid to the love of my life's weird secret life.

Hearing the top step creak, I sucked in a breath, my jaw twitching, I suddenly grabbed the glass of bourbon on her desk and downed the last bit of it. Letting out a puff of air as the alcohol bit at the back of my throat. I had to calm down before Victoria picked up on how much I really didn't want to do this and used that as an excuse to delay this talk. Maybe I should grab the big bottle of fancy bourbon she kept over the stove and have it ready for the both of us.

I went to do exactly that when Victoria walked into the office, a black laptop with a handful of papers on top in her hands, she looked at me. A painful smile on her face as she set the laptop on the desk near me, "Holly is out like a light." She met my eyes before traveling to the now empty glass on her desk. "I'll grab the bottle."

I nodded slowly, my eyes drifting to the black laptop and the curious stack of papers that looked an awful lot like the case files James always had strewn on the kitchen table in New York. The curiosity got to me and I reached for the top one. There was a strange logo on the front with the word classified stamped underneath it. Squinting at the logo, I recognized it as the one I had seen on Victoria's laptop screen from the one night I snuck downstairs to find her.

"I work for a company called Voltaire." Victoria's voice startled me and caused me to toss the file back on the desk. She smiled softly at me, handing me a glass of bourbon she had poured in the kitchen. "You know them as the fancy lingerie company you received a million catalogs from." She moved to lean against the edge of the desk facing me, setting the big bottle of liquor down as she cradle her own full glass of the amber liquid.

Victoria kept her head down, her brow furrowed in a pained manner, "That's one of their many fronts to keep the public and the government happy." She clutched the glass tighter. "Before I go any further, I need you to know that no matter what you hear, I love you, Alex." Victoria looked up, meeting my eyes with glassy, cloudy ones, "From the first second our eyes met to this moment, I have never loved anyone like I love you. You're the one true love of my life and the one person that saved me from myself and the world I was forced into it. A world that I never expected to find light in."

I swallowed hard, feeling the tears rise, why were we doing this? "I love you too, Victoria. So much."

She nodded, her face scrunching up in attempts to not cry. "I am a Professor at the Naval Academy, have been for many years. It was where Voltaire placed me after I recovered from my injuries while in captivity." She took a sip of the bourbon. It was clear she was struggling on how to start the conversation.

I moved to the edge of the chair, "Victoria, just tell me what you think you want to. I don't need to know everything."

She shook her head, lifting her head back up, "I don't want to lie to you anymore, Alex." She sucked in a slow breath, holding my gaze for a moment filled with awkward silence. "My operative name is Chimera. It was a name given to me by one of my direct bosses, the old man. I work for a black operations company that is a creative collaboration between the CIA and MI6, my bosses, codenamed the old lady and the old man are heads of each agency, respectfully. Voltaire is an attempt to unify the two missions of both agencies to control and eliminate mutual enemies."

I stared at the blonde. If I didn't know any better, I would think I was in the middle of a weird dream, but I wasn't. I looked at my glass, "What do you mean eliminate?" I had an idea of what the answer would be, but for some odd reason I needed, wanted clarification.

Victoria closed her eyes, "The after action report you read about my injuries and my rescue, the part where the psychologists noticed I had had a mental break, and that my PTSD was the cause. They were right. something snapped in me after all those days of torture and I came out a completely different person." She paused, setting the glass down. "Dani and I were pulled aside the day I met the president. Approached by the old lady, old man and a Colonel in the Army. They spoke of continuing the good mission of fighting evil and basically took advantage of my zombie like state. I agreed without thinking anything about it because I was still trapped in my broken mind. Dani agreed to come with me since she was the only person I trusted."

Victoria paused again, folding her arms and looking down at the floor. I moved closer to her, an overwhelming need to touch her as she spoke of things that could fill a spy novel. "So you work for the government as an intelligence analyst, Dani told me that much."

Victoria opened her eyes, catching that I was moving to touch her. She took a step away, "I don't analyze for them, I'm a field operative."

I frowned, hating her the walls were moving in. "Okay." I stood back up, "Victoria, I have told you a thousand times, I won't ever care what the secrets you hold are, I will always love you."

"I kill people, Alex." Victoria blurted it out, "I kill them in whatever manner my bosses suggest to me." She glanced at me, her eyes filling with pain. "I kill terrible people that sell, kill, mutilate and treat other humans as disposable currency." Her eyes were brimming with tears, "I'm a killer, an assassin, a contract hit woman. I kill people in the name of whatever convoluted idea of patriotism I'm supposedly serving."

I felt the wind get sucked out of the room and my body. I froze in my steps, staring at the woman I loved telling me what she just did. "Victoria."

She shook her head angrily, "No, Alex, let me finish." She grabbed the laptop and opened it, tapping on keys the screen lit up. "I was in Colombia the other day. Sent there to eliminate the head of a cocaine ring who was selling drugs and then using the money to overthrow the local government. An idea the CIA didn't like, so I was sent in. Last month it was killing a Ukrainian arms dealer and making it look like a suicide."

She pounded on the keyboard, her voice thick with anger and sadness, "I've killed congress members, oil magnates, drug dealers, arm dealers, human traffickers, sex traffickers, and I've done it all without a second thought other than how to make it look exactly how my bosses want it to look. I've killed a lot of people, Alex. More than I dare say, or it will bring an even harsher reality to what I am." Victoria shoved the laptop to the edge of the desk with a flippant flick of her wrist, pointing at it like I was one of her students. "It's all there Alex, in that laptop and in those file folders. I'm a killer for hire and I am one of the best, because I lack the humanity to falter when the time comes."

I stared at Victoria, taken aback by the hard tone that forced my eyes to the laptop flickering images of faces I half recognized from the news. I swallowed the rising upset in my stomach down, she wasn't bullshitting me, this was real. There were faces all over the laptop screen who I knew to be dead, the media having glossed over their tragic or celebrated demises.

"All I have ever known for the last ten years is how to live one life. One where I just change the mask from boring Professor to feared assassin who feels very little to nothing when I have blood on my hands." Victoria's voice was rising as it shook at the edges with tears, "Dani is my handler. She is my eyes and ears in the sky as she watches me dismember, choke, and murder the dredges of humanity. That's why we are so close, she saved my life and has every damn time I go out on a new job. Not because we were ever together in a romantic way, she's just always been the one person I could trust. Until you came into my life."

She sighed with a small smile on her face, her eyes clearing up for a second before she continued, her voice breaking more, "Before you even say it, I'm not a hero, a patriot serving the country I love. I'm a broken piece of what was a person, shattered by a war and by a fat arrogant bastard who sucked me into his world. I'm paid to kill people."

Victoria stepped a few more steps away, "I'm a killer, Alex. And I've lied to you to keep you away from that part of me. A part of me that I want to walk away from and never look back, but I can't. Not yet." Her tone became more and more distant with every step she took away from, as if she was trying to cut whatever cords that kept us together. Scaring the hell out of me that I was about to lose her even though what I was hearing was devastating and sickening.

I still had my eyes glued on the laptop, showing me images and snippets of case files that were confirming everything Victoria said, I felt the slow roll of sickness build. "Victoria, I." I almost said it was okay, but it would have been an automatic response to the pain Victoria clearly was in. I could find a way to forgive her, look past this. She was doing her part for the country, working for the government. She was no different than a soldier on the front line. This all could be justified and worked through, she was doing what she was asked to do by a higher power for a greater cause.

"You need to hear it all, Alex." Victoria's voice was trembling, "I never expected to fall in love with you. I thought I had lost that part of my humanity, the ability to feel, around the fifth day of my torture."

Victoria's persistence was there, in her voice, in the pointed movements she made to bring up file after file of her work. The way her body shook with every breath, it appeared she was on the verge of a complete breakdown. I turned to focus on the horrid images instead of the blonde in front of me struggling with every breath. What I saw on the laptop, broke my heart. The crime scene photos all showed a person who was very meticulous in the task at hand, but frenzied as one who was starting to lose themselves and struggling to find the way out. I had seen it a million times while assisting the Medical Examiner at Bellevue. Victoria was clearly broken and as I turned to finally look at her, I could see her two worlds were coming apart at the seams. All because of me and my demands for the truth. The truth to hear her version of a reality that was better left buried in that laptop.

Victoria looked at me, tears rippling in her eyes, "I have to tell you the truth about the first time we met."

I shook my head, "You found me in the metro station and took me to the hospital." I smiled softly at her, "You saved my life." I went to move forward, hoping this would be the end of the conversation and I could hold her and tell her that I could and would forgive her. She was just doing her job.

Victoria held up her hand, frowning, "Please." She dropped her hand as a tear slid down her cheek, "I was sitting on the bench when you walked down into that station. I was wearing a hat, sunglasses and reading a magazine." She folded her arms tightly across her stomach, shrinking into a tight ball as she kept her head down, the dark clouds covering her eyes and forcing more tears to fall from the woman. It felt like she was in a confessional and I was the priest about to hear a multitude of sins I wouldn't be able to stomach.

I felt my heart drop when that night flooded back, the memories all piling up quickly in small pieces. I could see everything, smell everything and hear everything. In particular I could clearly see the person wearing the USN hat bent over a Popular Science. I closed my eyes, focusing on bringing that memory in clearer. I could now see the curves of Victoria's jaw, her long neck, the same neck I loved to kiss late at night while she was sleeping. "No." My gut twisted hard, sending sharp pains up to my heart.

"I wanted to so desperately not to get involved, to let fate cast its wind wherever it may." Victoria looked up at the ceiling, "You looked at me and smiled. I turned back to my magazine and urged the train to get there quicker so I could go home. I had just finished a terrible job and wanted to forget. Then those junkies thought it was a good idea to bother you." Victoria dropped her head back down, tears running down her face, "I wasn't going to get involved, until they hit you. Then I got involved."

I spoke up, my voice cracking, "You didn't. You killed those men?" I felt my heart tighten to the point I couldn't breathe, this was not what I expected and it knocked all of the wind out of me.

Victoria nodded slowly, "I did. All of them. I killed them without a hesitation or a second thought of what I was doing. I rarely ever do when I'm in that mode." Her face contorted, "I never thought I would ever see you again, Alex. I dropped you off at the hospital and disappeared, but I couldn't stop thinking about you. The way you trusted me when you opened your eyes in the car as I buckled you in."

She moved closer to me, reaching for my arm, "Alex, please look at me."

I stepped back, shaking my head as my anger came out of nowhere, "No, Victoria, don't." I didn't know what to think. I was better when she was telling me she worked for the government agency, but telling me she outwardly killed four junkies, innocent or not, I didn't know how to digest it. "You killed those men." I tried to look at her but couldn't, I would just see those crime scene photographs and immediately picture her as a monster.

She nodded, "I did, I killed them because they were going to kill you if I didn't do something."

"You could have just roughed them up, left them or left me." I closed my eyes, "The detectives, they showed me the pictures." I could see the immense amount of violence of those pictures. They betrayed the gentle, soft ways of the woman I loved, the brutality of those images weren't Victoria. They couldn't be her. She wasn't like that. She was the woman I loved implicitly.

"Alex, please." Victoria's voice was painfully soft, shaking like it had earlier. Victoria was struggling to hold it together, and it shattered more of my heart that I was angry at her and causing all of this.

I glared at her when my anger spiked suddenly, "And were you going to kill me? Is that why you sought me out?" I was spewing out the words faster than I could think twice about what I was saying. I just didn't know what to say or think. The woman I loved completely was telling me she was a killer and had murdered for me was sparking a strange rage inside of me. "No, that never was a thought in my head. Ever." Victoria moved closer, "I love you, Alex, I could never hurt you. I fell in love with you that night and no matter how hard I tried, I couldn't stay away from you."

She let out a shaky breath, "I tried to stay away, keeping you only as a friend, but I couldn't. You were putting my humanity and my heart back together and I. Oh god Alex, I never meant to hurt you. I never want to hurt you."

I let out a half sob, "So you chase after me, lie about who you are and hide the fact you did what you did, never once thinking that it might bother me, hurt me to know this side of you?" I pointed at the laptop, shouting back at her, "You could have given this up at any time, you could have told me the truth when we were friends or let me go at any point! Instead you let me fall hopelessly in love with you and then force me to beg for the truth. Why didn't you let me go that night you came to the hospital? That night when you sent the tulips and had me come here? You could have walked away and saved us both from the piles of lies you've told over the last year."

I felt the tears rolling down my face and wiped them away, shaking my head at no one. "I can't believe this." I was a whirlwind of emotions, and could only find anger as the most solid one to stand on. I was struggling to keep it together and not fall apart into a pile of sobbing screams. This wasn't happening, this couldn't be why Victoria was so shut down. This wasn't why Victoria was so secretive and hid from me for the last year.

Victoria blew out an agitated laugh, "Believe this? What I can't believe is that you telling me over and over that you will love me no matter what. All those times you looked at my bruises, my cuts, my broken ribs. All the times you saw through the flimsy lies I told and refused to look harder at the bold moments of truth I slipped out." She moved to the laptop, "I wanted to walk away. Save you from the miserable piece of shit I am, but I couldn't. I fought so hard not to fall deeper in love with you. Fought even harder to keep you out of my double life, but I failed."

"Don't you dare put this on me, Victoria." I scowled at her, "Don't play the you let me fall in love with you card. It's pure bullshit and you know it."

Victoria suddenly picked up the laptop and threw it across the room, smashing it in half as she shouted, "We're both to blame here. Maybe me more than you, but we're both to blame for fumbling around the truth when I should have just told you the day you crept into my office." She waved a hand in the air, "I can't change who I was, Alex, or who I am now, but for fuck's sake! I'm working on getting out of this mess and getting you out with me."

"Out with you? What the hell does that mean?" I glared at her.

"It means, no one in Voltaire ever gets to retire with a nice party and a supermarket bought cake." Victoria looked at me with red, tear riddled eyes, "I might have not wanted this from the start, but now that I have it and you, I will sacrifice everything I have to keep it and you safe." Victoria blew out a hard breath and walked to the desk where she scooped up the files and shoved them in my chest, "Read these and you'll understand what I mean. They will show you the person I was. The person I no longer want to be, or can be because of you."

She looked at me once more, before closing her eyes, "I will understand if you're not here in the morning, but I will always make sure you're safe." The tone of her voice broke my heart, but did little to curb the furious anger I felt towards her. I shoved the files away, letting them fall to the floor with a hard slap.

Victoria grimaced painfully and walked away from me, stopping at the front door to grab her car keys before opening the door and walking out. A few seconds later, I heard the BMW start up and squeal out of the driveway.

When she was gone, I fell to my knees, dropping the files Victoria had shoved into my chest to the floor and began uncontrollably sobbing. Sobbing to the point that I could barely breathe.

After a handful of minutes, I heard Holly barking upstairs, making my heart hurt more. I sat up and wiped at my sore eyes, looking at the mess in front of me I caught a name that I recognized. One I had read in James email reply to my question about Voltaire months ago. I scooped up the file and shuffled to the phone I had set on the kitchen counter.

Hitting his contact, I wiped away more tears. I didn't know what to feel about Victoria right now, I still loved her, but I wasn't sure about the other feelings circling that love. I would need time to sort this out, sort out everything she had told me. I was beyond lost, my entire world as I knew it had been a carefully crafted lie.

"Hey Alex! What's up? You okay? It's kind of late." James had a smile in his voice.

I cleared my throat, "James, I think I have some information." I paused. Telling James what I had in my hands, would compromise Victoria somehow. My gut was shouting at me not to spill her secrets. That if I did, safe was a word that would no longer apply to either of us. I grimaced as a soft sob crept out of my throat, "I'm sorry for calling."

"Alex? You don't sound okay. What happened?"

I sucked in a slow breath, "I don't think you'd believe it if I told you."

James chuckled, "I worked foot patrol for three years, I've seen a lot of things that no one could believe. So, try me."

I flattened my hand on the file, shaking my head as I took the easy route, "Victoria and I had our first big fight." I scooted to sit on the floor, crying softly as James cracked jokes about our old fights, and how he learned to just accept I was always right.

I half listened, looking up at the fridge and right at the picture taken on the night of the formal. Victoria and I standing next to each other with big genuine smiles, holding onto each other and so deeply in love.

I placed my hand over my heart, hating that it would always be hers no matter how angry I was at her, or how in this moment I wasn't sure what our future would be.

I would always love her.

I drove fast, pushing the BMW to do what I paid so much money for it to do. Get me away from my house quickly. My eyes were blurry from the endless crying. Every time I looked in the passenger seat I would see my black hooded twin looking at me, shaking her head in a I told you so way. No matter what, her and I would always be one, I would always be the monster who killed and failed at finding a life I wanted to live with the only person I ever loved.

I had no real idea where I was going until I pulled into a driveway on the other side of town and climbed out of the car.

I pounded on the front door until Dani swung it open, "Fucking stop already!" She paused, looking at my sad state, "Oh shit, I'm taking it didn't go well?"

I shook my head, shrugging when I found I couldn't speak. I knew it would take a few days for Alex to wrap her head around everything. A few more for her to even think about talking to me. Deep down, I knew she loved me, but I wasn't sure she could ever forgive the monster I was.

Dani grabbed me by the arm and pulled me into her house, "You have perfect timing, Victoria." Her voice was dripping with sarcasm.

"Fuck off." I pushed the words out in a hoarse whisper.

Dani rolled her eyes, guiding me to her study. The same one I had slept on the couch a million times over the years. "No seriously, you should have waited until morning."

I glared at her as she shoved me towards the couch before moving to the liquor cabinet and grabbing an empty glass. That's when I noticed there was a bottle of whiskey on her coffee table with two half full glasses.

I cleared my throat. "Am I interrupting something?"

"The exact opposite, Victoria. Danielle and I just put the final touches on our plan." Maggie's voice made my head spin around to see her walking in from the other room.

She smiled softly at me, "I take it the truth session with Alexandra didn't fare well?" Her English accent did very little to soothe me.

I scowled at the woman, "I don't want to discuss this."

Dani hustled over, handing me a glass full of bourbon, "You don't want to, but we have to talk about getting Alex to New York in the next three days."

I glared at Dani, her words sinking in, "You don't mean?"

Maggie nodded, moving closer to me and handing over a small envelope, "Your exit plan has been set in motion. We had one more week to go, but as you will read, the old lady and the Colonel have picked up on your desire to leave and have fixated on the woman you love. They've both set in motion very lucrative contracts on both of your heads, to prove a point to me."

I swallowed hard, ripping the envelope from the woman's hands, "How did they find out about Alex?"

"They're spies, Victoria." Maggie smiled as if that was the only answer in the world. She then moved to sit next to me, motioning to Dani's laptop on the desk, "We have the plan ready for you to review. When we set it in motion, there will be no return." She looked at me softly, "But I can promise if we go ahead with it, Alexandra will be safe, protected and no harm will ever grace her life."

I stared at the bright blue eyes, nodding slowly, "Show me what you have."

A wet, cold nose poking my hand woke me up. Holly was whining and licking me, staring at me with a head tilt and wide eyes. "Do you need to go out?"

The little dog barked a resounding yes and scampered off to the back door. I let out a sigh, blinking sleep filled eyes and rolled off the couch I had passed out on from pure emotional exhaustion. I had talked to James for a few hours, trying to find a way to tell him what really happened but without telling him everything.

So I went the route of asking my ex advice on how to deal with the first really big fight between Victoria and I. In the end, he just reassured me that no matter what it was, it was clear Victoria and I were very much in love and nothing would break that.

I shook my head, yawning, nothing but the fact that my girlfriend was a hired assassin who seemed to have a tendency to go rouge in the name of saving me. Frowning at the memory of last nights' fight and the flashbacks I had about the crime scene photos that detective shoved in my face, along with the small pieces I remembered from that night. I felt sick, sad, heartbroken and clueless at what was to come next.

"Here you go." I opened the back door, letting Holly charge out to the middle of the backyard and run free. I watched her for a few minutes, feeling a strange regret that I asked for the truth and got it from Victoria. She was gone and I hated being in this house without her. It didn't matter that I was angry, scared, and a thousand other things, I missed her. I wanted her to walk in the door and tell me it was all a silly prank or a bad dream.

When the clock on the stove told me it was almost early afternoon, I decided that I should do something with the rest of the day. Occupy my hands and my thoughts before they were overwhelmed and I broke down again on the couch, wallowing in the heavy fear of what could come next. I walked back through the den to head into the living room to find my phone, I caught a glimpse of the broken black laptop on the floor. I sighed moving towards it to pick it and the pieces up, the last thing I needed was Holly chewing on plastic.

I bent down, lifting the mangled thing full of secrets and lies, I felt the tears rise up out of nowhere. I shook my head, "And yet I still love her so much."

"And I still love you, Alex."

Victoria's voice startled me, I dropped the laptop and spun around to see her standing in the doorway to the den. She looked run down, tired, and her eyes were red and dry. She still made my heart skip a handful of beats in one look. I stood up, looking down at the mess, "I didn't want Holly to eat any of the plastic chunks." I cleared my throat, trying hard not to cry in front of her.

Victoria moved into the room, reaching down, she snatched up the laptop, "I will take care of it." She looked at me for a solid minute, "Alex, I…"

I shook my head, walking towards the living room, "Victoria, I think I'm going to go to my mom's for a few days. To think and figure things out." I knew if I stayed at the house with her, I would more than likely either forgive her for everything when deep down I knew I needed to work out the fact she had killed for me. "I can leave Holly here with you."

"We need to leave, Alex, together. Go to New York tonight." Victoria's voice was raspy, shaky.

I looked over my shoulder, "New York? Why? I don't think this is a time for a quick weekend getaway to work on our problems." I looked down at the front of her sweatshirt I was wearing, "I don't know what to think or do. For some strange reason, I was okay with you doing what you do in the name of protecting the country, but then you did those things at the station for me." I paused, wincing, "I can't get past that, and I so desperately wish I could."

Victoria set the laptop down on the edge of the desk, "It's not a weekend getaway." She looked up at me, "I understand what you are feeling Alex, and I will not ask you to get past the things I've done in the last ten years." She moved closer to me, "All I will ask of you is to continue to trust me. I love you, Alex, and it destroys me knowing I've hurt you when it is the last thing I ever wanted to do."

She looked down at her hands, "Voltaire, the old lady in particular has found out a few things that have made him upset. He's put it upon himself to come after me and the only way I can keep you safe is if you come with me. Dani and I have come up with a plan. When in New York, we will be leaving after a day or two there for Europe."

I stared at her confused, "Europe? I don't understand." I sighed, folding my arms, "Don't talk to me like I'm a fellow spy, I'm not Dani." I felt the anger returning quickly.

Victoria nodded, moving even closer and I wanted to move away from her, but my body betrayed me. Her warmth was something I had grown addicted to a very long time ago, and even now, it was my weakness. "Europe for a couple of weeks until I take care of a few things, then we'll come home and I will be out of Voltaire. Retired and freed from this second life I have been living." Her eyes turned glassy, "Then you can leave, carry on with your life as you see fit. I won't stop you."

I frowned harder, shaking my head, "No, I'm not going to Europe or New York with you, I can't be around you right now." I swallowed hard, hating that I was saying what I was, since it was all lies. I wanted to be around her, I wanted to run to her, be swept up in her arms and yell at her while she held me. I waved towards my head, "There's too much in here that I can't figure out, I can't think straight. Everything just leads back to what you did, for me." I looked down at the floor, I was literally being torn into two by everything and not being able to shake how deeply I felt for this woman.

Victoria was an arm's reach away, clutching the laptop. "There's no room for negotiation, Alex. You have to come to New York. You have to come with me whether you hate me or not." Her voice was firm, yet still trembled. The woman looked like I imagined she did after her incident in the desert and she was in safe hands. Frail, tired, broken, yet incredibly determined to stay strong.

I shook my head harder, "No, I do not have to do anything I don't want to!" I stared at her, "You can't come in here and tell me what to do, I don't even know who you really are."

I didn't realize I was almost shouting at her until I saw her flinch. "You need to give me more answers, Victoria, to all of the questions you left me with. You walked out of this goddamn house like it was nothing! Like I was nothing!" I knew the words spilling out were my emotions speaking for me, but I was worn down and couldn't stop when the floodgates open. "I can barely look at you without seeing the faces of those men."

"And I see their faces every goddamn night I close my eyes! Their faces and every single other face I have eliminated!" Victoria exploded, her voice ringing in my ears and throughout the room. "I don't have time to sit here and argue things I cannot change. As for who I am and knowing who I really am?" Victoria stared at me with glassy clear eyes, "I am still the same fucking woman who fell in love with you, who will always love even when all of this is said and done. So fuck these questions I cannot answer to meet your satisfaction. I fucked up and have fucked up for the last ten years, I cannot change that Alex. I'm not a fucking time traveler that can go back at the snap of a finger and fix all the things I have destroyed."

She blew out a harsh breath, squeezing the broken laptop until I could hear the plastic crack under the pressure. "Yes, you're right. You don't have to do anything I ask of, but I need you to trust me with whatever tiny bit of trust you have left. I need you in New York, that's it Alex. Trust me one last time, trust me with your life."

I swallowed down the tears, spitting back at Victoria, "No. I'm not going anywhere until you explain everything. Why am I going to New York? How do I explain being in Europe to my family and my job? What the fuck is going on?"

Things were becoming messy. All I wanted to do, was compelled to do muddled emotions, was stand my ground and scream at Victoria, fight with her and find the reasoning behind it all. "Why did you kill those men at the station? I feel like everything we are is a total and utter lie. What was I really? A cover for you to hide behind? A fun experiment to see if you could balance two lives? What the fuck was it, Victoria?" I found myself shouting at her again, unable to be calm about anything in this moment. My life was in total upheaval and it was pissing me off that she was so nonchalant about it all.

Victoria shook her head, "I will repeat, we do not have the time to talk about all of this." She met my eyes, digging in her back pocket and pulling out a small envelope and setting it on the desk next to her. "Your ticket is in there, with the itinerary and the address I will be at." She then turned away, her body shaking and with her voice, "I can't keep fighting with you, Alex, when I have to fight for you to keep you safe." She took one step out of the den, that's when I realized she was leaving again. Walking out on me.

"Don't fucking walk away, Victoria. Stay here! Talk to me!" I let the tears slip, she was infuriating me with her stone cold, unbending behavior, "Don't prove my doubts right." I was backwards bargaining with her, trying to get her to stay so I could exact all of my rage on her and hope she would give in before I did.

Victoria paused at the doorway, her back still turned to me, "Alex, you are and will never be nothing to me." She looked over her shoulder and met my eyes, tears streaming down her cheeks, "You are everything to me, but I can't waste any more time. We can't. I will be waiting for you in New York." She turned away and walked out of the den and out of the house.

I yelled at her, "I will not chase after you! I told you that the last time you did this." I stopped when I heard the front door click shut.

I screamed into the empty den, my hands balled up in fists as the sobs returned.

I would not chase after her. No matter what.

"Dani, I'll be at the airport in ten minutes." I choked out the words as I raced the BMW up the freeway. My heart was beyond broken, shattered and with every mile I drove away from our house, I felt the pain increase in my chest. I had done one of the hardest things I had ever done and walked away from the one person I loved with my entire life, and the one person who made me truly whole and human. No matter how much I justified that I had to walk away from Alex and go to New York, it did very little to heal any of the new wounds the last twenty-four hours had created.

I was sliding into the black hooded figure. The one who lacked emotions and cared for nothing and no one. There was a plan put into action, one that had little room for error or delay. I had set it motion the second I left Maggie and Dani at her house and went home in the hopes of convincing Alex to leave with me, but as I expected, she didn't. She stood her ground and fought me like she had all the other times I shut down. I wanted to tell her everything, the entire plan ahead of us. The reasons why she was going to Europe for a few weeks, why I needed her in New York tonight.

How do you tell someone you love that you need to make them disappear because there is a contract on their head? All because of your mentally insane boss, losing his shit that you no longer wanted to kill people at his discretion?

I had already overwhelmed her with the brutal truth of what I did to those filthy pigs who laid their hands on her, I saw no point in throwing more on her until we were safe. Safe and behind closed doors were I could tell her everything without fear, and now I knew I would never have that chance.

Alex made her decision and I respected it, she didn't want me around in her life because of what I was, but I still had to force her to understand that there was just more than a need to keep her safe.

There were things I didn't want her to see, hear, or experience. The only way I could make that happen was get her to the safe house and away from me with Dani as her escort.

What I was about to do in the next forty-eight hours would change so much.

"Is Alex with you?" Dani's voice was firm, telling me she was a bit distracted as she spoke to me, "I picked up some chatter. The old lady has sent out three contracts on you and your nurse. One for her to be captured alive and used as bait for you. A five million dollar contract to bring you in dead with a fresh catch contract set at ten million dollars. The fucker is serious about this. What did you do?"

I bit the inside of my mouth, "Alex is still at the house, I couldn't get her to come with me. I need you to go there and do what you do best. Piss people off and get them to do what they don't want to do." I paused, "I don't know what I did to piss the old lady off. I think he got wind of my want to retire and that the old man is helping me leave."

Dani blew out a breath, "Did you even try to convince her to come with you?"

I frowned at the condescending tone in her voice, "Fuck off Dani. I tried you know that, I just can't waste time with arguments I can't solve." I let out a sigh, "This whole plan is for Alex. Everything we put into motion is to keep her safe and give her the life I should have given her, not this life I dragged her into."

"I know, Victoria." She tapped on a distant keyboard, "I will persuade her to go to New York. She called that cop last night, he may be useful in said persuasion."

I pulled into the small private airport, "Dani, please. Get her to New York by tomorrow night, I need to know she is on an airplane out to Sweden by the next morning." I ran a hand through my hair as my stomach twisted thinking about what was going to take place tomorrow night and the fallout after. "Please, promise me...."

"Shut up. You know I will take care of anything and everything." Dani sighed, "Alex will always be safe, I will kill every single plumber that is stupid enough to seek out that contract on her."

I shut off the car and stepped out, "Please, just remind her that I will and have always loved her..." I stumbled over the words as a sob escaped, "That she was the reason why I had to stop all of the lies."

"Again, Victoria, shut up." I could hear the softness in her voice, "That dumb nurse who is far smarter than you deserve, loves you even though she probably hates the living fuck out of you right now." Dani chuckled lightly, "We will do this and it's going to hurt like hell but we will get through this. I promise you."

I nodded into the night air, "I'll see you in New York." I hung up on Dani, catching a glance of the picture of Alex and I with Holly in front of us I had taken the first night the small dog fell into my life. I smiled softly, whispering, "I'm sorry." To the picture before shoving the phone in my pocket and grabbing my bag to head towards the plane.

Chapter 25

I threw clothes in a bag with anger as an endless amount of tears threatened to spill. I had been on a strange emotional high for the last couple of hours. Angrily cleaning the house and then manically folding laundry until I gave in when I removed one of Victoria's t-shirts from the dryer. The anger and hurt overflowed and I couldn't stand to be in the house any longer. I threw her shirt to the floor as more tears fell and rushed upstairs to start packing.

I decided to go to my mom's house for the night to think about what Victoria had told me when she came back to the house, the strange trip to New York and the even stranger urgency in her voice. I couldn't think straight being in a house where everything around me reminded me of Victoria and our relationship. A relationship that was broken and now felt like it was built on lies.

I shook my head, tossing another one of her sweatshirts to the side to reach for one of my shirts. Holly laid on the bed watching me as she curled up on Victoria's pillow. The poor little dog looked confused as to what had happened over the last few hours, she wasn't the only one. I was very confused and incredibly lost.

Sighing I looked at her, stilling my hands with a pair shorts clenched in them, "I wish I could explain it to you, but I can't. I don't understand what's happening." I set my bag down, moving to head downstairs to grab a few pairs of scrubs for work, Holly close on my heels barking softly in her way of asking where Victoria had gone.

When I was back in the laundry room, I heard the front door open as Holly scampered off. My heart tightened and I pressed my neatly folded scrubs against my chest and left the laundry room. "Victoria before you say anything, I will be back in a few days after I've had some time to think. I was going to take Holly with me, but I can leave her here."

I walked around the corner to find Dani in the similar black uniform I had seen Victoria wear in the winter, standing in the kitchen with Holly in her arms while the dog eagerly licked her face. Dani chuckled, nodding at the clothes in my hands, "You're packing, good. We're already a few hours behind schedule."

I scowled at the redhead, "I'm going to my parents." I turned to head back upstairs, "And I would like it if you left now."

I heard her exasperated sigh, "Alex, I'm not leaving unless you're with me. I made a promise to Victoria."

She followed me, still holding the wiggly Scottie. "So that means I need you to get over whatever stupid shit you're thinking about and listen. Then I'm going to need you to pack a bag, get in my car and go to New York with me to meet Victoria."

I reached the bedroom, fuming at the way Dani was speaking to me, "I'm not one of your spies to command." I tossed the scrubs on the bed, "Get out of my house before I call the police."

Dani leaned against the doorframe, smirking and scratching Holly's head, "Technically it's Victoria's house and go ahead and call the police." She reached into her pocket, removing her cell phone. "Hit the last call button, James is waiting for your call. He's also waiting for your dumb ass to get to New York."

I spun around, glaring at the smirking woman, "How do you know about him?!"

"Did you pay attention to anything Victoria told you last night?" She bent down to set Holly on the floor, "I'm a spy, I know everything I shouldn't know." She stood back up, walking over to me, "You called him a bit ago, asking for him to go digging in dark corners that could have gotten him killed if it wasn't for me always watching."

My jaw twitched with even more anger, "Don't bring him into this. He's innocent, a friend and shouldn't…"

"Oh, but you brought him into this Alex, wasn't me who did this. I took the extra step to bring him in further to keep him safe." Dani pointed at me, "There is so much you're still very ignorant to."

I huffed, turning back to the bag. "Just go away. Go do whatever murdering you have to do."

Dani suddenly appeared next to me, snatching the bag from the bed and throwing it the floor, startling me. "Alex, watch what you say." Her hard green eyes tore through me. "There is so much you don't understand, so watch that mouth before it gets you killed." She tipped her head down, "Victoria is doing all of this for you, and she has from the first time she let you into this house, into her heart."

I stared at the redhead, mildly frightened by her as she stood very close, "She also killed those men for me." I closed my eyes, "This all feels like a lie. A carefully crafted lie to...to...I don't know." I sighed, feeling the tears escape from underneath my eyelids.

A warm hand fell to my back, "You were never a lie to her. Her love for you will never be a lie." Dani's voice was softer, "You have to go to New York. You have to do everything Victoria and I ask of you in the next few days. If you don't." Dani paused, "Just do it Alex, trust me. Trust Victoria one last time."

I glanced at her, "Why should I trust you of all people? Why should I trust any of you?" My voice was raspy, tired from fighting. Dani's words had hit deep in the one part of me that still loved Victoria unconditionally, the same part I had been struggling with since the truth came spewing out.

Dani searched my eyes, "Because, I've grown very attached to you nurse blue eyes and the way you've given my best friend a chance at something more than the shadows she's lived in since we left the desert. I promised her that I would always keep you safe no matter what." Her hand moved away from my back, "Get the rest of your things, your lovely neighbors will be over after we've left to take on babysitting the little one." The tone of her voice told me that I no longer had another option.

Dani stepped away, moving towards the closet. I heard the floor safe being opened followed by the rustling of papers. I stared at the empty closet, trying to decide if trusting this woman was the best idea. She scared me, but deep down I knew she would never hurt me, that her promises to Victoria would always come first. I sighed, scooping out the pairs of scrubs I no longer needed and placing them back on the bed, "Will I see Victoria when I get to New York?" It was a tentative question. I was divided on Victoria. I still loved her very much but I couldn't stand to look at her right now. When I did, I felt myself forgiving and hating her for the things she had done in my honor.

Dani appeared out of the closet, a large stack of envelopes under her arm and a black holster in her hand. "Chances are no, not right away. Like I said, you're a few hours behind and the plan was set in motion last night. Victoria has a few things she needs to take care of and will probably meet up with you in Sweden in a day or two." Dani stepped closer to me, setting the black holster with the .40 caliber handgun I had Victoria hide in the safe when she was home. "James told me you're a bit of a deadeye?"

I stared at the black blob of plastic and steel, "He taught me how to shoot, for protection since we lived in a rough part of Brooklyn for a few months." I glanced up at Dani, "Are you going to tell me what this plan is?"

"Probably not." Dani smiled at me, "Just listen to what I tell you to do and things will be fine." She tapped the gun, "Take this with you, you may need it as we move further along." She turned to look at Holly laying in her bed, "When this is all done, Victoria will be the one to tell you the entire truth."

She looked over her shoulder, "Ten minutes and then we leave." Dani walked out of the bedroom, leaving me in a daze.

Two hours of incredibly thick silence later, Dani and I arrived in New York City.

I had said a quick goodbye to Holly before handing her over to Dale as he and Mary pulled into their driveway right as I dropped my bag in Dani's car.

Mary grinned at me, telling me that Victoria had called her and told her all about the quick weekend getaway to the big apple. I just smiled and nodded, kissing Holly on the head before thanking the nice old couple for watching the dog. I then climbed into the car and said nothing to Dani the entire ride to a private airport where we boarded a private jet and left, in silence.

Now I was again sitting in a fancy black sedan with Dani driving. She had changed out of her uniform on the jet and into a pair of jeans and grey sweater. Her red hair was down into a loose ponytail, giving the frightening woman a gentler appearance. Not once did she ever try to start up a conversation or even really look at me. She would only engage with me when we landed and helped get my bag in the trunk. The thick silence brought even more weight to the situation in front of me, leading me to understand that this was not a joke or a ploy to get me to buy into what Victoria did. This was serious and it rattled me.

As Dani pushed her way through the late night city traffic, I finally broke the tension, "Am I in danger?"

"Yes, you are." Dani answered quickly, bluntly. "Our one boss is disgruntled with Victoria for filing her retirement papers early and doing it through our other boss. Needless to say, you've become collateral damage to the oncoming shit show." She didn't look at me as she turned the car into an underground parking structure.

I glared at her, "Explain everything, it's my life, I think I deserve to know. No more cloak and dagger bullshit."

Dani chuckled, shaking her head, "I won't tell you anything." She then bent her head down as the headlights casted over another black sedan in front of us, "But he can."

I looked out of the front windshield to see James walking around to the back of the other black sedan, he had a tense look on his face as he squinted around the headlights.

I felt my heart drop into my stomach and the two began to churn like a blender. "James."

Dani parked next to him and got out of the car quickly, moving towards the trunk. I took my time getting out of the car, folding my arms across my chest as Dani handed James a thin envelope before turning to me, "Alex, when you two are done talking. Take the elevator to the penthouse level. Go to the door marked with a six and I'll fill you in on what's next." She clipped the last few words as her phone rang, answering it quickly, "Maggie, the nurse is here." She met my eyes as she continued, hers turning cloudy, "You've got to be fucking kidding me, I took precautions."

Dani slammed the trunk shut and stormed off. I only caught a few more curse words with her telling the caller that she would get a Dave ready to go immediately.

I watched her disappear into the elevator, when James moved around to the trunk of Dani's car, "Alex, I know you have a lot of questions." James thick New York accent rolled over the hood of car and hit my ears like a long forgotten favorite song. It almost made me smile if it wasn't for the fact I was in the middle of a terrible spy movie plot.

I shook my head, dropping my eyes to the concrete floor, "James, what in the hell is going on?"

He chuckled softly, "Let's take a walk to the corner, get you some coffee. I can talk as we walk." He grabbed my upper arm, "Even though it's under terrible circumstances, it's really good to see you again."

I looked at him with bleary eyes, James had not changed in the last couple of years, just a few more grey hairs at his temples. But he was still tall, dashing, charming and looked like he belonged in English films and not humping the streets of New York fighting crime. His bright blue eyes smiled at me in the way that told me he was worried and going into protective mode. "Yeah, it is."

James tugged on me gently. "Come on Alex, I'll get you filled in on why we're both here."

I nodded slowly, dropping my arms to follow him.

I paced along the wall of windows that made up the large penthouse, I had been on edge since I landed in New York and met with Maggie. Our plan had been leaked somehow and the old lady was sending one of his best my way. "Can we get Alex out of here? Shift her to Sweden now?"

Maggie sat on a couch across from me, "We can't she just landed, so has Achilles. My insider saw him leave the airport twenty minutes ago." She tapped her phone on her leg nervously, "Danielle has been notified. She's getting things in place for this all to go as planned and plans have changed, as I just told you."

I stopped to stand in front of one pane that looked directly at the Freedom Tower, "You promise when this is all done, I'm free?" I kept my eyes on the top spire even as I caught the reflection of my black hooded twin standing next to me, begging to merge into one and shutting down the human part of me Alex had drawn out every day from the first moment I laid eyes on her. I would have to keep my humanity separate and tucked away for what was about to happen next. I couldn't falter no matter what.

"Of course Victoria, when we've completed it all, Chimera will become nothing but a myth again." Maggie stood up, her heels clicking on the hardwood floors as she walked to stand next to me, "It's time all of this returns to myths."

I looked at the woman out the corner of my eye, "Alex?"

Maggie patted my shoulder, "Alex will be taken care of. We've made sure of it, as it stands she should be walking with James for a cup of coffee and we can follow through without her knowing anymore. By this time in two days, she will be home, safe."

I nodded slowly, turning back to the spire as Dani rushed into the room, tossing a bag to the floor as she began rattling off at a million miles a minute.

I closed my eyes and leaned against the glass, soon this would be over. I took a deep breath and opened my eyes. Taking one step to the right, I merged my reflection with that of the black hooded twin, staring back at me.

"Dani is a scary woman." James walked next to me, "She showed up on my doorstep the next day after you first called, asking me to go digging." He looked at me as I walked with my hands jammed into my coat pockets, "She introduced herself as being from Naval Intelligence and the next thing I knew, I was staring at files I knew I shouldn't have access to. Then she started telling me everything, about Voltaire and how I needed to keep my mouth shut." He sucked in a slow breath, "Then two weeks later I was sitting in a basement in some old building in D.C. talking to these old Naval officers. Telling me that Voltaire was straying and they needed my help to reel it in. It was them who had be brought in as a liaison for the Office of Naval Intelligence, them and Dani."

I kept my eyes on my boot tips. James had told me so much that I stopped listening to from the third sentence, zoning out as I heard more spy talk that did nothing to ease my fears. It only invigorated the other emotions of anger and confusion. "Were any of them referred to the old lady or the old man?"

"I met the old man, Maggie. I've met her a couple of times in the basement, Alex. Seems nice, but a total ballbuster if you provoke her." James looked over at me, "Alex, what Victoria has done, it was in the name of serving her country. I read her file, the one with what happened when she was captured, tortured. The woman has incredible survival skills and to be brutally honest, I don't look down on her for killing those shit bags that tried to hurt you in the metro station." He sighed, "I read their files, they deserved what they got."

I furrowed my brow, dipping my chin deeper into my coat, "Please James, don't try to justify that. She did that not under orders…" I drifted off, hating that he had a point. If I put myself in her shoes on that night, I would have done the same or something similar. My love for her was whittling away my resolve to hate her.

"No, but she did it to keep you alive, she saved your life. If I was in her position, I would have done the same a hundred times over." James stopped walking, "Alex, what is in the past is the past, we can't go back and fix all of the mistakes made. Shit, if I could, I would have tried so much harder to keep us together, but I can't. Our mistakes led us to part and onto better things that we were meant to do, meet the people we love."

I kept my chin down. "I don't know if I."

James interrupted me, "Don't say it. You know if you do, it will be a bold face lie. You love that woman, she loves you. I saw it in her eyes when I met her a few hours ago. You're her entire life, and for what it's worth, forgive her Alex. Forgive the things she's done for the simple fact you love her and you can't change anything, not even that." James linked his arm in mine, "The coffee place is right up here, it's on me and as we walk back, I'll tell you as much as I can."

I scrunched my face up, refusing to look up as more tears rolled over my cheeks. James was right, I couldn't change how much I loved Victoria and even if I had a time machine, I wouldn't go back and change how we came to be. I looked up, wiping away the tears with the back of my hand, "James, I always hated when you were right."

He laughed, leaning into me, "And I always hated when you left your scrubs on the bathroom floor."

I half smiled, shaking my head as he held the coffee shop door open for me to enter.

Dani sat across from me, her laptop open, as her hands flew around the keyboard like lightning, "I don't like doing this last minute without having a few diagnostic tests run, but it will work." She glanced up at me as I shrugged on the black hooded running jacket. "Achilles is a block away. Maggie's insider dropped a beacon on him at the airport, the good ole oops I spilled my energy drink on you trick." She tapped a few more times before standing up.

I watched her move around the desk towards me, "How much time?"

"Ten minutes, but knowing how good you are, you'll be done in eight." She smiled at me, "You kill Achilles and it will send a clear message to the old lady to back the fuck off." She motioned to Maggie sitting at the large kitchen table, typing away on her own laptop. "Old steel balls over there will make sure he understands."

I nodded, zipping up he jacket before feeling for the knives I had tucked in the interior, "Dani, when this is done. Let's have a drink?" I looked up at her, knowing I had glassy eyes.

Dani smiled genuinely, "Of course." She nodded towards the door, "Get going, I'll have your back."

I smiled back at the redhead, patting her shoulder, "Thank you."

With one last deep breath, I walked towards the front door. When my hand was on the handle, I heard Dani, "He's about to be in the alley in five. Hide in the shadows next to the dumpster. He never checks the shadows like the dumbass he is."

"That's his Achilles heel, isn't it?" I rolled my eyes at my own joke and pulled my sunglasses down before exiting the penthouse.

Clutching the coffee with both hands, I looked at James as he kept talking, this time actually listening to what he was saying. "There's this Colonel Aves I've been helping the OIN investigated. Some mysterious Army Colonel who really has no record, well one that isn't covered in black marker. He supposedly died a handful years back in Syria during a rebel uprising, but then Dani and the one old Navy Admiral with his advisor, showed me pictures of the Colonel bopping around New Jersey."

I furrowed my brow, "It must be that fat bird man Victoria and Dani would mention in their drunken ramblings." I turned to the sidewalk ahead, the building I was staying at was a few steps away. "They have a serious distaste for him."

"I don't blame them. A lot of people do. Including the CIA, MI6, NSA, FBI and any other intelligence agency you can think of. Seems Aves has done his fair share of shitting on everyone." James laughed, "Man, Alex I never thought this spy shit was real, only thought it was for the movies."

I shrugged, "I wished it was only in the movies." I sipped at the hot coffee. I had begun to settle down and listen to James, realizing why Dani had brought him in. He was a sensible honest man who wanted nothing more than to fight crime the best he could. Listening to him talk and tell me the things Victoria had tried to tell me, I felt terrible for not listening to her instead of lashing out at her. I still didn't feel at peace with the metro incident, but after James showed me the case files he had gotten from Metro D.C. police, I found it harder to feel for the four junkies.

Now all I wanted was to see Victoria and apologize.

James suddenly grabbed my arm like he used to when his cop instincts warned him, "Alex, wait."

I looked at him, he had thrown his coffee cup to the ground and reached for his sidearm. "What is it?"

He motioned to the alley in front of us, "I hear someone fighting." He gently shoved me back, "Stay back here, I'm going to take a quick look. Then we'll head back to the front door, get you inside and safe."

I nodded slowly, tossing my cup to the side I balled my fists and tucked up against the wall and watched James head into the alley.

I heard him shout. "Stop! Police!"

I moved closer when I heard him shout it again, then I heard his gun clatter to the ground with a large bang followed by him making a heavy oomph sound.

Then I heard Victoria's voice shouting at someone, "Leave him alone, it's me you want!"

My feet moved on my own and I ran to the alley, coming around the corner to see James knocked out with blood on his forehead, curled up in a ball next to the brick wall of the alley. I went to run to him, but froze as I also saw Victoria, dressed all in black, facing down a larger man wearing half of a black mask, covering his lower jaw. "Oh, I do want you. The price on your head is far worth more than a stupid lazy cop." He lifted his right hand and pointed a gun right at Victoria. I covered my mouth, preventing a loud gasp to escape. I wanted to run and stop this, but I was frozen by fear.

Victoria suddenly laughed, grabbing his right hand and bending the wrist until it snapped liked a dry twig, the man screamed out as she ripped the gun free. "Achilles, you're a goddamn idiot, always have been."

Her foot shot out, making contact with the man's kneecaps, dislocating both of them in a blink of the eye, rendering the man useless.

I watched as she stripped the guns into pieces, throwing each piece around the alley. She moved to the man who was now on his knees, "It's a shame the old lady thought you were the best to come after me, I will make sure he gets the best parts of you." She quickly grabbed his other arm, snapping it like she had the first.

"Fuck you, Chimera." He then drew his eyes to move past Victoria and fall on me standing like a damn gawking fool at the entrance of the alley. He laughed, raising his chin my way, "Looks like we have an audience."

Victoria turned slowly my way, her hard cloudy grey eyes landing on me without showing a hint of emotion, "Alex, get out of here! Now!"

I shook my head, "Not without you." I swallowed hard, fighting the need to scream, vomit. I took one step towards her when I felt a pair of strong arms wrap around me, lifting me up as a raspy female voice spoke against my ear.

"Oh Chimera and Achilles, didn't even notice me while you two were playing in your sandbox like shitty little children." The arms pulled me tighter as I clawed at them to free me. "Looks like I'm about to collect big time from the old lady." The voice against my ear, sounded eerily familiar, but I was in too much of a panic to think clearly and place it with a face.

Victoria stood up straight, "Dante, put her down. If you don't, you'll regret it." Victoria met my eyes, the clouds shifting away for a split second to show a minute amount of fear.

"I will in a second, maybe, but first let's dispose of the trash." The woman dropped me to the ground and I fell to my knees. I lurched to get to my feet, but was met with a hard backhand that knock me woozy and back to the ground. I could barely see what was going on as the woman, also dressed in black with dark black hair in a tight bun, removed a small silenced handgun. My head wouldn't allow me to stand up or get my limbs to move, but I could still see what was going on.

She didn't blink an eye as she fired three shots right into the laughing man's head, silencing his laughter immediately. The smoke barely hit the air when she attacked Victoria, striking her hard across the right cheek with the butt. Victoria stumbled back, but came up hard with a side angle kick to the leg, making the woman buckle. "Dante, leave now before I kill you."

The woman laughed, kicking Victoria in the stomach, "And miss out on a nine million dollar pay out?" She barreled into Victoria, shoving her hard against the brick wall, "Not a chance sweetheart."

The back of Victoria's head hit the brick with a loud crack, drawing a reaction out of me, "Stop it! You're hurting her!"

I rolled to my side, cringing as my head felt like it had split open. I pawed at the ground, slipping on a puddle, "Stop it!" I shouted again and looked up. I was able to focus the other woman's features, I squinted harder as my gut began screaming at me.

Victoria turned to the sound of my voice, and it was the split second her opponent needed.

I only saw the quick glint of the blade before it was buried into Victoria's stomach with so much force I heard her grunt as she slammed against the brick wall again. I screamed, trying to throw the other woman off but it didn't work, I kept screaming and forcing my body to move.

"NO!" I scrambled harder, gathering myself to my feet, looking up to see the bloodied blade leave her and slam back in. "NO!"

The other woman started laughing as she leaned against Victoria's ear, whispering something I couldn't make out, before shoving the blade in once more and dragging the blade upwards, in what I knew to be a deadly stroke.

When I finally was on my feet, the woman stepped away from Victoria, letting her slide to the ground, clutching at the blood pouring out of her stomach. The woman pulled a hood over her head, snapped a picture with a cell phone of Victoria and the other man on the ground and ran out of the alley, only pausing to look down at me, "You're lucky, she was worth more dead then you are alive."

That's when I saw her full face in the street light. Victoria's killer was that creepy EMT, Angela Diablo. She stared at me for a second as I struggled to get up, my vision blurry and the world still spinning. "Who the fuck are you? Is this why you've been following me?" I rasped the words out, "Why have you done this?" I found the air to raise my voice and reach out towards the woman.

I went to grab the Diablo's arm, but she easily shoved me away. She bent down and looked at me, "Let this go, nurse Ivers." She shoved me back on my ass and ran out of the alley. Leaving me to look at Victoria.

What I saw shattered me, not only for the fact that I was a nurse and I had seen this similar scene a thousand times and they all had one outcome, but because it was Victoria. I rushed towards her, stripping off my coat and falling to my knees in front of her. I shoved my balled up coat against the blood pouring out from the gash in her jacket. "Victoria, look at me, please."

Victoria was turning pale, slipping into shock with every breath. The blow to her head had disoriented her. I shouted at her as I saw her eyes roll into the back of her head. Her breathing was raggedy and bubbly, blood was filling her lungs quickly. I shook my head, fighting the nurse trying to tell me there was no hope in what was before me and reached for her cheek to get her to look at me.

Her skin was cooling with every second, "Oh god, no! Victoria, please, look at me." I fumbled for the zipper on her jacket and tugged it down, revealing exactly what I feared was underneath.

I gasped out a choked sob, "Oh fuck no." There was a large, precise laceration from her belly button up to the base of her sternum. With a surgeon's precision, the other woman had sliced open Victoria's major abdominal artery. She was bleeding out faster than I could stop it. I began uncontrollably crying, shoving my hands over the wound trying to push the blood that was pouring out, back into her body. "You cannot do this! You cannot die on me!" I shouted at Victoria, she was unresponsive, her eyes wobbling around in her head. Looking around at the sound of my voice but never looking directly at me. I knew the truth. The hard cold scientific truth of this injury and what the only outcome could be, but I wouldn't accept it. I could save her, I had to save her.

I grabbed her face again, slapping her cheek to get her to look at me, wake up out of the shock she was falling in. "Victoria, it's Alex, please look at me. Wake up and help me." I sobbed, looking over my shoulder at the sound of a groan. James was waking up, reaching for his head.

"James! I need help! Call an ambulance, Victoria's been stabbed and she doesn't have time!" I turned back to Victoria, her slate grey eyes latched on mine groggily before her head fell to her chest. "No, no, no, no. Oh god no, don't do this." I shouted again for James to hurry.

He got to his feet and rushed to me, looking down at the blood covering my hands, he whispered out, "Oh God." And pulled out his cell phone, shouting that he was a NYPD Sergeant and he some sort of a ten code and that he needed an ambulance and more police units immediately. He then placed his hands on top of mine, helping me to stanch the never-ending blood that was rushing out of Victoria. "Alex, they're coming, but I don't think she has enough time."

"Don't you dare say it!" I looked up at him through blurry eyes, I could hear the sirens in the distance getting closer, "She'll make it, she has to. She will." I nodded at him, crying harder as I turned back to Victoria, lifting her head so I could look at her, "I have to tell you I'm sorry, for everything." I whispered it, "Please, Victoria. Stay with me."

Everything became muted and distant, as if I was really watching from the sidelines. The ambulance showed up and I was shoved to the side as paramedics and police officers arrived. Scooping Victoria's limp, pale body onto a stretcher. They covered her stomach with rolls of gauze, trying to create pressure to get the bleeding to stop. I was pushed into James's arms and he pulled me to the entrance of the alley as more police officers swarmed the lifeless body of the man with bullet holes in his forehead.

"Alex, we should get out of here. I'll tell the detective to come find us at the hospital." James held my cheeks, looking in my eyes, "She's going to be okay."

I sobbed, looking over his shoulder to see the back of the ambulance doors close. A paramedic climbed on top of Victoria to start chest compressions. I fell forward into James arms, sobbing and screaming as I buried my face into his chest. He held me for a second, before picking me up and carrying me to the closest NYPD patrol car. James set me in the passenger seat in a ball and took off after the ambulance, full lights and sirens blaring.

James half carried me, half walked me into the emergency room. He waved at a nurse, "Hey, unit 745 brought in a female with a stab wound, I need to know where she is." He flashed his badge when the nurse gave him a shitty look. She rolled her eyes and pointed down the hall, "Trauma bay three, they're still working on her."

James nodded and walked me to a series of chairs right outside of the trauma bay, "Alex, I can't get you in there, so sit here. I'll be right back."

I nodded lazily, I was in shock and felt like I was in a dream state. Everything was numb, my hands were cold and stained in dried blood. I let him guide me to a chair and sit me down, I folded my arms across my chest and started rocking back and forth in the chair. This wasn't happening. This couldn't be happening. It had to be a dream. I would wake up, roll over and see Victoria with Holly on her chest, both asleep.

I smiled softly at the image and closed my eyes, my heart beat slowly as if it didn't want anything more to do with this night. It suddenly stopped for a few seconds, making me open my eyes and clutch at my chest. Something was wrong.

James suddenly pushed through the trauma bay doors, and looked at me with glassy eyes. His face contorted as soon as he saw me, and I saw him swallow hard. I shot to my feet, shaking my head, "Don't you dare." I knew that look, it was the same look he had when one of his friends was killed in the line of duty.

"Alex, I'm sorry." He reached for me.

I shook my head, stepping back, "Get away from me! Don't you dare say it."

James moved quickly and grabbed me by the upper arms, "Alex, she's gone. They couldn't stop the bleeding in time and…" He paused, looking down at the floor as if it would help him in this moment, "Victoria's gone." He looked up at me slowly, his eyes brimming with tears.

"Fuck you! No she's not." I slapped his hands away from me and charged through the trauma bay doors. I saw a tired doctor pull back the curtain, I shouted at him, "Where is Victoria Bancroft?"

The doctor gave me a dirty look, "Excuse me, you shouldn't be back here. Go back out front, a nurse can help you there."

I charged towards him, "Where is Victoria Bancroft! Answer me." I almost shoved him when I heard James two steps behind me.

"Doctor, this is her girlfriend." His voice was somber as he said it.

The young doctor's face changed as he nodded, "In here." He stepped to the side and held the curtain back for me.

I moved through and when my eyes landed on the sight before me, my knees buckled to the point James had to steady me.

"Ms. Bancroft had a severe stabbing wound, two of the three strikes she received bisected her aorta. Causing her to bleed out at a very rapid rate." The doctor continued on in a very clinical monotone voice, "She hung on for a bit, then as we inserted a chest tube to relieve pressure, she crashed."

"No more." I whispered the words out, "I don't want to hear anymore." I took a step towards the bed Victoria laid in. The nurses were starting the process of cleaning her up, they had covered her with a clean white blanket. A stark contrast to all of the red blood on the floor and on her face. There was a tube still in her mouth, taped to the side where the ambulatory bag had been used, and the silenced heart monitors showed a flat line. All hard facts I couldn't deny.

I moved closer, reaching for her hand sitting on top of the blankets with IV needles still inserted in the top of her hand. My fingertips ran over ice cold skin, making me tremble and shake, "Victoria." She was so cold, so lifeless and I felt my heart crack at the sight.

The doctor cleared his throat, "The official time of death was 10:25 p.m. I'll give you a minute." He squeezed my shoulder as he mumbled to the nurses behind us, wanting to get the cleanup process started.

I stared at her and reached for hand when James gently grabbed my elbow, "Alex, we need to step out. The detectives want to talk to you and the medical examiner is here. They have to take the body for criminal processing." He frowned at the cold, professional speech.

I looked up at him, "This isn't real." I went to step towards Victoria, but was shoved back by a few nurses and two people wearing windbreaker jackets with medical examiner in bold white letters on the back.

James tugged me gently, "The ME promised me I could take you down when they get her situated, but the evidence is still fresh." He winced again, looking at me, "Please Alex, we need to find who did this."

I was shoved back and out of the small curtained area. James held onto me and whispered that we should step outside to let them do their job. I was so deep in the grips of shock, that I mindlessly followed him, latching onto the fact that he was right. The evidence was fresh and would get us to who killed Victoria quicker.

Then it clicked in my head. I grabbed James hand, "Angela Diablo. Look her up, she worked at my hospital in D.C. She's the one who stabbed Victoria, I saw her. I saw her face." My mind started racing, "I can describe exactly what she looks like."

James looked in my eyes, nodding and pulled out his phone, "Sit tight. I'll call it in and get an artist down here." He smiled tightly and pushed through the bay doors.

I let out a shaky breath and turned back to the curtained area, my heart limping in its chest. I wanted to go back and say my goodbyes. Hold Victoria and tell her everything I didn't have the chance to. I relented and took a few steps back to the curtain, maybe I could plea with the nurses and the techs to let me have that moment.

The curtain whooshed open and the techs started pushing a stretcher with the ubiquitous black thick plastic body bag on it. I gasped and covered my mouth as my adrenaline was replaced by heartbreak. The nurses scattered away, leaving the two techs to silently roll the woman I loved away. I suddenly found my voice, and rasped out, "Please, can I say goodbye?"

The one tech, a young black male met my eyes then nodded to his partner, a younger woman with thick glasses and her hair tucked up under the ball cap she wore. I stepped closer, "Please, just a minute." The young man looked at his partner again as I continued to move closer. "She's my girlfriend."

I was two steps away when the woman turned around and grabbed my upper arms, ushering me into the corner of the bay. "Alex, leave this."

I looked up and gasped when the voice matched the dark eyes of Diablo. She glared at me, holding me tight as I went to shove her back. "No, you fucking murderer!" I clawed at her hands and turned to scream out for help. A strong hand covered my mouth and drew my eyes back to Diablo's. Her jaw twitched as she held my eyes before leaning in closer and whispering, "Let this go, Alex. Let her die, it's the only way you and Victoria will come out of this alive."

I screamed against her palm, scrambling at her hand to remove it. I wanted to shout at her, what the hell did she mean? Victoria was dead, by her hand, and now she was issuing riddles. That's when it sunk in, the idea that this wasn't real. This was a plot to allow Victoria to escape. I clawed harder, trying to free my voice so I could ask if this was what this all was. A way for Victoria to leave her second life.

Diablo looked over her shoulder, motioning to her partner. She looked in my eyes, a flicker of recognition of what I might have figured out, as I silently pleaded with her to let me speak. The young man rushed over as she bent down to my ear again, "No one will believe you, Alex. Let her die, so you both can live."

I screamed when I felt a pin prick in the side of my neck. I quickly felt drowsy and limp in Diablo's arms, barely hearing her call out for a nurse to help her.

The world went hazy as I was handed off to a nurse and James's voice filled my ears, dragging me out into the fresh air of the city outside.

I made it three wobbly, unassisted steps outside before collapsing onto my knees. The cold concrete biting through my jeans as I broke down again, James rushing to my side and lifting me up.

I looked at him, choking out, "She's not dead. Victoria can't be dead." It came out in a strange questioning way. I had to question it now, Diablo's words struck a deep chord inside of my gut. Telling me to accept her words as truth over the facts in front of me.

He nodded slowly, "She is, Alex. I'm sorry." He stopped, not knowing what else to say as I broke apart again, shaking my head and mumbling out words. I was still woozy from whatever injection Diablo gave me.

The only thing that wasn't woozy in my head, was that I had to prove Victoria wasn't dead. That it was a lie. Another lie to protect me.

Chapter 26

~Three days later~

"Your mom is already at the house, waiting. She just put the meatloaf in the oven." James looked over at me, setting his cellphone in the middle console. He had small smile on his face before turning back to focus on the road.

I didn't move, I kept my head pressed against the passenger window, blankly staring out at the world passing us by. The three hour drive back to Annapolis had been silent on my part. James tried filling the car with idle conversation but it was fruitless. I wasn't listening no matter what stupid jokes he offered up, the concerned questions about my state, or whatever he just spoke to my mom about for the last fifteen minutes.

I was still numb from the night Victoria died. My mind absorbed all of the facts given to me the next morning by James as I laid in a ball on his couch. He even set down the full medical report on the table in front of me, knowing that it was hard facts that couldn't be denied. Today was the first day that I hadn't started crying out of nowhere, sobbing, screaming and throwing things out of anger, confusion. It grew worse when he told me that an Angela Diablo died in 1946 at the ripe old age of eighty-five. There was no trace of the young Hispanic woman who stalked me at the hospital, or the woman I watch stab Victoria. She didn't exist, even when James reviewed hospital camera footage. He could see the top of her head and then carrying me after I fainted. There was no proof of anything. Angela Diablo was a figment of my imagination.

I now felt completely numb. Numb like I had been sitting in a freezer for days. Numb, cold and empty. My thoughts would drift from it not being real, to being very real when I remembered all of the clinical facts presented to me. The way she looked laying there motionless and pale, but all of those things could be faked. All of those things could be altered and regurgitated in a way that everyone believed it.

I read the final report from the hospital and the medical examiner's autopsy report. Victoria was dead. She died from massive internal bleeding. She had died within the five minutes it took for the blade to enter her abdomen and fall to the ground where my nursing skills became useless. These were the facts, printed in bold, clinical black and white. Signed off by the New York Medical Examiner's office.

But I didn't dare believe those facts, my gut begged me not to.

"Alex? Did you hear me?" James placed a hand on my shoulder, shaking me gently to acknowledge him.

I turned, squinting very dry, tired eyes his way. "What?"

He smiled tightly, "I said we're about ten minutes away from home. Is there anywhere you want to stop?"

I shook my head, frowning deeply as I shifted in the seat and sat forward. "Have you heard from Dani?"

He sighed, "Not yet, I left her message and she texted me back this morning. There's some serious fallout from what happened on top of organizing getting Victoria home." He cleared his throat, squeezing my shoulder, "Alex, I know I've said it a million times, but…"

"Just don't, please James." I looked up at him, my voice cracking for the thousandth time in the last three days. I dropped my eyes down to look at my red, sore hands. I had been washing them excessively since James brought me back to his apartment that first night. Sobbing uncontrollably, scrubbing the dried blood off of my hands with boiling hot water and all the soap he had in the house. Every time I looked at my hands for a second too long, I would see all of her blood on them. Staining my skin, the fingernails and they would begin to tremble and my mind would spiral out of control. I was fighting off the shock from losing Victoria and the confusion of the things Diablo said. I couldn't think straight.

I quickly tucked my hands into the front pockets of my jacket after catching her class ring still on my finger, "Keep calling her, leave her a message that she needs to talk to me." I cleared out the crack in my voice, turning to look at the freeway signs pointing the way home. "I need answers." Dani would know the truth. I would corner her, and demand that she tell me what actually happened and why Victoria felt she needed to do it this way.

James nodded, returning both hands to the steering wheel, "I will, Alex."

I closed my eyes, pressing a hand over my heart trying to feel if it was still beating, even that felt numb and cold, but it continued to beat. Pressing on with living while I struggled to find the answers why what happened and what I was going to do next.

"We're home." James leaned forward, turning the rental car up into the driveway.

The lone sight of the house had my throat tightening. This was her house and it became ours, but now it only reminded me that she was never coming home. I sucked in a ragged breath, tears welling up, I almost asked James to back up and take me anywhere but here.

Then I saw my mom step out of the front door, a tight comforting mom smile on her face as she held a wiggly Holly. I gasped out a quiet sob, pushing the car door open, I ran straight towards my mom. I ran right into her open arms, burying my face in her shoulder as the dams reopened and I sobbed harder than I had the first night. She whispered, kissing the top of my head, "Oh Ava, I'm so sorry."

She squeezed me harder while Holly yipped to get in between us. I cried until I couldn't breathe, holding on to my mom as she tried her best to comfort me. I could only close my eyes and choke out, "She's gone mom."

"I know, Alexandra. I know." The tears were thick in her own voice, echoing how much was really lost to us all in this world now that Victoria was dead.

I held onto my mom for as long as possible until Holly became too forceful in her determination to get closer to me. My mom handed her off to climb in my arms and helped me into the house. All I could do was hold the little dog close to my chest and hide my face in her fur. I didn't want to look around the house as I walked in. I didn't want to see the remnants of our fight I never bothered to clean up, the empty glass in the sink from Victoria and her bourbon, the grocery list on the fridge with her handwriting all over it. More than anything, I didn't want to accept that this house would never have Victoria step inside. Have her sit outside on the patio drinking coffee while she watched me water the lone tulip plant, meet her in the living room on Saturday nights for popcorn and movies. I would never have her near me anywhere in this house and it smothered my heart to the point it struggled to keep beating. Even if she faked her death, I wasn't sure I would ever see her again. There was a reason why she left me.

"I'm going upstairs." I mumbled the words out, hearing James greet my mom and set the bags down next to the laundry room.

"Okay Alex, if you need anything. I'll be here for a little bit longer. I'm staying at the hotel down the road for a few days while I try to work on things." James kept his soft tone, "If you need anything, I'm a phone call away."

I nodded with my back still turned to him and continued up the staircase towards the bedroom.

My eyes remained closed as I walked down the hall, I couldn't even look at the excited puppy in my hands, she was just another reminder and another face I would have to tell why her person was never coming home. Pushing the bedroom door open, I snapped my eyes open and saw the bedroom exactly as I had left it three days ago. A messy bed, clothes on the comforter and on the chair as I rushed around packing.

I bit my lip hard, desperately trying to hold back the never-ending rush of tears, and set Holly down on the floor to let her scamper off to her bed, barking happily. I stood in the middle of the room, looking and immediately picking out everything that was her.

Her half-finished fiction novel with one of my business cards sticking out as a bookmark. Her black framed glasses sitting next to it and her watch. Over in the chair under my folded scrubs, laid the last thing she slept in. A Navy rugby shirt and baggy sweat shorts. I covered my mouth to keep some of the sobs inside, and walked towards the bed and sat down on her side.

It still smelled like her. Her shampoo scent soaked into her pillow and the blankets, giving life to the ghost in the room. I grabbed the pillow with a trembling hand and crushed it into my body, trying to capture whatever was left of her. I fell to my side and let go, let go of the contained sobs and curled into a ball and cried heavily. I murmured in between sobs until Holly ran back to the edge of the bed and jumped up. She crawled over to me, poking her nose under one of my balled up fists, her way of checking on me. I glanced at the bright brown eyes of the little dog, and shook my head, "She's not here, Victoria's not here."

The dog stared at me for a second before crawling over me and flopping down right next to my head, slowly licking my cheek and whining softly. I cried more, running my hand over her head before pulling her into my arms. "I'm so sorry, this was my fault that she's not here." I sighed hard, struggling to catch my breath.

My mom appeared in the doorway, "Alex, James left for the day." She paused looking at me, her face fell as she moved to kneel in front of me. Brushing some of the hair that started sticking to my cheek from tears, she searched my eyes, "He told me what happened."

I scrunched my face up as the memories stuck fresh knives into my heart, "I never got to say I loved her one more time. She died thinking I was angry at her and that I didn't love her anymore." I met my mom's eyes, "She laid in my arms, thinking I hated her." I squeezed my eyes shut, huffing out a strangled sob. I let the grief overcome what little rational thinking I had left. I was tired, exhausted and confused. I wanted nothing more than to cry in my mother's arms.

"She knew, Alex. She knew exactly how much you loved her. You never had to tell her, she could always see it. We all could see it, you two were something incredible." My mom paused, realizing the tense she was using. Blowing out a quiet breath, she pressed a palm against my cheek, "We'll get through this. It's going to hurt like hell, but she'd want you to live." She smiled tightly, nodding at Holly, "The both of you. Live the life she fought for you to have."

I shook my head, wanting to tell her that I found life pointless now that I lost most of my heart. That life would never ever feel the same without Victoria next to me. Regardless of the lies, the deception and what she had done, Victoria was my one and only true love, and there would never be a replacement for her.

~Five Days Later ~

"Bill is coming down tonight. He was wondering if you'd be up to going out for dinner." My mom smiled at me over a frying pan full of eggs. "Get out of the house for a minute."

I shrugged, staring down into the blackish brown depths of the coffee in front of me, "I guess, but not too far. James called this morning to tell me Dani finally contacted him. Told me to expect her to drop by."

I clenched my jaw. I had not left the house in a week and had no plans to in the near future. I would only move around the house, shuffling room to room in pajamas holding Holly or staring at pictures of Victoria in the house. My mom would move around me, cleaning up after me, cooking for me, taking Holly for walks and then sit next to me to try and get me to talk, but I wouldn't. I was focused on getting answers from Dani. I had James calling her incessantly while he met with the Naval Intelligence Officers to be debriefed on what we both witnessed. It was the one thing that kept me from falling apart every three minutes when I saw another piece of Victoria, or stared at her ring for too long.

I had also started my own digging and placed a call to my contacts in hospital security. They were digging around in Angela Diablo's files and all of the security footage they had of her. It was going to take a few days, but I was promised I would have something by the end of the week.

I hadn't slept much, finding it hard to sleep in the empty bed without a warm body next to me. Holly tried her best to fill some of that void, but it wasn't the same. I would lay in the middle of the bed staring at the ceiling and cry on and off. I was so tired, but every time I closed my eyes I would see that night. Watching Victoria die followed by the sight of Diablo carting her off. It only made me restless and angry, so I remained awake before I exhausted myself and could fall into a dreamless sleep.

"Okay." My mom wiped her hands, pushing a plate of eggs and toast my way, "I'm going to take the girl for her walk. I'll be back in a half hour." She smiled, walking over to me and kissing my forehead, "I love you Ava."

"I love you too, mom." I poked at the eggs with a fork, sighing I shoved them away and held my face in my hands. I begged my head to stop spinning and my heart to start beating normally again. I begged anyone who would listen to tell me what I was supposed to do next, or at least tell me how I was going to live the rest of my life like this.

I heard the front door open and Holly bark like a maniac, like she always did at people she saw on the street. I heard my mom shush her and then whisper to someone that I was in the kitchen. I raised my head up, wiping my eyes, "James, give me a minute."

"I'm not him, but I'll give you two minutes, Alex."

I spun around at the sound of Dani's voice. She was standing at the edge of the kitchen dressed in a dark blue uniform with all of her ribbons and gold cording around the sleeve. She had her white hat tucked under one arm and a thick wooden box with an envelope tucked under the other. She looked at me with red rimmed green eyes and a tight painful smile on her face. The sight of the woman in front of me twisted my stomach into knots.

"What are you doing here?" I rasped the words out angrily, sliding off the stool to face her. "Why haven't you bothered to call me back for a week? What the hell happened?" I shook my head, my eyes welling up quickly, "You have so much to answer for."

Dani smiled tightly, dipping her head down, "I know, Alex." She moved to the island I stood in front of, "There was things I had to take care of, for her." She paused, her jaw clenching tightly, "I couldn't call you or see you until now."

"The fuck you couldn't. You were her best friend. I know she would want you to tell me everything." I shook my head, "Start talking." I glared at her, "Who is Angela Diablo and why did Victoria fake her own death?" I spoke the words quickly, hoping to gain any kind of reaction out of Dani. I got nothing but a solemn sigh and sad green eyes.

Dani let out a slow breath, "I need to do this one last thing." She set down the envelope next to me and moved the wooden box. "Victoria had specific requests about what to do if, this ever happened. Things she made me promise way back in the desert." She held out the wooden box. "She never had any family or real friends to speak of, until you, but the Navy acts quickly when there is no family." Dani cleared her throat, "Victoria was buried at sea three hours ago as requested. Over in the middle of the Pacific, where she was laid to rest." Dani looked away from me as she spoke the last few words.

I shook my head, "No, stop. Stop it and tell me what the hell happened! Who is the woman who stabbed Victoria? Does she work with you?" I was enraged, the stupid Navy and this infuriating redhead had taken so much from me.

Dani looked up at me, a lone tear rolling down her cheek, "I can't tell you anything. I have no idea who killed Victoria. James and I spoke about that woman you are suspicious of, but there's nothing there, Alex."

She sucked in a breath, "Victoria is dead. I've read all of the reports, watching the video and it was bad luck. Our bad, shitty luck coming back to strike." Dani sniffled and held out the wooden box, "On behalf of the President of the United States and the Chief of Naval Operations, please accept this flag as our symbol of our appreciation of Victoria's service to this...."

I lunged at Dani, shoving her back at the shoulders, shouting, "Stop it! Go! Leave! I can't hear this!" My eyes blurred with more tears, "I don't need more proof of what I already know. I need proof and answers that Victoria is still alive, I know she is alive. She's too smart and too strong to let this happen to her." I shoved Dani again, harder. "Why can't anyone ever tell me the fucking truth?"

Dani let out a breath, and when I came at her again she dropped the flag on the stool next to me and grabbed my upper arms to stop me, "Alex, trust me. This is the last fucking thing I ever hoped to do. This wasn't supposed to happen like this. We had a plan, and it got fucked up at the last minute."

She tipped her head down, "I made a fucking promise to my best friend, let me fulfill what I can, Alex." She looked back up, tears rolling freely down her cheeks. "Please, Alex. I'm so incredibly sorry that this happened and there wasn't a thing I could do to stop it, stop her."

I shook my head, struggling to break out of her grip, "You could have called it off, convinced her to find another plan!" I shouted at the crying redhead, "You could have done a million other things without orchestrating all of this! You could have taken me to Sweden instead of New York!" I stumbled, "I was the reason why she lost her focus, why she felt she had to do this."

I bent my head down, gasping for air, "It was my fault." I rasped the words out, "I shouldn't have been there." I looked up into teary green eyes, "Tell her, tell her to come back. I'm sorry and I'll forgive her."

Dani's grip loosened on my arms and slowly pulled me into a tight embrace, "Alex, I can't bring her back. She's dead." She stumbled over the words in a whisper, before clearing her throat, "This was not your fault. None of it. Never blame yourself for any of this. If anyone is to blame, it's me. It's Voltaire's fault, but it will never ever be your fault." Dani held me tighter, "You gave Victoria back her humanity, the chance at love and the fire to fight for it." She sighed as I resisted her hug, "She loved you, very much. Her last words to me were, I will always love her, please make sure Alex knows that."

Dani leaned back to look in my eyes, "Her love for you was never ever a lie. Remember that, Alex." She smiled painfully, stepping away to smooth out the front of her uniform to regain her own composure, "I will continue to find out answers, for you, Alex. I will always keep you safe as long as you live and I promise you, none of these people who did this will live to see the light of another day." She wiped at her cheeks with the back of her hand as more tears fell, "I have to go."

With that, the redhead spun around and rushed out of the house. Leaving me standing in the kitchen even more heartbroken and confused. I glanced at the flag before catching Victoria's handwriting on the front of the envelope.

I let out a shuddering sigh and reached for the envelope. I pried it open and shook out the contents to fall on the countertop. I recognized them immediately as last will and testament paperwork. I frowned, "Victoria, why?" I sniffled, hating the fact that Victoria seemed to know that this day would come at some point. Her double life demanded it of her to have this sort of preparation, even if it felt like an over orchestrated lie that just hurt me more.

I went to pick up the small folded piece of paper when I heard Holly bark her way into the house, my mom quickly following behind. "I just saw a redhead back out of the driveway, was that Dani?"

I nodded, "Yes. She dropped a few things off." I tucked my arms across my chest, my eyes falling to the flag in the box, "Victoria was buried at sea this morning. Another moment passed where I couldn't tell her the things I needed to." I picked up the wooden box and shuffled to the den where the rest of her Navy things remained untouched. I stood next to the desk looking over her box of medals, her certificates and everything that was that part of her life. I ran my hand over the glass, "Why did this have to happen?" I grimaced at the sinking feeling that I was buying another lie like it was candy.

"Alex? Did you look at this?" My mom rushed into the den holding up the papers from the envelope.

I shook my head, "No, I don't think I want to."

My mom held out the papers, "You should, the girl left you everything she had. This house, her car, her savings and everything imaginable." She then handed over the folded piece of paper when she saw my continued lack of interest, "At least read this."

I frowned taking the note as she rushed back out to the kitchen to read over the paperwork.

My heart skipped when I saw my name in her handwriting, bringing tears I didn't think I had back up.

"Alex,

I will always love you. I'm sorry for everything I did, but I would never go back and change a thing because it led me to you.

The one piece of my heart that made me human.

I love you forever.

Victoria."

I closed my eyes, clutching the paper and slid into the leather chair before resting my head on the desk top.

If I could go back in time and change things, I would. I would go back and tell Victoria it didn't matter what she did for me, that I would love her just as much as I always have.

Maybe if I could, I would have her here with me and not just a flag in a box and a few scribbles on a piece of paper. I would have my heart and soul back.

~Four years later ~

"Yes Stacy, I will stop by later tonight after I drop off the rest of the things I'm donating." I grinned as I held the phone sitting on the floor and sorting out books. "Yeah, I'm finally doing that spring cleaning my mom and you have been hounding me about for the last couple of years." I stood up from the box I had filled with old textbooks.

I rolled my eyes, "Maybe I'll tell you what happened with Diana." I bit my bottom lip, "I think I scared her off, I need to tell her that I'm still working on things."

I closed my eyes, listening to Stacy rambling about the latest gossip at the hospital I no longer worked at. How the whole nursing staff had changed and that I should do her a solid and get her a job with me. After another five minutes of her gnawing my ear off, she hung up to take a code call, giving me reprieve from my friend's endless gossiping.

Tucking the phone in the back pocket of my jeans, I looked around the den, smiling at the progress I had made. Holly jogged into the room with a ball in her mouth, plopping it down at my bare feet. I smiled at the dog who was now a far cry from the tiny little girl I first bought four years ago, she was now the same size as Annie and my forever sidekick. "Not now, I still have a few things to do." I picked up the ball and walked towards the patio door, "Go outside and play for a bit and then we can go for a car ride."

Holly barked excitedly, hopping on her back legs as I tossed the ball out the back door, laughing when she took off like lightning to chase after it.

When I closed the door, I caught my reflection in the glass pane. I smiled at myself, brushing my hair that now fell to the middle of my neck, back. I looked better than I had over the years, I was starting to fall into a semblance of happy, or complacent with how my life was now.

I had made a tremendous amount of changes in the last six months as I tried to find a life again. I left the hospital and moved to the Naval hospital at Bethesda to work on my Master's degree in occupational therapy, and move away from the blood and guts of being a trauma nurse. I had lost my desire for it after losing Victoria and couldn't handle seeing patients come in with stab wounds or any type of wound that would throw me back to that night when I lost her.

I went to Ward a few weeks after Victoria's death and asked for him to help me get into Bethesda, he stared at me for a minute before agreeing and when I left his house, he was the hundredth person to tell me how much Victoria loved me. That they all could see it in her eyes by the way they lit up and had no hint of the sadness she carried for so long. His words left me crying in my car for twenty minutes before I finally managed to gain enough composure to drive home.

It had been a hard road to take after Victoria died, I changed and was still trying to find pieces of myself to put back together and live a normal life. She had made sure I was taken care of, leaving me more money than I would ever see in my life. I had the house, the BMW and a few investments that James had investigated and found like her savings, were free and clear of any traces of wrong doing. Victoria had earned her money, and earned it properly. Although I rarely touched most of it, only using some of it for repairs on the house or pay of some bills. It only left me missing her more and more when I saw her name on the joint account heading.

Then there was the fact that I became vigilant in proving Victoria's death was a hoax. I had spent that first year, hounding James with every little idea I had. I sent Diablo's sketch all over the internet in hopes someone would know who she was. All I got in return was weird emails of a sexual nature and nothing else. I dug in all of Victoria's boxes, looking for answers about Voltaire and her past, but there was nothing but painful memories. My family and friends began to wonder about my sanity. I was always discounting them when they would recite the scientific evidence that Victoria had died that night. I would smile and listen to them and take it into consideration. Then I would go back to digging into the deep shadows the woman traveled in. I had uncovered most of the media and news articles about the deaths she was responsible for, proving to me that she might have been a killer for hire, but she was doing the world a service. I was obsessed with proving Victoria was alive somewhere, so obsessed that my mother did an impromptu intervention last year and sent me to a therapist who specialized in PTSD.

I played the game with the therapist, giving her the answers she wanted to hear, but never gave up hope Victoria was alive and faked her death. I still investigated it when I could, only moving it to the basement and in a closet where no one would see it. Digging in the depths of a world that no one even knew existed. A world where people killed to save the rest of us from evils we never knew could exist. In time, I had become a closet expert about contract hits, black ops organizations, the secret missions and recruitment of soldiers during the war, and how the government used them to do very dirty work.

I even went so far to dig in my own incident at the metro station using James stolen login for the entire criminal database system for the country. I found my file, the investigative work Detective Scarlett did and the following investigations. I would spend hours looking at the crime scene photos next to the photos taken of me at the hospital. My bruises and cuts a stark contrast to the utter chaos of blood and death on that platform.

After reviewing the evidence and the case files, Victoria had killed those four men to save me and also saved many others from the havoc they would have caused. Those four men were nothing but pure evil, waiting to strike at whim.

When I was done, I slowly forgave Victoria for what she and I thought she was. She wasn't a monster. She was a product of her environment. A human bred and trained to kill for her country, but the humanity never left her. It was only buried under a disguise handed to her by Voltaire. I just hoped I could find her, tell her that I was sorry and I believed her.

I moved back to the den sealing up the last box of Victoria's textbooks. I had taken a week off from the hospital right before final exams to finally take on the task of cleaning out the house and clearing away most of the things I had left untouched of hers. It had been four years and it was time. My investigations and leads were rolling to a dead end for the last eight months. Slowly making me believe that maybe I was crazy. Crazy and unwilling to believe what everyone else did, that Victoria had died that night in the alleyway and my adrenaline crafted some creative ideas and visions to compensate for overwhelming grief.

So, it was time to make a change and try to move past the years long mourning I had put myself through. I wasn't trying to get rid of Victoria, I was trying to find a life without her, and the only way I knew how to do that was by packing things up and storing them away. Stacy had told me her therapist mentioned the only way one can move past grief is if they make large changes that force them into living outside of grief.

So I cut my hair, went through the closest and packed up her clothes. Only crying once or twice when I caught a muted scent of her on a buried t-shirt. I missed her, that was the one thing that never changed over the years. I missed the woman I had fallen in love with and was still in love with even as my world shifted.

I put the BMW up for sale and emailed Dani to come over this weekend to take most of Victoria's Navy things to store at her house. I needed to move on in life, I had to or my grief of losing her would amplify the insanity I felt I was on the brink of.

I didn't want to forget Victoria, and I did my best to keep her with me. I had a few pictures in the house and still wore her class ring. I had tried to take that off and throw it in the Potomac, but I never got it off my finger. I would cry and push it back down the knuckle before whispering into the wind that blew in the direction of the Pacific, whispering how much I loved her, hoping somehow she would hear it.

It was only Holly and I living in this house, I would not let anyone that wasn't family in the house. I felt that it betrayed Victoria and the home we had made together. Not even Diana was allowed in the house yet, not until I cleared out some more of Victoria's things. I had to take Holly's lead, she had buried the angry stuffed goat last fall in a mud pile and left it there. I saw it as her way of realizing Victoria would never come home, no matter how long she sat at the front door and stared at it, waiting. Victoria would never walk back through the door.

Diana was an orthopedic surgeon at Bethesda and my way of burying my own angry goat. She was a Navy officer with chestnut hair, light blue eyes, beautiful with a very persistent way about her when it came to me. She was a stunning woman and I maybe latched onto her because she was a Naval officer and had certain familiar characteristics.

It took her a year to get me to take the offered coffee she would bring me on late nights of studying in the hospital library before I started the even later intern rotations with current occupational therapists. I was grateful that the Master's program was keeping my mind busy and active and off of old memories.

Diana continued to be persistent and I finally bent a month ago and had dinner with her. During that dinner I found her nothing to be like Victoria and it was different, new, and she relaxed me. Even taking notice of the ring I still wore, she smiled at me, tapping it before grabbing the bill, "Whoever they were, they are lucky to have you wear their ring. Tradition runs deep and I hope I'm not stepping on anyone's toes."

I smiled softly, twisting the ring, "I am, I was the lucky one." I tucked my hand away on my lap, looking up at Diana to quickly change the subject away from anything related to my past.

That dinner led to casually dating Diana here and there over the last month. She would drop me off at the house with a polite hug, then a polite kiss on the cheek, that became a very polite, but intense kiss one night. Leaving me mildly breathless and bringing many forgotten sensations back to life inside of me. I had missed human contact and living in general. Then one night, last weekend, we both drank a bit too much and she kissed me on her couch, things grew in intensity and next thing I knew we were in her bedroom, naked.

Although it was great sex, it didn't feel right. I would only close my eyes and try not to cry at the way Diana touched me. It was nothing like the way Victoria touched me. The way she knew exactly where and how to touch me and feel things that went beyond this earthly plane. Sleeping with Diana only brought up more wounds that I thought were buried, and it left me feeling like I had cheated on Victoria. I left her house in the middle of the night while she slept with a smile on her face. I called her in the morning to apologize and ask for a little more time, time to sort out the lingering feelings of a dead girlfriend from four years ago. The girlfriend I loved with everything I was and still did to this day.

Walking out to the mini with a box of books in my arms, I smiled at Dale, taking the trash out, "Afternoon Dale!"

The older man grinned at me, leaning on the fence, "Hey there Alex, looks like you're doing some late spring cleaning?"

I nodded, setting the box into the rear hatch before closing the shiny candy apple red door. "Yeah, taking a few things to the Academy library for their book drive." I wiped a few fingerprints off the red paint, "I don't think I can ever tell you enough times what an amazing job you did on the old girl. She still runs like she came straight from the factory."

Dale flicked his hand at me, "Ah, it's nothing. You did your fair share and I'm just happy you like it." He glanced at the house, "I'm heading to the hardware store, you need anything?"

I smiled, "Nope, I'm all good. I fixed the gutters last week and so far they're holding up." I winked at him, "Thank you for that as well."

"No problem, I like to help my neighbors." He pushed off from the fence, "See you later, Alex."

I waved to Dale and headed back inside. The old couple had become a second family to me and a crutch as I dealt with everything after. Between them and my parents, I was always fed and the house was cleaned until I found my legs to do it all again for myself.

Back in the house, I heard Holly barking at the fence like a fool. I huffed and grabbed an iced tea from the fridge before heading out to the patio to see what she was fussing about.

"Holly, settle down!" I hollered at the dog only to find Mary bent down petting the dog at the gate that divided our yards. "Oh hello there Mary!"

Mary grinned at me, ruffling Holly's fur, "I was looking for you, found this eager one first who demanded I throw a tennis ball a few hundred times." She stood up, tossing the ball across the yard. "Do you have a minute?"

I smiled, "Of course. I could use a break from cleaning the house." I pointed at the small patio table, "Did you want something to drink?"

May shook her head, "Thank you, but no." She sat down, setting a thick white envelope down on the table. "How are things lately, Alex?" The way she asked it, I knew she was still concerned about my wavering mental state. I internally rolled my eyes at myself, embarrassed. I had spent many an afternoon explaining my theories to Mary about how Victoria was very much alive and in hiding.

I shrugged, knowing what she was asking, "They're moving forward. Slowly, but surely." I opened the tea bottle, "James is still working on a few leads in New York off the scene evidence. Dani pops in and out once in a while, but it seems she moved into a different intelligence office, at least that's what Ward tells me." I spun the bottle cap, "It's been frustrating to not have any answers in four years. I know that it's all deep covert secrets, but I wish someone would tell me something, anything to give me some sort of closure." I turned to look at the blooming tulip plants under the far tree, Holly poking her nose in them. "Maybe if I had an answer to something, I could move on."

Mary smiled softly at me, her eyes dropping to the class ring on my finger. "Answers are a funny and tricky thing. They never come when you want them and wash over you like a summer downpour when you don't expect it." She turned to look at the same tree I was, "I had to hide a lot from Dale when we met, right before he shipped off to Vietnam. It was difficult, but at the time I was more in love with the job of keeping secrets than him."

I slowly turned to the older woman, my brow furrowing in confusion, "What secrets did you have to hide as a secretary for the Navy recruitment office?" Mary had told me a long time ago how she met Dale at a Navy recruitment fair at a high school to find volunteers to join the Navy and head to Vietnam. "Aside from social security numbers and personal information."

Mary turned to look at me, her hazel eyes piercing me in a way that shook me for a split second, "I had to hide the secret I was not a secretary and that I was keeping more secrets than the run of the mill intelligence officer." She took in a slow breath, "Dale is going to be gone for an hour, so please listen closely and never ever tell him what I'm telling you. He still doesn't know much and after almost fifty years of marriage, I'd like to keep it that way."

She paused, pushing the envelope towards me, "My codename is Raven and in the Office of Naval Intelligence and with the CIA, I'm still one of the top intelligence agents they've ever seen and one of the most dangerous, working for both of them for thirty five years. Granted as I've gotten older, I've shifted into an advisory role, but I know everything. You can look Raven up in the world wide web and see that I was quite the feared ghost. The male world leaders thought I was a vicious man, not a delicate lady sitting behind a desk for most of her service. Yet, I knew how to extract secrets." She looked at me with intensity, "Extract them in a similar way Victoria did." Mary's eyes clouded over quickly like Victoria's used to whenever she glossed over the things she did.

I felt my heart race and I unconsciously scooted away from the table, "Are you making this up?" I felt like this was a trick, a bad dream or a shitty joke planned by Dani.

Mary chuckled, "No my dear, I'm not. Nothing happens as a coincidence." She set her hands on the tabletop, "I've known about Victoria for many years, since she bought this house and every day after. I had been monitoring Voltaire from a distance as an outside advisor for the CIA. Keeping tabs on that foolish asshole Arthur as he bounced between sane and insane, dragging that girl in to his mess. I knew what Victoria was doing and near the end, I was working with MI6 to advise them on how to pull her out, pull her away from that madman. I even went to Danielle and James after an intel breach inside Voltaire to bring them into the fold of safety and help Victoria get out unscathed."

She laughed softly at the look of disbelief on her face, reading mind immediately, "Before you ask, James only saw me from afar in shadows, an old spy trick I learned way back in the sixties."

I glared at the old woman, "Why didn't you?" I was astonished and furious at this woman for so much. She could have helped me sooner, stepped in and told me all of this a long time ago and maybe prevented Victoria's death. She could have prevented my own spiral into a cracked mental state.

"Stop that mess that happened in front of you? Because no one in the world other than Victoria, Danielle and one more set that plan in motion. I found out about it when you came home, devastated and searching for answers." Mary leaned back in her chair, "James has been working with me and many others and finally some answers fell into my hands last night." She slowly pushed the envelope towards me, "I found someone in Scotland, at the University of Edinburgh who has more information on Voltaire and the woman responsible for Victoria's death."

Mary stood up, "Your flight leaves tonight if you want to go. The details are in that envelope along with a plane ticket." She then glanced at Holly running towards her, "Go to Scotland, Alex. The answers you've been searching for and needing to move on, are there."

She folded her arms across her chest, "If you don't want this. Burn that envelope and we will never speak of this again." She turned to walk towards her gate, "But remember, I never spoke to you about anything other than the weather and book donations."

Mary left my yard with a smile and a knowing look.

I stared down at the white envelope before curiosity took hold and ripped the thing open. There was a plane ticket as Mary said and a thin sheet of paper with a name scribbled on it.

E.A. Lamont – Medieval Studies - University of Edinburgh.

I blew out a slow puff of air, looking up at the bright blue sky and the sun shining down. I would wait until nightfall to start up the fireplace to burn the ticket and the note.

I had to move on, but chasing secrets from old spies was not the way to do it. It would only send back to the closet of secrets I had created in search of the truth.

Twelve hours later and a lengthy nap to chase out the jet lag, I was standing at the admissions desk of the University of Edinburgh, listening to a young girl with bleach blonde hair and a thick Scottish accent look up where I could find a E.A. Lamont. Telling her I was sent by an old Professor back in the states to search out this one to help get me set up for the fall semester.

"Och, here we go." The girl scribbled on a pad, "Third floor, second door to the right is Professor Lamont's office."

I took the piece of paper, smiling tiredly, "Can you tell me what it is that Professor Lamont teaches?"

"Aye, it says Ancient Medieval History." She grinned at me, "Perfect place to learn that here, so many old castles about."

I laughed and nodded, "True." I held up the piece of paper, "Thanks again!"

I then walked towards the staircase and climbed up the old wooden staircase, smiling at the way the creaked under my feet and how insane this was of me. Fly across the ocean and search out a complete stranger who my secret agent next door neighbor told me about. It was ridiculous and as I stood over the fireplace, ready to toss the envelope in the bright orange flames, my gut spoke up. It had recently fell into silence as I drifted into a form of silent living, but as I lifted my hand, it shouted at me to wait. Take a chance and follow Mary's trail. The least that could come of it, I would find out the whereabouts of the woman who killed Victoria and maybe pass it onto James.

My gut wouldn't stop until I boarded the Loganair flight and settled in for the journey. I would do this one last thing, follow this silliness and when it became more twisted secrets, I would go home and finish packing up and maybe call up Diana for an apology dinner.

I shifted my bag on my shoulder as I reached the third floor. There were two glass paned doors to my right, each had the ubiquitous name plate next to the door. First a *R. Maxwell – Theology* and then came *E.A. Lamont – Ancient Medieval Studies.*

I sighed, folding the piece of paper up to tuck in my coat pocket before reaching for the door to knock. The door was cocked open and I could see someone sitting at the desk through the frosted glass.

"This is stupid." I rolled my eyes and tapped lightly on the glass with my knuckles and opened the door a bit more, "Excuse me, I'm looking for a Professor Lamont?"

I plastered a pleasant smile on my face as I stepped in and looked up when the Professor stood from the desk. "Hi, my name is Alex...."

All of my words fell to nothing the second I made eye contact with E.A. Lamont, my heart doing a freefall into the bottom of my stomach. Her slate grey eyes sparkling as they glassed over. Her hair was a slight shade of strawberry blonde, but everything else was exactly as I last saw her before that fateful night.

When she was alive.

I clutched my bag strap, swallowing hard as my eyes welled up, "Victoria?" Her name came out barely above a whisper. I blinked a few times to clear away the tears, she was still standing there, pulling off black framed glasses and smiling that same soft smile that captured my entire being so long ago. Victoria was standing in front of me, smiling at me, very much alive and breathing. Her cheeks turning a soft shade of pink the longer I stared at her.

She licked her lips, nodding, "Hello Alex."

Chapter 27

Some would say that four years is a long time, but to me it passed in the blink of an eye.

I sat in the small old office, reading over essays and daydreaming as I looked out the even older paned glass windows. I had arrived at the University of Edinburgh six months ago, returning to the role of Professor and oddly enough it was bringing me much needed peace. The old man had placed me here for many purposes, to keep me in MI6 jurisdiction while I continue to seek out the Colonel.

I had spent four years hunting and dismantling Voltaire from the inside out starting that night in New York when I gave up so much to keep her safe from Arthur and the Colonel. I fell quickly into the old version of me in the black hood and shoved all emotions away as I killed ruthlessly and with a deep conviction fueled by revenge for everything that greasy man and his fat cohort had put me through.

After I killed most of Arthur's plumbers, all of them caught with their proverbial pants down as news of my death spread throughout the company, I continued on. Each gruesome death I handed down, revealed more and more secrets that drove me harder to find the end to Arthur and the Colonel. Maggie stayed out of my way, only providing the tools and transportation to keep my hands freshly covered in blood. Then six months ago, she put a halt to my activities, stating that I was drawing unwanted attention by the CIA and the NSA. She placed me in the University, let me choose my cover name and told me to wait for the seas to calm and I would be set free again. Free to carry out my personal vendetta against the Colonel and everything he had done to me and Dani. Things that grew to be horrible, manipulative truths of how I was captured and the true nature of my torturing.

Some of which I extracted from Arthur while I pulled his fingernails out one by one until he babbled like a child crying for his mother. When I was done with him, I continued dismantling the organization that created me, handing over their files to Dani and James and the ONI to sort through and put to good use.

Dani was by my side for most of it until recently when the ONI pulled her completely into their employment, and I met Raven. My dear old neighbor sitting in front of me sipping tea next in a small café outside of London.

I was shocked but not completely surprised that the older woman was one of the best spies in the business, and as she explained how she found me and that she had leads on the ever slippery Colonel Aves, I could see she was hiding another agenda for finding me. I said very little in that impromptu meeting, only staring at her and Dani as they drew out the Colonel's movements. The only question I asked during the whole thing was where Maggie was and why she wasn't a part of this meeting.

Mary smiled at me, "One thing at a time, Victoria. Secrets like these needs to be unraveled one at a time before you can act upon them."

I glared at the woman, "I don't care about secrets, I just care about death certificates." I grabbed the map of the Colonel's movements in South America and walked out of the café. The next day I was sent on a flight to Scotland instead of South America and handed keys to the office I now sat in.

Over the last six months when I had nothing staining my hands but dried ink, chalk and dust from old books, I let my mind relax and started to pull back the black hood.

My thoughts fell to what I left behind, who I left behind.

Alex.

I bit the inside of my cheek, indulging in a rare handful of minutes to think about the woman I loved so much, still to this day. I didn't remember much from that night in New York when the plan started. My system was so full of the cocktail of drugs Dani and the tech team concocted to allow me to medically "die" and it screwed with my memories. I wouldn't even allow Dani to tell me the aftermath, even when she met me at her house in her dress blues, fresh from attending my funeral and delivering the package to Alex. I would shake my head and look away from her, telling her to keep it to herself until this was all done.

Mary was the only one to corner me and ask why I did what I did, leave Alex behind like I had. When I looked in her eyes, I had seen clearly the suffering I had put Alex through and the myriad of emotions she had suffered from being in the wrong place at the wrong time. I looked away from Mary, focusing on the white porcelain tea cup near her hand, "They were going to kill her. Contract or not, they were going to kill her out of spite. Arthur hated she was the reason why I was leaving him, leaving Voltaire and upsetting all of the work he put into creating me.

Dani had pulled the chatter and contracts that Alex was going to be murdered in my house the second we returned from Sweden." I swallowed hard, cringing at the memory of how the contract suggested her death would look like. "So, we changed the plan. I had to destroy my entire life, destroy her heart so she could be safe. If they thought I was dead, they would never think to look behind their shoulders. Giving me the opportunity to slice every one of their throats and watch them bleed out as I stood over them." I paused, feeling my heart tighten, "I did all of this for her, as morbid as it may appear to you. It was all for her."

Setting down the pen I had been using to write tomorrow's class notes, I closed my eyes, rubbing at my temples. I missed Alex. I missed the piece of my heart that she held and I hoped she had found a way to move on. Find a life past the monster I brought into her life when all of my secrets came spilling out like a torn, overflowing grocery bag. She had made it clear that last night that what I was, was unforgivable and in a way it solidified that I and my black hooded twin would forever be one. More now than ever since I had stained my hands with so much blood over the last four years.

I opened my eyes when my cell phone vibrated in a circle, Dani's name flashing at me. I scooped it up, tapping the green answer button, "What?"

"Someone's cranky this morning." She huffed, "I thought we had gotten to a good place over the years, then I remembered how moody you are."

I rolled my eyes, tugging at the edges of the thick sweater I wore, "Get to the point, I have a class to finish preparing for."

"And how is your Scottish accent coming along? Last I heard it was bordering more on Scotty from Star Trek." Dani chuckled, annoying me more. Dani and I had grown closer over the four years, but there was new tension over the last six months since I was on stand down. She began to look at me and hint about home. It was her way of trying to open the door to talk about Alex. As much as I wanted to know nothing, I also wanted to know everything about Alex and what she had been doing over the years. I had only heard bits and pieces, seen a picture or two of her at Bethesda hospital as Dani and James continued to sort with the mess that was the now dismantled Voltaire files.

"Your point, please." I ran a hand through my hair, squinting at the strawberry blonde tones I added in when I became E.A. Lamont.

"The point is this. Raven called me yesterday, concerned about Alex." Dani paused, waiting for my angry refusal to hear anything about her. "As you know, Alex has been very determined in proving your death was a hoax. To the point that her mother almost had her admitted to the crazy house." She sighed, "I still hate you for making me lie to her that day. You have no idea how much it hurt to pretend that she was crazy with grief, not dead onto the truth."

I dropped the strands of hair, interrupting Dani, "Concerned about what? Last you told me, she was fine. Off anyone's radar, living a quiet life." I felt my stomach and heart slam into each other, "Dani, you know I can't."

"You can, because this is serious. I'm sorting through the encrypted intel, the shit is thick and practically unbreakable, but trust me when Raven is concerned, I take it seriously. Something fishy is hanging around Alex and Raven went to her last night. Told her that if she wanted answers for all those questions left from New York, an E.A. Lamont would have them."

Dani paused again, "Alex boarded a Loganair flight a few hours ago. She's coming to you, Victoria." She chuckled, "Way to be lame with your codename, using your middle name, Alex's middle name and grammy boozers last name. It's like you have been begging her to sniff out your trail. Should have stuck with the one I gave you, Laverne DaFazio."

I felt the bile in my stomach demand to be released, my hands trembled as I interrupted Dani's annoying jokes, "Why the hell did Raven do that?" I stood up from my desk and moved to the window, "You explained why I had to remain a ghost to her right? That I have to find the Colonel before I can go back to being alive." I looked down at the old wooden window sill, there was a double meaning in that last sentence. "I can't...."

"I know Victoria, but maybe it's time. Time to rise up from the dead and finish what we started. The intel Raven gave me is pointing to someone targeting Alex for something and none of us can decipher what yet." Dani sucked in a slow breath, "Raven is doing this because she thinks bringing you back together will shed some light on the creepy back chatter."

I shook my head, "No, god dammit no." I felt my eyes well up, "I'm not the woman she knew." I was the monster I was before her, the killer who only found solace when there was fresh blood being spilled.

"You are, and you know it. You will always be the woman she brought out." Dani sighed, "Anyway, heads up if you want to blow off class and hide in that fancy apartment Maggie paid for. But knowing Alex, she will find you somehow. E.A. Lamont. She came close a handful of times that first year."

Dani hung up, leaving me to stare at the knotty window sill. "Fuck." I threw the phone on the desk and moved to pick up the silver laptop Dani gave me when I arrived in Scotland. Since I was no longer tied to an agency, she was able to hook me up with a free agent status with the ONI, allowing me a high security clearance to navigate through their files and add more about Voltaire as I continued to eliminate the remaining members.

I tapped open the waiting email from Dani, reading the case notes sent by Mary and Dani. It was a total encrypted mess and there were some key words that popped out. Alex's name being one and then a bunch of gibberish.

I spent a half hour reading over the notes, trying to pull out any little things that would point to the Colonel or was a Voltaire trademark. I had set the seas into turmoil with my frenzied dismantling of Voltaire and killing Arthur like I did, and in reality I should have expected some sort of splashback.

I continued glossing over gibberish when I heard a soft knock on my door, I slapped the laptop closed and stood up as the visitor pushed open the door and spoke.

"Excuse me, I'm looking for a Professor Lamont?"

My lungs seized with my heart when I heard her voice. God it had been so long since I heard her voice this close, it swam through my ears and cradled right around my heart. I gripped the edge of the desk to steady myself as she entered into the office, "My name is Alex...."

Her bright blue eyes met mine and I watched them shift from curious to stunned to flooded with confused shock. She ran her eyes over me quickly, the knuckles on her right hand turning white around the strap of her bag.

"Victoria?" My name came out in a ragged, broken whisper.

I bent my head down, removing my glasses as I blushed involuntarily from the way she looked at me. Forcing air to move past my vocal chords, I licked my lips, "Hello Alex."

I glanced up to see her eyes fill with tears as she shook her head, "No, this….this can't be." She swallowed hard, letting out a heavy breath. "You're…I watched you." She scrunched her face up, her cheeks and face turning a bright red as furious anger became the primary emotion. She blew out an irritated laugh, "And they all thought I was insane."

I took a step towards her, drawn to her like I had always been when we were together, "Alex, it's me." I paused, "I know this is a unique situation." I frowned, there was no way I could explain anything to her right now. I had died in her arms, then disappeared into the wind to never be seen in four years and now here she was standing in front of her supposedly very dead girlfriend who faked her death to go on a massive killing rampage. What words in the world's dictionary are there to put together to explain this moment?

As the heavy silence fell, I took a moment to stare at Alex. She was still beautiful even though her hair was shorter and she looked a bit thinner, she was ridiculously stunning and it made my heart skip against my will. She continued to look at the floor and clench her jaw, making me wonder why the hell did I do what I did to this incredible woman who I loved liked no other.

"I always carried with me that I never got to say goodbye, that the last thing I ever said to you was telling you how angry I was with you for what you did." Alex's voice was raspy with unshed tears, "That you died without ever knowing that I had forgiven you." She suddenly looked up, tears slipping down her cheeks. "I wish this was just my mind playing tricks on me, or one of Dani's silly spy tricks, but as I look at you, you're standing in front of me, very much alive." Alex stopped suddenly, staring at me harder as if she was trying to convince her mind that I was standing in front of her and it wasn't a trick. "I knew you were lying to me, laying on that stretcher. Playing dead." She glared at me, "I don't understand."

I nodded, "It's me, yes, and I know that there's a lot I have to explain." I took one step towards her, wanting so desperately to touch her and convince the both of us this was really happening. That after four years, what I felt for her, I still felt deeply.

I was an inch away from grabbing her arm when a bolt of lightning struck the side of my face, a hard slap sound ringing in my ears. I blinked and grabbed my left cheek, looking up at Alex glaring at me with an intense fury.

"Fuck explanations, Victoria. Do you have any idea what you put me through?" She yelled at me, "I had to watch you die, say my goodbyes in a morgue and then live my life regretting I never told you how much I loved you? That I would never get that chance again?! You took that from me, you took my goddamn heart with you and left me with a gaping hole to survive off of."

She stepped closer to me as I rubbed my cheek, searching my eyes, "Four goddamn years. Four agonizing empty years where I shuffled through life finding reasons to keep living. Living in our house, sleeping in our bed alone and seeing you everywhere, begging to anyone who would listen, wishing I could go back in time and have five more minutes to tell you everything I didn't. Never mind the fact that I was on a mission to prove to the world that you were still alive. That bitch, Diablo, she told me something as she rolled you away. It stuck with me, I knew you were still alive no matter what the doctors and lab reports told me." Alex stopped suddenly, sucking in a large breath of air.

She then let out a hard sob, "You...were the love of my life and I fucking hate myself that as I stand right here in front of you, everything I felt for you is rushing back like you were never gone."

I squeezed my eyes shut, feeling a few tears of my own escape, "Alex, you weren't meant to be there." I shook my head reaching for her, grabbing on to her arm and shivering at how warm she was, "I had to disappear, and everything changed at the last minute. I did this to keep you safe." I closed my eyes when I felt her tense up and slowly remove her arm from my grasp.

"You lied again. Another lie that didn't have to be told." She turned to face the window, "I hate you, Victoria, I hate that...." She swallowed down another sob, "I can't do this." She turned to walk away when I grabbed her again. My resolve was breaking apart, had broken apart the second I touched her. "At least I finally know I was right. You're alive, always have been, but it was just another lie."

"Alex, wait."

She shook her head, "No Victoria, I'm done. I can't do this, I have a life back home, I have someone...a life I'm finally trying to move on with." She glared up at me, "Fuck you for all of this, fuck you and all of your lies. Fuck making me think I was losing my mind." The words came out with slow and steady venom and I cringed, trying to not let my jealousy rear its head. To be jealous of anyone in Alex's life would be even more selfish of me, but it didn't stop the anger from building.

I sighed hard, my anger filling my voice quickly, "Alex, I did what I did to keep you safe."

She rolled her eyes and tried to yank away from me, I held tighter, "Stop and listen. I'm about to tell you all the fucking truths of why I had to fake my death and leave you in a million broken pieces. If I hadn't done what I did, you were going to be murdered in our bedroom in a very horrible way. Leaving a vicious messy crime scene that would have haunted everyone you ever loved. My fucking shitty boss planned it from the second he found about you and my want to retire. He set out two very lovely contracts on our heads. I found out at the last second that it was a ruse and even if I was dead and my contract was collected, you were going to die." I held her eyes for a second to make sure I had all of Alex's attention.

"So, I gave up my life, the one I found with you. I gave up the one true love of my life, the one person who made me human and so damn happy, and replaced her with the monster in the black hood. After I died, I sought out every single person who was ever named in the plot to go after you and killed them. One by one, in manners that will one day come back to haunt me as my mind fails and I am no longer strong. After they were all dead, I sought him out and killed him slowly and painfully as he told me more secrets of how my monster was created." I paused as my throat tightened, "Secrets and lies, the foundation of my creation, and apparently my life blood."

Alex huffed at me, "I don't need to hear any of this. I got what I needed, I don't understand why Mary did this. It served no purpose."

I cringed at her flippant tone and let go of her arm, moving one step closer to her as I cried, "I need you to hear this Alex, because you standing here in front of me, is whittling away the façade I have kept for so long. The things I know, the truth of how I came to be, it's destroying me." I understood exactly why Mary sent Alex to me, she needed me to find my humanity again before I continued on with whatever she and Dani had found. I had to find a reason to protect Alex with everything I had, but I needed to find my humanity and face the truth of my creation.

"Just like you destroyed me." Alex folded her arms, "I don't want to do this, keep your stupid spy secrets to yourself. Let me go, Victoria." Her voice trembled with uncertainty, it was the last thing she really wanted me to do.

I looked up at the old wooden ceiling, rubbing the sting away on my cheek from her hard slap, "As I tore his finger nails out one by one, demanding him to tell me who was coming for you, he laughed in my face and fell into a delirious state from the pain. He told me that my capture in the war was planned. It wasn't the fallout of being behind enemy lines, it was a perfectly planned operation to seek out female candidates for what was to become Voltaire."

I looked down at Alex, her eyes welling up, "You see, I was handpicked to go into the warzone. My capture, and the death of my teammates, was all planned. Down to the last hot steel spike they drove into my skin. My torture was a morbid job interview of sorts and I was not expected to survive, since the other ones had died within the first few days, but then I survived. Their torture worked and I proved to be a strong candidate to move on to the next stage of a selection process I had no idea I was a part of."

I shrugged slowly, "What they didn't expect was my mind to fracture as it did and kill with such ease. That was a bonus for them, and they cashed in on it." I stared at her, "People died, good people died all because two old men wanted to create their own living killing machines to do their bidding." I sniffled, hearing Arthur's screams as I broke every one of his fingers in a blind rage after he told me I was nothing but a pawn in his chess game. "I am a product of that. A broken monster who had no cage."

I looked away from her, not wanting to keep on about Arthur as I sensed it was falling on deaf ears, "You were my weakness and my greatest strength. They feared you, Alex. They feared you because you were the reason why I wanted out. Falling in love with you was the best thing to ever happen to me."

I smiled softly, "I think I know why Mary sent you here, but I will let you go as you asked, let you move on with your life. After four years I can't expect you to hold on and wait for me." I moved to the door to open it for her, "But I will always love you with everything I am, I will never ever regret it or that I still love you so much, Alex." I smiled painfully, "I don't think I ever really deserved you." I closed my eyes at how close she was to me, her body warmth mixing with her perfume to swarm all of my senses. I was still so very much in love with her and she was the only thing in this world that could break through all of my defenses like a wrecking ball. I hated Mary for doing this, reigniting four years of a stale life I created to protect the woman in front of me.

I sighed reaching for the door, when Alex's hand covered mine, my class ring still on her right middle finger, "Victoria, wait."

I looked up in glassy blue eyes, Alex let out a breath before she closed the small space between us and kissed me hard and angry. I was startled by the impact but quickly melted into it and kissed her back like no time had ever passed between us. Her hands tangled in my hair tightly, yanking as she kissed me harder for a minute longer before breaking it off.

She panted with her hands still wound in my hair, "I hate you so much right now, Victoria." She slowly moved her eyes to meet mine, "But I can't ignore how in love with you I still am."

I could see the intensity in her eyes, the confliction of emotions she felt for me. This was a newer side of Alex I had never seen before, the strange almost dangerous intensity in her eyes as she spoke.

I licked my lips, swallowing slowly and whispering, "I know, I don't expect you to forgive me."

Alex sucked in a slow breath, "Not until you tell me everything. Everything, Victoria. No more lies, no more secrets, no more." She closed her eyes, "I need to hear it all."

I nodded slowly and reached for Alex, pulling her back into my arms, I held her. Sighing internally at the way she felt in my arms. God had I missed the way she fit with me. The way she squeezed the life out of me in an angry, loving embrace, I rasped out, "Where do you want me to start?

~ A little about the author ~

I started this journey writing fanfiction a handful of years and found that I had a lot in my imagination that needed to be shared with the world. The result was my first novel, Redemptio Animae, which I hope you have read and thoroughly enjoyed! This book will have a sequel that will answer questions and carry the two leads on their journey to reclaim their lives and love! So, look forward to that in the coming year!

I also thank you for purchasing and supporting an independent author!!!

If you're interested in keeping tabs on me and the future works that will certainly follow this debut novel, head on over to Facebook and find me at Sydney Gibson at Facebook.com/sydney.fivesixthree

And then to enjoy some of the nonsensical tweets and updates with future novels and the ongoing fanfiction I still occasionally putter with, find me on Twitter at Syndey563a.

There is also an author page on Amazon where you can follow me and be updated when the next book is going to be published.

Website is coming soon!!!!

Thanks to all of you!

Syd!

Made in the USA
San Bernardino, CA
13 December 2019